Little Ragdoll: A Bildungsroman

by

Carrie-Anne Brownian

This book is a work of historical fiction. Apart from the well-known actual people, locales, and events which feature in the narrative, all references to historical events, real people, or real places are used fictiously. All other characters, events, incidents, and dialogues are products of the author's imagination. Any resemblance to actual events, locales, or persons, living or dead, is entirely coincidental.

Published by Purple Tarantula Press
ISBN 978-1-927967-21-8 (paperback)
ISBN 978-1-927967-22-5 (hardcover)
ISBN 978-1-927967-19-5 (Kindle)
ISBN 978-1-927967-18-8 (Nook, Kobo, iBooks)

10 9 8 7 6 5 4 3 2 1

E-book cover design by Jaz Johnson; print cover design by Carrie-Anne Brownian

My generous thanks to the Hal Leonard Corporation for granting permission to quote from "Crackerbox Palace" (© 1976 George Harrison via Harrisongs) and "Be Here Now" (© 1973 George Harrison via Harrisongs).

The concluding lines of "The Last Question" (© 1956 Isaac Asimov) are respectfully quoted under fair use doctrine.

All other quotes are public domain due to age. The lyrics of "Benedictus" (© 1964 Paul Simon) are from the Latin Mass, and thus also public domain (in contrast to the actual sound recording).

http://www.facebook.com/pages/Little-Ragdoll-A-Bildungsroman/
435227226506660

To the real little girl who inspired The Four Seasons' song "Rag Doll"
and
To anyone who was ever a dark horse or different from the others.

Credit where credit is due. I couldn't have written this book without my wonderful soundtrack of The Hollies and The Four Seasons.

All events are linked together in this best of all possible worlds.
(Oft-repeated maxim of Pangloss in *Candide*, Voltaire)

Benedictus qui venit in nomine Domini. (Blessèd is the one who comes in the name of God.)
("Benedictus," fifth track on *Wednesday Morning, 3 A.M.*)

Cast of Characters:

Our main family:

Mrs. Dolores Beulah Troy (née Goossens), born 1923, a disgrace to motherhood, a drug addict, and a horrible worker, descended from Dutch-speaking Belgians who immigrated in the late 1840s

Mr. Antoine Norbert Troy, born 1923, marginally more intelligent than his wife but still a pretty awful person, with his only somewhat redeeming quality being a tip-top work ethic, descended from Huguenots who immigrated in the 1680s

Gemma Léonie Troy, born February 1942, the oldest of the nine Troy children, a rather aloof, spoilt princess till being forced into an unwanted marriage at eighteen

Carlos Ghislain Troy, born February 1943, the family dunce, who spends most of his time drinking, using drugs, or stealing, even at work

Allen Théodore Troy, born on D-Day (June 6, 1944), the only sympathetic Troy brother, who eventually realizes his goals of getting off of drugs, quitting drinking and smoking, moving to a nice neighborhood, finding a respectable job, and marrying a nice girl

Lucine Camille Troy, born January 20, 1946, very devoted to her younger sisters and the idea of going to college, who longs for the chance to be a normal teenager

Emeline Rosalie Troy, born May 14, 1948 (the same day Israel declared its independence), very bookish, quiet, intelligent, interested in history, languages, world religions, and older film stars, another substitute mother to her little sisters, eventually becomes a hippie, and dreams of becoming a librarian

Ernestine Zénobie Troy, born April 11, 1952, very brash, outgoing, unafraid of speaking her mind, which Emeline attributes to her Sun sign of Aries, and gutsy enough to make her own destiny away from their depraved parents no matter how young she is

Adicia Éloïse Troy, born July 11, 1954, our shero, a very sensitive, sweet, imaginative girl who dreams of leaving poverty and finding a guy from the outside world who'll love her just the way she is

Thomas Albert Troy (Tommy), born February 1956, the apple of Mrs. Troy's eye and a spoilt, entitled, coddled brat, though not incapable of demonstrating very, very slow progress in becoming a decent human being who doesn't think only of himself

Justine Anastasie Troy, born March 2, 1959, the family baby and the darling of her siblings' eyes, a bit like Phronsie Pepper without being spoilt or shielded from real life

Sarah Miriam Katz, born 1927, a Holocaust survivor from Baden-Baden, Germany, in America since 1947, since which time she's been an exploited live-in nanny, servant, and surrogate mother for the Troys

Friends and neighbors:

Girl Ryan (later Deirdre Apollonia), born April 8, 1952, Ernestine's best friend, the oldest of four siblings who've grown up squatting, full of Irish-American pride, and never afraid to share her radical power-to-the-people, Socialist, folkie, or feminist beliefs with anyone

Boy Ryan (later David Edgar), born June 13, 1954, the only Ryan boy, a good sport about having to be the man of his family so young but eventually fed up by being the only boy among three sisters and many female friends

Baby Ryan (later Fiona Líobhan[1]), born May 19, 1957, a very sweet, sensitive, inquisitive child, a rare en caul birth[2], often sings, dances, and plays a tambourine in Greenwich Village to earn money, and still wears her hair in ponytails even into her late teens

Infant Ryan (later Aoife Saoirse[3]), born April 20, 1959, the baby of the four Ryans, Justine's best friend, and not spoilt or shielded from real life either in spite of being the precious family baby

Julie Claire Spirnak, born May 10, 1954, one of Adicia's best friends, who grows up with Ernestine and the Ryans, and remains rather childlike, sweet, and sensitive in spite of her traumatic early childhood

Lenore Eve Hartlein, born June 25, 1947, originally from Greenpoint, Brooklyn, whom Allen and his sisters meet in late July of 1962, when she's running away from an abusive father, and immediately taken into their hearts and home as unofficial family

---

[1] Lee-VAHN

[2] Born entirely within an unbroken amniotic sac, as opposed to being born in the caul, when part of the broken sac is over the head or face.

[3] EE-fa SEER-sha

Betsy van Niftrik, born March 1952, an only child, the across the hall neighbor of Ernestine, Julie, and the Ryans after they move to the Meatpacking District, somewhat of a free spirit and radical due to her free-thinking parents

Mrs. Gloria Ruth van Niftrik (née Reinders), born 1929, Betsy's mother, a hippie and attachment parent by any other name before her time, just as unafraid as Ernestine, Betsy, or Deirdre to speak her mind on controversial subjects

Mr. Arthur Lawrence van Niftrik, born 1929, Betsy's father, also a free-thinker and political radical before either of those streams of thought gained popularity

Mrs. Suzanne Mary Doyle (née Bowstead), born 1932, the Troys' across the hall neighbor during their seven years in Hell's Kitchen, who has never given up hope of being reunited with her daughter from her first marriage

Mr. Benjamin Isaac Doyle, her second husband

Matthew Doyle, born August 1960, Mrs. Doyle's oldest child from her second marriage and a close friend of Justine's

Caroline Julia Doyle, born July 1964, Mrs. Doyle's second child of her second marriage

Meredith Clarissa and Graham William Doyle, born March 1970, Mrs. Doyle's final children

Marjani Washington, born 1954, one of Adicia's best friends, from a Black pride, progressive family, who wears cornrows, eats a lot of African food, and uses the word "Black" in lieu of "Negro"

Subira Washington, born 1951, Marjani's older sister

Zuberi Washington, born 1957, Marjani's little brother

Mr. and Mrs. Washington, their parents

Father Warren Ambrose Murphy, born 1920, a very liberal Episcopal priest who lives in Yorkville and runs a boarding school for disadvantaged young girls

Mrs. Iris Murphy, born 1920, his wife, who finds Lucine in their church when she runs away at sixteen and gives her the chance to get a real education

Giovanni Edoardo Monterastelli, born June 1961, Gemma's birth son from her unwanted first marriage, adopted at a year old by the childless Father and Mrs. Murphy

Warrick Grover Carson (Ricky), born July 15, 1952, a young man from a rich Syracuse family who moves up the street from the Troys. His unlikely love for Adicia changes her life forever.

Mrs. Enid Marsenko, born 1919, the owner of Upper East Side Beautiful Brides, an upscale bridal salon. She never forgets the awful Mrs. Troy or her unhappy daughters.

Mr. Nathan and Mrs. Adara Straussler, both born 1916, a German-Jewish, first-generation American couple who runs the bakery below the Troys' new apartment when they move back to the Lower East Side

Enemies:

Mrs. Luigina Rossi, Mrs. Troy's friend and former co-worker, Gemma's once-aunt-in-law, a fellow tenant of the Troys' original residence, a judgmental, busybody gossip with a mean streak

Francesco Monterastelli, born 1922, Mrs. Rossi's repulsive overage bachelor nephew, married to Gemma against her will in October of 1960, very abusive and controlling, with serious mother issues

Jacob DeLuise, born 1927, a creepy drug dealer whom the Troys plot to forcibly marry Lucine to

Ethan Pitskowski, born 1934, a grotesque drug dealer whom Mrs. Troy hatches a monstrous deal with to keep herself from going back to prison

Mr. Willoughby Aristotle Carson, Ricky's father, a rich snob with more money than sense, and lacking in basic human decency

Mrs. Georgiana Christiana-Helen Chantelle Whitestone Warrick Carson, Ricky's mother, who has a real mean streak, lacks just as much basic human decency as her husband, has nothing but hatred and disgust towards Adicia and her family for their poor origins, and who wears ridiculous hats

Seth Oswaldtwistle, born 1914, an ex-convict whom Mr. and Mrs. Troy plan to forcibly marry to Adicia

The second generation of Troys and assorted others:
Irene Lily Troy, born June 6, 1967, Allen and Lenore's firstborn
Amelia Katherine Troy, born October 18, 1969, their secondborn
Oliver Leo Troy, born September 5, 1972, Allen's long-awaited boy
Heinrich Rosen (Henry), Sarah's long-awaited husband, a fellow German survivor whom she meets at the City College of New York in 1964

Friedrich (Fritz) Rosenkatz, born August 1965, Sarah's firstborn
Nessa Tzipora Rosenkatz, born June 7, 1967, Sarah's daughter and Irene's best friend
Zachary Martel, born 1946, Lucine's husband, a fellow French-American, whom she meets while studying for her master's degree in social work at Hunter College in 1970
Simone Juliette Troy-Martel, born Halloween 1972, their firstborn child
Tyrone Duffy, born 1947, Gemma's second husband
Adrienne Nicolette Duffy-Troy, born March 30, 1973, their firstborn
Veronica Zoravkov, a Bulgarian-American midwife and former nurse who delivers Sarah's children and Allen and Lenore's daughters
Radana Zupan, a Slovenian-American midwife and former nurse who delivers Adicia and Ricky's firstborn
Robert Allen Rudolph Carson (Robbie), born May 6, 1973, Adicia's darling firstborn
George, Emeline's cat, a runt whom she adopts in June of 1972

Part 1: Meet the Troys
(September 1959–October 1960)

Through me is the way to the City of Woe:
Through me the way into the eternal pain;
Through me the way among the lost below.
Righteousness did my maker on high constrain.
Me did divine Authority uprear;
Me supreme Wisdom and primal Love sustain.
Before I was, no things created were.
Save the eternal, and I eternal abide.
Abandon all hope, ye who enter here.
(Lines 1-9, Canto III, *Inferno*)

Chapter 1: A Trip to Woolworth's

In the world Adicia Éloïse Troy is from, life is more like a Grimms' fairytale than a Disney fairytale. But sometimes even the darkest, most twisted fairytale has a happy ending, even for a poor girl from the Lower East Side.

Adicia peers through the wrought-iron bars of the eighth floor fire escape balcony as she holds her six-month-old baby sister Justine on her lap, a gentle September breeze giving them some relief from the heat of the concrete jungle. She wiggles her filthy toes, savoring the feel of the breeze against her skin.

"One day we're gonna leave this place and have a happy life far away, no matter how long it takes," Adicia says in her strong Manhattan accent. "We'll have a real house, lots of toys, new clothes, and a car. But you'll always be better to me than a thousand dolls." Adicia turns her head at the approaching saddle shoe footsteps.

"Have you forgotten we're supposed to go to Woolworth's this afternoon?" thirteen-year-old Lucine asks. "We'll have to start walking soon to get there in time."

Adicia pulls herself up, careful not to drop her real-live baby doll, and heads back inside. Eleven-year-old Emeline has her nose buried in a book as always, and seven-year-old Ernestine is having her hair brushed by their surrogate mother Sarah. They all wear clothes handed down from their oldest sister Gemma, with a marked progression from gently-worn on Lucine to worn-out rags on Adicia. Their three brothers have escaped hand-me-downs since the older two are only a year apart in age, and the youngest, three-year-old Tommy, is spoilt rotten by their mother.

"I can't walk all the way to Woolworth's in those," Adicia protests when Sarah extends a dirty pair of socks with several holes and snags. "I'll get blisters. My shoes are already worn enough."

"You do what you must when you have no choice," Sarah tries to soothe her, in the distinctive German accent she still has after twelve years in America. "I had to walk so many miles in tight wooden clogs and no socks, every day for weeks, before the soldiers rescued me."

Adicia sighs and pulls on her socks and shoes, then takes Emeline's hand as they begin the perilous flight down the crooked, broken, rotted staircase, which is missing a number of steps. Despite this tenement having been built in 1920, it's still not as safe or modern as some of the residences up by Tompkins Square Park. The landlord's family abandoned the building years ago, leaving their comparatively large living quarters just in time for the Troys to move in.

Sarah puts Justine in her old, worn-out, hand-me-down stroller, and they proceed down Avenue A. After they cross Houston Street about a block later, Avenue A turns into Essex Street, where Adicia's two older brothers are leaning against a dilapidated old storefront and smoking marijuana. Sixteen-year-old Carlos, who's also taking swigs from a bottle of vodka, pays them no regard, but fifteen-year-old Allen smiles at them.

"Going for a walk, ladies?"

"Woolworth's," Lucine says. "I hope you've taken care of buying your own school supplies, or will soon. They don't buy themselves."

"Did Adicia hurt herself? She's limping."

"Just socks with holes. It's not a big deal when it's not a huge walk."

Allen reaches into his pockets and hands Adicia four dull quarters. "Here you go. Enough for round-trip subway fare. You, Ernestine, and Justine ride for free, since you're so short. The nearest station's on the corner of Delancey and Essex. Since you don't hafta worry about walking no more, why don't you go to onea the stores uptown? They've mostly got the same goods for the same prices, but it's nice to get outta the neighborhood when you can."

Adicia slips the coins into her pocket and waves at her favorite brother as she continues down Essex Street. After the short walk to the station, she takes Lucine's hand and makes her way underground. Once they've gotten to the front of the line, Adicia stands on her toes and slides the coins across the counter in exchange for six tokens, three for the trip there and three for the trip back, plus a dime in change. Then they wait in line again at the turnstile. Lucine has to help Adicia with pushing it around, while Sarah hands Justine to Emeline and hoists the stroller over before going through. Adicia stays close to Lucine as they press through the crowd before the doors can close. They're lucky to find seats instead of having to stand and hold onto poles or straps.

Adicia takes Emeline's hand when they reach their destination on the Upper West Side. The subway lets them off near the Museum of Natural History, by Central Park, so they have to walk about two blocks east to get to the Woolworth's at the corner of Broadway and 79th Street. Adicia marvellingly looks around at the beautiful buildings they're passing, and the nicely-dressed people in the streets. If they have to shop at a bargain store, it's nice to do it uptown instead of downtown.

"Wouldn't it be nice to live here?" Ernestine asks as Woolworth's looms in front of them. "I bet Upstate is even nicer, since it's not as crowded. It must be nice to live in your own house and see grass, trees, flowers, streams, and mountains instead of brick, steel, concrete, and traffic jams. I can't wait till I'm old enough for college so I can make my dream come true."

"With what money?" Lucine asks. "I wanna go to college too, but Mother and Dad would never let me hear the end of it, and might even sabotage it. I can just imagine the hateful comments they'd make about how I'm getting above my raising and thinking I'm better than them and all our ancestors."

"Trust me, I'll make it happen. And I'll do it all by myself. I'm not gonna rely on a knight in shining armor on a white horse to rescue me." Ernestine opens the door.

Adicia shyly hangs back from the well-dressed girls and their mothers. Some of them have patent-leather Mary Janes, and they all have pretty, unfaded dresses, shiny satin hair ribbons, and freshly starched, ironed blouses.

"If it isn't the raggedy Troy girls," Jeanie Mraz says snidely. "I see your unpaid nanny came instead of your real mother. I suppose your mother knew she'd get kicked out if she came here drunk or smelling of drugs."

"Our mother works, unlike yours," Lucine says. "It must be too hard for you to understand some women work and don't have the luxury of spending the day at home."

"Your mother doesn't have a real job, like a nurse or secretary. She doesn't do important work. What's her record for holding a job, a month, two months?"

"Does that Kraut think she's fooling anyone?" Linda Jones asks. "Just call her what she is, a slave who works for peanuts. Maid and nanny, my eye. I bet your dad the Kraut-lover hired her. He shoulda been thrown in prison for sitting out the war. All the rest of *our* dads served our country and did the right thing."

"My father's not a draft-dodger," Lucine snaps. "He showed up when he was drafted, but he failed his medical tests. It's not our fault he was 4-F."

"How can you go out in public without long sleeves or a bandage covering that thing?" Mrs. Jones asks Sarah. "That's not decent, particularly not for little children. There's no decent way to explain that to them."

"Your attitude says more about you than me," Sarah responds. "My girls know what my tattoo means, and they don't think it's shameful or dirty. Are you uncomfortable to see evidence that not everyone has a life as perfect as yours?"

"Is this one starting kindergarten?" Barbara Stevens asks. "She looks like a dirty, ugly, torn-apart Raggedy Ann."

Adicia hides behind Emeline, too shy and scared to say anything.

"Do you have a boyfriend yet, Lucine?" Helen Johnstone asks. "All the boys are fighting over me and competing to ask me to the dances. Nice boys prefer girls who wear new clothes and don't live in tenements. Imagine that."

"Unlike you, I have more interest in school than getting a date," Lucine says. "I want a real diploma, not my Mrs. degree."

"Why do you and your raggedy sisters have such stupid old lady names?" Sharon George asks. "What's the baby's name, Eunice? And the name Ernestine belongs on a smelly old lady who has fifty cats!"

"I'd much rather be the only Ernestine at school than lost in a sea of Lindas, Barbaras, Susans, and Debbies," Ernestine retorts. "I like being unique. No one will ever forget my name."

"Our baby's name is Justine," Lucine says. "A very pretty French name."

"What's the little ragdoll's name?" Nancy Jenkins asks.

"Her name is Adicia," Emeline says. "It's an ancient Greek name, the Latinate form of Adikia, who was a goddess." Though Emeline typically bubbles over with her wealth of knowledge, she leaves out the fact that Adicia was named for the goddess of injustice because their parents thought it was an injustice to be saddled with a seventh unplanned child and yet another girl in a row.

"Ew, Greek mythology is so boring. I'd rather read fashion magazines and love stories, not stupid stories about made-up gods and goddesses thousands of years ago," Linda Hopkins scoffs. "And I love having the same name as a lot of other girls. It means I'm popular and boys will pay attention to me."

"Oh, people will pay attention to these losers too," Karen Becker says haughtily. "How could you not notice their ragged clothes? I can't believe they had the nerve to think they belong in a nice store. Did any of you even bathe today?"

"You look like a broken ragdoll," Sharon repeats to Adicia. "I can only imagine how those clothes will look when it's that baby's turn to wear them."

"Justine is our real-live baby doll," Ernestine protests. "She's more special than ten thousand fancy, expensive porcelain baby dolls at a toy store for millionaires."

"You seriously think that little rat is the last urchin your pathetic parents will produce?" Barbara asks in amusement. "All the poor trash have babies until they can't make them anymore, and we're the ones stuck paying for you."

"You don't pay for our family's rent and food. Our parents and our older brothers pay for everything."

"We're not on public assistance," Lucine says. "We work honestly."

"Our mother was given an operation to remove her womanly organs after she had Justine," Emeline says. "The doctor didn't want her to have any more kids."

"Thank God," Mrs. Hopkins says. "He deserves a gold medal for doing that, though he should've done that years ago instead of waiting till her ninth child."

"All five of you will be just like your mother," Jeanie says. "You're dreaming if you think you'll ever do better. By the way, decent girls don't go to college to get an education and find a job. They go to find husbands and drop out once they've got the Mrs. degree, or only get a degree so they can support their husbands through graduate school."

"Maybe you're only going to school to find husbands, but I want an education so I can have a better life," Lucine says. "Gemma works because she has to, not because she wants to find a boyfriend or have something to do before she gets married. She's not the type who expects a husband to take care of her. She doesn't even want to get married till she's at least twenty-one."

"Girls, shall we finish what we came here for?" Sarah asks. "You're not here to have fights *mit* mean girls."

"Why do you work for Mr. and Mrs. Troy when they don't even pay you?" Mrs. Jenkins asks. "My children's nanny is always paid nicely on a weekly basis. I don't give her five dollars every six months."

"I love Lucine, Emeline, Ernestine, Adicia, and Justine. Allen is also a nice boy when he's straight. The Troys aren't as horrible as the Nazis."

"It's not fair," Adicia complains as they wander into the next aisle. "All the other girls get new clothes for school. My clothes are twelve years old."

"Those girls won't look twice at their new clothes in six months," Emeline predicts. "They'll throw them away, or give them to charity if they have any sense, when a newer fashion comes along. They don't care about getting clothes that last for a long time."

"School isn't a fashion show," Lucine says. "You can wear the most expensive, newest clothes in the world, but it won't matter if you're not using your brain."

Emeline picks up a fancy calligraphy pen and lovingly strokes it. "I wish I could have a real pen to write all my important assignments. All the other girls have real pens."

"You'd break the nub off and get wet ink all over your hand. At least I could use a pen like that if we had the money for it."

"Why don't people make stuff with us in mind?" Ernestine asks. "It's not nice to discriminate against people who happen to be born with all their strength in the left hand."

"Be thankful schools have evolved enough so you, Emeline, and Allen weren't beaten and forced to switch like Dad was. Maybe in another fifty years, there'll be more specialized merchandise for lefties."

Adicia begins shaking. "Is my teacher going to beat me or yell at me when she sees I'm writing left-handed?"

"Not in this day and age. Most schools in this country don't do that anymore, even if a lot of teachers give lefties failing marks in writing. Part of me wishes I were a southpaw like you, Ernestine, Emeline, and Allen, but then I remember I don't need even one more reason to stick out and be made fun of."

The girls forlornly go along with their budget, dutifully choosing the cheapest notebooks, pencils, pens, folders, and loose leaf paper. They're expected to have the same pencil cases, lunchboxes, inkwells, and schoolbags year after year, instead of trading the old models in for new. Even by Woolworth's standards, the things they're getting are painfully cheap. Since this Woolworth's is in such a posh neighborhood, there are nicer, more expensive things than usual, which makes passing them up even more painful. Most painful of all is having to forego the lunch counter and its tempting smells. Next to their frequent diet of sardines, bacon grease on toast, roadkill, overripe vegetables, stale bread, and the leftover meat no one else wanted, things like ice-cream soda, apple pie, three-decker sandwiches of egg salad, ham, bacon, tomato, and chicken, cheese sandwiches, and hot chocolate with wafers and whipped cream are five-star offerings. The nicest meal Adicia ever had, besides her holiday meals at the Bowery Mission, was when Sarah took her and Ernestine to breakfast last May and they ate Belgian waffles with whipped cream and thick maple syrup. Adicia's had strawberries on top, and Ernestine's had blueberries.

The cashier recoils a little when their little band of ragamuffins gets to the head of the checkout line, but says nothing and dutifully rings them up. Their total comes to a paltry $2. Lucine is given the job of carrying the paper bag home.

"Losers," Jeanie says smugly as she skips off to her automobile.

"I wish we could get a cab," Lucine grumbles. "This bag's gonna get heavy, even if it's only a few blocks to the subway and then a few blocks home. Going up the stairs will probably be the worst."

"My apartment has an elevator and an elevator operator," Nancy says. "I'm surprised you could even afford subway fare instead of walking."

"Ignore them," Sarah says as they walk down 79th Street. "Worst thing that can happen is they call you names. You're going to school to learn, not meet boys and be popular. My girls have what it takes to go to college and find good jobs. Just think of it as being one year closer to leaving the old neighborhood."

"You can be come with us!" Ernestine promises. "It would be so nice if you had your own kids too."

"I already have five *kinder*. There are more ways to be a *mutter* than giving birth."

Adicia holds hands with Ernestine on their way to the subway station, while Lucine struggles with the bag. This time, Emeline has to help her with the turnstile, while Lucine puts the bag on its side and pushes it through. Adicia watches the subway pulling into the station with apprehension. She hates to leave the nice part of the city, where she isn't surrounded by old, run-down buildings and people who've lost hope of moving up in life. When she takes a seat, she feels the Upper West Side disappearing behind her and the run-down Lower East Side coming back. If only she could be as confident as Ernestine that this life isn't going to be forever and that when they're older, they'll be able to leave this far behind.

Chapter 2: Going Fishing

It's a Sunday in September, and the Troys' laundry is hanging on a line strung from the living room to the fire escape. The hot water was shut off for failure to pay the bill, so Sarah heated several large tubs of water on the old gas stove, lugged them onto the floor, and put in soap powder. Adicia thinks it's mean that her parents make Sarah do laundry by hand and don't even pay her, but Sarah tries to make her look on the bright side by saying she doesn't have to lug all that laundry down those dangerous stairs, transport it to a laundromat, and lug it back home and back up the stairs. After all, twelve people produce a lot of laundry.

Mrs. Troy stands in the kitchen cursing under her breath. "Can someone explain to me why we don't got no meat? Someone needs to start preparing supper in a few hours, and I ain't gonna pass off bacon grease on bread and vegetables with mold cut off as a meal for the third time this week."

"There wasn't no roadkill when I went out." Carlos puffs on a cigarette. "Usually there's at least a few pieces."

"I can hustle up some fish in the East River," Allen volunteers. "I just got a fake fishing license. Who wants to come with me to spot for cops, hold onto me so I don't fall in if I'm reeling in a big feisty thing, and carry the fish in a bucket?"

"Are you allowed to fish in the river?" Emeline asks. "I thought gangsters dumped bodies in there."

"That's why someone's gotta be there to spot for cops. Give me credit for having a fishing rod. Some people have to catch fish with their hands. I took out the reel and moved it to the left so I could reel with my stronger hand."

"Emeline will spot for cops, Adicia will carry the fish, Ernestine will kill the fish, and Carlos will hold onto Allen so he don't fall in," Mrs. Troy decides. "You'd all better be back by six."

"We're gonna have yummy fish for dinner!" Tommy says in a very annoying singsong voice. "Do I get the best piece, Mommy?"

"My darling little prince always gets the best of everything."

"I'm Mommy's angel," Tommy taunts his sisters. "I'm special because I'm the first boy after four stupid girls in a row."

Carlos swings the fishing rod at his baby brother. "Anyone ever tell you you're a little brat? What about special treatment for me as the golden firstborn son?"

"You're not cute and cuddly, Carlos, and we need you to help us with money and other things," Mrs. Troy says. "Tommy, on the other hand, earned the right to be spoilt and treated like a prince because he's the baby boy. I won't make him work even when he's old enough. You should know better than to question your responsibility as one of our breadwinners."

"I hope he falls into a gutter or gets eaten by a rat," Carlos mutters as they start the trek down the stairs.

During their walk down to the river, Carlos buys some narcotics from a friend and tries to look discrete as he injects himself. His sisters hang their heads.

"What kinds of fish swim in the East River?" Emeline asks when they reach the East River Park.

"I don't care, so long as they fill our stomachs tonight!" Carlos says. "Do you think I care if we eat fancy salmon or lobster versus bass or trout? I wouldn't know which fish is which from looking at it, would you, Allen?"

"Beats me." Allen plops onto the grass and swings his line into the water. "As long as it's not that godawful tuna fish in the can. That stuff's supposed to be cat food, not people food."

Ernestine stares in confusion at the first fish Allen unhooks ten minutes later. Carlos finally hands her a jack knife.

"You never offed a fish before? Most people smack 'em over the head, but you can gut it too. They don't have to be completely dead, so long as none of 'em are lively enough to leap outta the bucket."

Ernestine wants to throw up as she pokes the knife into it. "I'm sorry we have to kill you, Mr. Fish, but our family is hungry and needs your sacrifice. I hope you can understand and forgive us."

Carlos rolls his eyes, then injects himself again. "Is that what they're teaching you in second grade, that you have to talk to dumb animals like they're people before you kill 'em for food?"

"The Indians did that when they hunted deer, moose, and other animals," Ernestine says, oblivious to his intended nastiness. "They asked the animal for forgiveness and never forgot Great Spirit, or God, gave and took away all life."

"What do you need to learn about Indians for? All you need to know is they used to live here, then the superior white man came and killed most of 'em or sent 'em to reservations. I'm so glad I'm gonna drop outta school soon if this kinda nonsense is what they teach nowadays. All I ever needed to learn was accomplished by fifth or sixth grade—basic math, how to read and write, and a little science. Our kind don't need fancy advanced book learnin' like Indian history, Greek literature, and algebra."

"I like Indian history. It's neat. They're teaching us New York State history, and Indians lived here a long time before the Dutch made New York into a colony. I like that my teacher doesn't pretend American history begins and ends with white men."

Allen throws three more fish at Ernestine. "Once I got one, they all started coming! I hope I have enough grub in my sack to get enough to feed all of us!"

Adicia looks away from the dying gutted fish flopping around in the bucket. She hopes her small arms and hands will be able to carry the final weight back home. If she were to trip, fall, and lose the fish, her mother would be pretty mad at her, and she doesn't want extra reasons to be resented and mocked.

Emeline looks behind her and sees a cop. "How many fish before we call it a day?"

"You bored already?" Carlos snorts. "If we were real fishermen, we might be out in our boat in the middle of the lake for hours! Half the fun of fishing is being with your friends and waiting for fish to bite."

"But we're not fishing as a fun hobby, we're fishing because we have to eat, and there's a cop nearby."

"Don't worry. If he does come up to us, we act normally. Here, take a look." Allen pulls his fake fishing license out of his back pocket. "Doesn't it look like it could pass official inspection? You don't get something that looks this official in someone's basement!"

Five more fish have been added to the bucket by the time the cop comes closer. The girls don't know whether to pretend they don't know the boys or run away as fast as they can. Adicia hopes he takes pity on them and nicely looks the other way, the way she's been told cops in the movies sometimes do. Not that she's ever seen a movie. She knows the names of some of the really famous moviestars from Gemma's posters and celebrity magazines, like Marilyn Monroe, Elizabeth Taylor, Cary Grant, and William Holden, but has never seen any of them in action. Movies are a luxury the Troys can't afford when they live from penny to penny.

"Do you have permission to fish in these waters?"

"My sister can show you my license," Allen says confidently.

Emeline holds out the fake license. The cop examines it closely and then looks at Allen, then back at the license.

"Do you mean to tell me you're twenty-five and your name is Fernando Gómez?"

"Don't discriminate. My brother here is named Carlos, and he doesn't look Spanish either. Our mother just liked the names. Haven't we all known people who didn't look like the popular image of their names?"

The cop notices Carlos spinning around and talking to himself under his breath. "Excuse me, but can you tell me when your brother was born? I'll love to hear if it matches the birthdate on this license."

"Oh, easy. Allen was born on D-Day," Carlos says proudly, not realizing he's talking to a cop. "It's one of the few historical dates I remember from school, since my brother just so happened to be born that day."

"Allen? Isn't your brother's name Fernando?"

"Who's Fernando?" Carlos turns away and pulls down his pants so he can relieve himself into the river.

"I was in the war. I well remember we stormed the beaches of Normandy on June 6, 1944. So if your brother really was born on D-Day as you claim, he's only fifteen. Nice try at passing for an adult with this phony fishing license, though." The cop throws it on the ground.

Allen turns around slack-jawed at Carlos's idiocy. He's so annoyed and distracted he doesn't realize right away that he's getting another tug at his fishing rod. Carlos and the cop do nothing as Allen is pulled in and starts thrashing around in the strong waters of the East River.

"Let go of the rod and we can pull you in!" Emeline shouts.

"I paid for this rod! This ain't stolen! Do you know how hard it is for a guy like me to get a decent fishing rod?"

"When we studied geography last year, they told us it's not a good idea to swim in the East River," Ernestine says. "Why couldn't you go to a place normal people use for fishing, like Long Island?"

"Oh, yes, and then we would've gone back to our fancy mansion on the Upper West Side, given the fish to our cook to prepare on our fancy new electric stove and serve with five-hundred-dollar china and three-hundred-dollar silverware, and watched television in our leather armchairs while we waited for supper to be called," Carlos says sarcastically. "All you girls are in for a rude awakening when you get older and realize none of us are going nowhere and we'll always be society's underdogs."

"Mr. Policeman, is it true gangsters dump bodies in here?" Emeline asks. "I also read that during Prohibition, people used to go out in little boats and board big boats to get alcohol, then row back to shore with their contraband."

"This one reads too much," Carlos says derisively. "Thinks she's gonna be a librarian when she's a grownup. I don't know how she bears to read all those boring books about history and mythology."

"Yes, I have seen bodies in the river," the cop admits. "And I'll have you know my great-great-grandparents were poor Irish immigrants and my family was poor for many generations. Unlike you, I wanted to do better than how I was raised. Looks like your sisters are going to go somewhere in life because they're not afraid of going to school and thinking of themselves as more than poor people with no higher ambitions." He walks away.

Allen manages to throw the rod onto the grass, the fish hooked to it, and continues struggling against the strong waters. Emeline leans over as far as she can without falling in. Allen grabs onto her arm and she struggles to pull him back onto dry land, falling flat on her back. At least Allen isn't heavy, since they don't eat well enough to be even average weight.

"Now what are we gonna do for dinner?" Carlos whines. "We can't feed twelve people with just ten average-sized fish."

"We'll look through garbage cans," Allen says. "And Justine only eats baby food and formula. She can't eat solid food yet."

"Why do we spend money on formula when we could save so much by getting it for free?" Emeline asks. "Not that I'd want Mother to nurse her when there'd usually be drugs in her milk, but if she were straight, it'd be cheaper. A lot of the old books I read talk about rich children having wetnurses, or women nursing their own babies instead of fixing bottles."

Carlos grimaces. "Only low-class women nurse. Even we have some pride and respectability. Besides, do you ever see a baby drinking from anything besides a bottle? I didn't think so."

"It might come back in fashion. A new decade is coming."

"Where does she get these crazy ideas?" Carlos asks Allen. "She's read way too many books and gone goofy. Maybe it's true girls are ruined by too much education."

"No, I definitely think you're the biggest idiot in this family," Allen says. "Even I'm not that dumb when I'm using drugs. Thanks to you, we only got ten fish. My fake birthdate was May third, 1934!"

During the walk back home, they scavenge in garbage cans and add their unlikely loot to the bucket of fish—ten raw potatoes, three turnips, a loaf of stale bread, four soft apples, and a tomato with a little patch of mold. It's nothing compared to the nice holiday meals at the Bowery Mission. They serve things like real chicken, turkey, beef, mashed potatoes, cranberry sauce, stuffing, real fish, yams, chocolate cake, French onion soup, ham, and applesauce.

"Look." Emeline points to a shop several feet away. "That's a kosher butcher. Maybe he'll have some ritually impure meat to give us instead of throwing away."

"Why would a butcher throw away good meat?" Carlos asks.

"Meat isn't kosher if it has a defect, like a scarred lung or blood-spotted liver. Perhaps we can get some before they throw it away or donate it." Emeline skips into the shop.

Adicia and Ernestine look longingly at the chicken, duck, goose, turkey, lamb, and beef. Not all of them are choice cuts, but they all look better than the bottom of the barrel meat they're used to. They wonder if the butcher gets his meat at a reduced rate because he runs the store. Thanksgiving, the next time they know they'll eat decent meat, seems so far away.

"Excuse me, Sir, do you have any meat that was unqualified from being kosher? I hate to beg, but we only caught ten fish and can't make an entire meal for twelve people on just some fish and stale vegetables."

The butcher looks at Allen. "What happened to you?"

"I fell into the river when I was fishing. Our other brother was too out of it to bother holding onto me when the fish tugged too hard."

The butcher gets off his stool and walks over to a pile of random meats lying all over a long table near the back of the store. "This is where I keep the meats marked down for lower-quality or separated out when they're found to be unkosher. I usually donate the unkosher meat to the Bowery Mission, but I'll let you have some since you look like such nice children. All of you except for that young man spinning around like a top. Is he drunk?"

"He's on drugs," Ernestine says. "We all think he's the idiot of the family too. He'll probably end up in jail or a loonybin."

The butcher wraps up a generous portion of beef in old newspaper and puts the parcels into several paper bags. "Here you go. Have yourselves a feast tonight. The cow had a damaged lung, but the meat can still be used to feed someone not obligated by the laws of kosher. There's a teaching that there are sparks of holiness in everything, even inanimate objects like tables and chairs, but it's up to the individual to elevate the sparks and not just use the objects for mundane purposes. The animals we eat give up their entire lives to elevate these sparks of holiness, and this cow's sacrifice shouldn't be in vain just because there was something wrong with its lung. It's just going to be used in a different way than originally intended."

"That's a really nice teaching," Emeline says. "I'll have to remember that when I feel like I'm surrounded by unholiness and try to transform bad into good."

Mrs. Troy is wringing her hands and pacing back and forth like a caged animal when they return. Her eyes light up at the sight of the overflowing bucket and the bulging bags. Carlos begins singing an Elvis song and dances out to the fire escape.

"We got some discarded beef at the kosher butcher since it was found to be unkosher," Allen beams. "There are also ten fish, a bunch of vegetables, and stale bread."

"Why are you soaking wet, Allen?" Lucine asks.

"I fell into the East River, wouldn't you know it."

"Boys, you're geniuses!" Mrs. Troy proclaims. "What a great idea to scavenge for discarded meat there!"

"Actually, it was Emeline's idea. She was also the one who pulled me outta the river."

"You didn't have to agree to her idea, since she's only a girl. My boys are geniuses. I'm so glad that, if I had to be cursed with so many girls in a row, at least I got two of my boys second and third. Imagine if you were Tommy's age. We'd all be sunk."

"Girls stink!" Tommy shouts.

"Ignore them," Allen whispers to Emeline. "You'll be outta here soon enough and won't have to deal with them anymore."

Adicia and Ernestine go into their tiny room and look at a book they got from the Tompkins Square Library last week, until their father comes home from the box-making factory and their mother calls everyone to dinner. Once again Mrs. Troy loudly praises Allen and Carlos for finding the beef, ignoring the fact that it was Emeline's idea and initiative. As the beef is passed her way after making its rounds about her parents, Tommy, and her six older siblings, Adicia wishes her mother had fallen into the East River, and wouldn't have been pulled out. Even if she leaves home early, Adicia feels like those years will last forever.

Chapter 3: Halloween 1959

"Look what I've got for you, Tommy!" Mrs. Troy dangles a sack in front of her pet child. "My friend Mrs. Rossi let me use her sewing machine so I could make you this darling little Halloween costume!"

"Did you make the rest of us Halloween costumes too?" Adicia asks eagerly, wondering if perhaps her mother is growing a heart.

"Of course not. I can't waste my hard-earned money on fabric and thread to make costumes for eight other children. I ain't one of them television mothers, June Cleaver or Donna Reed. You know very well I hate homemaking and don't coddle children besides Tommy."

Adicia's heart sinks. Her mother is as self-centered and mean as always.

"You watch television, Mother?" Ernestine asks. "Do you watch it at work?"

"Some of my co-workers and employers discuss their favorite programs. I know as much about the popular shows as if I watched them every week. Anyone who wants to can pitch in to get me and your father a television for Christmas so we don't have to learn about them from the weekly updates at work."

"Television costs a fortune!" Emeline says. "It's more than a few weekly paychecks for both of yous!"

Tommy rips open the sack. "I love you, Mommy! I'm going to be a red crayon and collect lots of candy!"

"Can we go trick-or-treating too if we get our own costumes?" Adicia begs.

"You mistakes can do whatever you want, but I'd just make you turn over all your candy to Tommy. You don't deserve candy and chocolate."

"What if Tommy gets so many cavities all his teeth fall out?" Emeline asks. "Can you afford the dental bills?"

"You think I care if all his teeth fall out? My golden boy prince has earned the right to eat a million pieces of candy in a row if he so wants. Most people have a lot of false teeth and fillings. Only uppity rich snobs waste money on a foolish luxury like going to a dentist every year. Ain't it enough you all have toothbrushes?"

"If my teeth fall out from eating lots of yummy candy, the Tooth

Fairy will visit me and put money under my pillow!" Tommy crows.

"The Tooth Fairy never visited me any of the times I lost my teeth," Adicia complains. "She's never visited anyone else either."

"The Tooth Fairy doesn't exist," Emeline says. "It's a feel-good myth parents tell their children, like Santa or the Easter Bunny, so they won't think their parents are the ones leaving money or presents. If any of those figures really existed, they'd visit all of us, not just Prince Tommy."

"Tommy, we're going to carve a spooky jack-o-lantern together," Mrs. Troy goes on, tuning out her daughters. "You'll have a cute little plastic jack-o-lantern to collect your candy, and I'll carry a big pillow-case to hold the surplus. We'll trick-or-treat all through the Lower East Side and try to get to at least one other neighborhood. How could anyone not want to give such a sweet little angel an extra share of candy?"

"I'll know if any of you dumb girls steals my candy!" Tommy warns his sisters.

Everyone in Adicia's school except a few odd people from extremely religious families celebrates Halloween. Allen, Carlos, and Gemma's high school and Lucine's junior high are having Halloween dances and parties, and Emeline, Ernestine, and Adicia's elementary school has announced costume contests in each classroom, class parties, and a big Halloween parade all around the school. Adicia and her sisters will look and feel like outcasts when they show up wearing their usual ragged hand-me-downs instead of Halloween costumes. Sarah would love to make them costumes, but there isn't enough money for fabric and thread, nor enough time to sew them by hand. The Troys don't own a sewing machine, so Mrs. Troy uses their neighbors' machines on the odd occasion she makes something like Tommy's Halloween costume or the baby animal-themed quilt she gave Tommy for his third birthday.

Most of their classmates will also be bringing in food for the parties, food made by their loving, attentive mothers. A lot of it will be Halloween-themed, like cupcakes outlined with little ghosts, cakes frosted with bats and spiders, and hollowed-out pumpkins filled with autumnal vegetable soup. Those mothers take pride in their cooking and homemaking. Mrs. Troy can't understand the idea of asking children to bring in food for parties, and says it's just a way for mothers to compete with one another in who makes the best baked goods. She wouldn't know what to do with a box of pre-made cake or brownie batter if it dropped into her lap along with the mixing bowl, baking pan, whisk, and wooden spoon.

"Do you think we'll get punished by our teachers when we show up tomorrow without costumes?" Adicia asks Ernestine on Thursday after dinner, when they're in their tiny bedroom.

"We live in a historically poor neighborhood," Emeline speaks up. "Our teachers will be idiots if they send us to the principal's office because we didn't wear costumes. My teacher never said it was a required assignment."

"Maybe we can take some of Gemma's makeup," Ernestine suggests. "She sometimes leaves her handbag lying around. We could take a little money from it and buy something."

"Gemma would notice we stole her makeup and her money."

"How can Mother call herself a real mother?" Adicia protests. "Real mothers love all their kids and do nice things for them. She only loves Tommy, and only likes Carlos and Allen 'cause they're boys and they help with money."

"Like Sarah says, giving birth to a child doesn't always make you a mother. And there are more ways to be a mother than having biological children. Some teachers and nuns have more kids than people who just happened to reproduce."

Out in the living room, Gemma is spinning around in her ballerina costume and whining about how it doesn't fit as well as it did when she bought it. Sarah has been pressed into commission letting out the waistline.

"I think someone had a few too many cream puffs on her last date," Carlos sneers. "Or you're overeating on your lunch break at your big fancy job."

Gemma steps into her room quickly to take it off and put her normal clothes back on. When she returns, she dumps the costume on Sarah's lap.

"I had a sundae on my last date with Johnny Jefferson, and he was nice enough to let me eat most of his too. We had steak for dinner and went out again for apple pie before he walked me home."

"Men don't like a woman who overeats," Mrs. Troy proclaims as she lights a cigarette. "Nobody loves a fat girl."

"It's called a healthy appetite, Mother, and why shouldn't I eat my fill when I have the chance? You'd prefer I keep to our pathetic roadkill and spoilt turnips diet even when I'm outta this place?"

"She's getting above her raising," Carlos says derisively. "Next thing you'll know, she'll be moving into a swank mansion on Long Island with a millionaire husband and putting her three kids in private schools."

"I'd love to move to Long Island or one of the nicer neighborhoods uptown, and I do intend to only have a few kids as opposed to a huge pile of brats. I bet your stupid self will be in jail or a sanitarium when I'm a proper society woman with a respectable husband. How many times have you gotten high or drunk this week, Carlos? At least my cigarettes aren't bad for my health or something only degenerates and delinquents use."

"We'll find you a husband as soon as we can," Mrs. Troy promises. "He won't be as bad-off as us, but he won't be a rich man neither. I hope you get all this teenage foolishness outta your system by the time you need to settle down and be a full-time wife and mother."

Gemma dismissively waves her hand at her mother. "I'm the Class of 1960, a woman of a new decade. Your worldview will be a relic before you know it. I'm gonna have fun, not saddle myself down to a guy you want me to marry when I'm not even old enough to vote yet."

"Do you think you expanded your waist for another reason besides overeating?" Allen asks.

Gemma turns bright red. "What kind of immoral, loose woman do you take me for? Maybe you and Carlos do those things with girls, but I value my reputation. God, I'd kill myself if I got in trouble."

"Sometimes I wanna kill myself just for living in this tenement. But unlike you, other people depend on me to help take care of them."

Carlos wanders over to the kitchen, where the drugs are kept. He wishes his sisters would all shut up about how the money they've poured into drugs could've been used to buy better food and clothes, or to get a nicer home. Carlos expects all of his younger sisters to take up drugs and alcohol, for the same reasons he, Allen, and their parents did. They weren't motivated by a love of breaking the law and putting potentially dangerous substances into their bodies so much as they wanted an easy, reliable escape from the hard life they were born into. It remains a surprise that Gemma's never touched drugs, and that Lucine hasn't expressed any interest either, despite being about the age he and Allen were when they started dabbling.

In the morning, Adicia, Emeline, and Ernestine head out to school, wearing their usual hand-me-down rags. Ernestine tried to wear her pajamas and pass that off as a costume, but Mrs. Troy wouldn't let her leave the apartment like that. Emeline thought of dressing like a boy, in pants and an old shirt belonging to her older brothers, but couldn't find a hat to tuck her hair up under. At least Lucine isn't expected to wear a costume to school, despite the class parties.

"What a surprise, the dirty Troy girls couldn't afford costumes," one of the Debbies in Emeline's class taunts when they get to the schoolyard.

"They did dress up, as their ragged selves," one of the Barbaras in Ernestine's class says.

"How often do you brush your hair?" Theresa Mladsky starts walking around them. "All three of you have hair full of rats' nests."

"Our nanny brushes our hair," Ernestine says. "It's harder to untangle when it's not brushed every day."

Adicia looks around with a mixture of jealousy and wonder. All the other children are in Halloween costumes—witches, wizards, cowboys, cowgirls, Indians, monsters, princesses, kings, queens, princes, ballerinas, Chinese girls, outlaws, circus animals, cereal boxes, scarecrows, Vampyres, and Frankenstein's monster. Their mothers probably spent a lot of time sewing their costumes, and making the special Halloween-themed baked goods they'll be eating at their class parties.

"I don't think girls without costumes should get any candy or food at our parties," Jody Krause says.

"And I don't think people who are so rude and mean to the faces of people who never did anything bad to them deserve to go through life with so many nice things," Emeline says. "Why are any of yous so mean to us? Are yous just offended we're different from you, and that difference makes yous uncomfortable? I was reading a book our nanny recommended, and it says when you hate someone, you hate something in that person that's part of yourself, since what isn't part of ourselves doesn't disturb us."

"Stupid bookworm," Jeanie Mraz says as she walks into the building.

"I bet you need glasses before we graduate sixth grade," one of the Lindas in Emeline's class says. "I'm shocked you don't need them yet from all that squinting at books you do. No boy wants to date a girl with glasses or who knows more than he does."

"Can I read that book after you're done with it?" Ernestine asks.

Emeline smiles down at her. "I don't know if it's at your reading level. It's a book from the adult section of the library. Sarah says the author won the Nobel Prize in Literature in 1946."

"I wish I read well enough to read grownup books."

"You can borrow some of my other library books. I'm working my way through the Five Little Peppers series and am on the second book. It's not the greatest writing, and it's really obvious it's from the Victorian era, but they're nice, classic children's books at heart."

The children start filtering into the school when the principal appears on the steps. The Troy girls join hands and slowly walk to the steps leading up to the girls' entrance. Emeline grumbles under her breath about how stupid it is that schools have different doors for boys and girls when it's practically 1960.

"We'll meet back on the playground for lunch," Emeline says. "I'm sure we'll have a nice Halloween celebration of some type with Sarah, Justine, and Lucine tomorrow, when we'll have the apartment to ourselves."

Adicia sits through the day miserably, watching the other kindergarteners walking about in their wonderful costumes and helping themselves to the cupcakes, cookies, cakes, tortes, pies, and other wonders whipped up by mothers who enjoy being mothers and treating their children in a special way. She and her sisters are in a very small group that has to stand off to the side when the costumed students put on their big parade around the entire school. The teachers could've had only students with the best costumes go on the parade, instead of making them feel even more shunned. Adicia can hardly stand the thought of sweet little Justine, almost eight months old, going through this same ordeal when she's in school.

Saturday is Halloween. The apartment is indeed emptied out for Adicia and her sisters, as Gemma is at her party, Carlos and Allen are out with some girls, Mrs. Troy is taking Tommy trick-or-treating, and Mr. Troy is picking up a few extra shifts at the factory. As depressing as their surroundings are, it's nice to have privacy for awhile.

"I'm going to make lovely Halloween costumes for my kids when

I'm a mother," Ernestine declares as they gather under the table, the lights dimmed, to tell spooky stories. "I'll have a nice, modern sewing machine instead of that ancient black thing Mother uses when she makes stuff for Tommy."

"I would've loved to be something historical," Emeline says. "A Pilgrim, a Colonial girl, a pioneer, a Medieval princess, something that lets me express my love of history."

"Did you celebrate Halloween in Germany, Sarah?" Adicia asks.

"Halloween is an American holiday. I never saw anybody celebrate it. All I know about it, I learnt since I came to this country."

"Halloween started in Ireland thousands of years ago," Emeline says. "It's only relatively recently gotten more and more popular in the West, mostly America and Canada. It's celebrated in a more traditional fashion in Spanish-speaking countries. If the high school taught Spanish, I'd be looking forward to learning about how it's celebrated in the various parts of Latin America."

"In any other family, you would've been enrolled in a special school for gifted youth or skipped a grade or two."

"My teachers always knew I'm advanced for my age and that I've read my way through almost all the books in all my classrooms' libraries and the main school library. It'll probably be awhile before I get through every book that interests me at the Tompkins Square Library and Hamilton Fish Park Library. That'll have to do for now."

"It's colder than usual," Adicia says. "Can someone put the stove on?"

The lights go out as Sarah gets up. Lucine picks up the flashlight and starts looking for matches and candles. The fuse box is in the basement and only supposed to be accessed by the landlord, who usually only has anything to do with his tenants when he's evicting them, demanding back rent, or shutting off utilities.

"Do you think our cheapskate parents didn't pay again, or is it just a blackout?" Lucine asks. "Usually they don't shut off utilities at the end of the month. It's usually a week or two after the first of the month."

"It's probably a blackout," Emeline says. "We can live without electricity for a little while. How do you think people functioned before gas and electricity?"

Ernestine goes to the fire escape door and looks outside. "The people across the street don't have any lights either. It must just be a local thing."

"Can you tell us a scary story, Sarah?" Adicia asks. "But don't make it too scary."

"Oh, you can't scare us that easily," Ernestine boasts. "We're not babies, and we live with scarier stuff than some ghosts and witches that don't exist."

Justine begins fussing on Sarah's lap. Lucine shines around the flashlight to locate the bag with diapers, diaper pins, bottles, Enfamil, and other baby supplies. Since Justine's birth in March, her own mother has never changed one diaper or administered one feeding. When Sarah came along in 1947, she handed off the care of her first four children, and has only been actively involved in mothering Tommy since. Mrs. Troy held Tommy nice and close while she fed him a bottle of Similac she heated up, lovingly burped him, bathed him, rocked him, changed him. All because he was a boy.

"I'll tell you a story from *Grimms' Fairytales*," Sarah says as she sits back under the table and guides the bottle into Justine's mouth. "Emeline is very familiar *mit* these stories, but I don't know if she's read all of them."

"It was the first book I ever read," Emeline says. "Our parents caught me reading it when I was three, and I got scared and pretended I was just looking at the pictures. I didn't get caught knowing how to read till I was four, but Sarah knew most of that time I could read."

"I wish I could've learnt to read all by myself that young," Lucine says. "I think you're some kind of savant for just waking up one day and starting to read from an adults' book, no previous reading lessons."

"Let me tell you the story of the boy who went to learn what fear was," Sarah begins. "Once upon a time, a *vater* had two sons. The younger son was asked by his *vater* what he'd like to learn to make a living, and said he wanted to learn how to shudder. A man at church said he could teach him. After he learnt how to ring the church bell, he was sent at midnight to ring the bell, and the church man appeared dressed as a ghost. The boy wanted to know what was going on, and when he didn't get an answer, he pushed the man down the stairs. His *vater* was very upset, and made him leave to learn how to shudder. All the time the boy complained he didn't know how to shudder. Then he was advised to spend a night under the gallows, where seven men were hanging...."

Adicia and Ernestine sit wide-eyed as Sarah tells the story of the little boy who was so arrogantly fearless he wasn't scared by things that would scare the pants off any other child, like seeing a ghost, spending three nights in a haunted castle, sleeping under a gallows with seven dead bodies dangling from nooses, being attacked by dogs and cats in the darkened castle, seeing half a man falling down a chimney, witnessing a game of bowling played with skulls and severed legs, and being attacked by a man who comes back to life in a coffin. The story is pretty scary, but they can't help but wonder if they'd react in a similar apathetic, annoyed fashion if they were dealt with some of these terrifying things. Sarah went through a lot of horrible, scary things too, and she's said she became numb to it all after awhile. It's only fitting the first book Emeline ever read contained this and other grim, disturbing stories. They all know better than to believe life is like a Disney fairytale. Where they're from, life is more like a Grimms' fairytale.

Chapter 4: Thanksgiving 1959

"Do you think the mission's Thanksgiving dinner will be as yummy as it was last year?" Adicia asks as she and her sisters change into their relatively nicest dresses.

Every year on Thanksgiving, Sarah takes Lucine, Emeline, Ernestine, and Adicia into The Bowery, one of the neighborhoods bordering the Lower East Side, and they eat a wonderful meal at an old mission bearing the same name as the neighborhood. Mr. and Mrs. Troy have no part of it, feeling that eating a decent meal on special occasions raises their expectations and makes them feel even worse when they have to go right back to eating roadkill, stale bread, and over-ripened tomatoes the very next day. Carlos typically shares their views, and spends holidays engaging in his usual delinquent behavior. Allen is staying home for a terribly lousy version of a Thanksgiving dinner.

"They've been feeding people and doing lots of other great stuff to help our kind for almost a hundred years," Emeline says. "Do you really think they'd let us starve?"

"Will they have baby food for Justine? She can't eat solid food yet."

"I'm sure they'll have special food for her, like mashed turkey and carrots. You don't need teeth to eat mashed potatoes and cranberry sauce," Lucine says.

Out in the living room, Gemma adjusts her new rabbit fur hat and puts on her knee-length dark red wool coat. She's been invited to spend Thanksgiving with her friend Shirley Hamilton, who lives with her parents and younger brother in a walk-up brownstone in the northern portion of the neighborhood. Most of the mean girls at the younger girls' schools live in that part of the Lower East Side, which has developed into more of an artistic, gentrified area in recent years. Adicia wishes they lived in the northern section, where some people have houses. It must be nice to live in a real house instead of a tenement. The Hamiltons probably have their own yard, a fireplace, a dog or cat, maybe both, carpeting, and a dining room. Gemma says respectable people eat in a dining room instead of in the kitchen.

"I got some turkey breast lunchmeat at the deli for seventy-five percent off since it was two days past the expiration date," Mrs. Troy says proudly. "Our darling baby Tommy will eat even better than us. I found some turkey meat at my job the other day. These rich people who eat at that hotel never ask for their leftovers to be wrapped up, so the wait staff throws the excess food in the garbage. People who throw food in the garbage are fools. I bet they'd have heart attacks if they knew poor people like us are getting free meals thanks to their pompous stupidity."

"How much turkey meat is there?" Allen asks excitedly. "I hope it can feed all of us!"

"You ain't getting none. That meat is for Tommy and Tommy only. You're only my third-born; Tommy is my precious baby boy and the first boy after four girls in a row."

"But what if there's leftovers? You really think a three-year-old kid can eat a full adult-size serving?"

"Tommy can get as chubby as he wants. It means my baby's staying warm with extra body fat even if we can't afford a rich boy's coat. Now shut up and start setting the table."

"I guess now ain't the right time to ask why you and Dad always seem to have enough money for drugs and alcohol but not enough money to buy decent groceries." Allen stalks over to the cupboard and pulls out four chipped white and orange plates from a tableware set his parents got as a wedding gift in 1941.

"You drink and use drugs too, Allen! You even sell them sometimes so we can get rent money!"

"At least I ain't higher than a kite as much as you and Carlos! I like the buzz as much as any of you, but we're still gonna lack decent food when the mood passes."

Sarah leads the girls out to the door and isn't a bit surprised when neither Mr. or Mrs. Troy turns around to bid them goodbye or acknowledge they're going out. As a thirty-two-year-old spinster, she feels like the true mother of five children. The girls' children will probably call her Grandma.

Lucine carries Justine as they go down the stairs. Ernestine almost falls down two steps and is caught by Emeline. They're joined on the stairs by some of the other residents going to the Bowery Mission for their Thanksgiving meal. Adicia takes a little heart from seeing these people joining them. They're poor and working-class too, yet they don't have a bad attitude towards accepting charity, and they seem happy in spite of not being rich. Adicia cannot understand the attitude her parents and Carlos have, that only snobs want to "get above their raising" by getting a good job, wanting a higher education, and moving to a better neighborhood.

Adicia knows the walk to The Bowery very well, though she usually only goes there on Thanksgiving, Christmas, and Easter. Ever since she can remember, Allen has made his sisters memorize the route, in case anything worse than usual happens at home and they need a safe place to run to. Sometimes when he's sober, Allen walks with them back and forth to make sure they know how to find their way there. He's taken them on this walk after dark a few times, so they recognize the way and the landmarks at night instead of only in the daytime. Adicia hopes she never has to go there by herself or run away in the middle of the night.

The scents of delicious food are overwhelming when they enter the dining hall. Adicia eagerly rushes over to a table with five available chairs and place settings, making sure it's near the end of the table so they have space for Justine's stroller.

"Do you mind that you never eat kosher meat, Sarah?" Emeline asks as they're being served.

"You eat what you can when you don't have money. Besides, I wasn't from a religious family. Most German Jews weren't religious. My family wasn't anti-religious, but we weren't Orthodox either."

"Judaism has different denominations like Christianity? I haven't read many books on world religions. I don't even know what denomination my family's supposed to be, just that we were baptized some type of Protestant."

"I don't know either," Lucine says. "Why did our parents bother having us baptized if we only go to church on major holidays?"

"There are four major branches of Judaism," Sarah says. "Then there are many different communities in the Orthodox world, and small branches like Karaites. We can look for a good book about it next time we go to the library."

Adicia practically inhales the feast set before her. Roast turkey, mashed potatoes, cranberry sauce, stuffing, yams, vegetables, pumpkin, pecan, and apple pie, applesauce, and piping-hot rolls. The volunteers and mission workers are very special for buying, preparing, and serving all this food to so many people, and then cleaning it all up. Her parents and brothers don't know what they're missing, though she does feel sorry for Allen. He probably would come to eat with them, but feels an illogical need to appease their parents and go along with their lifestyle. Emeline says Allen's a Gemini, the astrological sign of the twins, Pollux and Castor. One of the common characteristics associated with Gemini is acting like two different people, a pull in two different directions. Adicia doesn't understand some of these things Emeline knows so much about from all her prolific reading, but she does know she feels very sorry for Allen, stuck in the tenement with their horrible parents and the insufferable Tommy. Mrs. Troy didn't have to be so rude and mean to him just because he dared to ask for some turkey meat. Adicia hopes Tommy eats so much of that leftover turkey from the garbage that he chokes.

Sarah is holding Justine on her lap and feeding her a bottle of Enfamil when one of the mission volunteers brings more food. The volunteer squeezes Justine's little hand and smiles down at her. Justine's blue eyes light up at the extra attention.

"If you'd like, we can bring some baby food to your little girl. We have food even for the littlest guests who come to our tables. You don't want to only drink baby formula on a big holiday, do you, sweetie?"

Sarah doesn't correct her. As it is, the four middle girls are fellow brunettes, and she goes out with them more than their own parents.

"Our baby's named Justine Anastasie," Ernestine volunteers proudly. "Our dad's French, so we all got at least one French name. She's gonna be nine months old next week, since she was born on March second. March to December equals nine months."

"Are we having a nice party for Justine's first birthday?" Adicia asks as the volunteer fetches some baby food. "Even if she won't remember it, it'd be a special thing to do for her."

"Do any of us besides Gemma or Tommy ever have a real birthday party?" Lucine asks. "Where would we get the money for cake, presents, balloons, and party favors, and who would come over?"

"Justine could meet other babies if she went to daycare," Ernestine proposes. "If Sarah went to classes to get her high school diploma and then went to college, she could take Justine with her. Don't schools for grownups have to have daycares?"

"Would Tommy go with them?" Lucine asks in amusement. "And would our hateful mother approve of Sarah going back to school?"

"The bad guys in Germany didn't let her finish going to school.

Why should our mean mother not let her get a diploma? We won't need a nanny forever, and maybe she could go to college to be a teacher or something else where she gets paid real money to take care of kids. She can do that as a real job."

"You dream too much."

"It doesn't hurt to dream. Some dreams do come true."

The volunteer comes back with the baby food. "You can take any extra home."

"Can we get baby food for Justine when we come again on Christmas?" Adicia asks.

"You can get baby food whenever you come here. This place is open all the time for anyone who needs a meal, not just on holidays."

Adicia hates to leave the mission when dinner is over and people start clearing the tables. She knows they have beds, baths, and other things for people who need more than just a hot holiday meal a few times a year, and wishes her parents weren't so stupid and proud they shun all forms of charity. Emeline says the Bowery Mission offers help with education and job training too, which everyone in their family would easily qualify for. They could go to summer camp in the mountains or get money for a nice college, but because of their parents' warped attitudes, they have to suffer in silence.

"Do you think they'd pay us if we stayed and helped wash the dishes?" Lucine asks.

"I'm pretty sure most of these people aren't getting paid for their efforts," Emeline says. "Unlike Gemma, I don't think we'd be allowed to keep our own money. Allen and Carlos always turn whatever money they make over to our parents. But you can ask if you wanna."

"I think they like me more than the rest of you. They weren't totally beaten down by too many kids when I was born, and I don't need to tell them I made some extra money." Lucine walks off towards the kitchen.

Sarah and the other girls wait off to the side near the door. Five minutes later, Lucine reappears, looking somewhat dejected.

"They said they wouldn't think of letting their needy guests do any dishwashing, but they did give me five dollars and said we can use it to have a happy Thanksgiving."

"Five whole dollars?" Ernestine asks excitedly. "That's even better than doing some boring dishwashing for a few hours!"

"We could buy a doll with that!" Adicia says hopefully.

"We're not buying a doll," Lucine says. "We're using this to buy something we need, like food or mittens."

"Can I go to the kitchen and ask what you just did?" Ernestine asks. "Some kids make money by begging or washing car windows. I hope they're not too suspicious if I do it right after you."

"You're not doing that. Of course they'd be suspicious, and think we might be running some kind of begging scam. You look so much like me, they'd probably guess we're sisters. You can beg on your own time."

"Will I ever get a doll?" Adicia asks sadly as they begin walking home. "I know Santa doesn't exist, so I won't get one for Christmas like all the other girls in my class."

"Maybe someday," Lucine says half-heartedly. "But in the meantime, Justine is our sweet real-life baby doll, and you're our precious real-life ragdoll."

"And unlike those snobby mean girls at school, we won't get tired of our sweet real-life dolls and demand new ones in six months or a year," Emeline says. "Remember that book I read you this summer, *The Velveteen Rabbit*? The stuffed rabbit was so loved by the Boy in spite of how he wasn't as fancy as the other toys, and he told his nurse the rabbit was Real and not a toy. When the Boy got sick with scarlet fever and the doctor told his parents to burn all the toys and give him a new velveteen rabbit, the rabbit became a real rabbit hopping in the field with the other rabbits. The Boy's love made him more than just another toy. The moral of that story is someone or something that's been made fun of or dismissed because of a shabby appearance can be appreciated and given a whole new life because of the power of someone's pure, selfless, undiscriminating love."

"You really think someone will see past my ragged hand-me-downs and wanna be my friend or, when I'm big, my husband?" Adicia asks.

"You'll know anyone who does really loves you for you. Someday we'll all have friends who accept us just as we are and won't care about our impoverished origins."

Chapter 5: Christmas 1959

All the girls and boys at school who celebrate Christmas have been talking for weeks about what their families are going to do and what presents they want. Every time Adicia walks through the streets, she sees houses, businesses, and apartments all lit up and decorated, eye-catching holiday displays in store windows, and Christmas trees in stores and house windows. There's a very big Christmas tree at the center of the city, in Rockefeller Center, where she and her sisters like to go on weekends when they feel up to taking a bit of a walk. It's a bit over three miles away, so they have to allow enough time to get there and back, and then the time they like to spend walking around. Every time they go on one of their longer weekend walks, Adicia can hardly believe Midtown is part of the same city as her out-of-date tenement. She loves the sights of Rockefeller Center, Times Square, Broadway, the Chrysler Building, and the Empire State Building. Her eyes almost fall out of her head every time they stroll down Fifth Avenue and see all the expensive stores, fancy mansions, and luxury apartments.

But Adicia knows she won't have a lavish Christmas dinner and that she'll be eating her holiday meal at the Bowery Mission again. There will be no beautifully-decorated Christmas tree with piles of colorful presents underneath on Christmas morning, no stockings stuffed with oranges, chocolates, and marbles hanging on the mantel above a fireplace that doesn't exist, no visits to a department store Santa to tell him what they want, no milk and cookies left out for Santa to eat. Gemma will celebrate with friends, and Tommy will certainly get at least one present, but for the rest of them, there will be no real Christmas.

Though the Troys are generally twice-a-year churchgoers, Mr. and Mrs. Troy are very strict about their offspring being home by 6:00 so they can get ready to go to church and be there on time for the Christmas Eve service. The Troys never go to the same church twice, which adds to their children's confusion about what religion they're supposed to be. The older children wonder if they were all baptized in the same denomination, the way their parents hop from church to church.

"Why can't we have real winter clothes like Gemma?" Adicia

complains as they suit up to walk to Midtown after breakfast. "I'd like a nice warm rabbit fur hat too, and a pretty fur muff instead of these raggy mittens."

"We could've had those things passed down to us if they were properly taken care of," Lucine says bitterly. "Princess Gemma thinks only of herself, and not the fact that her clothes are gonna be passed down to five girls after her. You're supposed to store fur in a certain way and have it specially cleaned if you want it to last a long time, like regularly cleaning diamonds. Not that any of us will ever wear really expensive furs. Rabbit fur's probably as upscale as we're ever gonna get."

"How much does something like mink or silver fox cost?" Ernestine asks.

"About three hundred dollars. I wouldn't want one myself. It's gross how some furs have actual animal faces and paws. I'd wanna throw up if I had to wear something with part of a dead animal attached to it."

"It's not fair," Adicia repeats. "Can't our parents ever buy us our own clothes?"

"They don't even wanna save money by making clothes. Only Prince Tommy gets that luxury. I hope that little brat is beaten up when he starts school."

Carlos is strutting around in the living room, wearing the closest thing he has to formal clothes. The suit jacket is bone-thin, the tie is a bit too small, and there are a few holes worn in the pants, but in his mind, it's a formal suit that makes him look dashing. Every so often, he drinks from a bottle of whiskey.

"Is it okay if Allen and I have girls over here while the rest of you people are out doing your thing before church?"

"So long as you don't contaminate my bed with those girls while I'm at work," Gemma says in revulsion. "Say what you want about me, but I've never sullied my reputation by doing things with a boy outside of marriage. How often do you go to the doctor to get checked for venereal diseases? I also wonder if either of you has ever gotten a girl in trouble."

"Allen and I have our own bed. As for going to a doctor, I could care less if I have a hundred diseases or got a hundred girls in trouble."

"How are you gonna get girls in trouble?" Tommy asks.

"Nothing you need to know about at your age," Mrs. Troy says. "Your brothers are big boys and do big boy things with their girlfriends. When you're a big boy and start having girlfriends too, you'll understand."

"I'd care if I got a girl in trouble," Allen says. "Though I hope that never happens until I find someone who's marriage material, not just someone to have fun with for a little while."

"Then why do you do those things with girls you don't wanna be with in the long run?" Gemma asks. "All the guys I've dated were good to go on dates and have some fun with, but not the types of guys I'd wanna be bonded to forever because of some stupid mistake."

"I'd give her money to take care of the mistake," Carlos says, uncaring his three-year-old brother can hear everything he's saying. "Who wants to get married and ruin his life?"

Tommy and their parents are going to spend the afternoon at the movies and have an early supper at a deli. The girls take cold comfort in the fact that their father isn't spending his Christmas bonus on drugs and alcohol. His boss probably good-heartedly assumed he'd use the extra money to buy nice presents for his nine children, take everyone to supper at a fancy restaurant, or fix up his apartment, not have it stolen by his wife to spoil her already-spoilt-rotten youngest son. Mrs. Troy frequently takes Mr. Troy's money to buy things for Tommy. Some of that money was used to buy Tommy an extra present as well. It's a complete mockery of Christmas for only the favorite child to get presents.

Dressed in worn-out mittens, coats that don't do much to keep the chill out, worn hats, and boots in need of repair, Sarah and the girls start the walk up to Midtown. Emeline pushes Justine's stroller. Justine, wrapped up in blankets and a baby-sized coat Lucine bought with the five dollars she got at Thanksgiving, is the warmest one in their party. Adicia wonders if her baby sister understands what filth and degradation they're surrounded by, or if she doesn't think to question her surroundings because she's taken care of so well by Sarah and the girls. Right now she's babbling away in her babytalk, for all the world a happy baby.

Adicia loves looking into the store windows. Christmas must be a fun, happy holiday to those who celebrate it properly, judging from the wreaths, boughs of holly, mistletoe, lavishly-decorated trees, happy red stockings, bright lights, and large plastic statues of Santa, reindeer, elves, and snowmen. All the toys look so enticing too. If Adicia were a rich girl and believed in Santa, she'd write him a letter asking for every toy. Emeline is more intoxicated with the books, while Lucine admires clothes and jewelry. Ernestine's favorites are the mechanical toys and building sets.

"I'd love to be dressed in soft cashmere," Lucine says dreamily, gazing at a mannequin wearing a two-piece pink cashmere suit, a rose-shaped brooch, and black patent-leather high heels. "I'd take such good care of it, dry-clean it regularly, and put moth balls in the wardrobe. I'd take good care of the shoes too, polish them, and store them in their original box when I wasn't wearing them. If a strap broke, I'd repair it instead of throwing the shoes away for a new pair."

"That's a pretty pin," Ernestine marvels. "If I had a million dollars, I'd buy a different pin for every day of the week. I'd get ones shaped like a heart, a dog, a cat, a frog, a star, a flower, and a moon."

"I wish we could go into one of these stores so we could gaze at the jewelry, but the manager would probably think we were thieves, and would easily tell we have no money to buy anything."

Ernestine's face lights up when they pass a toy store on Fifth Avenue, with a large, ornate electric train running around a big Christmas tree. Real smoke is coming out of the stack. Around the train is a beautiful miniature village set, with figures caroling, ice-skating, sitting on park benches, and walking their dogs. Each figure has had a lot of attention paid to its face, body, and wardrobe.

"If we had a Christmas tree, we could buy that train and little village! We'd have so much fun putting it together! I'd be even more excited to see a real train. It'd be so fun to spend an entire day riding a real train all around the Five Boroughs, looking out the windows at the scenery, and soaking in the nice feeling of being a real passenger on a train."

Emeline wheels the stroller a little farther and gazes into the windows of a large bookstore. "How lovely it'd be to have a real house and my own huge room for a library. I'd fill it from floor to ceiling with nothing but books, old magazines, and newspapers in protective wrappings. I wish we were able to own books besides our schoolbooks. There are so many nice books I'd love to reread whenever I wanted to. Our parents would probably use them for firewood when our heating gets shut off, or sell them for drugs."

"Is it okay to not like a book character you think the author wanted you to like?" Ernestine asks, looking at a display of children's books she wishes she could find under the tree tomorrow morning.

"Who are you talking about?" Emeline asks.

"Phronsie Pepper. She's a little spoilt brat like Tommy, only she doesn't lord her favored status over everyone else. When her family celebrated their first real Christmas, that little brat got the best presents of all. Adicia and I would love a beautiful doll like Phronsie got. What kind of dumb name is Phronsie anyway?"

"It's short for Sophronia. I'm not a big fan of nicknames myself. She isn't so bad as the series goes on. She gets a bit more mature, self-aware, and likable as she gets older, in spite of everyone around her treating her like a helpless infant and overgrown baby her entire life."

"She went wandering off three times in the first book and almost got killed by horses one of those times, and no one punished her or yelled at her! I know we love Justine a lot too because she's our baby, but I'd be embarrassed if we always treated her like a helpless baby who can do no wrong and rushing to apologize if anyone dared get her a little bit upset or accidentally did something that hurt her. I liked Joel and Dick best."

"Our parents would care less if one of us wandered off or was almost killed," Adicia agrees. "They'd be happy if one of us got lost."

"What book are you on in that series? I only read the first book so far. Everyone is always shouting, screaming, crying, or getting too excited over nothing."

"So far I've read *Five Little Peppers and How They Grew*, *Five Little Peppers Midway*, *Five Little Peppers Abroad*, *Five Little Peppers at School*, and *Five Little Peppers and Their Friends*. I'm also currently reading *Five Little Peppers Grown Up*. I have six books left to go, though I was told most of the rest of 'em aren't sequential and were just written to give readers new stories about the Peppers. If you decide to read more books in the series, prepare to be annoyed at how much they oversentimentalize their 'little brown house days.' Me, I won't glorify and sugarcoat our current lives a bit after I'm a grownup and have a nice job and live in a nicer place. It's like they conveniently forgot how horrible it was to be that dirt-poor."

"They really wanna relive being poor?" Ernestine asks in shock.

"They even take vacations back to that stupid 'little brown house' of theirs, and eventually rent it out to people, I'm told. The more books I read in the series, the more I dislike Polly and Jasper and the more I like Phronsie. She grows up more, and they act like stupid children. Kids back then grew up faster and were miniature grownups by their teens. Polly was a lot more mature in the first book, which starts when she's only ten, than she is in the book I'm reading now, when she's twenty."

"I feel like a junior grownup myself," Lucine says. "Our crummy parents did everything they could to cheat us outta a childhood, and now I'm being cheated outta my teenage years. I read a few of those books when I was younger, and they annoyed me too. If I came into money and found out we had a wealthy long-lost relative who just happened to be the son-in-law of our unlikely benefactor, you can bet I wouldn't wax on and on about how great it was to be poor and take vacations to our tenement like it was a hotel."

Adicia walks over to the next store window and presses her nose against the chilly glass. There are beautiful porcelain and china dolls on display, with velvet robes, silk dresses, patent-leather shoes, blonde, brown, and red ringlets, fur muffs, rosy pink cheeks, curly eyelashes, and stylish hats. They're so much more beautiful and detailed than the new Barbie dolls, which many of the girls in kindergarten have been clamoring for. Adicia doesn't think she'd have much fun with a plastic doll that isn't big enough to hug, cuddle, or sleep with, and outfits that are so small in comparison to the pretty clothes on the larger dolls. Even a larger plastic doll would be fun to play with, though Adicia would be very careful if she got one of these beautiful china or porcelain dolls. She'd never drop or break it. Besides, she doesn't like the name Barbie, since it's a nickname for Barbara, and there are too many Barbaras at school to keep track of. Adicia loves seeing pretty, less-common doll names, like Juliet, Annabelle, Amandine, Dorothea, and Cordelia. She likes how she and her sisters don't share their names with any of the other girls at school. Even their middle names are special and unique. Emeline has told her most girls get thoughtless, default middle names like Anne, Marie, Elizabeth, Jean, and May. Even if they're poor, no one could ever forget someone with a name like Ernestine Zénobie, Justine Anastasie, or Adicia Éloïse.

"I'd like a hula-hoop," Ernestine says from a store window a few doors down. "All the other girls in second grade have them, and they always have contests during recess to see who can keep spinning longest."

Adicia skips over to another store window. "Oh, I'd love to have one of those toy horses! When I'm a mother, I'm gonna buy my kids a beautiful rocking horse that looks as nice and fancy as the horses on a merry-go-round."

"I'd love to have some of those boardgames," Lucine says. "We could have fun playing them on weekends."

"Tommy would probably demand to play them too, and Mother would let him cheat," Emeline says.

"Can we go in a department store before we look at the tree?" Ernestine asks. "I'm cold."

"As long as it's not Macy's. Gemma pretended to not know us the last time we went there, and I know she's arrived at work by now."

"We'll blend in even if she does see us," Lucine asserts. "She probably won't notice us in the crowd. A lot of people wait till Christmas Eve to buy presents."

They head towards Macy's, where Gemma has been working as a salesgirl in the perfume department for the past year. Gemma works every day after school and on weekends, taking the subway instead of walking. She loves making her own money, and fully expects to continue working after she marries. She'd be bored stiff if she were home all day changing diapers, preparing formulas, washing and ironing clothes, and preparing meals. She works not only because she has to, but also because she enjoys it.

"See, lots of people are here," Lucine says when they enter. "They won't even notice some ragamuffins in the crowds. They're probably mostly thinking about getting those last few presents before the clock runs out."

Macy's contains a world of possibilities. They marvel, wide-eyed, at the things the other half can buy. Beautiful china and porcelain tea sets and tableware, with flowers, roosters, exotic birds, moons, suns, and stars, kaleidoscopic geometric patterns, and festive Christmas designs. Iron, copper, steel, enamel, and aluminum pots, pans, skillets, frying pans, French onion soup pots, saucepans, soup pots, strainers, sieves, colanders, teakettles, cake pans, pie pans, cake molds, cookie cutters, mashers, meat grinders, roasters, toasters, skimmers, ladles, casserole bowls, and muffin tins. Shimmering crystalware and shiny silverware. Regal four-poster canopy king-sized feather beds with silk sheets, comforters, and pillows stuffed with goose down. Televisions, radios, record players, washing machines, refrigerators, color cameras, stoves, sewing machines, hair dryers, electric shavers, irons and ironing boards, vacuums, dryers, and clocks. Dazzling displays of jewelry and watches. Elegant clothes featured in fashion magazines. Colorful makeup and aromatic perfumes, with Gemma thankfully nowhere in sight. Soft, fluffy towels and washcloths. Curtains made of beautiful fabrics. And, best of all, the most amazing toys.

"We should find a bathroom before we see the tree," Lucine says. "Justine might need a diaper change and another bottle."

"I heard Johnson and Johnson make diapers you can throw away after one use," Emeline says. "Wouldn't that be nice if we could afford those instead of washing diapers by hand and carrying around the soiled ones in a plastic bag?"

"I don't think management would be happy if they caught us washing a dirty diaper in a bathroom sink," Ernestine says. "Though they might let us mix a bottle in there."

"They probably have a changing room," Lucine says. "That's different from a regular bathroom."

"They'd better have a changing room," Emeline says. "I'm sure the flagship Macy's of all places has at least one changing room. We're not in some backwoods town in Iowa or Idaho. Surely the management and store designers realize not all women stay home all day with their babies."

Ernestine boldly goes over to a nearby woman with three children and a baby to ask if she knows where the nearest changing room is. The woman looks over at Sarah and the other girls, smiles, and gives Ernestine the directions. The other girls often marvel at how bold and outgoing Ernestine is, how she can have such ambition at such a young age, in such a downcast environment. The best reason Emeline can come up with is that Ernestine's astrological sign is Aries, whose defining characteristics include being optimistic, outgoing, friendly, fearless, and impulsive.

Sarah is used to being mistaken for the girls' mother, and lets the strange woman believe she's out on some last-minute Christmas Eve shopping with her five daughters. She doesn't care the woman probably assumes she celebrates Christmas. After Ernestine repeats the directions, they head off towards the changing room to fix Justine's bottle and change her diaper.

"Aren't these things a pain to change in public?" another woman asks. "Some of my friends have a diaper-cleaning service that takes away the dirty diapers and delivers new ones. My aunt used one during the war, when she had to work and couldn't be at home all day taking care of her children."

"I heard Johnson and Johnson make diapers you throw away after one use," Emeline says. "I hope more companies have them and they're more popular when I have kids someday."

"Only girls?" a second mother asks. "No boy yet to carry on the family name?"

"We have three brothers and another sister," Ernestine supplies. "Our oldest sister works in the perfume department as a salesgirl. She's graduating high school in June."

Sarah gives thanks she looks older than only thirty-two, after all the hard living she's been through. She'd be mortified if any of these respectable women thought she were a disreputable woman who started having children as a mere teenager.

"Let me fix the bottle," Adicia pleads. "I watch you doing it all the time and know how much water and formula to put in."

Sarah hands her an empty bottle, a measuring cup, and the Enfamil, and Adicia scampers off to a sink to pour in the water and measure the powdered formula.

"The older ones were fed *mit* Similac. The baby gets the newest formula. Only the best for our baby, right, Justine?"

"Where are you from?" one of the women asks. "My husband was an immigrant too, and hasn't lost his accent after over fifteen years."

"Germany." Sarah refuses to lie and pass her accent off as Swiss, which Lucine has counseled her to do a few times.

"She's not one of the bad Germans we fought the war against," Emeline says. "She came here to escape from the bad guys."

"Oh, my brother-in-law immigrated from Germany too," another woman jumps in. "He gets some dirty looks and negative comments, as though some people think anyone with a German accent was automatically a Nazi, and like there weren't a lot of German immigrants before the war started."

Adicia comes back with the bottle and gently guides it into Justine's small mouth. Justine is used to getting room temperature bottles, and reaches out her hands to hold her bottle. Adicia is glad Justine's too young to understand what Christmas is all about or to feel cheated when there are no presents under a tree and there's no special Christmas breakfast waiting for them, like apple cinnamon French toast with apple pie on the side, Belgian waffles with fresh fruit, whipped cream, and maple syrup, or chocolate chip pancakes with sunny-side-up eggs, bacon, and fresh oranges, with freshly-squeezed orange juice, hot apple cider with cinnamon sticks, or warm eggnog.

On their way out, they pass the Macy's Santa. Without having to be told anything, none of the Troy children ever believed in Santa. It doesn't take a genius to figure out, even at three years old, that Santa would come to every home that celebrates Christmas and deliver presents for all children who've been good, instead of skipping the poor families, or only providing presents for one child. Santa is supposed to be a loving, kindly, jovial grandfather figure, not a black-hearted, mean-spirited miser who only rewards select children with presents. At least, Santa is supposed to be a grandfatherly figure. Adicia's grandfathers, Pierre Troy and Norman Goossens, are as bad as her parents and Carlos, but she knows real grandfathers are supposed to be very special people.

"Would you like to come sit on my lap and tell me what you want for Christmas?" the Santa calls.

"With all due respect, Sir, we don't believe in Santa," Emeline says. "I know the real meaning of Santa Claus is supposed to be a good feeling in doing good things for others this time of year, but we don't get any holiday spirit at our home."

"If Santa was real, he'd bring all of us presents, not just our bratty little brother and spoilt oldest sister!" Ernestine agrees.

"We've never gotten any Christmas presents," Lucine says.

"I'm not their *mutter*. I'm their nanny," Sarah jumps in. "If I were their *mutter*, I'd give them *wunderbar* Christmas presents."

"No Christmas presents ever?" the Santa asks in disbelief.

"Santa doesn't come to our tenement on the Lower East Side, where everyone's poor or lower working-class," Lucine repeats. "Maybe our spoilt three-year-old brother Tommy believes in Santa since our mother buys him gifts, but none of the rest of us ever believed."

"Even when we have nicer lives when we're grownups, we still won't tell our kids there's a Santa," Ernestine goes on. "It's not nice to lie to kids."

"I'd feel like a big hypocrite if I let my kids believe in something I was never led to believe in, though I do intend to give any future kids as nice of a Christmas as I can."

The Santa looks at them sadly as they continue making their way out of Macy's.

After another small walk, they reach Rockefeller Center and see the large tree all lit up. Adicia and Ernestine feel dwarfed by its huge size, and wonder how many people it took to cut it down, transport it, and string it all up with lights and the star on top. After gazing at the tree for awhile, they walk around the plaza to look at Radio City Music Hall, the RCA Building, and the Roxy Theatre before turning around to walk back downtown. Adicia hopes her little legs are able to keep pace and make it home by 6:00 so her mother won't get mad at them.

When they get home, Mr. and Mrs. Troy are smoking cigarettes while Tommy scribbles in a coloring book they just bought him. Magic Markers of various colors are rolling, uncapped, all over the filthy floor.

"Hey, no fair. None of us ever got a coloring book and markers," Ernestine protests.

"And I'm getting more presents tomorrow!" Tommy shouts happily.

"My girl tonight was a real wet blanket," Carlos grouses. "I thought she was a real woman, not a scaredy-cat. Allen took her side and pulled me away from her."

Allen glares at his older brother. "Clearly you misunderstood what type of girl she was when you asked her out and invited her here. Maybe you were too drunk or drugged up to realize she was a nice girl."

"What do you mean, what type of girl?" Adicia asks.

"I don't go out with girls who don't put out," Carlos rambles on, uncomprehending his younger sisters don't understand what he's talking about. "Allen ruined my fun by coming to this future old maid's defense and wrestling me away from her before I could do what I wanted. Meanwhile he got to do his thing with his girl!"

"Unlike you, I've never tried to do that with a girl who didn't want to!"

"Everyone gets to take a five-minute bath, and we have to reuse the water," Mrs. Troy starts directing. "Tommy gets the first of the hot water, and then your father and I will go. Gemma is next, then the boys, and then the rest of the girls go by twos."

"But we won't have any hot water left by that time," Adicia says.

"Like I care. Sarah, start drawing water and heating it up. I'll get Tommy undressed while we're waiting."

"Can I use my bath toys?" Tommy begs.

"We could use those stupid bath toys to get money for drugs," Carlos whines. "None of us ever had bath toys!"

"Tommy does. When will you realize he's the favorite child and you didn't do anything to earn being spoilt?"

The water is freezing and filthy by the time Adicia and Ernestine get in the tub thirty-five minutes later. Neither of them feels very clean when they get out of the bath, and they feel even dirtier when they attempt to dry themselves off with the bone-thin towel that's been used by everyone else. At least Justine gets to have a bath in the kitchen sink instead of waiting around for everyone else to finish and getting the worst of the water supply.

This year Mr. and Mrs. Troy have decided to go to a Lutheran church. Last year they dropped into a Methodist church, and the year before that, the first year Adicia can remember, they went to a Presbyterian church. As usual, they sit in the back row and tell anyone who asks if they're new or visiting that they're trying out various churches until they find a spiritual home. Adicia knows that's a lie. Her parents don't have a Bible or any type of other religious book, never talk about anything related to religion, have no religious decorations or crosses hanging up, never say Grace before meals or make their children pray before bed, and laugh at the idea of sending their children to Sunday school.

Some of the other children sitting near them start laughing about how Adicia and her sisters smell bad. Ernestine wishes she could stand up on the pew and scream at them that they'd smell bad too if they'd just taken a bath in freezing, dirty bathwater and been made to dry themselves with a towel eight other people had just used, but she knows it's very wrong to raise one's voice or act up in church. Instead they all keep staring ahead at the pretty Christmas tree on the pulpit and the verdant wreaths hanging all around, festooned with bright red velvet bows and boughs of holly.

Other children go to bed expectantly on Christmas Eve and put out milk and cookies for Santa. The Troy girls have no illusions about what's going to happen in the morning, and go to bed wearing their ragged pajamas, on their shabby mattresses that don't have pillows or sheets. Except for the mattress Lucine shares with Gemma, that is. They get a real bed, though Gemma chafes at sharing her bed, or bedroom period, with anyone. That bed has a full set of real sheets and pillows, a box spring, and a wooden bedframe. Emeline is looking forward to Gemma leaving home so she can be moved into that bedroom and sleep on a real bed, even if she'll have to share with Lucine. At least then she won't have to go through the indignity of sleeping two to a twin mattress. One faces the foot of the mattress, and the other faces the head. None of them enjoys having feet near her face all night long. Cold comfort is that Sarah has told them that when she was a prisoner of the Nazis, she had to sleep ten to a wooden plank. It could always be worse, and they could be forced to sleep on the floor.

Morning dawns and there's no Christmas miracle. Breakfast is the usual lumpy gray porridge and dirty tap water, served in the usual beat-up bowls and cups considered part of a nice tableware set back in 1941, when Mr. and Mrs. Troy got them as a wedding present. Tommy has a stocking stuffed with oranges, chocolates, candies, firecrackers, crayons, and several presents in fancy wrapping paper. His sisters are sickened to see him unwrapping a football, a set of Lincoln Logs, and a couple of Matchbox cars. Then Mrs. Troy wheels out a bright red tricycle and Tommy goes nuts with excitement.

"Are you crazy?" Allen demands. "The money you spent on this little brat's presents coulda been used to pay our utilities or buy better food! What does a three-year-old need with a football or Lincoln Logs?"

"I have a tricycle and you stupid girls don't," Tommy taunts his sisters.

Allen pulls out a cigarette and his lighter, then stalks out into the hallway. Carlos quickly joins him, carrying a bottle of vodka and a bag of drugs. He's already forgiven his brother for coming to his date's rescue last night. Gemma is next to leave, heading off to her friends in the nice northern part of the neighborhood.

Adicia and her sisters spend the afternoon reading books before scrubbing up and heading to the Bowery Mission for a nice dinner. That meal is the one thing she looks forward to every Christmas. This year they're served mouth-watering roasted vegetables, ham, bread rolls, chicken, yams, applesauce, stuffing, and mashed potatoes. For dessert they're served pumpkin and apple pie, fruitcake, sugar cookies, and a pretty cake that looks like a log, which Emeline says is called *bûche de Noël*. Though she doesn't celebrate Christmas, Sarah has come along for the decent meal, skipping the ham.

Adicia is cheered up when Sarah says Chanukah begins tonight, and they can light the chanukiyah with her for the next eight nights. When they get home, they gather in the tiny bedroom and light the first candle. While watching the candlelight dancing, Adicia crawls onto Sarah's lap and falls asleep, dreaming of a miracle in the darkness being performed for her and her sisters the same way the Maccabees witnessed the miracle of the oil lasting for eight days instead of only one.

Chapter 6: A New Decade Still in Poverty

Mrs. Troy and Carlos come rushing into the tenement on New Year's Day, carrying a bunch of crates making a lot of noise. Adicia looks up from a game of marbles with Ernestine and Emeline, wondering what in the world they've brought home with them.

"Carlos and I were looking for roadkill for a nice New Year's meal tonight, and found something even better!" Mrs. Troy says breathlessly. "A poultry truck heading to the slaughterhouse had just driven by, and these crates fell off. Now we have chickens for meat and eggs!"

"Are you crazy?" Mr. Troy asks. "Where are we gonna get the money to pay for chicken feed or a coop?"

"They'll eat what we eat, and they don't need a coop. They'll wander around like a dog or cat. Mrs. Nankin on the second floor told me her grandmother used to raise geese and chickens in this very neighborhood, and a lot of her grandmother's friends and neighbors also raised poultry in the tenements."

Mr. Troy spits on the floor. "I'll never be able to sleep with those damned things clucking and screaming all night long! I bet they'll get feathers all over everything, even our food, and answer the call of Nature whenever and wherever they feel like it!"

"Free eggs and chicken meat, Antoine! You don't need a rooster to get chickens to lay eggs, and once the chicks grow big enough, we'll kill 'em for meat! Just think of how delicious it'll be to have toast, vegetables, and soup made with chicken broth or fat! My grandparents swore by goose fat, and my parents raised me on chicken fat whenever they could find some. I won't hafta embarrass myself at the butcher's no more, begging for the worst cuts or getting mostly bones and fat."

"They'll peck me to death in my sleep! And you don't know if those birds have diseases!"

"Can we get a goat or cow too?" Tommy begs. "I want ice-cream, pudding, cheese, and milk too!"

"Goats and cows don't just fall off the back of trucks," Allen says.

"Even if they did, they wouldn't be welcome in this home!" Mr. Troy goes on. "A cow would break the floor and smash up everything in sight!"

"I had a girl once who spent summers on a farm with her aunt and uncle. The cows and goats had to get pregnant about once a year to produce enough milk for people. Good luck finding a bull to sneak in here to do its thing with your cow."

Mrs. Troy ignores her husband and second-born son and starts rummaging around under the sink to find a crowbar to pry open the crates. She and Carlos go around freeing the chickens, who promptly start fluttering around their strange new surroundings. Tommy rushes to pick up the feathers and throws them at the chickens.

"Are we gonna have eggs for breakfast every day?" Adicia asks.

"You get what's left after Tommy, your other brothers, your father and I, and Gemma have eaten them. It's pathetic how you keep forgetting how low on the totem pole you are in this family."

"Girls are stupid." Tommy sticks his tongue out at his sisters.

Adicia had been looking forward to the new year starting, since her kindergarten teacher had explained several times to the class how they'd be witnessing, for the first time in their young lives, not only the beginning of a new year but also of a new decade. Some of the children had had a hard time understanding there'd never be another year called 1959 again, and they'd have to wait another century to see another decade called the Fifties. Adicia was worried about accidentally writing the wrong date on her schoolwork after the switch, but the teacher told the class a five can be turned into a six very easily, a lot more easily than when other decades end and new ones begin.

Gemma went to Times Square with her well-bred friends to watch the big aluminum ball drop at the stroke of midnight, then went to the penthouse suite of one of her work friends for a party with champagne, hors d'oeuvres, chocolates, a crackling fire in the fireplace, and dancing to records. The rest of the family spent the dawn of the new decade doing exactly what they've always done. Adicia wishes she didn't have a reason to believe the Sixties will be just as crummy as the Fifties.

"Do you think I'm gonna get in trouble with my teachers when I go back to school?" Ernestine asks. "We hafta do an English assignment on what we got for Christmas or Chanukah, and I have nothing to write."

"A good teacher should give alternate assignments, like if you don't wanna dissect animals," Emeline says.

"I already got in trouble with her once. I dared to challenge her on something she marked wrong on a test about titles. I don't care I had to wash chalkboards because I refused to write something stupid a hundred times."

"You got away with sassing a teacher?" Lucine asks. "Some of my grade school teachers hit kids."

"She marked me wrong because I didn't identify the married women as Mrs. Husband's Name. Mother never calls herself Mrs. Antoine Troy! It's always Mrs. Troy or Dolores Troy. Why should her own name be erased?"

"I'd want my name to be erased if I were named Dolores," Emeline says. "It means 'sorrows' or 'pains' in Spanish. I don't know why it was so popular when Mother was born."

"I told my teacher my name will always be Ernestine, even if I get married. She said no decent boy would ever wanna marry me if I don't want the gift of his name, and I said maybe I'd have to marry another girl if that's how boys really feel."

Emeline laughs. "Your big mouth is gonna get you in real trouble someday if you don't learn when to keep quiet."

"The Orthodox kids haven't had their Christmas yet," Lucine says. "They won't have anything to write about either."

Mr. and Mrs. Troy have yet again taken advantage of the fact that Orthodox Christmas hasn't arrived, and have put up a tree salvaged from the garbage dump. Half the needles are gone, the trunk is wilting, and there's no water stand to keep it green and hydrated, but all that matters is the respectability of having a tree like other people. The night it was dragged in, Mrs. Troy and Tommy decorated it with cheap ornaments kept in a box under the bathroom sink. It's not as nice as other trees, trees hung with brightly-colored tinsel, popcorn, cranberries, shiny glass and metal balls, real candles, artificial birds, berries, flowers, and fruits, tiny musical instruments, pinecones, Santas, snowmen, and reindeer. There's also no manger scene underneath. While normal families are thinking about taking down their Christmas tree and decorations, the Troys are just putting theirs up.

"Can we go to the East River Park and go sledding?" Ernestine asks.

"So long as you're home by dinner." Mrs. Troy is sweeping up chicken feathers.

"Why can't we go to Cedar Hill?" Lucine asks. "We went there on a class trip last year, and it was really fun."

"Why walk all the way up there when you can go somewhere in the neighborhood?" Emeline asks.

Adicia wonders what it'd be like to go sledding down a real hill like Cedar Hill or Pilgrim Hill in Central Park, with a real wooden sled. The girls in her class who live in the northern section of the neighborhood have talked about going sledding on handsome wooden sleds with iron runners, decorative curlicues, and a leather or rope rein to stop the sled if it's going too fast or the hill is too steep. Even nicer would be a ride in a big sleigh. Adicia has seen some of those big sleighs when they've been up to Midtown to see the Rockefeller Center tree. They're pulled by horses, and the people riding them usually have nice, warm blankets over their laps. The people who ride in big sleighs and go sledding on actual sleds would probably never consider using a garbage can lid as a sled.

"Did you hear Carlos tried to join one of the local gangs?" Lucine asks as they're walking to the park. "He was whining they rejected him because he drinks and does drugs too much. They couldn't trust he'd be quick enough on his feet during a fight with a rival gang."

"Why do we have to live in *this* neighborhood?" Ernestine asks. "It's one thing if you only have enough money to live in a place like this when you're young, but people who have kids are supposed to wanna move uptown, where they don't have gangs and tenements."

"Part of me kinda likes living in a neighborhood with such a rich history," Emeline confesses reluctantly, stepping over a dead rat. "So many immigrants settled here, and a whole culture of tenement living was created. At least our tenement isn't a nineteenth century one, with only one or two rooms, no running water, no gas or electric lights, no bathrooms, and only one small window. You can see almost an entire street of those nightmarish buildings if you walk down Orchard Street."

"Would you still say that if we lived in one of the other apartments?" Lucine asks. "Ours is the only one with so much space, because the landlord and his family used to live there before they wisely abandoned it for a real house or apartment."

"We're not as poor as some of the other people here. Dad gets a dollar an hour, and works every day, full-time. Some people don't have work every day, or can't find work period. And Mother works on and off. Those boys Carlos wanted to join a gang with are probably a lot worse off than we are."

"I don't understand how our parents always seem to have money for drugs, alcohol, and junk for Tommy, yet we're always getting our heat and hot water turned off because they can't or won't pay the bills," Ernestine says. "I'd have so much fun building stuff with Lincoln Logs or riding a bike. Tommy's too young for them."

"What about that football?" Lucine asks. "Who's he gonna play with, and where's he gonna play with it? At least we don't have china and crystal to worry about breaking."

"Maybe he'll throw it into someone's yard and the person won't let him have it back. One of the boys on the sixth floor said he and his cousins were playing with a bouncy ball, and one of them accidentally hit it over someone's fence. The man who lived there refused to let them on his property and wouldn't give it back to them."

A number of other people are walking through the park when the girls arrive, carrying their garbage can lids. When the weather's nice, people come there to take walks, run, play tennis and other sports, bike, fish, and have picnics. They can also see the Brooklyn Bridge and the Manhattan Bridge from the park, and have an up-close and personal view of the Williamsburg Bridge, which runs down the center of the park. Adicia wishes they could walk across any of those bridges and get away from the toxic dump they call home, and go to a nicer place Upstate. She's heard from girls in her class who've gone to summer camp or visited relatives that there are beautiful lakes, forests, mountains, rivers, and fields up there, and people aren't forced to be compressed into multi-story buildings. The only people who think Manhattan's so romantic and glamorous must either not live there and get all their information from movies and books, or are fortunate to live uptown and not exposed to the reality of downtown poverty, crowding, gangs, and hopelessness.

Ernestine climbs into her upturned garbage can lid and lets Lucine push her down the hill. Emeline climbs into hers and pushes herself down. Lucine gets into hers with Adicia on her lap and goes down last. They land in a heap at the bottom and climb back up to do it again over and over again. Adicia wonders if one of the blessings in disguise of being poor is that her much-older sisters genuinely enjoy spending so much time with her and Ernestine. A lot of her classmates from the northern part of the neighborhood don't have such close relationships with their much-older sisters, who wouldn't be caught dead with them. Lucine and Emeline are closer to one another the same way Ernestine and Adicia are, but the four of them ultimately have the type of close relationship most sisters don't always have unless there's only a year or so between each of them. Adicia wonders if they'll still be together to become a quintet when Justine's a little older and able to do things with them. She can't bear the thought of being separated.

When they go home, the usual disgusting fare is waiting for them. Mrs. Troy has typically dressed it up like some sort of feast, as though almost-spoilt vegetable garnishes on possum roast make it into a gourmet steak at a fancy five-star restaurant. Adicia would prefer liver, tongue, eyeballs, brain, heart, and intestines to wild animals run over by cars or who died of diseases or injuries. The nice mission people at the Bowery would never dream of serving roadkill to their needy guests. Adicia wishes she could stay over at the mission to experience even more hospitality and learn what it's like to sleep in a real bed with sheets and a headboard, take a hot bath with enough soap and a warm fluffy towel to dry herself off with, and put on brand-new clothes, freshly laundered and dried in modern machines instead of washed by hand the old-fashioned way. They probably have a hairbrush she could use to brush her chestnut-colored hair, and toasty flannel pajamas and bunny slippers to wear at night.

The first day of 1960 is also the last night of Chanukah this year. Though Sarah doesn't have the money to buy ingredients for traditional Chanukah foods, she always invites the girls into the tiny room to light the candles with her at night. Every year since Adicia can remember, they've been plain white or yellow candles. Sarah says back in Germany, they had beautiful candles of all types of colors and designs, and the more upscale Judaica shops here in Manhattan have prettier, more artistic candles too. Adicia dreams of a day she and her sisters will have a big Christmas tree covered in beautiful lights and decorations, with a train set, miniature village, and heaps of presents underneath, and Sarah will have a beautiful work of art for a chanukiyah and the prettiest candles she can find.

One of the Chanukah blessings Sarah says when lighting thanks God for performing miracles for her ancestors. Adicia wishes she could be witness to a great miracle in her own lifetime and not just have to hear about miracles that happened in the ancient days of the Bible.

She wonders why so many miracles only seem to have happened in those long-ago days instead of in the modern era, when people still need miracles. It's hard to believe so many religions have holidays emphasizing lights at this time of year, as a way of keeping hope and happiness alive in the darkness and cold, when she knows as soon as Christmas and Chanukah are over, hopelessness and darkness will descend again. No great miracle happened when 1959 changed to 1960 at midnight. Her parents and Carlos don't care a new decade has begun, aren't upset they're still in the same place they were ten or fifteen years ago. What was good enough for their ancestors is good enough for them. They've never questioned why they have to live in a squalid tenement, work terrible, low-paying jobs, and eat food from garbage cans and the side of the road.

"Do you think any of us will come into any luck during the Sixties?" Ernestine asks.

"I'll graduate high school in 1964," Lucine says. "And damned if I'm ever coming back to this neighborhood or this building. I don't know how I'll do it, but I'll make something happen. I wish I could take all of yous with me."

"Four years is a long time to wait for something. I'm not gonna rely on anyone else to rescue me. I don't wanna wait till I'm outta school. I hope our chances to get away from this place come soon."

"We'll have to wait and see what happens," Emeline says. "There's a world of possibilities in this brand-new decade, and even if our parents and Carlos are determined to stay down in the muck and mire, we have the opportunity to get above our raising and start better lives for ourselves. None of us should forget that, even when it seems like we're surrounded by nothing but darkness, misery, and filth."

Chapter 7: Cindy Visits

Adicia and her sisters are at the kitchen table reading their new library books on Valentine's Day, Sunday, when Allen comes in with a girl. They can't imagine why he'd bring a date here for Valentine's Day. It's not as though it has the atmosphere and amenities of a fancy restaurant or theatre.

"This is my current girlfriend, Cindy Valentino." Allen goes to the fridge for a beer. "I met her two weeks ago at Tompkins Square Park. We were both smoking marijuana and found out we like to get our stuff from the same dealer. Oh, and she's in my English class."

"English is the only class besides biology I really like," Cindy says in a very heavy Manhattan accent.

"Help yourself to some booze or drugs. We've got lots of drugs in the kitchen."

"Aren't you worried about what'll happen to you if you do too many drugs?" Emeline asks.

"I do them in moderation. You know I ain't higher than a kite as often as Carlos or our parents." Allen opens a little box and pours some cocaine into a paper wrapper.

"Haven't I heard your date's last name before?" Ernestine asks. "It sounds so familiar."

"You probably have heard Cindy's last name before," Emeline says. "Rudolph Valentino was a famous moviestar when our grandparents were teenagers. He died here in New York City when he was pretty young. I read a couple of the books his movies were based on. I'd love to see the movies themselves, but we don't have a movie theatre nearby showing old stuff, even if I had money for the movies."

"Were they good books? Would you recommend them to me?"

"They were all grownup books, I'm afraid. My favorite was *The Four Horsemen of the Apocalypse*, by Vicente Blasco Ibáñez. It's about an Argentinean family of French origin who moves back to France around World War I, and Julio Desnoyers joins the army in an attempt to prove his bravery and manhood, after he's lived the life of a pampered artist and had an affair with the wife of one of his dad's friends. It has a very powerful anti-war message."

"You ain't never seen a movie?" Cindy asks. "My family's poor too, but we always sneak in when we wanna see something. Tickets are usually under a buck, so you can do something to scare up money on your own. My brothers like to go into other neighborhoods and beg. They pretend they're blind, or need money to get an operation for our mother." She quickly jumps away as the chickens come running into the kitchen. "What in the hell are them things doing here?"

"My mother and goofy brother Carlos found 'em on New Year's Day," Allen says. "They fell off the back of a poultry truck heading to the slaughterhouse, and no one came back to pick up the lost crates. My mother's hoping to use 'em for eggs and meat. So far, ain't none of 'em laid eggs."

"Would Mother read a book on raising chickens if I got one out of the library for her?" Emeline asks. "Though I don't think we need a book to be told chickens usually don't lay eggs when they're not in a coop with warm bedding and safe perches. These poor things have been fluttering all around the tenement since they came here. I'm surprised none of them's died yet."

"Do chickens have breeds like dogs and cats?" Ernestine asks. "Maybe these are a breed that's mostly for show, not to lay eggs."

"They're plain white chickens," Lucine says. "I'd assume the breeds that are more for show or specialty eggs would have fancy colors and feathers."

"What kind of meat is this?" Cindy asks from the open refrigerator door. "It don't look like beef, poultry, or lamb."

"Your guess is as good as anyone's," Allen says. "Might be leftover possum, maybe raccoon. It's not small, so I know it ain't squirrel or rabbit. Sometimes we get groundhog or badger."

"That's different. My family eats the leftover meat the butcher don't like to sell to his rich customers. It has lots of bones, gristle, and fat."

"That's the kind of meat we get too," Lucine says. "Or we get the garbage cuts most people don't want, like dark meat and necks."

"My mother brought home actual turkey meat on Thanksgiving," Allen says. "She fished it outta the garbage can at the hotel she worked at then. They throw away the leftovers in the hotel restaurant, and she snuck around to find stuff to take home. Of course, only my bratty baby brother Tommy got to eat any of it."

Mrs. Troy, as per her usual track record, didn't hold the job at the hotel for long. She was fired in mid-January when she was caught smoking cocaine instead of vacuuming the carpets. Now she's employed at a gas station, a job she's held five other times in the past. Her longest-running job was a five-month stretch as a coat-checker at a restaurant in the Financial District in 1950. She lost that job when she was caught using narcotics. Her most common reasons for being fired are being caught drinking and using drugs. A couple of jobs she's lost because she was lazy, messed something up very badly, or routinely showed up late. Mrs. Troy barely cares she's had over one hundred fifty different jobs over the past fifteen years she's been working. It's not as if anyone in their neighborhood has a résumé. The types of jobs Mrs. Troy applies for and temporarily works aren't the types of jobs that require such a thing, since they don't much care she doesn't have a high school diploma or GED.

"So you met Allen two weeks ago?" Emeline asks Cindy. "How soon did you begin calling each other boyfriend and girlfriend?"

"It's assumed after a few dates. I know some people who go through a stupid formality of asking someone to be their guy or girl. What's the point of that if you already know you're exclusive and it's been more than three dates?"

"Two weeks is too soon to declare yourself boyfriend and girlfriend," Lucine says. "Maybe after two months I'd consider it."

"Have you kissed her yet, Allen?" Ernestine asks.

"Of course. You're supposed to do that by the third date, if not on the first date. You get a reputation as a cold fish and a tease if you're a girl, or an unmanly guy, if you don't put the moves on someone by then."

"Then why'd you come to the rescue of Carlos's date when he wanted to do things with her and she didn't?" Emeline asks.

"There's a big difference between doing something you both want and tryna force someone to do something only you want. I'd be upset too if a girl tried to make me do stuff when I didn't want to."

"Do you think she's marriage material?" Lucine asks. "And have you done your adult things with her?"

"I do that with most of my girlfriends," Allen says, embarrassed. "But no, I've never had a girl I'd wanna marry. I probably won't date Cindy for that long. She's just someone to date and get physical with until someone else comes along."

"So you're gonna do your thing here and then go on a date? I hope yous close the door if you're planning to do that."

"No, I brought Cindy home for a nice Valentine's Day supper. It's nice to have guests for special occasions."

The girls hate when there are guests. Mr. and Mrs. Troy always insist on having what they think of as a fancy formal meal, which is almost always roadkill steak. They also drink twice as much, with the wine and champagne they somehow have money for while neglecting their utility bills, and do more drugs than usual too. Mrs. Troy has a beat-up dirty vase she fills with the rank tap water and puts wilted flowers into for a centerpiece when the weather's nice. These flowers are never from an actual florist's, of course, nor are they from a real garden in a backyard that doesn't exist. Mrs. Troy picks them from other people's property without permission, or pulls up flowers widely considered weeds, like dandelions. She doesn't care when there are bugs discovered crawling on the flowers.

"What did Allen give you for Valentine's Day?" Ernestine asks.

"A week-old bouquet the florist sold for ten cents. It's pretty. Ain't it nice to get bargains? Your brother would be a fool if he shelled out five bucks or more for a huge bouquet of fresh red roses."

"If I ever have a boyfriend, I'd want him to buy me chocolates and flowers on Valentine's Day," Adicia says.

"I'd like pretty jewelry," Emeline says. "As it is, even if we could afford jewelry, our parents and Carlos would probably pawn it for drugs."

"We didn't get any valentines when our classes exchanged them on Friday," Ernestine says. "At least Lucine's too old to do that and was spared that humiliation."

"Yeah, but I am old enough to have a guy ask to be my valentine, and none of the boys are interested in me," Lucine mopes. "Not that I think I need to have a boyfriend, but it'd be nice if even one guy showed interest in me. I'm not that unattractive, am I?"

"You shouldn't care what eighth grade boys think of you," Emeline says. "They're not the kinds of boys you'd wanna date if they care only about where you're from and what you look like. Let them go to the stupid girls who make fun of us. Think of it as a much nicer guy being saved for you when you're old enough for a serious relationship, a guy worth waiting for. I'd rather wait to be a woman so I can date a grown man than start dating immature guys in junior high."

"Gemma's current boyfriend got her a big box of chocolates, perfume, a red mink stole, and a big bouquet of twenty peach-colored roses," Ernestine says. "I'd love for anybody, boy or girl, to get me such nice presents."

Cindy rolls a cigarette and goes onto the fire escape with Allen. The girls marvel at how they're so cavalier about having a relationship and doing physical things after all of two weeks. Gemma has repeatedly stated she'd never do those adult things, which none of them quite understand the meaning of, with a guy she didn't intend to marry, and that her reputation would be ruined if she acted like that. Cindy's from a family just as poor as theirs, yet she doesn't share Gemma's views. Adicia wonders if maybe that means only girls who intend to get above their raising, like Gemma, are that selective about boyfriends, and if girls like Cindy don't have anything to lose because they don't exactly come from a family with money and a great reputation. Still, Adicia hopes someday when she's older, she isn't expected to go out with boys if she'd prefer to wait till she's ready.

Mrs. Troy comes home at 7:00 and heads right to the living room to take off her shoes and coat. She catches sight of Cindy when she's filling up a pipe in the kitchen. By this time, Cindy and Allen are a little bit buzzed from their drugs.

"We're havin' a guest tonight for Valentine's Day, Mother," Allen informs her. "This is Cindy Valentino, my girl of the past two weeks."

Mrs. Troy looks Cindy up and down. "Another decent choice Allen made. I trust you're from our part of the neighborhood, not that uppity section. Our family is Lower East Side people for generations, and if we ever leave the neighborhood, we'll stay in downtown Manhattan, where our kind belongs. I'll tell our Yid servant girl to make a feast fit for a guest. Do you like raccoon?"

"I can't say I've ever eaten it, but there's a first time for everything." Cindy hopes it's true most unfamiliar meat tastes like chicken. "Allen didn't say yous had a servant."

"Oh, she ain't paid regularly. I just use her to take care of my kids, clean the house, cook, do laundry, and other odd jobs. It's a cake deal, Miss Valentino. She came here when she was all of twenty years old, barely spoke English, had no friends or family, didn't have a high school diploma, and was desperate for work and a place to live. She's stuck here, whether she likes it or not. Who's gonna hire her with no legit work experience? She's got no money to go back to school. I'm set for life with this woman."

"That's mean to talk about Sarah like that," Adicia says.

"I don't care what you think about what I say about that Yid, you stupid mistake. Sarah, come out here and make a raccoon roast. Allen has a guest, so we're having a special supper tonight. You'd also better clean up after us and wash all the dishes. I don't wanna see no dried food on any dishes like I found last week."

Sarah comes out of the tiny bedroom, carrying Justine. "Look, Mrs. Troy, your baby is cutting her fifth tooth!"

"Like I care." Mrs. Troy pulls the foil-wrapped raccoon meat out of the refrigerator. "Make sure to put all the garnishes on this—tomatoes, peppers, onions, mushrooms, carrots. And put all the alcohol and liquor on the table."

"Cute baby," Cindy says. "How old is this one?"

"Eleven months," Adicia says proudly. "Justine is our real-life baby doll."

"Thank God, I won't be having any more unplanned rats after this one," Mrs. Troy says. "My doctor finally took out my reproductive organs."

Sarah hands Justine to Emeline and Lucine before going into the kitchen. The girls begin playing with her, while Mrs. Troy lies on the davenport to smoke her cocaine.

The smell of roasted raccoon wafting through the tenement as suppertime draws near is disgusting. All Adicia can think about is how raccoons look, those bushy tails, all that fur, and how they like to climb in garbage cans. Meat animals are cows, sheep, pigs, chickens, ducks, turkeys, and maybe goats, not wild animals. Even people who live out in the country and hunt wild game only eat deer, bears, moose, rabbits, and reindeer. If her parents enjoy wild animals so much, they should move to the countryside instead of picking up gross dead animals from the road.

Mrs. Troy looks very pleased as she sits down to supper, while Sarah slaves away putting the raccoon roast on the table and cutting up the meat. Having guests is one of the highlights of her existence, since it proves she's a respectable woman, with a respectable family, and their tenement is a place where guests are showered with hospitality and fine meals. She's sent Carlos out to steal some flowers to put in the middle of the table, and put out a worn linen tablecloth with cigarette burns in several places.

Adicia has always been repulsed by her parents' poor table manners. Her father's particularly bad about it. Mr. Troy doesn't seem to register what it means that there's a guest present, and swills his drink as always, burps loudly, scratches himself, chews loudly, picks up and eats food that falls on the floor, and gets food all over his face and shirt. Napkins are unheard of in the Troy household. All while they're eating, the chickens run around underfoot, clucking and pecking.

Cindy can't decide which is worse—the drugged-out Carlos stabbing his fork at the air; the fact that there isn't enough silverware for everyone, forcing some of the Troys to eat with their hands; the worn-out tableware; the tablecloth with cigarette burns; Mr. Troy's table manners; Mrs. Troy's bizarre pride at showing off her tenement and serving a roadkill roast; her treatment of Sarah; her attitude towards her daughters; Tommy's obnoxious blather; the chickens; the raccoon meat; or Gemma's condescending facial expressions and talk. Even her family isn't that terrible, and even she doesn't use as many drugs as Carlos and Mr. and Mrs. Troy. At the end of the meal, she gets her coat and leaves by the fire escape to avoid going down the stairs, which are worse than the stairs in an amusement park's haunted house. Allen follows after her to walk her home to her apartment on Rivington Street.

"She wasn't that bad," Adicia says as she and Ernestine are lying on their sheetless mattress that night. "Allen usually dates nicer girls than Carlos."

"Did you see the look on her face?" Ernestine laughs. "She couldn't get outta here fast enough!"

"I'd expect nice food if I was a guest at someone's home, not garbage. Mother can dress up roadkill as much as she likes with vegetables and wine, but it's still roadkill."

"Why are Allen and Carlos able to bring friends and dates over without asking ahead of time? If I had any friends, I'd want them to come over to play, but Mother hates us, so she'd probably say no."

"That must be nice to have friends," Adicia says dreamily. "Do you think we'll ever have real friends?"

"I know we will. Emeline said anyone worth your time is worth waiting for. She was talking about boys, but it's the same idea. If someone really wants to be our friend, she won't care what we look like or where we've been. Who cares how much time it takes to find real friends? At least we're not so desperate to have friends we'd go around with the mean girls at school."

"I don't think our parents wanna have money. They act like having money is horrible, and that we'd be bad people if we got rich and moved uptown. Why do they wanna live in this crummy neighborhood forever and have bad jobs?"

"It was good enough for their parents, grandparents, great-grandparents, and further back. They probably think we're saying they're bad people because we don't wanna live like they do. Maybe it's a blessing in disguise they don't want anything to do with people who have money and nice lives, since they'll never bother us after we're grownups and get to move away."

"You really think we'll have real houses someday, real food every day, real beds with sheets, backyards, and new clothes?"

"I know we will. You've gotta stop imagining these things and start believing they'll happen. These things and more will happen for us someday because we made them happen."

Chapter 8: Facts of Life

While Mr. and Mrs. Troy are out drinking on the St. Patrick's Day weekend, Emeline talks to her sisters about the educational filmstrips she saw that day.

"I'm dying to know what kind of film the boys saw. They made us see different films, though I'd think the information's the same. I sorta knew some of it, but some of it I've never run across in any book."

"Are these the films telling you about the joy of becoming a woman?" Lucine asks. "I don't feel any joy when I fasten that damned belt around my waist every month and hook sanitary napkins onto the belt. At least I knew what was happening to me when it happened, since I share my room with Gemma and had seen her using that stupid belt since I was eight."

"What's a sanitary napkin?" Ernestine asks. "And when do either of you wear belts? Belts are for men."

"It's a kind of belt you wear under your clothes. You'll see these filmstrips in four years, so you don't need to know about these things for awhile."

"I'd die of embarrassment if I got blood on my clothes and anyone saw it," Emeline says. "Do we have the money for a belt and napkins?"

"Mother would be embarrassed too if you bled in front of her. She'll buy you a belt and napkins to avoid dealing with the sight of it and the reminder that she has six daughters and only three sons."

"We also saw a film talking about how babies are made. I had a vague idea for awhile, but I didn't really know *that's* what Carlos and Allen do with their girlfriends. Although the filmstrip didn't make everything very clear. Are they afraid if they give us specific information about how this stuff works, we'll wanna run out and immediately do it?"

"Did you see educational filmstrips when you were in school, Sarah?" Ernestine asks. "We see them at least twice a month, and most of them are so boring and stupid."

"That must be an American thing. And I wasn't in school long enough to learn some of the things you older girls do."

"I still wanna know more details about how to prevent babies. The films just told us about how human reproduction works and what happens when a girl starts becoming a young woman. If you do that to show love and you're in a marriage, and not just fooling around with random people like Allen and Carlos, surely you don't have a baby every single time. The world would be filled with trillions of people if you always make a baby from doing that."

"Mother got her female organs removed," Lucine says. "That's one way. And she's used other methods, as we all know so well. I don't know what some of those things exactly are, but I know of them."

"What exactly is a diaphragm? I know from the story that I was a failure of it, but the only kind of diaphragm I know about is the big muscle inside your chest."

"I don't know what it is either. Don't you love how vague those filmstrips are? It's like someone describing an elephant without using real words that let you visualize it in your mind."

"Do you think Mother would put aside money to buy me a bra? I never asked if you wear ones handed down from Gemma."

"Sadly, yes. When we were no longer the same size, Mother bought the most unattractive bras she could find. Gemma's bras were at least pretty, even if they were used."

"What's a bra?" Adicia asks.

"It's a modern form of the corset," Emeline says. "It doesn't crush your bones and organs, and only covers your breasts. You and Ernestine don't need to worry about them anytime soon."

"Don't you love how those films act as though only respectable married people do those things?" Lucine asks. "It's not a big secret Mother was pregnant with Gemma at her wedding. I don't think there are only two alternatives, being pure and chaste until marriage or automatically getting venereal disease, ruining your life, and having an unwanted baby if you wanna do that before you're married."

"I'm glad they don't show us films in kindergarten," Adicia says. "But you still didn't tell us why yous need to wear a belt under your clothes."

Emeline hesitates, then shrugs. "Kids a couple hundred years ago were routinely exposed to things that are today considered too grownup for them. I don't get why so many people in so-called refined, respectable society think we're such delicate little flowers who can't handle certain information. We've all seen and heard our parents having physical intimacy, even if we didn't know what in the world they were doing. Maybe people only think kids from well-bred families in the suburbs need protecting from this information, and we slum kids are trash and don't count. Lucine, do you wanna show them your belt?"

Lucine goes into the bedroom she shares with Gemma, who's out on a date for the holiday, and brings out a white elastic belt with metal clasps and safety pins in the middle.

"We'll have to wear onea those someday?" Ernestine asks.

"They make special underwear you can attach napkins into, but that's an expense Mother can't deal with. She'd rather buy each of us a belt and be done with it, instead of being bothered to buy enough pairs of sanitary underwear. Some girls use applicators, but I'm sure Mother thinks those things are only for disreputable girls and married women because they're worn inside the body. She buys a big box of Modess napkins every few months and dumps it in our room. Gemma says she never talked to her about it, just came home with the box and a belt one day and told her she expected she'd start to become a woman soon."

"You're as bad as those filmstrips! Neither of you are telling us what exactly you need those things for!"

"When you start to develop into a young woman, your reproductive system releases an egg every month, and it comes out of the body as blood. That's why Gemma and I wear the napkins and the belt, so we won't make a mess all over our clothes."

"Why can't that happen when you're a grownup and wanna have a baby? Isn't it silly for your body to do that when you're not an adult? It's probably a waste of good eggs too."

"You can ask those questions if you have a school nurse who comes in to talk to you about that when you're old enough."

"They gave us these booklets from Modess." Emeline pulls hers out of her schoolbag. "I only looked through mine and didn't read it all the way, but I was shocked at how graphic some of the pictures were. I guess we need to know what our female parts look like, both inside and out, but even our science textbook doesn't have this kind of detail!"

"The woman on the front cover is so ugly!" Ernestine laughs. "It looks like a man in a dress and a wig!"

"'Essence of Womanhood'?" Lucine laughs. "The ones we got

were called 'Very Personally Yours' and from Kotex, and we saw a really loony film from Disney called *The Story of Menstruation*. They made it seem like we were really looking forward to it, like it's such a beautiful, romantic thing. They glossed over things like really bad cramps, and made it seem like all normal girls will be able to carry on doing normal things like dancing and exercising, and that we have to smile even if we feel like garbage. I'm not in the mood to do much else but lie around and read or do schoolwork during that time of the month, and I don't care if the people who put together those stupid booklets and filmstrips think that makes me unladylike or abnormal."

"The booklet I got only uses male pronouns when talking about doctors," Emeline says. "Aren't there any female doctors who specialize in women's issues? I'd hate to have to expose myself like that to a strange man when I'm having a baby, having really bad cramps, or haven't menstruated yet by the time I'm seventeen."

"There probably are. God, I can't stand these stupid booklets and filmstrips. They were clearly written and made for girls from the right side of the tracks, not girls like us. How can we relate to hypothetical girls who have great relationships with their parents, get to wear make-up and nailpolish, go on dates, go dancing, have lots of friends, dream of growing up so they can wear womanly clothes and get married, and live in actual houses?"

"Did you use that calendar in the back, Lucine? I can't imagine I'd mark off the days of my future menses. I'd rather read books or work on my schoolwork. I don't care what days of the month it comes and how long it lasts! It's not like I need to plan ahead, since we don't go on vacations and don't have any friends. As long as it comes each month, I figure I'll be normal."

"I didn't see the point of it. I also wanna know the names for the outer parts of our reproductive organs. They named all the inner parts in the film and the booklet, but not the parts we can see. I was too embarrassed to ask, and none of the other girls volunteered either."

"Our booklets don't show or name those parts either. Do they think we're not supposed to ever look at ourselves there and wonder what those things are called? One of the filmstrips said you grow hair there, and under your arms, when you become a young woman, but the booklet doesn't show any hair there either. Is it part of a plan to keep girls ignorant about their bodies and leave everything up to male doctors?”

“I honestly can’t believe any real women wrote these things or produced these films, but maybe I can, since you know what happens when a girl doesn’t keep smiling and acting happy and sweet even if she’s anything but. I get so many comments because I speak my mind and don’t play nice when I’m not in a happy mood. My goal in life is to go to college and have a real career, not just a job, and maybe get married if the right guy comes along when I’m old enough and we can afford to set up a household and have kids. They look at me as though I have nine heads when I say I don’t think my utmost fulfillment as a woman will come through getting married, taking care of a man, and birthing babies.”

“What do you expect?” Sarah looks up from watching Justine try to walk on her unsteady, wobbly little legs. “When you’re poor, you have to work and don’t have the luxury of sitting around as a pampered *hausfrau*. You grew up surrounded by working women. Those mean girls grew up *mit mutters* staying home and *vaters* working. Women in their world usually only work before marriage, since it’s not considered respectable for a married woman to work.”

“Is our baby trying to walk?” Adicia asks excitedly, bored of the grownup conversation Lucine and Emeline are having. “Maybe she’ll be walking by Easter.”

“No real steps yet. Hopefully she’ll be able to take a few steps soon.”

“Mother won’t care,” Ernestine says. “She didn’t care when you told her about the teeth she’s cut either. What kind of vile mother doesn’t care about her baby’s special firsts? She can’t even pretend to be happy and excited!”

“Do you think she’ll say her first words soon?” Adicia asks.

“Most babies say their first word around their first birthday. If she’s like you and your sisters, her first word will be ‘Mama,’ and I’ll have to train her to not call me Mama, just like I had to train you, Ernestine, and Emeline. Allen says Lucine’s first word was ‘bottle.’”

Carlos comes stumbling into the tenement, on drugs as always, with some sort of metal clip on his nose. Lucine rushes to get rid of the menstrual belt, though Carlos might not known what it is, either in his drugged state or because he has nothing to do with female matters. Allen comes in after him, a bit tipsy but not falling-down drunk.

"That green booze was nasty. I can't believe how many of my friends were swilling it down. One of my non-drinking friends asked for a green milkshake instead, and that looked hideous too."

"Why do people make green drinks for St. Patrick's Day?" Ernestine asks. "My class cut shamrocks out of green construction paper and read a story about leprechauns."

"How the hell are you drinking at a bar, Allen?" Lucine asks. "You're only fifteen."

"The bartender's our buddy. He doesn't care a lot of us are underage. It ain't a snotty wine bar for uptown snobs, so he knows mosta the customers are underage." Allen bends down to Justine. "Is she trying to walk?"

"She is a year old now," Emeline says. "Isn't it fun watching her grow up? While I'm glad Mother won't be having any more kids, it's kinda sad this is the last time we'll be able to watch a sibling going from a newborn to a baby to a little person. It always happens so fast."

Allen picks Justine up and tosses her up in the air a few times. "You're a pretty baby. It's nice to have another hair color in the family besides brown."

Carlos ambles over to the table and picks up Emeline's booklet. "What the hell is this? 'The Essence of Womanhood'?"

"It's nothing," Emeline lies, turning red.

Carlos flips through the pages. "Check out these illustrations! They never gave me pictures like this when I was in school!"

"Come on, Carlos, leave her alone. She's in sixth grade, and schools like to give those facts of life films and pamphlets to kids at that age," Allen says, cuddling Justine.

Justine is making contented baby noises and smiling a big smile, overwhelmed at the surprise attention from her one sympathetic brother. Usually the only people who play with her and talk to her are Sarah, Lucine, Emeline, Ernestine, and Adicia, and sometimes the people at the Bowery Mission when they go there on holidays.

"I didn't need none of this nonsense when I was in sixth grade," Carlos goes on, fumbling around for a refill of whatever drug he's got clipped to his nose. "I learnt the birds and the bees story from our parents, and they didn't need to show me pictures or give me technical names. Why, I can tell the exact story they always tell, word for word, about how each of us was created. We all know we was mistakes. They never tell you that in them films and booklets, do they, that not all kids are planned or wanted. Hell, I knew exactly how it was done years before I started doing it, since I'd seen our parents going at it so often! They never chased me outta the room or told me I was a bad boy for seeing that. All perfectly normal and natural."

"Carlos, please," Allen begs. "Ernestine's only seven, and Adicia's five. They don't need to know these things until they're older."

"Nonsense. They've seen our folks going at it too. If we was any poorer, we might all sleep in the same room or bed, so there wouldn't be no secrets there neither. Only uppity snobs from the other side of the tracks think it's bad to let their kids know about this stuff at that age." Carlos sits down, almost missing the chair. "I'm telling the story, whether any of yous like it or not. Gemma was made in the backseat of a stolen car, in the parking lot of a motel. Our folks didn't use nothing, since they figured it couldn't happen the first time. Since they couldn't afford an abortion, they had a shotgun wedding. Me, I was the product of too much drinking. When you're that drunk, you don't think about using no rubbers or diaphragm. Allen was the result of a broken rubber. Personally, I don't use them things. They get in the way and are impossible to open without ripping. A sadist must've designed them."

"Carlos, that's enough."

"Lucine was a failure of pullin' out. I use that method sometimes, but it cheats me outta pleasure. If my girl of the moment's smart, she'll use her own method or take care of it with enough money. I don't care if I get a girl pregnant. That's her problem for not using a diaphragm or douching."

"What does all that mean?" Ernestine asks. "You're talking to us like we understand what you're saying."

"Nothing our parents ain't told yous many a time already."

"But we don't understand it when they say this story either."

"Whatever. Emeline was a failure of a diaphragm. Mother got fitted for one after Lucine, but never was able to put it in properly. The baby she lost between Ernestine and Emeline was caused by failure of a vinegar-soaked sponge. I'm glad I'm a guy. I can't imagine shoving vinegar in my nether regions."

"I secretly hoped she'd die when she fell down the steps," Lucine confesses. "I'm probably the only four-year-old who wanted her mother to die when she had an accident instead of hoping she'd be okay and get well soon."

"Ernestine was another diaphragm failure. Mother had outgrown it by the time she started using it again. Guess she was too lazy to get refitted for a new one. Adicia was another diaphragm failure. You'd think she would've sworn that thing off after it already failed her twice. Tommy's story is the funniest. Our parents was doing it on the fire escape, on drugs, fell off, and landed in a pile of leaves. They was so drugged they kept doing it. Justine was a pessary that didn't wanna stay in place. As far as I'm concerned, they both shoulda gotten sterilized after Lucine and kept it to two of each. Kids are a damn nuisance and eat up all your money and time. Who wants to raise kids when normal people are done?" Carlos pulls a cigar out of his back pocket.

"Normal parents and big brothers don't go around telling their kids and younger siblings stories like that!" Lucine shouts. "I don't know why anyone would want to do *that*, for either babies or love!"

"I hope you ain't such a cold fish by the time you're in high school. I don't want the reputation as the older brother of a prude."

"You already have a reputation, Carlos, a reputation as a drug addict, a drunk, a lowlife, an idiot, a poor boy, a thief, and a terrible student."

"Like I care." Carlos wanders into his room and throws his clothes on the floor before getting onto his sheetless mattress. "Have a great night, everyone."

"How many times do we have to hear this story?" Adicia asks as Carlos begins snoring loudly.

"Our spiteful mother will always remind us we were all mistakes," Lucine says. "Notice we still don't know what exactly a diaphragm or pessary is after hearing that story so many times."

"The booklets and filmstrips don't mention them," Emeline points out. "There's a lot adults don't tell us, in an attempt to keep us ignorant and innocent. Do they think only bad girls would have those questions?"

"Guys rule this world. Girls and women are second-class citizens, the same way we're not as high on the totem pole in this family as our brothers."

"I don't think you're second-class citizens, even if I am a guy," Allen protests, putting Justine down so she can try walking again.

"You've got the power to bring life into the world, which I don't have. Onea the things going for me with the girls is that I have six sisters. When they hear that, they're like flies to honey."

"Carlos has six sisters too, and I doubt that makes girls like him," Emeline says.

"When I'm old enough for one of those belts, can mine be purple?" Ernestine asks.

"I'd like a blue one," Adicia says. "Dark blue is my favorite color."

"Mother will get the ugliest, cheapest belts she can find," Lucine says. "Maybe you can dye them, though I never thought about dyeing mine a different color. I try to avoid anything to do with that time of the month as much as possible."

"If this bleeding thing you get when you're a teenager is so bad, we should try to make it a little fun," Ernestine says.

"You'll have to start shaving extra hair on your body too," Emeline says. "I hope Mother doesn't get me an old, rusty razor, or doesn't expect me to use the same razor Dad and our brothers use."

"She got a pack of razors for me and Gemma," Lucine says. "You'll probably have to share ours."

Lucine and Emeline suddenly seem a lot older than Adicia and Ernestine. When Adicia starts first grade and Ernestine starts third grade in September, Lucine will be going off to high school and Emeline will be starting junior high. She and Ernestine are nowhere near getting bizarre booklets and seeing strange filmstrips, nor are they worrying about things like menstrual belts, shaving razors, bras, and human reproduction. Adicia hopes this won't be the beginning of a divide between them as the older half of their foursome become young women.

Chapter 9: Easter 1960

All the girls at Adicia's school were very excited when April came, since that meant Pesach and Easter were coming very soon. This year, Pesach began on April 11, and Easter will be April 17. Since they live on the Lower East Side, many of the girls are Jewish, and they talked about the housecleaning preparations their families undertook; how their parents put away their ordinary dishes and took out two sets of dishes, one for milk and one for meat, only used during these eight days once a year; the pretty new dresses they wore at the Seders; and how they got to stay up late at the Seders.

The Christian girls talked all about Easter, both the Western Easter and Orthodox Easter, which are on the same day this year. They too will be getting pretty new dresses to wear to church, special hats, and Easter baskets. Adicia knows Santa and the Tooth Fairy don't exist, so she doesn't believe in the Easter Bunny either. Tommy of course will get an Easter basket, and Gemma will have holiday fun with her friends, but no one else will have a real Easter other than the obligatory church service and a meal at the Bowery Mission. Adicia wishes she had friends so she could have an invitation to an egg-roll. She's heard the White House has an egg-roll on its lawn every Easter, and has day-dreamt about how wonderful it'd be to be a personal guest of President and Mrs. Eisenhower. President Eisenhower was a big hero of the war, when he was General Eisenhower and not the president.

Mrs. Troy is about ready to give up on the chickens, since they haven't laid any eggs yet, and kill them for the meat. If they were laying eggs, Adicia would have so much fun decorating them, and painting hollow shells an older person got the yolks out of without breaking the fragile shells. Emeline says the Russians and other Eastern Europeans used to have beautiful decorated eggs. Some of them are on display in museums. Adicia wonders why everyone says so many bad things about the Russians if they created such beautiful artwork. She'd rather look at pictures of their art than do stupid duck and cover drills because the teachers think the Russians are going to attack America.

Adicia can only imagine how wonderful it'd be to get a real Easter basket. The other girls in class say they're lined with a special type of artificial grass, and filled with Easter eggs, chocolate eggs, chicks, and rabbits, oranges, nuts, jellybeans, gumdrops, colored marshmallows in the shape of rabbits and chicks, stuffed animals, and sometimes real pet rabbits, chicks, goslings, or ducklings. Their families go to churches where they're established members, wear nice new clothes and hats, and have a scrumptious lunch and supper, usually featuring ham or lamb, cornbread, candied yams, casseroles, and hot cross buns. They probably have delicious Easter breakfasts too, like bacon, scrambled eggs, smoked fish, omelettes, hash browns, fresh fruit, French toast, and coffeecake.

Mrs. Troy is in the living room admiring a large hand-woven basket when the girls get home from school the Friday before Easter. Without being told, they know it's Tommy's Easter basket.

"I was fired from the gas station, so I used my extra time I woulda been working to pick this up at a boutique on St. Marks Place. Don't yous dare go into the bags over there. They're full of goodies for Tommy."

"Wouldn't your first thought after getting fired be to look for a new job, not to spend money on stuff you don't need?" Lucine asks.

"Jobs are like trains; they come along every fifteen minutes." Mrs. Troy lights a joint and kicks off her shoes.

"Why were you fired this time?" Ernestine asks.

"I cursed out a customer who thought I didn't fill his tank up all the way. He got the manager over, and he took the customer's side."

"Did you fill it up all the way?" Emeline asks.

"Of course not! That way they'll come back to us sooner and make me more money! I ain't some sucker who gives all the gas to these uppity rich folk who can afford to drive around in fancy automobiles!"

"What kind of church are we going to for Easter?" Adicia asks. "Can we try a Catholic church this year?"

Mrs. Troy grimaces. "Ain't none of us speak Latin, do we? The Papists have their entire service except the sermon in that dead language, and the priest don't face the congregation. I also don't want people staring at us and talking when we don't take Communion."

"What's Communion?" Ernestine asks.

"It's also called the Eucharist," Emeline supplies. "Are you ready to learn some pretty big words? Catholics and Orthodox Christians believe the wafers people eat during services literally turn into the body of Jesus, and that the wine turns into his blood. That's called transubstantiation. Most Protestants believe Jesus's spirit is with the wafers and wine, but isn't transformed into them. That's called consubstantiation. Other Christians believe it's just a symbolic act."

"So it's like cannibalism?"

"Not to people who believe in it. I can tell you more when I read some more books about Christianity and its different forms."

"You'd better prepare to look for a man who can take care of you with a decent job like your father," Mrs. Troy lectures. "As it is, you'll never get hired when you read useless books all day long."

"I'm going to be a librarian when I grow up. I don't want to depend on a man for money, and I don't want to flit from job to job like you."

Mrs. Troy goes to the davenport to lie down. "I raised you better than to get above your raising. I'll look bad in front of everyone if you do that. It's bad enough Gemma's graduating from high school in two months and working at an uppity department store. But take note, all of you, she's gonna be brought back to earth whether she likes it or not. She's dreaming if she thinks she's gonna go to college and move to Long Island."

Gemma has been accepted at Hofstra College in Hempstead, with her B average and 1100 SAT score. She wants to study business so she can open her own store, and plans to join a sorority and as many clubs and organizations as she can fit into her social calendar between studying. Mr. and Mrs. Troy are aghast anyone in their family would go to college, instead of being proud she's the first one on either side to do that. They're prouder of Carlos for announcing his intentions to drop out and start a job at a cereal factory. His sisters think he couldn't be stupider, getting that close to finishing school and throwing it away because of a bizarre idea that only disreputable people do well in school and graduate. Allen, who barely shows up at school more than Carlos, is pulling Cs and Ds, in contrast to Carlos being proud of getting Fs, Us, and very low Ds on everything he's ever done since grade school.

"Can we have an Easter egg hunt here?" Adicia asks. "Maybe the chickens will lay eggs as an Easter miracle."

"Miracles don't exist, you dumb mistake. If miracles existed, I wouldn't have been saddled with nine children, six of 'em girls. At least I lost the baby between Emeline and Ernestine. I'd go crazy if I had children into the double digits. I would've ripped out my womb myself and not waited for my doctor to give me the operation."

"What would you have named that baby if it survived your accident? Did they tell you if it was a boy or a girl?"

"You talk to me like I'm onea them pampered uptown mothers who give a damn when their children talk to them. I don't wanna be friends with any of yous but Tommy. You're mistakes, dirt. Go away so I can smoke in peace."

"What a disgrace to motherhood," Lucine mutters under her breath as they head off to the tiny bedroom.

Instead of spending the rest of Friday and Saturday looking forward to Easter like all the other girls at school, Adicia and her sisters go through the same old, same old they always do. There are no Easter eggs hidden through the tenement, no egg-rolls to go to, no pictures to be taken with the Easter Bunny, no special Easter brunch with the Easter Bunny, no Easter baskets to dream about finding on Sunday morning, no pretty new dresses and hats hanging up in the closet. Just as on Christmas morning, the smells wafting through the tenement on Easter morning are those of lumpy gray porridge and bacon grease.

This year the Troys have decided to go to an Episcopal church, figuring they've exhausted all the mainstream Protestant churches in the neighborhood and that Episcopalians won't have Latin services. Since they're going to a 9:00 service, everyone is rushed in and out of the bathtub just like on Christmas Eve, and the water is freezing and dirty by the time Adicia and Ernestine are allowed in. While Gemma struts around wearing a pretty pink straw Easter bonnet, pink patent leather shoes, white silk knee-high stockings, and a pink chiffon dress, the rest of the family is bedecked in old, worn-out, ragged clothes.

People stare at them as they make their way to church. Everyone else has nice clothes, instead of looking like a band of ragamuffins. While Lucine pushes Justine's stroller, one of the wheels breaks off. She folds up the stroller and carries it the rest of the way, handing Justine to Emeline. Maybe back at home they'll be able to screw the wheel back on.

"Who's that on the cross?" Tommy asks loudly as they enter the church, staring up at the large crucifix hanging above the altar.

Mrs. Troy bursts out laughing, unable to control herself even as everyone around them stares. She doesn't care her pet child has exposed them as twice-a-year churchgoers.

"That's Jesus," Emeline tries to explain. "He was a teacher and spiritual figure who lived a long time ago. His teachings formed the basis of Christianity."

"I didn't ask you, stupid bookworm. I was asking Mommy."

"What she said," Mrs. Troy manages to say between hiccups of laughter.

"We've never been to an Episcopal church before, so you haven't seen a crucifix. Protestants usually have a plain cross. Catholics, Episcopalians, and related denominations emphasize the Crucifixion, and most Protestants emphasize the Resurrection."

"I don't know what that means, and I don't care." Tommy runs over to the pew farthest in the back and begins walking on top of it.

"That thing is scary," Adicia whispers. "Why do they want a statue of a man with blood all over him, nailed to a cross, and wearing a crown of thorns?"

"We can read about it together in a book on religion from the library," Emeline whispers back as they walk over to the pew Tommy claimed. "Sometimes things look strange to us when they're very normal or beautiful to people who believe in them. These people don't see a tortured, dying man, but a symbol of the sacrifice they believe he made."

"I'd never wanna sacrifice myself for anything," Ernestine says.

"Why did he sacrifice himself?" Adicia asks.

"I think you'll hear more about that during the service." Emeline takes a seat and sits Justine next to her.

Lucine looks through the church bulletin during services. It seems like a lovely church, and makes her wish she belonged to something like that, maybe not a church, but some type of organization, like a French-American club. She's envious of the people publicly acknowledged in the celebrations page, for graduations, weddings, engagements, births, baptisms. The church has a youth group too. Being in a youth organization would give her the perfect chance to meet other teenagers and do things outside of school, even if it wouldn't make her the most popular girl in school. Since turning fourteen in January, she's increasingly wished she had peers to do things with, like Gemma and her older brothers.

After the service, the Troys shuffle out quickly while everyone else stays to chat with their friends. Lucine picks up the folded stroller and looks back at the happy church community they're leaving, knowing the festive Easter bonnets, gloves on the women, smiling children, and pastel-colored spring-themed dresses represent a world she and her family will never be a part of so long as they remain in their pathetic tenement.

Lunch consists of fried bologna, fruit so soft it's on the verge of rotting, vegetables with moldy parts cut off, stale bread, and old creamed corn soup thickening into a pudding-like texture. Adicia and her sisters are glad they're not eating roadkill as their holiday meal.

"Why do our parents take such pride in eating this terrible food?" Ernestine asks as they walk to the Bowery Mission that evening for supper. "Even those stupid Five Little Peppers didn't eat stale vegetables, overripe fruit, and roadkill. They were a loving family and didn't wanna be poor their whole lives, though it annoys me when they go on and on about their stupid 'little brown house days.'"

"This is all our parents know," Lucine says. "They don't know how people with money really live. They think everyone with money is automatically rich and an uppity snob, and don't understand that some people who live comfortably and own their own houses are middle- or working-class. They think it's a betrayal of how we were raised and how our family lives when we talk about college, careers instead of jobs, and moving away. Just look at some of these old buildings and businesses. They're abandoned or run by new owners. A lot of people who used to live here moved away when they got more money. We're still an immigrant neighborhood in some ways, but not the same way we were fifty years ago."

"Are there any nice neighborhoods downtown?" Adicia asks.

"Greenwich Village and the West Village are pretty nice, from what I've heard. A lot of artists, poets, and musicians live there."

"I'll live here as long as I have to, but I don't think I'll wait till I'm eighteen or even sixteen to leave," Ernestine announces. "Kids in the old days often left home when they weren't much older than I am."

"Now you're really dreaming. You just turned eight. What are you thinking, you'd leave home at twelve? Where would you go? How would you get money? What if the police found you and made you return home? This isn't the eighteenth century!"

"Where there's a will, there's a way. I want it to happen, so I'll make it happen. The universe will open up a way for me, and I'll take the first chance I get."

Adicia skips into the mission ahead of her sisters and Sarah and runs over to the nearest table with five empty place settings. She can't wait to be served dinner, since it'll probably be her last decent meal until Thanksgiving. The sight of the other Bowery guests makes her happy, knowing here they won't be judged for not having pretty new Easter bonnets and dresses, or asked to compare Easter baskets.

Ernestine goes over to one of the mission workers, carrying the stroller and the wheel. "Excuse me, is there anyone here who can fix my baby sister's stroller? One of the wheels came off when we were walking to church this morning."

Justine smiles and coos at the mission worker from her snug place in Sarah's arms.

"Of course we can find someone to fix it. We never turn away anyone who comes to us in need, particularly not on the holiest day of the year. I'll get one of our handymen, and we'll come find you when it's fixed." The woman takes the wheel and stroller. "How old's your sister?"

"Thirteen months," Ernestine says proudly.

"You sure know how to make attractive girls," the woman tells Sarah, smiling. "Are there any more besides these four?"

"Our other sister's sitting over there." Emeline points. "We've also got some brothers and an older sister, who didn't wanna eat here."

"Our oldest sister's celebrating Easter with friends, and our brothers are too proud to accept charity," Lucine says.

"Our little brother made a big scene in church this morning," Ernestine says. "When we walked in, he asked loudly, 'Who's that on the cross?' We went to an Episcopal church, and we usually go to Protestant churches, so he'd never seen a crucifix before. I still don't know how he could not know that was Jesus, even if we only go to church a few times a year. That's supposed to be one of the first things you learn at church!"

"I'd like to go to church more, but the other people always judge our family when we go," Lucine says. "On Christmas Eve, the other kids laughed about how we smelled bad. If they'd bathed in cold water a bunch of other people had already used, they'd smell bad too. And they always look at us funny because our clothes aren't as nice as theirs."

"I'm very sorry to hear that. I hope you know no one at this mission judges anyone for not looking a certain way."

"We love your mission!" Ernestine says.

Emeline leads the others over to Adicia. Soon they're being served delicious candied yams, cornbread rolls, lamb, hot cross buns, some kind of dish made with eggs, roasted vegetables, chicken, mashed potatoes, candied orange slices, milk, fruit juice, and sparkling water. Adicia always finds it hard to believe so much delicious food exists in such a dismal part of the city.

At the end of the meal, someone delivers the stroller, whose wheels are now all firmly attached. The mission worker also gives Justine a stuffed white rabbit. Justine doesn't know what to do with it at first, since she's never had any toys before. Then she figures out it's meant for hugging and cuddling, and falls asleep holding it as Sarah wheels her back home.

Mr. and Mrs. Troy are out drinking when they come back, and Carlos is hanging over the fire escape in his usual drug-induced state. Sarah puts Justine on a blanket on the floor to see if she needs her diaper changed.

Justine wakes up and smiles up at her sisters and Sarah. "Mama."

"Did our baby just talk?" Emeline asks excitedly.

"Our baby just said her first words!" Ernestine echoes.

Adicia looks at her sadly. "No, not Ma-ma. Sa-rah. Our real mother is that other woman who lives here, the mean one who looks like she rolled outta a garbage dumpster."

"Mama," Justine repeats.

"She'll learn soon enough, the way the rest of us did," Lucine sighs.

"Maybe you can adopt us and take us away from this nasty place," Ernestine suggests. "Justine can grow up seeing you as her real mother and not know about the horrible woman who really gave birth to us."

"None of us will leave here anytime soon, unless a miracle happens," Sarah says.

Emeline jumps up and runs into the bathroom. "Can anybody help me?" she calls. "I think I need a sanitary napkin, and I don't have a belt!"

"Are you sure?" Lucine asks. "You're only eleven! Gemma and I were both twelve and a half, and some of the girls in my classes haven't gotten their first menses!"

"I'll be twelve next month. Those goofy booklets and filmstrips said some girls are younger than others. I've been developing a bustline since I was even younger than this."

Sarah gets two extra safety pins out of Justine's diaper bag and goes to help Emeline. Lucine ducks into her bedroom to get a Modess pad from the big box Mrs. Troy buys every few months and embarrassedly dumps on her oldest daughters' bed.

"Can't you borrow Lucine's belt?" Adicia asks.

"That's not sanitary," Lucine says. "It's like borrowing underwear."

"Will Emeline be able to go swimming with us in the summer if she's bleeding from that part of her body?" Ernestine asks.

"Not unless she uses an applicator. According to the booklets and filmstrips, we're not supposed to be in cold water or get chills, but I refuse to believe that's true. Not too long ago, people thought you'd die if you bathed or exercised, and that was proven total bunk."

Adicia doesn't understand much of what her older sisters are talking about. She hopes with everything in her that their happy little quartet will continue as it always has, though Lucine is soon to go to high school and Emeline has undergone the strange and secretive process that turns a girl into a young woman. The one constant in her life, the friendship she shares with her sisters, means everything to her. Without it, she'd have to figure out a whole new way to navigate the rough hand she was dealt when she was born into a family plagued by poverty for generations.

Chapter 10: The Sacrifice of Gemma

Adicia and her siblings spent the first day of summer vacation at the Hamilton Fish Park Pool at East Houston and Pitt Streets. Gemma, Carlos, and Allen used the diving pool and played tennis with their friends, while Adicia, Tommy, Ernestine, and Justine used the wading pool and playground. Lucine and Emeline swam in the diving pool but didn't have the nerve to use the diving board. Adicia was jealous and resentful to see Tommy using the pool toys and equipment their mother bought him instead of using the money for groceries or bills, but happy she got to enjoy a day having fun and able to cool down in the water. She was so glad to get away from the stifling, depressing mood of the tenement, she was able to somewhat overlook Tommy's sassing remarks and how he several times stuck his tongue out at her, her sisters, and Sarah.

Gemma's swimsuit is brand new. Many of the boys flirted with her, probably because of her red bikini. Adicia can't believe Gemma's wearing something that looks like underwear in public, but Gemma swears it's what all fashionable women wear and that only squares and wet blankets wear one-piece swimsuits. Carlos and Allen also have relatively new bathing trunks. Carlos has green trunks, and Allen has blue trunks. Tommy of course also has new bathing trunks, red with little black stars all over. The rest of them have hand-me-downs, which Mrs. Troy insists are perfectly fine so long as they're washed well before being handed off to a new owner. Lucine's is somewhat fashionable, since it's only a few years old, but the rest of them hate wearing suits last considered fashionable in the late Forties and early Fifties.

"Whose car is that?" Gemma asks as they walk up Essex Street. "It's not bad. You think we have a new neighbor?"

"Most people who live here can't afford cars," Carlos points out. "Maybe it's an undercover cop tryna bust the place for overcrowding or some other violation of the housing or fire code."

"Nonsense," Allen scoffs. "There are mobsters living in the building. They always slip the cops money if they come to investigate."

When they get to their tenement on the eighth floor, a greasy man with a cold, hard face is in the living room, talking to their parents and Mrs. Troy's former co-worker Mrs. Rossi from the third floor. He turns to Gemma and smiles at her in a way that makes her sick to her stomach and gives her a foreboding of something very bad about to happen.

"Gemma, this is my bachelor nephew Francesco Monterastelli. I was just visiting him and his parents the other day and remembered your lovely parents wanna find a husband for you. I thought he'd be a nice match."

"Monte-what?" Gemma asks. "Didn't most people with long names have them shortened when they got off the boat?"

"Get used to saying, writing, and spelling it, since you're gonna be saying and writing it a lot in the near future," Francesco says. "Don't you modern women wear clothes anymore? I don't want my future wife walking around in a bikini. Go put some decent clothes on." He walks over to her and smacks her on the behind very loudly. "Hustle it up, woman."

Gemma looks at her parents and Mrs. Rossi in horror. "If this is supposed to be a joke, I don't find it at all amusing. Yous can end your creepy farce now."

"You heard your future master, girl. Go to your room, change outta that revealing thing, and put on decent clothes," Mr. Troy says.

"Okay, in case any of yous forgot, I'm going to Hofstra College on Long Island this fall, joining a sorority and as many other clubs as I want, and majoring in business so I can open my own store when I graduate. I'm not gonna be a little eighteen-year-old bride like some of the other girls in my class. I don't wanna be married till I'm at least twenty-one, so I can have some fun before settling down."

"No woman of mine is gonna go to college." Francesco spits on the floor, narrowly missing one of the chickens, who've finally begun to lay a few eggs. "What kind of disreputable institution is this that they admit girls? Next thing you know, they'll be teachin' cows to drive!"

"It was founded in 1935 as part of NYU and gained independence as its own college in '37," Gemma says, reciting what she memorized from the promotional pamphlets she read while deciding between applying to Hofstra, Hunter, and Barnard. "And where have you been? Almost all schools admit women today."

"I don't approve of higher education for women." Francesco slaps her on the behind again. "Nor do I approve of bikinis. After you change, I'll go through all your clothes and pick out the stuff I won't allow you to bring to our new home together."

Gemma, reeling from disbelief, runs to her room, closes the door, takes off her bikini, throws it on the floor, and opens the door of the wardrobe she shares with Lucine, one of the Troys' few pieces of furniture worth more than a few dollars. After what seems like forever, she finally picks out a brown calfskin skirt falling to her mid-calf, pink leather sandals, and a pale green silk blouse with sleeves extending to the wrists and a neckline covering her collarbone.

Francesco smiles a partly toothless grin at her when she emerges. Gemma wants to vomit when he coarsely grabs her face and forces a French kiss on her. While this is happening, her parents and Mrs. Rossi stand by without saying a word or moving to pull Francesco off her. Suddenly her happy day at the Hamilton Fish Park Pool seems like a distant memory that happened to someone else entirely.

"How dare you do that!" she yells when he releases her. "I'm a good girl, not a common whore who does that with any man who happens along!"

"Oh, nonsense, Gemma. We all know you've kissed more than a few boys," Mrs. Troy says.

"Boys I wanted to kiss, not strange men who forced kisses on me! And I certainly never let a boy put his tongue in my mouth!"

Francesco goes into Gemma's room and opens her closet, pawing through all the clothes on hangers and throwing random things on the bed and floor. Gemma is seething.

"No woman of mine wears pants. Only tramps wear pants. Those skirts and dresses are too short. I only want you wearing clothes that come at least to the mid-calf like that skirt you have on now. These blouses show too much arm and cleavage. I don't want my friends and relatives to think I'm marrying a hooker. And you can forget all about wearing makeup and nailpolish. Only whores wear that. My dear sweet mother never painted her face and nails. She'll teach you a true example of womanhood."

"How old is Francesco?" Emeline asks, feeling sorry for Gemma for the first time ever.

"He's thirty-eight," Mrs. Rossi says.

Gemma stifles another urge to vomit. "I've said I'd like to marry an older guy, but I meant five or six years older, not twenty years older! He's old enough to be my father!"

"So? He's old enough to have some money in the bank, and has a decent job in a bar. As soon as he heard he'd be married soon, he and his parents went to look for an apartment, and he signed the paperwork for a nice one-bedroom apartment you'll be moving into as soon as the wedding bells ring. It's in Two Bridges."

"What kind of square lives with his parents at almost forty? Is he able to function without his mommy and daddy doing everything for him?"

"That's gonna be your job from now on. You'll be a replacement for his mother and will cook, clean, and do whatever else needs doing. Now would be an ideal time to start shadowing Sarah when she cooks and does laundry, since it's gonna be all on your shoulders soon. It's perfectly normal to live at home until marriage in the Italian community."

"We're not in Italy. We're in the good old U.S.A. I'm not even Italian. I'm half-French and half-Belgian, and *my* people have been here since the 1680s on my father's side and the late 1840s on my mother's side. Are his mommy and daddy gonna pay us visits every single day to check up on their overgrown baby and tell me everything I'm doing wrong?"

"If you're a good housekeeper and wife, they won't need to visit that often," Francesco says. "But we will have weekly family meals, and my mother expects to visit our children whenever she wants, and to move in when each child is a baby, so she can make sure you're being a proper mother and show you how to take care of a baby properly."

Gemma looks at her parents desperately. "Why are you letting this happen? It's illegal in this country to force a woman to marry someone! This isn't India. I'll only marry a man of my choosing, after I'm at least twenty-one and have experienced life and had my youthful fun. I certainly don't intend to give up makeup and fashionable clothes for the sake of a brute who thinks it's still the Middle Ages."

"You were getting above your raising, that's why," Mrs. Troy says. "You were not raised to wanna go to college, have a career, and move away. You'll only be moving a stone's throw away. He ain't transplanting you to a foreign place like the Upper West Side or Chelsea. You should be thankful we ain't marrying you off to someone who lives in a tenement and that he earns a bit more money than your father. You're marrying up."

"The O'Connells on the fifth floor let us use their phone so we could book an appointment at a bridal shop tomorrow at eleven," Mrs. Rossi says. "My sister and her husband will pay for your wedding, so you don't have to look at the cheapest dresses. Your sisters can be the bridesmaids, Tommy can be the ring-bearer, Adicia can be the flower girl, and one of your friends can be your maid of honor. You can order a nice bouquet of roses or colored daisies, instead of picking wildflowers or using a wilted thing the florist was about to throw out."

"I look through your *Seventeen* magazine each month when it arrives, to check for any indecent content, so I know they have ads for china and other things every newly-engaged girl needs for her future household. Francesco took a look at some of the back issues while you were at the swimming pool, and he got some ideas for an engagement ring from their ring ads. Even your magazine knows all proper girls your age should be getting married instead of going off to college."

"If that's what you think *Seventeen* is all about, you're reading it very selectively," Gemma says darkly. "They have those things for their readers who *are* getting married, not saying all their readers are automatically getting married fresh outta high school or you're a square if you're going to college and don't wanna get married right away."

"About your posters and records." Francesco spits on the floor again. "They won't be coming with you when you move in with me. Elvis can't sing or act his way out of a paper bag, and the only man you need to be dreaming about will be me, not Elvis, William Holden, Cary Grant, or Rock Hudson. You won't have time to go to the movies or listen to your trash records when you're running a household and birthing babies."

"Am I supposed to wear an apron and a hairnet while I slave away in the kitchen?" Gemma snarls sarcastically.

"That would be fantastic. I hope you don't have none of those stupid ideas some modern women have about wanting to plan children. I want the babies to start coming immediately, one after the other, just like your own parents did. You'd better produce me a boy on the first try."

"And what if I run to girls like my mother, you'll beat me?"

"I'll beat you anyway if you act uppity or get outta line. It's a proper man's duty to regularly beat his wife. Oh, and you'll need to convert to Catholicism for my priest to marry us. Start thinking about a baptismal name. What's your middle name? Maybe that can be your saint's name."

"It's Léonie," Mr. Troy supplies. "All my kids got at least one French name. We've got Gemma Léonie, Carlos Ghislain, Allen Théodore, Lucine Camille, Emeline Rosalie, Ernestine Zénobie, Adicia Éloïse, Thomas Albert, and Justine Anastasie."

"My mother makes delicious lasagna, ravioli, gnocchi, and minestrone. Those are my favorite foods. You'd better be able to make them as good as she does. When you visit my parents, you can learn how to make pasta dough. We also love goat meat. Don't worry, I'll give you money to go to the market to buy the things I need to eat. Tomorrow I'll drop by again with a list of chores you must do every single day, and a list of recipes you'll need to prepare for me. Expect an engagement ring by the end of the week."

Gemma's mouth hangs wide open as Francesco leaves with Mrs. Rossi. "What was that? You're not seriously forcing me to marry this grotesque bully, are you? Normal parents wanna protect their children from bad guys, not happily send them into the lions' den!"

"Bridal shop tomorrow at eleven," Mrs. Troy repeats, ignoring Gemma's pleas. "Be glad we care enough to find you a decent husband before you got stuck with someone you liked but who ain't necessarily the best provider like I did. I did defend you to Mrs. Rossi when she suggested Francesco's parents would ask you to go to the doctor to prove your virginity. I said you insist so obnoxiously over and over again you ain't the type who puts out. Someone who ain't a virgin wouldn't be that sincere and vocal about it, particularly not when your brothers make no bones about doing that with their girls."

"We're having supper with the Monsterellis, or whatever their name is, tomorrow," Mr. Troy goes on. "Francesco's the oldest of thirteen, and all his siblings except his sister Antonia, who's a few years older than you, will be there with their families. Antonia's studying to be a nun."

"Right about now I wish *I* were a nun," Gemma mopes.

"They found a priest who'll do your conversion in less than six months for enough money," Mrs. Troy says. "Most priests want you to study for at least a year, but some respect money enough to rush people through conversions for the sake of marriage. I wish you didn't hafta join the Papists, but it ain't as though you'll be becoming one where it really counts. You're just doing it for the sake of appearances. I don't expect to ever visit you and find you praying to Mary or the saints. A pity my grandchildren by you will have to be raised Papists, though."

"When's the wedding?" Ernestine asks.

"That depends on how soon the priest can rush through Gemma's conversion. We're hoping it'll be sometime in the early fall. Lucine, you always whine about wanting more fashionable clothes and makeup, so you can take all the clothes Francesco has forbidden Gemma to bring into their new household, and all her makeup, nailpolish, posters, and records."

Gemma glares at Lucine when her face lights up in a huge smile.

"We'll have to use the O'Connells' phone again tomorrow to call Hofstra and say you won't be enrolling," Mrs. Troy continues. "Any money you may have given them will be your loss, though perhaps you can be refunded since the school year didn't start yet. A girl going to college, indeed. You should've been like Carlos and dropped out."

Carlos goes into the kitchen for some methamphetamine. "You wouldn't catch me dead graduating high school. I have more important things to do with my time, like hustle drugs, drink, and start a real job. I get to eat for free on the job too. The rich people at home will never know their cereal box don't have as much cereal as it's supposed to."

"I always liked having a last name that was easy to spell, pronounce, and remember," Gemma mopes. "I wanted to marry a guy with an equally simple name, like Jones, Miller, or Smith. What's his name again, Montestarelli?"

"Monterastelli," Mrs. Troy says.

"It sounds like a name Chico Marx would use!"

"Who's Chico Marx?" Adicia asks.

"A member of a comedy team that stopped making movies awhile ago. One of them hosts a quiz show now." Gemma turns back to her mother. "Am I supposed to cut off all my beautiful blonde hair and put it up in an old lady bun too? Will he make me cover my hair entirely?"

"We'll have plenty of time to discuss all these things before your big day in the fall. Now who else is looking forward to a delicious Italian supper tomorrow night?"

The bridal shop Mrs. Rossi and the Troys selected is on the Upper East Side, so Mrs. Troy has decided it'll be better to take the subway instead of walking over an hour to get there. The next morning, she, Sarah, Mrs. Rossi, Tommy, and the girls set out for the subway station, wearing some of their relatively nicer clothes. Mrs. Rossi has a large wad of cash in her purse, given to her by her sister and brother-in-law. Adicia is so excited about traveling uptown and going to a bridal shop, she loses track of how unhappy Gemma is and how beastly unfair their parents are being by forcing her to marry a repulsive much-older man.

Adicia's eyes light up at the sight of all the beautiful dresses, and all the lovely shoes, veils, and other accessories. She'll be the flower girl, which means she'll walk up the aisle as she sprinkles flower petals from a basket. Even if she only has a chance to wear this dress one time, she'll finally get to know what it's like to wear a brand-new dress. She might get pretty new shoes and stockings too, and have her picture taken in group wedding photos. Adicia has only ever had her picture taken in group school photos. Even if her parents could afford the regular solo pictures for the yearbook, they wouldn't want pictures of their daughters. Adicia only knows what she looks like from looking in the dirty, cracked mirror in the tiny bedroom.

Mrs. Troy does the talking. "Hello. I'm Mrs. Dolores Troy, and this is my friend and neighbor Mrs. Luigina Rossi. My oldest daughter Gemma's getting married in the fall to Mrs. Rossi's nephew Francesco Monterastelli, and she needs a nice dress. My son Tommy's gonna be their ring-bearer, my daughter Adicia will be flower girl, and the other girls will be bridesmaids. Gemma hasn't selected her maid of honor, so we may be paying another visit a bit later."

"I get to wear a special suit and carry rings on a fancy pillow!" Tommy shouts excitedly.

"Is this other woman in your bridal party?" the salon owner asks.

"Oh, that's only Sarah, my kids' nanny and my servant. I imagine she'll come to the wedding too, since she helped raise Gemma, but she'll be in the audience and won't require a special dress."

Sarah lifts Justine out of her stroller to let her toddle around on her newly confident walking legs. Now fifteen months old, Justine took her first steps in May and has been toddling around everywhere ever since. She's also saying a few simple words and using her own baby words for other things, like calling her bottle a "baba." Mrs. Troy barely notices her youngest child is toddling and saying words, and cares less she's almost completely uninvolved in watching these developmental milestones for the final time.

Gemma is taken into the dressing room by the owner as an associate is dispatched to find a couple of dresses in her size. She sinks down onto the bench and takes off her shoes, still in total shock.

"When did you meet your fiancé?" the owner asks.

Gemma breaks down sobbing. "Yesterday! I spent the day at the Hamilton Fish Pool, and when I came home, this strange man was there with Mrs. Rossi, and she and my parents told me we'd be getting married! He slapped me on my behind twice, ordered me to take off my new bikini and put on less-revealing clothes, and when I came back in more modest clothes, he grabbed me and forcibly kissed me! He even stuck his tongue in my mouth! I admit I've kissed more than a few guys, but I never let any of them put a tongue in my mouth! I certainly never let any guy kiss me on only our first date! I'm the kind of girl who likes to wait till at least the third date!"

The associate, who's come back with four dresses, stops in her tracks upon hearing this story. Her mouth drops open and the dresses slide to the floor.

"I have to convert to Catholicism too! I'm not particularly religious, but I'm not against religion in general or Christianity in particular. If I did wanna change my religion, it'd be because I wanted to and I believed in their ideas about God and the Bible and what have you, not because I was forced to convert for appearances' sake just to marry a bully twenty years my senior."

"Why are your parents making you get married?" the associate asks. "Is it part of your culture?"

"My parents don't want me to go to college, and they're punishing me for tryna do better than they did. My intended is thirty-eight and still lives with his parents, and expects me to be his substitute mother! Well, they may succeed in forcing me to marry this brute and have children with him, but I'll never accept it, and I'll escape this bizarre family and get the last laugh on them if it's the last thing I ever do."

Mrs. Troy thinks she hears Gemma sobbing, blubbering, and carrying on, but shrugs it off. Even if Gemma is telling everything to the saleswoman and the owner, she'll still have to go through with the marriage. She and Mr. Troy decided Gemma needed to be married, and immediately selected Francesco, so it must be done.

When Gemma comes out in the first dress, Mrs. Troy stands up to closely critique her.

"Chantilly lace is perfect for any bride," Mrs. Rossi says. "It flatters every woman. Though the arms are a bit short for Francesco's style."

"I'm not wearing body armor just to please that brute."

"The neckline is a bit high," Mrs. Troy says. "I don't think there's anything wrong with exposing your collarbone."

"While Gemma's trying on the other dresses, why doesn't someone find bridesmaid dresses?" Mrs. Rossi asks. "And Tommy needs a small suit."

"I'm sorry, but we don't carry suits. I can give you the addresses of several nice menswear shops nearby if you'd like." The associate pulls a small blue dress off a rack. "What was the flower girl's name again, Alicia?"

"Adicia. She's named after a Greek goddess," Emeline says. "Not a name you hear every day, is it?"

"Do you have a color scheme?"

"Color ain't important," Mrs. Troy says. "So long as everything fits and looks decent. The gowns don't have to match each other or the flowers."

"Dark blue is my favorite color!" Adicia says. "Can I please have this dress?"

"Can I pick my own dress, since we don't care about having the same color?" Ernestine asks.

"Can I have high heels?" Lucine begs.

"Can we wear jewelry?" Emeline asks.

While Gemma tries the other three dresses on and holds her tongue as her mother and Mrs. Rossi debate how fashionable they are, if Francesco will approve of them, how tight or revealing they are, and how plain or elaborate they are, her sisters have a blast trying on dresses and shoes. They leave at 1:30 with a dark blue satin dress for Adicia, a red chiffon dress for Ernestine, a green taffeta dress for Emeline, a violet organza dress for Lucine, leather shoes matching each girl's color, with a pair of low heels for Lucine, a long heavy lace veil Gemma hates, a pair of white high heels with binding ankle straps, and a floor-length ivory Chantilly lace wedding gown with a long train and a lot of beading on the bodice.

A stop at a menswear store a few blocks down produces a small suit and bowtie for Tommy, who annoys all the staff by running up and down the aisles, pulling things off racks and shelves, and loudly prattling about things no one cares about. All the salespeople are relieved when the little terror leaves.

The Troys, Sarah, and Mrs. Rossi return at 5:00. Carlos opens the door, smoking methamphetamine and holding a small stack of papers.

"Gemma's man stopped by to drop off a list of his husbandly requests. He also left a package on her bed. Don't worry, I didn't pry into it. I had better things to do with my time, like get high."

Gemma grabs the papers and rushes into her room. Her stomach lurches when she opens the box. Francesco bought her a bunch of ugly, utilitarian, grandma-style bras and underwear, presumably to replace the pretty ones she has now. The list is handwritten in very sloppy printing. Gemma isn't too surprised to find Francesco doesn't know how to write cursive. Her youngest sisters can print better than that, despite being at least thirty years his junior.

"Look at this." She tosses the papers at Lucine when she enters the room to hang her new dress up in the wardrobe. "This is what that premodern fool expects me to do after he's forcibly married me."

Lucine can't decide whether to laugh or cry as she starts reading. "He wants you to clip his fingernails and toenails, brush his hair, bathe him, dress him, and light his cigarettes?"

"He won't let me smoke my own cigarettes, according to this! And what if I don't know how to cook his precious goat meat or lasagna exactly as his stupid mother does? I've never eaten goat meat or seen it at a restaurant!"

"If he likes everything exactly as his mother does it, why doesn't he just marry her or keep living at home?"

"He might be living at home at almost forty, but that violent kiss he gave me yesterday was not his first kiss. That could not have been beginner's luck. He definitely knew what he was doing. He must've had a bunch of girlfriends already, but they didn't marry him for good reasons. I wonder if he plans to have a couple of mistresses."

"I care less if your father's ever been unfaithful to me," Mrs. Troy says. "So long as I'm the woman he comes home to at the end of the day."

"Can we wear our new dresses to supper at the Monsterellis' house?" Adicia asks.

"Only on the wedding day. But do wear nicer clothes than usual. We want to impress them, not make them think we're slobs or trash."

"Do I have to sit next to this bully at supper?" Gemma asks.

"In time you'll learn to love him. Besides, even if you find his manners repulsive, he could always make up for it in other ways, if you know what I mean."

Gemma runs to the bathroom to vomit at the idea of Francesco touching her, seeing him naked, and sleeping with him. Had she known she'd be forced to marry such a creature, she would've slept with one of her more serious boyfriends instead of insisting on waiting for marriage. Now she has no choice but to give up her virginity to this disgusting thing, someone she doesn't even like, someone who won't do anything to make it special for her. She almost wants to lie she's pregnant by her last boyfriend so she can have a shotgun wedding to someone she likes.

Mrs. Rossi told them to be at the Monterastellis' house in Little Italy for supper at 7:00, and Mrs. Troy makes sure to have her brood bathed and dressed properly before they set out for the walk. Gemma drags her heels the entire way and stays well at the back of the line, dreading entering that house and having to see Francesco again.

"Welcome to our lovely home!" Mrs. Monterastelli says in a friendly tone of voice when she answers the rowhouse door. "Yous can come right into the kitchen. Supper should be out of the oven in just a little bit. We made goat meat, beef lasagna, and minestrone soup."

Adicia peers into the kitchen. "Can we help you put away your dishes, Mrs. Monsterelli?"

Mrs. Troy looks in to see what she's talking about, and stands back in embarrassment. A big pile of pots and pans is stacked on top of the stove and the shelf next to it, and a large number of dishes, cups, and utensils are in the drainboard and next to the sink. Even in the Troys' pathetic kitchen, dishes are always put away in the cupboard before the last person goes to bed.

"I'm so sorry, Mrs. Monterastelli. We didn't know you hadn't finished cleaning up before we came over. We'll sit in the living room while you finish up."

"Oh, that?" Mrs. Monterastelli looks behind her. "That's how our kitchen is organized. We use our cupboards for other things. Come on and sit down."

"You already have a leg up on this woman," Mrs. Troy whispers to Gemma. "A good housekeeper is proud of her home, even if it is a tenement, and never lets guests or strangers see a mess or don't put away her dishes after she washes them."

"What do you and your husband do for a living to afford a house?" Ernestine asks. "And how much money do you make?"

"I don't work. Respectable women don't work. Gemma ain't gonna be working when she marries Francesco. My husband's the co-owner of a restaurant, and Francesco's a bartender."

"Do you have drugs?" Carlos asks. "I'm dying for some drugs, any kind, right about now."

"Will alcohol be enough to tide you over until you get home?"

"If respectable women don't work, do you think Mrs. Rossi, your sister, is a bad person for working?" Ernestine asks.

"Some women have to work. At least she's only a cleaning lady in a hotel, not a woman with an actual career. It's too bad she couldn't marry a man who could take care of her so she wouldn't have to work."

"I wanna work," Emeline says. "I'm gonna be a librarian when I'm older."

Francesco comes into the room and grins at Gemma, pinching her breasts. "Come sit down, woman. My family's waiting to meet your family. All of us are here except Antonia, who's a postulant at a convent at the church you'll be converting through."

"What's a postulant?" Adicia asks.

"It's the first level in becoming a nun," Mrs. Monterastelli says. "After your postulancy, you become a novitiate. Then you take your vows."

"Somea the girls at our school are Catholics," Ernestine says. "They say most Catholics go to private school, and only Catholics without money go to public school."

"Gemma and Francesco will send their kids to Catholic school without a doubt. We can't wait for the first baby to come. All my kids except Antonia have married and had babies by now."

Gemma is swept along to the table by Francesco and his mother. She's shown a seat near the head of the table, a good distance away from her family. Meanwhile her siblings are so busy inhaling the hot home-cooked food they barely pay any attention to Francesco's leering at and groping of her. Several times she slaps away his hand when he tries to slip it underneath her skirt.

"We can't wait for you to start having babies," the oldest daughter, Sophia, says. "All us sisters and sisters-in-law have done it so many times, we can recommend the best obstetrician in the area."

"Isn't it a bit early to think about doctors when we're not married yet?" Gemma asks nervously.

"Nonsense. Most people have a honeymoon baby. Our doctor is so God-like it's unbelievable. We just put all our trust in him and let him do the dirty work. I think all of us have fallen a little in love with him. We feel so safe and protected under his care. I didn't even question it when I awoke from a few of my deliveries with no skin on my wrists or around my ankles. I just knew it was something he did for my own good."

"Before the babies comes marriage, and before marriage comes conversion," the second sister, Maria, says. "The priest who'll do yours ain't our normal priest, but our regular priest insisted on taking at least a year. We can't have a delayed wedding, can we? You'll learn more as you go along. So long as you get the basics in before the wedding."

"Can we quiz Gemma on what she already knows about the one true faith?" one of the older nephews asks. "Does she know who our current Pope is or the names of the Twelve Disciples?"

Gemma is sick to her stomach over Francesco's nauseating behavior and the endless supply of heavy food being pushed on her. She's made to finish five large pieces of lasagna, a huge slab of goat meat, three bowls of minestrone, a huge serving of salad, and three long, thick breadsticks. Dessert is some sort of cake, of which she's made to eat four slices. She cares less that for once her mother isn't lecturing about how ladies only eat so much for fear of gaining too much weight and not being able to attract worthwhile men. There's a big difference between a healthy appetite and overeating to the point of being sick.

"Your food was yummy!" Adicia tells Mrs. Monterastelli. "Can we come over here and eat anytime we want after Gemma's married?"

"We loved your goat meat!" Ernestine says. "We were afraid it'd taste terrible since we never had it before, but it tasted really good!"

Carlos looks into the living room. "You people got a television? How long did you have to save up for that?"

"We put aside a little money each month for a year or so. It ain't hard with the right job and proper budgeting and saving," Mr. Monterastelli says.

"I'm starting a job soon. Maybe I'll be able to afford onea them things too, though I'd rather spend all my money on drugs and alcohol before getting me a status symbol like that."

Gemma cannot believe Francesco's entire family is acting just as bonkers as her parents, as though it's so normal to arrange a marriage like this and as though her own feelings don't count. Even societies with arranged marriages don't do it like this. Instead they're carrying on about seeing the priest, shopping for furniture, and choosing a doctor. Gemma is terrified after hearing Sophia had no skin on her wrists or around her ankles after having a few of her babies, with no idea how that happened. Perhaps the only kind of people who'd accept such a shocking thing as normal are the same kind of people who'd celebrate a forced marriage.

Mrs. Troy has decided to quit her latest job, clerking at the post office, to devote all her time to planning Gemma's wedding. With Francesco's parents footing the entire affair, it won't matter how much money is spent. Instead of going to work at Macy's, Gemma is dragged along to the church where it was decided she'd be converted. In the span of only three days, her entire life has been turned upside-down.

"I'm Father Raimundo," the priest greets them. "You're the young lady converting for your upcoming marriage?"

"It doesn't matter what I want, since my parents and Francesco's family decide everything from now on," Gemma grumps.

"That's the spirit!" Mrs. Troy says excitedly. "Turn everything over to us and it'll all go better. Now Father, I ain't really a fan of the Papists, but if it's only for the sake of marriage, it ain't as though she's really becoming a believing member. I assume the Monterastellis already paid you to rush her through conversion?"

"I do dozens of these quickie conversions every year. I teach them basic Catholic history and beliefs, a couple of major prayers, the most important saints, and the titles of various spiritual leaders in the hierarchy. Gemma, you can start by telling me what you already know about Catholicism."

"You have a Pope in Rome who tells yous what to do, yous don't approve of birth control and have at least twelve babies, you don't believe the Protestant teaching that Mary later had blood children with

Joseph and wasn't a virgin forever, you have a different version of the Bible, and you think the Communion wafers and wine turn into Christ's body and blood."

Father Raimundo looks at Mrs. Troy and Mrs. Monterastelli for validation. "Well, it's a start. Some of 'em come in here only knowing we have a Pope and pray to saints for intercession."

Mrs. Monterastelli waves at someone walking near the front of the church. "Father, may we have permission to speak to Antonia? We ain't seen her since she started her postulancy, and Gemma should meet her sister-in-law when she has a chance."

"What, you need permission to talk to someone or have a visit when you're a nun?" Gemma asks.

"Some convents relax it a bit after you're a fully-vowed nun, but all self-respecting mother superiors make their postulants and novices follow strict rules. At least Antonia ain't becoming a cloistered nun."

"It doesn't matter what the mother superior thinks. She's only a woman," Father Raimundo says. "I override her. Why I could order all the nuns to walk around naked down Houston Street, and they'd have to obey me."

Gemma realizes in depression that this priest is no man of God, and that he won't be an ally for her either. Right about now she wishes she'd been nicer to her sisters and Sarah. They could've helped her escape had she cultivated a good relationship with them over the years. Carlos is almost always off in his own drugged world, so he'd be no help even if she liked him, and Allen's only sixteen, even if he doesn't drink or get high as often as Carlos. She thinks darkly that if Allen ever went straight, he'd probably be able to do something to get at least some of their sisters away from their horrendous home life and protect them from their parents. As it stands now, the formerly golden firstborn child is being offered up as a sacrifice.

Gemma rushes off to talk to Antonia, hoping someone who's only a few years her senior will be a modern woman like she is, and can suggest something, anything, to get out of this impossible situation. Antonia got away from her family, and wasn't forced to leave the convent.

"You don't know me, but I'm being forced to marry your brother Francesco," Gemma blurts out breathlessly. "And I'm being forced to become a Catholic, quit my job, and withdraw from the college I was accepted to!"

Antonia looks back at her mother and Mrs. Troy, the latter of whom looks as trashy and ill-kempt as always. Even when Mrs. Troy puts on relatively decent clothes, she bears the look of a woman far older than only thirty-seven because of all the hard living, drugs, and alcohol she's done, and has a permanent mean look. Sarah looks older than her age too, but she has a sympathetic face and hasn't hastened the aging process by imbibing a lot of drugs and alcohol or having nine children and ten pregnancies in seventeen years.

"My parents finally found a woman for that gross bully?"

"The match was suggested by your aunt Mrs. Rossi! What modern woman in her right mind wants to marry a guy who's twenty years older and expects her to wait on him hand and foot, even clipping his nails and bathing him? I wanna vomit every time I think of how I'll hafta go to bed with him! And meanwhile everyone is smiling and acting like this is so normal!"

"Francesco's a big mama's boy, but he always bathed himself and took care of his own personal hygiene. He's had a lot of girlfriends, but none of them marriage material. I hope he doesn't give you something like syphilis from the philandering I'm sure he'll do even after marriage."

"You're religious. You believe in God, Jesus, and the power of prayer. Is there any special prayer I can do to get outta this nightmare?"

Antonia smiles weakly. "I'm afraid you can't do much short of running away and making sure no one ever finds you. But there are always ways to get out afterwards. Saint Rita's the patron saint of impossible causes. Maybe if you take her as your saint's name and pray to her every day, she can intercede with God on your behalf to save you. Perhaps you can prove Francesco is an unfaithful husband and get a divorce, or have him committed to the loonybin because of how much he drinks. Put all your thoughts toward escape, and God will open up a way to salvation."

Gemma is so beaten-down after only three days of horror, she feels she has no choice but to accept Antonia's advice. If she stops fighting and gives the impression she accepts her fate, things won't be so hard to endure. She'll lead everyone to believe she's "come to her senses," while all the while secretly plotting a way out of this mad dream. That way, it'll make it harder for them to discover what's really going on inside her mind, and she'll be able to get the last laugh.

***

After spending what had been planned as her last summer before college studying for an insincere conversion with a nasty priest, shopping for furniture and other household items for an apartment in a neighborhood she hates, and planning a wedding, Gemma has been told the wedding date will be October 2, Sunday. Mrs. Troy and Mrs. Monterastelli had been hoping to finalize the agreement by the first of the month, but Sarah protested that that day was Yom Kippur and she wouldn't be able to attend the wedding.

The wedding won't be much, by Gemma's standards, but her parents are convinced it'll be the wedding to rival all weddings. She supposes people who think roadkill is fine eating and buy wilted flowers intended for the garbage can instead of fresh flowers for full price would be impressed by a three-star hotel and a bland supper of scalloped potatoes, beef, garden salad, and spaghetti.

The engagement ring Francesco bought her at the end of their first week of engagement is a platinum band topped by a square-cut diamond solitaire. Gemma thinks it's the epitome of boring, but has said nothing to keep as much peace as she can while figuring out how she's going to eventually make her break. Later, when she's free and has a man of her choosing, she can ask for a ring with colored side stones, or a colored gemstone in the middle with diamonds as accents.

Being in a wedding is the highlight of her sisters' whole year. Before they leave for the church, Lucine excitedly folds and hangs up all the clothes that are now hers, unable to believe she'll walk into school on Monday wearing first-run fashions instead of hand-me-downs. She's looking forward to finally wearing makeup and nailpolish too.

The social hall is closed off so the bridal party can change. Gemma mutely lets her mother and Mrs. Monterastelli help her into the dress she didn't choose, then pulls on her stockings and shoes. Only very reluctantly did Francesco agree to let her wear makeup for the ceremony, since the photographer told him it'll show up better in pictures.

"Remember, it goes better if you relax," Mrs. Rossi whispers a bit too loudly.

"What goes better?" Adicia asks.

"Your big sister's wifely duties she'll have to start doing tonight,"

Mrs. Rossi responds vaguely. "Nothing you need to concern yourself with for at least twelve more years."

"You mean cleaning and cooking?" Ernestine asks.

"That's enough of this conversation," Gemma says nervously. "Let them stay little girls as long as they're supposed to. It's bad enough they've been cheated out of real childhoods so far."

"Childhood is a luxury for the rich," Mrs. Troy proclaims. "Adicia, remember not to throw all your petals on the carpet at once. You need to toss them slowly as you're walking. Maybe some parents think it's cute or funny when their daughter messes up, but I won't. And the rest of yous, walk slowly. Turn and smile at people instead of looking straight ahead."

"Can we hang up our bouquets so they dry and keep forever?" Emeline asks.

"If you want." Mrs. Troy puts the veil over Gemma's face. "Are we all ready to walk down in the order we rehearsed?"

"We can't wait!" Adicia picks up her basket of red rose petals.

Gemma stands back as the wedding processional starts. First Father Raimundo, Francesco, and the best man enter from a side door and walk to the altar. Then Gemma's sisters walk down with the groomsmen, who include Carlos and Allen. Carlos, who was somehow prevailed upon to be sober and off drugs for the day, is Lucine's escort, and Allen is Emeline's escort. Ernestine is escorted by one of Francesco's nephews. Then comes Gemma's maid of honor, her former co-worker and classmate Diane Gaffney. Tommy comes next, holding a pillow made by one of Francesco's sisters, with plain yellow gold rings tied on with a ribbon. Finally, "Here Comes the Bride" starts, and Adicia walks in front of Gemma and Mr. Troy, happily scattering petals along the carpet and smiling at everyone. She can't believe her luck, wearing a beautiful new dress for the first time in her life, the center of attention for a little while, and going to go to a party after the wedding.

Gemma grins and bears it as she's walked down the aisle by her father, knowing she really is literally being given away to become Francesco's property. There's nothing she can do about it now but plot revenge while pretending to smile and keep sweet.

Though Gemma's entire being wants to run out of the church then and there, she responds in the affirmative to the vows, including a

vow to obey Francesco. Her stomach churns at the conclusion of the
ceremony when Francesco grabs her and violently French kisses her,
but she continues to play the part so no one will suspect the charade.
To escape the lions' den, she has to slide out slowly and put on the
greatest acting job of her life. If she does escape successfully, perhaps
her sacrifice will have been worth it, and will serve as the one good
thing she's done for her sisters.

Part II: Dramatic Developments
(March–December 1962)

I have always believed, and I still believe, that whatever good or bad fortune may come our way we can always give it meaning and transform it into something of value.
(*Siddhartha*, Hermann Hesse)

Perfer et obdura; doler hib tibi proderit olim.
(Be patient and tough; someday this pain will be useful to you.)
(*Amorum*, Ovid)

Chapter 11: Ernestine's New Friends

Ernestine is kicking a ball down the street one afternoon when she notices a strange girl and boy about her age climbing into a garbage dumpster and putting food and other items into a large flour sack. They don't live in the tenement, and she's never seen them at school or around the neighborhood.

"What are yous doing digging through our garbage dump? That's for my family and our neighbors to get food from!"

"What, you own this dumpster?" the boy challenges her in a Manhattan accent even stronger than Ernestine's.

Now in fourth grade, Ernestine still has no friends. She'd do almost anything to make a real friend and have someone to talk with who isn't related to her. "What are your names? And where do yous live?"

"They call me Girl. I'll be ten next month. That's my brother Boy. He's gonna be eight in June." She has the same heavy Manhattan accent.

"Your names are actually Girl and Boy?" Ernestine is very sad they have such uncaring parents who couldn't be bothered to name them properly. At least her parents gave all their children special names.

"We have two little sisters named Baby and Infant. Baby's four and Infant's two. Our parents didn't want kids, so they named us by what we were. The name Girl was already taken, so they called the next girl Baby and the third one Infant."

"How long have you been here? I've lived here my whole life, and I've never seen either of yous around."

"We live in a squat in The Bowery. It's more like a communal village. All the walls were knocked down, so it's one huge living space where we all share and help each other."

"What's a squat?"

"An abandoned building, or any place really, that someone doesn't have permission to live in. We ain't lived there forever. We used to live in a huge hole in the road, but the cops chased us out when they came to fix the road and found people living in it. We've also lived in an abandoned subway tunnel and the basement of an abandoned factory."

"You're not scared the cops are gonna find you and arrest you?"

"Nothing that ain't happened before," Boy says. "We always find a new place before long."

"But what do you do if the cops catch you and you have to run away fast? Do you go with just the clothes you're wearing?"

"You get what you can grab before they grab you," Girl says. "Where do you live?"

Ernestine points three buildings behind her. "I live on the eighth floor."

"By the way, what's your name?"

"I'm Ernestine. Say, do you go to school around here?"

"We've never gone to school. I don't think we even have birth certificates. I don't think they let you write 'Girl' or 'Boy' on the name line. We weren't born in hospitals. I was there when Baby and Infant were born."

"Do you know if you have a last name?"

"Sure. It's Ryan. I was seven when our parents disappeared, so I know some things about them."

"If you don't go to school, do you know how to read and write? I love school, even if there are a lot of mean girls who make fun of me and my sisters for being poor."

"People in the squat read newspapers and magazines to us. We don't know much math, but we don't need that if we never become math teachers or scientists. Though I'd like to learn more. I wanna go to college someday, and they'd never accept me with the education I have now."

Ernestine thinks of a brilliant idea. "How would you like me to tutor you? I can bring my schoolbooks over to your squat after school or on weekends and show you what we're learning in fourth grade. My sister Adicia's in second grade, so she can lend her books to your brother."

Girl climbs down from the dumpster. "Would you like to be friends? There ain't any girls my age in the squat, and it's boring sometimes to only be with Boy and our little sisters. We love the grownups, but we can't talk about kid stuff with them."

"I don't have any friends either, just my little sister Adicia and our older sisters Emeline and Lucine. Emeline's in eighth grade and Lucine's in tenth grade. Our baby sister Justine's three, but she's a little young to do things with us. We also live with our substitute mother

Sarah."

"Why don't you come over to visit us? The Bowery ain't a far walk from here, so you can be home by supper."

"Sure, I'll just have to tell Sarah." Ernestine runs up to the tenement and goes up the fire escape.

Inside the tenement, Carlos and Allen are smoking cocaine and imitating the Three Stooges. Ernestine tries to ignore them as she goes over to Sarah.

"Sarah, is it okay if I go to visit a new friend? I promise I'll be back by supper."

"You made a friend?" Adicia asks. "Is she from school?"

"I just met her and her brother digging through the dumpster. They live in a squat in The Bowery, and invited me to visit. Since they don't go to school, I volunteered my tutoring services."

"You're going to a squat?" Lucine asks in horror. "Don't you know squatters are breaking the law? What if the cops came and raided the place while you were there?"

"I care about having a potential new friend, not what might happen if cops come. They say cops have chased them outta their homes before, and they always found a new place. So can I please go, Sarah? I've never visited someone else's home before!"

"Are you sure this is safe?" Emeline asks. "And do their parents know you're coming?"

"Their parents left them after they had their last child, and they're being raised by the other grownups in the squat. I don't think they care I'd be visiting. It's not like I'm a spy who's gonna tell the cops."

"Be back by supper," Sarah says. "I know how much you want a girlfriend."

Ernestine happily scampers back down the fire escape.

"You let her go?" Lucine asks. "We don't even know these kids' names or the address!"

"Can I run after her and go there too?" Adicia asks. "Maybe there are other kids my age who live there."

"Do any of us really have many options for friends?" Emeline asks. "They're probably nice people, and we know they're not fake friends laughing at Ernestine behind her back because of how poor we are. Maybe we can we invite them for supper sometime."

"Have you forgotten where we live and who our parents are?" Lucine asks. "They think roadkill is gourmet food guests will love."

"Adicia can go too if she wants," Sarah decides. "You all need to get out of here more often and play *mit kinder* your age."

Adicia jumps up and runs down the fire escape, following after Ernestine walking off in the distance with her two new friends. She catches up to them as they're turning onto Houston Street and takes Ernestine's hand.

"I wanted to meet your new friends too, and Sarah said I could. Though Lucine was worried you didn't tell us their names or address."

"I'm Girl, and this is my brother Boy," Girl introduces herself. "I'll be ten next month, and he'll be eight in June. What's your name?"

"Your real names are Girl and Boy? Your parents are worse than mine!"

"If you think that's bad, wait'll you meet my little sisters Baby and Infant. My full name is Girl Ryan. My parents didn't care enough to give us even common middle names like Marie or John, but I do know our family name."

"I'm Adicia. Adicia Éloïse Troy. My middle name has funny marks on some of the letters. Ernestine, our oldest sister, and our favorite brother also have middle names with French accent marks. Our father says if it had no accents, it'd be pronounced El-WAZ instead of Éloïse. I don't speak French yet, so I take his word for it."

"Is your dad from France?" Boy asks. "Our last name's Irish, and our mom's maiden name was Irish too, but I don't know if our parents are purebred Irish or mutts."

"His family's been here since the 1680s," Ernestine says. "They were something called Huguenots, Protestants who were treated really mean in France. Most French people are Catholics, so they didn't have freedom to worship. They kept it in the family until he married our mother, who's Belgian. He figured she was close enough, since some Belgians speak French. I think our mother's family name is Dutch, though. Goossens. Her family came from the northern part of Belgium, where they speak Dutch. We're not boring you, are we?"

"We don't go to school," Girl says. "This is education for us. What else would I wanna talk about, movies and television shows I didn't see and music I didn't hear, or stuff that lets me learn about new things?"

"We don't see movies or have a television or radio either. Our oldest sister had to leave her records and record player behind when she got married a year and a half ago. Her husband doesn't approve of Elvis and the other singers she likes. Our sister Lucine uses the record player now."

"Is having a big family as grand as they make it seem in all the books?" Girl asks as they cross into the boundaries of The Bowery.

"No way." Ernestine wrinkles her nose. "Our oldest sister was always a snob and acted like a princess, until our parents forced her to marry that guy. That was the first time we ever saw her acting like a real human. I don't think she's happy even so much time later. She's not even happy about having a baby. Our two oldest brothers are drug addicts and drinkers, though the younger one, Allen, is really nice when he's straight. Our little brother Tommy's a terror. Our mother spoils him rotten and lets him act like a brat and a bully to everyone. That leaves five of us girls to be part of that happy big family myth."

"There it is." Boy points. "Our squat. We've lived there for four years."

Girl leads them over to the front entrance and knocks with one short knock and three louder knocks. A man wearing a yellow beret opens the door.

"This is my new friend Ernestine, and that's her sister Adicia," Girl says. "They're gonna visit us for awhile."

The man waves them on to the staircase. Adicia can't believe how nice the staircase is for an abandoned building. The stairs in the tenement are in serious disrepair and always scary to navigate, and at least a hundred people currently live there and have a landlord. This building has no landlord and isn't supposed to be inhabited, yet it's in much better shape.

"We're on the third floor. This was a mansion in the last century, when this neighborhood wasn't a slum. By the time we moved in, the walls had already been knocked down to make each floor a big open space. We have a communal kitchen area, mattresses on the floor, and some couches and tables in the living room area."

A small girl with dark brown ponytails runs over to them. "Who are your friends? Are they gonna be living here?"

"These are Ernestine and Adicia Troy. They live on the Lower East Side and came to visit. They might be coming to visit regularly, since they go to school and can teach me and Boy things in their schoolbooks." Girl turns back to them. "That's my little sister Baby. The blonde toddler over there is Infant."

Adicia looks at the things hanging on the walls. Though most of them are pictures and stories cut from magazines and newspapers instead of posters or artwork, it makes the place seem nicer than the tenement. Nothing hangs on the walls at home, except for the posters left behind in Gemma's room. Even the refrigerator doesn't have anything stuck to it with magnets.

"You've got a picture of President Kennedy?" Ernestine asks jealously. "I like him. I wish we had a picture of him in our place."

"We all love him here," Girl says. "He cares about poor people. Ike mighta been a war hero, but that didn't mean he was a great president. I don't think any of the grownups here voted for Nixon in the last election."

"Can I have something to eat?" Adicia asks. "Our supper won't be for awhile, and it won't be anything great. I think we're having leftover possum and bacon grease on toast tonight."

"You can buy possum meat in the store?" Boy asks. "Is this a foreign food store?"

"Our parents and oldest brother like roadkill," Ernestine says. "We eat skunk, possum, badger, groundhog, squirrel, and raccoon. It doesn't taste too strange, but knowing where it comes from makes most of us wanna throw up."

"We have great food here," Girl says. "Most of the grownups work, even if they don't earn a lot of money, and they're able to buy enough food to feed all of us decently. Sometimes they send people out to scare up some food in garbage cans and dumpsters, like we were doing. Everything belongs to everyone else here, so the dishes and cookware are communal. Maybe someday when we all have some money saved up, we can move Upstate and start our own community. Onea the adults told me they used to have something called utopian villages there about a hundred twenty years ago."

"Our nanny Sarah says they have something like that in Israel too," Adicia says. "It's called a kibbutz."

"Where do you get your clothes and furniture and stuff from?" Ernestine asks.

"We get 'em from the garbage dump, or sometimes someone buys cloth and thread to make clothes. We have a few sewing machines. Onea the women made us beautiful quilts and pillowcases."

Ernestine and Adicia look at the rows of mattresses. Each has sheets, a quilt, pillows in pillowcases, and a mattress pad.

"Our beds don't have sheets or pillows," Adicia says. "The only real bed belongs to our two older sisters."

"What do you do about the bathroom or taking a bath?" Ernestine asks.

"This building was built before people had electricity or indoor toilets," Girl says. "We use candles or lamps without plugs, and go in onea the outhouses out back. There are a couple of bathtubs, mostly on the second and fourth floors. I usually bathe about four times a week, and take my sisters with me. Boy goes in the mornings, usually, about four times a week too."

Infant toddles over to them, holding a doll. "I need to go to the outhouse."

Girl reaches down for her hand and leads her over to the door. "I'll be right back. We'll have a snack when we return."

Adicia gapes. "Your little sister has a doll? We never had dolls or toys, except for a stuffed rabbit our baby sister Justine got at the Bowery Mission one Easter."

"Onea the ladies who lives here, Mrs. Bailey, made her for Infant. Yous really never had any toys? Even in our squat, we have toys!"

"It ain't hard to make your own toy," Boy says. "My sisters have dolls made from wooden spoons, with string and ribbons for hair, buttons glued on for eyes and a nose, and red ink for a mouth. With enough cloth and cotton, you can make a ragdoll too."

"Onea the men here, Mr. McAllister, made me doll furniture," Baby says. "The grownups don't let me and Infant go outside much unless it's to use the outhouse, since this is a bad neighborhood, so we hafta do something all day. We play with our toys and have people read stories to us. Sometimes we put on shows and play dress-up. Once we had a tea party with someone's old tea set."

Ernestine looks around in wonder. "Your place is awesome. I wish I lived in a neat place like this. Instead we live in a stupid tenement. Our family lives in the apartment that used to belong to the landlord's family, a long time ago. Everyone else lives in two or three rooms. We have a living room, a kitchen, a bathroom, three bedrooms, and a tiny room we use as a bedroom for me and Adicia. Our nanny Sarah and our baby sister Justine sleep in the living room. Our sister Emeline used to sleep in the living room or the tiny room too, until our oldest sister moved out and she got to sleep in a real bedroom."

"This place is a lot cleaner than ours," Adicia says. "It got even dirtier when our mother and oldest brother brought some dumb chickens in. They took months to start laying eggs, and they never laid any eggs that turned into chicks. They were hoping to raise them for meat too."

"Do you ever get freezing dirty bathwater when you bathe after a lot of people on your bath day?"

"Why would that happen?" Boy asks. "We don't reuse bathwater. We have running water, and since we ain't paying for it, it don't matter how much we use. Your parents really make yous reuse bathwater?"

Ernestine barely comprehends this is an abandoned building, without electricity or toilets, in a dangerous neighborhood even poorer than her own, and full of people breaking the law by squatting. It's a paradise in comparison to the tenement. Everyone seems to be happy, everyone shares everything, the children have toys, the beds have sheets, covers, and mattress pads, the food is said to be marvelous, and people aren't crowded together. Part of her wishes she could live here.

When Girl comes back with Infant, they have a snack of cherries, apples, and graham crackers. The fruit is fresh and ripe, and the graham crackers aren't stale. Ernestine is even more impressed when Girl gets out glasses and pours grape juice from one of the old iceboxes in the kitchen area. Girl says they keep their drinks and perishables fresh and cold with chunks of ice from the local iceman.

As they're talking over the snack, Girl explains part of their reason for living in a squat isn't just because they're poor, but because they want to make a statement about the gulf between rich and poor. They could move into one of the run-down tenements or shacks in The Bowery or one of the adjoining neighborhoods which are just as ill-off, but that would mean paying money to a landlord who only cares about making money off of people living hand to mouth, someone who wouldn't care about helping them out of poverty. They're also squatting because they believe in taking a stand against what Girl calls the status quo, which she says means authority, or the established way of doing things. This has been their home for the past four years, and if the cops crack down on them, they'll simply be made homeless again and have to find someplace else to live where they don't have to pay rent. The cops will be punishing them for being poor and not having much formal education. They've made this building their respectable home, while the original owners and tenants have long since abandoned it.

Ernestine also learns their birthdays are only days apart. Girl's birthday is April 8, and Ernestine's birthday is April 11. Girl says when she and her siblings have a birthday, a baker in the squat makes a cake using beets and carrots to color the frosting. They get birthday presents too, wrapped in either newspaper or colored tissue paper. Last year, Baby got a homemade dollhouse, Infant got a stuffed cat, Boy got a piggybank to keep the change he finds on the street, and Girl got a crocheted afghan.

While Girl is showing Ernestine and Adicia her multicolored afghan, Baby takes a seat to Ernestine's left. Ernestine smiles down at the middle Ryan sister, who's very cute with her dark brown hair in ponytails.

"Why do you have a bump on your finger?"

"Everyone has this, my sister Lucine says. It's a writing callus. Adicia's getting one too."

Girl drops her afghan and sits in front of them, smiling. "Are you a southpaw? Me and all three of my siblings are too. A lot of the grownups tell us teachers do awful things to lefties to try to force them to switch. I'm glad I don't go to public school if that's what they do. You're brave to not let them change you."

"Adicia is too, and so are our sister Emeline and brother Allen. It looks like our baby sister Justine's also a lefty. It runs in our family, since our dad was born a lefty but let his teachers change him."

Girl takes Ernestine's hand. "You shouldn't have a callus if you hold your pencil properly. One of the grownups taught me, Boy, and Baby how to write so our hands won't hurt and we won't slant or smudge. I'd be glad to teach you and Adicia our secrets of good left-handed writing. Our teacher said schoolteachers don't understand you have to hold your pencil differently when you're a lefty, form some letters in a different direction, and put the paper at another angle. Now I have something I can teach you in exchange for you tutoring me!"

When 6:00 comes and it's time to start walking home, Ernestine feels as though she's leaving a veritable slum paradise, the type of world she never knew could exist in such a downtrodden place. As she and Adicia walk home, she keeps casting longing glances behind her at the old brick building. Adicia likes the squat too, but knows their parents would never hear of moving to such a place. The thought of being caught by the police and having to live so secretively also worries her. She cannot share Girl's disdain at the status quo and the gap between rich and poor, even if Girl is probably right. Adicia is only seven and a half, and cares more about where her next meal comes from than starting a utopian community or getting revenge on authority.

That night, as they lie on their miserable bare mattress in the tiny room, Ernestine can't stop thinking about Girl and the squat. She promised Girl she'd come by the next day with her schoolbooks so she could start tutoring her, and that Adicia would bring her schoolbooks for Boy. It seems as though it'll be forever until she can go to the squat and see Girl again. She cares less Lucine is horrified she intends to make a habit of visiting a squat and that they require a knocking code to gain entry in case it's a cop. For reasons Ernestine cannot put her finger on, but only unexplainably sense, she feels a whole new life is just beginning.

Chapter 12: Lucine's Would-Be Husband

Shortly after Easter, in the last week of April, Mrs. Troy stands up at supper and says she'd like to make an announcement. Lucine's stomach turns into icy knots from the way her mother's looking at her. Mr. Troy seems to be in on it too, from the equally creepy way he's looking at her.

"We ain't an uppity family who takes delight in sending kids to college. Gemma tried to do that, and your father and I brought her back to earth by marrying her off to one of our own kind. Carlos dropped out rather than graduate high school, and with any luck, Allen will fail his senior year instead of being allowed to graduate. Lucine, I've decided not to waste no time or prolong the inevitable. Instead of starting your junior year in the fall, you'll get married and drop out."

Lucine's fork falls onto the floor. "What! I'm only sixteen!"

"Exactly. We can't waste anyone's time by letting you think you stand a chance of going to college or graduating high school. I'm afraid you won't be marrying up like Gemma, though he ain't as poor as we are. He's a salesman in a furniture store and sells drugs on the side."

"I'm not marrying a drug dealer, or marrying anyone at only sixteen."

"Since he'll be my brother-in-law, can he fix me up with free drugs?" Carlos asks. "What type of drugs does he sell?"

"Cocaine, meth, heroin, marijuana, uppers, hallucinogens. Maybe he'll introduce Lucine to the wonderful world of drugs."

"How old is this drug dealer you intend to marry me off to? It was disgusting how you made Gemma marry someone twenty years older."

"He's thirty-five. I met him while I was getting an emergency refill of cocaine, and we got to talking about how much he loves teenage girls. I told him he could marry one, since I'd begun looking for a husband for my second daughter. Don't worry, you'll get as nice a wedding as Gemma. I've been embezzling from the bank I work at so we can afford this."

Allen stares at her. "You've been embezzling? Don't you know they could lock you up if they discover you've been committing a crime? And don't you think it's really alarming when a guy that age talks about how he loves teenage girls? If I had a teenage daughter, I wouldn't introduce her to a creep like that, let alone suggest he can marry her!"

"Were you by any chance drunk or high when you met this man?" Emeline asks.

"Both. He's gonna come by this weekend so he can see Lucine and decide if he likes what he sees. If he likes her, the wedding's on for the first week of summer vacation. Thankfully, he's a fellow Protestant, so this time we don't hafta worry about that nasty business of a conversion for the sake of marriage."

"I don't think Gemma's happy in that marriage you forced her into," Lucine says. "At least you and Dad seem to care about each other."

"I don't give a damn if Gemma is happy or not. All I care about is that she's back in her station in life, not away at college getting above her raising. Life ain't supposed to be happy. Justine can be the flower girl, and Gemma can be your matron of honor."

"If you see him again before the weekend, can you tell him to bring some drugs?" Carlos begs.

"What's embezzling?" Adicia asks.

"Taking money that doesn't belong to you," Emeline says.

"So what? I falsify the books when someone makes a deposit, and pocket the rest. You'd be surprised at how much money I've saved up this way. Not like the rich snobs will notice money missing. They've already got enough."

"Mother, believe it or not, not everyone who has enough money to live in a nice neighborhood and have nice things is rich," Lucine says.

"Why don't you want Allen to graduate?" Ernestine asks. "He can always repeat the year if he fails, or take failed classes over the summer."

"My kids don't go to college. Gemma was uppity enough to graduate and get accepted to a college, but thankfully we set her straight. Carlos dropped out like a proper boy of our class. Lucine will get married and drop out before things get that far. Allen likewise shouldn't get above his raising by graduating. At least he's getting mostly Cs and Ds instead of rich boy grades like Bs and As."

"I'd like to go to college someday," Allen protests. "Not right away, since I wanna work for awhile and save up money for college, but someday. Maybe by the time I'm twenty-five."

"Join me at the cereal factory," Carlos says. "You get to eat for free on the assembly line. No one's caught me, and it ain't like rich people will notice or care the boxes ain't as full as they're supposed to be."

"I want a real job, not mindless factory work. I don't know what yet, but I hope I find a real job after I graduate."

Carlos gasps. "You plan to work in an office or God forbid have an actual career like a teacher or banker? I hope you flunk out instead of graduating. No one wants to hire guys like us for real jobs. Besides, uppity rich snobs won't want someone who drinks and does drugs teaching their kids, working in their office, or handling their money."

Allen lets the conversation drop. It's no good trying to convince Carlos or their parents that getting a higher education and having a real job is important if he wants to do better than how he was raised. As for his substance abuse issues, he'll fight one battle at a time. Alcohol and drugs help him deal with this awful life.

The next day after school, Ernestine and Adicia take their schoolbooks over to the squat to give Girl and Boy their daily lesson. Lucine is still concerned about their frequent visits to a squat in one of the city's worst neighborhoods, but they enjoy spending time with their new friends and being in a place where everyone gets along and doesn't use poverty as an excuse for eating the worst food possible or being stingy about spending money on necessary things like bedsheets and curtains.

"Come right up!" Girl greets them. "I'm afraid you'll hafta stay away from Baby and Infant for the next week or so. They got the measles from a grownup who never had it as a kid."

Baby and Infant are lying on their mattress, which has been moved to the far end of the floor. A large platter of food is at the head of the mattress, and they're both clutching their dolls.

"I hate being sick," Adicia says. "I had the measles when I was four."

"Have you two had it yet?" Ernestine asks.

"Yeah, we got it when we lived in the basement of the abandoned factory, a little before we came here. Boy and I also had mumps, chickenpox, and rubella. Some of the grownups took us to get polio and DTP shots at a public free clinic, so we don't hafta worry about that. Did you get those shots?"

"Our mother figured it'd be worth the trip to avoid the shame and extra expense of raising crippled children, and didn't wanna be disturbed by several months of whooping cough. Though she wasn't the one taking care of us when we had measles, mumps, chickenpox, and rubella. Sarah took care of us." Ernestine opens her schoolbag and shakes out the books. "What would you like to study today? We're starting to learn fractions in math and are reading *Charlotte's Web* for English."

"We're starting decimals in my math class," Adicia says. "We're learning about planets in science."

"What are fractions and decimals?" Boy asks.

"A decimal is a dot in a number. When it's in a certain place, it means something's in the hundredth, thousandth, or tenth place. Ernestine says fractions are two numbers with a line between them."

"Our teacher says fractions will come in handy when we're at a store and there's a sale," Ernestine says. "You can figure out how much something will cost if it's half or a third off."

"Is it okay if I have a snack?" Adicia asks as she sits down with Boy to look at the math book. "I don't wanna take your food, but I'm hungry."

"We've got grapes, peaches, and vanilla wafers," Girl says. "Your parents should be ashamed of themselves for not giving their kids an after school snack. What are they spending all their money on if your dad gets a buck an hour and works twelve hours a day mosta the week, and your mother usually works some kinda job too?"

"Rent for our seven-room piece of junk, alcohol, drugs, the worst food they can find, and sometimes utilities if they have money left over," Ernestine says. "Sometimes they budget for stuff that can't be avoided, like school stuff. Our mother spends a lot on gifts for Tommy too."

Adicia begins wolfing down the fruit and wafers Girl sets in front of her. Girl and Boy look at her in sympathy.

"Our mother confessed the other evening she's been stealing money from the bank she works at," Ernestine says. "She was so matter-of-fact about it, like there's nothing outta the ordinary about committing a crime and letting your whole family know about it."

"Why is she stealing money?" Boy asks. "And is she using that money for a good thing at least?"

"She used a fancy word for it. Embezzling, I think it was. It's so our sister Lucine can marry some thirty-five-year-old guy at the end of the school year. Lucine's only sixteen, but our parents decided behind her back she'd get married and drop out."

"What!" Girl shrieks. "Does she intend to trade away all six of her daughters like cattle?"

"The way she's going, I wouldn't be surprised. It didn't bother us very much when they forced Gemma to get married, since it was so fun to be in a wedding, and we never liked her very much, but we love Lucine. We don't want her to marry an old guy she doesn't know and be forced to leave school. And Gemma says having a baby was a nightmare. They did awful things to her, like tying her down to the hospital bed. She has no memory of anything that happened after a mean nurse gave her a shot. She awoke no longer pregnant, the baby in the nursery, and bruises and rubbed-off skin on her body. That sounds really scary. Maybe that's why she doesn't enjoy having a baby, since she can't remember giving birth and wasn't allowed to hold him until they left the hospital."

"Our mother gave birth to Baby and Infant here in the squat. Boy was born in the subway tunnel, and they say I was born in an abandoned store my parents lived in till I was a month old. A lot of doctors treat the poor like trash, the grownups say. They've told me people didn't use doctors or go to hospitals till very recently in history, and that doctors were always meaner to poor patients than rich ones."

"Do you have any ideas for how Lucine can get outta this?" Adicia begs. "We don't wanna lose her."

"The guy she's supposed to marry is a furniture salesman and a drug dealer, and he loves teenage girls," Ernestine says. "He's supposed to come over this weekend to decide if he likes Lucine."

"When Gemma's husband came over the first time, he slapped her bottom twice and forced a kiss on her. I don't want this guy to treat Lucine like that. Lucine has never kissed a guy or been on a date. She'd rather do well in school than spend her time dating guys she won't marry. That would be really mean if she had to be kissed against her will by this terrible person when she's never had a chance to do that with a nice guy she likes."

"Why doesn't she tell this guy she has a cold?" Girl suggests. "I don't suppose she still hasn't had onea the childhood diseases."

"Could she fake scarlet fever or having chickenpox again?" Ernestine asks. "I've heard some people get chickenpox twice."

"Have her wear her most unattractive clothes and not comb her hair. A lot of guys won't touch a woman who looks ugly. Would she get in trouble if she cut off her hair?"

"Can't she run away?" Boy asks. "She doesn't have to stay in your home if she's being made to do something she doesn't want. Your parents sound so awful I'd run away too."

"But where would she go, and how would we find her again?" Adicia asks.

"You won't be at home forever either," Girl says. "There are always ways to find people. Couldn't she look in a phonebook? I know it'd be sad to lose onea your sisters, but what other choice does she have? Your parents didn't back down when they made Gemma get married. I doubt they'd agree to call it off this time."

"If our parents intend to do this to all of us, my turn is in six years," Ernestine says. "I'm not waiting around that long for them to force me to marry an old bully who does drugs. I wish I could live here."

"You're welcome to join us. We've got enough space for a new person."

"Can we get back to tutoring?" Adicia asks. "This talk about splitting up my family is making me really sad."

"Sure. We'll talk about this more after the weekend, after you meet this prize your parents wanna bring into your family."

***

Mrs. Troy ordered Sarah to make badger burgers for supper on Saturday, on stale rolls, with a side of sweet potatoes. The tablecloth with cigarette burns is draped over the table, and a place of honor is set for Lucine's intended fiancé. The familiar smell of roadkill is wafting through the tenement when a knock sounds at the door at 6:30. Excitedly, Mrs. Troy rushes over to open the door and usher him inside.

"Everyone, this is Jacob DeLuise. He's gonna be our supper guest and hopefully Lucine's husband very soon. Jacob, come have a look at Lucine and see if she's your type."

Lucine squirms under Jacob's gaze. Whereas Francesco just looked greasy and mean, Jacob looks downright demonic and creepy, and gives off a very strange vibe. She shies away when he tries to run his fingers through her hair.

"Teenage girls are the best. I have my way with plenty of my teenage clients, but I ain't been lucky enough to marry one yet. Your mother says you're gonna be dropping outta school to marry me. Just what I'd like, a nice, obedient girl at home all day doing housework and producing children."

"I'm not about to have a child when I'm only sixteen," Lucine retorts. "And I certainly won't be having one anytime soon, no matter my age, after what happened to my older sister."

"Gemma is being a spoilt princess as she always has been when she opens her mouth to complain about what happened to her when she had Giovanni," Mrs. Troy says. "The same thing happened to me every time I gave birth, and you don't catch me whining about that unpleasant but necessary business. You'd think she expected to give birth in a Swiss spa, waited on hand and foot."

"We served you badger burgers for supper," Carlos says as he ambles up. "Did you bring drugs for me? I don't have a favorite, so it don't matter what you've got on hand."

"So do you like Lucine?" Mr. Troy asks. "We'd love to get rid of this one. She's as willful as Gemma, thinking she can get above her raising by graduating high school, going to college, and having a career."

"I'll take her," Jacob says, revealing a mouth missing even more teeth than Francesco's. "I've got a nice one-room apartment in Tribeca, and it'll be perfect for moving a little wifey in. Does Lucy like drugs?"

"My name is Lucine. No one calls me Lucy."

"Naw, she's as straight as an arrow," Carlos says disdainfully. "Though maybe after she lives in the real world with you long enough, she'll be converted to the wonderful world of drugs. Ain't no way a person of our class can get through life without drugs and alcohol for distraction."

"Combined with your money from drug dealing and my money from embezzling, we'll be able to put on a great wedding," Mrs. Troy purrs. "Everyone needs to come sit down and eat."

Lucine is physically sick from having to sit next to Jacob, whose table manners are just as appalling as Mr. Troy's. She feels relatively lucky Jacob isn't trying to fondle her the way Francesco did to Gemma.

As soon as supper is finished and the table has been cleared, Lucine bolts off to her room, followed by her sisters and Sarah. Jacob, who's been smoking methamphetamine on and off during the meal, barely notices, and continues sitting at the table with Carlos and Mr. and Mrs. Troy, who are also smoking it. Realizing no one's paying attention to him, Tommy amuses himself by throwing his football around the living room. Allen sits on the ripped davenport to smoke a cigarette.

"There's no way I'm marrying him and dropping out of school. Not that I'd mind living in Tribeca, but I'd wanna live there on my own or with potential friends, not a drug dealer old enough to be my dad."

"He looks so creepy!" Emeline says. "I can't quite place it, but there's something really odd about him."

"He gives off a really bad energy," Ernestine says. "Girl told me people project something called an aura, an unseen energy field. Most people can't see auras, but you can usually feel really positive or negative energy."

"I'm jealous you have such an intelligent friend. I wish I had someone to talk about stuff like that with. All the other girls in eighth grade think I'm a square for reading and talking about stuff that doesn't relate to movies, music, boys, or fashion. It's nice to meet someone who's deeper than her age. It's amazing she's never had a single day of school and is that intelligent and mature for her age."

"Girl's awesome. I hope you can meet her sometime. You'd probably have a lot to talk about."

"How am I supposed to get outta this?" Lucine asks. "There's no way I'd become a sixteen-year-old bride even if I had a real boyfriend. I won't even be able to vote for another five years. I'm way too young."

"Gemma went from a mean snob to a melancholic sad sack after our parents forced her to get married," Emeline says. "I don't want that to happen to you too. Gemma probably hates us because we didn't do that much to protest."

"Gemma hated us anyway," Ernestine says. "Though maybe that awful thing turned her into a human being with real feelings."

"You cannot stay here if you're going to be forced to marry him," Sarah says decisively. "Gemma was forced into a marriage she didn't want. It should not happen twice in the same family. You'll have to get as far away from here as you can. Your parents might hate you, but they also hate being humiliated and looking disreputable. I wouldn't put it past them to send out the bloodhounds all over downtown Manhattan to search for you. Do you remember how to walk to Midtown?"

"That walk is over an hour long!" Lucine protests. "This time there wouldn't be any pretty Christmas tree in Rockefeller Center to look forward to!"

"Couldn't she go to the Bowery Mission for the time being?" Emeline asks. "We don't know anybody who lives midtown or uptown, and they'd probably immediately recognize Lucine isn't one of them from her clothes and the lost look on her face."

"A church would never turn anyone away," Adicia says. "Even if the other kids always laugh at us when we go to church, the minister and his wife would understand and help you. You can go into the first church you see when it starts getting dark."

Lucine looks out the window in consternation. "There's no way I'm making that long of a walk when it's dark! I don't wanna leave this crummy neighborhood and our horrid parents that bad!"

"You might not wanna run away at night, but I will," Ernestine declares, standing up. "I'm not waiting around for six years for our parents to make me give up my dreams and marry a random guy they find. I'm packing my stuff and moving into the squat."

"What! You're only ten! How are you gonna move away from home? What if that place is discovered by the cops? You've only known these people for about a month and a half! And aren't you scared to walk to The Bowery at night?"

"My future is with the Ryans, whether or not they stay in the squat. We all know there's no future here. I might as well make my own future by getting away while I can. Don't worry, I'll still go to school." Ernestine goes into the tiny bedroom and starts gathering her ragged clothes, schoolbooks, and school supplies.

"Is she really serious?" Emeline asks. "Is anyone gonna stop her?"

"I don't wanna lose both of yous," Adicia begs. "It'll only be me, Emeline, and Justine if both of you go away."

"Will our parents care?" Lucine asks. "They'll probably see it as one less daughter to have to trade away."

"There'd be more room in this accursed tenement, if you wanna look on the bright side," Emeline says. "There'll only be nine people."

Ernestine goes into their parents' bedroom to take Mr. Troy's suitcase, which he hasn't used since they moved here when Lucine was a baby. He probably won't notice it missing. Suitcase in hand, she goes back into her room and puts her scant belongings into it. After closing it, she goes back to her sisters and Sarah.

"This is goodbye. Lucine, I'm counting on you to do the right thing, before those awful people force you to marry that loser. Lookit them. They're so drugged they don't notice what's going on here. Adicia, I'll still see you every day because you're tutoring Boy. Emeline, you're welcome to come visit us. Sarah, thank you for being such a good substitute mother. Justine, you'll always be our baby, even when we're grownups. I hope you manage to get outta here before you get that much older and don't have to grow up so poor, in such a crummy neighborhood."

None of them can find their tongues as Ernestine walks to the door, the suitcase knocking against her legs. Jacob, Carlos, and their parents don't notice Ernestine leaving. Tommy continues playing with his football, caring less one of his hated sisters is on her way out.

Allen, who's been nodding off to sleep with his cigarette in his mouth, jolts awake when he hears the door opening. To his great surprise, he sees his ten-year-old sister turning the knob and holding a suitcase.

"Where in the world are you going at this hour?"

"I'm leaving this hellhole for my friends at the squat. I'm not gonna wait around for our parents to force me to marry some jerk. Don't try to stop me."

"You're walking to The Bowery at this hour? And you're going to a squat instead of the mission, where you know you'll be safe at all times?"

"I'm always safe at the squat. Girl said they have a place for me. It's the most wonderful place I've ever been to. It's sorta like how Sarah describes a kibbutz."

Allen looks over at the four people at the table, still drugged out of their minds, one of whom is supposed to marry Lucine in a bit under two months. "Fine, I'll walk you there. You're probably safer there than here."

Ernestine triumphantly takes his hand as they begin the perilous descent down the stairs and walk out into the night. She doesn't look back at anything, and hopes she never has to set foot in the old neighborhood ever again. Allen throws his cigarette into a sewer as they cross into The Bowery.

Ernestine gives him the directions to the by-now familiar six-story brick building with a yellow wooden door and three concrete steps. As she knocks in the special code, she notices lights on.

"That's strange. This place was built before electricity, so everyone uses candles or lamps that don't need plugs."

A big-boned woman in a pink gingham dress opens the door. "You're friends with the Ryan kids on the third floor, ain't you?"

"Yes I am. I'm moving in tonight. This is my big brother Allen. He's not moving in. He just walked me here 'cause it's dark."

"Go on up."

Ernestine eagerly pulls Allen up the stairs to the third floor and knocks on that door next. "It's me, Ernestine!"

Girl flings the door open. "What's going on? What did you come so late for?"

"I'm moving in. I had to. I'm not sticking around for my parents to barter me away like a cow. People here aren't drug addicts who feast on roadkill and treat girls like dirt." She sets her suitcase down. "So, what's the story with these electric lights?"

"It was a big surprise. Onea the first floor residents is an electrician, and he secretly worked on rigging the building for electricity. Now we're just like other people. Ain't it fantastic to have electricity at night? I'd gone so long without it, I didn't remember what I was missing." She looks up at Allen. "Are you Ernestine's brother? Why are you here?"

"This is Allen. He walked me here 'cause it's so late."

Girl smiles at him. "You're kinda cute."

"Don't get any ideas," Allen says embarrassedly. "I'll be eighteen in June."

"Don't worry," Boy says. "She'll be alright here. The way Ernestine and Adicia describe your place and your parents gives me the chills."

Ernestine rushes over to Girl's mattress. "I can't believe I'm gonna finally sleep on a real bed with sheets!"

"Would you like to spend the night too?" Girl asks Allen. "If I was you, I wouldn't be in a hurry to get back to your awful parents."

"No, I have to go back there. I'm graduating high school, I hope, and I'll do what I can to find a job and a decent place to live. In the meantime, I'm needed at home."

Ernestine watches from the window after Allen goes down the stairs. She strains her eyes till she can no longer see him departing in the distance. Then she goes back to the mattress, opens her suitcase, takes out her pajamas, and goes behind one of the dressing curtains to change. Ernestine is very proud of herself for escaping the lions' den first of all her siblings. Her parents no longer have any power over her. She's out of the Lower East Side. She's free.

Chapter 13: Meet Julie

A new resident moved in during May. He and his young daughter live across the hall, though Adicia has never seen the girl at school or leaving the building. She wonders why the girl has no mother, but hasn't had the nerve to ask. Adicia would love to ask the girl to be friends, but is afraid to go there because the girl's father gives off a very bad energy, and just gives her the creeps.

Carlos has been going there on a regular basis, though. Like Jacob, this man is also a drug dealer. Unlike Jacob, however, he doesn't seem to have another respectable job. If they all stopped using drugs and spent their money on something worthwhile, they wouldn't be so poor. It's one thing if her parents genuinely choose to be poor, but she and her siblings weren't able to make that decision for themselves.

Adicia is thinking about writing a note asking the girl to be friends and slipping it under her door when Mrs. Troy comes home from work late Saturday afternoon, dropping her beat-up tan leather purse on the shabby davenport and waving around a huge chunk of cash.

"Everyone, we're getting on the subway as soon as we can and going to the lovely bridal shop on the Upper East Side we used before! It's time to select your dresses!"

"Is Gemma coming too?" Emeline asks. "You said she'd be maid of honor."

"Matron of honor. A maid of honor is an unmarried virgin. A matron of honor is a married woman."

"What about Ernestine?" Adicia asks. "Is she still gonna be in the wedding when she doesn't live with us anymore?"

"Not that I give a damn what she does with her life, but she'll need to be in the wedding. You can run over and get her so we won't be late. I used the O'Connells' phone before work to tell them we were coming at six. I called Gemma too. Sometimes I wish we had a phone. Gemma's lucky we married her to a man with a phone."

"I wish you'd told us we were going there before just now," Emeline says.

"You never do nothing you'd need to reschedule. Let's go, everyone. Adicia, you go get Ernestine, and we'll meet at the subway station as soon as we can. You should feel lucky, Lucine, that I care enough about giving you a proper wedding to embezzle so much money."

"Can't we save money by reusing our bridesmaid dresses from Gemma's wedding, and me wearing her dress?" Lucine asks, well aware there'll be no wedding if she has her way. "Emeline can probably fit into my dress, Adicia can wear Ernestine's, and probably only Ernestine would need an entirely new dress."

"Normally I'd agree with you and think you're being very sensible, but I don't want people to think I can't put on a decent, respectable wedding where everyone wears nice new clothes. Maybe the shop will give us a discount for being return customers."

Jumping at any excuse to get out of the apartment and the depressing neighborhood of Two Bridges, Gemma threw Giovanni in his stroller and hopped on the next subway for the Upper East Side. She arrived at the bridal shop twenty minutes early and is now in the lobby while the party ahead of her family debates which dress the bride-to-be looks best in. To keep busy, she thumbs through a magazine and shoves a bottle into Giovanni's mouth, ignoring his cries to be held. Eventually Giovanni realizes his mother isn't going to pick him up to feed him and quiets down.

"Gemma Troy?" a woman entering the shop asks. "What a surprise to see you!"

Gemma looks over at her. "Lorraine Neiman! I haven't seen you since we graduated high school!"

"I'm a student at Hunter, and just got engaged to a man named Joe Wickline. I'm studying English, and he's studying chemistry. My parents encouraged me to continue school so I can support our new little family while he puts himself through graduate school down the road. They think it's foolish and premodern how a lot of girls drop out once they find a man." Lorraine looks down and notices Giovanni. "It looks like you're married! What's your new name?"

"Mon-te-ras-tel-li," Gemma sounds it out. "My sisters have never gotten it right and just call my in-laws the Monsterellis. Frankly, that's a better name for the family I was forced to marry into. This is Giovanni. I wanted to give him a nice all-American name like Bobby or Jimmy, but he had to be saddled with an in-your-face Italian name. I hate my husband so much. I've been trying in vain to find a way outta this unwanted marriage, and I'm so tired of pretending to be a devoted wife and daughter-in-law."

Lorraine sits next to her. "Your parents forced you to marry some-one? Isn't that against the law?"

"I came home from the first day of summer vacation and there he was. My parents and his whole family acted like nothing was loony. He drinks, hits me, rapes me, won't let me do anything outside the apart-ment but buy groceries, can't cut the apron strings at forty years old, constantly criticizes my cooking because it's not exactly like his saintly mother's, cheats on me, and thinks I'm not a real woman because I haven't gotten pregnant again. I never wanted a baby at this age. I feel no connection to Giovanni because I have no memory of his birth and couldn't see or hold him till we left the hospital four days later. That was the worst experience of my life. I was humiliated and abused, and Francesco's sisters and sisters-in-law act like I'm a horrible woman for daring to not share their glowing opinion of that pathetic doctor they recommended so highly. Right now I'm waiting for my mother and sisters. My sister Lucine, who's only sixteen, is being forced to get mar-ried too, and to drop out. There's gotta be a way to save her, and to save me from this nightmare of a marriage. At least I'm safe from pregnancy. I wish the Pill had been available two years ago."

Lorraine sees how lifeless and haggard Gemma looks, as though she's aged at least ten years instead of only two. Her lack of interest in her own baby is also frightening. All the other young brides and moth-ers she knows are a lot happier and more engaged.

"Gemma, my father's a lawyer, and he might be able to find a way to help you." Lorraine pulls his business card out of her purse. "He's handled some tough divorce cases. I'm sure any judge in his right mind would grant a divorce or annulment based on what you've told me, that your husband's abusive in more ways than one and your parents forced you into marriage."

"They forced me to withdraw from Hofstra too! I have no higher education to fall back on! I care less what happens to Giovanni. Francesco's family can take him for all I care. I hate the engagement ring he gave me too. It's so boring, like he randomly selected it from a catalogue, not taking my tastes into account."

Lorraine holds out her left hand. "Joe got me a white gold band with three diamonds and four sapphires. I love how it incorporates both diamonds and colored stones, so it stands out in a crowd."

"My ten-year-old sister Ernestine recently moved out, and our parents barely blinked an eye. She's in a squat in The Bowery, with new friends she and my seven-year-old sister Adicia are tutoring. Squatting in an abandoned building is better than living in that horrid place we came from. Our parents aren't there, the food's better, and people care about each other."

Gemma stops talking when her family comes in. Adicia and Justine rush over to Giovanni, more interested in playing with him and talking to him than his own mother. Gemma doesn't step in to make sure they're holding him correctly as they lift him out of the stroller, like most new mothers would.

Shortly after the group ahead of them departs, the owner comes out to greet them and freezes in her tracks. Gemma's appearance horrifies her. She was a fresh-faced eighteen-year-old two years ago. Now she looks like she's at least thirty, and has no animation in either her bearing or her face.

"Oh, good, it looks like you recognize us," Mrs. Troy says. "My daughter Lucine is getting married, and we also need a matron of honor dress, three bridesmaid dresses, and a flower girl dress. I'm sure you have plenty of wedding dresses for teenagers, from all the shotgun weddings there are."

Lucine looks lost and confused as she walks off with the owner and a sales associate. She instructed her sisters to choose dresses they don't like, since they won't be wearing them, and Mrs. Troy will have to return them in humiliation. Mrs. Troy, who smoked cocaine on the subway home from the Financial District, and smoked some more on the ride uptown, doesn't sense anything suspicious as the girls pull out dresses in colors that aren't their favorites, in styles that aren't the prettiest or most flattering.

"This marriage is not going through," Lucine whispers to the owner when they're in the dressing room. "My mother is paying for these dresses with criminal money. She's been embezzling from the bank she works at to afford this. I wish I could turn her in without getting in trouble with her. My sisters and our nanny say the only way for me to get out of the fate my older sister had is to run away."

"Oh, I remember your older sister very well. She was the unhappiest bride-to-be I've ever had. What's that odd smell on your mother? She had a funny smell the last time she was here too."

"She's a drug addict. Her favorite is cocaine, which she was doing on the way up here. She claims she never did drugs while pregnant, so none of the doctors or nurses would report her and to avoid the cost of a sickly baby."

"I'll ask one of the salesgirls to find a couple of dresses we usually sell to older brides. If you won't be walking down the aisle in it, get one you'd never choose. Your mother is a disgrace to motherhood, and I look forward to her coming back here in humiliation when she returns all the dresses."

***

When Sarah and the Troys come home, the new girl across the hall is in the hallway playing jacks with herself. Adicia hands the box with her dress to Emeline and stays behind to try to make friends.

"Hi. I'm Adicia. My brother Carlos visits your dad sometimes. What's your name?"

"Julie Spirnak. I just turned eight. You look like you're my age." The girl has soft blue-gray eyes and slightly wavy dark blonde hair. Though she's slightly taller than Adicia, she has a similar petite frame.

"I won't be eight till July eleventh. I'm onea the youngest girls in second grade."

"That's nice that you go to school," Julie says wistfully. "I never went to school. My daddy won't let me. My mommy wanted me to go to school, but she divorced my daddy after she tried to tell the cops about bad things he does."

"You mean how he sells drugs?"

"No, other things. The cops told her it was a private family matter, and that no one would believe her if she tried to tell people. Respectable people don't air their dirty laundry in public, and nobody believes a woman's word over a man's."

"What are those funny noises always coming from your place? I wanted to go over to your place and ask to play with you since you moved in, but I was afraid because your dad doesn't look like a nice person, and those noises really scare me."

"I hate them too, but my daddy says I hafta live with it as long as he's around. Do you know how to play jacks?"

"Is it like marbles? We have a set of marbles my older brothers used to play with. It's the only thing we have to play with, since we don't have dolls or toys."

"You bounce the ball and pick up a jack before the ball can

bounce again. You pick up two on your next turn, and three the next, and keep doing that till there are no jacks left. The person with the most jacks wins."

Carlos steps into the hall. "Outta my way, you brats. I gotta buy me some coke from Mr. Spirnak. I can't last much longer without some."

"What's the worst that would happen if you went a little while without any drugs?" Adicia asks. "People don't die or get sick when they stop drinking."

"You ain't been introduced to the wonderful world of drugs yet. I fully expect all of yous to join us when you're old enough." Carlos pulls a joint out of his pocket, lifts his new green lighter to it, and starts smoking. "A day without drugs is a day without sunshine."

Mr. Spirnak steps outside. "Glad to see you, Carlos. You're my best new client. Julie, get back inside. I told you not to talk to any of the children here or to leave our apartment. You know what time it is after I give Carlos his drugs?"

Julie starts shaking. "It can't be that time again already, Daddy. It was already that time three hours ago."

"What time is it?" Adicia asks.

Mr. Spirnak glares at her. "None of your business, you stupid girl. What happens in a man's home is his private business. It was laughable enough when my ex-wife tried to rat on me to the cops."

Carlos strides into the Spirnaks' apartment and impatiently waits for Mr. Spirnak to follow him, dragging Julie by her left arm. Adicia stands there baffled as the door closes.

Allen comes out, smoking a cigarette. "Did Carlos just go to get a refill on coke? We have plenty, and even if we were out of it, it ain't like he needs more right this second."

"Have you ever been in there, Allen? Mr. Spirnak looks so mean and scary, like that guy our parents want Lucine to marry. I just met his daughter Julie, and there's something really strange about how she talks about him, and how he treats her."

Carlos and Mr. Spirnak complete a drug transaction, and then Julie starts whimpering, saying "No" loudly and repeatedly, and finally begins screaming. Allen tries the door, but it's locked. Adicia is sick to her stomach, though she has no idea what's going on, when Mr. Spirnak starts making those strange noises again.

"Why are all those sad noises coming from their place? They sound like the noises our parents make sometimes, but scarier."

"We've got a degenerate for a neighbor, and not just the usual type of degenerate this piece of garbage attracts. Unfortunately, cops don't touch cases like that."

"If he's beating Julie up, why is Carlos just sitting there doing his drugs and not tryna save her?"

"Carlos is a vile excuse for a human being. He only cares about himself and drugs. Don't you remember how he complained because I came to the rescue of his date when he was tryna do things against her will? But no, I don't think he's beating her up. He's doing something even worse."

"Why can't we break their door down or call the cops if he's doing something so awful? Can't you go to jail for doing bad things to your kids?"

Lucine steps outside. "What in the world are those new neighbors making those noises for again? I'm tryna do homework, and can't concentrate with those disturbing noises."

"That guy is scary! He has bad energy, like Ernestine says. He's even worse than our parents."

The Spirnaks' door opens and Carlos comes out smoking his cocaine and swinging a large brown paper bag filled with more. Julie is violently trembling and has her arms around herself, her head down.

Allen pulls some cash out of his back pocket. "You've gotta get that girl away from this man," he whispers to his sisters. "I'll buy some drugs from him, and you take her into our place while I keep him busy. You can take her to the squat and have Ernestine's new friends take care of her."

Mr. Spirnak smiles broadly at the sight of a new client, overlooking Julie going into the hallway again. He shuts the door to begin showing Allen his vast cornucopia of drugs and quoting him prices.

Julie looks around tentatively, her eyes wide, as Lucine takes her hand and leads her across the hall. Adicia's eyes also widen when she sees Julie leaving a trail of blood.

"Lucine, isn't someone my age a little too young to mens—menst —what's that long word again for when a girl bleeds every month?"

Lucine looks down and turns green. "Julie, you run right into our apartment and go into the wardrobe in my bedroom. It has a pink quilt on the bed. You stay in there until we come get you. Adicia, you get a wet washcloth and bring it right back to me."

"What's a wardrobe?" Julie whispers.

"It's a long, dark wooden thing you hang clothes in, like a big cupboard without shelves."

Julie runs into the Troys' apartment and Adicia goes to run a washcloth under cold water. Lucine fights the urge to vomit as she cleans up the drops of blood scattered across the hallway. The fact that Mr. Spirnak looks so much like the creepy man she's supposed to marry makes her even more determined to do something, anything, to get far away from this dead-end life of poverty, crime, and degeneracy Carlos and her parents revel in.

"My daddy's gonna be very mad when he sees I'm not there," Julie says. "He'll come into your apartment and look for me, and your parents will probably be mad at you too. He told me I have to stay with him till he dies."

"My sister Ernestine left home recently to live with some friends, and our parents didn't care too much," Adicia says. "Why do you wanna live with your dad when he does bad things to you?"

"The cops will make me return to him. They wouldn't let me go with my mommy when she divorced my daddy, because they said she was making up lies about him and airing our dirty laundry in public."

"The cops haven't made Ernestine come home. Our parents seem glad she left, since they have one less girl to deal with. Our mother hates girls."

"He's gonna see me leaving the building and will run after me. And I don't wanna walk alone at night. I don't even know what street goes where."

"I'll take you to Ernestine. She lives in The Bowery. That's a neighborhood to the west of ours and also sorta inside of ours. Part of Chinatown is also in The Bowery. We studied maps of Manhattan in school this year."

"We used to live in Hell's Kitchen. I have no idea where it is on a map or how far away it is from here."

Lucine comes into the apartment to wipe up the rest of the trail of blood, still sick to her stomach. Part of her wonders if Jacob is depraved in that way as well.

"Adicia, you're gonna go down the fire escape with Julie and run to the squat. It's a bad place to walk after dark, but she can't stay here overnight. Our parents won't care you're gone for a little bit so long as you come back."

"Does Julie need one of those belts?"

"No, I'm afraid that's not why she's bleeding. Her father is a very disturbed man who's apparently done this to her many times before, and she needs to get away from him before he can do it again. Please hurry and try to be back within an hour."

Adicia takes Julie by the hand and goes down the fire escape in the darkness, too concerned about getting to the squat and back home quickly to have time to think about what'll happen when Mr. Spirnak notices Julie missing. She runs as fast as she can, knowing the walk by memory, even if some of the landmarks aren't familiar in the dark. Julie looks around and takes in all the sights, glad to breathe fresh air and see new things after years of being locked in squalid apartments and forbidden to go outside.

Adicia gives one short knock and three long knocks before a tall man in faded brown pants and a worn yellow shirt opens the door. She identifies herself as Ernestine's sister and runs to the third floor.

"Ernestine, it's me, Adicia. I've brought a new resident. She and her dad moved across the hall, but we had to sneak her outta there because her dad's a bad guy."

Ernestine opens the door. "Do our parents know you're here?"

"Allen went into his apartment to buy drugs so he could be kept busy while Lucine cleaned up blood in the hall and I brought Julie over here. Her dad's a creep who sells drugs."

Girl goes over to them. "Welcome to our humble squat. I'm Girl Ryan, and that's my brother Boy and our sisters Baby and Infant. Yes, those are our real names. How old are you? I'm ten."

"I'm eight," Julie says shyly. "Is it okay for me to take a hot bath? My body hurts after what my daddy did to me."

"Our bathtubs are on the second and fourth floors, by the fire escape door. I had crummy parents too, but at least they never hurt us. In case your dad's looking for you, you can stay here. There's a lot of stuff to do here. Just ask my little sisters."

"This place is awesome," Ernestine says. "It's like a slum paradise."

"Julie doesn't go to school," Adicia says. "Maybe we can tutor her too. She'd be in my grade if she was in school."

"I think you should get going," Girl says. "You don't want your parents to get suspicious if you're gone too long, and your brother can't be over at that guy's place to stall him forever."

"I didn't bring anything with me," Julie says. "What am I supposed to wear?"

"You can wear some of my old clothes."

Julie waves to Adicia as she goes back down the stairs. Adicia is a bit jealous yet another person has escaped the depressing life they were all born into, and wonders if it'll ever finally be her turn to escape.

Chapter 14: Gemma Gets Out

"Who the hell are the lunatics running this asylum?" Francesco demands, storming into Planned Parenthood. "I just found a package of those new-fangled birth control pills in my wife's nightstand, with the prescription information saying it was given to her here! Last I checked, a respectable woman needs her husband's permission for birth control devices! She can't just go out and get them on her own like a common whore! No wonder our only child is a year old and she ain't gotten pregnant again!"

"We practice doctor-patient confidentiality here, Sir," the receptionist informs him. "We cannot tell you anything about your wife's personal medical history without her written consent."

"That's nonsense! As her husband, I control her and make all her decisions for her! She don't get a say in what she does with her body! I'm demanding you look up Gemma Monterastelli in your records and tell me who her doctor is, so I can go in and have a man-to-man chat with him about how he violated my marriage by giving these pills to my wife. Plus we're Catholics, so we can't use them. My wife's conversion wasn't sincere if she can so casually go against the teachings of the Pope."

"Not that I'm going to tell you anything confidential, but I do remember a woman named Gemma coming here recently to get her prescription renewed and to have her yearly doctor visit. Her doctor is a woman, not a man."

Francesco is beside himself with amusement. "A woman doctor? Next thing you know, they'll be teachin' cows to be doctors! Our son was delivered by a proper male doctor whom all my sisters and sisters-in-law sing the praises of. My wife alone thinks this man is evil."

"Look, Sir, if you can't respect the privacy we practice here and show yourself out, I will call security and have you escorted out. We take very seriously what we do here, and unlike a lot of places, we respect a woman's right to decide her own medical care."

Francesco grumbles in Italian under his breath. "Fine, have it your way for now, but you ain't heard the last of me. There's a big family celebration tonight, and after I use that opportunity to scold her in front of everyone, I'll be back here with a lawyer to get ahold of her medical records. Remember, men are always superior to women. Just because they have the vote now don't mean they can do whatever they want without their husbands having a say."

Mrs. Troy has carefully planned the celebration this evening. School has just let out, and she's going to use the occasion to have a festive supper in honor of Lucine and Jacob's supposed upcoming marriage, and to celebrate Giovanni's first birthday. She's also ordered Ernestine to come over. Little does she know Lucine went into her room and stole her suitcase, now packed and sitting under Lucine and Emeline's bed. She also has no idea Gemma's planning to use the occasion to give a piece of her mind to her family and to deliver some shocking news to Francesco.

There are more people than usual at supper, so Mrs. Troy has ordered Sarah to pull the kitchen table into the living room. The coffeetable is a pretended table extension for the people on the davenport. The "festive meal" is roadkill as usual, raccoon stew, with stale vegetables and suspicious-looking cheese on the side.

Carlos is wandering around smoking meth as the guests start to arrive. He flops down onto the davenport when Gemma and Francesco arrive with Giovanni. Giovanni has a bottle stuffed in his mouth, and Gemma is smiling for the first time in a very long time. Mrs. Troy believes it means Gemma has finally "grown up" and now accepts her station in life and the marriage forced upon her.

Jacob arrives next, after buying drugs from Mr. Spirnak. He's shown to a seat next to Lucine, and given a larger portion of stew.

The only relative of Francesco's who was invited is Mrs. Rossi. Gemma can barely stand the sight of Mr. and Mrs. Monterastelli, and Francesco's sisters and sisters-in-law have treated her like a pariah since Giovanni was born and she began complaining about what happened to her in the hospital. It's just as well. She wants Francesco to be the one to explain things to them after the firestorm she's going to unleash tonight.

"I'm so glad you're all here," Mrs. Troy begins as she pours herself a glass of wine. "Exactly a week from today, Antoine and I will give Lucine in marriage to Jacob DeLuise. We all appreciate your humble wedding gifts. They'll be moving to Jacob's apartment in Tribeca, where he works as a furniture salesman and drug dealer. Lucine will devote herself entirely to homemaking and raising children, since she'll be dropping out of school. Even if she ain't reconciled to her fate now, it's Antoine's and my hope that in time she'll come around and accept what's expected of a girl of her social class. Gemma tried to fight her own marriage, and today she's a content wife and mother, living in a poor neighborhood, no more uppity ambitions about college and working."

Francesco throws Gemma's birth control pills onto the table. "If that wench is so reconciled to our marriage and her fate as a poor woman, what in the hell is this?"

Adicia stands on her chair to look at the strange object. "Gemma, are you sick? What are you taking those pills for?"

"Oh, I'd be quite happy to tell everyone," Gemma says, standing up. "Those are birth control pills from Planned Parenthood, where I see a female doctor and have my concerns taken seriously. Apparently Francesco snooped through my nightstand and found my little secret, but I'm glad it's out now."

"You shouldn't snoop through other people's things," Ernestine says.

"I'm her husband! I've got every right in the world to make her business my business! I remember her taking a vow to obey me, not a vow to keep secrets and lie to me!"

"You thought I was being serious when I said 'I do,' you brute? I faked my way through the ceremony the same way I faked my way through that conversion! At least not all of that conversion was fake. I chose Rita as my patron saint since she's the saint of impossible causes, and I've prayed to her every single day to intercede with God on my behalf to save me." Gemma turns to her sisters. "Part of me did it for the five of yous. I sacrificed myself knowing I'd eventually escape, and serve as an example to yous that it's possible to leave the class you were born into. Now I know how Jesus felt, sacrificing himself for the greater good of mankind."

Francesco turns purple. "You dare compare yourself to Jesus Christ, you vile betrayer? A better comparison would be to Judas!"

"Yes, I do compare myself to him. Are you gonna stop me from my own personal feelings, you bastard? You've certainly crucified me enough times in our unhappy life together. Everyone, I want yous to know this horrible excuse of a man beats me, curses at me, gets drunk all the time, cheats on me with women of ill repute, forbids me to do much outside the home except go grocery shopping or visit my family, ignores the baby I didn't want, rapes me, doesn't cover himself up to protect me from possible venereal disease from all those whores he philanders with, and let's not forget to mention his crazy Oedipal complex!"

"Gemma, that's enough," Mrs. Troy says. "We're among company. This ain't the time or place. Now be a proper wife and shut your mouth."

"What's an Oedipal complex?" Adicia asks.

"It's when a man is way too close to his mother," Gemma says, continuing on her rant. "When we were first married, we must've gotten fifteen phonecalls a day from his mother! Now it's dwindled to about three a day. He makes us go over there at least once a week for supper. The only reason I haven't gained a hundred pounds is because I spent so much time running back and forth from the bathroom! Yes, I get that Italians love to feed people and show off their hospitality. That does not mean your family has to force-feed me when I'm beyond full. Do you know how sick I am when my stomach's already about to pop and I'm not allowed to say no to a fifth slice of lasagna, a third plate of ravioli, another serving of goat meat, and a tenth slice of peach pie? And when we're at home, he constantly criticizes *my* cooking, because it's not exactly like his precious mother's. Well, I say, damn your mother! God*damn* your mother to *Hell*!"

"How dare you speak like that about my dear sweet mother! She carried me in her body for nine months and raised me till I was thirty-eight!"

"Cut the damn apron strings already, you overgrown mama's boy! I wanted to marry a man, not a little boy who's dependent on his mommy and daddy for everything! I'm surprised you could bathe or use the toilet by yourself when I met you. What normal man forces his wife to clip his nails, bathe him, comb his hair, dress him, and light his cigarettes? Speaking of, does anyone have a cigarette?"

"I've got one," Allen volunteers, pulling one out of the package in his pocket and handing the cigarette and lighter down to her.

Gemma lights the cigarette and starts blowing smoke into Francesco's face. "That feels great after almost two years without a cigarette. Modern women smoke, you bully. Why are you allowed to smoke, but I can't?"

"Decent women don't smoke, either in public or private! Only fifty years ago a woman would be arrested for smoking in public!"

"Well, it's 1962 now, you bully. Modern women also don't wear clothes covering as much as women of a hundred years ago. We've had the right to wear knee-length skirts and short-sleeved blouses for awhile. They even make pants for women, and let us wear makeup. But what other attitudes should I expect from someone who was born in 1922?"

"You ain't a modern woman no more! You're my wife, and I decide what you wear! When we get home tonight, I'm throwing those poisonous pills down the toilet so we can finally start working on our second child."

"I'm not coming home with you tonight, and I certainly won't be having a second child, by you or anyone else, for quite some time. Not after how I was treated in the hospital last year."

"Oh, get over it!" Mrs. Rossi shouts. "That's what happens to all women! Do you know what childbirth was like before we had modern doctors and hospitals? Now we can just go to sleep and forget the pain, and wake up with a baby."

"Of course I'm not suggesting we go back to the times when many women and babies died. What kinda crazy person do you take me for, Mrs. Rossi? I did want medicine for pain relief, but I shouldn't have been totally knocked out to achieve that! This bully's sisters and sisters-in-law treat me like I'm an awful, awful woman because I think their precious, God-like obstetrician is an evil man who got into that field of medicine because he hates women and enjoys controlling us. I wanted a female doctor because I didn't feel comfortable letting a strange man see and touch intimate parts of my body, but no, that medical practice I was forced to go to has no female doctors. I asked over and over, at every single prenatal visit, for explanations of what he was doing, and what would happen when I gave birth. He never explained anything, and got quite annoyed I wasn't a meek woman who lets the doctor do whatever he wants because he's supposed to know best. He even patted me on the head and spoke to me in a very patronizing manner when I raised serious concerns, like bleeding or cramping."

"The doctor always knows best!" Mrs. Troy says. "You're being as stubborn and willful as always when you act like a doctor has a right to explain anything to you. I never gave a damn to know why my doctors did anything to me.”

"Francesco's sisters and sisters-in-law couldn't believe I was angry over what happened to me. Can anyone tell me why in the hell I'd need to be tied down and given medicine to slow my labor because the doctor was going out to dinner and the movies and wouldn't be back for eight hours? Why did they wrap gauze around my head, shave my pubic hair, and force me to have an enema? I lay in my own waste for hours, and the nurses kept yelling at me like I was an awful, awful woman for feeling humiliated and abused! When the doctor came back, one of those mean nurses gave me a shot of something. The next thing I knew, I wasn't pregnant anymore and Giovanni was in the nursery. I couldn't see or hold him till we went home four days later. I was given a shot of something to dry up my milk, though I wanted to save money by using my own milk instead of formula. Why did I wake up with bruises all over my body and rubbed-off skin around my wrists and ankles? Why do I have no memory of giving birth? I read a book by Dr. Grantly Dick-Read, about giving birth naturally and without fear, and everyone laughed at me when I suggested some of the things I read there. Apparently it's crazy for a woman to do her own reading and not let the doctor handle everything.”

"That's how all women give birth nowadays. I gave birth all nine times put to sleep, and was also asleep when they removed the pregnancy I lost. You should be thankful modern women are able to be knocked out and can't remember such a painful experience.”

"I feel no connection to that baby because of what happened to me. I might be a happy mother if I could only remember giving birth to him and had been able to hold him afterwards. Instead I hate that damn baby and wish he'd never been born.”

"You're gonna get a beating tonight for this scene you're causing,” Francesco says. "This is not proper behavior for a wife of mine.”

Gemma looks around at the people gathered there. Her parents, Mrs. Rossi, Tommy, and Jacob look horrified, and Carlos is too drugged to understand much of what's going on, but Sarah, Allen, and her sisters seem to be smiling. Taking heart from the fact that the people she's most causing this scene for are paying attention, she blazes on.

"And did yous know my name isn't Gemma anymore? No! It's Mrs. Francesco Mon-te-ras-tel-li! I always knew a girl's name changes when she gets married, but I planned to marry a guy with a name as easy to pronounce and remember as mine, like Smith, Jones, or Johnson! And I only changed my last name, not my first name! Why did my first name hafta disappear when I married this brute? Why can't I be called Gemma Mon-te-ras-tel-li or Mrs. Mon-te-ras-tel-li, not Mrs. Francesco Mon-te-ras-tel-li? That's just Francesco's name with the title Mrs. in front! It's like saying I'm the wife of Francesco, without the important information that is my actual name! Mother, no one ever calls you Mrs. Antoine Troy, and I've certainly never heard you calling yourself that or signing your name that way! All the women in Francesco's family and the women I've met in my boring life as a housewife act shocked when I introduce myself as Gemma, not Mrs. Monsterelli, as my sisters call his family. Monsterelli is frankly a better name for them. Carlos is too drugged to ask anything to, but Allen, do you expect your future wife to call herself Mrs. Allen Troy?"

"Probably not. I don't think that's a convention most women of our class follow. It's more a thing upper-class women do."

"Lucine, you do not have to follow in my footsteps and marry this loser. You don't wanna end up like I did. But thank God, I no longer have to deal with Francesco after tonight. I'm gonna go out and enjoy the resta my youth. I want to dance, go to parties, work, go to college, join a sorority, wear nice clothes, and do the things all normal, modern twenty-year-old women do. Do you hear that, Francesco? I'm free!"

"What the hell are you going on about, woman?" Francesco spits. "You're still my wife, and I still control you! You ain't going out in public for a long time after this."

Gemma reaches into her purse and pulls out a piece of paper. "Think again, you brute. You see your signature on this line? And you see my signature? This is the document that says we're divorced."

Mrs. Troy looks like she's having a heart attack. This is the ultimate humiliation, after she worked so hard to find a husband for Gemma and to marry her off in a nice wedding. This is not good publicity for her family on the eve of Lucine's supposed wedding.

"How the hell could we get divorced if we never appeared before a judge, you stupid cow? And how the hell could I have signed that thing? Did you forge my signature?"

"I just so happened to see my old school friend Lorraine at the bridal shop last month, and told her of my troubles. Her dad's a lawyer, and I discussed our marriage with him. He prepared a case in my defense, that you were an abusive husband, a cheater, and a drunkard. What, you never responded to the notices you got in the mail to appear in court? I was certainly there. The judge ruled you in contempt of court for refusal to appear, and gave me the papers. It's not my fault you didn't open your mail or refused to come to court."

"I never got any such notices in the mail! I certainly would've shown up had I known you were trying to divorce me!"

Gemma threw away the letters so Francesco wouldn't appear in court and the judge would decide in her favor, but prefers to let him think the letters went unread or ignored for another reason. "You know how sometimes you get so drunk you act like a madman. Maybe you tossed 'em out the window or used 'em as toilet paper in your drunken state. And from the look on your face now, I wonder if you came here half-drunk."

"That still don't explain how the hell my name came to be on these papers unless you forged it!"

"I got you rip-roaring drunk last week and had you sign it. You were so drunk you didn't know or care what you were signing."

Allen and the girls burst out laughing. Francesco is so shocked he can no longer find his tongue to yell at Gemma, and just stares around stupidly.

"You can take this ugly engagement ring, and the wedding ring too. Do any of you girls want this boring diamond ring that wasn't chosen with my likes or personality in mind?"

The girls shake their heads in unison.

"Good, then I'm chucking them both." Gemma goes over to the fire escape door, twists both rings off, and throws them into the street below. "You can take that kid too. I don't want anything more to do with him. No, on second thought, you'd just give him to your overbearing mother to raise, and he'd turn out another version of you. Sarah, would you like to take this baby?"

"We're done raising babies here," Mrs. Troy speaks for Sarah. "We can keep him here for a short while, but if you don't want him, we can turn him over to an orphanage."

"Well, whatever you do with him, tell the orphanage people his name is Bobby. I wanted him to have an all-American name like Bobby, Jimmy, or Johnny, but no, he had to get an overly Italian name like Giovanni."

"What if his new parents don't like the name Bobby?" Tommy asks. "And he knows his name as Giovanni for a whole year. He might not answer to Bobby, and if his name is changed again, he'll be confused."

"Oh, babies don't care what their name is. It's not like he's your age." Gemma goes back to the table. "And another thing, Mother, before I leave. The way you treat Sarah is disgusting. I'm sure it's a form of slavery to only rarely pay a live-in servant, and only pay her very small amounts, while using her for fifteen years to raise your kids, cook, clean your home, and do everything else you're too lazy, drunk, or drugged to do yourself. Emeline, Ernestine, Adicia, and Justine all said 'Mama' as their first word, to Sarah, not you. You should be embarrassed your own children didn't recognize you as their mother. Sarah, you're thirty-five. Wouldn't you like a husband and kids, instead of being a slave to my mother? She barely treats you better than the Nazis did."

Sarah hesitates, afraid of Mrs. Troy's reaction, then goes ahead. "Yes. I'd love to have my own baby before I'm too old. I have no family. It's only me. If I don't marry and have at least one baby, my whole family line will die *mit* me. My survival will have been in vain. There's more than one way to be a *mutter*, but raising someone else's *kinder* won't continue my family bloodline and memory."

"Are you happy knowing that, Mother? Sarah thought she was coming to a new life of freedom and second chances in the best country in the world, and was almost immediately enslaved again. If she'd run into any other woman looking for a nanny and household help, she probably would've been able to go to night school and have a diploma by now. I may hate having a baby, but I've never pawned him off on anyone else to raise." Gemma goes over to her old room. "Now I'm gonna take some of the things Francesco wouldn't let me keep, like my posters and records."

"Where are you gonna stay?" Mr. Troy demands. "You ain't welcome here after this stunt, and I'm sure Francesco's family won't accept you back neither."

"My friend Lorraine Neiman, who goes to Hunter and lives in a three-bedroom apartment with friends on the Upper East Side. Her dad rescued me from this horrid marriage, remember? Lorraine said I can sleep on the sofa bed, and if I still need a place to stay, I can take over her room after she gets married in October. I'm also going to reapply to Hofstra."

Gemma shuts the door and begins taking down her posters and rolling them up in their cardboard tubes, still in the wardrobe. She tosses the posters into the duffel bag she brought over, unplugs the record player, and carefully puts it in the bag. Next she picks up the cardboard box of records and sets it next to the bag so she doesn't forget it on the way out. Her radio is the next thing she puts in the bag. Finally she goes into the wardrobe for some of her old clothes and finds most of them gone.

Gemma pokes her head out the door. "Lucine, can you come in here? I need your help with packing my clothes."

Lucine leaves Jacob and goes into the room. "Do you really want your clothes back? I know they were never mine to begin with, but I like wearing them."

"Are they all in the wash?" Gemma whispers. "I can't find the lot of them."

Lucine kneels down and pulls the suitcase from under the bed. "I packed everything up a little while ago," she whispers back. "I'm gonna run away before our parents can marry me off to that repulsive drug dealer out there. Did you know he's friends with another drug dealer who moved across the hall last month, a man so degenerate he was raping his own daughter? Thank God we were able to sneak her to the squat where Ernestine moved."

"Where are you going? At least I know where I'm going and have a place guaranteed when I get there."

"Midtown, I think. It's over an hour on foot, but it's the farthest away from here I know how to walk to. I'll go into a church before it gets dark and hope for the best."

Gemma reconsiders the matter of the clothes. "You need the clothes more than I do. I have clothes back at Francesco's, even if they're not as stylish as these. I can always buy myself new clothes after I start working again."

"Will I ever see you again? I can't believe I'm asking you that, but I feel bad for you after what happened to you. I'm already upset because I don't know if I'll ever be able to find Sarah, Allen, or our little sisters again after I run away."

"We might run into each other sometime. I'm never going downtown again if I can help it, so if you're gonna be hanging around up-town or midtown, I'll probably bump into you eventually. If you really wanna know, you can look up my friend Lorraine in the phonebook and ask her. Her new name's gonna be Wickline, and her future hus-band's name is Joe. I think I'll be fine, though. I've got all my stuff I wanted to pick up, and all I've got left to collect are my pills on the ta-ble. Then I'm going to Francesco's to get the resta my stuff. I wish you luck in your own escape."

Mr. and Mrs. Troy make obscene gestures at Gemma as she walks out with the box of records, the duffel bag over her left shoulder. Gemma ignores them and picks up her birth control pills, dropping them into her purse. Mrs. Rossi gives her a dirty look, as Francesco still looks around stupidly.

"Do you need money?" Allen asks.

"Allen, don't try to aid and abet this traitor, or we'll wash our hands of you too," Mrs. Troy says.

Gemma leans down to look at Giovanni one last time. "He's not a bad-looking baby. Someday I'll have another kid when I'm married to a guy I like and wanna have a kid. Maybe the next time I'll be able to remember giving birth and won't be treated like a cog on an assembly line. Be good for your new parents, Bobby."

"His name is Giovanni!" Mrs. Rossi yells. "You can't take this boy's name away from him when you ain't sticking around to be his proper mother! He's half-Italian, and deserves a name that shows who he is!"

"And he's all American, and deserves a name that reflects where he was born. At least some ethnic names blend in instead of sticking out like a sore thumb." Gemma goes to the door. "Goodbye, everyone."

"Where are you going?" Carlos asks.

"You mean you didn't pay any attention to the big scene Gemma just made?" Mrs. Troy asks. "She went behind Francesco's back to get a divorce I'm surprised is legal, is abandoning her child, is moving up-town, and was carrying on about things all decent women accept as the natural course of things, like being identified through their hus-bands and giving birth knocked out."

"And she compared herself to Jesus!" Mrs. Rossi says.

"Damn, I missed that?" Carlos whines. "Guess I was too high to notice."

Gemma goes down the dangerous steps for the last time and turns around to look back at the ten-story tenement she called home for fourteen years. She quickly begins walking southeast to Two Bridges to collect the rest of her things, breathing in the air of freedom. Part of her wishes she'd done this two years ago, but what's past is past. At least it happened better late than never. From this point on, she can only look forward to the future.

Chapter 15: Sarah Gets in Trouble

Carlos comes home early from work three days before the wedding that's never going to happen, smoking a joint and ranting up a storm.

"Can you believe my bastard boss fired me for eating on the job? I said I've been doing that since I began working there, and he said if he'd known that, he woulda fired me a long time ago! Now I gotta find me another job! Just when I was planning to find me my own place, too!"

"You can't eat when you're at work?" Justine asks.

"Not according to this fat cat! He also said I won't get paid for the days I already worked this week!"

"Carlos doesn't eat at work like you're thinking," Lucine says. "He's allowed to take a lunch break. He was stealing cereal from the conveyer belt instead of putting it in cereal boxes."

"It ain't like the rich snobs who buy that cereal in their fancy grocery stores would notice some missing! They've got enough money to afford ten boxes of cereal to make up what's gone!"

"Are you really moving out?" Adicia asks excitedly.

"I was hoping Allen and I could find a place together. Guess I'll hafta sell drugs full-time to afford it. Do you know if any factories or stores are hiring?"

"How about going to night school for your high school equivalency diploma?" Lucine asks. "Then you can go to a vocational college to help you get a real job."

"You're a high school dropout too. Whether you like it or not, you ain't going back to school after you marry DeLuise. It's bad enough both Gemma and Allen got high school diplomas."

"Hopefully Gemma will be able to go to college in the fall, the way she'd planned to before our parents derailed it. Allen plans to go to college someday, after he's worked awhile."

Allen graduated high school by the skin of his teeth, passing with Cs and Ds in all his classes and finals. He's been spending a lot of his time going through the male help wanted ads, hoping to find a decent job that isn't mindless or demeaning like the jobs Carlos and their parents have worked. Some of the female help wanted ads seem more interesting, like being an artist's model and setting up the window displays in a tea room. It's unfair the want ads are separated by sex, though he dares not say this to his mother, who thinks her own sex is inferior and should continue letting men tell them what to do.

"Look, Giovanni's trying to walk," Emeline says. "Don't you wanna play with our nephew?"

"Don't get too attached to that kid. He's only here for a few more days, and then he's headed to the orphanage. Besides, playing with babies is for girls." Carlos goes to the kitchen and fumbles for another joint.

"You'll feel sorry you spent all your time doing drugs instead of doing things with Giovanni. You really don't want any final memories of our firstborn nephew?"

"It's so fun having a baby again," Adicia says. "Are you sure we can't keep him?"

"I wish we could, but your *mutter* said he goes to the orphanage in a few days," Sarah says. "I'm sure he'll have nice new parents. Don't you want him to grow up *mit* a nice family, in a nice place?"

"Do we really hafta tell the orphanage people his name's Bobby? Robert's a nice name, but it's not the name he was given, even if Gemma hates that name."

"Giovanni's a lovely name," Emeline says. "A couple of famous artists had that name, and the writer of a very old book called *The Decameron*. All the librarians told me I was a little too young to read it, though I've read adult books before, and it's not a dirty book."

"Yes, it is," Lucine says. "It's a very dirty book, from what I've read of it. A lot of the stories are really raunchy—cheating spouses, clergymen breaking their vow of chastity, intimacy before marriage, lots of stuff not meant for children's books, or even for someone your age. You could try reading it, but I don't think it'd make sense if you don't know what some of these things mean. It's like how when you were Adicia's age, you didn't know what menstruation or sexual relations were. It didn't make sense if you heard people talking about it."

"I'll help you *mit* adult books to read at our next library trip," Sarah says consolingly. "You've liked Hermann Hesse's books. How many have you read so far?"

"The first one I read was *Demian*, in sixth grade, and then I read *Gertrude, Beneath the Wheel*, and *Peter Camenzind*. The subject matter of some of his other books looked a little out of my league."

"Just because you're only fourteen doesn't mean you can't like and understand them in your own way. You appreciate and understand a book in a different, more mature way when you reread it as an adult, or at a different time in your life. You'd like *Narcissus and Goldmund*. You love history, and it takes place during the Middle Ages, including an outbreak of Black Plague. You'd also like it because Goldmund's an artist, and you love art and art history. It does have adult material, but it's not explicit or tasteless. You might like *Siddhartha* too, since you love reading about world religions. It's a story about Buddha and how he achieved enlightenment."

"Who's Buddha?" Adicia asks.

"He was a spiritual leader and teacher, like Jesus," Emeline says. "He lived in what's today Nepal, and was born a prince. He gave everything up because he felt sick at seeing the differences between his pampered life in the palace and the horrible things the poor people outside the palace gates went through. He wandered around for a long time, trying to find the meaning of life and how to gain enlightenment, which is sort of like getting close to God. He denied himself everything but basic necessities, but he found out happiness and enlightenment don't come from starving yourself or wearing rags. When you're older, I can help you find library books on Buddhism and the other Eastern religions."

"Why do you care about other religions?" Carlos sneers. "I barely care about Christianity except to show up at the obligatory two services a year."

"It's neat to learn about how other people believe. It's embarrassing so many Americans don't know or care much about how people in the rest of the world live. My teachers think I'm a little strange because I wanna take more than one language and enjoy taking out library books on other languages. Most Europeans know at least three languages fluently instead of only taking one language for school because they have to."

"I knew French and Italian in addition to German," Sarah says. "I probably should've taught you German, but it was very important for me to learn English. Maybe I'll have a bilingual child if I ever have my own baby."

"How old is too old to have a baby?" Adicia asks. "I've heard of women in their fifties who have babies."

"It can happen, but it's harder over forty. Most women who have babies so old are very religious and have been having babies for a long time. They didn't just start at forty-eight or fifty."

Mrs. Troy comes into the apartment grumbling. "The bank manager asked me to leave early and wouldn't tell me why. He'd better not be about to fire me so soon before Lucine's wedding. I need to embezzle more money to pay for everything."

"Isn't embezzling a crime?" Adicia asks.

"Like I care. You mistakes should be thankful I'm using it to pay for Lucine's wedding and not my own things."

"I was fired today," Carlos announces. "Damned boss caught me helping myself to the cereal."

Mrs. Troy lights up a cigarette. "You'll get over it. I've lost count of how many jobs I've had. They're like buses; they come along every fifteen minutes."

"But I liked my job," Carlos whines. "What other job lets you sneak food when you're supposed to be working?"

"Why do you need to eat on the job?" Lucine asks. "Don't you get your fill of raccoon stew and badger burgers here?"

"I was gonna move out, too. I hope I can afford rent from just selling drugs. Can I move into Gemma's old place, now that Francesco's moving back in with his parents?"

Allen tosses the want ads at him. "Sure, if you enjoy living in the worst neighborhoods in the city. Me, I'd like to have my first home in a nice place like Greenwich Village."

"There are a lot of niggers and spics in Two Bridges," Mrs. Troy says. "Francesco got what he could afford for his ungrateful wife, but I wouldn't feel safe near them."

"What's wrong with living near Negroes and Spanish-Americans?" Emeline asks. "You're friends with people of Italian and Irish ancestry, and people useta have racist attitudes toward them."

"Mother just used very bad words," Lucine tells Adicia and Justine. "We don't want to hear you using those words. Negroes and Spanish-Americans will be very upset if you use those words."

"I don't give a damn what the coons and spics think about what I call them! I'll call them whatever I please! I can call Sarah a kike and a Yid too if I feel like it!"

"Why are you so mean?" Adicia asks.

Mrs. Troy reaches into the refrigerator for a bottle of beer. "My own children won't allow me to talk how I want in my own home. I'll be drinking in my room if anyone needs me. Sarah, I want you to start supper at five. Today it's gonna be lamb. I found a cut of meat the butcher threw out because it had worms in it, and he gave it to me for almost free."

"I don't wanna eat meat that had worms crawling in it," Adicia whispers to her sisters.

"'Had'?" Emeline asks. "There might still be worms crawling it in, and they're all over the other food in there!"

"What can we do?" Sarah sighs. "We need to eat."

"I'm not eating it," Lucine declares. "I'm tired of pretending roadkill and bad meat are so tasty. I'd pretend to forget about the time and burn it if I were you."

"Well, we've got some time till you have to start supper," Emeline says. "Can we go to the library and get new books? We have to return some books, and you promised you'd help me look for new adult books I'd like."

Sarah looks around. Mrs. Troy is drinking in her bedroom, Tommy is taking a nap at the foot of her bed, Carlos is doing his usual thing, and Allen is looking through the want ads. No one needs her, and there are no chores that need doing till 5:00.

"Sure, we'll go to Tompkins Square Library. It's closer than Hamilton Fish Library, so we can get home quicker." Sarah picks up Giovanni and puts him in the stroller. "Let's leave by the fire escape."

"You can push a stroller down the fire escape?" Adicia asks.

"He's a year old. He's a little too heavy to risk carrying down those nightmare front steps."

Emeline goes to get their library books and library cards. "I can't wait till I have my own house and can fill up an entire room with books from floor to ceiling. I hate always having to return books I like instead of keeping them for always."

"Can we get a baby book for Giovanni and read it to him while he's still here?" Adicia asks.

"We can get whatever books we want. I'm sure Giovanni would love being read to by his aunts before he has to go to the orphanage."

***

Sarah and the girls are not looking forward to seeing, touching, or eating worm-infested meat. On the way home from the library, they hatched a plan to destroy the meat so no one has to eat it. They don't care if they get in trouble or Mrs. Troy throws a fit.

Lucine goes to the cupboard and pulls out a baking pan big enough to accommodate the foil-wrapped lamb Sarah takes out of the refrigerator. They don't bother pouring Crisco on the bottom of the pan like they usually do, since no one's going to eat it. Sarah leaves the meat in the foil, afraid to peel it open and see the worms, dead or alive. At least there are no holes in the foil.

Emeline turns the oven all the way up to 500° and opens the door for Sarah to slide the pan in. Tommy is up from his nap and occupying himself with his Lincoln Logs, not paying any attention to what's going on in the kitchen. Carlos has wandered off to meet some friends, and Allen is on the fire escape smoking marijuana. Mrs. Troy is still holed up in her room drinking and smoking meth, and probably won't emerge till Sarah calls supper.

"What are we gonna eat instead?" Adicia asks.

"We'll find something," Lucine says. "We always do."

"Now we walk away and ignore the oven till we smell the lamb burning," Emeline says. "I'm going to read Giovanni the books we got him."

Lucine sits on the davenport and pulls Justine onto her lap to read her *The Cat in the Hat Comes Back*, while Emeline takes Giovanni into her room to read him *The Poky Little Puppy*, *Curious George*, and *Harold and the Purple Crayon*. Adicia has checked out *The Cricket in Times Square* and *Strawberry Girl*, and asks Sarah to read them to her. They periodically look over to the kitchen area to make sure there isn't any smoke coming out of the oven.

When the meat has been in for forty minutes, Sarah gets up to check on it. She pulls on a pot glove and tentatively peels away a little of the foil to see if the lamb's turning black yet or if it can stay in a little longer. She's so focused on carefully inspecting the tainted meat, she doesn't hear Emeline shouting in the background, "Oh, look, he's walking!"

Sarah hears baby noises coming from behind her and turns around to see Giovanni heading towards the open oven at a remarkable speed. Without having time to think, she instinctively shouts, "*Nein! Sehr heiss!*"

Giovanni starts crying at the loud noise in a strange language, stopping in his tracks. Sarah scoops him up and cuddles him as she paces the floor.

"What the hell did I just hear in my own American house?"

Everyone stops to look at Mrs. Troy, who's just bolted out of the bedroom, a bottle of whiskey in her hand. She looks furious.

"I just heard Kraut words spoken in my American house. If that baby needs to hear any language besides English, it should be Italian, and spoken by Francesco's family! Give me my grandson. You ain't capable of taking care of him."

"Why can't we keep him?" Tommy asks. "I want a little brother."

"Why are you such a racist?" Lucine asks. "Don't you know what city we live in, and what neighborhood? You're so proud of our Lower East Side roots, and you act like a foreign-born American is horrible for speaking her own native language?"

Mrs. Troy goes over to the living room and looks at the new library books on the coffeetable. "I see Emeline has gotten herself books by a Kraut writer too. Did you tell her Kraut writers are superior to Americans? Not that I like her reading so much to begin with, but if she's gonna be a hopeless bookworm, at least point her towards native writers!"

"Hermann Hesse's Swiss," Emeline says. "He was born in Germany, but moved to Switzerland when he was young. Later he moved back to Germany, but was back in Switzerland a long time before the war. The Nazis banned his books because he didn't write about things they liked. Sarah recommended his books because she liked them, and she knows I'm interested in a lot of the things he writes about. Unfortunately, one of the books she recommended hasn't been properly translated into English yet, so I had to take out some of his other books today."

"You're talking to me like I give a damn. I want the Kraut books out of my house."

"This isn't your house," Sarah says, still holding Giovanni. "You rent an apartment in a tenement. You may live in the only apartment *mit* seven rooms, but you're just an ordinary tenant. Since you often don't pay utility bills, you have heat, hot water, and electricity shut off by the landlord."

Mrs. Troy looks derisively at another book on the coffeetable, a book about Hinduism. "I don't tolerate pagan religions in this house. Why do you need to know the details of how heathens bow down to their idols?"

"You burst out laughing when Tommy asked who the man on the cross was when you went to an Episcopal church! You don't educate your own *kinder* on your own supposed religion!"

"Sarah took us to her synagogue once, and it was nice," Adicia says.

Mrs. Troy's eyes light up with anger. "You went behind my back and tried to indoctrinate my children into your religion?"

"We were curious. We just wanted to learn. Nobody tried to convert us. They didn't laugh at us like they do in the churches you take us to."

"You are a horrible *mutter*. You only care about your *kinder*, except Tommy, when it comes to looking good among your friends and neighbors, or just to say you're a *mutter*. No respectable *mutter* gives her *kinder* to a nanny to raise full-time. I was the one who gave them bottles, changed their diapers, bathed them, dressed them, helped them *mit* schoolwork, and everything else. I was the one who was there when Lucine and Emeline started to menstruate. You just dumped a box of napkins and a belt on them."

Mrs. Troy starts sniffing furiously. "Is that our supper for tonight? Do I smell our beautiful lamb burning? I paid a half-dollar for that, a bargain considering other five-pound racks of lamb at that butcher's go for at least three dollars!"

"You paid that price because it had worms in it. Decent *mutters* don't feed their *kinder* food that can make them sick."

Allen wanders back into the apartment. "What's all the yelling going on here for? I was tryna mellow out."

"I'll tell you what's going on," his mother informs him. "Sarah is fired."

"What!" Lucine shouts. "You can't fire Sarah! Who's gonna look after Justine all day when no one's home?"

"Who's gonna cook and clean while your lazy self is getting drunk or smoking cocaine, marijuana, and meth?" Emeline asks.

"Who's gonna protect my little sisters and be the one sympathetic adult in their lives?"

"Why are you firing her?" Allen asks. "Are you that high or drunk you're gonna kick out the best thing going for my sisters, and your own almost-free source of housecleaning and cooking?"

"Didn't you hear her shouting something evil in German at my grandson? And she's encouraged your pathetic bookworm of a sister to check out library books written by a Kraut and to get books on foreign religions. I just now found out she also took them to her Yid church once."

"I'm glad Giovanni's going to a new family soon," Lucine says. "He'll be raised by people who care about bettering their lives instead of people who love wallowing in poverty and look down on anyone who dares wanna do better for themselves."

"She didn't say anything evil to Giovanni," Emeline says. "She just said, 'No! Very hot!' Would you have preferred he walk right into an open hot stove?"

Mrs. Troy gasps when she sees how high the oven's been set to. "Who the hell cranked it up to five hundred degrees? Someone, pull that thing outta there and throw it in the garbage before it starts a fire."

"I did it on purpose," Sarah says. "No one wanted to eat meat *mit* worms in it. That is beyond disgusting."

Allen shuts off the oven and pulls out the pan with a pot glove. Mrs. Troy rolls her eyes when she sees the foil still wrapped around the lamb. Parts of the foil have melted and become stuck to both meat and pan. She'll have to clean this up all by herself tonight.

"Sarah, pack up your things and get outta my house. Don't try to contact my children again if you know what's good for you. Here's some money for subway fare to Brooklyn. I hear that's where a lot of your kind live now, after mosta 'em left this neighborhood."

Adicia and Justine run after her as she goes into the tiny bedroom, still holding Giovanni, to start putting her meager possessions into her suitcase. Emeline and Lucine are too stunned to do or say anything.

"Maybe she'll change her mind tomorrow and beg you to come back," Adicia suggests. "She can't live without you."

"I won't change my mind ever," Mrs. Troy calls nastily. "If I have to, I can always pick up another young dumb girl at work or in the market."

"Sarah isn't dumb! She's helped us with our schoolwork and learnt along with us! It's not her fault she was kicked outta public school when she was only eleven!"

"Sarah might have a German accent, but she speaks better English than you!" Lucine agrees. "Whoever taught her English didn't teach her to use the word 'ain't' or double negatives, or any of the other butcheries of the English language you and Dad employ!"

"You think I don't know I don't speak proper English?" Mrs. Troy snorts. "I ain't as dumb as you girls think."

Sarah folds up her clothes and lays them in her suitcase, then puts in her chanukiyah, some family photos she found after the war, a couple of books, including Emeline's first book, an English translation of *Grimms' Fairytales* with illustrations, a few hats, her shoes, and the girls' class pictures from over the years, the only pictures she has to remember them by. Mrs. Troy paces back and forth in annoyance, getting impatient at how long it's taking.

"Where are you gonna go?" Emeline asks.

"I don't care if she sleeps on the street!" Mrs. Troy rants. "I want her out of our house! If I have to, I can find another stupid immigrant to exploit for housework and childcare."

"Can Sarah still come to Lucine's wedding?" Tommy asks. "Since Gemma ran away, Lucine needs a new maid of honor."

Mrs. Troy thinks for a minute. "Allen, do you or Carlos have a girlfriend we can use as a maid of honor?"

Allen snuffs out his joint. "Mother, do you have any common sense left in your head after all those years of drinking and drugging? If I asked my girl of the moment, whom I've only been seeing for two weeks, to be the maid of honor in an unwanted wedding for a complete stranger, she'd either laugh in my face or dump me!"

Sarah looks over at Allen desperately as she slowly makes her way to the front door. "After Lucine leaves, you'll be the only adult left to protect your sisters. Please promise me you'll get a job and move to a nicer neighborhood once you get enough money saved up. Your sisters deserve better. Maybe you can finally meet a nice girl who's marriage material, and she can take my place as their substitute *mutter*."

"We only want you, Sarah!" Adicia pleads. "We don't want anyone to take your place!"

Mrs. Troy points to the door. "Show yourself out. And don't forget the subway fare." She throws the coins at Sarah.

Emeline rushes to pick up the coins and puts them in Sarah's purse. "Can I carry your suitcase down the stairs for you?"

"You do and you'll be kicked out too."

Justine and Adicia run to Sarah and hug her tightly, bursting into tears. Mrs. Troy taps her foot on the floor in annoyance. Emeline and Lucine go over to hug her next. Giovanni starts crying, upset by all the commotion.

"Look on the bright side," Emeline says unhappily. "Maybe you'll finally be able to find a husband and have your own baby."

"Will we ever see you again?" Adicia asks tearfully.

"If God is just, we'll meet again someday. When people are meant to be together, they always find a way back to each other. You have to be good and listen to your big *bruder* Allen. He'll take care of you after Lucine leaves. Remember, good people always come out on top and bad people are punished, even if takes a long time for justice to be served."

***

Ernestine looks up in surprise. "Sarah! What are you doing here?"

Sarah sets her suitcase down and sits next to Ernestine on the mattress. "Your *mutter* fired me, and I wanted to say goodbye to you before I leave the area."

Ernestine's mouth falls open. "That evil wench fired you? Was she drunk or high? If she was, I bet she'll be desperate for you to come back tomorrow!"

"Come join us for supper," Boy says. "We're gonna start very soon. Tonight we're having chicken soup and peppers stuffed with rice. Our communal table's over there, and I'm sure we have an extra chair for you."

"Where are you going after this? The mission?"

"I want to spend the night here. I don't want to walk alone in downtown New York. But to answer your question, I'm going to the place I should've gone when I came to this country, the Hebrew Immigrant Aid Society. They used to be nearby, but they might've moved."

"I can get you a phonebook," Girl volunteers. "We don't have any phones, but it's helpful to look up addresses."

"Why did she fire you?" Ernestine asks. "Did you break a bottle of her precious alcohol or mess with her drugs?"

"She wanted to serve lamb *mit* worms for supper. Your sisters and I made a plan to ruin it by putting the oven up too high and letting it burn in the foil. Your *mutter* was in her room drinking and drugging when she heard me speak German to Giovanni. He was getting too close to the stove, taking his first steps, and I got scared and shouted the first thing that came into my head. Then she got mad because Emeline got out a library book on Hinduism and some books by a German-Swiss writer she likes, books I recommended to her. When she smelled the meat burning, we got in a fight. She's also angry I took you girls to synagogue once. She gave me subway fare for Brooklyn, but I'm not leaving Manhattan."

"Ain't there an abandoned baby there?" Girl asks. "Why didn't you take him with you so he won't hafta be sent to the orphanage?"

"What would I do with a one-year-old boy? I'm sure he'll find nice new parents soon. Gemma's a better *mutter* than Ernestine's, since she knew she didn't want a baby and couldn't take care of him like he deserved. She didn't keep him just to say she's a *mutter* and to avoid looking bad."

"Our parents left us to the community 'cause they had no interest in kids. If I ever met Mrs. Troy, I'd give her a piece of my mind."

"That woman will be left alone and miserable one day. Even Tommy will get sick of her when he realizes the *mutter* who spoils him rotten is a drunk and a drug addict who expects him to stay in poverty as some sort of ridiculous birthright."

"Why did she give you subway fare for Brooklyn?" Ernestine asks. "That's gotta be a lot more than the fifteen cents it costs to go anywhere in Manhattan."

"She says I'd find more of my kind there. She also used bad words for Negroes and Spanish-Americans when Carlos suggested moving to Two Bridges. She won't feel safe near them."

"And that's the evil woman my sisters are stuck with now that you're gone. Why don't they have a license for having kids?"

Baby climbs onto Sarah's lap. "Why do you have a tattoo? I never met a woman who had a tattoo before, only sailors and bad guys."

"This is my sister Baby," Girl says. "She's five. Our baby sister Infant's over there pretending to help in the kitchen. She's three."

"When I was your age, very bad people took over my native country and did very bad things to my people. When I was sixteen, I was taken to a very bad prison for people the bad guys hated. We had our names taken away and replaced by numbers. This was my identification number. America and many other good countries fought a big war to defeat the bad guys and their friends."

"That sounds worse than what happens here sometimes," Baby says. "Girl says sometimes good people go to prison just because they're poor and can't afford a nice lawyer, or because the jury thinks they're guilty just because they're poor."

"Are you gonna go to college after you get your high school equivalency diploma?" Ernestine asks. "What do you wanna study?"

"Probably teaching. After fifteen years taking care of children, it seems natural to become a teacher and get paid for it."

"Are you sure you can't stay here?" Julie asks. "Everyone's so nice. I can't forget about the bad things my daddy did to me, but being treated so nicely helps take my mind off it a little bit."

"I'm sure this is a nice community, but my life wasn't meant to be here. I'm going to go back to school, find a job, and hopefully find a husband and have a baby or two before I'm too old. I don't think I could do that here, do you?"

"I guess not," Ernestine admits. "But it's nice to have you here before you hafta say goodbye. I can't believe my wicked mother did that."

"Don't feel bad about what you did," Girl encourages her. "No decent mother expects her kids to eat worm-infested meat. You did the right thing by burning it."

Infant comes running over to them. "The grownups told me to tell yous supper's ready."

Ernestine takes Sarah by the hand. "Let's go have a nice supper, and then we'll make plans for what you're gonna do tomorrow. Whatever happens, I'm sure it'll be the start of a lovely new life for you, far away from this cesspool of a city and my insane mother."

Chapter 16: Fire!

Lucine is extremely nervous about what she must do to avoid being forced into marriage to this horrible creature tomorrow. She's going to slip out at night and walk to the mission, then at the break of dawn start walking to Midtown and find a church. By tomorrow at this time, she'll be far away from the tenement and the dead-end generational poverty her parents and Carlos are convinced is their birthright instead of something to work their way out of.

"We still ain't found a replacement maid of honor," Mrs. Troy frets as she puts lunchmeat on a platter at 6:00. "Where's Carlos? He could hustle up a random girl, and I'd pay her with somea the money I've embezzled!"

"How much money exactly have you embezzled?" Emeline asks.

"Enough to pay for a nice wedding and have some left over for nice things for myself. Some people's embezzlement schemes last for years before they're caught. That almost makes me wanna work this stupid job long-term instead of quitting or letting myself get fired."

"Won't you go to prison if they catch you?" Lucine asks.

"Tomorrow at this time we're gonna be celebrating your wedding, and two days from now you'll be in your new apartment in Tribeca with Jacob. Don't worry about what might happen to me."

Carlos comes into the apartment, smoking meth. "I was just down in the basement tryna fix the fuse box. My friend Nick on the fourth floor got his electricity shut off 'cause he and his wife didn't pay their utility bills, and I was tryna tinker with it and undo what the landlord did. That damn fat cat took out the penny I shoved in the socket last time I fixed it, so I put another one in. We're paying him to live in his building; the least he could do is let us have electricity all the time."

"Sockets are supposed to prevent overheating or short circuiting," Emeline says. "We learnt in my science class this year that it's dangerous to stick coins in them."

Carlos rolls his eyes. "Whatever. I've done it before many a time."

"You've also gotten drunk and done drugs many a time, but that doesn't mean the next time couldn't be the time you die, get sick, get arrested, or hurt yourself."

Carlos ignores her. "I also got a new job today. I'm an auto mechanic at a car repair and service shop on Twelfth Street."

"What do you do there?" Adicia asks. "Are you an assistant?"

"No, I'm a real mechanic. I came in off the street when I saw a sign in the window that said they was hiring, and I said I was the man for them. They won't care I lied about having three years of experience working in an auto repair shop. What they care about is that I show up and do the job."

"But you don't have experience," Lucine says. "I don't think you know the first thing about fixing cars."

"It can't be that hard. I've broken into lots of cars in parking garages to steal stuff and break them so their snobby owners won't be able to drive 'em no more. If I can break 'em, I can fix 'em."

"What's the basement like?" Adicia asks. "It looks so dark and scary."

"I didn't have no flashlight, so I used a match to see around. You'd think that cheapskate would at least put windows in. Some people use the basement for storage. There's a bunch of garbage on the floor too."

"I hope you're gonna steal stuff from the cars you fix," Mrs. Troy says. "We could use a lot of the stuff rich people leave lying around their cars."

"I won't let a day go by without taking what I can. It ain't my fault those rich bastards leave stuff in their cars instead of keeping it at home. I've found some great stuff in cars—maps, flashlights, money, movie tickets, cigarettes, clothes."

"But stealing is wrong," Adicia says. "They're leaving their car there with the trust it's gonna be fixed and not stolen from. How would you like it if you had a car and a mean mechanic decided to steal something from it?"

Carlos waves his hand dismissively. "Not my car, not my problem."

"You were just fired 'cause you were caught stealing," Lucine says. "Why are you doing that again? You might get a reputation as a thief, and if word gets around, no one might want to hire you someday."

"That'll never happen," Mrs. Troy declares. "Look at how many jobs I've been fired from for tardiness, stealing, laziness, not showing up, or being caught drinking and using drugs. People still wanna hire me. Carlos will do fine."

Tommy picks up a piece of bologna and jams it into his mouth. "I hope we're having a nicer supper than lunchmeat at the wedding."

"Of course we will," his mother soothes him. "It's just that I ain't a very good cook, and I had to whip up what I could with minimum preparation. We'll be eating lots of hotdogs, casseroles, and sandwiches till I can find another girl who's dumb enough to agree to work for almost no money and only be paid once every few months."

"What did you cook before you had Sarah?" Tommy shoves a slice of turkey into his mouth.

"I just told you. Mostly hotdogs, sandwiches, and casseroles. Sometimes I made recipes from a rationing cookbook someone gave us, like pasta with melted cheese and hamburger meat."

"Don't we got any roadkill?" Carlos whines.

"I forget how to cook meat. You and your father always skin the meat. I never cooked exotic game when I still cooked."

The chickens begin running around in circles and clucking furiously. Mrs. Troy tries to shoo them away, though they keep running back to the kitchen. She curses the day she and Carlos took them home. The amount of eggs laid over the last two and a half years is a drop in the bucket in comparison to the hundreds of eggs she expected them to lay every month. They never were able to breed either, with the lack of a rooster.

"Do you think they wanna go outside?" Adicia asks.

"I'd love to put them outside and have them never come back," Mrs. Troy grumbles. "They've been more trouble than they're worth."

"I smell something funny. Maybe they're smelling the same thing."

Mrs. Troy looks out the fire escape door and doesn't see anything out of the ordinary. She opens the front door and sees the lower few levels of stairs on fire, with the line of fire steadily coming up the steps.

"Someone, fill up a bucket! The front steps are on fire!"

Everyone rushes to the front door to look. Carlos starts laughing.

"I guess I did that. I had a canister of gas I siphoned off from a car to give Nick, and some of it spilled when I set it down. When I was done with the fuse box, I tossed the match onto the floor. I guess the puddle of gas caught up to it."

Allen and the girls look at him in wide-eyed horror, unable to believe what he's admitting, and the fact that he's so nonchalant about it.

"And you put a penny in the fuse socket!" Lucine reminds him. "Thanks to you, the building is on fire!"

"Hey, we're up on the eighth floor. The firemen will get to it before it reaches this far."

"How are we gonna call them? The O'Connells are the only people we know with a phone, and they're on the second floor, whose stairs are engulfed in flames!"

Emeline rushes to the fire escape and cranes her neck downwards. Flames are creeping up the side of the building and look to be at about the fourth floor by now.

"We all need to grab what we can and get outta here," she says. "There's no time to waste packing up everything or waiting around for the firemen to arrive."

Mrs. Troy looks at her husband. "Let's go get our stuff, Antoine. If the fire ain't put out before it gets up here, we can see about renting Gemma's abandoned apartment. Carlos made the same suggestion earlier, but I wouldn't hear of it at the time because of how many spics and darkies are there."

Emeline is already stuffing her library books, her library card, some clothes, and a couple of her other possessions into her schoolbag, while Lucine rushes to join her. As soon as their parents are in their room, she'll grab the packed suitcase under the bed and make a run for it.

"Does anyone have a bag I can put the drugs in?" Carlos asks.

Adicia goes to look out the front door again and feels a very hot wave of air in her face. By now the flames are up to the sixth floor and are spreading fast. The other tenants are streaming down the fire escape, and the air is permeated by screams, crackles, pops, and shattering glass. Her heart racing, she takes Justine by the hand and runs into their room.

Tommy starts crying. "Where are we gonna go, Mommy? All our stuff is here, and I don't wanna move to a new place!"

"The apartment where your traitor oldest sister used to live!" Mr. Troy snaps.

"I don't know how to walk there by myself!"

Lucine looks both ways to make sure their parents are in their room and their door is locked. Her heart pounds as she heads to the fire escape, carrying the suitcase, Emeline at her side.

"We're going to Tompkins Square Park," she whispers. "We'll decide what's gonna happen there. I'm not going to Gemma's old apartment on my life."

Tommy screams as flames come through the front door and start spreading to the living room. Carlos looks up from dumping drugs into a brown paper bag and begins cursing. Not willing to risk being trapped by flames, he takes the bag and heads for the fire escape. He's promptly knocked over and loses the entire contents of the bag. When Carlos tries to get up, he feels a host of people walking all over his head, arms, legs, and back. Nobody tries to help him up or even notices him.

Adicia has all her library books and some clothes, including her pretty flower girl dress, stuffed into her schoolbag, and is huddled on the sheetless mattress with Justine, who's clutching her stuffed rabbit. Everything happened so fast, they're only now starting to understand what's going on.

Mrs. Troy has finished dumping her favorite clothes and shoes on her bed, and is now crawling around on the floor in confusion. "Where in the hell are our suitcases, Antoine?"

"Maybe we sold 'em for drugs and can't remember?"

"But how are we gonna take our things outta here without suitcases? I can't remember selling 'em or lending them to anybody!"

"Shut your yap, woman, and just get outta here! Our tenement's on fire, and you're chattering away like we have all the time in the world to get the hell outta here!" Mr. Troy grabs a few articles of clothes and charges out of the room, ignoring the bawling Tommy and Giovanni huddled on the floor by the door to Carlos and Allen's room.

Mrs. Troy stumbles out of her room with some clothes tucked under her arm and her purse over her right shoulder. Also ignoring Giovanni, she grabs Tommy by the hand and runs to the fire escape.

Adicia hears retreating footsteps and can't believe no one is coming for her and Justine. When she tries to open the door, she screams at how hot the doorknob is. Justine also screams when she sees the entire wall on their right is consumed by fire.

"Is anybody here?" Adicia screams. "We can't open our door!"

"Nobody loves us," Justine sobs. "Our parents left us to burn."

"Nobody dies by burning, Emeline told me. She said the people who were burnt as witches died of breathing in smoke. They were dead long before the fire reached them."

"Why did Carlos set our building on fire? He's so stupid!"

"Carlos never thinks about anybody but himself. He even laughed when he realized he started the fire."

They begin screaming as loudly as they can when they hear footsteps after what seems like an eternity. Maybe the firemen have finally come to the rescue.

"Who's here?" Allen shouts.

"It's us, Adicia and Justine! Everyone else ran out, and the doorknob is too hot to touch!"

It seems to take forever until Allen is able to kick the door down and get in there to save them. Justine is hysterical with sobs and clutching her rabbit for dear life as he picks her up and grabs Adicia's hand, running as fast as he can for the fire escape. Adicia finds it hard to run fast enough to keep pace with the weight of her schoolbag. She clings onto his hand for dear life, and Justine is afraid to let go of his neck for fear she'll fall and be crushed by the mob on the fire escape or die of smoke inhalation.

"We forgot Giovanni!" Adicia screams as they're halfway down the fire escape, throngs of people pushing past them. "Gemma's baby is going to die!"

"Why did our parents leave us?" Justine sobs.

Allen deposits them on a street corner in front of the tenement, where they watch the building going up in flames as he runs back up the fire escape. Adicia deep down is kind of happy to see that building destroyed. Her entire life, as long as she can remember, she's been hit by waves of hopelessness and sadness in there, a strange feeling she can't put into words. Maybe the invisible energy fields Girl believes in apply to things too, and she sensed negative energy.

Giovanni has toddled into the master bedroom, where Gemma dumped the bag with his baby supplies. When Allen dodges back into the flaming apartment, Giovanni is sitting by the bag and bawling. Not wasting a second as pieces of the flaming rafters start coming down from the tenth floor, Allen grabs his nephew, puts him in the bag, and darts out moments before the entire Troy apartment is engulfed in flames.

Adicia is holding Justine's hair back as she vomits from a mixture of fear and smoke inhalation when Allen rejoins them, depositing the bag with Giovanni on the curb. Everyone has been steadily walking past them, not stopping to ask where their parents are or if they're okay.

"We're going to Tompkins Square Park. Lucine and Emeline are probably there. If so, we'll say goodbye to Lucine and decide what's gonna happen."

"I don't wanna say goodbye to Lucine!" Adicia protests as they start walking. "We just said goodbye to Sarah!"

"We have to say goodbye to Lucine. If we don't, she's gonna be forced to marry that DeLuise scumbag tomorrow. You don't want her to be forced to drop outta school and marry some thirty-five-year-old jerk when she's only sixteen, do you?"

"Will we ever see her again?" Justine asks.

"I don't know for sure, but at least we know she's gonna have a chance to have a decent life. She can continue going to school, go to college, land a nice job, and someday marry and raise kids in a much better place. Manhattan's only a nice place to live if you've got the money to live uptown. The only people who think our neighborhood is so swell and romantic never lived here, and are only listening to the good parts of the stories their grandparents and great-grandparents tell about immigrant life."

"The Lower East Side stinks!" Adicia shouts as they watch the burning tenement recede in the distance.

Lucine and Emeline are on a park bench near the playground when they see Allen and their two little sisters approaching. Lucine leaps up and runs toward them. Justine and Adicia let go of Allen's hands and run towards her open arms, all of them sobbing. Emeline rushes to join the group embrace.

"It's a good thing I checked for any stragglers," Allen says. "I had to kick a door down to get them."

"Where were you?" Justine asks. "Why didn't you save us before there was so much fire?"

"I went up to the ninth and tenth floors to warn people and tell them to get out. I came back to make sure everyone was out."

"Allen went back to save Giovanni too," Adicia says proudly. "I remembered halfway down the fire escape that he was still there. I guess Mother took care of getting Tommy out, since we didn't see him when we ran out."

"Meanwhile Carlos was saving his stupid drugs!" Emeline says.

Lucine reaches down to pull Giovanni out of the baby bag. "Hey there, little man. You'll probably never see him again, but your uncle is a very brave guy who risked his life to save you."

"He's such a cute baby! I'm glad he looks like Gemma instead of that brute Francesco."

"I heard Mother carrying on about how her and Dad's suitcases were missing," Adicia says. "Dad thought they might've sold 'em for drugs and forgotten."

"It works for me," Lucine says. "I'm glad Ernestine and I took their suitcases. They didn't deserve to save any of their stupid possessions in those suitcases. They're in better hands now."

"At least Sarah and Ernestine are safe," Emeline says. "I can't believe Carlos was our unknowing arsonist. Somehow I always thought even *he* couldn't possibly be that stupid, careless, or unthinking. Who throws a lit match on the ground where he spilled gasoline, and shoves a penny in an old fuse socket?"

"Is it bad if I hope Julie's dad died in the fire?" Adicia asks.

"Part of me wishes our parents had died."

Lucine's eyes widen. "Yous guys, I just came up with the best idea. When I don't show up, our parents might believe I died in the fire. It couldn't have come with better timing."

"We're supposed to pretend you're dead?" Adicia cries. "It's bad enough you're gonna leave us and we won't know where you are!"

"You're not saying goodbye to Ernestine before you go?" Justine asks.

"The Sun sets about 8:30 this time of year," Allen says. "You'd better get going if you wanna reach Midtown before it gets dark. It's a bit over three miles away, and you know how long that takes on foot."

Lucine kisses and cuddles Giovanni, then tightly hugs each of her sisters and shakes hands with Allen. Emeline holds Giovanni and waves his hand for him as they stand at the edge of the park, watching Lucine walk up the street and toward what they all hope will be a chance at a better life. Knowing she'll be a target if she appears scared, sad, or lost, Lucine keeps her head up, her gaze confident, and her steps steady.

"What are we doing now?" Adicia asks.

"Emeline and I are going to Gemma's old place, where our parents, Carlos, and Tommy probably are by now," Allen says. "Adicia and Justine, yous stay here with Giovanni until it gets dark. You can hide

among the elms. You're gonna walk to the mission from there. You remember how to get there from here after I showed yous so many times."

"Why can't we walk there now, when it's not dark?"

"Someone might recognize you, or for all we know, our folks are
looking for us. It has to be under cover of darkness. I don't know what
our plan is from here, but it doesn't involve you going right back to our
parents. I'll see what I can do about getting a job and finding an
apartment in a nicer neighborhood, and hopefully yous can move in
with me. As for Giovanni, I don't want him going back to our folks either, ever. Gemma may have abandoned him, but she's a better mother
than ours. I'm sure the people at the mission will find a nice family to
raise him. Knowing our folks, they would've found the worst orphanage or sold him on the black market to a desperate couple willing to
pay a thousand dollars for their own baby."

"What do we do in the meantime? It's awhile till it gets dark."

"You put your new library books in your schoolbag, right?" Emeline asks. "You can read them to Justine. I think she'd enjoy *A Cricket in
Times Square* a little bit more than *Strawberry Girl*. And here, I put the
books we got for Giovanni in my bag. We'll see you again as soon as we
can. Don't worry, we're not leaving like Lucine."

"You'll be good girls and do exactly as you're told, right?" Allen
asks. "The people at the mission will be good to you. I'm jealous you'll
get to sleep in a real bed and have real food tonight. I have no idea
what's waiting for us in Two Bridges, but I'm sure it ain't four-star
cooking or a nice, warm bed with fresh sheets."

"Giovanni just began walking," Adicia says. "He won't be able to
keep up with us."

"Carry him in your schoolbag, and put your things in his baby
bag. He's about twenty pounds, and it'll be easier to carry his weight if
he's on your back like a papoose. Remember to hold Justine's hand the
whole way and look both ways before crossing streets. New York drivers are crazy."

Adicia looks at Emeline and Allen, whom she knows are depend-
ing on her to listen to them and look after Justine and Giovanni. "Yes,
I'll do my best, so long as it means we'll all be together in our own
home soon."

***

Lucine has been steadily walking for about an hour and a half, remembering to keep her eyes peeled and to not slow down. As the light starts to fade from the sky, she passes Times Square, Broadway, many of the famous high-rise buildings, Rockefeller Center, and St. Patrick's Cathedral. If it weren't so important to keep moving and find a place to take shelter before the Sun sets, she'd spend more time taking in all the sights and sounds.

Taking a chance, she enters the next church she passes, an Episcopal church. She doesn't notice anyone in the sanctuary or walking in the halls, so she takes a seat in a pew and sets her suitcase down. Lucine wasn't raised religious, but she's certain someone will help her in the morning. Religious people are supposed to be kind, thoughtful, and helpful towards the less fortunate. As Lucine looks at the beautiful Crucifix up front, she hopes her own sacrifice, albeit on a much smaller scale, will be worth it.

"Hello. I'm Mrs. Murphy, the priest's wife. May I help you, my child?"

Lucine bursts into tears. "I've just run away from my parents after our tenement burnt down and I was supposed to marry a thirty-five-year-old drug dealer tomorrow and be forced to drop out of school! I don't know if I'll ever see my little sisters again! And we agreed to let our parents think I died in the fire!"

Mrs. Murphy looks at her sympathetically. "You've come to the right place if you're in need of sanctuary. My husband and I run a boarding school out of our church for disadvantaged young ladies, not too far away from here. The Lord didn't bless us with children, so helping these girls is our way of having children. Have you come very far? I don't recall seeing smoke or fire in the distance, or hearing any fire engines."

"I came from the Lower East Side. My family lived up by Tompkins Square Park, not the lower part near the Financial District."

Mrs. Murphy stares at her in amazement. "That's got to be a long walk! And you walked all by yourself? You must be exhausted!"

"Is it okay if I sleep in your church tonight? I'd love to go to your school, but I assume it's only for Episcopalians. My parents baptized me, but I don't know what denomination. I think they baptized all of us in different denominations. We never went to the same church twice for Christmas or Easter. The other kids laughed at me and my sisters because of our ragged hand-me-downs, and how my youngest sisters smelled bad after taking a bath in dirty, freezing bathwater. Would I have to get rebaptized to be accepted at your church school?"

"If you were baptized once, you're already a Christian. Some people like to be rebaptized as adults, after becoming religious, but I don't see the need for that. Just because they weren't practicing or believing Christians doesn't negate their original baptism, though some people choose to reaffirm it. Jesus never said anything about denominations. But first things first. I was just about to go home when I saw you, and I'd hate to leave knowing someone in need is sleeping on the couch in my husband's office and going hungry instead of sleeping in a proper bed and having a nice supper. Please be our guest tonight, and we'll talk about sponsoring you for our school in the fall. What's your name?"

"I'm Lucine. Lucine Camille Troy."

Mrs. Murphy notices her French pronunciation of Camille. "I take it you've got some French blood?"

"I'm half-French on my dad's side. All of us got at least one French name. I'm one of the ones who got two French names. Our mother's of Belgian ancestry, though from the part of Belgium where they speak Dutch, not French."

"My husband's very interested in tracing family history. Maybe sometime after we get to know each other better, you and he can talk about your family histories. Now, let's go and have some supper. Please let me carry your suitcase."

Lucine almost thinks she's dreaming as she follows after Mrs. Murphy and gets into a taxicab going to Yorkville. The apartment she's ushered into is on the third floor of a cheerful yellow building that looks relatively new, in comparison to the tenement, which was built in 1920. Her incredulity increases when a doorman greets them at the door and an elevator operator greets them at the elevator. If she didn't know any better, she'd think she really did die in the fire and is now in Paradise.

"Warren, this is Lucine Troy. She's sixteen. She walked to our church all the way from the Lower East Side after her building caught on fire, and she's interested in going to our school and becoming a member of our church. Her parents were planning for her to marry a thirty-five-year-old drug pusher against her will tomorrow and to make her drop out of school. You won't mind if she joins us for supper and stays overnight, do you?"

"Of course not. Come right in, Miss Troy. You can sit on our davenport and have some of the mixed nuts in the jar on the coffeetable while we heat up some supper. We'd love to talk to you over supper about what's brought you to us."

Lucine can't believe what a nice apartment she's been taken to. There's carpeting on the floor; the furniture's in good shape; it appears as though the place is dusted, vacuumed, and cleaned on a regular basis; there are framed photos on a table, a record player, television, radio, and phone; the windows have pretty curtains; and the kitchen table has a real tablecloth instead of an old piece of junk with cigarette burns. The plates Mrs. Murphy sets on the table are blue and white china, the kind of tableware Lucine and her sisters used to admire when they window-shopped in Macy's, and the silverware is shiny and in good condition. The glassware also shines, and has no chips or cracks. So this is how the other half lives. No wonder Gemma ran back to this kind of life as soon as she got the chance.

"May I ask what kind of meat this is?" Lucine asks after supper is called and Father Murphy has said Grace.

"It's beef stew," Mrs. Murphy says. "Have you ever had it before?"

"Oh, I know what beef tastes like, it's just that my parents' choice of meat was usually roadkill instead of normal meat. Sometimes my mother bought real meat, but it was usually the worst, cheapest cuts she could find—bones and fat, dark meat, turkey neck, or meat that was thrown away or about to go bad."

"Roadkill?" Father Murphy asks in disbelief. "Your family ate roadkill?"

"Raccoon, possum, badger, groundhog, squirrel, rabbit, skunk, fox. They thought it was fine eating, and always served roadkill steak or stew when we had company. The taste wasn't too bad, but it made most of us sick thinking about where it came from."

"Don't worry," Mrs. Murphy says. "You'll never have to eat roadkill again. The cook at the school serves wonderful food from good farms and markets."

The Murphys cannot believe the stories Lucine tells over supper and dessert, each one worse than the last. If Allen hadn't come back, their two youngest daughters and one-year-old grandson would've died, and they doubtless wouldn't care.

"Do you think someone from your church would like to adopt Giovanni?" Lucine asks hopefully. "My youngest sisters are taking him to the Bowery Mission tonight, but I don't know if they handle adoptions. I know he'll be better-off with any new family, but he's not a newborn. He recognizes us as his family, and if he was able to regularly see one of us, it might be easier for him to adjust to a new family."

"I almost want to adopt him!" Mrs. Murphy says. "I always felt reconciled to not having children because of our work with the school, but maybe there's a place with us for raising a child too. What a shame your sister wanted to change his name to Bobby when he's got a beautiful name like Giovanni."

"You can look up the mission in the phonebook and call them if you're interested. I guess they'd have to get my sister to sign over her rights. As far as I know, neither she or her ex-husband signed any kind of document giving up their parental rights and granting permission for someone to adopt him."

"Well, whatever happens, you and your little nephew will be well taken care of from now on. Leave everything to us, and you'll both have wonderful new lives where no one will ever harm you again."

***

Adicia sees the small sliver of a Moon visible in the sky as she, Justine, and Giovanni crouch among the majestic elms in the park. Giovanni fell asleep after she mixed him a bottle with the Enfamil in the bag and water from a fountain, and only briefly opens his eyes as she lifts him into her schoolbag. Justine puts the books into the baby bag, half-asleep herself.

"Hold my hand, Justine, and don't let go of it. We hafta look both ways before we cross streets. We're going to the mission, remember? They'll give us nice hot food and a bed, and we'll go to Ernestine in the morning. Allen and Emeline will pick us up from there. You can go back to sleep as soon as we eat something."

"Is Giovanni too heavy for you?" Justine asks as Adicia slips the bag over her small shoulders.

"Allen said he's about twenty pounds. I'll probably be able to carry him the distance to the mission. It's not as big of a walk as the one Lucine took. I guess it's better we didn't save the stroller, since some jerk might try to grab him in the night. Allen thought our parents might've sold him to someone like that. Some people pay money for babies instead of getting them through an orphanage, even if it's against the law." Adicia kneels. "Dear God, if you exist, please help us get to the mission safely and don't let anyone come after us in the dark."

Justine clings onto her hand as they start walking, as Adicia walks a little slower with the extra weight. Though most people take public transportation, there are an awful lot of cars out, even for a poor and working-class area. Some of the drivers don't pay any attention to stop signs or red lights and cruise right through them. A number of people are also sleeping in the streets, and a few times the girls have to duck behind a corner or garbage can when they see drunks or other bad people approaching. All the while Adicia keeps thinking of their goal, to get to the mission, and doesn't let herself give into fear. After being trapped in their room and thinking they were going to die of smoke inhalation and burning alive, this isn't that frightening.

They start running when they see the mission coming into view. Adicia carefully removes her schoolbag, pulls Giovanni out, moves her belongings from the baby bag back into the schoolbag, and bangs on the door. They have to wait a little while before they hear approaching footsteps and see a light being turned on.

"Our tenement burnt down, and we need a place to stay. I'm Adicia Troy and I'm almost eight, and that's my baby sister Justine, who's three. We brought our nephew Giovanni Monsterelli too. I hope you're not mad I carried him in my schoolbag, but I couldn't carry him and hold my sister's hand at the same time. He only started walking this week, so he couldn't keep up with us if we'd made him walk."

"Is it true we can sleep in a real bed here?" Justine asks. "We always go here for supper on Thanksgiving, Christmas, and Easter, but we've never stayed the night before."

"Come right in, dear children. We'll get you something to eat and find a bed for you. I'll see if there's a crib for the baby. Did you lose your parents in the fire?"

"They're at our oldest sister and her ex-husband's apartment in Two Bridges," Adicia says. "Our sister left that bully a week ago, and he moved back with his parents. Our parents and oldest brother think we can move in till they find a better place, though our other brother Allen wants to move us in with him when he gets his own place and finds a job. Our parents aren't very nice people. They left us to burn. Allen came back after he warned the people on the floors above us, and had to kick our bedroom door down to get us. He ran back into the building to get our baby."

"We're not keeping him," Justine speaks up. "Our big sister wants him to be adopted. Can you find a nice new family for him?"

"Let's get you girls something to eat first. Has the baby eaten recently?"

"There's baby food in his bag, but we didn't have a spoon, so I made a bottle with his formula and water from a fountain," Adicia says. "I'm good at mixing bottles. I watched our old nanny Sarah do it all the time, and she let me make Justine's bottles sometimes."

The mission worker looks at them sadly. "Someone your age shouldn't be mixing baby bottles. That's supposed to be a parent's job, not a little girl's."

"Our mother is a bad mother. She got Sarah to work for her for almost no money fifteen years ago. Sarah was the one who raised us. Our mother has nine kids, and she's only a real mother to our six-year-old brother Tommy. She fired Sarah recently, which I guess is for the better, since she was saved from that awful fire."

The woman ushers them inside, carrying Giovanni. "You know where the dining hall is. Someone will serve you supper shortly, and then we'll find you a nice warm bed."

"I've never slept in a real bed before!" Justine says. "Our beds at home had no sheets. They were just bare mattresses."

"We don't really do adoption work, but we can easily get in touch with an adoption agency. Did your big sister put any paperwork in this bag that would give the agency the legal right to put her son up for adoption?"

"I looked in there, and she put in his birth certificate and a booklet that listed how much formula he drank as a newborn and what shots he got, but I didn't see any papers about adoption," Adicia says. "She's staying uptown with a friend named Lorraine Neiman. You can look her up in the phonebook, though Gemma said she never wanted to come back downtown. Could you travel uptown to meet her and do it there?"

"Here, let me take your schoolbag. We'll put it on the bed. In the morning we can figure out what we're going to do about this poor baby."

"We're going to our older sister Ernestine after breakfast. She lives in this neighborhood with some friends. Our brother Allen and sister Emeline are gonna pick us up there."

They walk to the dining hall and find empty seats. Their mouths water as a server brings chicken, roasted vegetables, fresh bread, apple pie, and baked potatoes. This is definitely better than the pathetic platter of lunchmeat their mother was preparing to serve.

After eating, the girls are shown to the sleeping quarters and given pajamas. Justine tucks her stuffed rabbit into the bed before they change out of their clothes, which still smell somewhat of smoke and ash, and into the new pajamas. They can hardly believe their luck as they crawl into the freshly-made bed with a mattress pad, sheets, a comforter, and pillows in pillowcases. Before long they'll probably be sleeping on a bare mattress again, but it's nice to savor the feeling of sleeping in a real bed while it lasts.

***

At 1:00 the next day, Allen shows up at the mission, wearing the same clothes he wore yesterday. One of the workers gets the door for him and invites him in, wincing at his smoke-stained clothes and the patches of ash.

"My name's Allen Troy. I'm looking for my little sisters Adicia and Justine, who are seven and three. They were supposed to come here last night with our baby nephew Giovanni. Adicia's a brunette, and Justine's a blonde. Justine would've had a stuffed white rabbit."

"Yes, I remember the two little girls you're talking about. The baby's still here, but the girls left after we served them breakfast. They said they were going to their older sister Ernestine, who lives in this neighborhood."

Allen clutches the wall for support. "What? That was never part of our plan! They were supposed to wait here for me! Ernestine's only ten, and she lives in a squat. The place seems safe and secure enough, but they would've been safer staying here till I came for them!"

"I'm sure they're safe. God watched over those three precious children and saw them safely to our mission last night, and he'll continue to watch over them. Is there anything we can do for you? Would you like lunch and fresh clothes?"

Allen looks a little embarrassed, then decides to speak up. "I just graduated high school with pretty bad grades, and I've been looking for a decent job so I can afford an apartment in onea the nicer downtown neighborhoods and hopefully move my little sisters in with me so they'll be away from our horrific parents. Do you have vocational training or someone who could help me look for a job or an apartment? A guy like me will probably never have a white-collar job or go to a fancy university, but I'd really like to go to some kinda college eventually and have a decent career that can pay my bills, help get me outta this neighborhood, and give me a chance to have a better life. I wanna meet the right girl someday and have kids, and I don't wanna raise my kids and let my future wife live in a bad neighborhood where everyone's proud of being poor and doesn't want their kids to do better."

"We'll do what we can. We have people who can help you look for work and find housing. A number of the people who come to us need help becoming self-sufficient after they've been homeless or lived in substandard housing arrangements. Do you know how to use the 'For Rent' section of the paper?"

"I ain't gotten that far yet. I've just looked at the help wanted ads. Most of 'em are either too outta my league or stuff I'd be embarrassed to do. I know too many people in the old neighborhood and my family who started jobs like factory work or dishwashing, thinking they'd graduate to better jobs after enough time, but ended up in those pathetic jobs for years, or went from dead-end job to dead-end job."

A man comes into the front entryway. "We just received a call from a lady uptown about a baby who was brought here last night. Do we know anything about who this baby is?"

"My nephew Giovanni? My sisters brought him here. Does someone want to adopt him already?"

"I told her we can't do anything till we locate an adoption agent and have the parents sign over custody. Do you know where we can locate the parents?"

"His dad's in Little Italy, and my sister's on the Upper East Side. I don't know if her ex-husband has any interest in signing anything, but my sister will sign over her maternal rights in a heartbeat. She was forced into marriage, and never wanted a baby at her age. Did my sisters leave any of the paperwork in the baby bag with you?" Allen turns to the man. "Who's this woman who wants to adopt him? How would she know about my nephew being here?"

"A young girl she took in last night said her baby nephew was here.

The lady's still on the phone, if you want to talk to her."

"That was my sister who ran away yesterday. I'm glad to know she's safe. I'm still interested in vocational training or job coaching, but I need to pick up my sisters first."

"Can we expect you back here at this same time tomorrow?" the woman asks. "I can tell you've been through a lot, and you've got a kind face. Remember, no one in need who ever comes through these doors is turned away."

Allen feels a small measure of triumph as he walks out of the mission and towards the squat. He might not ever be as successful as the people uptown, but he's going to do something better with his life than what his parents did. Knowing he'll get above his raising and not be pulled into the muck and mire of the generational poverty his parents revel in means the world to him, and gives him a glimmer of hope that perhaps his adult life won't be as depressing and dead-end as his first eighteen years.

Adicia and Justine are playing marbles with Ernestine, Baby, and Boy when Allen comes into the third floor of the squat. Julie and Girl are reading the funny papers, and Infant is having a tea party with her dolls.

"I never told yous to come here. You were supposed to stay at the mission."

"Please don't be mad at us," Adicia begs. "We thought you'd know we'd go here. We had a place to go when it was light out, and didn't wanna take away food and a bed from people who needed it more."

"Where's everyone else?" Ernestine asks. "I hate our parents even more now. What kinda cold-hearted people leave their kids to fend for themselves in a fire?"

"Your brother Carlos is a dunce," Girl says, looking up from the paper. "Are you sure he wasn't dropped by the doctor or didn't have his head squeezed by forceps?"

"What are forceps?" Adicia asks.

"A metal instrument that looks like salad tongs. Doctors use 'em to pull babies out. Sometimes they miss or clamp too deep or tight. I wouldn't be surprised if that's why he's so stupid."

"We went to the Monsterellis first," Allen says. "Francesco ain't done moving out, so he still had his key. He left mosta his furniture behind and said we could have it. Our parents and Tommy took the bed, Carlos and I slept on the pull-out sofa bed, and Emeline slept on the guest bed. There was food in the fridge, chairs, and a table. Rent is fifty bucks. Mother was cursing up a blue streak 'cause she lost all the dresses and the receipt."

"Those dresses were ugly!" Ernestine says. "Lucine told us to pick colors we don't like and styles that look bad on us, since we wouldn't be wearing 'em."

"I hope Lucine got to where she needed to be," Girl says. "Even when you're from a rough area, it ain't safe for a girl alone at night."

"All those walks to Rockefeller Center and Midtown to see the Christmas tree and Macy's paid off," Allen says. "She made it up there and then some."

"How do you know?" Adicia asks.

"When I was at the mission, a man came into the main hallway, saying he was on the phone with a woman uptown interested in adopting the baby who was brought over last night. She heard about Giovanni from a young girl she took in last night. That could only have been Lucine."

"Maybe she can adopt all the rest of us too, and we can be together again with Lucine!"

"I don't think it's gonna work out that way. We need to find Gemma to get her to sign over her rights before anyone can adopt him. Since the Monsterellis washed their hands of Gemma, I bet Francesco won't be too against signing his over."

"But we'll be able to find out where she is, right? I can't wait to write her a letter or talk to her on a public phone!"

"I don't think that's a very good idea, at least not for now. We're supposed to pretend to our parents she died in the fire. Knowing anything about her whereabouts might not be safe. If they find out, we might all get in trouble, and they might try to go after her and force her back home. You don't want Lucine to be taken away from the nice new life she's starting, do you? I'm sure we'll be able to find her eventually, when it's safer."

"Do we hafta go to Gemma's apartment? There's gonna be eight of us with only one bedroom."

"We'll make do. Tomorrow I have a meeting with a vocational counselor at the mission. With any luck, you, me, Emeline, and Justine will be in a nicer place soon. Ernestine, you're welcome to live with us too."

"Not on your life," Ernestine declares. "I like my new life here. Besides, I won't go anywhere without the Ryans or Julie. We're a packaged deal."

"But who's gonna keep an eye on you?"

"I'll look out for myself. Yous all know where I am if you wanna see me."

Adicia puts her schoolbag on her back and takes Justine's hand. As they follow after Allen, she thinks about how rotten it is that their family is so split up. Normal families aren't supposed to be in so many places.

***

Mrs. Troy is still delusionally counting on marrying off Lucine to

Jacob, in spite of the destroyed wedding clothes and the missing bride. Her eyes darken in embarrassment when she sees Allen with only Adicia and Justine in tow. Without Lucine, there will be no marriage to a man she very much wanted to bring into the family because of his drug connections and slightly better financial situation. She'll also have lost thousands of dollars it'll take awhile to embezzle again, and will look bad in front of her friends if this wedding she put so much thought into planning is cancelled at the last minute.

"Where's the brat?" Mr. Troy asks. "He burn up in the fire?"

"He's at the Bowery Mission, waiting for an adoption agent. Someone's already interested in adopting him, though they need to find Gemma to get her to sign over her rights," Allen says. "Francesco will need to sign over his rights too."

"Why did you run out with only Tommy?" Adicia asks. "You left sweet little Giovanni behind. He would've died if Allen hadn't come back."

"Tommy is my favorite child, my beautiful baby boy," Mrs. Troy says as she lights a cigarette. "Giovanni, or Bobby, as Gemma insisted he be called, is only the first of many grandchildren. Gemma didn't want him, and after she disgraced our family, we don't want nothing to do with her neither. That includes her kid. It's too bad them pesky mission people got involved. I coulda fetched a pretty sum on the adoption black market for a healthy one-year-old blonde baby boy with green eyes. Girls and dark-haired kids usually don't go for as much money as he would've."

"It's a good thing I ain't in need of medical attention after what happened to me!" Carlos whines. "Everyone was stepping all over me when someone knocked me over, and no one bothered to help me up or tell people to clear outta the way! Plus I lost all my drugs! I've been going through crazy withdrawal without 'em!"

"I've been without drugs too, and I ain't climbing the walls," Allen scoffs. "Unlike you, I don't make it a habit to get higher than a kite several times a day."

"We've got plenty of cigarettes, and there's booze in the fridge," Mr. Troy volunteers. "Don't worry, we'll get more drugs as soon as we can."

"What about new clothes!" Emeline shouts. "We lost mosta our clothes, and some of you only escaped with the clothes you were wearing! Just look at Allen's sooty clothes!"

"Is that my problem?" Mrs. Troy asks. "I wasn't the one who was foolhardy enough to run back into a burning apartment not once but twice. One of our sources of income coulda gotten killed by that foolishness, and we can't support eight people on only three poverty-level incomes."

"Forget about that for a minute!" Mr. Troy shouts. "Where's Lucine? She's supposed to get married today, and Jacob will be very displeased if his teenage bride has vanished!"

"I didn't see her," Allen says truthfully. "Maybe she was trapped by the fire, or lost consciousness and couldn't cry out when I came back to check for people."

"Are they gonna publish a list of victims?" Carlos asks. "I hope the firemen came before it spread to other buildings."

"I don't give a damn about anyone who mighta died except Lucine! If she escaped and cowardly decided not to join up with us, she ain't welcome in this family no more. If she ain't physically dead, she's as good as dead in our hearts," Mrs. Troy declares. "The one thing I can't stand is looking like a fool! We had that wedding planned for months! If we had the money for a P.I., I'd reach for Francesco's phone to send out the bloodhounds!"

"Why don't you reach for that phone and do something we actually can do?" Mr. Troy asks. "You have the business card for the bridal shop in your purse. Call them and ask about getting your money back. I hope they understand the receipt and the dresses were all burnt."

"Can they do that over the phone?" Emeline asks. "Why not take the subway over and do it in person?"

"I'll have to do that anyway. At least this way she'll know I'm on my way over." Mrs. Troy dials the operator, beside herself with glee to have a telephone at her disposal. She sits smoking and smiling as she gives the phone number to the bridal shop.

"Hello, Enid Marsenko of Upper East Side Beautiful Brides speaking," the owner says when she picks up the phone.

"Yes, my name is Dolores Troy, and my daughters and I was in your shop not that long ago. My daughter Lucine was supposed to get married today, but yesterday our tenement was destroyed in a fire, and all the dresses were destroyed, along with the receipt. The would-be bride has also vanished, though we can't be sure if she died in the fire or ran away like a little yellow-bellied coward. I'd like to know when I can arrange an appointment to get my money back."

Mrs. Marsenko bursts out laughing. "Yes, I remember you and your unhappy daughters well. It serves you right to lose your money and one of your daughters. Our store warranty does not include acts of God. You're out of what, three hundred fifty dollars? Maybe if you'd taken out insurance on the dresses, I might be able to reimburse you."

"Who takes out insurance on clothes? All I know is I'm out of all that money I worked so hard to get, and I'm going to look like a fool when there's no wedding tonight and I have to announce the bride is either dead or ran away!"

"Your daughter told me you were embezzling to get that money. If I knew what bank you worked at, I'd report you immediately. Now stop wasting my time and let me get back to my clients. I'm helping brides who actually want to get married and who aren't being forced by their parents to marry much-older drug pushers." Mrs. Marsenko hangs up.

"Can you imagine her nerve? How am I gonna get that money back? That was like taking good money and throwing it down the latrine!"

"That ain't our problem," Allen says. "No one told you to embezzle all that money, and you, Dad, and Carlos was the only ones who wanted that farce of a marriage. Last I checked, it's illegal in this country to force a minor into marriage to a grownup. It ain't like Lucine wanted to marry a boyfriend and asked your permission. Do you plan to marry the rest of your daughters off to older guys too?"

"Of course. There ain't nothing they can do about it. They're only girls. If my parents had set me up with a decent husband, I might've had a better life. It's nice to be stuck married to someone you like, but love don't pay the bills."

"Why don't you find a wife for Carlos?" Emeline asks. "That'd be a better use of your time. Knowing Carlos, he'd want to marry a drug dealer or prostitute, so that'd be a source of easy money for you and Dad."

"Carlos will find a wife in his own time. Right now he's working hard at selling drugs and that new job of his. Besides, a girl needs a husband more than a man needs a wife."

"Look, there's gonna be no wedding," Allen says. "Why not get your humiliation over with and start telling people the wedding's off? You can start by calling the reception hall and the church."

"It'll look worse if people show up and there's nothing there," Mr. Troy agrees. "I think they'd understand, given what happened yesterday."

Mrs. Troy grumbles and reaches for the phone again. Allen and her daughters are surprised she has that many friends to break the news to. She doesn't have many long-lasting friends from her endless parade of short-term jobs, and they have no idea where most of their former neighbors are. Jacob himself hasn't shown up to inquire after his promised bride. He'll probably write off his losses and find a young girl desperate enough to marry him, or another woman black-hearted enough to trade off her underage daughter for drugs and a boost in reputation.

***

Giovanni sits on Lucine's lap at the meeting with the adoption agent and the judge whom the mission workers contacted as soon as they could. Francesco and his family were eager to wash their hands of Gemma, so he had no problem signing the document he was presented with a few days earlier. Gemma, sitting across the table from her sister, her son, and the Murphys, still feels no connection towards Giovanni. There are no regrets or second thoughts.

"This is gonna be the last time I sign my name as Mon-te-ras-tel-li," Gemma says firmly. "I didn't have the time or money to change my name back to Troy, but after today, I'm going back to Gemma Troy. No more Mrs. Francesco for me!"

"Your ex-husband sounds horrible," Father Murphy says. "Your parents aren't the kind of people I'd want to meet either."

"The priest who did my quickie conversion was a beast too. He said he could do whatever he wanted and people would have to obey him, like if he asked the nuns to walk naked up Houston Street or made the altar boys crawl around on the floor and gobble like turkeys."

"I hope your ex-husband never remarries or has another child," the adoption agent says. "Just from visiting him and his parents, I could tell something's not right about him."

"Oh, he won't be able to remarry, since we only have a civil divorce. We didn't get an annulment, though I'm sure any judge or priest in his right mind would grant that too, given how I was forced into this marriage and Francesco was a cheater and abusive in multiple ways."

Gemma reaches for the paper and signs her name in the indicated places. She looks at the document and smiles when it's all over, knowing this closes that nightmarish chapter in her life. July 2, 1962, Monday isn't just the day she signed over her maternal rights to Giovanni Edoardo Monterastelli, henceforth to be known as Giovanni Edoardo Murphy, but the beginning of the rest of her life.

"We can take care of that name change next," the judge says. "After the terrible things you've been through, I'll do it for free."

Gemma's face lights up. "Why, thank you! After what happened to me, I don't think I'll wanna get married again till I'm at least twenty-five. My name won't be Troy forever, assuming I remarry someday, but it'll be nice to have my old name back in the meantime. Next time I'll be able to pick the man I marry. I never would've voluntarily picked a man whose name I have to sound out in my head every time I say or write it."

"We still call your ex-in-laws the Monsterellis," Lucine says. "That's a better name for them than whatever their real name is."

"Are you going back to your friends' apartment after this?" Mrs. Murphy asks. "If you are, my husband and I will pay for your cab. Your place is closer to here than our place, so it makes sense to drop you off first."

"Don't worry about Giovanni," Father Murphy says. "My wife and I have been married for twenty years and never had children. We made up for it by running a boarding school for disadvantaged young ladies and sponsoring select girls like your sister. But now we realize perhaps we were meant to have our own child, and your sister was sent here by God to facilitate this adoption. I'm sure you'll remarry someday and have another child when you want one and are ready to be a mother. Maybe by the time you have another child, the hospital procedures will have changed, and you won't be treated like part of an assembly line and will be able to see your baby right away."

"I'm so glad no one after me will have to go through that," Gemma says. "Ours is the last generation who'll just shrug and accept being born into poverty and all it brings with it. Giovanni is the first generation who'll never grow up knowing what poverty and hopelessness feel like, and for that I'm very grateful."

Chapter 18: Carlos's Accident

"Mommy, can I play with Benny and Sammy down the hall?" Tommy begs. "I promise I'll be home when you tell me, and I'll listen to their mommy."

"Hey, no fair," Adicia protests. "None of the other kids in the building have asked to play with us."

"Guess I'm more popular than you stupid girls." Tommy sticks his tongue out at his sisters.

"What are they?" Mrs. Troy asks. "I've seen darkies and spics in this building. There ain't much we can do about it till at least October, but I don't feel safe letting you play with foreigners."

"What do you mean, what are they? They're kids. I don't know what spics or darkies are."

"She means Negroes and Spanish-Americans," Emeline says, looking up from *The Journey to the East*.

"Oh, those people. Benny and Sammy have brown skin, so that probably means they're Negroes. Can I still play with them?"

"Absolutely not," Mrs. Troy declares. "Ain't there any decent white children in this building you can play with?"

"Not fair! I want new friends to play with, and we already had fun playing Candy Land in the front lobby!"

"You got to play a boardgame?" Emeline asks. "I wish we'd been invited to play too."

"Why don't you like Negroes and Spanish people?" Adicia asks.

"I don't want my kids associating with inferior races. We might be poor, but we still have standards. Tommy may not play with darkies."

"This summer vacation stinks!" Tommy shouts, throwing himself on the floor. "First our apartment burns down, then we hafta move to this crummy neighborhood and an apartment even more crowded than our old one, and now you won't lemme play with my new friends!"

"Why don't I enroll you in Cub Scouts or another club for boys your age?" Mrs. Troy tries to soothe him.

"That's not fair either," Adicia protests. "You never suggested any of us could join Girl Scouts or Camp Fire Girls."

"I ain't got the money, time, or interest to invest in my dumb mistake daughters joining social clubs. Tommy, however, has earned that right. I won't hold scout meetings in my home, but I will pay membership dues and go to all his public functions. I'll even sew on all his badges."

"Can we join a 4-H club?" Emeline asks.

"Look at yourself," her mother says derisively. "Even if I gave a damn about giving you extracurricular activities, you know damn well your head is buried in a book mosta the time. You'd never get along well in a social group that required you to interact with a lot of other kids and do stuff that didn't involve being a bookworm."

The doorbell rings, and Tommy gets up to answer it. "I bet it's my new friends. They're wondering why I didn't come back yet from asking my mommy permission to play with them."

Mrs. Troy opens the door, expecting to see either Tommy's new friends or their mother. Instead a police officer greets her. Allen, kneeling in a corner by the open window, quickly stuffs his cocaine pipe under his shirt.

"Are you Mrs. Dolores Troy, mother of nineteen-year-old Carlos Troy who works at Mighty Mike's Mechanics on Twelfth Street?"

"Yes I am, Officer. What's the reason for this visit? He ain't already in trouble at work, is he?"

Allen discreetly stands up and shakes the remainder of his cocaine out of the window, kicking the pipe underneath the radiator. The last thing he wants is to get in trouble for using drugs if Carlos is in trouble for the same offense.

"Earlier today, his boss found objects in his locker that exactly matched items recent patrons complained were missing after they took their cars in for service, but that's not the reason I'm here. I came from Beekman Downtown Hospital to report Carlos was injured in an accident at work. He was fixing a car, and it fell on top of him."

Mrs. Troy screams. "What! How could that happen! Didn't anybody try to help him?"

"The jack wasn't tightened all the way, and the car fell down while he was underneath. He had wide bloodshot eyes and clammy skin, which seemed to indicate he was on some sort of drug recently. Do you know anything about your son taking illegal drugs?"

"His favorite drug is meth!" Adicia pipes up. "He also likes cocaine and marijuana. Sometimes he uses narcotics too."

"Carlos likes to smoke cigarettes and drink too," Justine joins in.

"Mrs. Troy, are you aware of the fact that your son is using drugs?" the cop asks. "Your young daughters know all about it."

"Is Carlos in trouble for using drugs?" Adicia asks. "His other job is selling drugs."

The cop looks sternly at Mrs. Troy. "How much do you know about your son's involvement in the drug life? He's done it at home often enough for these girls to know about it, so I can't imagine his own mother would be blind to it. The theft, and using and selling drugs, are offenses we'll deal with after he recovers. Consider yourself warned, he could be arrested as soon as he leaves the hospital."

"Do we have to visit Carlos in the hospital?" Emeline asks. "He's not a very good big brother."

"He was incoherent when he was pulled from under the car, his boss said. Knowing he's indeed a drug addict, I wonder if he didn't fasten the jack all the way because he was too drugged to know the difference. Be warned, Mrs. Troy, we may bring more officers here later to search the premises for drugs. Now we're going to get in my car and drive back to the hospital. A subway, bus, or cab won't get you there as fast as I can."

"Will seven people fit in the car?" Emeline asks.

"The little girl can sit on your mother's lap. Let's go."

"I hate that child," Mrs. Troy says as they follow after the cop. "My oldest daughter Emeline can take her. God must hate me, to give me six girls and only three boys, and then to do this to my firstborn son. That boy is one of our four sources of income, and we can't afford to lose him!"

Adicia looks excitedly at the police car when they get out on the street. She's never been inside a real car before, not even a taxicab. Justine stands back in amazement too, unable to believe they're about to take a ride in a real car.

"How come your car has safety belts in front but not in back?" Emeline asks.

"That's how modern cars are designed. Not too long ago, a lot of cars didn't have any," the cop explains. "Would one of you girls like to ride in the front with me?"

"Justine has to sit on my lap. Let Adicia sit next to you."

Mrs. Troy glares at Allen as they get into the car. She expected he'd remain behind to cover up any traces of drugs.

"Your car is neat, Mr. Cop," Tommy says, looking out the back driver's side window. "Where's the hospital?"

"Beekman Downtown Hospital is on the corners of Gold, Beekman, and Spruce Streets. We're in the southeastern part of the city, so we'll be driving slightly west, past the Brooklyn Bridge. It's not too long of a drive."

"Are you allowed to use this as your personal car, or can you only drive it when you're working?" Adicia asks.

"It's a business car. I have my own car at home, though I take the subway to work. My family and I live in Tribeca."

"Our mother was trying to force our sister Lucine to marry a drug dealer who was way too old for her who lived in Tribeca. She disappeared after a fire at our old tenement."

Mrs. Troy is turning purple in embarrassment at all these unwanted revelations. "I hope you don't judge me unfairly, Officer, based on these wild stories my daughters are telling you."

"Believe me, Mrs. Troy, I doubt these are lies. Children are remarkably honest and understand better than some adults what's going on around them. It seems you're the one who wants to pretend there's no drug use in your home."

When they reach the hospital, the cop ushers them inside and tells the receptionist who they are. Mrs. Troy and Allen are the only ones allowed to see Carlos, while the girls are made to stay in a waiting area in the hallway. Adicia and Justine stay close to Emeline in their chairs, too scared to walk around in the halls and see sick people. Tommy doesn't care about bumping into patients and runs up and down the hall making aeroplane noises, even after he runs over several nurses who scold him.

From behind the closed door, they hear their mother screaming over and over again. Allen emerges several minutes later, looking very shaken.

"Is Carlos dead?" Emeline asks.

"No, but he's as good as dead. He's paralyzed and drifting in and out of consciousness. Mother's also upset about losing one of her sources of income probably forever, and how she doesn't have the money to keep him here indefinitely."

"Paralyzed?" Adicia asks. "Doesn't that mean he can't walk?"

"He crushed his spinal cord when the car fell on him. They also think he took too many drugs shortly before it happened, since he has a very high heartrate, wide, bloodshot eyes, very pale skin, and shortened breath. If he comes to and stays conscious, and is discharged eventually, he's gonna be arrested for using and selling drugs. He's also in trouble for stealing from his customers."

"You don't look so good yourself, Allen," Emeline says in concern. "You're not standing straight."

Allen struggles to sit down and falls out of the chair. His sisters and Tommy crowd over him as he begins gasping for breath and trying to unbutton his shirt. They can hear his heart almost beating out of his chest.

"Someone, help us!" Adicia screams. "Our big brother is having a heart attack!"

"I mighta smoked too much cocaine," he gasps.

Mrs. Troy rushes to the door in time to see her other older son being loaded onto a stretcher and wheeled down the hall. She begins screaming hysterically again and faints. Emeline rushes after Allen, ignoring the hospital's supposed policy against minors being allowed to see patients.

The cop comes back into the hallway and stares at the scene. He helps Mrs. Troy into an empty chair and waits for her to come back to herself, noticing Adicia and Justine seem more upset by what happened to Allen than their mother. Tommy is the only one visibly upset and asking if his mother will be okay.

"Mrs. Troy, does your other older son also do drugs?"

"What makes you think that?" she snaps irritably. "Allen is one of our four sources of income, and damned if I'll let you take him away from us too!"

"I'm asking because it's very rare for a young man his age to have a heart attack, unless he has a bad heart already. Sometimes excess doses of drugs produce rapid heart palpitations and shortness of breath. You already have one son whose life is ruined because he used drugs; it won't be a huge surprise if you tell me this one also uses drugs."

"Don't take Allen away from us," Adicia begs. "He saved me, our baby sister Justine, and our baby nephew Giovanni from a fire last month. He's gonna move us in with him when he gets a job and finds an apartment."

"At least Carlos ain't in trouble for arson," Mrs. Troy mutters.

The cop stares at her. "Arson? Did I just hear you say the word arson in relation to the young man in that room back there?"

Mrs. Troy buries her head in her hands and weeps.

"Carlos started the fire that burnt our tenement down," Adicia says. "He spilled stolen gas in the basement and threw a match on the floor after he was done using it to see the fuse box. A friend of his had his electricity shut off, and he asked Carlos to fiddle with the fuse to try to make it work again. Carlos also stuffed a penny in the socket."

"Was this reported to the police, or did you just let it be assumed an accident?"

"Why would I be stupid enough to get my own son in trouble?" Mrs. Troy snaps.

"That's one more thing to charge Carlos with. I'll ask again, is your other son using drugs? Hell, are *you* using drugs?"

"Please don't take Allen away from us," Adicia repeats. "He's not perfect, and he uses drugs sometimes, but he's a nice guy when he's sober. He wants to make something of himself and take care of us."

"She's right," Mrs. Troy finally admits. "Allen does use drugs, but as he always likes to rub in our faces, he don't get higher than a kite as often as my husband, Carlos, and I do. He don't drink as often as us either. I think his favorite drug is marijuana, though he also enjoys cocaine from time to time. I don't think he really likes meth, though that's Carlos's favorite. Cocaine is my own favorite drug."

"Are you going to arrest our mother and make us go to an orphanage?"

"As much as I want to punish everyone who does wrong, I can't take a mother away from her young children, even if she is using drugs. Your oldest brother's still under arrest as soon as he leaves the hospital, though. If your other brother truly is a lesser user, we can probably find a counselor with experience in drug withdrawal. It's bad enough one already ruined his life at only nineteen; the other one still has a fighting chance if he goes straight in time."

Emeline stands off in a corner as several doctors hover around Allen and push a mask over his mouth and nose. A nurse listens to his heartbeat through a stethoscope, while someone else shines a light into his eyes. Nobody tells her anything, which frightens her even more. Finally, after what seems like hours, the doctors and nurses leave, with one nurse left behind to monitor him. No one says anything to her on their way out, nor do they acknowledge her presence.

"Why am I in the hospital?" Allen asks. "I thought we only came here because Carlos got hurt."

"You were having a hard time breathing, and your heart was beating really fast," Emeline reminds him. "We thought you were having a heart attack."

"I need help. I'm as sick as Carlos. I shouldn't use drugs if I'm serious about finding a real job and getting outta this area. I thought I was okay since I didn't use them as often or as much as Carlos and our parents."

"I don't want to live with you if you use drugs, even if you do find a place in a nicer neighborhood. You especially don't want little Justine to be around your drugs."

"It helps me deal with the tough life we were dealt. I ain't no addict."

"I'm sure Carlos thought that starting out too, and now look what's happened to him. He'll never walk again, and that means he'll probably never work again either. How are you gonna take care of us if you're dead or paralyzed? And don't you wanna have your own family someday? Kids don't deserve a druggie for a father, and a nice girl would never go out with a drug addict or alcoholic."

Adicia and Justine tiptoe into the room. Mrs. Troy stands in the doorway, fuming over how much embarrassment this'll bring to her family. She'll never live down having a firstborn son who can't walk and is facing a number of criminal charges. If Carlos's hospital stay isn't totally covered under charity, she'll be seething at how much money she has to come up with. At least she isn't in trouble for embezzling, she thinks darkly.

"Is our brother coming home today?" Adicia asks the nurse.

"We need to monitor him for at least another day. Don't worry, he'll be okay. He just had a big scare from using too much cocaine."

"Will I need to stay here for a long time if I'm quitting drugs?" Allen asks. "I've heard people quitting cold turkey go kinda nuts before they get it all outta their systems."

"If you're dumb enough to want to quit all drugs, you know we don't got the money to afford fancy rehab," Mrs. Troy lectures. "Just make sure not to overdo it like Carlos. Your father and I only get high maybe once a day, and only use one drug at a time. Follow our example and you'll be fine."

"Mrs. Troy, are you seriously encouraging your own son to continue using drugs after what just happened to him and his brother, and in front of a medical professional no less?" the nurse asks.

"We live what we know where we're from. That means not going to college, working low-paying jobs, staying in the area, and using drugs. Are you going to challenge my family's traditions?"

"Your so-called traditions are dying with our generation, in case you hadn't already noticed," Emeline says. "Like it or not, we're tryna make good and not stay in your cesspool."

"I ain't coming back home, Mother," Allen says. "After I get discharged, I'm going to the vocational counselor I've been meeting at the Bowery Mission, getting a real job, and finding a nicer place to live. I'll come home to collect my stuff, but I won't come back to live. You'll have to support everyone with your and Dad's salaries, and hope Carlos can find decent work as a cripple."

"Will you really give up drugs and let us live with you?" Adicia asks.

"Will it be in a nice neighborhood like Greenwich Village?" Emeline asks.

"Will you make us nice food and buy us pretty clothes?" Justine asks.

"I can't promise it'll be the nicest place in the world or that it'll be easy, but I can promise I'll do my best to take care of yous and give yous a better life."

Mrs. Troy storms back to Carlos's room, hoping there won't be any more unpleasant surprises in store in the near future. She's already weathered so many humiliations in such a short timespan, and doesn't know if she can handle any more. Even poor people care about their reputation, and there can't possibly be room for much respect now. She sincerely cannot understand why so far all her daughters and her middle son want to get above their raising. This is one floodgate that doesn't seem likely to shut anytime soon.

Chapter 19: Allen Steps Up

"How's this for an eighth birthday present, Adicia?" Allen asks. "You, Emeline, and Justine can move into my new place in the West Village today."

The girls had been sitting on the front stoop and people-watching on the hot July day when Allen came by in the early evening. He's a little jittery from being off all drugs cold turkey, but otherwise he's slowly starting to look healthier. The girls are glad his primary drug of choice was only marijuana and not Carlos's favorite, meth, or their mother's belovèd cocaine. He's even quit smoking cigarettes, since nice girls wouldn't want to get close to a guy who smells like an ashtray.

"Are we really gonna move in with you today?" Adicia asks, her eyes wide. "Will we have a real birthday party?"

"I can't promise a birthday party, but my bakery gave me a free cake when I said onea my little sisters turns eight today. You girls ain't seen my new place yet. It's a two-bedroom apartment that came partly furnished, on the fifth floor. It's maybe ten years old. There are lots of windows, a real elevator, an electric stove, a laundromat three blocks away, and it's close to Hudson Park Library."

"You work at a bakery?" Emeline asks. "We haven't really heard anything from you since you were discharged from the hospital."

"The nice people at the Bowery Mission helped me with the classifieds, budgeting, and job interviews. Thanks to them, I found a place for only forty bucks a month. They also gave me a loan of three hundred bucks. I used it for rent and mattresses. There's a sofa bed, but I figured you'd wanna sleep on a real bed."

"What do you do at the bakery?" Adicia asks. "Do you cook?"

"I set up window displays, wrap up orders, make brownies and cookies, and frost cakes. Ain't the most glamourous job in the world, but it beats a box-making factory."

"Can we really, truly move in with you and not hafta live with our witch of a mother anymore? It's too good to be true!"

"I don't know if she'll be okay about it long-term, but we should all hope for the best. I don't think she'd care after she gets over the shock. She and Dad barely cared when Ernestine moved into the squat."

"Are we gonna have balloons and streamers?" Adicia asks as they walk up the steps and into the building. "I've never had a real birthday before."

"Just a cake for now. Have you ever had real cake before?"

"I can't remember if I ever had real cake except at Gemma's wedding. Do I get to have the biggest piece?"

"Of course. You're the birthday girl."

"I'm surprised you remembered Adicia's birthday, Allen," Emeline says. "Do you know the rest of ours?"

"You're May fourteenth. Sarah said you were born the same day Israel declared its independence. You both turned fourteen this year. Justine's March second, Ernestine's April eleventh, and Lucine's January twentieth. Give me some credit for remembering my sisters' birthdays."

As Adicia and Emeline are loading up their schoolbags with their clothes, library books, and sparse possessions, Mrs. Troy comes home in a huff. Tommy looks up from playing with the new Matchbox cars she bought him a few days ago, confused as to why she's home earlier than usual.

"I was fired," she announces as she kicks off her shoes. "That damn bastard wouldn't tell me why, though he was giving me funny looks all day. All the way home, I felt like I was being followed. They had better not be on my tail for you know what." She reaches for her cocaine pipe and starts filling it up. "Allen, what are you doing back? You told me you was moving out and wouldn't come back after you picked up your stuff."

"I'm taking my sisters to my new place. We're also having a little celebration for Adicia's birthday. Did you know she's eight years old today?"

"No, and I don't care neither." Mrs. Troy takes a good long puff on the cocaine.

"Can Benny and Sammy come over for supper tonight?" Tommy asks. "They keep asking me to have supper with them, but I know you don't like me to play with them or go to their apartment when you're home."

"I don't want you going over there *period*! The only nigger I'd tolerate in our apartment would be a house nigger."

"What's a house Negro?" Adicia asks, correcting their mother's racial epithet. Lucine said that was a very bad word and she should never use it, in spite of their mother's insistence on using bad words for people of other races.

"A servant, like a maid or cook," Emeline says. "It's an expression from the days of slavery, when the higher-ranking slaves were allowed to work in the house instead of doing the really terrible work in the fields."

"Tommy, you are not to go over to the apartments of any darkies or spics in this building while I'm at work from now on, is that clear?" Mrs. Troy asks. "I'll buy you your own game of Candy Land to make up for it, and we can have fun playing it together as often as you want."

Tommy is jumping up and down and wailing in protest when the door opens. The man who didn't even knock comes into the living room and grabs Mrs. Troy's arm. Tommy stops mid-tantrum and runs over to the man.

"Leave my mommy alone! She was just fired from her job and said a strange man followed her home!"

"I am that man. My name is Officer James Gallaghan, and I'm an undercover cop. I was asked to observe your mother at work starting about a month ago, because the bank manager thought there was suspicious activity going on. There have been a number of complaints from customers about missing money they know they deposited. Today we finally got the last bit of evidence we needed. Dolores Troy, you're under arrest for embezzling. I hope you have a good place for your kids to stay till your husband gets home from work."

"I was just taking them with me, at least the girls," Allen says. "I'm moving them into my new apartment in the West Village so they can get away from this wretched woman who bore us. Tommy can stay with his friends down the hall till our dad gets home."

"I can stay with Benny and Sammy?" he asks excitedly.

Mrs. Troy fumes but knows she can do nothing to forbid it at this point. "Ain't there a rule against charging more than one person in the same family at the same time? My oldest son is going to be arrested himself as soon as he leaves the hospital!"

Officer Gallaghan takes a whiff of what's coming from Mrs. Troy's pipe. "That's not tobacco, is it? We're also charging you with drug use and possession."

"The cop who took us to see our oldest brother in the hospital said there might be a police team coming over soon to search for drugs," Emeline says. "Our parents had a lot of drugs in our old place. They haven't had time to restock much, but I'm sure you'll still find plenty of drugs lying around."

Mrs. Troy curses her life as Officer Gallaghan leads her outside and handcuffs her. Tommy rushes to the window to see her being led into a police car parked around the corner, then loses interest and runs down the hall, banging on the door of his new friends. Allen finds a notepad and pen and writes a note for their father, taping it to the front door before he and the girls leave.

"Is Mother going to jail?" Adicia asks.

"I hope so," Emeline says.

"She's not a real mother," Justine says. "Sarah was our real mother."

"Allen, will you find us another woman like Sarah?" Adicia asks. "We can never have another Sarah, but we might need someone to look after us."

"I can't afford a nanny or live-in servant. Unlike Mother, I believe in paying hired help a decent wage, on a weekly basis. Besides, it wouldn't go unnoticed if a woman moved in with us. People have funny ideas about single women living with guys they're not related to, even if they're not boyfriend and girlfriend."

Adicia doesn't understand what that means, so she changes the subject. "Are we taking the subway?"

"I like to take the bus. It lets me see more of the city instead of keeping me underground. It's a little bit more expensive, but I like it."

The girls look askance at some of the people in the bus stop. Some are smoking cocaine and meth, and some are talking to themselves. Adicia stays as close to Emeline and Allen as she can while they wait for the next bus to roll in. She wishes someday she didn't have to live in the city and could go from place to place in a real car, instead of taking long walks, the subway, or the bus. It'd be nice to have her own bicycle too, without worrying about crazy drivers running her over. When Tommy had his tricycle, he was only allowed to ride it around the tenement and on the nearby sidewalks, instead of taking it for a real ride around the neighborhood.

Adicia follows Allen onto the bus and nabs a seat by the window, dumping her schoolbag on an empty seat with Emeline's. Justine climbs onto Emeline's lap and holds her rabbit up to the window so it can see the streets, buildings, and people going by. Allen takes the seat with the schoolbags and holds them on his lap. He wants to believe this is the last any of them will be seeing of the gritty working-class section of downtown Manhattan.

"That's it." He points as the next bus stop comes into view. "The blue building two blocks down from the stop. We're on the top floor."

"Can we play on the roof?" Justine asks.

"I'm afraid there's no playground or swimming pool on this roof, but you can walk around on it and play there if you want. If it gets hot enough, you can sleep on it. There's a fire escape on the other side of the building, and it leads up to the roof."

The people walking in the streets look like nice people. Adicia thinks about the invisible energy fields Girl believes in, and feels a happy, positive energy coming from this neighborhood. She never got that kind of sensation from the Lower East Side, The Bowery, or Two Bridges. The stores are also a lot more cheerful and inviting. Several offer handmade crafts and artwork, as opposed to being fishmongers, butchers, pawn shops, and dimly-lit grocery shops. An open-air market is across the street. It doesn't compare with the opulence of uptown, but Adicia feels she's come to a very special area.

Allen opens the front door, and they walk into a small entry hallway. Adicia and Justine's eyes light up in excitement when they see a real elevator. They're too excited over the prospect of having an elevator in their very own home to care it's self-operated instead of manned by an elevator operator.

"It's unit 515," he tells them when they get out of the elevator. "Emeline, you can pick up my mail while I get the door."

Allen flicks on the lights after opening the door. The girls eagerly walk into the living room and set their schoolbags on the blue davenport, then start walking around to inspect everything. Justine narrates everything she sees to her rabbit.

"Does your rabbit have a name?" Allen asks as he pulls Adicia's cake out of the fridge. "Is it a boy or a girl?"

"I don't know. It's just a rabbit. What do you think its name is?"

"The Velveteen Rabbit didn't have a name either," Emeline says. "It was just the Rabbit, like his owner was the Boy."

"Oh, it's got little flowers in the middle!" Adicia says happily. "Are they real or frosting?"

"They're miniature rosebuds. Just 'cause I'm in charge don't mean I'll let you eat junk food. Too much frosting is bad for you, particularly considering it has no healthy content."

"The Five Little Peppers made a birthday cake for Mamsie with real flowers in the middle in the first chapter of the first book, remember?" Emeline asks. "Their cake was homemade with a wood-burning stove, not store-bought like this one."

"You still remember that?" Adicia asks. "It was a long time since you read that series."

"Not that long. Only a few years. I don't remember everything from every book I've ever read, just the ones I liked best or thought were most interesting. Like Mother says, I'll never get a so-called real job because I remember things like all the presidents, things that happened in a bunch of books, important dates in Civil War history, and words in foreign languages, instead of things that'll get me a job that earns money. At least my kind of knowledge will pay off in the library studies field."

"Are you gonna get a telephone and television? I've never talked on a telephone before, not even a payphone. Mother was the only one who got to use the phone in our new place."

"Sure, I'll buy a phone eventually, when I have the money saved up to pay for a phone bill each month," Allen says. "I'd like to save up for a record player and a television too."

Emeline sits at the table. "Did they really give you this apartment with furniture in it?"

"Sometimes they come furnished or partly furnished. I had to buy our beds, but they left the sofa bed, the table and chairs, and a couple other pieces of furniture. I bought a few plates, cups, and utensils for the meantime, but I'd like to pick up more pieces at onea the outdoor markets. They sell household goods, not just artwork, clothes, and books. I'll give you some money for it." Allen starts fidgeting. "I could really go for a joint about now. You don't know how difficult it is to give up both drugs and alcohol cold turkey. I can't even have my precious cigarettes anymore either."

"Why can't you have cigarettes?" Adicia asks. "They smell bad, but Gemma said they're good for you. They're not like drugs. She said even doctors smoke."

"I can't be too sure. It's best to kill two birds with one stone and quit all of it. Like Emeline said, nice girls don't like guys who drink, smoke, or use drugs. How can I get a girl to wanna get close to me if I smell like cigarettes?"

"I've heard some doctors think cigarettes are unhealthy," Emeline says. "They're one and the same as drugs or alcohol, only more accepted by polite society. I can't stand that gross smell. It makes me cough."

"What's for supper?" Justine asks.

"Will you like leftover chicken soup and roasted potatoes?" he asks. "I ain't as poor a cook as Mother, but I ain't a chef either. I have to learn to cook better, since I don't wanna starve or eat crummy meals like bacon grease on toast or melted cheese with noodles and hamburger meat."

"We had creamed chipped beef on toast last night," Adicia says. "That looks like dog vomit."

"No roadkill ever?" Emeline asks.

"Not in this home. Besides, I don't know how to skin it, nor do I want to. I'd feel like a damn butcher if I had to skin my own meat."

"Do we have candles for my cake?" Adicia asks.

"Not this year. Don't worry, someday you'll have a nicer birthday celebration than just a cake with some flowers on it."

"That's okay. Coming here to live with you is enough of a birthday party for me. I've never had a real birthday, so I don't have anything to compare this to."

"You're the best big brother ever!" Emeline says. "Meanwhile Carlos is paralyzed and half conscious on a hospital bed because he's such a loser!"

Adicia eagerly laps up the chicken soup and practically inhales the roasted potatoes after they're done being reheated in the electric oven. The water from the tap in the kitchen sink also doesn't smell funny like the tap water she's used to drinking. Most exciting of all is the birthday cake. Allen cuts her the largest slice, and lets her have a second slice after she finishes the first. This is even better than the squat, she thinks happily as Allen washes the dishes and she and her sisters jump on their new bed.

"I hafta be up for work at seven o'clock," he calls in to them. "Try to get to bed by ten."

"Can we walk into town tomorrow?" Emeline asks. "I wanna go to the library."

"We can do that on the weekend. Maybe yous can go to Washington Square Park tomorrow. I'll write down the directions in the morning so you don't get lost."

"I can't wait to start our new life!" Adicia says.

After they change into pajamas, Emeline reads Adicia and Justine a bedtime story. They go to sleep curled up together under the covers of their beautiful new bed, almost delirious with joy at getting to sleep in a real bed and not have to give it up in the morning. Even the guest bed at the Two Bridges apartment wasn't as big or comfy as this. The only thing that would make it even happier would be if Ernestine joined them, Adicia thinks as they lie there snug as bugs in a rug. And even in spite of Lucine having to go away, Adicia is very thankful Emeline is still with them and doesn't think spending time with her little sisters is beneath her. She hopes they can stay like this for always.

Chapter 20: Introducing Lenore

About two weeks later, while coming home from a day at Washington Square Park, rain starts pouring down. Allen and his sisters immediately rush into the bus stop for shelter once their bus comes to a stop. As soon as the rain clears a little, they'll make a run for it in the dark.

A forlorn-looking young girl is sitting on a suitcase, seemingly uncaring rain is coming down on her. Adicia and Justine feel sorry for her and decide to go over and introduce themselves. Something about her reminds them of the place they were in not so long ago.

"Hi. My name's Adicia, and that's my baby sister Justine. What's your name?"

"Why are you all alone?" Justine asks. "Do you want to hold my bunny to make you feel better?" She extends her stuffed white rabbit.

Emeline trails after them. "You're gonna catch cold if you stand in the rain. You don't wanna be sick during summer vacation, do you?"

The strange girl looks at Emeline with a sad smile. "They were just tryna cheer me up. I don't think they meant any harm. I do look sorta out of place here." She speaks with a very strong Brooklyn accent.

Emeline notices the girl is about her age. "Are you visiting relatives for summer vacation?"

"I'm sort of running away," she whispers. "I had to escape my father. I'm from Greenpoint, Brooklyn, and I came here on the subway with money I stole from my mother's pocketbook. I switched to the bus in case anyone was following me. I'm trying to get as far away from Brooklyn as I can, though I think I only have enough money left for another bus ride."

"Why don't you stay with us tonight?" Adicia volunteers. "This is a really nice neighborhood. You'll probably find someone who can help you in the morning. Do you know where you're going?"

"I don't care. I figure I'll find a job and a place to live when I get to the end of the bus line. As long as my father doesn't find me."

Allen pushes through the crowd. Seeing a young girl alone with a suitcase reminds him of Lucine, and his heart floods with pity. As he takes off his lightweight jacket and kneels down to put it over her, he notices what beautiful dark green eyes she has, how naturally beautiful her skin is without any makeup, what a pretty, small mouth she has, and her long, flowing, raven hair. A strange feeling overtakes him, unlike anything he's ever felt.

"I'm Allen Troy," he says, struggling to find his tongue. "What's your name?"

"I'm Lenore Hartlein." Lenore shrinks back. "Could you please not touch me? I'm only fifteen, and I don't trust strange men. My father was an abusive son of a bitch, and it's gonna take awhile to forget what he did to me."

Allen immediately steps back. He'd never ask out a minor, nor would he try to do anything with someone who's been hurt or abused by a man, but the funny feeling continues. He stands back, his mind racing, as another bus pulls up.

"Wait," he calls, tugging on her sleeve. "Would you like to babysit my sisters? You need a safe place where your father can't find you. This is a very progressive neighborhood, and people won't think anything funny about you staying with us. It's a two-bedroom apartment, and the sofa bed is free. I won't charge you a penny or make you do any chores. Plus, you're only a year older than my sister Emeline. She'd love to have a real friend her own age. I promise I'll be a complete gentleman and won't lay a hand on you."

"You can trust Allen," Emeline says. "He's got six sisters. Guys with lots of sisters are usually more respectful towards women. He just moved us into his apartment so we could get away from our horrible parents. Would Allen have taken us outta that cesspool if he weren't a nice guy?"

Lenore looks at them uncertainly. "I don't know. I'm not sure I can trust anyone at this point."

"Allen once came to the rescue of our other older brother's date when he was tryna force himself on her. Allen pulled him off her and escorted her out of the building. He always dated nicer girls than our other brother, and he never forced himself on anyone. He's not going steady with anyone now, since his only priorities are taking care of us, working, and saving money. Allen recently quit drugs, alcohol, and cigarettes cold turkey, though he never used them as frequently as our parents or other older brother."

Lenore starts to look at Allen a bit more kindly. "I guess your sister's telling the truth. You probably wouldn't have done all those things if you were a hoodlum."

"You'll love our apartment!" Adicia says. "It's only two blocks down from here. We're on the top floor."

"Will you be our new Sarah?" Justine asks, holding out her small hand.

"Sarah was our nanny," Emeline says. "She was with our family since a year before I was born, and was fired last month, for the stupidest reasons."

"Please come with us and be our friend!" Adicia begs.

Lenore looks at them and thinks for several minutes. Then she looks at the unfamiliar, darkened streets and the departing bus. This isn't as far away from Greenpoint in particular or Brooklyn in general as she'd hoped, but she has to agree this is a nice neighborhood, home to many artists, poets, musicians, and free-thinking Bohemians. This'll probably be a safe haven for the time being. Besides, the girls seem so eager to be friends. Perhaps some of that enthusiasm for life will rub off onto her and help her get better. Last but not least, Allen has a kind face, and she can't help noticing he's kind of cute.

"Okay. I'll stay with yous until I can find something better. Maybe tomorrow we can take a walk together or go shopping. You can introduce me to this neighborhood and get me settled into your apartment."

"Oh, hooray!" Adicia shouts. "We're going to have a new big sister!"

"Let me carry your suitcase for you," Allen volunteers. "You must be awfully tired from all the traveling you musta done. If I had an umbrella, I'd ask you to take it, or share it."

Justine and Adicia hold hands with Lenore as they run the two blocks to the apartment. Emeline unlocks the front door and holds it open for them.

"You live in a building with an elevator?" Lenore asks in wonder.

"Our first building with an elevator," Emeline says. "There's no operator, but it's enough we don't hafta walk up and down stairs all the time. You should've seen the stairs at our old place. They were like something outta the haunted house at an amusement park, only more nightmarish."

Allen pushes the button and holds the door. Lenore steps into the elevator, marveling at what a reversal in fortune she's had since she ran away a week ago. She's gone from sleeping on park benches and subway platforms to being put up in a real apartment in a beautiful neighborhood with two charming little girls, a girl who's just about her age and perfect for making friends with, and their cute older brother. It's almost too good to be true.

"Are you by any chance named after the dead woman in Edgar Allan Poe's 'The Raven'?" Emeline asks as they enter 515. "I'm a huge bookworm, and I just have to ask that."

"Yes, I was. My mother had a book of poetry, and she thought it sounded like a pretty name. But please don't call me Nora or Lennie. I like my full name better."

"We don't use nicknames in our family either," Adicia says. "Only our little brother Tommy goes by a nickname."

Lenore counts on her fingers. "Just how many kids are in your family?"

"Nine, six girls and three boys."

"Would you like something to eat?" Allen asks from the kitchen. "I was gonna make my sisters a light supper. Would you prefer baked potatoes with roasted vegetables or chicken soup with dumplings? I'll serve either with fresh rolls from my bakery. I get to take home the leftovers."

"May I have the soup?" Lenore asks.

"Sure thing." He pulls the covered pot out of the refrigerator. "It needs to get hot for a little while on the stovetop. While you're waiting, you can go into my sisters' room and change into warmer clothes. There are towels in the bathroom, so you can put your wet hair up."

Lenore heads towards the smaller bedroom, Emeline carrying the suitcase. "Is it okay if I borrow some of your pajamas till I can buy my own? I don't have any."

"Don't have any pajamas?" Adicia asks from the living room. "Do you sleep in your clothes?"

"My father had his own reasons for not letting me wear pajamas," she says cryptically as she shuts the door.

Allen is sick to his stomach. Lenore's father was just like Julie's. Mr. Troy is father of the year in comparison to those degenerates.

Emeline pulls one of her nightgowns out of the chest of drawers that came with the apartment. "I hope you like this. We lost mosta our clothes in a fire last month, but we had some given to us by charities. They're nicer than our old clothes. We had to wear stuff handed down from our oldest sister. Not only were the clothes old by the time they got to most of us, but they were also out of fashion."

"I think it'll fit. You look about my size. You can borrow some of my clothes if you like too. I'm an only child, so I never had to wear hand-me-downs." Lenore takes off Allen's jacket and folds it up on the bed, then opens her suitcase and starts removing her wet clothes. After wearing them for an entire week, they're full of road dust and sweat.

Emeline is bending over the suitcase and taking out Lenore's clothes to put away in the empty top drawer when she catches sight of something that's not quite right for a girl Lenore's age. Dropping her voice to a whisper, she asks, "Are you sick? Do you have cancer?"

"No, I'm not sick, as far as I know."

"I'm sorry, I didn't mean to look, but I happened to see that out of the corner of my eye. You can't have delayed puberty, since you have a bustline, and I assume you're menstruating by your age."

"Oh, that." Lenore looks down at herself, then slips a long green dress over her head. "My father sort of wanted me to look like a child even after I started growing up. He couldn't control my growing breasts, so he made me shave so I wouldn't look like a young woman."

Emeline is queasy. "Can't you have your dad reported to the cops for doing those deranged things? If my mother can be arrested for embezzling and drugs, your dad can be arrested for child abuse and rape!"

"Cops never take cases like that," Lenore says in resignation. "They only take real cases like murder and theft, and they never believe those things. They'd think I was tryna ruin my dad's reputation and that I was a liar. Nobody believes women when they accuse guys of crimes. Just lookit the Bible. A woman needs a bunch of witnesses to successfully bring her husband to court for cheating, while all a man has to do is say his wife is guilty and she can be convicted much more easily. It also says a woman wasn't really raped if no one heard her cry out or if she didn't try to fight back. That was onea the few books we had at our place, and I read a little every day. I'm not much into religion for that reason."

"Most religions have anti-woman aspects, but those aren't the only things in there. I love reading about world religions. Buddhism's pretty nice to women. Buddha taught women as well as men and didn't say a woman had to totally serve her man to become enlightened. What are you, by the way? We're some kind of Protestant."

"I was baptized Catholic, but my family didn't make a habit outta going to church."

"We don't go to church a lot either, only twice a year. We never went to the same one twice. I don't pray, though I think there's probably a God, and I think of Jesus as a teacher and spiritual leader who'd be horrified if he came back to Earth and saw all the horrible things people have done in his name over the years."

Adicia knocks on the door. "What's taking yous so long? Allen put our supper on the table, and we're waiting for you to eat."

"Just a minute," Emeline calls.

Allen smiles and pulls out a chair for Lenore when she comes to the table with Emeline. "Serve yourself first. You can have the whole pot if you like."

"Allen's a good cook!" Adicia says. "Our parents made us eat nasty things like roadkill and moldy vegetables. Now we eat real meat, fresh fruit and vegetables, and even dairy products."

"Would you mind if I moved to the end of the table?" Lenore asks. "I'm a southpaw, and I don't wanna bump anyone's elbow."

Allen smiles at her, and his eyes light up. "So are all the rest of us. Left-handedness runs in our family. Our dad was born a southpaw, but he gave in to teachers tryna switch him. Our sister Ernestine's also a lefty, and so are four of her friends. You'll never have to worry about bumping anyone's elbow here."

"All four of you plus another sister are lefties? And four of her friends too?"

"You're really one of us!" Adicia says. "Now we know you belong here!"

Lenore ladles soup into her bowl and takes a roll from the plate in the center of the table. She gulps the soup down ravenously, somewhat embarrassed at how the Troys are eating with a bit more decorum. After supper, Allen offers her a slice of cherry pie, and she accepts, trying not to smile at him. He'd probably laugh if he thought she had a crush on him, and she doesn't want to encourage this crush besides. After what she just escaped from, it's going to be a long time before she can bring herself to trust any guy to be more than friends.

"Here, this is where you'll be sleeping," Allen says after supper, unfolding the sofa bed. "Emeline, get the spare pillows and sheets in the hall closet."

"I can do that myself," Lenore protests. "I know how to make a bed."

"I think we all know, to varying degrees, you've already been through enough. Let us help you while you're getting better." He smiles at her, and Lenore thinks he's got a really cute smile.

"Tomorrow we can shop for groceries," Adicia says. "We'll show you the grocer we like to go to. Then we can buy more tableware. We haven't bought more than what we need most."

"I'll leave you money and a shopping list," he says as he makes the sofa bed. "Our shopping bags and baskets are in the kitchen closet. You can use a payphone to call me at work if there's an emergency. The number of the bakery is on the paper with important phone numbers on the fridge. Since tomorrow's Monday, I need to get to sleep early to be up for work on time. I like my sisters to go to bed by ten, and you'll probably wanna hit the hay by then too, after the ordeal you've been through."

Lenore goes back into the girls' room to change into the night-gown Emeline lent her, then walks back out to the sofa bed. Justine tries to offer her the stuffed rabbit again.

"No, sweetie, you can keep your little friend. I know you want to make me feel better, but I'll be fine without a stuffed animal. You'd probably miss your bunny tonight."

"This is her only toy," Emeline says. "She must really like you if she wants you to borrow her bunny. It was an Easter present from a Bowery Mission volunteer when she was thirteen months old. It means a lot to her, and now even more so because she saved it from the fire."

"Justine's bunny is Real, just like the Velveteen Rabbit," Adicia says. "Do you know that story?"

"I can't say I do," Lenore says. "Is that a movie or a book?"

"Oh, no, we've never seen a movie. It's a story about a stuffed bunny a boy gets for Christmas, and how the bunny becomes Real over time because the Boy loves him so much, even if he isn't the most ex-pensive or fanciest toy he has. Then the Boy gets scarlet fever, and his doctor tells his parents to burn all his toys and bedding, and to get him a new bunny. The bunny becomes a real bunny hopping with other bunnies, and when the Boy gets better and comes home, he thinks the Rabbit looks just like his old bunny he thinks was burnt."

"Maybe someday we'll become Real too," Justine says. "When someone loves you enough, even if you're poor and don't wear nice clothes, you become really special and different."

"The Boy loves the Rabbit just the way he is. I hope we find someone from outside our family who loves us just the way we are."

"I'm sure you will someday," Allen says. "But now I think it's time for you to leave Lenore alone and let her sleep. You can get to know each other plenty tomorrow. What was your last name again, Lenore?"

"Hartlein. It's a Southern German name meaning 'brave little one,' a pet form of the word for brave or strong."

Allen smiles at her again. "Well, I'll let you get a good night's sleep, brave little one. Girls, I trust you won't disturb Lenore while she's tryna sleep."

Justine puts the rabbit next to Lenore's pillow before she tiptoes to their bedroom. Adicia and Emeline make sure to tuck the sheet and quilt in before they join Justine. As soon as he finishes washing the dishes, Allen turns off the lights and goes into his room. As he drifts off to sleep, he can't shake the feeling he just found his future wife at the bus stop of all places. He's never had such an indescribable funny feeling from meeting any other girl before. The idea of waiting three years to ask her out is a hard pill to swallow, coupled with her fear of being touched by a man so soon after what she escaped from, but he consoles himself with the thought that it might teach him patience, and make him appreciate a relationship more because he'll have to earn it. He never had to work for any relationship before, never asked permission for a kiss or to make out. In the meantime, regardless of his strange immediate attraction to her, he's glad to have found a substitute for Sarah to take care of his sisters.

In the morning, Adicia and her sisters go into the kitchen for cereal. Adicia and Justine pour milk onto theirs, still not over being able to have milk whenever they want, but Emeline likes her cereal dry. She tried it with milk a few times but hated how soggy it got. The only fruit left in the fruit bowl is one peach, which Emeline washes, cuts up, and splits three ways. They make toast with a frying pan, since Allen hasn't been able to afford a toaster yet, and put cherry preserves on top. There's some homemade orange juice left, and the girls all use a strainer, since they hate pulp. Justine always puts her rabbit in the empty chair so it can eat with them, but now she lets Lenore continue sleeping with it. They try to keep as quiet as possible as they eat, and periodically send sympathetic looks over to Lenore, still out like a light and curled up in the fetal position, her long jet black hair flowing on the pillow next to her.

They're afraid running water might wake Lenore, so they tiptoe back to their bedroom to get dressed instead of taking their morning baths. Allen isn't strict about making them bathe at a certain time or even every day, so long as they don't routinely go several days between bathing. Adicia loves taking a bath with hot water, washing with a thick bar of soap instead of a bar cobbled together from various slivers of the cheapest soaps her parents could find, and drying herself off with a fresh towel, but it won't be too bad to wait a little bit and have her bath in the later afternoon or early evening, after they're through with their errands.

The girls are sitting quietly on their bed and reading when Lenore finally wakes up at 11:00. She goes into the bathroom and runs a bath, and is in there for a long time. They don't blame her for taking such a long bath after she probably hasn't bathed in a week. They take their books into the living room to read on the davenport when they hear the tub being drained and Lenore opening the door. She deserves privacy while she dresses.

"What are you reading?" Lenore asks when she emerges in a knee-length yellow calico dress. "I always wished I could read more, but we didn't have many books, and I wasn't allowed to leave the apartment much, let alone to go to the library."

"I'm reading *The Last Battle*, the final book in the Chronicles of Narnia series, by C.S. Lewis," Emeline says. "I like series books. You get to know the characters and follow them over a long time instead of only knowing them for one book. Adicia's reading *Little House on the Prairie*, by Laura Ingalls Wilder. Justine can't quite read yet, so she's looking at *Green Eggs and Ham*, by Dr. Seuss, and trying to sound out some of the words. We taught her her ABCs when she was two, and we hope she'll start reading on her own by the time she's four."

"Emeline's been reading since she was three!" Adicia says. "Her first book was *Grimms' Fairytales*."

"You want us to make you breakfast? We're got cereal, eggs, and bread, though we're all outta fruit."

"We also have oatmeal and honey."

"I'd like eggs and oatmeal. I haven't eaten too much the past week, and I want to fill my stomach up. I hope your brother doesn't mind if I eat too much of your food."

"I'm sure he won't mind." Emeline smiles. "If I didn't know any better, I'd almost think he has a crush on you. Did you notice the way he was looking at you last night?"

Lenore blushes. "It's just your imagination. Why would an experienced eighteen-year-old wanna bother with a fifteen-year-old? I've never even kissed a boy. No guy wants a girl who needs to be taught how to kiss or doesn't wanna do anything physical."

"If a guy likes you enough, he won't care how many beaux you've had or haven't had, or how long you wanna wait to be physical. I'm waiting till I'm at least eighteen to date, so I can concentrate on school. I might wait longer than most girls to find her man, but I'll end up with the man who's worth waiting for." Emeline pours a thin layer of Crisco into the frying pan and cracks two eggs into it. "But don't worry. Even if he really does have a crush on you, he'll keep to his promise to not lay a hand on you. My brother respects women. He even complained because the help wanted ads have different sections for men and women, as though you need to be a certain sex to do certain jobs."

Adicia dips a clean pot into the canister of oatmeal and holds it under the faucet until the water covers it just slightly. She puts it on a free stove burner and lets Emeline heat it up.

"Allen saved me and Justine from a fire," Adicia says while Lenore's breakfast cooks. "Our stupid parents ran out and abandoned us. Our mother only thought to save our little brother Tommy. Allen went up to the top two floors to warn people, then came back to check for anyone left. He was very brave. He kicked down our bedroom door to save us. Then he ran back into the burning building for our baby nephew Giovanni. Emeline says he was as heroic as a character in the Five Little Peppers series, Joel Pepper. I haven't read all the books in it yet, but she says in the last book, there's a fire on a ship, and Joel stays behind till very last to save a lot of people."

"Are you really gonna stay with us and be our new Sarah?" Justine asks as Emeline slips the dippy eggs onto a plate and pours the oatmeal into a bowl. "We all thought Sarah was our mother when we were babies. Our first words were 'Mama,' and we said it to her, not our real mother."

"Strangers have never been so nice and welcoming to me ever before. And I always did want sisters. I guess I will stay."

"Goody!" Adicia shouts.

After Lenore finishes breakfast, they take the shopping bags and baskets and go out to pick up the items on Allen's shopping list. At the local grocery, they buy tomatoes, blueberries, strawberries, peaches, raspberries, oranges, peppers, cheese, and several boxes of uncooked pasta. Their next stop is the nearest butcher, where they buy two chickens and five pounds of ground hamburger meat. After that, they visit the fishmonger to pick up two pounds of salmon.

They return to the apartment to refrigerate the perishables, then sit down to lunch. Emeline fries some of the hamburger meat and serves it with fried peppers and rolls. Lenore continues to be taken aback when they offer her the first serving, and the largest portion.

"Do you have a toothbrush?" Adicia asks as she trots off to the bathroom. "We lost our old ones in the fire, but Allen bought us new ones."

"I didn't unpack it yet. It's a boring black color."

"Allen got us pretty toothbrushes," Justine says. "Mine's purple, Adicia's is blue, and Emeline's is green."

"After we brush our teeth, we can get the extra tableware and cookware we need," Emeline says. "Allen thinks they might have some for sale in onea the open-air markets. This is such an amazing neighborhood, an entirely different planet from the eastern side of the city."

"Can we take our baths when we get back?" Adicia asks. "We didn't bathe this morning 'cause we didn't wanna wake you up."

"How does your brother afford all this?" Lenore asks as the Troy girls brush their teeth.

Emeline rinses her mouth out. "He works six days a week at a bakery, and makes three bucks an hour. He also got a loan of three hundred bucks from the Bowery Mission people. He used some of it on rent and our beds, but there's still a bunch left. We have two bucks left of the money he gave us today, so we'll probably be able to find tableware we can afford."

Justine picks up her rabbit and waits by the front door for Lenore and her sisters to finish. She gives her hand to Emeline when they walk over, smiling a big smile at her. Lenore finds it surprising and refreshing to see a teenager who's so close and loving with her little sisters. Emeline doesn't seem bothered or put out at all by holding hands with them, reading to them, making food for them, or helping them dress or brush their teeth. She doesn't seem to realize or care she's given up a normal teenage life. This is all she knows how to do.

A table sale starts ten blocks away, with books, tableware, cookware, clothes, gadgets, jewelry, toys, artwork, and records arranged on tables on the narrow streets. Adicia wishes they could buy it all and make their new home even more perfect, but two dollars can only buy so much. Emeline wishes they could take all the books, though they don't have a bookshelf yet, and there wouldn't be enough room for that many books. Justine would love to buy all the toys, though she doesn't have a toy chest, and she knows it's not nice manners to leave one's toys lying about.

"How much are your plates?" Emeline asks the woman at the kitchenware table. "We also need pots and pans."

"How much can we buy for two dollars?" Adicia asks.

"This is a bag sale," the woman explains. "Whatever you can fit into a bag goes for one dollar. Are you shopping for your parents?"

"Oh, no. We live with our big brother Allen, and this is our new friend Lenore."

"Lookit this!" Emeline calls. "A waffle iron! We could make Belgian waffles for breakfast every day if we had onea these!"

"Those waffles were yummy! Can we really buy it?"

"We can get whatever we want for two bucks if we fill up our bags as much as we can!" Emeline pulls Justine back from the table. "Don't touch anything, sweetie. These things are heavy, and others are fragile. We don't want anything to break or hurt you."

Justine steps back and sits on the front stoop of an apartment behind them, narrating everything she sees to her rabbit. Adicia holds out the bags as Emeline and Lenore fill them with pots, pans, silverware, cups, glasses; pretty plates decorated with flowers, animals, leaves, butterflies, birds, hearts, and Christmas designs; a serving platter with blue swirls, casserole dishes, the waffle iron, bowls, and a large and small roasting pan. They pack the bags with the courtesy tissue paper and pieces of cardboard so nothing breaks, scratches, or rubs against one another. Most of it isn't as nice as the things they used to admire at Macy's, but it's several steps up from the hideous kitchenware they used before. They don't care none of the sets are complete.

It's not like they're going to have supper parties or guests who find mismatched tableware scandalous. They're just glad to find such nice things at such an affordable price.

After they get home, Emeline and Adicia put the things away in the cupboards while Justine narrates the pictures in her Dr. Seuss library books to her rabbit. When the kitchenware is all put away, Adicia takes Justine into the bathroom. Lenore can hardly believe an eight-year-old is comfortable taking a bath with her three-year-old sister. Most girls Adicia's age want the bathtub to themselves, and only young children want to bathe with a baby sibling. She hears them splashing around and having an animated conversation, having a great time in spite of their lack of bath toys.

Emeline takes a bath after her sisters are finished and enough time has passed for the hot water to come back. Adicia offers Lenore her pick of Emeline's library books.

"Most of 'em are grownup books, but you're probably too old to wanna read my books. Emeline read me and our other sister Ernestine somea the earlier Narnia books, and we really liked them. I useta wish our old wardrobe had a secret door to a magical fantasy world like the one in the book, so I could escape that tenement. I don't know if this one would make a lot of sense to you, though. It's the last one in the series, and you don't know any of the characters. Emeline said the lion king in the book is supposed to represent Jesus, though they don't seem like religious stories to me."

"What about this other book? The one by the writer with a German-sounding name."

"He's really Swiss, Emeline says. He was born in Germany and now lives in Switzerland. He won a Nobel Prize for writing in 1946. She read this one a few years ago and wanted to read it again. Our old nanny Sarah recommended it to her. Emeline likes this writer. This one, *Demian,* was the first one by him she read. She says it's about how it's a really special thing to be different from other people, and that the Mark of Cain mentioned in the Bible isn't a bad thing, but the mark of someone who's brave enough to think for himself and not be just like everyone else. Maybe when I'm older, I'll understand it more. I'm not an advanced reader like she is."

"Does your brother like to read?"

"He's not much of a reader. He reads the newspaper or popular magazines sometimes, but not really books. At least he reads more than our other older brother, who's in the hospital and will never walk again."

Lenore's eyes widen at how matter-of-factly Adicia says this. "What happened to your other brother?"

"Oh, he was on drugs at work when a car fell on him. He didn't tighten the jack all the way 'cause he was so high. The weight of the car crushed his spine. He's going in and out of consciousness. The cops are gonna arrest him as soon as he's discharged. They don't care he's gonna go to jail in a wheelchair. He did a lot of very bad things, like using and selling drugs, and accidentally burning down our tenement."

"That's the same brother who was tryna do adult things with his date when Allen came to her rescue?"

"The same one. Carlos is a very bad boy. I'm happy he won't be coming around anymore, though I kinda feel bad he's paralyzed. He's only nineteen, too young to spend the rest of his life in a wheelchair, however dumb he is."

Emeline finishes her bath and dries off, reaching for her clothes. She hangs the towel back up over the towel rack and brushes out her wet hair. Before she leaves the bathroom, she checks the medicine cabinet and under the sink to make sure they don't need a refill on anything. She's particularly glad the box of Modess pads Mrs. Troy bought her after the fire still has enough left for another month or two. Emeline is embarrassed at the thought of asking Allen to pick up more sanitary napkins, or explaining why she needs a little bit more money than usual for shopping. Even a guy with six sisters can't be that immune to feeling awkward about that subject.

"I hope you're okay with Modess napkins, Lenore," she calls. "That's the brand our mother always bought for us. They're under the sink. Did you bring your belt?"

"I brought all four of them, but I have to wash them."

"You have *four*? My mother only bought one each for us!"

"Of course I need more than one. They usually get a little bloody, and you need a fresh belt while the other one's waiting to be washed. Your mother made yous wear the same belt your entire menses?"

"Boy, I'm glad it's gonna be at least four more years till Adicia needs a belt. I can't imagine asking Allen to buy one for her, or to ask for money to buy one. I wonder how our sister Ernestine's gonna handle it when the day comes."

"Why did your parents let her move out at only ten years old?" Lenore asks as Emeline comes out to the living room. "I'm sure my parents are searching all over for me by now. I hope they think I went somewhere in Brooklyn and not that I escaped to the next borough over."

"They barely cared. They figured it was one less daughter to hafta deal with, one less mouth to feed. She's probably doing alright with her new friends, but we miss her. At least she knows our door's always open."

Allen usually comes back from work at about 6:30. Tonight, he isn't home at his usual time, so Emeline decides to start supper and not wait around for him. If he's picking up an extra shift to make more money, so much the better.

Adicia sets the table with the new plates with butterflies, silverware with fancy swirls on the bottom, sepia-toned glasses, and the serving platter. Emeline opens a few cans of vegetables and dumps them into a casserole dish, mixing them with leftover pieces of chicken and peeled potatoes. She'd prefer to make a casserole with flour or noodles, but she doesn't know how to make dough, and Allen doesn't want them boiling water when he's not around to supervise.

Emeline is pulling the casserole out of the oven when Allen comes home at 7:30, carrying a festive red bag with green ribbons as handles. He approaches Lenore and hands her the bag, smiling at her.

"I know how much Justine loves that rabbit, and I'm sure she'd miss it if she gave it to you every night. I thought you could use your own friend to keep you company at night and make you feel better. I went to a toy store after work and picked this out for you."

"You bought me a present?" Lenore asks in shock.

"I don't think a girl is ever too old to sleep with a doll or stuffed animal until she's a married woman. You probably never had one growing up, did you?"

Lenore pulls out a very soft tan dog with big floppy ears, a short tail, large black eyes, a couple of brown spots, and an endearing smile. "That was very nice of you, but you shouldn't feel like you hafta spend your money on a stranger."

"You were a stranger last night. You're not a stranger now. Come on, I know you like it. You looked really happy when you saw it." Allen smiles at her again, and Lenore feels butterflies in her stomach.

"It is really cute," Lenore admits. "No one ever gave me a present or treated me so nice before."

"Then it's all yours. Maybe someday, you can give it to your little boy or girl when he or she wants a stuffed animal to feel better at night."

"Come join us for supper after you wash up," Emeline says, noticing how smitten her brother looks. He's smiling a lot more than usual, and his eyes almost seem to have a sparkle. There's no doubt left in her mind he's got a crush on Lenore.

"Tomorrow we can make strawberry pancakes," Lenore says. "How would you girls like to help me make them for breakfast?"

"Instead of cereal or oatmeal?" Adicia asks. "We usually have that or bacon and eggs for breakfast."

"We've got everything we need for pancake batter. All you need to do is slice the strawberries very thinly and add a little vanilla to the batter to make it sweet. We can make blueberry and raspberry pancakes next. All that fruit we bought today needs to be put to good use, doesn't it?"

"You know how to cook?" Allen asks, looking like a happy little boy.

"I had to help my mother in the kitchen all the time. I can cook or bake almost anything but exotic recipes, and even those I bet I could get the hang of with a cookbook and enough practice."

"I think you're a keeper!" Allen flashes her a lovestruck grin.

***

The next Sunday, Allen wakes up to the smell of Belgian waffles. His sisters are in their pajamas and sitting at the table as Lenore pours more batter into the waffle iron. A big bowl of strawberries, blueberries, and sliced peaches is in the center of the table, as the girls take turns dipping a big spoon into it and putting the fruit onto their waffles. A small bottle of maple syrup and a small bowl of homemade crème Chantilly are also on the table.

"Lenore made us Belgian waffles for brunch!" Adicia calls excitedly. "Come join us before all the batter runs out!"

"I'll need to get dressed first. It's not proper for a gentleman to let an unrelated lady see him in a state of immodest dress."

"Since when do you care about modesty, Allen?" Emeline teases him. "You're fully clothed. No one cares you're wearing pajamas."

"As long as the waistband is secure and not in danger of accidentally falling down, I don't think I mind," Lenore says, taking in how cute his tousled hair looks first thing in the morning.

"We've got new squeezed orange juice too, and Lenore strained all the pulp out of it before she poured it into the pitcher!" Adicia says.

"She wouldn't let us have any eggs or bacon, just waffles," Emeline says. "She said Belgian waffles are more like dessert than breakfast, and she doesn't want us to overeat or have too much unhealthy food at the same meal."

Allen eagerly takes a seat, and Lenore pours him a glass of orange juice and puts the just-finished waffle onto his plate.

"Would you like fruit, syrup, or crème Chantilly?"

"You don't hafta serve me." He smiles, wishing he could touch her on the arm or hand instead of only having to look. "It's swell enough you made this nice brunch for my sisters."

"Isn't Lenore the best ever?" Adicia asks. "No one will ever take Sarah's place, but she's great in other ways."

"Yes, she sure is." Allen grins stupidly, trying not to gaze at Lenore too much.

"You've been smiling a lot more than usual since she came here, Allen," Emeline says. "I'd say you found a substitute of your own, for drugs, alcohol, and cigarettes. Doesn't she have a wonderful effect on all of us?"

"She's the nicest thing I've ever found at a bus stop." Allen fumbles with his knife and almost drops it on the floor, too preoccupied with gazing at her.

"I wish we had a camera so we could take a picture," Adicia says. "I think this is what a family picture is supposed to look like."

"I think it is," Allen agrees, taking his eyes off Lenore reluctantly. "I don't know if this arrangement will last forever, but we've got a wonderful new little family here, and a great new friend we've invited into our unconventional family."

Chapter 21: A Short-Lived Reunion

It's just getting dark on a night in late August, and Allen, Lenore, and the girls are on the fire escape, taking in the cool air and watching stars come out, when a small group of people runs down the street. One of them is dragging a pile of mattresses with a rope, and several are carrying suitcases. In the gathering darkness, Allen could swear one of them is Ernestine, and the one pulling the mattresses is Girl Ryan.

"How long would it take to get here from The Bowery?" he asks.

"That's kind of a random question," Lenore says.

"Not when I think onea those people is my other little sister Ernestine."

"Why would Ernestine be here, and at night?" Adicia asks.

"I have no idea, but I'm sure it ain't good if it is her." Allen starts down the fire escape.

Emeline strains her eyes, positive Allen's just seeing things, but soon enough makes out the familiar form of the fourth-born Troy sister. Her mouth drops open.

Allen catches up to them and clamps his hands on Ernestine's shoulders, stopping her dead in her tracks. She looks up at him with a mixture of fear and relief.

"I'm sure you're wondering what in the world we're doing here at this hour, or doing here period," Girl begins. "We had a real tragedy today. We lost our lovely home, and had to get out before the cops could get up to the third floor, arrest the grownups, and throw us into an orphanage."

"We're homeless now," Infant says sadly.

"The cops raided our squat," Boy says. "While they was on the first floor arresting people and acting like jerks, we heard what was going on and grabbed whatever we could. One of the grownups tied our mattresses together and put our clothes and toys in a big sheet that was tied shut. What couldn't fit in the sheet went into our suitcases. We escaped by the fire escape before they got up to the third floor."

"We ran here 'cause it was the only place I could think of," Ernestine says. "It was only a mile or so. We don't know where everyone else went, or if we'll ever see any of them again."

"We'll just go right back to squatting," Girl says. "When the cops go after us for squatting, they make us homeless all over again and force us to take up residence in a new place in secret. It doesn't solve our problem. If they really cared about people, they'd help us with free or cheap housing, give us decent jobs and training for jobs, and improve the school system. I hope they sleep horribly all night, knowing they made at least two hundred people homeless."

"Do you plan to sleep in the street tonight?" Allen asks. "Ernestine's of course welcome to stay here, but I don't have enough room or money for all six of yous."

"Oh, we don't intend to impose on you. We'll find a new place to squat nearby. In the meantime, can we come up and try to figure out what's gonna happen next?"

Allen takes the rope and drags the mattresses over to the front door, sighing in resignation. He pulls the keys out of his left pocket and hands them to Girl.

"Bronze opens the front door, and silver opens our apartment, 515."

Ernestine, Julie, and the Ryans gasp in delight and shock when they see the elevator in the front lobby. Infant, who's riding on top of the mattresses, closes and opens her eyes several times to make sure that's what she's really seeing.

Allen is none too thrilled about the prospect of putting up six extra people for at least one night as Girl unlocks 515. After he maneuvers the mattresses through the door, he surveys the living room and looks into his sisters' bedroom to see if there's any space to stick them all.

"Ernestine, you're really back!" Adicia says excitedly, rushing over to hug her favorite sister. "Are you here to stay?"

"These are pretty nice digs," Girl says, looking around. "Maybe someday we'll be able to squat in a place like this."

Emeline and Justine run over to hug Ernestine next. They hadn't been entirely sure they'd ever see her again, at least not anytime soon.

Ernestine looks at Lenore in surprise. "Who's this, Allen, your girlfriend?"

Allen blushes. "No, she's just a friend we met at the bus stop last month. She's sorta a replacement Sarah. She and Emeline are also becoming great friends."

"You met her at a *bus stop*?" Girl asks in amusement. "What was she doing there? I don't think someone waiting for the next bus would agree to move in with a bunch of strangers!"

"Her name's Lenore Hartlein, and she's a lovely girl. Are you implying she's a girl of ill repute? I'd never let a prostitute or drug dealer move in with my little sisters."

"I was running away from home," Lenore jumps in to defend herself. "Adicia and Justine came over to me because they felt sorry for me, all alone and rain falling on me. I ran away from Brooklyn to escape my disgusting father. He did awful things to me."

Girl lowers her gaze. "I'm sorry. I wouldn't have known. It's just that you usually don't think of a bus stop as a place to make new friends or find babysitters. Our friend Julie here also had horrible things done to her by her dad and ran away from home too. Adicia snuck her over to our old squat while Allen bought drugs from her dad to stall for time."

Allen can't decide which of their stories is sadder. All he knows is the lot of them aren't the types of people polite society wants to be associated with or acknowledge the existence of. Young people from their world would never be portrayed in a movie, television show, or book. The anti-vice societies would jump all over that, as though their real lives are an offense against decency.

"Would yous like something to eat?" he asks. "We already ate our supper, but I can heat up leftover tuna casserole or beef stew."

"That's gonna deplete a lot of our food!" Emeline protests. "Ernestine and Julie I can understand taking in, but I'm sure the Ryans can fend for themselves. They were fending for themselves long before Ernestine moved in with them."

"I don't wanna put them up more than a day or two either, but they're here now, and probably don't have any other safe place to go. Would you rather they sleep in the street or go from building to building looking for a place to squat at night?"

"Is your basement free?" Girl asks as Allen heats up the food.

Allen turns around to look at her in disbelief. "Did I just hear you correctly? Are you thinking of squatting in the basement?"

"Well, yes or no? Are there any apartments down there, and are they free, or is it a regular storage basement where we can find space to live and sleep?"

"You are not squatting in the basement, and to answer your original question, it's a normal basement, not a storage area or floor of apartments."

"Good. We can move our stuff there and set up house."

"No, you are not. I ain't about to get in trouble with my landlord. I'm already worried about having eleven people in a two-bedroom apartment. That's gotta violate the housing and fire codes."

"The tenement violated both, and no one ever tossed us out," Ernestine points out.

"Where else would we go?" Girl asks. "I liked that big hole in the road. It was like onea those war bunkers. I liked the subway tunnel least."

"We won't bother you by taking up all your room," Baby says sweetly. "We can pull our mattresses up to your roof. It's August, so we won't freeze to death overnight."

"I want Julie to sleep on the sofa bed with me," Lenore announces. "The poor little thing could use a friend who can relate to what she went through, much as I wish that kinda thing didn't hafta happen to anyone."

"We go to bed around ten," Allen says. "You'll hafta figure out what you're doing about sleeping arrangements soon. I bought a double-sized bed for my sisters, but now that Ernestine's here, I'll hafta use more of my loan money to get a second bed to make bunk beds. Adicia and Justine can sleep on the bottom, and Emeline and Ernestine can sleep on the top. Four girls can't sleep on one bed."

"We're getting out of here as soon as we can," Ernestine assures him. "We don't want you to get in trouble with your landlord."

"We don't hafta stay here," Girl says. "The Meatpacking District's just above us, and I'm sure we can find an abandoned stable or slaughterhouse to squat in."

"I don't care where you're squatting!" Allen implores. "It's still breaking the law, whether or not it's unfair to poor people! You can argue the politics of rich versus poor to a judge till you're blue in the face, but you'll still be found guilty. At least at your old squat, there were lots of adults with jobs. How are you gonna scare up enough money, and how will you get heating, running water, and electricity? Do yous know how to cook, and would there be any icebox or refrigerator if yous set up shop in an abandoned slaughterhouse? How would you cook? Most importantly, what's Ernestine gonna do about school?"

"We can beg, wash car windows, pickpocket, do odd jobs like deliver papers and sell lemonade," Boy says.

"That won't make enough money for even one person to live from hand to mouth. Child labor is illegal in this country, so none of you would be able to find real jobs anywhere."

"We'll get by like poor kids have always gotten by," Girl insists. "When you grow up homeless and squatting, you learn a thing or two about how to depend on yourself and make ends meet. Why only a few hundred years ago, girls my age were considered only a couple years away from marriage."

Allen stands by helplessly as they wolf down the casserole and stew, wiping their mouths on their sleeves instead of using napkins. He doesn't offer them the peach pie Lenore baked the other day, afraid they'll eat it all and leave none for the five pre-existing residents. Luckily, they don't think to ask for dessert, since they're not accustomed to having such a meal except on very special occasions.

Ernestine tries lying on the bed with her sisters, but there's not enough room for four people. She and Girl lug their mattress into the room and put it next to the bed. Girl helps Baby and Infant set their mattress up on spare space in the living room, while Boy pulls his near the kitchen. Julie gets onto the sofa bed with Lenore, still taking in her new surroundings with wonder and amazement.

"Did your daddy make you stay in your apartment too and never go anywhere?" Julie asks. "I wasn't allowed to go to school or play in the hallway."

"I could barely leave the apartment," Lenore says. "I didn't go to school either, or church. I only left for my forced weekly visits to the doctor."

"Why did you have to go to the doctor once a week?" Adicia asks. "I don't think our parents ever took us to the doctor, except to get polio and DTP shots at a free clinic. They didn't want to spend their money on it."

"He was friends with the doctor, who was a real creep and probably hated women. He wanted to make sure I didn't have any grownup diseases or problems. You're too young to understand. I hope you never have to go through anything like that."

"Why would you have diseases?" Justine asks. "And why would you need to be checked for sickness every week?"

"This was a doctor for grownups and teenage girls with certain problems. Why don't you trot off to bed with your bunny and dream of nice things now?"

After Boy and the girls have gone to bed, Lenore sets her stuffed dog next to Julie and tiptoes out to the fire escape. Allen notices her missing when he's going to the kitchen for a glass of water before bed, and finds her on the fire escape, bent over and crying.

"Are you gonna be okay? Whatever that son of a bitch and his doctor friend did to you, you're safe from them both now. Someday it'll seem like a distant nightmare, I promise you."

"That sweet little girl reminds me so much of me at that age. I'm jealous of her because she got away at only eight. I endured seven more years of that hell. Is it true you made a disturbance so your sister could sneak her away from that creep?"

"He was a degenerate. I wished he could've been castrated instead of only losing the target of his perversion. We found out he died in the fire, by the way, so he won't ever come back after her. My dad might be a drug user and drinker, but at least he never laid hands on any of my sisters or any other young girls. He's probably cheated on my mother at least a few times, but he sticks to adult women."

"I can't get that image outta my head now. I had to see that doctor once a week from the time I was only twelve. I wasn't allowed to have any clothes on, and a mean nurse held me down so I wouldn't move away from the doctor. He copped a feel on me too, and thought I was a whore to be in there all the time, like it was my fault my father's a pervert. My father wanted to be sure I wasn't pregnant or hadn't gotten any diseases from his philandering. The thought of ever going to any kind of doctor ever again gives me the creeps." Lenore starts gasping for breath.

Allen looks at her hesitantly, knowing Lenore doesn't want to be touched by a man anytime soon. When she continues to struggle for breath and sounds like she's having a panic attack, he gently starts to rub her back, telling her, "Breathe in, breathe out," until her breathing returns to normal.

"I wish I could give you a hug," he says sadly.

"You're a really nice guy, Allen," she says, just as sadly. "Maybe someday I'll let you hug me. One day, when the memory of my father isn't so fresh in my mind."

"I'll wait for you. That is, if you're still interested in living with me and my sisters."

"I really like it here," she says as she walks back to the sofa bed. "Don't worry. Tomorrow we'll work out something about our guests."

In the morning, Girl heads into the kitchen to see what's for breakfast. She surveys the choices that present themselves—eggs, bacon, oatmeal, cereal, fruit, bread, jam, smoked fish. There was never such a big variety of meal choices at the squat. After spending a good five minutes agonizing between all the delicious breakfast options, she finally decides on bread with raspberry jam, scrambled eggs, and bacon. She knows smoked fish is a bit of a delicacy, and doesn't want to upset Allen any further by eating his expensive foods.

"What are we gonna do today?" Ernestine asks as she plops down at the table. "I still say we should squat in the basement till we find something more permanent."

"I'm gonna scout for abandoned buildings and apartments," Boy says. "I'll keep scouting as long as it takes us to find new digs."

"We also need to make a sign to use when we go begging. Boy, you have a pretty voice. You could sing in the streets for money."

"What would our sign say?" Julie asks.

"Something about how the cops made us homeless and that we have no parents, and that we need money and a new place to live."

"I have a mommy somewhere. She wanted to keep me when she divorced my daddy, but the judge and the cops wouldn't let her have me. I don't know if she still lives in Hell's Kitchen, though."

"What was your mommy's name?" Baby asks. "I like you and don't want you to leave us, but if you found your mommy and you know your daddy's dead now, it ain't right to stay with us longer than you have to."

"Our name is Spirnak, but I don't know if she remarried since she divorced my daddy. Her first name is Suzanne."

"Maybe your grandparents on her side are still alive and we could search for her through them?" Ernestine suggests. "What was your mom's maiden name?"

"Her what name?"

"The last name she was born with," Girl supplies. "I don't like the term 'maiden name,' since it's been a really long time since the average bride was an actual maiden, fourteen or fifteen, and it also assumes every woman will change her name. Somea the women back at the squat told me stories about interesting famous women who kept their birth names after marriage, like Lucy Stone and Olive Schreiner."

"I got in trouble at school once for defending my answers on a test about people's proper titles," Ernestine says. "I didn't identify any married women as Mrs. Husband's Name, which sounds really dumb and silly, and the teacher marked those questions wrong. I tried to argue my case with her, and she said no decent boy would ever want to marry me if I didn't want the gift of his name. I said maybe I'd hafta marry another girl if most boys are that stupid."

"I don't think most women do that where we're from. Only rich or middle-class women call themselves Mrs. Husband. I understand if they wanna have one family name, but it's only her last name she's changing, not her first."

"My sister Gemma raised a fit about that. All the other married women looked at her like she was crazy when she introduced herself as Gemma, not Mrs. anything."

"My mommy's name before she married my daddy was Bowstead," Julie says. "But there are so many people in this city, and we don't know if she moved. She might not even be in the phonebook."

Emeline comes into the kitchen, holding Justine's hand. "Have yous decided what's gonna happen now?"

"Exactly what I said last night," Girl says. "We're squatting in the basement till Boy can scout out another building. I'm sure the landlord won't be too mad if he finds us. Everyone here is so Bohemian, I don't think anyone would care. They'd probably agree with our cause."

Ernestine smiles when she sees Lenore waking up and coming over to the kitchen. "So, what's really the deal between you and my brother?"

"I help with Adicia and Justine while he's at work, and I help with cooking for your sisters. He's also giving me a nice place to stay where my father can't find me."

"Not that. I heard that part already. I mean the part where you're an attractive girl and he's a good-looking guy, you're both in the same home, and you're both the right age to do whatever it is teenagers and grownups in relationships do."

Lenore blushes. "I'm only fifteen. Allen's eighteen. Guys his age don't go for younger girls like me. Hoodlum types don't care, but he's a nice guy. And he's already had a bunch of other girlfriends. Experienced guys don't wanna bother with a girl who doesn't even know how to kiss a boy."

"None of Allen's girlfriends lasted long. He dated for fun and then they broke up. I think his longest girl was five months. He knew nonea those girls were marriage material. He did adult things with a lot of them, but he wasn't in love with any of them. I saw how he was looking at you last night. I might be only ten, but I've seen how guys look at their girlfriends when they really like them."

"How do they look like?" Adicia asks. "I don't notice any special look."

"Like she's the only person in the world, like nothing else matters."

"I hope a boy looks at me like that one day. Do you think a boy from the nice part of the world would ever like me?"

"Don't depend on any man to take you outta this life. I wanted to get away from our parents, and I did, all by myself. I'm not waiting around for a knight on a white horse to come riding in and rescue me."

"We're more concerned about how you're gonna get outta the mess you're in," Emeline says. "You're welcome to stay, and perhaps we'll keep Julie here too, but there's no way we're keeping six people. Children can't get by on their own in this country, in this century. Even if you did find a new place to squat and weren't caught, you still hafta go to school, and you all need money."

"We'll find ways," Girl insists. "Just watch us."

"Then you're a fool."

As he's walking home from work at 6:15, Allen comes upon a crowd of people gathered in the street. A cardboard box is in the center of the crowd, filled up with a substantial pile of coins and bills. He does a double-take when he sees Boy dancing as he sings folk songs, while Baby beats a tambourine and dances. Infant is in the shade, propping up a sign reading, "We were just made homeless last night when cops raided our commune in The Bowery. We have no parents and are looking for money and odd jobs so we can get by when we find new living quarters. Sincerely, Ernestine Troy, Julie Spirnak, and the Ryan children."

"Won't you spare some change for six poor children?" Baby asks as he comes up to them.

"I already put yous up in my home and fed you last night, and I'm sure you all helped yourselves to breakfast and lunch in my kitchen to-day too!"

"We moved our mattresses down to the basement after lunch, so don't you worry we're stealing your food or taking up your living space. We'll buy food that doesn't need cooking till we find a place with a stove and refrigerator."

"You can do whatever you want with or without anyone's permission, but my sister ain't gonna be a part of your squatting schemes. She can visit you all she wants, but she's going to live with her family. She had a reason to move in with yous in April, but now there's no more worry about needing to get away from our parents. Ernestine's coming back where she belongs."

"You can't take our friend away from us!" Boy protests. "She and Girl are best friends!"

"I'm supposed to sit by idly as my ten-year-old sister takes up squatting in a basement, with no adults and no way to earn money outside of this shameless begging? You'd feel the same, I hope, if you were a lot older than Baby and Infant. It's my job to protect and take care of my sisters, since my parents failed to do it."

"Ask her and see what her answer is. I don't think she'll wanna leave us and go back to you."

Allen rushes past them and down the remaining blocks to the apartment. When he gets in, Ernestine and Girl are reading the newspaper, Julie is playing marbles with Adicia, Justine, and Emeline, and Lenore is putting a rack of lamb on the table. That lamb will never feed eleven people unless they use the starvation-size servings Mr. and Mrs. Troy used to insist on to feed a dozen people.

"Ernestine, do you really intend to move into the basement to squat with the Ryans? We all want you to come back to live with us. There's a nice elementary school in Greenwich Village you'd be attending in the fall with Adicia. I know you really like your friends, but your place is with your family."

Ernestine looks up at him and shakes her head. "I'm sorry, Allen, but my place is no longer with you. My place is with Julie and the Ryans now. Maybe we'll find Julie's mother someday, but even if Julie were to go back to her own family, I'd still stay with my new family. It's not that I don't miss my sisters, but I've started a new life with the Ryans. I can't go back to how it used to be. Of course you're all welcome to come and visit me."

"In the basement?" Emeline asks. "How are we supposed to sleep at night, knowing you're in the basement squatting?"

"I can't live with you and know the Ryans are struggling to make ends meet, knowing I'd be getting nice, full meals while they have to beg in the streets and do odd jobs. It's like having an adventure. I like that more than this boring, predictable life you've got now. It's nice of you to care so much, though."

"That's her final decision," Girl says.

"Can I still go to school in the fall? I don't wanna stop going to school."

Allen feels like his head is about to explode. "Fine. Have it both ways. Just understand one thing. If any trouble arises again, you're coming back with your family. I'll make bunk beds, and you'll come home at a normal curfew, obey all my rules, and eat the food that's served. As soon as the new year comes, I'm gonna use some of my savings to go to the court to have Emeline, Adicia, and Justine legally put under my guardianship, and you too will be put under my guardianship. Is everything understood?"

"I don't like having our family split up so many ways," Adicia protests. "Ernestine, please stay with us!"

"I'd break up your new family if I stayed here with my friends, the same way my new family would be broken up if I stayed here. I'll only be in the basement. Boy hasn't started scouting for a new abandoned building to squat in yet. I'll try to stay as close as I can, so we'll be able to visit regularly," Ernestine tries to reassure her.

"We don't wanna impose on your brother," Girl says. "We can have a weekly supper together."

Adicia used to worry about Lucine and Emeline growing apart from her because they were so much older and starting to become young women with new concerns and interests. Now Ernestine's the one breaking apart their family, just when it seemed it was starting to come back together again. It's not fair Ernestine would choose her friends of only four months over her own family, even if they're only going to be in the basement. All she can do now is hope nothing more happens to disrupt her life after it finally seems like things are going right for a change, after so much chaos in the last few months.

Chapter 22: Christmas Calamity

After the lease ended in October, Mr. Troy and Tommy moved to a three-room apartment on the fourth floor of an old tenement in Hell's Kitchen renting for twenty dollars a month. Mr. Troy cares less there are frequent gang fights in the neighborhood and that he has to pony up subway fare every day to go to his job at the box-making factory on the Lower East Side. He knows Mrs. Troy won't be happy to come back to a building and neighborhood she constantly complained about. As for Carlos, he let the hospital declare him a ward of the state and washed his hands of his oldest son. If he ever regains enough of his senses and is rehabilitated enough to leave the hospital and stand trial for arson, petty theft, and selling, using, and possessing drugs, the authorities will notify Mr. Troy.

Mrs. Troy took a plea bargain to avoid going to trial and was put in prison for only four months, contingent upon paying back the entire $5,000 she embezzled, being on probation for the next ten years, and regularly submitting evidence to the court that she's making steps to get and keep a steady job, be a mother to her children, and turn her shoddy life around. Full well knowing she'll probably never be able to do any of those things, but knowing what would happen otherwise, she agreed to the plea bargain and hopes the court will forget about her over time. There are enough murders and robberies in New York City that any judge in his right mind would lose interest in following up on a run of the mill crook and drug user.

The only people who greet her when she's released from prison two weeks before Christmas are Mr. Troy, Tommy, and Mrs. Rossi. Tommy is the only one who rushes to hug and kiss her. Mr. Troy regards her almost as a stranger, having lost interest in his wife for everything but sexual intimacy years ago. Mrs. Rossi looks very flustered and starts chattering a mile a minute while Tommy is still snuggling with his overindulgent mother as though he hasn't seen her in years.

"Oh, for the love of God, Luigina, let me cuddle my baby for the first time in five months before you tell me something I probably don't care about!"

"Dolores, did you know your son Allen found a girl at a bus stop and moved her into his apartment with your three underage daughters?"

Mrs. Troy abruptly releases Tommy and stands straight up. "What in the world! When did this happen, and how did you find out?"

"I found a new job in the Meatpacking District, and one day after work I went to stroll in the West Village. Who should I see but your son and four of your daughters with a strange girl!"

"Four? I'd better not be about to find out the fourth was Lucine! If she ain't physically dead, she's as good as dead in our hearts, and she ain't welcome in this family no more!"

"It was Ernestine. I guess the cops was tipped off to that squatting situation and cracked down on it, so she went to your immoral son. I didn't inquire into the specifics, since I was more interested in what this strange girl was doing with your kids. If she's just Emeline's friend, they wouldn't have been taking what looked like a family walk together."

"Did Allen get a girl in trouble and not marry her?" Mr. Troy demands. "We raised him better than that!"

"I didn't see any pregnancy midsection. If he did get her in trouble, it's too soon to tell. Well, little Adicia and Justine recognized me, and I told them I was going for a stroll and window-shopping after work. I asked them who their new friend was, and they said she was a substitute for Sarah. I thought she was too young and attractive to just be a live-in nanny and servant, and besides, respectable women don't live with men they ain't related to, at least not without another woman or a relative. I guess people don't care about their reputations and proper decorum in that damned Bohemian wildland."

"What does Bohemian mean?" Tommy asks.

"It's someone who cares more about stupid stuff like art, poetry, and music than earning a living, and who does whatever he feels like, even if it goes against the established rules of proper society," Mr. Troy says.

"How did you find out this girl was living with them instead of just a girl Allen was having at the moment?" Mrs. Troy asks.

"Adicia and Justine are so stupid, they'll tell an enemy classified information. Kids are too honest and just speak their minds to anyone, like they don't know you don't share certain things with certain people. They told me they met her at a bus stop one night, and invited her to live with them to do what Sarah used to do. She's also a great cook and

Emeline's new best friend. They're only a year apart in age. This girl is fifteen."

"Allen's getting his jollies off an underage girl?" Mr. Troy asks in horror. "We raised him better than to be a pervert and deviant! He could be arrested for that!"

"Then how come you made Gemma marry an older guy and were tryna make Lucine marry another older guy?" Tommy asks.

"That's entirely different," Mrs. Troy defends herself. "Gemma was eighteen and overdue for a husband, and Lucine was sixteen, old enough to be married with parental permission. A respectable marriage is much different from a grown man having his way with an underage girl. I care less he's having intimacy outside of marriage, but to actually have the girl living with him and his minor sisters! That just boggles my mind!"

"Men don't pick up respectable girls at bus stops, Dolores," Mrs. Rossi says. "You don't solicit random strange girls there if you're serious about finding hired help or a nanny. Men go to bus stops to pick up hookers and score drugs, not to meet respectable girlfriends and live-in servants."

"So Allen was out hustling for a hooker and took my minor daughters with him? It's bad enough I'm going to look like a bad mother in the new neighborhood 'cause only one of my children still lives with me!"

"Why don't you take some time to get settled into our new place first?" Mr. Troy asks. "Then you can confront Allen and demand the girls come home. I don't want people to talk about us either. Just about the only thing we can say we're good at is having kids, and you don't want the new neighbors to immediately think you're a horrible mother because you let most of your kids move out underage."

"You can lie to them that Allen was taking care of them for you while you was in prison," Mrs. Rossi says. "I sure as hell wouldn't want any of my kids exposed to such an immoral living situation. You can't afford any more shame in your family, Dolores. I hope to God he's taking measures to not get this girl in trouble."

"In the meantime, I'm in desperate need of a drink or some cocaine. I was frantic to get back to my drugs and drinking all them months they had me in the clink, but now I need a drink or a puff of cocaine even more. I cannot believe Allen would disgrace our family

like that and expose his own sisters to that filth and perversion."
***

Adicia and Ernestine are now in third and fifth grade, respectively, at an elementary school in Greenwich Village, and Emeline's in her first year of high school. During the day, while Allen's at work, the girls are at school, and the squatters are begging, performing for money, and working random odd jobs like picking up trash and walking dogs, Lenore watches Justine. Justine loves having Lenore all to herself, and always looks forward to their daily walks around the neighborhood or to one of the local parks. It almost makes up for losing Sarah.

For the first time, Adicia is going to celebrate a real Christmas, though Allen doesn't have enough money for a big, fancy Christmas tree dripping with ornaments, lights, tinsel, and strings of popcorn and cranberries, decorating the apartment within an inch of its life, ingredients for only the finest meals, or expensive presents. The most important thing is that she's going to be together with her brother and three of her sisters, and they'll exchange presents and have a modest tree. Allen promised they'd take the bus to see the big tree at Rockefeller Center. They'll go ice-skating at Central Park afterwards, look around at Macy's, and have hot chocolate with crème Chantilly when they get home. She can hardly wait for Christmas morning, when, for the first time in her life, she'll wake up to a pretty tree with presents underneath, and stockings full of nuts, chocolates, candies, oranges, and small presents.

"Do you think next year we'll be able to buy real ornaments?" Adicia asks as they assemble cut-out ornaments from magazines.

"I hope so," Emeline says. "I think 1963 is gonna be our best year ever."

"Julie and the Ryans are invited to our Christmas too," Allen tells Ernestine. "Tell them they can bring up their mattresses and sleep here over Christmas Eve. I wouldn't dream of having five of the members of this family miss out on what's probably their first real Christmas too."

Ernestine smiles a big smile. "You really consider them part of our family now?"

"They're your friends and your new makeshift family. They're our family now."

"Do you have presents for all of them?" Justine asks.

"Are we all exchanging presents?" Adicia asks. "I don't know if they can spare any money for presents. They need money for food more."

"I'll find trinkets for them," Allen promises. "I'm sure none of us expect presents in return. By the way, Ernestine, are yous all warm enough?"

"We moved our mattresses next to the coal heater. When the coal deliveryman fills it up every week, he sees us sometimes and doesn't care. He's one of the good guys. He knows how the system exploits the poor and working-class, and that not everyone's lucky enough to have real housing. He came by once with a load of heavy blankets to make sure we won't freeze. Sometimes he slips us chocolates, fruits, and cheeses."

"Are we going to church for Christmas Eve?" Emeline asks.

"I like the Church of St. Luke in the Fields. They're Episcopal, and they hand out bread after Sunday services. I hear they have a Christmas pageant and Easter egg hunt every year."

"I don't want people to laugh at us because we don't have the nicest clothes or smell like perfume," Adicia says.

"Your clothes are nicer now," Allen says. "The ones you got from charity after the fire ain't that old. If I was you, I'd be happy all those ancient ragged hand-me-downs was destroyed in the fire. And you don't hafta take baths in freezing dirty bathwater or use the same towel as ten other people no more."

"Allen, in the new year, could one of your resolutions be to try to start using proper English?" Emeline asks. "Your speech doesn't make you a bad person, but if you're serious about going to college someday and having a higher-paying job, either higher up in the bakery or somewhere else, you might wanna make an effort to stop saying 'ain't,' using double negatives, and improperly conjugating verbs. It makes you look less educated, and it might make your teachers or employers think you're not worth hiring or helping with schoolwork."

"Why do you, Carlos, and your parents speak improper English when your sisters don't?" Lenore asks.

"They cared more about school and read a lot more. I'd probably speak better English if I'd given more of a damn about paying attention in school and read more books. When you read a lot and have teachers correcting mistakes, you probably learn quickly what's proper spelling and grammar, and what ain't."

"Do you mind if we correct you every time you use bad English?" Emeline asks.

"Probably wouldn't hurt. I do wanna be a good example. I'd hate to think you don't respect me as much 'cause I don't use proper English."

"Are we gonna rent ice-skates?" Adicia asks. "I don't want you to spend all your money on that if you need it more for food and rent."

"It'll be my treat. I don't know if Julie and the Ryans will wanna join us, in which case it'd cost a lot more."

"How about sledding?" Ernestine asks. "I always wanted to go sledding in Central Park, with a real sled. I guess we can always use onea the hills at Washington Square Park or St. Nicholas Park."

"You'll get a real sled someday. I have to repay the Bowery people their loan first, and save up money for a telephone, a bike or scooter, maybe more furniture, and a bookcase for Emeline."

"We won't be poor anymore in the new year!" Adicia says happily. "I can't wait for 1963 to start!"

***

Christmas Eve started out like any other day for Adicia. She woke up happy and excited about the memory of ice-skating at Central Park the other day, when she, Allen, Lenore, and her sisters put on skates and glided around on a big rink for a few hours, for the first time in their lives rubbing elbows with the other half of society as more than just onlookers. They belonged on that skating rink as much as anyone from a middle-class or rich family. Adicia took turns holding hands with everyone, and a few times was brave enough to skate around on her own. Even little Justine had a good time, either holding hands with someone or being held by Allen or Lenore. Afterwards they looked at the big Christmas tree and window-shopped at Macy's. Part of her wishes she believed in Santa, because this year she's going to get Christmas presents, and it couldn't hurt to ask for something Allen might not have bought. When she lived on the Lower East Side, she knew Santa didn't exist, but now that they're moving up in life, she's more inclined to believe in at least the message of the Santa myth.

They're sipping hot cocoa with Lenore's delicious homemade crème Chantilly when someone starts loudly banging on the fire escape door. Allen puts down his drink and gets up to peer through the window on the door. His eyes bug out when he sees his mother.

"Open the damn door, Allen Théodore Troy! I'm your mother!" she screeches.

Adicia's stomach turns to ice. She grips Emeline and Ernestine's hands under the table as Mrs. Troy storms in, looking livid.

"So you're outta the clink already, or did you break out?" Allen asks nervously.

"I sat in jail for a month while waiting for my case to be heard, since no one was decent enough to pay my bail, and I spent another four months rotting in prison. Thank God, I'm out now, in our new home in Hell's Kitchen with your father and dear little Tommy. I have no intentions of fulfilling any of the conditions of my release and parole, but I'm sure the criminal justice system will forget about me soon enough. It ain't like we live in Mayberry."

"I suspect you didn't come here to wish us a Merry Christmas. How did you find out where I live?"

"You remember Mrs. Rossi, my friend and former co-worker, and Gemma's former aunt-in-law? She ran into the lot of you on a walk after work one day, and told me all about what she discovered. I merely looked your address up at the post office. Now I'm here to break up this house of sin and take back my underage daughters."

"'House of sin'?" Girl laughs. "Boy, are you one crazy woman."

Mrs. Troy fixes her gaze on Lenore. "Is that the whore you picked up at the bus stop, Allen? The hooker you moved into your own home with your minor sisters under the same roof? I cannot believe you up and solicited sex at a bus stop, with your own little sisters there, and moved your whore into the apartment with them! If you had to get your jollies off an underage girl, at least you could do it in private, and not live with her outside of marriage! You could be arrested for having intercourse with a minor! I hope to God you're pulling out or making her use them new-fangled birth control pills! I suppose all these strange children are Ernestine's scruffy friends from her misadventure in squatting."

Girl is laughing hysterically. "You're so out in left field it's funny, Mrs. Troy. You don't know how wrong you are about everything. Lenore sleeps on the sofa bed, and she babysits Justine. Ernestine, our friend Julie, me, and my siblings live in the basement. We have a weekly Sunday supper, and Allen was nice enough to invite us to sleep over on

Christmas Eve so we can all have a nice Christmas tomorrow. Don't worry, Ernestine's still in school. She ain't begging and doing odd jobs with us."

"Lenore's our new Sarah!" Justine defends her nanny. "And she's Emeline's best friend."

"For the love of God, Allen, if you was that desperate for a nanny and live-in servant, you coulda put out a want ad, not used your catch of the night to do double duties! Girls, how often have you seen or heard your immoral brother going at it with his whore?"

"Lenore is not a whore, Mother, and I haven't laid a hand on her all these months she's been here. She ran away from home because her father was an abusive degenerate. We've provided her with a nice place to stay and be safe."

"Only disobedient children run away from home. Decent children who respect their parents and are brought up properly let their parents do whatever the hell they want to them till they're old enough to move out. That means putting up with any beatings, incest, or whatever the hell else some parents choose to do in the privacy of their own homes."

"Are you a nutcase?" Boy asks. "Why are you jumping to these wild conclusions? Where's your evidence that Allen and Lenore are going steady?"

"Why the hell should any child have to put up with a parent who beats or rapes her?" Allen yells. "Someday that's gonna be a criminal offense, not something you're supposed to keep a shameful secret and unable to press charges against!"

"You're ruining our Christmas Eve," Adicia says in a small voice.

"I don't give a damn if I ruin your whole week, you stupid mistake. You and your sisters are coming with me, and we're gonna live in the new tenement your father found for us in Hell's Kitchen. There are three rooms, a bedroom, kitchen, and living room. Your father brought Francesco's old phone, so after we save up a little money to afford a phone bill, we'll have that hooked up. You'll get used to the new place soon."

"I'm not coming with you," Ernestine says. "I'm staying with my friends. You already washed your hands of me in April."

"I can explain away your absence to my new friends and neighbors, but not the absence of my other three minor daughters. People in the new building talk about me. They think I'm a bad mother because only one of my children still lives with me, and because I let four of my daughters out of my custody. It's bad enough I've weathered so many other scandals this year."

"I have a newsflash for you, Mother. You *are* a bad mother!" Allen shouts. "You're one of the worst mothers I know of! Real mothers love their children and take care of them instead of forcing them to marry men twenty years older, exposing them to drugs and drinking, purposely living in the worst buildings and neighborhoods, calling them names, telling them every chance you get that they were all mistakes, and feeding them garbage like roadkill and meat with worms! Just to let you know again, Lenore is not a whore. We met her at a bus stop one night while we were waiting out the rain, and my sisters decided to make friends with her. When we found out she was a runaway and had been abused by her father, we offered to let her move in with us. She's so good with the girls, just like Sarah, and she's a great cook too and a wonderful friend for Emeline. What the hell kind of crazy guy do you think I am, Mother, to take my sisters with me when I'm going to pick up girls of ill repute? I've never been with a hooker! Why would I move a girl of ill repute into the apartment with my little sisters? Why would I court trouble by being involved with a minor? None of these wild fantasies you're spinning make any sense!"

"We take the bus instead of the subway so we can watch the city going by," Adicia says. "She looked lonely, so Justine and I went to talk to her. Allen's never gone out on a date since we've lived with him. Lenore doesn't date anyone either."

"Was you born this mean, Mrs. Troy, or did something happen in your life that made you such a bitch?" Girl asks. "My parents might've abandoned me and my siblings, but at least they left us in the care of people who wanted to raise us in the community, and they recognized they didn't wanna be parents. You meanwhile seem to think merely reproducing nine times means you're a good mother, and that it's your right to treat your kids however you want. My mother never once called us stupid, dumb, annoying, idiots, fools, or mistakes. And what's so wrong with meeting a new friend at a bus stop? You act like it's a cocaine den or a brothel, and at three in the morning, not a normal evening hour. Sometimes people meet at the unlikeliest of places, and new friendships or romances blossom. I suppose you're too mean and cynical to believe in the concept of destiny."

"Allen doesn't smoke cigarettes, drink alcohol, or use drugs anymore," Emeline says proudly. "He gave them all up cold turkey so he could be a good example for us and improve his health."

Mrs. Troy looks at him in disgust. "You've turned into a first-rate pansy, Allen. Living in a Bohemian wilderness instead of among your own people, only living with girls, and going straight. You need drugs, smokes, and alcohol to deal with the bad life we was born into. And what kind of red-blooded American man can live with a pretty girl like that and not jump her bones every chance he gets?"

"Now I really know you're crazy," Girl says. "Just a moment ago you was bawling Allen out 'cause you assumed he was being intimate with an underage girl outside of marriage."

"Let's go, girls," Mrs. Troy barks. "Emeline, Adicia, Justine, collect your things and come with me. We're going to the subway, and we'll be home in time for church services. Your father and I picked a Lutheran church this year."

"We're going to an Episcopal church here, St. Luke in the Fields," Adicia says. "Tomorrow morning we're going to open presents. See how pretty we decorated our tree?"

"Boy, are you getting above your raising if you think you're entitled to a real Christmas like them uppity rich kids uptown. Don't make me call for the cops to drag yous away from here. Allen, have fun shacking up with your whore now that there won't be no one else left here. You can screw her whenever and wherever you want, without worrying the girls will walk in or overhear anything."

"That's not fair." Justine starts to cry. "We were looking forward to our first real Christmas."

"Oh, cry me a river, you dumb mistake. Get that white rabbit you always carry around, put your coat on, and wait for me on the fire escape while your sisters are packing."

Justine runs for her rabbit and then runs for Allen, who picks her up and holds her tightly. Mrs. Troy stomps over and tries to pull Justine away from her brother, uncaring her youngest child is screaming and sobbing hysterically.

"You can have my baby sister when you pull her out of my cold dead hands, you evil bitch. I don't know how such an evil woman could produce so many decent kids. Even Gemma turned out decent. That makes seven outta nine kids who don't wanna stay in your belovèd cesspool of poverty."

Adicia and Emeline are stuffing their clothes and other belongings into their schoolbags, their whole bodies shaking. This was definitely not the Christmas Eve they were hoping for, and tomorrow will be just another day yet again. 1963 is going to be an awful year instead of their best year ever.

"Leave your schoolbooks behind for Allen to return, girls," Mrs. Troy calls as she's still trying to tug Justine out of his arms. "You'll be going to new schools in your new school district."

"You're a disgrace to motherhood," Ernestine says.

"Our Christmas presents for you are under our bed," Emeline says as she walks out wearing her coat, her schoolbag over her back.

"Maybe you can boss around those two, but Justine's only three and a half. She deserves to stay here and not have to grow up in bad neighborhoods, with almost no money for anything decent," Girl begs.

"She's my kid, and I'll raise her however the hell I want to!" Mrs. Troy gives one final yank, and Justine slips out of her grip. She cares less Justine falls on the floor and screams.

Lenore rushes over to her. "Are you okay, sweetie? Where does it hurt?"

"So your whore is also a nurse, Allen?" Mrs. Troy asks. "I still can't get over a son of mine hustling for sex at a bus stop!"

"I won't waste my breath explaining to you again that that ain't what I was doing there, and that even if I was gonna look for a hooker, I'd never take along my little sisters." Allen goes into his room and comes out with three packages wrapped in tissue paper. "You can open them tomorrow. I wish you could open them here on a proper Christmas morning, instead of in a hole in the wall in a terrible neighborhood."

"I got you presents too!" Ernestine says. "I put them in the hall closet."

Justine clings to Lenore's neck and looks at her mother with terror. "Do I have to go?"

"You're going whether you like it or not, you stupid mistake. This foolishness here has gone on long enough, and I'm putting a stop to it today."

"What foolishness, me raising my sisters in a healthy environment and giving them a chance to do something in life besides marry young, pop out nine kids, work crummy jobs, make almost no money, and live in the worst places possible?" Allen asks. "Why would you wanna live in a neighborhood with a name like Hell's Kitchen?"

"You're going to Hell, Mrs. Troy," Girl says. "I ain't religious and probably wasn't baptized, but I believe there are punishments in the next life for people who was evil in this life. And I believe the soul lives on, and bad people have to come back to atone for past mistakes or misbehavior. I hope to God you come back as a neglected child yourself."

"I feed, clothe, and house my kids. I don't beat them, rape them, or starve them." Mrs. Troy yanks Justine away from Lenore. "Someone get this little brat's coat. I ain't about to look like a bad mother in public by carting around a kid without a coat in winter."

"It takes more than the bare minimum to be a good mother. Why should you consider yourself a good mother if you only do the basics? A good mother goes above and beyond. She puts her kids in good schools, buys them nice things, makes them good meals, spends lots of time with them, encourages them to make good in life, and raises them in a nice neighborhood. You don't need money to do them things either. There are lots of good mothers who are poor and working-class. They're different from you 'cause they love their kids and do as much for them as they can with what they've got."

"Is Justine going away?" Infant asks sadly. "She's my friend."

"I'm more of a mother to my little brother and sisters than you'll ever be to any of your nine kids. I would ask how that makes you feel, but then I remember you don't have human emotions. You don't give a damn when anyone points out inconvenient truths. You just keep on insisting on living in Mrs. Troy fantasy land, where things are exactly as you paint them, in spite of all the evidence pointing to the exact opposite truth."

Boy goes to fetch Justine's coat and puts it on her. "I hope you're happy you ruined your kids' Christmas, you witch." He hugs Justine. "Remember all of us love you. That oughta matter more than that one evil woman who hates you and treats you so mean."

"Say goodbye to Allen, his whore, and Ernestine and her scruffy friends, girls," Mrs. Troy says. "Emeline, you carry Justine. She won't cooperate if I try to go anywhere near her."

"You know where I live if you ever wanna visit," Allen says as

Mrs. Troy drags Adicia by the hand and Emeline carries Justine, who's still crying and screaming. "Don't ever forget I did right by yous while you were here."

"Allen was gonna go to a judge and have us put under his legal guardianship in the new year," Emeline says. "You ruined our lives just when they were starting to look up."

"You talk to me like I give a damn about any of you. When will you get it through your heads I don't love or even like you? I only love Tommy."

The eight people left stand at the fire escape balcony and watch as Mrs. Troy leads the girls off towards the nearest subway station. Adicia and Emeline carry the presents Allen and Ernestine gave them, while Justine clutches her rabbit. Allen feels close to crying, but remembers it's not considered proper for men to cry. Ernestine clings to her brother's leg and looks on sadly.

"If you want, I can live here from now on," she offers. "I don't want you to feel lonely, and you need someone else here so it won't look like you're living in sin with Lenore."

"I don't have to stay here," Lenore says. "People will talk even here. We all know what's really going on, but strangers won't. I can find a job for a fifteen-year-old with no formal schooling, and move into a cheap place. I have to find a job anyway, now that there's nothing left for me to do all day."

"I'm not about to turn you out in the cold on Christmas Eve," Allen says. "I know it's unconventional and what it looks like, but I want you to stay here. You're my friend, and friends don't abandon their friends."

"Why did Justine's mommy spoil our Christmas?" Infant asks forlornly.

"She was born mean, I'm sure," Girl says. "The only thing we can do now is hope they'll find ways to get away from that poisonous woman."

***

Justine is still crying when they get off the subway. She and Adicia are both terrified of living in a neighborhood named Hell's Kitchen. At least the Lower East Side and Two Bridges had a friendly, home-like quality, in spite of being so run-down. The people they pass in the streets don't look friendly at all, and the buildings and shop fronts look scary as well. Emeline wants to gag when the new tenement comes into view. This is a big downgrade after Gemma and Francesco's apartment. She would've thought her mother had gotten a taste for living in a real apartment instead of mutely accepting their father's decision to move into an old tenement. At least this building looks like it were built in the twentieth century, after new tenement laws came into place, and isn't one of the older ones Jacob Riis wrote about in *How the Other Half Lives*, which she read through the Hudson Park Library last month.

"After we go back to school after Christmas vacation, who's gonna watch Justine during the day?" Emeline asks as their mother turns her key in the front door. "God knows you'll be working for the next thousand years to pay back all that money you embezzled."

"Do you feel stupid now, knowing you went to jail for that and embezzled for nothing?" Adicia asks. "There was never any wedding, so it was all a waste."

"Can Dad use some of his extra money to pay for a nanny or daycare?"

"I'm sure I can find a desperate young thing to take advantage of, the same way I found Sarah. I don't want people to think I'm a bad mother 'cause I put my kid in daycare."

Justine is still crying as they walk up the narrow, crooked, broken stairs, which are at least several levels above the stairs at the old place. When they reach the fourth floor, they bump into a woman holding hands with a dark-haired little boy and carrying a pocketbook. Adicia notices her eyes are the same blue-gray color as Julie's.

"Are you gonna be one of our new neighbors?" Adicia asks.

"I've seen her from time to time," Mrs. Troy says. "She lives across the hall. There are five apartments on each floor. I'm very sorry you have to be subjected to my brat of a youngest child's tantrum. Little mistake thought she was gonna have an uppity, pampered Christmas. I nipped that fantasy in the bud by taking these girls away from their delusional older brother who was tryna teach them to get above their raising."

The woman looks very uncomfortable with Mrs. Troy's abusive language towards her own children. She stoops down to Justine's level and smiles at her. "I'm Mrs. Doyle, and this is my son Matthew. Would you like to come over for milk and cookies sometime? I'm going out for last-minute Christmas shopping, but I'm usually at home, since my only job is homemaking and being Matthew's mommy."

Mrs. Troy's eyes light up. "You don't work? Would you mind having this brat dumped on you during the day? I ain't got no money to hire a babysitter or nanny, and daycare would make me look like a bad mother."

"You have milk and cookies?" Adicia asks excitedly. "Can I come over too?"

Mrs. Doyle smiles at her. "How old are you, darling? I had a little girl once, but then I lost her. You look like you're about the same age she'd be if I still had her."

"I'll be eight and a half next month."

"My daughter was the same age." Mrs. Doyle looks very sad.

"Did your little girl die of a disease or have an accident? How long ago did you lose her?"

"I don't think I want to discuss that. Just seeing you reminded me of my own little girl I used to have."

"Well, will you or won't you babysit this youngest brat of mine?" Mrs. Troy demands. "I ain't got all day to wait for an answer!"

Mrs. Doyle turns to Matthew. "Would you like a new little friend to play with, sweetie?"

Matthew smiles and waves at the girls. "I like new friends."

"Good. That problem was solved quickly." Mrs. Troy unlocks their door and marches in, impatiently waiting for the girls to follow her.

While Allen, Lenore, Ernestine, Julie, and the Ryans go to a nice service at St. Luke in the Fields, Mr. and Mrs. Troy, their three remaining daughters, and Tommy head off to a random Lutheran church for Christmas Eve services that evening. Once again the girls had to suffer through dirty, freezing bathwater, although at least now they have separate towels, thanks to Mr. Troy cleaning out all of Francesco and Gemma's belongings. Mrs. Troy makes comments under her breath about all the Puerto Ricans in the neighborhood as they walk to church.

"Do you happen to know what religion Allen's bus stop whore is?" she asks loudly as they walk into the church.

"You don't care how many times it was explained Lenore isn't a whore and that's not even close to what we were doing at the bus stop," Emeline sighs.

"Lenore was baptized Catholic, but she's not religious, and her parents didn't go to church much," Adicia says.

"Allen's not only in bed with a minor and a whore, but a Papist too?" Mrs. Troy shrills.

"Thank God you girls are safely away from his disgusting web of influence!" Mr. Troy says. "I'm still waiting for the revelation he's a pederast, after all the other shocking revelations we've heard! Would you no longer be surprised to hear he's a pederast too, Dolores?"

"What's a pederast?" Emeline asks.

"A man who has sexual relations with boys," Mr. Troy says matter-of-factly.

Emeline thinks that's disgusting, and can't imagine her brother doing something so immoral and disturbing. After her mother's scene at Allen's apartment, though, defending him is useless. Her parents have their minds made up Allen is a depraved individual and Lenore is a whore, and no amount of contrary evidence will convince them otherwise.

***

On Christmas morning, Tommy opens a toy robot, a new football and set of Lincoln Logs, a box of ten Matchbox cars, Candy Land, and an Etch a Sketch. His stocking contains roasted chestnuts, chocolates, candybars, candied fruit slices, oranges, and a rubber tarantula. Mrs. Troy spent her first paychecks from her new job on presents for Tommy instead of paying back the $5,000 she embezzled. The seriousness of meeting her parole conditions means absolutely nothing to her.

Adicia and her sisters sit on their bed, which also was taken from Two Bridges, as they open their presents. Allen got Adicia a rabbit fur hat, which she always wanted; Ernestine got her a gray scarf cut from some of the extra material on one of the blankets from the coal deliveryman; and Lenore got her a green crocheted cozy for her cups of hot chocolate and tea. Emeline and Justine got the same things from Lenore and Ernestine, only Emeline's cozy is red and Justine's is purple, and Emeline's scarf is tan and Justine's is white. Allen bought Emeline a pair of white flannel pajamas with candy canes on them, and he got Justine a rabbit fur muff. Their stockings are stuffed with nuts, chocolates, candies, oranges, and small trinkets.

"You won't be getting no Christmas presents next year, unless Allen and his whore want to ship them here." Mrs. Troy takes a puff on her cocaine pipe. "Don't you dare get used to the idea of celebrating the holiday like rich kids."

"I guess we really are in Hell now," Emeline mutters to her sisters.

Back in the West Village, Allen and Lenore are unwrapping the presents Adicia and Ernestine made in their art classes. Adicia's third grade class made picture frames with buttons, seashells, rounded pieces of glass, bits of ribbon, and rhinestones glued around the edges. Ernestine's fifth grade class made hand-painted terracotta pots filled with dirt, with an envelope of assorted flower seeds. Emeline made a storage box for spare change, recipe cards, sewing supplies, pens and pencils, bills, and other odds and ends. From Justine, there's a large pinecone Lenore helped her glue colored plastic beads onto.

Ernestine unwraps a red wool jacket with little jingle bells along the waist from Allen, a flowered gingham coin purse from Lenore, a jar of potpourri covered with a lace doily from Adicia, a decorative bar of soap from Emeline, and a family picture Justine drew with Magic Markers. Their mother made a mockery of that family picture when she came marching in there the other day, ruining their Christmas and breaking up their family.

"You think we'll ever be able to be a family again?" she asks glumly as she holds up Justine's picture.

"We're still a family," Allen tries to reassure her. "We're just a family in different places now. Someday, when we're older, we'll all be together again."

"Why does your mother have to be so mean and heartless?" Girl asks. "Decent parents want their kids to do better than they did, not punish them for tryna make good. Why would she want her whole family for every generation to be poor and think that's the best they deserve?"

"They think it's a rejection of them. When you say you wanna go to college, move outta the old neighborhood, and work a steady job that pays well, that's saying not graduating high school, living in crummy places, and making beans for wages ain't good enough for you even though it was good enough for them. It makes them think they're bad people or losers."

"I'd like to go to college when I'm a grownup. My parents would probably be happy about that, if I ever ran into them again. Then again, my parents were better parents than your mother for knowing they didn't wanna raise kids. Your mother thinks all a good parent has to do is have her kids in her custody, while she does jack to take care of 'em."

Allen unwraps a plain white shirt from Lenore, on which she embroidered "#1 Brother" in large characters. Like Justine's family picture, this gift too now seems like a tragic joke.

Lenore unwraps a red cotton apron with black swirls from Allen. He wanted to get something that wasn't too impersonal and wouldn't make it look like he likes her, so he settled on something practical she could use on a regular basis. He's too glum to smile about the thought of Lenore cooking for him and only him.

"We can look on the bright side," Girl says. "One of the grownups at the squat, who studied literature in college, once told us a story about a man who goes to Hell and then goes up through Purgatory and Paradise. He had to go to the lowest place possible before he could start his journey up to happier and prettier places."

"You mean Dante's *Divine Comedy*?" Allen asks.

"I'll take your word for it. You're the one with the high school diploma, not me. The moral of that story was sometimes you have to sink to the worst place possible before you can get better. You might appreciate things more when you've already been through the worst, instead of taking everything for granted or having an easy answer to a bad situation."

"Why don't we put on our coats and take a walk in the park?" Lenore asks. "No use sitting around moping on a holiday."

The usual walk in Washington Square Park does nothing to cheer Allen up. All he can think about is that three of his sisters are in Hell, taken away from him by a spiteful, hateful, black-hearted, vindictive mother whose only claim to them is that she gave birth to them. Emeline is already fourteen and Adicia is almost eight and a half, but Justine is only three and a half. Even if Mrs. Troy succeeds in cheating her older daughters out of what's left of their childhoods, there has to be some hope Justine can be saved before it's too late. If there's any justice left in the world, Justine won't have to spend her entire childhood in the same impoverished, dead-end circumstances the older Troy siblings have been condemned to. If Gemma's sacrifice helped to save Lucine, maybe the sacrifice of Emeline and Adicia will someday save Justine.

Part III: The Conjoined Twins of Agony and Ecstasy (January 1964–December 1969)

Under heaven one can see beauty as beauty only because there is ugliness.
All can know good as good only because there is Evil.
Therefore having and not having arise together.
Difficult and easy complement each other.
Long and short contrast each other; high and low rest upon each other; voice and
sound harmonize each other; front and back follow one another.
(*The Tao Te Ching*, Chapter 2)

Some times are good, some times are bad;
It's all a part of life.
("Crackerbox Palace," ninth track on *Thirty-Three & 1/3*)

Chapter 23: Ernestine and Her Friends' New Home

"Remind me again why I'm doing this?" Allen asks Ernestine as she climbs into the passenger's seat of the bakery's delivery truck.

"Because you're a good big brother, and you love me and care about my friends, even if you're too manly to admit it."

It's the first day of 1964, and Ernestine, Julie, and the Ryans are moving to the Meatpacking District, a small neighborhood just north of the West Village. They've finally found a nice place they can call their own, thanks to Boy's undeterred scouting. They'll be on the fourth floor of a five-story building that used to be a factory of some sort, in a wide-open space like the squat back in The Bowery. Boy crawled in through an open window last week and found this living space, one of two potential living quarters on the floor, all boarded-up on the outside, with signs telling potential intruders to stay out and that it's not for rent. The people who lived there before, whenever that was, left behind a record player and records, a radio, a refrigerator, a stove, several small tables, chairs, a davenport, and a kitchen blender. Boy tested the record player with Pat Boone records, and reported the electricity works. As for what they'll do for money, they'll continue begging, singing, dancing, and doing odd jobs. Ernestine and Girl will be twelve in April, so they'll soon be able to do basic jobs that can earn more money.

"So now you're *really* gonna be alone with Lenore," Girl teases him as she settles down on the pile of mattresses in the back of the truck. "You think you'll finally tell her how you feel about her soon?"

"She's only sixteen and a half. That was still underage last I checked."

"It ain't like you're thirty or she's thirteen. There are only three years between yous guys. Ain't you afraid she'll get interested in another guy? Who knows, maybe she thinks you prefer men since you've never gone on a date in all the time she's known you."

"I couldn't even hug her when President Kennedy was assassinated. I told her I wished I could, and she said she wished she could too, but even a tragedy like that couldn't make her comfortable with being touched by a man, even in a non-threatening way."

"I'm glad I'll still go to the same school," Ernestine says. "I don't wanna switch schools twice or have my sixth grade graduation ceremony with a bunch of strangers."

"I wish I could go to school," Baby says. "What grade would I be in if I went to school?"

"First. Most kids start first grade when they're six, and turn seven during the school year. Infant would start kindergarten in the fall if she was in school."

"Why can't I start school?" Infant asks as Allen starts driving.

"We have no parents or guardians, no real permanent address," Girl says. "And we have no birth certificates or real names. Our parents couldn't even be bothered to give us names like Mary, John, Elizabeth, and Jane."

"Are you gonna give our new address to our sisters?" Ernestine asks. "We won't be that far of a walk from them."

"Of course I'll let them know," Allen says.

"Who's gonna be closer to Lenore's job now, us or them?" Boy asks.

"She's about midway between yous guys. I'm glad she never has reason to go into their crummy neighborhood, since my mother's still up in arms about her existence. Emeline told me on the phone last week that our mother still calls her 'the bus stop whore.' Maybe our parents would only go to a bus stop for drugs or a hooker, but normal people use them for their intended purposes."

Lenore got a job writing press releases for an art gallery a few months after Mrs. Troy ruined Christmas 1962 for her children. The people who run the Chelsea gallery didn't care she's never had a day of formal schooling. The most important thing is she knows how to write good descriptions of art and how to entice people to come to the shows and auctions. In the evenings, when she's not at work, she goes to night school in Greenwich Village to earn a high school equivalency diploma. Allen feels a little inferior to her, since the marks she gets in her classes are mostly higher than the ones he got in high school, though she does struggle a little in her mathematics classes.

"Are we gonna enter and exit by the windows?" Julie asks. "I don't want people to think we're breaking in, find out we have no parents, and throw us in an orphanage."

"I cut a door-size opening in some of the boarded-up front wall on my second trip there," Boy says. "It blends in perfectly. You'd never notice it was there unless you looked really closely and carefully. Plus the building is so old it don't need a key."

"Did the building look very occupied?" Baby asks. "I don't want anyone getting suspicious."

"I think the cops are more concerned with real crime like murder and robbery than cracking down on a couple of young squatters," Girl says. "It ain't like we'll be making enough noise to wake the dead."

"My mother has the same attitude," Ernestine says. "She hasn't paid back a single penny of all that dough she embezzled. If I was the judge, I'd demand each paycheck automatically goes to the bank she stole from, instead of letting her get the paycheck and do whatever she wants with it. Last I heard from Adicia, she's using it to buy drugs, alcohol, cigarettes, and presents for Tommy."

Girl starts laughing. "I'm sorry, I know it ain't funny, but I can't help but laugh every time I remember your mother's bizarre ranting when I had the misfortune of meeting that evil bitch. She has such ridiculous, selective morality. She don't even realize what a silly hypocrite she is. It's like those people who think it's a sin to end an unplanned pregnancy, but don't have a problem with getting pregnant outside of marriage in the first place."

"Can we hang up pretty pictures on our new walls?" Infant asks. "I miss the pretty pictures and other things we hung up at the squat."

"We'll hang up whatever we want and make it a nice home for ourselves. When we break even with our money, maybe we can buy records, books, and knick-knacks."

As they get closer to the new building, Boy stands up and cranes his neck to try to see out the front window. He begins pointing as a large brick building comes into view. It's the third building on a quiet, nice-looking street. Several people in nice clothes are walking, and a few other vehicles drive by. There aren't many cars parked on the nearby streets, and all the neighboring buildings are well-kept, no broken windows or dilapidated fronts. It looks almost like the now-familiar street settings of the Village. They smile upon realizing they haven't downgraded.

"How are we gonna move our stuff in without being exposed as squatters, though?" Girl asks.

"It's New Year's Day," Boy says. "Ain't barely any people around to catch us. Most people go away this time of year. Even if people say hello to us, I don't think they'll be so rude to ask if we're squatters.

Ain't nonea their business, and I don't think they'd assume we are right away. For all I know, somea the other residents are squatters too. So long as the landlord don't find out there are unauthorized tenants."

Allen finds a free space to parallel-park. "Anyone up to helping me hoist the mattresses outta the back? It's not good to let them get wet with snow. It'll take a long time for them to dry."

Ernestine, Girl, and Boy scramble out and lift the other end of the mattresses. No one stops to stare at them or seems to think this scene is anything out of the ordinary. Anyone who glances their way assumes they're new people moving into the building.

"Look at the nice big elevator we've got," Boy points out proudly when they get inside. "They musta needed all this elevator space when the building was a factory."

"I like it already," Baby announces. "It's older than the basement, but it's old in a good way."

When they get up to the fourth floor, Boy shows them where he discreetly cut the door-sized opening in the boarded-up outer wall of the abandoned apartment. He swings it open, and Allen unties the mattresses so he can fit them in the door one by one. Infant and Baby stay behind to get acquainted while the others go back out to the truck for the rest of their things.

"What's this?" Infant asks.

"Girl says that's called a record player," Baby says. "It plays music on black round things. The old owners left somea their records behind, but Girl says they're boring old people music. When we break even with money, we can buy music by popular singers. Won't that be nice? We can listen to music while we eat our supper or play games in the evening."

"How come they left so much of their stuff behind?"

"Maybe they was evicted, or they had to run away, and no one ever came back for their stuff. Too bad for them. It's ours now."

Ernestine steps out of the elevator first, carrying what used to be her father's suitcase, when she and the others come back carting the rest of their belongings. As she's walking to their apartment, a girl across the hall walks out and approaches them. She has long brown hair in braids, deep brown eyes, and is wearing a blue dress.

"You're moving into that boarded-up place? I didn't know it was for rent or sale."

"Yup, we're your new neighbors," Girl says, trying to sound as nonchalant as possible. "There's me, me brother, my two sisters who are already inside, and my two friends here. The older guy is my friend Ernestine's big brother Allen. He's only helping us move, and won't be living here."

The girl looks at them a bit sadly. "You don't have parents, grandparents, or any other grownups living with you? Did a rich relative leave yous guys money, and that's how you can live by yourselves?"

"We'll get by. We always do. My friend Julie has a mother somewhere, but she's with us in the meantime."

"So you're orphans?"

"Not exactly," Ernestine says. "I left home the month I turned ten, and Julie joined us about a month later. My folks are sorry excuses for parents, Julie's father was a degenerate who's now dead, and my other friends' parents had no interest in kids and left them in the care of their community. We just moved from my brother Allen's basement because we wanted a place all our own. This isn't far from where he lives."

"Our last name is Ryan," Girl says. "They call me Girl, and my brother's called Boy. Our little sisters in there are Baby and Infant."

The girl from across the hall looks at them with pity. "Those are your real names? Your parents couldn't even call you something common like Mary or John?"

"What they called me is the way I'm staying. At least for now. They might make me take a real name when I go to college and they need something grownup to call me."

The girl looks at them hesitantly for a minute, then holds out her hand. "I'm Betsy van Niftrik. If you want, you can come over and visit me if my parents say they're okay with it. I can ask them if it's okay for me to visit you too. I think we're about the same age. I'll be twelve in March."

"Ernestine and I will be twelve in April," Girl says, unexpectedly excited at the thought of a new friend already. "Julie and Boy are nine, Baby's six, and Infant's four."

Betsy disappears into her apartment and comes back with her parents. Allen hopes they aren't about to ask where these children are getting the money to rent the place on their own, or why they're living alone without any grownups.

"Hello. I'm Mr. van Niftrik, and this is Mrs. van Niftrik. Betsy told us we're getting new neighbors about her age. She asked if she could go over and visit them, and if they can return the favor. We'd be delighted to invite you over. All Betsy's friends are from school, since there aren't any children her age in the building."

"Hello, Mr. and Mrs. van Niftrik," Ernestine says cheerfully, shaking their hands. "I'm Ernestine Troy, and these are my friends Julie Spirnak and Girl and Boy Ryan. The older guy is my big brother Allen."

"Those are really their names, Mom and Dad," Betsy says. "Mr. and Mrs. Ryan couldn't be bothered to give their children real names before they left them."

"Betsy mentioned you have two other sisters," Mrs. van Niftrik says. "Would you like to invite them over too? We'd love to serve yous guys hot chocolate and fresh chocolate chip cookies."

"My mom's a good cook," Betsy says invitingly.

"Can Allen come too?" Ernestine asks. "We can wait a little while to finish unpacking and setting up our new home."

"I wouldn't dream of issuing an invitation to some people and not others. You can come over for hot chocolate and cookies too, young man. You're awfully handsome. I'm sure you have your pick of the ladies."

"Allen likes one girl in particular, but he's too shy to tell her he likes her." Ernestine grins at her brother. "He's liked her since he first laid eyes on her a year and a half ago."

"She's three years my junior." Allen blushes. "She's sixteen and I'm nineteen. If I still like her when she's eighteen, I'll tell her how I feel then."

"You're not only good-looking, but a gentleman too," Mrs. van Niftrik says approvingly. "We can tell our new neighbors are of good stock."

Girl goes into their new apartment and comes back holding hands with Baby and Infant, who look curiously at their new neighbors. Mrs. van Niftrik smiles down at them, feeling sorry they have no mother.

"We're really invited for cookies and hot chocolate?" Baby asks. "But we don't even know you."

"It's our neighborly duty to give a warm welcome to newcomers," Mr. van Niftrik says. "Maybe tomorrow, after you've unpacked and settled in, you can join Betsy, Mrs. van Niftrik, and myself when we go sledding in Central Park. Betsy just got a wonderful new sled from her uncle for Christmas."

Ernestine and her friends look at one another in astonished disbelief. They can hardly believe their good luck at finding a new friend already, and that she has such nice, understanding parents. Maybe this is how real parents are supposed to be, and they have no familiarity with them to know the difference. Ernestine wishes she had parents like Betsy's.

"I want cookies," Julie says. "My mommy used to make really good cookies. She used to always invite neighbor kids over for milk and cookies when my daddy was out. I lost her when she divorced my daddy and the judge wouldn't let her have me. They took my daddy's side even though he was a very bad man. They thought my mommy was lying about how awful he was."

"Then it's settled," Mrs. van Niftrik says. "All seven of yous are coming over for something to eat, and we can get to know each other a little better."

***

The next night, when they've finished unpacking and have settled into their new living quarters, Ernestine lies on her mattress with Girl, unable to believe the great good fortune they've walked into. They haven't downgraded at all. This is even better than the squat. It would be wonderful if they could stay here in peace for the next six and a half years, until Ernestine graduates. The icing on the cake is that they have a new friend across the hall, and her parents don't seem to care they live by themselves. They probably will never starve, even if they don't pick up enough money to buy food every week, since Mr. and Mrs. van Niftrik have invited them to come over and eat any time they want to.

"The stars are pretty from our new windows," Baby says. "One of the grownups at the squat said stars look different when you're in different places."

"She meant when you're in different parts of the world, sweetie," Girl says. "We're just in a different place in the same town. They'd look a lot different if we was in a place like South America, Australia, or India."

"The sky's so bright and pretty, even if the stars are the same.

Sometimes we can't see the stars so good 'cause there's too much light or smoke getting in the way."

"It's nice to know we're under the same night sky as my four favorite sisters," Ernestine says. "No matter where we are, we're under the same stars. We're not really that far apart if we're all looking at the same stars tonight and are all in each other's hearts."

Chapter 24: Emeline Escapes

January 20, Monday, is Lucine's eighteenth birthday, and she wants nothing more than to talk to her sisters again and to know they're alright. The party thrown for her by her friends at the Murphys' school is the kind of thing she used to dream of back in her tenement days—dinner at a private room in a nice uptown restaurant, dancing to records by popular singers, going to a new movie and sitting on one of the balconies, then back to the boarding school, where they have pigs in a blanket, deviled eggs, bite-sized chocolates, egg creams, and soda pop while Lucine opens presents. Though it's a school night, they're allowed to stay up a bit late because it's Lucine's coming of age birthday, something that only comes once in a lifetime.

Lucine can't call her sisters even if they have a phone, since their parents are supposed to believe she's dead. Her only hope is Allen. While her friends slowly drift off to bed so they can be up in time for school tomorrow, Lucine asks the house mother if she can look in the phonebook and use the phone.

To her surprise, she sees Antoine and Dolores Troy listed. She wonders how many drugs they had to sell to afford a phone and a monthly bill, or if they stole the phone at Gemma and Francesco's place. Come to think of it, they probably did steal everything they could from that apartment. She wonders if they stayed only for the remainder of Francesco's lease, or if they remained there a bit longer. Then she sees Allen Troy listed. She hopes this is indeed her one good brother, since most men with that name spell it Allan or Alan. If it is, it can only mean he's moved up in life enough to be able to afford a monthly phone bill, presumably through legit means instead of selling drugs or embezzling.

"Hello?" she hears a strange female voice asking after the operator connects her to what she hopes is Allen's number.

"Oh, I'm sorry, I must have the wrong number. I thought this was Allen Troy."

"Allen lives here. He just went to bed, but I can bring him to the phone. Who shall I say is calling?"

Lucine's mind boggles at the thought of her brother having a woman in the apartment overnight, and wonders if this is a live-in girlfriend or just a girl he's having at the moment. "I wanna surprise him. Just tell him it's someone from his past."

Lenore feels a twinge of jealousy, wondering if this is one of Allen's many ex-girlfriends who might want to get back together with him. She quietly opens his door and softly calls his name. When he doesn't answer, she timidly sits on the bed and starts gently shaking him awake. He looks like an angel with his eyes closed, and she wonders what it'd be like to sleep next to him instead of in the girls' old bed, which she switched to sleeping on after Mrs. Troy ruined everyone's Christmas.

Allen slowly opens his eyes, somewhat annoyed at being woken up until he realizes Lenore is on his bed and touching him. Living with a girl he's had feelings for for an entire year and a half and not able to act on his feelings is a special kind of torture. If only she were already eighteen and weren't so traumatized by what her sick father did to her, he'd tear her clothes off and have his way with her, finally able to channel that past year and a half of pent-up frustration.

"Is something the matter?" He hopes she doesn't hear his heart beating so loudly.

"Someone called on the phone for you and said she was someone from your past."

"At this hour?"

"She said she wanted to surprise you, and didn't give me a name."

Allen gets out of bed and goes to the phone. "Hello? Who's calling me this late?"

Lucine starts crying at the sound of her brother's voice. She didn't know for sure if she'd ever see or talk to any of her siblings ever again, apart from a few times she saw Gemma that first summer uptown.

"Who is this, a crank caller?"

"It's me, Lucine," she manages to choke out.

"Lucine?" he asks in shock. "Where are you?"

"I'm in my boarding school in Yorkville. My friends and I just celebrated my birthday, and I wanted to try to get in touch with someone from our family to make my greatest birthday wish come true."

He looks over at the calendar and notes the date. "I guess it is your birthday today. Happy eighteenth birthday, little sister."

"Thank you. Can you make my birthday even better by telling me the rest of our sisters are safe with you and not with our awful parents?"

"I can tell you Ernestine's in a safe place, but unfortunately, the other three are with our parents in Hell's Kitchen. I tried my best to keep them, but our witch of a mother came over here after she got outta prison, on Christmas Eve 1962, and dragged them away from me."

Lucine gasps. "Mother was in prison? They're in Hell's Kitchen of all places now? And she had the audacity to destroy Christmas for her own children? Now I really know she has no heart or soul."

"They came to live with me on Adicia's eighth birthday, and we had it really good for five months. I even found them a substitute for Sarah, the girl who answered the phone. They were going to school in the Village, eating great food, doing fun things, and having a great time for the first time ever, till Mother put a stop to it. Ernestine and her friends came here a month after us, when their squat was raided. They squatted in my basement till a few weeks ago, when they moved into an abandoned apartment in the Meatpacking District. Don't worry, they have it real good there. They made friends with a girl across the hall, and the girl's parents are very friendly and sympathetic. They're not about to turn them in to the authorities, and they often invite them over to eat and do things with them, like sledding or skating in Central Park."

"What's that you said about Mother having been in jail? When in the world did that happen?"

"She was arrested by an undercover cop on Adicia's eighth birthday, just as I was taking them outta there. We sent Tommy across the hall to friends till Dad got home. He was just gonna arrest her for the embezzling, but then he smelled what was coming from her pipe and charged her with using and possessing drugs too. She served only four months, unfortunately, and hasn't paid back any of the five thousand bucks she embezzled. She hasn't fulfilled any of the other conditions of her release either. She got ten years probation. Carlos was supposed to stand trial for arson, drugs, and petty theft, but he's still in the hospital, so they can't do anything about charging him or sending him to jail."

"What are you talking about? Why is Carlos in the hospital, or don't I wanna know?"

"He'll only be twenty-one next month. Even if he did cause this by his own drug use and stupidity, I can't say I envy him being crippled at such a young age. He was high at work, and didn't fasten a car jack tightly enough. While he was fixing a car, it came crashing down on him and crushed his spinal column. Dad let the hospital declare him a ward of the state while Mother was in the clink, so he wouldn't have to be stuck with his hospital bills. He was drifting in and out of consciousness for a long time, and finally regained his senses a few months back. Mother went to see him recently, and he was carrying on like a madman. Since he was in and out of it for so long, it never got a chance to sink in that he's a useless cripple who's gonna spend the rest of his life in a wheelchair."

"Wow. I never liked Carlos, but even I don't think he deserved to be paralyzed, and so young too." Lucine is trying to take in all these facts one at a time, but can't wrap her brain around some of them. "I'll give you the number for my school. The Episcopal priest and his wife who run it are sponsoring me, and adopted Giovanni. I've talked to them a few times about Emeline coming here and being sponsored too. I want so much to see her again, and for her to have a chance to go to a real school and do something with all her smarts. Someone who's so intelligent and well-read doesn't deserve to suffer through terrible public schools in the worst parts of the city. She'll be sixteen in May, so our parents will probably be chomping at the bit to marry her off to a repulsive guy twenty years older. You've gotta help me save her."

Allen reaches for a notepad and a pencil to write down the numbers and addresses Lucine gives him. "It probably won't be easy, but I'll do everything in my power to get Emeline to you. She should have a chance to make something of herself at a nice school while she's still got a few years left to be a teenager."

"Do you think little Adicia has what it takes to be the oldest sister, if Emeline can escape? Since Ernestine no longer lives at home, Adicia would be forced into the role of the biggest sister a lot earlier than she's probably ready for it. She's only nine and a half, and has already been cheated outta most of her entire childhood."

"Does she really have a choice? She'll have to get used to the role, whether she's old enough or not. I think her love for Justine and her commitment to protecting her will help her. Maybe she'll save our baby sister from this black hole of despair our parents thrive in."

"I hope so. Listen, I have to get to bed soon, but I have one more question for you. Who was that woman who answered the phone? You said she was like a substitute for Sarah, but that doesn't explain why she still lives with you! Did you decide to make her your girlfriend and shack up with her?"

"She's three years younger than me. We're just roommates. Mother thinks differently, and is convinced she's a whore because we met her at the bus stop. She thinks I was out hustling for sex and had our sisters along with me, and moved this so-called hooker into the apartment. What type of completely immoral degenerate does she take me for? This girl was running away from her abusive dad, and we gave her a safe home. Her name's Lenore, and she's Emeline's best friend." He pauses. "I hope I didn't ruin your birthday by telling you so many depressing things."

"Knowing our family, I didn't exactly expect to hear positive reports. I didn't expect you'd lie to me to protect my feelings. Well, have a good night's sleep, and give your friend my thanks for taking care of our sisters. I'll talk to you again soon, I hope."

"That was your sister Lucine?" Lenore asks after he hangs up. "Is she in a good place? Where is she?"

"She's in an Episcopal boarding school up in Yorkville, run by the couple who adopted my baby nephew Giovanni. They took her in when she ran away. Today's her eighteenth birthday."

"You said something about taking Emeline to her? How are you gonna do that?"

"I can't be implicated. My mother would never let my sisters visit or talk to us ever again if she thought I was the one who helped Emeline run away. I work six days a week, so I can't go there in the middle of the week or even on Saturday. Our mother doesn't hold a regular job, since she's always getting fired or quitting after a few weeks or months, so we can't predict her schedule and plan around when she'll be outta the tenement. Probably the only way would be to do it in the middle of the night, though I don't like the idea of walking around unarmed in that neighborhood after dark."

"You'd go into Hell's Kitchen by yourself in the middle of the night? Aren't there gang fights there?"

"The alternative is worse. I'm not about to sit by as my little sister is forced to quit school and marry an abusive drug dealer twenty years her senior. The girl is a walking encyclopedia, learnt to read when she was all of three years old, without anyone teaching her, and has always read several grade levels up. In a decent family and a decent school, her brilliance would've been recognized years ago, and she would've skipped a grade, maybe even two grades. If she can get into this school, she'll thrive and be given work that's up to her advanced level. Who knows, she might be able to start college early too."

***

Emeline is now a high school sophomore, and bored and unchallenged as always in English, history, art, and French. Her geometry and chemistry classes give her a bit of a hard time, but then again, math and science haven't been her strong suit for awhile. Home economics is absolutely boring, but she gets good marks in that class as well. When she's not doing homework, she goes to the Columbus Library and gets as many books as her card allows, taking Adicia and Justine with her so they don't fall behind in their reading and self-teaching. Adicia, now in fourth grade, reads about two grade levels up thanks to all the encouragement she got with reading and being read to over the years, and Justine, who'll be five in March, now reads simple books on her own. Emeline and Adicia are glad Justine won't be alone when she starts kindergarten in September, since Adicia will be in the elementary school for two more years and be able to protect their baby sister.

They're sitting on their bed and reading their newest library books in the middle of the week, Emeline putting off her boring math homework, when the phone rings. Half-expecting it to be a drug dealer, a debt collector, or Mrs. Troy's parole officer, Emeline gets up to answer it.

"Emeline, are our parents home, or is it safe to talk openly?"

"Oh, it's only you, Allen. We're always scared it's someone of ill repute or someone who wants back rent, since our parents don't have many legit friends. Is everything alright?"

"You're alone? Is Tommy there? Knowing him, he'd blab everything to our immoral mother."

"He's with friends on the second floor. Mother hates that they're Puerto Rican, but she can't do anything about it when she's not home."

"I have very good news. I got a call from Lucine a few days ago on her birthday. She's in boarding school in Yorkville and is doing fine. She wants to know if it's possible for you to join her."

"Lucine's okay? It's been so long since we heard from her, I was starting to wonder if we'd ever find her again!"

"Allen heard from Lucine?" Adicia asks excitedly. "Is she with him?"

"Do you have her contact information? I'd love to see her again, but I can't abandon Adicia and Justine when they're so young. Who'd protect them from our parents and serve as a buffer?"

"Look at the facts, Emeline. You'll be sixteen in four months, and you know what that means. You don't wanna be forced to drop outta school and marry an older swine, do you? Your whole life should be ahead of you at this age, not about to end prematurely."

Emeline looks over at her little sisters, who are only nine and four. They depend on her for so much and probably won't know what to do without her to protect them and encourage them to do well in school, but then again, they're pretty resilient. They've adapted to a lot of things most children from the other side of the tracks wouldn't be able to handle, and would probably eventually learn how to get along by themselves, no more older sisters to look out for them and make sure they're doing okay. Children from families like theirs don't grow up expecting anything to be handed to them on a silver platter.

"What do I have to do?" she asks, her voice shaking.

"We can only do this in the middle of the night, since our parents would never be outta the tenement at a time when I'd be able to help you. Do you know how to leave without waking our parents up?"

"I can leave without making much noise, but I'm not about to walk around in this violent neighborhood in the middle of the night."

"I'll be waiting for you so you won't have to walk alone."

"I can't do it without you. Can you sneak into the tenement?"

"I can't sneak in there without causing a disturbance. Even if you left a window open, it's the middle of winter, and there's only one bedroom. Our parents might wake up and see me, and blow our cover. Don't worry, I'll be waiting for you in front of the tenement."

"I suppose I won't be able to disclose my whereabouts to anyone."

"You're going away?" Adicia asks sadly. "Why are you leaving us?"

"When are we gonna do this?" Emeline tries her hardest to ignore Adicia's questions.

Allen looks at his calendar. "February first, Saturday night. Don't our parents usually go out drinking or drugging on the weekends after work? That gives you a little over a week to do what you need there and say goodbye."

"In the middle of the school year?"

"Your school doesn't teach you beans. It's not for smart kids like you. You'll join Lucine's school. It's run by an Episcopal church, but they're a pretty cool group. The church I go to, St. Luke in the Fields, is very progressive, not the type of church that tells you you're going to Hell for every little perceived infraction. I don't think they're gonna demand you become a full-blown, practicing, believing Christian."

"Do I have to pay them back? Boarding school isn't free."

"Lucine spoke to the priest and his wife about you being sponsored like she is. You'd go there on a full scholarship. It's a school for disadvantaged girls, so they don't expect their students to pay thousands of dollars, and to immediately repay any loans."

Emeline looks at her sisters. "I don't wanna leave, but I know you're right about what'll happen if I stay much longer. I'll be ready by the first of next month."

Adicia and Justine look at her sadly after she hangs up. They can barely believe Emeline would think about deserting them, after they already lost Lucine, Ernestine, and Allen.

"Lucine wants me to join her at her boarding school uptown. I won't have to pay anything, and I'd finally be in a school where my talents are respected instead of ignored."

"I'm too young to be the big sister," Adicia protests. "I'm only nine and a half."

"You can go see Ernestine if you ever need anything."

"I don't wanna live in this bad place alone. I've always been the little sister. I don't know how to be the big sister."

Emeline looks at her sadly. "I know you'll do fine. You'll learn how to be the best oldest sister you can be before you know it. You've already been a super big sister to Justine her entire life. You did great taking her and Giovanni to the mission."

"Hell's Kitchen makes me miss the Lower East Side, The Bowery, and Two Bridges."

"Will we ever see you again?" Justine asks.

"We'll see each other again someday. It might seem like a long time, but I've read that when you're a grownup, time passes a lot quicker. Five or ten years is no big deal to a grownup, though it seems like forever to us."

"Are we supposed to pretend you're dead too?"

"Not unless there's another fire. Just let them think I ran away and you had no idea where I went. Allen's gonna help me, so don't worry I'll be walking alone in the middle of the night."

"Does this mean I have to run away when I'm older?" Adicia asks.

"We'll have to wait and see what happens. But whatever does happen, I have to count on you to be very brave and to look after Justine. You'll be the only one left to take care of her and protect her."

"I'd never leave Justine." Adicia squeezes their baby sister's hand. "She's our baby, and we love her too much to throw her to the wolves."

"When will we see you again?" Justine asks.

"I have no idea, but we have to believe we'll all meet again in better times. You're a grownup a lot longer than you're a kid or a teenager, though it seems like forever we've been stuck in this crummy life. All of us will have the best grownup lives we can dream of, and we'll make up for how we had such rotten childhoods."

"You'll never get to find out if Mrs. Doyle has a boy or a girl," Justine protests. "Today she told me she has a baby in her belly. Matthew will be a big brother."

"I'll have to catch up on everyone's news when it's safe for all of us to be together again. I won't go away right now. I have about a week and a half left."

"You'll never forget us or stop thinking about us, will you?" Adicia begs.

"I'll never forget my sweet little sisters as long as I'm on this Earth. Don't think of it as goodbye, but more like till we meet again."

***

Emeline watches the clock as February first, Saturday, turns into February second, Sunday. She spent the day packing her clothes and paltry other belongings into her schoolbag, now quite worn after ten years, and putting anything extra into her pillowcase. Only Mr. and Mrs. Doyle across the hall know what's going to happen at about 1:00 in the morning. True to form, Mr. and Mrs. Troy are both still out drinking at their favorite local bar. Most weekends, they don't come home till at least 3:00 A.M., and are always falling-down drunk and usually high as well. They won't notice right away that one of their despised daughters is missing without a trace.

Allen stands outside the tenement and notices almost everyone's lights out. The few lit windows are obscured by curtains. He creeps around to the back and goes up the fire escape, trying to avoid falling on icy patches in the dark. When he's at the fourth level, he knocks on the window, hoping he's got the right apartment.

A strange man pulls aside the curtains and opens the window. "You must be Allen Troy. The apartment you want is across the hall. Don't worry, we like your sisters and won't tell your parents anything."

"Would you like warm milk and something to eat before you go back into the cold night?" Mrs. Doyle asks. "Your parents won't be back for a few more hours, so there's no rush to get away."

"Oh, no, I don't wanna take your food and impose on yous in the middle of the night."

"I insist. In fact, bring all three of your sisters over here for warm milk and food."

Emeline is putting her bone-thin coat on as Allen knocks on their door. Tommy is out like a light and doesn't stir when the door opens and their older brother enters.

"We have an invitation with the Doyles to eat something before we go," he whispers. "Is that okay?"

Justine is very drowsy, but has kept herself awake because she didn't want to miss saying goodbye to Emeline. "Mrs. Doyle makes yummy food," she says from the davenport.

They tiptoe across the hall, Tommy still in a deep sleep. Mrs. Doyle is already heating a pot of milk on the stove and scooping chocolate pudding into another pot.

"My wife lost her daughter from her first marriage a number of years ago, and feels it's her duty to take care of any neglected kids she finds," Mr. Doyle says as he sets the table. "Adicia's just about the age her daughter would've been. She was born two months before Adicia."

"You were married to another man before Mr. Doyle, Mrs. Doyle?" Justine asks. "Are you divorced or a widow?"

"I'm divorced," Mrs. Doyle says uncomfortably. "We never mention his name. He was a very bad man."

"Our big sister Gemma's divorced too," Adicia comforts her. "She was married to a very bad guy too. I also have a friend whose parents are divorced, though her dad's dead now, and she doesn't live with her mother anymore."

"Maybe your new baby will be a girl, and you can get another chance to have a little girl," Justine suggests.

Allen looks embarrassed. "I didn't know you were expecting. You shouldn't exert yourself to serve us a snack in your condition."

Emeline gives him a look. "Oh, please, Allen. You're the third of nine kids, and you think a pregnant woman's an automatic invalid? You haven't been around many pregnant women lately, I guess."

"Pardon me for asking, Mrs. Doyle, but that rubella epidemic going around is really scary. Is your baby in any danger of being deformed?"

"Oh, no, I had rubella when I was twelve. Poor Matthew just got over it, but thankfully I was able to take care of him without catching it again as an adult. I'd do the right thing if I did get rubella while expecting, of course. I don't want a deformed or defective baby."

Adicia laps up the warm pudding and milk set in front of them. Emeline helps Justine with hers, since she's so sleepy.

"So are we taking the subway?" Emeline asks. "Not a lot of cabs come through here, 'cause they're afraid of the locals."

"I'll go with you," Allen says. "I'm not letting my fifteen-year-old sister walk alone in this seedy place at this hour, let alone take the subway alone period. Lucine said she'd be up to greet us. Just think, you'll get to see little Giovanni again. How old is he now, three?"

"A bit over two and a half."

"Giovanni must not remember us anymore," Adicia says. "Do you think he misses us?"

"He knows Father and Mrs. Murphy as his parents, and Lucine as his aunt. I'm sure they're not keeping his adoption a secret, and won't be upset if he wants to meet Gemma when he's older."

As soon as they finish eating, Emeline stands up and puts her coat back on, putting on her schoolbag backwards. She doesn't want to risk a tough cutting the straps. Allen carries the pillowcase and takes her by the hand.

"We'll see each other again someday, when all of our lives are better," Emeline promises Adicia and Justine as she hugs them tightly. "Remember, this isn't goodbye, just till we meet again."

Adicia and Justine stand at the Doyles' window waving goodbye to Emeline as she and Allen disappear into the night. It seems as though Emeline's going to another universe far, far away and that it'll be centuries before they meet again. Adicia longs for the time they lived on the Lower East Side, because however miserable their existence was, at least they were all together in one home as a family. Now, in the space of only a year and a half, their family has shrunken to only Adicia, Justine, and Tommy. Their former life might have been even harder, but it was comforting in its predictability. Now she can only hope she has what it takes to step into the role of biggest sister in her severely shrunken family.

Chapter 25: Magically Medicinal Music

"Wanna come over to my place and watch *Ed Sullivan*?" Betsy asks Ernestine as they play Aggravation, which Betsy brought over this Sunday afternoon.

"You mean watch television?" Julie asks excitedly. "Sure, I'd watch anything on television, even a station pattern!"

"I've never watched television except for in store windows," Ernestine says longingly. "Isn't *Ed Sullivan* a variety show?"

"He has musical acts," Betsy says. "It's on every Sunday at eight. Tonight there's a British group called The Beatles. They have the number one record in America right now. I have their single. It's called 'I Want to Hold Your Hand,' and it's very good. I can bring it over and play it on your record player now, unless you wanna wait for the show tonight."

"We haven't thought about buying popular records," Girl says. "We've been waiting to break even with our begging and odd job money before buying stuff we don't need to get by."

"I don't wanna miss it. I've been waiting to see this group in person since December. All of you are welcome to come over tonight to watch it with me. My parents will make us popcorn and egg creams."

"It might be fun," Ernestine concedes. "We do need a break from being miniature grownups sometimes."

"What kinda music do they make?" Boy asks. "I hope it ain't like this boring Pat Boone stuff the former owners left behind."

"They do rock music," Betsy says. "Like The Beach Boys or The Four Seasons. You've liked those bands when I've played their records."

"My oldest sister Gemma liked Elvis," Ernestine says. "Our parents thought he sounded like a cat in heat, whatever that means. Gemma's ex-husband said he couldn't sing or act his way out of a paper bag, which is a funny expression I don't know the meaning of either. She had popular records by Negro singers too, though our parents don't approve of Negroes."

"They don't sound like Elvis. I'm not such a big Elvis fan myself. My favorites are still The Four Seasons. Elvis seems like a nice guy, but his old records aren't my style. The records he cuts now are kinda boring, like he sold out to the people who useta complain he was too rough around the edges."

"Your parents are pretty neat for letting you listen to rock music," Girl says. "I've heard a lot of parents don't approve of popular music."

"My parents don't care yous guys are squatting. They're very open-minded and progressive about almost everything."

Infant reaches for a grape in the bowl of fruit on the coffeetable. "Will we really get to watch a real television tonight?"

"Yes, we'll watch television for the first time in our lives," Girl tells her smilingly. "We're going to watch a popular music group from England."

"Where's England?" Baby asks.

"It's across the ocean from us," Ernestine says. "It's an island that's part of Europe. There are two other countries on the same island, Scotland and Wales. England's in the middle. Together with Northern Ireland, they make up the United Kingdom. Betsy, do you know where in England this group is from?"

"Liverpool. It's a sailing city on the coast and along the Mersey River."

"I don't remember if I've ever heard a British accent before," Girl says. "I only remember one of the grownups at the squat once said an English person can make a shopping list sound like Shakespeare."

"What's Shakespeare?" Infant asks.

"He was the greatest writer of all time, at least in the English language," Ernestine says. "Emeline and Lucine read some of his sonnets and plays in their English classes, and they said it was almost impossible to understand without a lot of footnotes. He wrote in a form of English we don't use anymore. Emeline said his appeal over the centuries is more about how he was a writer for all time, with characters and stories that seem real in any era or place."

"English people drop their Rs and use long As," Betsy says. "They have funny pronunciations too, my mother said, like how they say 'aluminum' with five syllables instead of four, and pronounce schedule 'shedule.'"

"Do you know how old they are?" Julie asks.

"I've seen pictures. They're pretty young. Early twenties, I think. They're pretty cute too."

"So they're a little older than Allen," Ernestine says.

"Your big brother's cute. Do you have any other brothers where he came from?"

"My oldest brother Carlos is gonna be twenty-one this month. He's a cripple. Then I have a little brother, Tommy, who turns eight this month. He's the spoilt brat of spoilt brats. Allen's the only one with a lick of sense or decency."

"Isn't Carlos a Spanish name? What's the story with giving him a name that doesn't match with the rest of your names?"

"Who knows what my mother was thinking when she named him. She doesn't even like Spanish people."

"Why is he crippled? Did he catch polio, or was he born crippled?"

"He was in an accident at work in July '62. A car fell on top of him and crushed his spinal column. He was going in and out of his senses for a long time and only regained his senses a couple of months ago. I hear he's going crazy on account of realizing he'll be in a wheelchair the rest of his sorry life."

"He's not just any cripple, but paralyzed too," Girl jumps in. "Paralyzed people can't move their legs or anything else below where they was paralyzed. If you're paralyzed at the very top of your spine, you can't move your arms and don't feel nothing below the neck."

"Carlos was supposed to be arrested for arson, petty theft, and drugs, but the cops can't do anything when he's a helpless hospital patient. I feel bad for him for being crippled so young, but he was never gonna amount to anything anyway. It's not a huge loss to society. All he did was sell drugs and work low-paying jobs where he tried to get away with stealing. He was fired from his first job for eating cereal off the conveyer belt, and at his second job, the one where he had the accident, he was found out for stealing stuff from people's cars."

"No wonder you don't want anything to do with certain people in your family," Betsy says. "I'd move out young too if I were you."

"Is there enough room for all of us?" Baby asks. "A davenport only seats three or four people. I don't wanna sit on the floor my very first time watching television."

"My dad has a recliner, and my mom has a cushioned chair. Julie, Ernestine, and Girl can sit on the davenport with me, and we can find soft cushions for Boy, Baby, and Infant to sit on."

"I can't wait!" Infant says excitedly.

***

A little before 8:00, they trot across the hall and into the van

Niftriks' apartment. Betsy shows Girl, Ernestine, and Julie newspaper articles she cut out about the British group that's going to be on the show tonight. The girls think they kind of look similar, since they all have brown hair and the same haircut, but they agree with Betsy that they are pretty cute. Betsy is a little surprised at their long hair, but Ernestine tells her a number of men in the Village have long hair. Mrs. Troy would probably lecture them about being interested in male singers with long hair, but she's not here to spoil their fun. Someone born in 1923 doesn't know jack about what's popular nowadays.

"Here they are!" Betsy shouts as Mr. Sullivan is introducing them.

She, Julie, Girl, and Ernestine sit at rapt attention as the band begins their first song, "All My Loving." Girl's eyes light up when she realizes the bass player is a lefty, and she turns to Ernestine and her siblings with a huge smile. Ernestine and the Ryans are thrilled to see one of their own in such a public venue, and to see a grownup who stayed true to his left-handedness instead of giving in to attempts to shame and bully his out of his natural inclination.

Ernestine thinks it's pretty rude how the majority of the girls in the studio audience are screaming. Even if one really likes a band and is excited to see them perform, that's no excuse for screaming nonstop. They're probably making it hard for the band to hear themselves play, and are missing the entire show because all they're doing is screaming.

During the next song, a cover of what Mrs. van Niftrik says is a Broadway tune, "Till There Was You," there are closeups of each bandmember, providing each one's name. Ernestine rolls her eyes when a caption appears under John's name, saying, "Sorry girls, he's married." As though any of the girls in the audience or watching at home stand a chance of marrying someone that much older and that famous. She and Girl both think he's the handsomest, married or not. The others are cute, but John has a more mature face, like a handsome adult man, not carrying the look of a cute, soft-faced boy into early adulthood. Girl also feels a special energy coming from him, an aura she has a very good feeling about.

After the third song, "She Loves You," there's a commercial break, and then a magician named Fred Kaps performs tricks. Infant and Baby are more interested in the magic tricks than in The Beatles. Boy is more interested in the tricks too, feeling the musical stars of the evening are more for girls.

Performing next are some of the members of the play *Oliver!* After the opening musical act, Ernestine and her friends can't help but feel bored and anxious for The Beatles to return. A day ago, they never would've been so picky about what they did or didn't watch on television, never having watched it before, but now everything is somehow different, like a special kind of magic has been worked upon them by these cute visitors from across the ocean.

More boredom follows in the form of Frank Gorshin doing impressions of several actors, another commercial, Welsh singer and banjoist Tessie O'Shea, comedy duo McCall and Brill, and yet another commercial. Finally The Beatles return and sing "I Saw Her Standing There." Julie decides she thinks Paul is the cutest one during this song. Their final song of the evening is the one Betsy told them about, "I Want to Hold Your Hand." Ernestine, Julie, and Girl think it does sound fantastic, and hope they can buy their own copy if they hustle up enough money after they've bought food for the week.

The final performers of the night are Wells and The Four Fays, who do a comedy routine. Ernestine, Betsy, Julie, and Girl barely care about them at this point. All they can think about are the four cute young British musicians who stole their hearts and did something to them they can't find words to explain. All they know is they feel really different now.

"I don't feel sad anymore," Ernestine announces. "There's been such a black cloud hanging over everyone since we lost President Kennedy, but now it's like the bad spell has been broken."

"I feel the same way," Betsy agrees.

"Do they have a full LP?" Girl asks. "After tonight, I could listen to those fellows singing the phonebook!"

"They have an album called *Meet The Beatles*. I've been saving up my money so I can buy it. LPs are about three bucks, two bucks more than a single, but I like them so much, I don't care how much I have to pay."

"When can we see them again?" Julie begs.

"I think they're going to be on again next week."

"Can we come over again next Sunday night, Mr. and Mrs. van Niftrik?" Girl asks.

"You girls are welcome anytime you like," Mrs. van Niftrik tells them.

"Do you have a favorite, Betsy?" Ernestine asks. "I like John."

"So do I!" Girl says. "We haven't been best friends for almost two years for nothing! It's like we share a brain at this point!"

"I don't know who my favorite is," Betsy says. "I'll have to see them again and read a little more about them before I make my decision."

"Paul is cute," Julie says. "He has pretty eyes."

"I didn't know you was into that girly stuff," Boy says.

"What, just because we don't do other girly stuff means we can't do one girly thing in our lives?" Girl challenges him. "Why can't we fawn over cute guys in a band?"

"I don't think I've ever seen you looking this happy, Julie," Ernestine says. "The special magic these guys brought over the ocean with them healed even you."

"Maybe we can see them in concert!" Betsy says. "I'm sure they'll be playing in New York. They're right here in the city as we speak, in the CBS studio."

"Maybe if they're here over the summer, you can go to a show as a summer vacation present," Mr. van Niftrik says. "You deserve something nice as a reward for your sixth grade graduation."

"That would be the best present ever, Dad!"

"We'll step up our begging and odd jobs to earn money for our own concert tickets!" Girl says with bright eyes.

She, Ernestine, Julie, and Betsy look around at one another with happy expressions and the same special feeling in their souls. They have no idea exactly what just happened, but they do know they're never going to be the same again after tonight.

"Window-washing," Girl says. "I've scored so much money from it, I've been able to buy Beatles' records after we've bought our food for the week."

She, Ernestine, and Julie are sitting around talking to Adicia and Justine on a balmy day in June, while Boy, Baby, and Infant are begging and performing for money in Chelsea. Since losing Emeline at the beginning of February, Adicia and Justine have been coming over to see Ernestine fairly often. She's their only older sister left, and they always feel better after they visit her. Right now, Girl is suggesting ways they can make extra money over summer vacation.

"Don't the drivers get mad and cuss you out?" Adicia asks warily.

"A couple of 'em always do, but you gotta grow a thicker skin if you wanna make a living offa begging and doing odd jobs. Some don't curse me or honk, but they don't give me any money. Most of 'em are decent and give me a quarter. Sometimes I get a whole dollar. Though most New Yorkers take public transportation, there are still tons of cars. With daylight hours so long this time of year, you can hustle up plenty of unwitting customers each day. Whenever there's a red light or road delay, you go up to a car and wash the windshield, maybe the side windows if you got enough time. I guarantee you'll get plenty of change by the end of the day."

"Where do you work?" Justine asks. "Just in your neighborhood?"

"We make the rounds. Here in the Meatpacking District, Chelsea, the West Village, sometimes even up into your appropriately-named hellhole of a neighborhood."

"It's not such a far walk," Ernestine says. "Yous guys walk here often enough. All you need are a bucket of soapy water and a sponge or rag. We can demonstrate on onea the cars outside."

"But you can't really mess it up. Ain't no wrong way to wash a car windshield, so long as you don't accidentally use a bucket full of coal dust."

"Do I need two buckets?" Adicia asks. "I don't want people to get angry at me if I wash their windshields with the same dirty water I used on thirty or fifty other cars."

"You don't need one bucket of clean water and another of soapy water. So long as you wring out your sponge or rag before you wipe off the soapy stuff. I'm sure none of these drivers expect a professional carwash from a street urchin."

"Could we be reported to the cops for washing their cars without permission?" Justine asks.

"How would they get our names or addresses? The most they can do is honk or yell. They can't very well drive away when they're stuck at a red light or stopped in the middle of rush hour, and they'd be damn stupid if they up and walked out of their cars, leaving them abandoned in the middle of the road."

"So long as you don't make the mistake of washing a cop car," Ernestine says. "Then I'm sure there might be trouble."

"You think I might get extra dough if I washed a limo or fancy rich person's car?" Adicia asks.

"I've never seen a limo or an expensive car in our neck of the woods, but I'm sure it's possible," Girl says.

"Make sure you've got nice deep pockets," Ernestine says. "I use a purse too, just in case I get too much change for my pockets."

"Can I do this too?" Justine asks. "I'm so small, I don't think I could reach the windshields."

"You're a little bit too short, but Adicia's just the right size," Girl says. "She's small for her age. The drivers might not always realize someone's about to wash their cars when they get to a light. They'll suddenly see a hand coming up and will be stuck."

"It's sure easier money than begging or performing," Ernestine says. "You know for sure you've got money coming to you."

"Has anyone ever pulled a gun on you or yelled at you so bad you had to run away?" Adicia asks worriedly.

"Who could get mad at a poor street kid?" Julie asks. "They'll know by our ragged clothes and dirty faces that we're one of them, not privileged uptown kids. Who could say no to giving one of us urchins spare change? I got a whole dollar a few times too."

"So have I," Ernestine says.

"Ever get any five-dollar bills or anything above that?" Justine asks.

Girl laughs. "The drivers might take pity on us or do the decent thing, but they ain't nuts. You don't hand out five or ten bucks like candy to street kids."

"I don't know if we have a bucket," Adicia says. "Our mother never washes the floors or windows with anything besides a rag or mop."

"You're just in luck, since we have a supply of buckets." Girl goes over to one of the closets. "Me, Ernestine, and Julie each have one, and it looks like there's one more for you. All you do is fill it up at the beginning of the day and put soap powder in it, then drop a sponge or large rag in. Do you have any at your place?"

"My mother won't notice or care her cleaning rag's missing. We've got at least one sponge too."

"Perfect. If you notice the water getting too rank, dump it out and get a fresh supply at a fire hydrant or fountain. I carry around a little packet of soap powder in case that ever happens. I'm smart like that."

"Where do you store your money? I don't want my parents to discover my car-washing money and use it to buy drugs or booze."

"This is a pretty safe neighborhood and building, so I don't worry 'bout people breaking in and taking our money, but just in case, I store our extra dough in a hole in the davenport. Some people store their valuables in a hole in the bed, though I don't like the idea of destroying our beds."

Adicia is very excited at the thought of having money to keep and spend for her very own, and is full of nervous excitement and anticipation over going out to wash strangers' windshields and make it happen. Sarah once told her everything new seems scary the first time, but sometimes the nervousness makes it better or more exciting.

"I wouldn't get a piggybank if I was you," Ernestine says. "Our parents have no shame, so they'd probably raid it. Dad took money from Tommy's piggybank once and caught hell from Mother, but *she* wouldn't see anything evil about taking money from her daughters' piggybanks."

"I also recommend hiding money in furniture legs," Girl says.

Ernestine looks at her best friend's free-swinging breasts and laughs. "I know something else you need to buy with your car-washing money, and that's a bra. You could get arrested for indecent exposure if you walk around in public much longer with those things swinging around like that."

"Why should I wear onea them things? They're an updated form of the corset and Chinese foot-binding."

"Girls our age are supposed to wear bras if we've got bustlines. Emeline was sporting an ample bustline by our age too. She was even younger than us when she started sprouting breasts, as a matter of fact."

"Soon you'll both need belts and sanitary napkins," Adicia says. "What's that long word again for when you bleed every month?"

"Menstruation," Girl says. "Thank God, that ain't happened to either of us yet. Don't worry, I'm not so radical I intend to bleed into my clothes. We'll make our own to save money. We can get snaps for cheap at a home goods store, and stuff cut-out rags with cotton or old washcloths. Damn those stupid belts. There's a better way to handle that time of the month, and I ain't about to finance the fat cats who run those companies. I'm sure most of 'em are men, since a woman would probably never design such horrid things. Come on, wearing a belt and fastening a napkin to it with hooks or pins? That sounds like a form of Medieval torture!"

"We saw an awful filmstrip in my class this year about menstruation," Ernestine says. "Lucine and Emeline were right about how terrible those filmstrips are. The pamphlets we got stunk too. They were called 'Growing Up and Liking It,' from Modess. The time when I start to wear lipstick and go on my first date, what baloney. Poor kids like us don't wear makeup or have boy-girl parties, and I have more pressing things to do with my time than keep track of my menstrual cycle in that calendar."

"That pamphlet was a hoot. I lost track of how many times they used the words 'dainty' and 'daintiness.' Ain't nothing dainty about us urchin girls. Who wants to be dainty? Dainty girls and women are a waste of society. They don't do nothing to contribute to it. All they do is sit around putting on makeup, dancing, and throwing supper parties. A delicate girl would never last a day in our world."

"Can we get back to what we were talking about?" Adicia dreads the time when she too starts to become a young woman. "When can I start washing windshields?"

"Let's go outside and have a practice run on a parked car." Girl drags a bucket over to the kitchen sink, which looks more like a basin sink than a normal-sized kitchen sink. "You'll be a pro in no time."

"Remember to come back to us and report how you're doing," Julie says. "You're newer to it than we are. You might need advice, or wanna share how much dough you're raking in."

"Oh, yes, let's compare how much we're each making!" Ernestine says. "So far Girl is in the lead, but she's been a street kid her whole life and knows how to do these things. Julie and I haven't been in the business quite so long."

"We'll meet back here in a week to discuss how you've done your first week in business," Girl tells Adicia. "With a sweet face like yours, who could resist giving you extra change? You look like such a dear little ragdoll, someone everyone would feel pity and compassion for. You don't need to do nothing extra to act the part, since you were born to play it."

***

Adicia was nervous about starting to wash strangers' car windows and windshields, but quickly came to realize Girl, Ernestine, and Julie were right about how simple it is, and how many drivers would take pity on her and give her some change. So far, she's canvassed most of the blocks of Hell's Kitchen, and blends in pretty well. Tough-looking people leave her alone or at most glance at her before moving on. She's not a girl from the moneyed classes trying to pass herself off as underclass. At most, she's gotten a dollar when people don't have change, but usually she gets a quarter or a half-dollar. Some people have been cheapskates and only given her a dime, but they're far and few between. Her favorite place to get business is a light that seems to last for a good three minutes. With the cars forced to stop for that long, she has more time than usual to wash the windows. She tries to impress the drivers by how seriously she undertakes her endeavor, instead of smiling at them and making smalltalk. If they smile at her, though, she'll return the smile. Adicia wonders if some of them might've been in her shoes when they were young, and so feel obligated to help her out in the small way they can. She also wonders what they might assume about her. Maybe some of them think she doesn't go to school, is homeless, or is an orphan.

One day, not that long after she's begun her business, she sees a nicer car than usual pulling to a stop at the light. Not wasting a moment of the long light to admire the car, she immediately puts up her left hand to start washing the windshield. She hopes the driver thinks she's doing a good job with his nice car, and is glad he's not one of the drivers who's given her a strange look upon realizing she's a southpaw.

Though she isn't wasting any time in the three minutes she's got to do her job and make a good impression, she does notice out of the corner of her eye that the driver has a kind face. Hopefully he'll be a nice guy and give her a quarter or even a whole dollar bill.

As the light changes, she stands back and waits for him to give her her fair due. He reaches into his pockets to search for change, then hesitates when he pulls out a bill. Adicia hopes he doesn't want to cheap her out by giving her nothing or only change if a dollar bill is all he's got. Then, with cars starting to honk at him to get moving, he hands her the bill and starts to drive away.

Adicia glances at it, expecting to see the familiar face of George Washington, but instead sees a different face. Her eyes widen and she looks at the departing driver in pure astonishment when she realizes she's been given a ten-dollar bill. She can't decide if he's a millionaire or a local philanthropist who likes to give larger bills to needy children. At any rate, this is definitely the most money she's ever going to earn washing windshields, and a story Ernestine and her friends will probably never believe without the evidence.

***

"No way!" Ernestine gasps when Adicia pulls out the ten-dollar bill. "A guy in a fancy car gave you ten whole bucks just for washing his windshield?"

"I wish I'd been on that street that day and able to catch him too," Julie says jealously.

"Maybe he's a celebrity who's in town for the opening of his new movie or play," Girl says. "Or maybe he's a new resident with a little money. Boy, I hope the rest of us run into him too, and often."

"He hesitated a little when he first pulled it out, like he wasn't sure about giving me so much money," Adicia says. "Maybe that was all he had, and he felt bad for me and gave it to me anyway."

"Who cares why he gave it to you!" Ernestine says. "The most important thing is that he did give it to you! We need to decide what we're gonna spend our new fortune on. God knows, you don't get ten bucks for doing that every day."

"Betsy's going to a Beatles' concert in August. You, Girl, and Julie would love to go to that show too."

"Don't you even think about that," Girl chides her. "I ain't so crazy about them I'd use a friend's surprise fortune, which you'll probably never see again anytime soon, to pay for concert tickets. A concert is over in a little while and don't last like, say, a new dress or a sturdy pair of shoes. Even buying a nice meal at a restaurant would be better than wasting it on a concert."

"Ten bucks can buy a lot of candy," Justine says, propping her rabbit up on a pillow.

"It could probably also pay for a visit to the dentist after you rot all your teeth from eating ten bucks worth of candy. I say we should look at catalogues to determine average prices of stuff we need, and if there's any money left over, use that for something we don't need, like gumdrops or a record."

"Lucine got five bucks once from the Bowery Mission people when she volunteered to wash dishes after Thanksgiving supper," Ernestine says. "They felt bad for her and gave her money instead. She used it to buy a coat for Justine. She was the warmest of all of us that winter."

"It's a good thing your mother don't know about this. Knowing her, she'd make you give her your hard-earned money. Bad mothers like her have this attitude of what's yours is mine, and feel it's their right to take everything away from their own children. I hope that bitch rots in Hell or comes back to Earth as a neglected child herself someday."

"I probably could use new clothes," Adicia admits. "It's no fun wearing these ragged hand-me-downs my whole life. And I don't think I've had a new pair of shoes ever."

"With only about two bucks, we could buy milk, eggs, and bread," Julie says.

"We could buy a ticket to the World's Fair that's in town," Girl says. "It's only a buck for kids to get in."

"It's here in Manhattan?" Adicia asks. "I heard it was in one of the other boroughs."

"It's in Queens, so we'd have to take the subway."

"I'd love to go to the fair, but that'd be eight dollars for all of us. It wouldn't be fair if only some of us went."

"Where do you think the ticket money would go to?" Ernestine asks. "I'd feel uncomfortable if it's going to rich fat cats who live off of our sweat and blood."

"How about a belated birthday present for Allen, or a birthday gift for Lenore?"

"I'm sure they'd love the thought, but would insist you keep your money to spend on yourself. It's not every day you score so much money from washing a windshield."

"Speaking of Allen and Lenore, is there any word about whether they're finally more than friends?" Girl asks, grinning.

"Nope," Ernestine sighs. "I bet she wonders why a good-looking, nice guy like him hasn't been on a single date since she's known him."

"He said it'd feel like cheating on her if he dated someone else," Adicia says. "I like the idea of clothes, but I'm still growing. Those clothes and shoes would be too small for me in another year or two, and they'd be old by the time Justine fit them."

"Well, what else could we get that's practical?" Girl asks. "Get nice clothes. Don't think about how you'll outgrow them eventually. You get what you need when you need it. It's the same reason we spend money on food, even though before long the food turns into waste products."

Adicia suddenly looks worried. "Do you think the saleslady would think we stole the money if we come in there with a ten-dollar bill to spend? Kids like us don't just come into bills like that on our own."

"We'll wear our nicest clothes and scrub our faces and hands really well," Julie says. "If anyone asks, you can say you have a nice relative with money who gave it to you as a present."

"Let me start by brushing your hair," Ernestine says. "Then you'll scrub up real well and borrow one of Julie's dresses. You're about the same size, and she's got nicer clothes than most of yours."

"Julie's taller than me," Adicia protests.

"I know I'm a little bigger than you, but our body types are both little," Julie says. "That's called petite, right?"

Girl nods. "You both have small bones, even if you ain't the same height. Let's start getting you spruced up so we can go out to a store and look for decent clothes and shoes. You can buy the clothes a little bit too big, so you can grow into them and keep them longer. If we've got any money left over, you can buy a treat for yourself."

***

Since it gets hot in the factory turned apartment building, the van Niftriks have let their young neighbors borrow one of their electric fans for the summer. It's now July, and the sticky heat really bothers them, particularly Baby and Infant, who miss the pleasant coolness of the basement.

"Can we listen to something besides The Beatles?" Adicia asks as they lie on the floor and play records. "They sound nice, but I don't wanna get bored of them by listening to only them all day long."

"Sure thing. The Four Seasons are still my favorites, no matter how much I love The Beatles." Betsy stands up. "I'll go over to my place and bring back a couple of their records, and other non-Beatles stuff too. It probably is a good idea to break it up with other music."

"I hope you don't think I sound ungrateful," Adicia says as Betsy fetches the records. "I've never gotten to listen to our own records before, but I don't wanna get sick of listening to the same songs or band over and over again, no matter how good they are."

"It's a good point," Girl says. "I get sick of a song too when I hear it too much. You can have too much of a good thing."

"Do you have a favorite, Adicia?" Ernestine asks.

"A favorite what?"

"A favorite Beatle, of course," Girl says. "Though you ain't seen them on television like we have. You've only heard their songs and seen their pictures. Maybe it's easier to choose your favorite when you've seen them in motion and heard them talking. Ernestine and I both like John best, Julie likes Paul, and Betsy's favorite is Ringo."

"I never really thought about it. I have to live in that hellhole with my parents, so I have other things to occupy my time besides picking a favorite Beatle."

"You're probably right. We wouldn't have cared about that either only a short time ago."

Betsy comes back carrying a small pile of records. "Here you go. Some of them are a little old, but I hope you don't mind. The Beach Boys, The Four Seasons, and Ricky Nelson. I have a bunch more, but I didn't want to bring over too many."

Adicia reaches over for the record on top of the pile, *Rag Doll*, by The Four Seasons. The face of one of the bandmembers is oddly, eerily familiar, though she can't quite place where in the world she would've seen any famous person before. As she keeps staring at it, it dawns on her.

"What's wrong, Adicia?" Julie asks. "You look as though you've seen a ghost."

"That man, the one on the far left. He looks exactly like the fellow who gave me ten bucks for washing his windshield."

"What!" Ernestine says. "I really think you're imagining things. What would a member of a famous band be doing driving through Hell's Kitchen and handing out ten-dollar bills to street kids?"

Adicia paws through the pile of records and picks out the rest of the Four Seasons records. Each time she sees his face, the more convinced she becomes that he and the man whose windshield she washed are one and the same person.

"Betsy, this man, what's his name?"

"That one?" Betsy looks at the one Adicia points to. "That's Bob Gaudio. He plays the piano and writes a lot of their songs. Do you really mean to tell us you think *he* was the one who gave you that money?"

"I don't know. Maybe he just bears a resemblance. It could happen."

"That's probably all there is to it," Ernestine says.

Adicia still can't shake the feeling. "Betsy, do you have any other pictures of this band I could look at? I really wanna find out if I'm just seeing things or if this really is the same guy."

"Sure, they're my favorite band, I've got tons of pictures and clippings of them." Betsy jumps up again. "I'll be right back with my scrapbook."

Adicia sits shaking and confused while she waits what feels like forever for Betsy to come back from across the hall. While the *Rag Doll* record plays, she pores through Betsy's extensive scrapbook of The Four Seasons, looking at every picture and news clipping carefully. Her heart is racing by the time she gets to the last page.

"That's the man. The tall guy in that band is the one who gave me ten dollars for washing his windshield. I would swear on my own life that's exactly the same man. I'm more and more convinced with every picture I see."

"You're sure?" Julie asks.

"I'm positive he's exactly the same man. I've seen too many pictures to be seeing things or think it was another guy who looked similar."

Betsy looks at her with a slight grin, then breaks into a huge smile. "I am so jealous of you! You met one of the members of my favorite band and got money from him!"

"You met a celebrity!" Girl says excitedly. "I can't believe one of our kind met a real-life celebrity!"

"You washed a millionaire's windshield!" Ernestine says. "No wonder he gave you ten bucks!"

"Maybe he'll drive through again and give me fifty bucks next time," Adicia says hopefully.

"I don't think he lives here," Betsy says. "They record at a studio in the city, but when you're as rich and famous as he is, you don't hang around in a part of the city like this."

"I can't blame him. I wouldn't wanna live here if I had money either. I don't even wanna live here now."

"Isn't the title track a sad song?" Girl asks. "It makes me think of us. We're all girls from the wrong side of the tracks too, laughed at by the rich kids, wearing ragged clothes. We'll probably never be the wife or girlfriend of a boy from the nice part of town, since our kind ain't supposed to mix. If a guy from money did like one of us, his folks would never approve."

"It's number one on the charts," Betsy says. "A lot of people like it."

"If this is a new song, maybe he wrote it not long after he saw me," Adicia says. "Do you think it's possible he was inspired by me?"

"Okay, now you're probably dreaming," Ernestine says. "Good songwriters turn 'em out like candy. They get inspiration from all sorts of people and stuff. It's possible, but the odds aren't in favor of him writing that song because he saw you."

Adicia pulls herself up into a sitting position and hugs her knees. "I don't know. Even if he probably was thinking of someone or something else when he wrote it, it's nice to know some millionaires are nice people and that a girl like us can be written about in a song that goes to number one. I'll never forget how kind he was to me when he didn't have to give so much money, or any money, to a sad little girl who looks like a ragdoll."

Chapter 27: Letters to and from Lucine and Emeline

"Would you like to write to Lucine and Emeline?" Allen asks his sisters one Saturday afternoon in September when they're gathered at his place for lunch. "Lucine just went away to college, and I'm sure it'd make her whole semester to hear from her precious little sisters. I'll use the Xerox machine at work to make copies, so you can only write on one side of the paper."

"You have their addresses?" Ernestine asks. "I thought we couldn't know that."

"You can't, but I can. The most I can tell yous is Emeline is at that Episcopal boarding school uptown and Lucine just started Hunter."

"I'm still learning how to write," Justine says.

"We'll write for you if you're not up to writing by yourself yet," Adicia promises. "But I bet they'd both like to see something in your handwriting to know you're learning to write and not such a baby anymore."

"Maybe someday I'll save up for a typewriter, but for now all we have are plain paper and pens." Allen goes to the desk in Lenore's room, which she bought after saving up enough money from her job at the art gallery. "You don't mind if I steal some of your paper, do you, Lenore?"

"Go ahead. I already wrote to Emeline, and don't need any at this very minute."

Allen steals a glance at Lenore's body form under her rather clingy yellow dress before he turns his attention back to his sisters. All three of them saw what he just did and grin at him, unable to believe Lenore didn't notice how he was looking at her and practically devouring her with his eyes.

"We learnt in my English class that we always have to date our work, not just our letters," Ernestine says. "Can I start the letter?"

"You're the oldest sister now. Go ahead."

Ernestine grabs a green pen and begins composing a letter in cursive.

Saturday, September 19, 1964, West Village, Manhattan, New York City, USA

Dear Lucine and Emeline,

This is Ernestine writing. How are you? Me, Adicia, Justine, Allen, and Lenore are doing good, and so are my friends Julie and the Ryans. I have a new friend now too. Her name is Betsy van Niftrik, and she lives across the hall from us at our new apartment in the Meatpacking District. We've lived there since the first of the year, which you probably were already told by Allen. Betsy's parents are really cool, and let us come over anytime we like. Betsy is allowed to come visit us a lot too. Her parents feed us good food, let us watch television with them, and even paid for movie tickets for me, Julie, and Girl when we went with Betsy to see A Hard Day's Night *at the theatre in August. I'd never seen a movie before and sat in a real movie theatre! Are either of you Beatles' fans? Lucine, you might be a little too old for them, but Emeline might like them. We think they're awesome. Girl and I both like John best, Julie likes Paul, and Betsy likes Ringo. Adicia likes them too, but she doesn't have a favorite.*

We're doing pretty good for ourselves with money. We've been running a pretty profitable business of washing car windshields since May, and we got Adicia into it. I'll let her tell you all about her adventure in June, when she had a very special customer. Boy, Baby, and Infant are still singing and dancing in the streets for money, and begging. We also do odd jobs, like picking up trash, sweeping front stoops and verandas, and walking dogs. When winter comes, Boy will volunteer his snow-shoveling services. With the money we pick up from all this stuff, we can afford enough food for each week, new clothes from time to time, and records with our spare money. The people who lived at our apartment before us left a lot of their stuff behind, including a radio and a record player. The records they left behind were mostly junk, like boring old Pat Boone and other stiffs in suits who don't know beans about good music.

I'm in junior high now, in a very nice school in Greenwich Village. Betsy goes to the same school, though I never met her in elementary school because she was in a different classroom. We have a couple of classes together now. It's pretty awesome that I get to take a real school bus, instead of having to walk like I did in the old days. I tutor Girl every day, and Adicia tutors Julie and Boy when she comes over. Now that Justine's in school, she tells Infant about what she's learning in kindergarten. Baby sadly has no one to help her. Maybe someday she'll go to a real school, before she gets too old.

I got my first bra earlier this year. Lenore took me to Macy's and helped me pick it out. Girl has a bustline too, but she doesn't think she needs one. She came with us, and thought some of them were kind of pretty, so Lenore bought some for her too. Girl doesn't like wearing them, but she's agreed to put one on when she goes out in public so people won't arrest her for indecent exposure or think she's a girl of ill repute. She takes it off as soon as she gets home. She made sanitary napkins too, when that day comes. We won't need a belt, since Girl made them with snaps, cloth, and bits of washcloths for stuffing. We'll wash them so we can use them every month, instead of wasting money on a big box of Modess every few months.

Can you believe I'm already twelve? I guess big sisters always think of their little sisters as little girls in their minds, even when they start growing up. I can't believe you're eighteen and sixteen now either. Somehow I always picture us in my mind's eye as we were when we lived on the Lower East Side, when all of us were still together. I hope someday, when we're all able to be together again, I'll have a much happier picture in my mind to remember us by, though we'll probably all be grownups by then.

Love,

Ernestine Zénobie Troy

"Your turn," she tells Adicia.

Adicia picks up a blue pen and starts writing a little distance down from where Ernestine left off. She writes in cursive too, though her cursive hand isn't as practiced or steady as Ernestine's.

Dear Lucine and Emeline,

This is Adicia. I'm ten now and in fifth grade, still in a terrible school in Hell's Kitchen. Even the bad neighborhoods we lived in and visited before didn't have such terrible names. At least we don't live too far from the library. I hope you think I'm doing a good job as the big sister, though I'll never be as good as either of you. Tommy is a brat as always, but he's with his Puerto Rican friends on the second floor most of the time. Mother stews up a storm about how Tommy plays with whatever kids are friendly to him and doesn't care if they're Negro or Spanish-American. Tommy might be a brat, but he's not prejudiced against people of other races or colors. Justine goes to kindergarten in the morning so she can take the bus with me, and when she comes home, she spends the rest of her day with Mrs. Doyle across the hall. Mrs. Doyle's little boy Matthew turned four last month. Now she has a little girl too, born at the end of July. Her name is Caroline Julia. Mrs. Doyle used to have another little girl, when she was married before, but she lost her. Her first little girl was only two months older than me. It's very sad she lost her daughter (she won't tell us why she died so young), but now she has a new one. I hope it makes her happy to have another chance to have a daughter.

I met a real millionaire in June, and he gave me ten dollars! Ernestine, Girl, and Julie got me into washing car windshields for money this summer, and it was just as easy as they told me. I've done good business in Hell's Kitchen, and no one bothers me. They know I belong there and that I'm not a rich kid trying to pass for one of them. My favorite place to work is at a light that lasts for three minutes. One day, a nicer car than usual came up. When it came time to pay me when the light was changing, he gave me a real ten-dollar bill! I used it to buy nice clothes (a few sizes too big so I can grow into them), a good pair of shoes, a few secondhand paperback books, and a charm bracelet. The next month, I was visiting Ernestine and her friends again, and Betsy brought over records by The Four Seasons, who had the number one song on the charts that month. One of the guys in the band, who Betsy said is their songwriter and pianist, looked so familiar. After I looked at all the pictures in Betsy's scrapbook (they're her favorites), I was positive he was the one who was so nice to me. I can't believe a girl like me met a real-live millionaire and got to wash his car. I guess this means not all people who become famous and get money are jerks to us.

Justine and I are holding up as best we can with our parents and Tommy, but we're always waiting for the day when all of us can be together again. We can't wait to hear back from you.

Love,

Adicia Éloïse Troy

"You girls don't have to sign your middle names too," Allen says. "They know who you are already."

"I know, but it feels more formal, signing your whole name to a letter," Ernestine says. "What's the use of a middle name if you never use it except on a birth certificate, a diploma, a marriage license, or when you're in trouble?"

"Do you have a middle name, Lenore?" Adicia asks.

"Eve," she says, not taking her eyes off the book she's studying on the davenport.

"Like the lady in the Bible who got in so much trouble for eating the apple?"

"Yes, that's the same name. It means 'life.' Not that I believe Adam and Eve were real people."

"Justine, do you want to write a little something?" Allen asks. "They'll be thrilled to see you can write now."

"When do I learn to write all curvy like that?" Justine asks.

"Second grade, probably," Ernestine says.

Justine takes a red pen and starts printing in large letters, trying her best to look like a big girl with neat printing and not too much space between each word. She makes a special effort to use the special left-handed grip and hand position Adicia learnt from Girl, and to angle the paper properly.

Dear Lucine and Emeline,

This is Justine. I'm in kindergarten now. I ride the bus to school. I can't wait to see you again. I'm being a good girl for Adicia at home. I miss you.

Love,

Justine Anastasie Troy

"You know how to spell your middle name already?" Allen asks. "That's a pretty long name to memorize for a little kid."

"We all taught her," Ernestine says proudly. "The same way Lucine and Emeline taught me how to spell my name, 'cause it's so long."

"Can you take them to the post office first thing Monday?" Adicia asks. "I can't wait to hear back from them."

"I have to Xerox the pages at work first," Allen says. "Don't worry, I'll get them out as soon as I can."

***

Emeline and Lucine's reply letters arrive in the middle of October. Allen comes home from work before Lenore and heats up leftover goat meat for supper while she's at night school. Since the letters are intended for everyone, he opens them and reads them first. Emeline's comes from one of the Yorkville dorms on the boarding school grounds, and Lucine's comes from one of the Hunter dorms on the Upper East Side, where she's a sociology major. Allen hopes Lucine will be able to help a lot of people and make a difference in the lives of disadvantaged people when she gets her social work license.

Lenore gets home several hours later and puts her textbooks away before going into the kitchen to heat up the remainder of the goat meat. Allen is on the davenport, reading *The Village Voice*.

"Lucine and Emeline's letters came today," he informs her as she pulls the meat out of the oven.

"That's good to hear. The girls will be so happy to read them." Lenore pours a glass of milk. "By the way, Allen, could I ask you a personal question?"

"What do you wanna know?"

"Since I've known you, you've never had a girlfriend or gone on a date, and I know you had a lot of girls before. Are you afraid to bring girls here because of what they might think of you having a female roommate? I hate to think I'm keeping you celibate so long."

He hopes she doesn't see him blushing as he struggles to find an answer that doesn't involve confessing the truth. "I'm sort of in love with one girl in particular, and I'll probably never be able to have her. I'd feel like I was cheating on her if I went on a date with another girl."

Lenore feels a stirring of jealousy. "Oh. Is she a co-worker?"

"I'd rather not tell you too much about it. It's embarrassing enough a guy like me is so hung up on a girl. By the way, have you met any guys you like?"

"No one I want to date." She hopes her voice isn't shaking. "I'm not ready to do anything with a man yet. There was one guy I thought I liked, but he's not interested in me."

Allen's eyebrows shoot up. "You liked a guy and none of us ever heard about it? How long ago was this?"

"He'd never like a girl like me. He's too old and experienced. I must've been dreaming if I thought I had a chance with him." Lenore starts stabbing at her meat with her knife.

"Wow, I never suspected someone like you would have a thing for an older guy with lots of experience after what happened to you. Would I know this guy?"

"That's none of your business," she snaps.

"I guess you don't wanna talk to me about it since I'm not a girl. I know how it feels to be in love with someone who'll probably never love you back, but I don't know how it feels when you're a girl dealing with that. Me, I'm just an unlucky guy who fell in love with an unattainable girl the first and only time I was in love."

"If I were your girl, Allen, I'd never treat you like that," Lenore says sadly.

"You're a nice girl. Whoever gets you as his girl will be a very lucky guy."

"Thank you," she says in a small voice.

Lenore retires to bed early and starts crying herself to sleep on her pillow as soon as she knows Allen is asleep. She can barely stand to look at him over the ensuing days, believing his heart belongs to another woman. Hoping to force herself to get over him, she begins treating him very coldly and frequently snaps at him for no reason. Allen meanwhile wonders what he's done to make her so mad at him, and like a hopelessly lovesick puppy puts up with all her verbal abuse and silent treatment. Lenore forces herself not to feel sorry for him when he looks at her with his big brown eyes looking so sad and wounded.

She had a beautiful dream of Allen approaching her when she was old enough to be viewed as a real woman, not a teenage kid, and asking her if she'd like to go out with him, but his eyes were on another girl all along. Most twenty-year-old guys would laugh at the thought of a seventeen-year-old thinking she stands a chance with someone so much older, particularly when she has absolutely no experience with men.

When the girls come over on Sunday to read the letters, Lenore is quietly doing her schoolwork at her desk while Allen mopes around in the kitchen, really torn up about how he did something, he doesn't know what, to make the girl he loves so angry at him. As the girls take their places at the kitchen table, he sends a few longing looks towards Lenore's room.

"What's wrong, lover boy, have a fight?" Ernestine whispers.

"I don't know what I did to her," he whispers back. "All I know is she's been treating me like a dog for the last few days, and I can't stand thinking I did something to make her sad or upset."

"Lenore, why are you mad at Allen?" Justine calls, not bothering to keep her voice to a whisper.

"He knows what he did, even if he's not man enough to admit it," Lenore replies cryptically.

Ernestine leans over to him and starts whispering again. "Why don't you buy her flowers to apologize for whatever she thinks you did? Girls her age are supposed to love that stuff."

"That sounds like a good idea," he whispers, hoping Lenore will be so happy to see he got her a special present, she'll find it in her heart to forgive him for whatever he did and stop treating him so badly. He can't bear the thought of having done anything to make her so upset.

"Let's read Lucine's letter first!" Adicia says. "We haven't heard from her in over two years."

Ernestine reaches for the letter with Lucine's handwriting. Allen hid the envelopes so they won't see the return addresses. She positions it so they can all see it.

My dear little sisters Ernestine, Adicia, and Justine,

I'm so glad I have a chance to hear from you after so long! I'm very upset to hear our wicked mother ruined your Christmas and took you away from Allen, but at least you're not forbidden from visiting him. I'm glad Ernestine and her friends are doing so well for themselves, considering they're not old enough to have real jobs and don't live with any grownups. What luck the neighbors are so nice to you! I'm also glad you're in a much nicer neighborhood.

What a neat story about Adicia meeting the man from a famous band! That's the kind of story she'll tell her grandchildren someday. Our parents don't know what they're talking about when they insist everyone with money is a jerk who doesn't care about the underclass. I'm sure this man wasn't born having so much money, and even if he were, he still did something very nice for a sweet little girl without being asked. Good people will always do the right thing, no matter how much money they might have or where they live. Although hopefully you'll have a much better job someday and won't have to wash windshields for the rest of your life!

It's so exciting to hear little Justine is in kindergarten and can read and write! Our real-live baby doll isn't such a baby anymore if she's already five. I hope she doesn't get too much older before I can see her again. I'd hate to miss out on her entire childhood and not see her again till she's a teenager or grownup. I hope she stays just as sweet as she is, even if she's a lot older when we can be together again.

I got all As and Bs at boarding school. The Episcopal priest and his wife who run the school sponsored me, so I didn't have to pay any money or take out any loans. I was able to study things they never taught at that crummy Lower East Side high school, like Latin, Dante, Shakespeare, early English literature, famous artists from the Renaissance, psychology, and French literature. I lived in one of the dorms and made a lot of friends, all from disadvantaged families like ours. I was probably the poorest one, but they never treated me like a sad charity case. They wanted to be my friends because they liked me. We've had so much fun going to the movies and dance parties, having birthday parties, staying up late talking in our beds, playing popular records, and learning how to cook. (To answer Ernestine's question, I like Paul Anka, Gene Pitney, and Ricky Nelson best. Most of the girls my age aren't as into The Beatles as younger girls.) I didn't care we had to wear uniforms. No one could make fun of me for my clothes when we all wore the exact same thing.

The couple running the school, Father and Mrs. Murphy, adopted our little nephew Giovanni not long after the fire. The judge was nice enough to change Gemma's last name back to Troy for free after she signed her last name as Monsterelli for the last time. I saw Gemma from time to time that summer, and she was doing well. She reapplied to Hofstra and was accepted again, and took a job as a salesgirl in a local department store. She's studying business just like she originally planned. She's not a bad person at all. Her ordeal with being forced to marry Francesco and deal with his loony family taught her a lot of humility and made her into a more mature woman. She also agreed with the Murphys' request to write Giovanni a letter they'll give him when he's old enough, to explain why she gave him up for adoption and that she never meant him any ill will even though she never felt any motherly bond to him. When she's older and meets the right guy, I'm sure she'll have a much better second marriage and will love any future children.

I'm a freshman at Hunter College, free of charge, studying sociology. With my background, I felt I'd be a perfect match as a social worker. I think the people I serve will appreciate that I used to be one of them, and that I'm not an overprivileged rich kid who decided to study social work as a charity case mission to the underclass. I hope someday I can help people, make a difference in their lives, and make the impression of a real friend, the way the people at the Bowery Mission are always so nice to everyone.

I'm also now an Episcopalian. Mrs. Murphy told me I didn't need to get rebaptized just because I wasn't baptized Episcopal and didn't grow up religious, though I did have a little ceremony where I was welcomed to their church, along with other new members, in the fall of 1962, shortly after I started their school. I really like how this is a pretty progressive church and that they're actively involved in social justice and other modern causes. Don't worry, I don't think you're bad people for not being religious. If you're meant to become religious, it'll happen in your own time and when you're ready to do it.

I miss all of you and can't wait to see you all again!

Love,

Lucine Camille Troy

"I hope I get to go to college someday too," Ernestine says. "Gemma and Lucine are both college girls, so I know it's possible for a girl like me to go."

"I hope you get to go to college too," Adicia says. "I'd like to go when I'm that age, but I never thought about it as much as you did."

Ernestine picks up Lucine's letter, carefully folds it back up, and puts Emeline's letter in front of them.

To my sweet little sisters Ernestine, Adicia, and Justine,

I'm very glad to hear from you. I can't believe Ernestine is already in junior high, Adicia only has two more years left of elementary school, and Justine is in kindergarten now! I'm a junior in high school now, after being accepted to the same boarding school Lucine went to. They gave me tests to determine where I stood when I entered midway through my sophomore year, and I tested on a college level for English and history. They put me in advanced classes in those subjects, and I'm finally able to read adult, classic novels and study historical events I haven't already been studying since third grade. I'm also able to study Latin and German, not just boring French, and the home economics class we have once a week is fun, not dull and demeaning like the one I was taking earlier this year. The best part of studying here, though, is that we're not too far from Midtown and the central branch of the library. I thought I'd died and gone to Paradise the first time Lucine and I walked over there. There are two big stone lions on the front steps, and thousands of books inside. I've gotten so many wonderful books in the past nine months, a lot of them unavailable at the smaller branches. The librarians don't care I'm a teenager checking out mostly adult books. There aren't too many books written for teenagers, and I'm not about to read and reread juvenile books for the rest of my youth, until I'm old enough to read only adult books.

I've made a couple of very good friends at school. Not as many friends as Lucine, but I'm okay with that. I'd much prefer to read a book or do schoolwork than go to a party or talk about nothing for hours. It's more important to have quality than quantity with friends. I'm not unpopular; the other girls just recognize I'm the quiet, bookish girl and that my natural setting isn't a social setting. We're all friendly with one another, even if I don't have a dozen or more good friends, and no one judges me for my clothes anymore, because we all wear a uniform. It's kind of neat I get to wear a real school uniform. It makes me feel very professional and grownup. The clothes I wear on weekends and school vacations are a lot nicer than the ones I used to wear.

What a beautiful story about Adicia and the famous guy! I don't know if he'll remember her forever, but I'm sure she'll always remember him and how kind and charitable he was. I'm also glad to know she spent that money on important things and didn't waste it on something like candy or toys. It's not every day a poor kid gets handed a ten-dollar bill by a kind-hearted celebrity who just happens to be passing through town and happened to be at the right moment at the right time to get to do this good deed. Mother is wrong when she carries on about how everyone with money is an uppity snob who doesn't care about our kind.

To answer Ernestine's question, yes, I do like The Beatles (and I can't believe she's old enough to have celebrity crushes!). Maybe I'm a little too old for them, but it's not like I'm one of those screaming young girls who's only thinking about how cute they are and can't hear them singing or playing their instruments. Liking somebody's music has nothing to do with how cute they are, though it does help if someone is good-looking in addition to talented. My favorite is George. I guess it's because he's the baby of the group, and it makes me think of my own dear little sisters and how the baby of a family needs special mothering, love, and protection. Is it a good or a bad thing I feel such a strong mothering instinct at only sixteen? Besides, I know how it feels to be pegged 'the quiet one.' That label sticks, and people sometimes don't expect much of you since they think you're not talkative. But boy, will I prove to anyone who thinks I'm just another quiet, bookish girl that still waters can run deep when I go into the world and make something of myself!

Well, it was good to hear from you again. One day, before we know it, the time will come when we can all be a family again, the way we were two years ago, only in a much better place, without our horrible parents. I miss you all so much and think about you every day.

Love,

Emeline Rosalie Troy

"Emeline's gonna be a very good mommy someday," Adicia says. "I don't think it's sad she feels mothering towards George because he's the youngest. She doesn't know how to not feel mothering and protective after she was such a super big sister to us for so long."

"Someone her age in the other half of society wouldn't feel that way," Allen says. "She's had no childhood, and only has a few more years left to be a teenager. Not that she would've been a typical kid or teenager anyway, given how bookish and serious she is, but she might've had half a chance to have a life outside of being a big sister. She can't even admire a celebrity without bringing her mother hen instinct into it."

"At least she's at a real school and has a great local library," Ernestine says.

"She and Lucine didn't mention any boyfriends. I'm kinda glad they're focusing on school instead of dating. If they had serious boyfriends this young, they'd be more likely to continue our family cycle."

Lenore closes her door, refraining from slamming it only because the girls are there. She's committed to staying here until she finishes night school, but from now on is going to make herself as much of a shadow as possible. As far as she's concerned, Allen is just a roommate who happens to be good-looking. With her out of the way, maybe he can finally pursue that girl he mentioned, and she can move on with her own life. Her heartbreak won't be prolonged if she doesn't have to look at the guy she's foolishly fallen in love with every day. Maybe she'll leave the city, so she won't run the risk of bumping into him with a wife and kids someday. He can go bump into another woman at a bus stop the same way he found her. At any rate, her life with Allen is over in her heart, and by the coming of the new year, their life together will be over in every other way too.

Chapter 28: A Feverish Situation

Allen wakes up in the middle of the night on a very cold night in January 1965 with a strange feeling. He checks the locks on the doors and windows, which are all shut. Then he looks into Lenore's room and sees she isn't there. She's not in the kitchen, the living room, or the bathroom either. He's about to phone the police to report a kidnapping when he sees a note on her pillow.

Dear Allen,

This is goodbye. I can no longer bear to live with you when I know I'm keeping you from being a normal man and going out with girls. A good-looking young guy like you shouldn't be forced to be celibate for so long. Maybe now you'll finally have the courage to take a chance with that girl you're in love with. I also have to leave to avoid dealing with my own unrequited love. I hope you and your sisters have wonderful lives. You deserve it more than I do.

Regards,

Lenore

He has no idea how long she's been gone or how far she's gotten by now. Not wanting to waste a moment more, he goes to the closet for his coat, and discovers Lenore has left behind her coat, hat, gloves, and boots. Starting to panic, he pulls his winter clothes on, stuffs his keys in the coat pocket, and rushes out the door, down the hall, into the elevator, and out of the building. Snow is falling rather heavily, so there's little chance of following any footprints.

She probably couldn't have gotten far in this weather, so he starts heading in the direction of the nearest subway station and calling her name. Not many people are out at this hour, in this weather, so no one is able to help. He goes up and down what seems like every block in the Village and is starting to head up towards Chelsea three hours later when he notices long black hair contrasting with the whiteness of the snow still falling. He rushes up to the semi-covered form and immediately recognizes her when he looks into her face, his eyes having adjusted to the dark. She doesn't make any movements or open her eyes when he takes his hat off and puts it on her head.

"I don't know what you thought you were doing running away, but I've been looking all over for you since one in the morning." He takes his gloves off and shoves them over her hands before starting to push the snow off of her. "As soon as I dig you out of here, we're going home where you belong."

No one appears in the street to help as he shovels the snow off of her with his bare hands. As soon as most of the snow is cleared, he takes off his coat and puts it over Lenore's body. She doesn't show any sign she's aware of Allen's presence, even when he asks if she can hear him.

"If you can't talk, at least squeeze my hand to let me know you can hear me," he pleads, taking her small hand in his. "You're my whole life, Lenore. I don't know what I'd do without you to help me, take care of me, and keep me company. You're the only girl I want, I promise you."

Her hand remains limp in his. Allen grabs her wrist and finds a faint pulse. Hoping to get her inside before she catches hypothermia, he struggles to pick her up and carries her back through the snow-covered, darkened streets. It takes about an hour to get home.

Allen reaches into his pocket for the key and can barely turn it in the lock after the cold winds have been nipping at his hands for so long. While he opens the door, he struggles to keep holding onto Lenore. He encounters the same difficulty when he enters the elevator and 515.

Once finally back inside, he carries Lenore to her room, sets her on the bed, pulls the covers back, removes the winter clothes, pulls her up so her head is on the pillow, and tucks her in. At this hour, he doesn't expect any doctors to be in the office, and he doubts any doctors nowadays make housecalls. Lenore also would only be comfortable being seen by a female physician, and he's not sure how many female doctors practice in this immediate area. Still, he can't bear the thought of leaving the girl he loves unconscious and untreated for the next few hours while waiting for a doctor's office to open. He doesn't care at this point what a respectable doctor might think of their living situation.

All the doctors he locates in the phonebook are out. His next line of defense is to look through the services advertised section of one of the local alternative publications. Near the end of the list, he sees a naturopathic doctor, Dr. June Sviatko. He has no idea what a naturopath is, but he'd take any type of doctor at this point.

"Is this Dr. June Sviatko the naturopath?" he asks when the call gets through, his voice shaking.

"Yes I am. I've just arrived at my office and heard my phone ringing as I walked in the door."

"Do you make housecalls?"

"Not usually. Are you unable to get to my office?"

"My roommate fell unconscious in the snow, and I don't want her to die. She was out there for a couple of hours without any winter clothes. She'd never want to go to a male doctor or a traditional hospital after certain experiences. You've gotta come over here and help her. I love her too much to let her die so young and thinking I don't love her."

Dr. Sviatko looks around her office. "I have a few assistants and another doctor. I don't know if they'll get in at the regular time because of the bad weather."

"You might not have many patients today because they can't get through in the snow! We're over in the West Village, near the Hudson Park Library." He gives the address. "You can come up the fire escape, and I'll let you in. We're up on the fifth floor, number 515. I'd ordinarily wait at the front entrance, but I don't want to leave her alone for a minute."

She takes a few minutes to think about it. "You sound like a nice young man. I could make an exception and make a housecall just this once."

"Thank you, thank you, thank you. I'll pay you immediately for your inconvenience. You don't know how much this means to me."

Allen turns back to Lenore after he gets off the phone. Her eyes are still shut, though he feels a weak pulse and sees her chest going up and down from her weak breath intake. Forgetting everything he was ever taught about proper masculine behavior, he starts crying.

"You've gotta stay with me. After you get better, I'll do something special for you every single day. Forget what I said about being in love with another girl. I was talking about you but didn't want you to find out I like you. You can forget that guy you said you liked too. I'm the one who's wanted you for two and a half years. I'll make you my woman as soon as you're eighteen. You're the only one I've ever loved or wanted to marry. I knew from the first time I saw you that you were gonna be my wife someday. You're gonna be my respectable wife, and we're gonna have some little Troys. How does three kids sound to you? And when the time comes, I want to grow old with you and have grandchildren together. You're the only girl I've had eyes for in the last two and a half years. I love you so much it hurts to look at you some-times, knowing I can't touch you or tell you how I feel. I know you can't hear anything I'm saying, but I mean every word of it. I'll take off time from work to nurse you back to health. I don't care if I'm fired. I just don't know what I'd do if I lost you."

A little before 7:00, Dr. Sviatko knocks on the fire escape door. Allen jumps up and rushes to let her in, pointing the way towards Lenore's room.

"I woke up at about one and noticed she was gone. I looked for her for hours and finally found her as I was walking north toward Chelsea. I don't think anyone attacked her, since her clothes were undisturbed and there was no blood. She must've slipped on ice."

Dr. Sviatko listens to Lenore's heartbeat, shines a light into her eyes and mouth, looks into her ears, and takes her temperature. Allen wonders if this is what happened to Carlos. He hopes Lenore won't end up like Carlos, going in and out of her senses for almost a year and a half before recovering. It would be even worse if she were paralyzed, though he'd still want to be her fellow if she couldn't walk.

"There's no telling how long she was out of it before you found her, or if she broke her leg. We could only do an X-ray at a hospital or doctor's office. And her body has to absorb nutrients. She could only have IV feeding at a hospital, where they'd be able to monitor her and give her medicine. She also has a fever of one hundred five degrees and needs more medical attention than I can give her. My alternative remedies only go so far. Naturopathic medicine generally isn't meant for dealing with unconscious people."

"She can't go to a hospital," Allen pleads. "She had a real bad ex-perience with a creep of a doctor. She'd hate to wake up and find out I let her be taken to a hospital and poked, prodded, and seen naked by a strange man who might hate women. My older sister had a bad expe-rience with doctors and hospitals too, when she was having a baby. And they usually don't allow anyone in the room with the patient. When they find out she's unmarried and living with me, they'd assume we're living in sin, and would treat her like trash."

"I understand and agree with everything you're saying, but there's no other way to feed and treat an unconscious person. I'll have to call for an ambulance to take her to Beekman Downtown Hospital. You can come and sign her in."

"How can I sign her in when she's not my dependent?"

"Nobody has to know you're not really married. For all they'll know, you're a very young couple who couldn't wait to come of age to get married. The young lady isn't eighteen yet, is she?"

"She's seventeen. I'm twenty."

Dr. Sviatko goes to the phone and looks up the hospital in her little address book. "Yes, I need an ambulance. The young lady's husband found her unconscious in the snow. She needs immediate attention at a hospital." She gives the address. "Their name? I'm afraid I didn't have a chance to ask that."

"I'm Allen, two Ls and an E, and she's Lenore. Our name—I mean, my name—is Troy."

"Mr. and Mrs. Allen Troy. The young man tells me his first name is spelled with two Ls and an E." Dr. Sviatko puts her hand over the phone and turns back to him. "What's the young lady's birthdate?"

"June 25, 1947," he says, taking the phone from Dr. Sviatko.

"Is there any chance your wife could be expecting, Mr. Troy?" the woman on the other end of the line asks.

Allen blushes. "Absolutely not. There won't be any baby Troys till we're a little bit older."

"And does your wife have any pre-existing health conditions?"

"Not that I'm aware of."

"Okay, we're sending an ambulance over."

It seems to take an eternity before Allen hears the siren, after he's placed calls to his work and Lenore's work and night school telling them they won't be coming in today, and that Lenore will probably be out for longer than just a day. He stands back feeling helpless as the paramedics put Lenore onto a stretcher and wheel her out the door and down the hall to the elevator. He and Dr. Sviatko follow them into the ambulance, where one of the paramedics puts blankets over Lenore.

"She needs X-rays," Dr. Sviatko says as another paramedic puts an IV into Lenore's arm. "We don't know if she broke any bones, or if she just hit her head."

"Why wasn't the hospital called immediately?" one of the paramedics asks.

"She has a big fear of doctors and hospitals." Allen tries not to look at the needle in her arm. "I hoped we could treat her with a housecall from a doctor, the old-fashioned way."

"He's a young newlywed in love with his bride," Dr. Sviatko says. "I hope you can excuse the young man for not thinking with his head."

When they arrive at the hospital where Allen had his own close brush with death two and a half years ago, Lenore is wheeled down the hall and towards the emergency department. Allen is made to stay at the front desk and not given a chance to say goodbye. He can barely sign his name to the papers shoved in front of him, and has to remember Lenore is being passed off as his wife so he doesn't accidentally print her name as Lenore Hartlein. He's too overwhelmed with fear and despair to stop and think about how nice the name Lenore Troy looks.

"Do I have to pay a deposit?"

"We'll send you a bill when Mrs. Troy is sent home. It probably won't be within the day, so there's no need for you to sit in the waiting room. Someone will give you a call when she's ready to go home."

"Can I have any flowers or gifts sent up to her room?"

"When she's moved into her own room, you can send your wife all the flowers you want. We'll let you know when she's put into her own room."

***

Adicia, Tommy, and Justine were very excited when they woke up and saw all the snow, since that meant a snow day. They could barely hide their glee as Mrs. Troy grumblingly got ready for her current job, shelf-stocking at a record store in Midtown. Mr. Troy already left a few hours earlier for the box-making factory, where work is never cancelled and his wage has only increased incrementally over the years. Right now, it's only $1.25 an hour, and doesn't seem likely to shoot up anytime soon.

"Can I play with Pablo and Ramón?" Tommy asks Adicia after their mother has left. "I know you stupid girls are gonna stay with Mrs. Doyle."

"Sure." Adicia is secretly proud her eight-year-old brother is asking her permission for anything and deferring to her as the oldest sibling, even if she's only ten and not one of Tommy's favorite people. "Take your coat, hat, and mittens in case yous guys wanna play outside."

"If Mommy and Daddy are home late, can I have supper with the

Gómezes?"

"I don't think they'd approve of that even if you left a note. You know how Mother feels about your friends."

Tommy crinkles his nose. "Mommy's mean when she doesn't let me do stuff with my friends. What did a Puerto Rican ever do to her? She was mean about my Negro friends in Two Bridges too."

"Some people are prejudiced against other races or colors. You can't change a person who thinks like that. It's like having a fear of dogs or heights. It doesn't make any sense, but people still have those feelings."

Tommy goes to the closet for his winter clothes and heads downstairs. Adicia and Justine head across the hall and knock on the door.

"Come on in," Mrs. Doyle calls. "I'm feeding Caroline, but we're all girls here."

Adicia stops in her tracks when she sees Mrs. Doyle with five-and-a-half-month old Caroline at her bare breast. Matthew is playing with his toys on a little rug on the floor, seemingly oblivious to his mother exposing herself like that.

"Can't you afford Enfamil or Similac?" Adicia asks, remembering Emeline once said something about mothers in the old days feeding their babies in that way.

"We could probably afford formula, but I wanted to save money and nurse my babies with my own milk. I had a bit of an argument with the nurses at the hospital, but they finally let me nurse instead of making me get a shot to dry up my milk."

"That means Matthew can't give her bottles like I used to do for Justine. I even made a bottle for my baby nephew Giovanni once."

Mrs. Doyle looks at her sadly. "Such a little girl shouldn't have to take care of her baby sister like that. It's bad enough most of the kids in your family have had no choice but to assume so many grownup responsibilities so young and be substitute parents to so many younger siblings."

"I don't mind. It's just what we have to do."

"If I still had my first little girl, I'd never make her take care of Matthew and Caroline like she were their real mother."

"Did you name Caroline after her?" Justine asks.

"Part of her name, yes. I didn't have the heart to use the same name and have to hear it all the time, so I used another form of my first child's name as part of Caroline's name."

Justine hears the phone ringing across the hall. "Can I go answer that? Maybe it's our mother saying her job is closed and she's coming back home."

Adicia waves her on. Justine skips back into their living quarters and picks up the phone on the coffeetable. Adicia instructed her to never say their parents aren't home when she gets the phone, and to always ask who's calling first. This time, though, she doesn't have a chance to launch into her memorized spiel, and only is able to say "Hello" before being broken off.

"I hate to be the bearer of bad news, but I'd like to ask you to make get well cards for Lenore. She's in the hospital."

"Oh, no! Did she have an accident, or is she sick?"

"She fell down in the snow last night and isn't awake. They don't allow minors, especially not unrelated minors, to visit people at the hospital. I had to pretend to be her husband when she was taken there."

"Do we send the cards to the hospital? Oh, I hope Lenore is gonna get better and not be sick forever like Carlos!"

"You can send them to me, or maybe we can make them together and I'll take them there for her. I'll give yous money so you can buy her little presents. How does visiting on Sunday sound? We can make get well cards together, and pick out flowers if any florist has decent fresh flowers in stock."

"What if she went to sleep and will never wake up?"

"Then I'll be the saddest guy in the world. Hey, can you keep a secret? After Lenore gets better, she'll be almost eighteen. I only waited so long to tell her I like her 'cause she's three years younger than me, but I don't have to wait much longer. After a respectable period of going steady, I'm gonna ask her to be my wife, and I'd love for you to be our flower girl."

"I was supposed to be the flower girl when Mother was tryna force Lucine to get married."

"This time you'll get to be the flower girl in a happy wedding everyone wants. At least, I hope Lenore will have me. Maybe she thinks I'm too old and experienced for her."

"I want Lenore to be our new big sister! She'll be a great new sister!"

"I hope you're right," he says sadly.

***

Two weeks after the beginning of her hospital stay, Lenore flutters her eyes open. She has a terrific headache, her whole body aches, she feels hollow, her right leg smarts, and she feels very hot. As she grows accustomed to her strange new surroundings, she realizes she's not in her own home. She deliriously pulls the covers off and runs her hands along her body. There are no casts or large bandages, though there's a needle in her arm. She starts wiggling her toes to make sure she's not paralyzed, and is relieved when she can move them. Her next thought is to wonder what she's doing here. The last thing she can remember is slipping on black ice a few blocks away from the southernmost boundary of Chelsea. She hopes the hospital bracelet will tell her something, anything, about what put her in here, but it only provides her age, date of birth, approximate height and weight, and name. She wonders why in the world they have her name down as Lenore (Mrs. Allen) Troy, or how anyone would know her name or birthdate period if she can't remember coming here and didn't have any identification papers when she left.

"Oh, you've regained your senses, Mrs. Troy," a nurse says as she enters the room. "Let me check your vitals, and we'll see if you can be discharged to your worried husband soon."

"Where's Allen?" she demands, too delirious to question why these people think he's her husband. "Why did he let me come here? He knows I'm afraid of hospitals."

"You were taken here with your husband and a doctor who made a housecall. You were too far gone to be treated at home. We had to give you X-rays, run tests, feed you with an IV, and give you medicines through another IV." The nurse points to the nightstand. "Your husband brought you a beautiful bouquet of red and pink camellias. He and some of your younger sisters-in-law also made you get well cards."

"Can they come and take me home right now?"

"You're still running a fever, though if you can keep down liquids on your own and walk a little, they might be able to discharge you within the week."

Lenore reaches for the flowers after the nurse has gone. A small note among the flowers says simply, "For our beautiful Lenore. Love, Allen and the girls." She hopes she'll be discharged soon so she can get some answers to what in the world happened to her and how Allen could've taken her here when she left without a word.

Three days later, a nurse comes in with a bag of clothes. She informs Lenore her "husband" signed the paperwork for her discharge and sent a change of clothes. The nurse helps her with changing, then gets a wheelchair. She sets the cards, the flowers, and the stuffed frog Allen sent her yesterday in Lenore's lap and begins wheeling her out.

Allen is waiting for her at the desk by the exit doors. Lenore, in spite of her weakened state, can't help but feel butterflies in her stomach when he smiles his cute smile at her. He comes forward and squeezes her hand, looking the happiest she's ever seen him.

"I hope you'll excuse your husband for not kissing you in greeting, Mrs. Troy, but we told him you shouldn't have such close contact until you're off your medications. What a shame this happened to such a young newlywed couple."

"How are we getting home?" Lenore asks, still a bit dizzy and delirious.

"I called for a taxi," Allen says. "I'm not taking you on a bus or subway in this condition. I bet you can't wait to get home."

"Is there anything permanently wrong with me?"

"Your husband already asked that question," the nurse says. "You don't have a heart murmur or any other complications from your extended fever, and your right leg only got severely bruised. No bones were broken, and you didn't hit your head hard enough to have any kind of brain damage."

"You're gonna be okay." Allen smiles at her, taking the wheelchair from the nurse. "You're gonna have as much bed rest as you can. I'll make all your food and bring it out to you, so you don't have to walk back and forth to the kitchen while I'm at work. Only soft or liquid foods, like applesauce, chicken broth, tomato soup, yogurt, and gelatin. I got you a present you can entertain yourself with when I'm away at work. Just wait'll you see what I got you."

He wheels her down to the curb, where a cab is waiting for them. Allen opens the back door and puts the frog, flowers, and cards in a large bag on the floor, then helps Lenore in and climbs in after her. Too delirious to help herself, she lays her head on his lap so she doesn't have to be in a seated position. She smiles weakly when she feels him gently stroking her hair and face.

When the cab drops them off in front of their building, she lets Allen put his arm around her back to help her with walking, uncaring he's getting more up-close and personal than she's ever allowed any guy to get. As soon as they get home, Allen leads her over to a chair and opens the sofa bed.

"This is what I got for you." He lifts a heavy wrapped box. "Can you walk over here and open it?"

Lenore slowly walks about ten steps to the sofa bed and reaches for the package. She stares in disbelief when she realizes what she's unwrapping.

"Allen, I can't accept something this expensive! This must've cost a small fortune after you paid my entire hospital bill! What day is it? I don't know how long I was in there."

"I don't care if I have to spend a million bucks on you. I was planning to buy a television set anyway, once I had the money saved up. I just bought it a little sooner 'cause I knew you'd need something to keep yourself occupied all day. You'd probably get bored of just listening to records and reading. Today is February fourth, Thursday. You were in the hospital for more than two weeks."

"Is it still 1965?"

"Yes, you weren't in there that long, thankfully. I told your work and night school about what happened, so they don't expect you back immediately. If you feel well enough, someone can deliver your homework."

Lenore lies down, putting her head on the pillow. "How did you come to know I was in the hospital, and why did they think I was your wife? I didn't tell you I was leaving or where I was going. Did you search the hospital after I left?"

"I thought they told you you were taken there from here. I wanted to treat you at home, but the naturalistic doctor I found said you needed stuff only a hospital could provide. What were you thinking, going out in the middle of the night without winter clothes? What if I hadn't found you, or if bad people had found you before I did? I had to put my own hat, gloves, and coat on you to keep you from freezing!"

"I wanted to get as far away from you as I could. Maybe I didn't care if I did freeze to death. Now you're gonna hafta wait even longer to start dating again, since you'll be nursing me back to health." She looks up at him with sad eyes. "But you must really care about me if you went out in the middle of the night to find me, brought me back here, and got medical attention."

"Believe me, you're the only girl I want in my home. As for why they thought we were married, the home doctor told them. Didn't the nurses and doctors treat you really nicely 'cause they thought you had the title Mrs. in front of your name? A lot of 'em treat young unmarried girls like trash, and we all know what they would've assumed if they knew we're not married. Better they thought you were a seventeen-year-old bride than a teenage girl living with an older male roommate."

"But what about that girl you said you were in love with? Now you'll have even more reasons to not ask her out, and it's all my fault."

"Right now I'm more in love with her than ever before," he says as he gets extra blankets from the closet. "As for you, you can forget that fellow you said you were in love with. He doesn't deserve you. He probably never liked you in return. Say, would you like pudding or chicken broth? If you're not hungry, you should get some sleep."

"Pudding is fine," she says, her voice shaking. "I won't bother you anymore after I get better. I'll move out and let you resume your normal life. I feel like a monster for denying you the chance to get together with a girl you really like. I've already made you spend far too much money on me with hospital bills and a television."

"You're not going anywhere," he insists as he brings over a bowl of pudding. "It was bad enough I almost lost you when you tried to run away. What would I do without you to help me keep house, take care of me, and keep me company? Don't you like me anymore?" He helps her sit up to eat the pudding and puts the frog next to her.

Too weak to get into a long discussion about why she was trying to run away, and not wanting to seem ungrateful, Lenore mutely takes the spoon and eats some of the pudding. After she's finished, she lets Allen tuck her in and put the extra blankets over her. It vaguely crosses her mind that perhaps she herself is the girl he's said he's in love with, but she shrugs it off as ridiculous and an overactive imagination. Even if he were in love with her, he couldn't do anything about it now.

***

All through the remainder of winter and into the spring, Allen has continued nursing Lenore back to health. He'd put her breakfast and lunch in a cooler or crockpot within easy reach or a few steps of the sofa bed, and when he came home from work, he'd serve her supper first and then attend to his own. For over a month, all Lenore could bear to swallow or keep down was soft or liquid food. Very slowly, she was reintroduced to more substantial foods, like crackers, orange slices, and vegetable soup. Every weekend, Ernestine and her friends, Adicia, and Justine have come to visit her, sometimes bringing more get well cards and small presents. Lenore now has a small zoo on the sofa bed from all the stuffed animals Allen's bought her—a frog, a teddybear, a cat, a parrot, a snake, a chipmunk, a turtle, a tiger, a lion, a horse, a pig, and a dragon. He's also bought her a number of records, books, magazines, and small handheld puzzle games. She's embarrassed for him at how much money he's spending on her, but every time she broaches the subject, he just smiles at her and tells her he'd spend a million dollars on her if he had to.

By mid-April, Lenore is able to walk around the apartment and not feel overexerted, and by the beginning of May, she's able to go on short walks around the neighborhood. On the weekends, the girls join her, and they sometimes go to the parks. Ernestine, Adicia, and Justine fill her in on what's going on at school, and Julie, Girl, Baby, and Infant tell her about their adventures in making a living from odd jobs, begging, and performing. For Julie's eleventh birthday that month, she's able to frost the birthday cake Allen made, and to make cookies with the homemade cookie cutters Ernestine gave her as a Christmas present.

"Allen's birthday is coming up," Adicia tells her the last weekend in May. "I think his best present would be to see you back at normal. Why don't you surprise him by making a nice gourmet supper the way you used to, and set the table with the nicest plates and tablecloth? He'd be over the moon to see you got so better."

"He'll be twenty-one next Sunday," Ernestine says. "That's old enough to vote. I assume he'll register Democrat, like a sensible person. They're the only party that speaks for our kind."

"I'm gonna register Socialist when I'm twenty-one," Girl says. "They speak for us even more than Democrats. Though it's obvious Allen ain't poor no more. He's comfortably working-class if he can afford a television and all the other stuff he doesn't need to get by."

"Next Sunday will also be the twenty-first anniversary of D-Day," Adicia says. "I don't know what happened on that day, but I know

Allen was born on that day, which is supposed to be a big, historic event from the war."

"It was the turning-point in the war for America," Ernestine says. "We studied about it a little in seventh grade this year. A bunch of soldiers landed on French beaches and started the mainland invasion of Europe. Till then, they'd been fighting in Africa, the Pacific, and Italy."

"There's another war going on now," Julie says. "Betsy's parents don't think we belong over there."

"Of course we don't belong over there," Girl says. "All it's doing is killing poor boys who don't have the choice of going to college or working a high-class job. They join the military 'cause it's their only way to find a job and get money. Guys from the middle or upper classes are able to go to military schools like West Point and make a career out of the military, but they're usually not cannon fodder like our poor and working-class boys. From what I've read about it and seen on the van Niftriks' television, it don't make a lick of sense. At least I can understand why we was in the last war, the Civil War, and the Revolutionary War."

"Well, hopefully it won't continue too much longer," Lenore says. "Allen is just the right age if they started another draft. I'd hate to lose him."

Girl smiles at her. "It's obvious you really like Allen, and we'd have to be blind to not have known for a long time he's got a major thing for you. Why don't you tell him you like him? Are you afraid he'll laugh at you for being the one to tell him first?"

"What are you talking about? He's told me on a couple of occasions he's in love with this one girl, but he hasn't approached her about it 'cause he thinks she'd never have him. I also think he hasn't asked that girl out 'cause she'd never wanna go steady with a fellow who has a female roommate. He's been celibate on account of me for almost three years."

"He was probably saying he likes *you* without up and telling you he likes you," Ernestine says. "Didn't you tell him you liked another guy who'd probably never have *you*? God knows we all know you were referring to *him*!"

"You think I like him?" Lenore blushes. "Even if I did, he'd never be interested in me in that way. I'm too young for him, and I've never had a boyfriend. I think I'm healed enough from what my father did to me to feel ready to do things with a guy, but a guy who's had a lot of girls would never consider going out with a girl who'd need a lesson in how to kiss."

"Allen had his first girl when he was thirteen. He met an eighteen-year-old who invited him up to her place and taught him some things. We lost count of how many girls he had since then, but none of 'em lasted very long. Longest was five months. He never loved any of 'em. They were just girls to pass the time with. You'd be the only girl he really loved and waited for, instead of doing all that grownup stuff within the first few dates. If I had a boyfriend, I'd feel it was more special if he didn't kiss me or try to make out immediately. It probably means more when you've known each other for awhile and you saved it to look forward to."

"You're thirteen yourself. If Allen is any kind of good big brother, he'd never let you get away with doing things with boys at your age. Maybe he learnt from his mistakes."

"Boys are allowed to do that stuff at any age, pretty much, and go unpunished," Girl says. "Us girls get crucified if we do anything with a boy one second before marriage. I wanna know how guys are supposed to get all this experience they're allowed to have with girls before they settle down. Are they going around with all the same girls, or are these girls too afraid to admit what they've done?"

"What are we gonna do special for Allen's birthday?" Adicia asks, not quite understanding what Lenore, Ernestine, and Girl are talking about.

"How much money have you got in your bank account?" Girl asks.

"I'm not old enough for my own bank account, at least not without a co-signer," Lenore says. "I was always paid in cash, and I kept it in a jar in my room. There's probably enough to buy nice food and a decent present."

"Make him steak," Julie says. "That's a really nice meal, and something normal people don't get to eat every day of the week."

"You can buy him a suit," Ernestine says. "Allen doesn't have a formal suit. I'm sure he'd really appreciate getting his first real suit from the girl he loves. If he's gonna move up in the chain of command at the bakery, go to college eventually, or someday have another professional job, he'll need to dress the part. You don't have to shell out a fortune to get a decent suit."

"Make sure to include a necktie," Girl says. "Monkey suits look ridiculous on our boys, but if one of our boys is moving up in the world, he has to wear formal clothes from time to time. You can tie his tie for him if he don't already know how."

"White suits look ridiculous," Adicia says. "I don't think Allen would wear one even if he did wanna wear a suit. And black suits are too common. He should stand out in a crowd if he's gonna wear a suit."

"You could probably find one in dark blue or red. They also make 'em in gray and tan. All the formal clothes I've seen Allen wear is that old brown vest he sometimes wears with a button-down shirt and a bowtie. I think he got the dress pants he wears with that getup from a secondhand clothing store."

"He could use a new pair of nice shoes too," Julie says. "Maybe he'd pay us to shine his shoes."

"He bought you a television, paid for all your hospital bills, and bought you all these stuffed animals," Baby says. "The least you could do for him in return is buy him a good suit of clothes and make him steak for supper."

"We can all go shopping for it together," Girl says. "Do you know what his size is?"

"I used to take his laundry to the laundromat, but it's been so long, I've forgotten what his size is."

Infant rushes into Allen's room and comes back with a pair of pants and a shirt. Girl takes them and looks for the tags.

"He's a thirty-four-inch waist and a medium in shirts. Infant, put these back and bring us some of his shoes."

Infant goes to put them back in the closet, trying to make it look like nothing were disturbed, and picks up Allen's dress shoes. When she comes out to the living room, Girl takes them and holds them up to the light to see the numbers written on the bottom insides.

"Ten even. Not too freakishly large and not too small for a man. We'll have no problem finding stuff in his sizes."

"Say, Ernestine, have you or Girl started having menses yet?" Adicia asks. "I haven't heard anything from either of yous about it, though botha yous wear a bra now."

"Glad to say it ain't happened yet," Girl says. "I hope I'm onea the girls who makes it till age seventeen without bleeding. That would just get in the way of the things I do. How could I wash windshields or run around doing my odd jobs if I had to deal with that stuff every couple of hours? Getting it this young only made sense when people lived till all of thirty and had to have kids in their teens."

"Not yet," Ernestine says. "I've no longer got Sarah or our older sisters to help me when the day comes. Maybe I'd be more excited about the idea of getting it if we still had them, so they could help me and share their stories."

"Boy, I'm glad Justine and I are only six," Infant says. "All this grownup stuff sounds so strange."

"Getting older isn't that bad," Lenore says. "People take you more seriously when you're not a kid, and you get to do a lot of stuff you couldn't do at a young age. I could learn to drive a car if I wanted, and I can have a job. Allen will be old enough to vote next Sunday, another good thing about becoming a grownup."

"You're both also old enough to be married," Girl teases her. "How did you like being called Mrs. Troy at the hospital?"

Lenore buries her head in her hands and blushes.

"We know, Lenore," Ernestine says. "You like Allen. We'll see if you're still denying it after you make him his special birthday supper and present him with his fancy grownup suit and shoes next weekend."

***

Allen comes in after an afternoon with his friends on the Sunday of his birthday and smells steak. Adicia, Justine, Ernestine, Julie, and the Ryans are sitting around the kitchen table, which is topped by a blue and white linen tablecloth and set with some of the china, crystalware, and silverware Allen purchased last year, instead of the usual mismatched dishes they set the table with when they all eat together. Lenore opens the oven door and takes out the roasting pans where she's been cooking six steaks, baked potatoes, and vegetables.

"Look, Lenore got better enough to make a special supper for your birthday!" Justine calls.

"I can see," Allen says, looking at Lenore setting the food on the table. "She looks great."

"Come sit down!" Infant says. "You get the biggest steak!"

Lenore pulls Allen's chair out for him and puts the largest steak on his plate. The girls insisted she get the next-largest steak, while the rest of them split the other four. Justine and Infant, Adicia and Julie, Ernestine and Girl, and Boy and Baby divide theirs in two and fill the rest of their plates with the vegetables and baked potatoes. Julie, the only right-handed person, is on the right-most side to avoid bumping anyone's elbows.

"Does this mean you'll be cooking supper most of the time again?" Allen begs. "I really missed your cooking."

"I missed cooking for you," Lenore admits. "Now you don't have to make all my food for me and bring it over to me. Your nurse work is done."

"I'm glad," Allen says, unable to take his eyes off her. "Now you can take care of me again. Every man needs a good woman to take care of him."

All the girls notice Allen has his eyes more on Lenore than the steak. Adicia barely understands all this boy-girl stuff, but is very jealous. She hopes when she's old enough, she'll find a guy who's as crazy about her as her brother is about Lenore, and that he'll look at her with that same kind of love.

"Would you like to see the present I got you?" Lenore asks after they've finished supper and had the birthday cake Allen got for free from the bakery.

Justine and Infant get the boxes Lenore hid under her bed and deposit them in Allen's lap. Lenore looks away from him shyly as he opens them.

"We helped Lenore pick them out!" Justine says proudly.

Allen finds a new pair of black dress shoes, a necktie with diagonal blue, white, and red stripes, a dark blue suit jacket with matching pants, and a white button-down shirt with pale blue vertical stripes. He looks over at Lenore with an awestruck grin.

"You didn't have to spend so much money on me for my birthday. You haven't worked for almost five months. Besides, it wasn't that long ago you were really mad at me and wanted to move out."

"You've been so nice to me when you didn't have to be. This is the least I can do to repay you. Please don't think you have to get me something expensive on my birthday in return."

"Isn't Lenore still a keeper?" Adicia asks.

"She's the best!" Justine says.

"Yes, she is," Allen agrees. "Something tells me she'll be with us for a very long time to come. I think this is just the beginning of even better and happier times for our unusual little family."

Chapter 29: Allen and Lenore's Romance

"Would you like to go out to supper to celebrate your birthday?" Allen asks Lenore. "You deserve something really special to mark your eighteenth birthday after all you went through this year."

"You mean tonight? Isn't Friday night usually a date night? People might assume we're on a date."

"Today's your birthday, isn't it? We'll have a nice supper, and I can give you your presents when we get home. I can't wait to show you what I got you."

"What if that girl you like sees us and gets jealous?"

"No other girl is gonna steal me away from you. Stop worrying about whatever I told you about another girl. How'd you like to go to a Greek restaurant?"

"I don't think I've had Greek food before."

"Why we don't we go and try it out? I hear Greeks make excellent food. I'm sure you'll have a great time."

"Okay," Lenore finally agrees, secretly thrilled she'll be going on something that looks like a date with Allen, even if they'll only be going out as male-female roommates. "I guess I'm paying for my own meal."

"I'll pay for everything. It's not very chivalrous to take a girl out to eat and make her pay for it. It's my job to pay. Why don't you put on fancy clothes while I put on that suit you got me, and we can be going."

Lenore darts into her room to put on a green sundress, a lightweight dark green shawl, and yellow leather open-toed sandals. Allen puts on the dress shirt, dress pants, and dress shoes, leaving off the suit jacket since it's so hot. He wishes he could offer Lenore his arm as they start down the hall to the elevator.

"I don't look so bad without makeup, do I? I never got around to buying any when I was working."

"You're naturally beautiful. You're not onea those girls who needs to put on a bunch of makeup to make herself look good. You should feel proud of having such nice skin and features without needing any extra help."

Lenore blushes. "You really think I'm beautiful?"

"The most beautiful girl I know, both inside and out. I'm proud I'm gonna be seen out and about with you."

When they arrive at the restaurant, they're given an outdoor table. Allen pulls her chair out for her and seems to spend most of his time looking into her eyes. Lenore tries her best to shrug it off as gratitude she's still alive, though she can't help but feel like she's turning into a bowl of gelatin every time he looks at her. She wonders what it would feel like to be touched by him in a non-platonic way, and shivers with excitement at the thought of it.

For supper, Allen orders stuffed grape leaves and moussaka, and Lenore orders baked lamb and spanakopita. He won't hear of her ordering soup and salad to save money and avoid overeating. Even after she's regained her health, Allen is terrified of Lenore becoming sick all over again. Only hearty, substantial foods will do. He insists she try several bites of moussaka from his fork. For dessert, Allen orders karidopita, a cake made of crushed walnuts and soaked in syrup, and Lenore orders the closest thing to ice-cream, partially frozen Greek yogurt with honey and berries.

On the way home, Allen turns to her, his heart beating loudly enough for Lenore to hear. "Do you mind if I hold your hand?"

"Sure," Lenore says after thinking about it for a few seconds.

Allen reaches for her hand and takes it gently in his, trying not to look at her for the rest of the walk home. Lenore doesn't look at him either, though her insides feel as though they're on fire from the sparks of excitement. Most girls her age probably think of hand-holding as baby stuff, but when one's never done it with someone special before, it's electrically charged, marking a different kind of physical contact and maybe the start of a boy-girl relationship. But maybe Allen wants to hold hands as friends and never asked her before. Not everyone holds hands for romantic reasons.

When they're back home, Lenore sits on the davenport while Allen goes into his room to fetch her birthday presents. There's a tingling sensation in the hand he was holding. After what her father did to her, she never imagined she'd someday long for any man to touch her. Her whole body aches to be touched by him again, even if it's just hand-holding.

"Happy birthday, beautiful girl," he says as he sets the gifts next to her.

Lenore opens the larger box first. It contains yet another stuffed animal, a smiling monkey, along with a bottle of perfume and a pair of light blue ballet flats. Allen looks at her for approval as she encounters each item.

"These are very thoughtful gifts. I guess you found out my shoe size the same way I found out yours."

"I insisted they find me flat shoes instead of those high-up shoes all the girls your age are supposed to wear. I don't want you slipping and falling again with high heels, after you already slipped with regular shoes."

Lenore opens the small box next. A folded note is on top of a bracelet with dark green stones. She hopes she isn't blushing too much as she reads the note, "Happy birthday to the prettiest girl I know, Miss Lenore Eve Hartlein, on her 18th birthday, June 25, 1965, Friday. Love, Allen Théodore Troy."

"You can't really think I'm the prettiest girl you know. And my mother once told me it's improper for a man to get jewelry for a lady unless she's his mother, sister, grandmother, wife, or a very serious lady friend he's going to marry."

"You have really beautiful green eyes. I got you emeralds so they'd go with your beautiful eyes. Here, let me put it on your wrist for you."

Lenore feels butterflies in her stomach as Allen puts the bracelet on her left wrist. She's trying to put the idea of him meaning anything more than friendship out of her mind when she hears him asking, "Would you like to go to the movies on Sunday?"

"You can't mean as a date," she says in embarrassment.

"Would it be so bad if I were taking you out on a date? You're old enough now to go out with me. You don't have to go out with me if you don't want to, but it can't hurt to give it a try."

Lenore gives him a slight smile. "Yes, I think I would like to go to the movies with you. Can we watch television?" She hopes to shift the conversation away from the idea of going on a date and a potential relationship starting.

Allen pushes the on button and goes up through ABC, CBS, and NBC to find something to watch. After settling on NBC, he turns to Lenore and smiles at her again. "Is it okay if I put my arm around you?"

Lenore looks straight at the television set. "I don't see why not," she decides after considering it for several long minutes.

She settles into the crook of his arm as her heart beats a little faster, as they both continue to look at the television and not one another. By the time Allen gets up for a glass of water after the show ends, she's starting to feel very comfortable sitting there with his arm around her. He's always made her feel very safe and protected, though right now he's probably motivated by something other than mere goodness of spirit.

When he takes his seat after coming back with the water, he puts his arm around her again without asking this time. At the first commercial break, he reaches for a drink and fumbles the glass when he puts it back, almost dropping it. He turns to Lenore, looking very nervous, and starts stuttering and pausing when he addresses her.

"I was...thinking, maybe...if it doesn't bother you...maybe...I mean, would you mind...would you be okay...how would you like it...I'd like to...I really want to...I've never asked a girl for permission before...Can I kiss you?"

Lenore involuntarily smiles, too nervous and surprised to answer.

"Is that a yes? If you don't want to, I won't make you."

"I'm scared. When you're my age and you've never done that, it seems really scary when it finally has a chance to happen."

"Don't worry, I won't be rough." Allen knows better than to bring up the fact that he gave a number of his ex-girlfriends their first kisses, and that he was nervous too when he had his first girl, the eighteen-year-old who invited him up to her place when he was a mere lad of thirteen. That would be the last thing Lenore wants to hear, comparisons to other girls. "If you don't want to do that, it's fine with me."

"Yes, you can do it," she says, her throat getting dry and her palms sweating.

Allen reaches over and gives her a soft, gentle kiss on the mouth that only lasts several seconds. Lenore's heart skips a beat.

"You look really happy. That wasn't so bad, was it?"

She can only smile an excited smile.

"Again?"

"Yes, please," she manages to squeak out in a whisper.

The second time he kisses her for a little bit longer, while Lenore's heart beats very fast and she has a warm, fuzzy feeling. When he pulls away and asks, "More?" she nods excitedly again and this time closes her eyes. She can hardly believe her good fortune. A little under three years ago, she ran away from Brooklyn and found some charming little girls and their cute older brother at the bus stop, and now she's being kissed and held by her handsome older roommate, whom she's had a crush on almost since the beginning. Never in her wildest dreams did she think the older Allen would reciprocate her teenage crush on him. At her age, a twenty-one-year-old is an older man, not someone from her own age group.

"You have no idea how long I've been wanting to do that," he says when he comes up for air. "Do I pass your test?"

Lenore suddenly feels insecure and turns her head away. Perhaps it really is too good to be true and he feels sorry for her after her ordeal in the winter, or he just intends to pass the time with her until he finds someone his own age.

"Something wrong? Don't you like my technique?"

"That was wonderful, though I have no one to compare you to. It's not that. Why did you pick *me*, Allen? I'm only turning eighteen, and you're twenty-one. Why would you pick me over a woman your own age? I'm not the prettiest girl I can think of, and I have absolutely no experience with men. You're a good-looking guy and had a bunch of girlfriends already. You shouldn't want to be with a girl you have to give a kissing lesson to. I don't know how to kiss you back without embarrassing myself and showing you how dumb and inexperienced I am."

Allen puts his arm around her and squeezes her hand. "You don't have to try kissing me back till you feel ready. Do you know how hard it is to find a sweet, pure-hearted girl like you? You've been so wonderful to my sisters and have taken such good care of me, without being asked. Maybe I'm too old-fashioned and double-standardish, but it's refreshing to find a girl who doesn't have any ex-boyfriends to compare me to, who hasn't given away pieces of her heart and is able to experience everything with a fresh slate. I like the idea of being your first everything." Allen cups her face in his hands and kisses her again. "You're the only girl I've ever been in love with, from the first time I saw you. I had the strangest feeling, the kind I can't explain in words. Since I knew what your father did to you, and 'cause you were only fifteen, I waited three agonizing years for you to be old enough for me."

Lenore is even more convinced she's dreaming. "You really liked me all this time and never told me? I guess I was the girl you told me you liked so much but didn't ask out."

"The only girl I've wanted for almost three years. Would I have gone to find you in the snow and taken care of you while you were convalescing if I didn't care about you so much? I love you, Lenore."

She looks down in embarrassment. "Did you just say you love me?"

"I told you before, when you were unconscious. That's okay if you don't love me yet. You don't have to say it back just 'cause I said it. But I guess you at least like me. You're not a tramp who lets a guy kiss her if she doesn't like him."

Lenore continues hanging her head in embarrassment. "Almost since I met you. I thought I never stood a chance 'cause you're so much older and experienced, and you told me you loved someone else. You were the guy I said I liked who'd probably never ask me out. I ran away so I wouldn't have to look at you and feel my heart breaking every time, knowing you liked someone else. I still think I'm dreaming."

Allen looks at her with sad puppy-dog eyes. "It was my fault you almost died? Had I known you liked me back, I wouldn't have told you that. I was being too much of a gentleman by wanting to wait till you were eighteen. No one at the hospital thought I was a creep for being twenty to your seventeen. As the girls always told me, it's not like I was thirty or you were thirteen."

"Maybe it's not such a big age difference when you get older, but it seems like you're a lot older. I feel like the luckiest girl in the world, getting my dream man as my eighteenth birthday present." Lenore leans over and shyly kisses him, then hides her face and giggles nervously.

"Don't hide your face. That was as sweet as sugar."

"Did you say that to all the girls you ever dated?"

"It doesn't matter what I said or didn't say to any other girl. You're my girl now, the one who was worth waiting for. I still can't believe a guy like me went and fell so hard for a girl, or that you liked me back all along. At least, I assume you want me to be your fellow."

"Yes, Allen, I will be your girl."

***

Adicia, Justine, Ernestine, Julie, and the Ryans come by on Saturday afternoon, carrying a shopping bag with their birthday presents for Lenore. Lenore is a bit moony-eyed as she greets them.

"You seem different," Ernestine says. "Does that happen to everyone when they turn eighteen and magically become adults?"

"Did you feel different overnight when you turned thirteen and became a teenager?" Lenore asks her.

"A little. Girl says she didn't feel like a teenager right away."

Girl pulls up a seat at the kitchen table and sits with her head in her elbows, an annoyed look on her face. When Lenore offers them birthday cake, Girl gives a little sigh and accepts a thin slice. She says nothing as she slowly chews the cake.

"What's eating you?" Lenore asks. "You're usually so animated."

"She started menstruating last night," Ernestine tattles.

Adicia looks at Girl with a mixture of jealousy, admiration, and surprise. "Why'd you keep it a secret? You didn't say anything about that when Justine and me met yous guys at your place."

"I was not looking forward to this," Girl grumbles. "I wanted to hold out till I was seventeen. Lucky Ernestine still ain't gotten hers."

"She went across the hall to Mrs. van Niftrik for help when she realized what was going on," Julie says. "Mrs. van Niftrik thought her homemade washable napkins were ingenious, and so much more practical and thrifty than the Modess napkins and the belt she uses. Betsy turned thirteen in March, but she hasn't menstruated yet. I'm glad I have at least two more years left to not have it."

"What did Allen get you for your birthday?" Baby asks, glad she's only eight and too young to be dealing with such a situation.

"A stuffed monkey, perfume, blue flat-soled shoes, and an emerald bracelet," Lenore says. "He spends too much money on me."

"A guy only spends so much money on a girl when he really likes her," Ernestine says. "You think he'll come home from work with more gifts?"

"Even if he does, I'm not wishing for anything more! Your brother has already gotten me a miniature zoo, and now he's gotten me jewelry, shoes, and perfume!"

"Can we go to the park after you open your presents?" Infant asks.

"Sure, that'll be fun."

Lenore takes the bag from Boy and pulls out the presents wrapped in newspaper. Ernestine and her friends pooled their money for a mauve jewelry box with seashells and bits of rounded, colored glass for decoration; Adicia got her a compact mirror with rhinestones with some of her windshield-washing money; and Justine got her a green, white, red, and yellow potholder she made in kindergarten.

"Someday when we're older and have jobs, we'll get you presents as nice as the ones Allen got," Adicia promises.

"He took me to a Greek restaurant for supper and held my hand part of the way home."

"How romantic!" Ernestine says. "Hand-holding is very underrated."

"When we were watching television after we got home, he put his arm around me."

"How exciting!" Julie says. "I bet you didn't put up a fight when he did either of those things."

"He asked my permission for both things," Lenore says proudly. "A lot of guys would just make their move and not care if the girl wanted it. You should've seen how nervous he was about asking me if he could kiss me."

"What!" Ernestine gasps, a big smile appearing on her face. "My brother really kissed you, on the mouth I'd assume?"

Lenore giggles nervously. "It was very nice."

"What does it feel like?" Girl asks, suddenly interested in her surroundings. "Not that I wanna do that with anyone till I'm a bit older, but I'm curious. I should know what to expect."

"Like being tickled by butterflies. You feel invisible, electric sparks, and you get butterflies in your stomach."

"I don't know why anyone would wanna do that." Infant wrinkles her nose. "It's like chewing on someone's face. Older people do lots of stuff I think is goofy."

"You're only six, sweetie. When you're my age, you'll probably think a lot differently." Lenore picks up her purse. "Who wants to go to the park? I'll buy yous guys snacks or ice-cream if we pass a vendor."

"That's it?" Girl asks. "You're gonna drop the bomb that Allen kissed you last night and leave it at that? No other details?"

"I wouldn't want to bore you with details when you've never had your own boyfriend. I don't think you could really understand what I'm talking about if you haven't experienced it yet. Besides, Ernestine, Adicia, and Justine might be a little grossed-out if I go into more detail about their brother kissing me."

"You're right," Adicia says immediately. "I hope no boy kisses me till I'm at least eighteen."

"When you're eighteen?" Justine asks. "I don't want to do that ever, with any boy!"

"I told you," Lenore says.

Girl looks at her in awe as they file out of the apartment, as though she's a species from another planet. Lenore seems more than five years her elder by mere virtue of having a boyfriend. That's the kind of growing up experience she'd prefer to be having right about now, instead of stuck having her first unwanted menstrual period.

***

That evening, while Lenore and the children are sitting around watching television and eating supper, Allen comes in from work with a large bouquet of red roses. The girls look at the flowers jealously as Lenore takes them and puts them in a vase. As soon as she's put them away, Allen puts his arms around her waist, pulls her close to him, and kisses her. Adicia and Justine stare at their brother with wide eyes, while Infant, Baby, and Boy look away in disgust. Julie and Ernestine stifle their nervous giggles, while Girl stares as much as she can get away with so she can try to find out how they're doing it. She doesn't want to fumble in the dark when it's her own time to start doing that.

"Do you have to do that in front of us?" Adicia asks after her brother has pulled away from Lenore.

"How can I keep my hands off my new girlfriend after I've liked her for almost three years?"

"I hope you don't start doing that weird stuff our parents do whenever they want, even if we walk in on them. The stuff that makes babies."

Lenore turns bright red. "Don't worry about that. Decent people don't do that with company, and it'll be awhile till I wanna do that. Only disreputable girls do such things with guys they've only been going out with for a little while."

"Are you gonna use those pills that prevent pregnancy?" Ernestine asks.

Lenore turns even redder. "That's a very long time off I have to worry about that!"

Justine looks at her a little sadly. "Does this mean you're not gonna do as much stuff with us as before, now that you've got a boyfriend?"

"I'll still do things with you. It's not like I'm moving to another planet."

"Well, I hope you don't intend to do that in front of us every time we come over from now on," Baby says. "I never wanna kiss a boy. It looks like chewing on someone's face."

"You will someday," Girl tells her. "Sometimes stuff makes more sense when you're older, even if it seems really weird at your age. I hated getting that line when I asked grownups to explain confusing things, but now that I'm thirteen, a lot of stuff that confused me as a kid makes more sense. I didn't get the appeal of kissing either at your age, and though I ain't done it yet, I get why people like it so much."

"Shall we finish our supper now?" Allen asks. "I hope yous guys saved enough for me."

"Of course we've got enough left for our handsome man of the house." Lenore skips over to the kitchen to pull out what remains of the goat meat and stuffed mushrooms. "Take a seat, and I'll have it heated up for you in a jiffy."

Allen looks at Lenore adoringly, as though she's the only person there, or in the entire world. Though she finds boy-girl relationships very mysterious, Adicia feels a twinge of jealousy that Lenore found someone to love her and take care of her, someone who loves her just as she is. The day when she'll be old enough for such a relationship seems very far off, as does the prospect of finding a nice guy of her own.

***

The summer has been like a dream come true to both Allen and Lenore. Every weekend they've gone on a date—the movies, a restaurant or café, a picnic in one of the local parks, a jazz or folk music club, museums, and, best of all, the World's Fair in Queens. Lenore has also gone back to school to finish her high school equivalency diploma, and goes during the day so she can be with Allen when he gets home from work in the evenings. She hopes she can go back to work at the gallery in Chelsea when she has her diploma, since she really enjoyed working in the art world. Perhaps it won't be in the same position, but they might have other positions available.

Lenore still feels disbelief when she's on a date with Allen or when he hugs or kisses her just because. It doesn't make any sense that she of all people would catch the eye of a handsome older man. Every time a girl looks at her jealously because of her cute escort, she has a sense of satisfaction, as though she's won the ultimate prize. Poor girls from Greenpoint never win the hearts of men like Allen. Though they've only been going steady for a few months, she knows Allen is the type who'd stay with her in the long haul. Working-class men are supposed to take care of their families, as foreign as the idea seemed growing up. Perhaps it's second nature to him to be so respectful towards girls, having grown up so outnumbered.

One night in early October, while Lenore is lying on her stomach on Allen's bed as he gives her a massage through her clothes, the transition from their innocent hand-holding, kissing, hugging, and fully-clothed massages starts.

"Would you feel comfortable letting me touch you?" Allen asks uncertainly.

"You already are touching me," she says, although she already has an idea of just what he's trying to ask.

"We'll keep the lights on, so don't worry about that. I'm not asking if I can do everything right away. I won't touch you below the waist."

Lenore rolls over onto her back. "Do you want to take my blouse off or just touch me?"

"That's up to you," he says nervously. "Damn, I never asked a girl if I could do that. It was just assumed we both wanted to do that, so there was no need to go through the formality of asking her permission and negotiating what would happen."

Her hands drift to the buttons on his shirt. "Will you let me touch you too?"

He smiles at her shyly. "Go ahead."

Lenore timidly begins unbuttoning his shirt. "Can you warn me if you're really bushy?"

"I'm not a Neanderthal. I don't think I'm really a hairy guy."

Lenore giggles nervously when she finishes unbuttoning Allen's shirt. He pulls the rest of it off and throws it on the floor. Lenore tentatively touches his chest, hoping she isn't blushing too much.

"You're cute. You're not a girl who's done this a million times before. I've always considered you a virgin. If something happened to you against your will, that's a lot different than choosing to have relations. In your heart, you're still pure, sweet, and innocent."

Lenore tenses up a little when Allen starts undoing her buttons. He stops when he hears her nervous breathing.

"Relax. If you're that nervous, you can just go back to your room and we can say goodnight for tonight."

"No, I can't push things off just 'cause I'm a little scared of them at first. That makes them even scarier when they do happen."

She tries to relax and breathe normally as he unbuttons the rest of her blouse. Allen struggles to unsnap her bra in the back, so she does it for him.

"Am I pretty enough for you?"

"Every part of you is beautiful," he says reverentially. "May I touch you?"

She nods nervously. She remembers how her father used to grab her and how his creep of a doctor friend used to poke and prod her during her forced weekly visits, but that's now cancelled out by how badly she wants Allen to touch her. Her whole body fills with the excitement and anticipation of being intimately touched by him for the first time, and she purrs in delight when she feels his hands on her.

"That feels really nice. You have nice hands."

"So I'm not doing it wrong? I can continue?"

"You can touch me there all night, you handsome man."

Allen kisses her on the neck. "Your wish is my command, beautiful girl."

***

A few weeks later, Lenore is dusting when she runs across a new book on the small shelf in Allen's room. Her eyes widen when she sits down to look at it and sees all sorts of graphic pictures, accompanied by descriptions of sexual positions and how to give one's partner pleasure. It's not smutty, but she can't believe he'd buy a sexual advice book when he's had so much prior experience. It must mean only one thing, that he intends to sleep with her at some point. Lenore hopes Allen's respectful treatment of her continues and that he doesn't think she's a whore the morning after. She knows what happens to a lot of girls who are intimate before marriage. At any rate, though, a guy who'd buy *The Kama Sutra* probably isn't the type who'd pitch his girlfriend aside after a few rolls in the hay.

"Allen, what is this book all about?" she asks when he gets home from work that evening, not letting him hug or kiss her in greeting.

He blushes. "That's, um, a book I bought for future reference."

"So you can take me to bed?"

"Only when you want to, of course," he stammers.

"Why do you need a book teaching you how to do what you already know how to do? I assume you don't forget that kind of thing, even if you haven't done it in over three years."

"Hey, I never used that book with any of my other girls. Neither of us cared about anything but momentary pleasure. It didn't matter if we didn't do anything fancy or if the girl got any equal satisfaction out of it. I got the book so I can know how to give you all the pleasure you deserve."

She sets the book on the coffeetable. "What if your sisters or one of Ernestine's friends had found this? I know what it's about, but they're young and innocent. The older ones know what sexual relations are, to a degree, but not well enough to know there are entire books about positions and techniques!"

"If they'd found it, I would've explained calmly it's a guidebook for grownups in serious relationships. Hell, I probably could do a better job of explaining the facts of life to 'em than those stupid school filmstrips. How do they think kids will understand this stuff if they're given such vague, sugarcoated misinformation? My sisters know you don't have to be married to have a baby, since our parents were expecting Gemma at their wedding."

Lenore sits down. "If you intend to do that with me eventually, do you know if you have any venereal diseases from all those girls you were with before me? I'm pretty sure I don't have any venereal diseases, since I went to that pervert of a doctor every week, and I always got a clean bill of health."

"I don't have any diseases. I never slept with girls of ill repute like Carlos. Besides, I don't look sick, do I?"

"I want to know for sure. You never can be too sure. It's one thing for a girl to risk her reputation, but I don't wanna risk getting a venereal disease. A girl of our class doesn't have much of a reputation to give up, but I can't get diseases if we're only making out. I've heard about women with diseases being unable to have kids or dying."

Allen looks very uncomfortable. "If it means that much to you, I'll go to the clinic Gemma used. Hey, this must mean you wanna do that with me if you're so concerned about whether I have venereal diseases.”

"You'll have to wait and find out. Respectable girls don't do that after only four months."

"You're still respectable to me, and I've known you for over three years. It's not like we did that the very night I brought you home from the bus stop, as my mother is convinced it happened. If you do wanna do that with me, I want you to keep your reputation. You should go to that clinic with me and get those new-fangled pills my older sister took. My mother probably wouldn't have had nine kids and ten pregnancies if those things had existed then. I'd do the right thing if I got you in trouble, but it's not fair for a kid to grow up knowing he was a mistake and his parents only got married 'cause of him."

Lenore looks away, embarrassed at how adult their conversation is becoming. "Would they give me any birth control devices when we're not married? I thought it was against the law in a lot of places for un-married girls to get them unless they lie about being married. It was surprising enough the hospital bought the story about us being married without wedding rings."

"You have to remove all jewelry in the hospital, and I told them I don't like wearing rings. If they suspected anything, they never told me. But anyway, that place Gemma went to is called Planned Parenthood. It has branches in a few other places now, but the one here was the original clinic. It's pretty old, and they've always been about giving ser-vice to people who need it. It's not like other clinics where they look at us poor and working-class people like we're trash, or automatically judge unmarried girls as whores."

"So we don't have to make up names or pretend to be married if we go there?"

"I don't want my girl getting in trouble, and it's only fair to have myself cleared for venereal diseases. You never can be too sure about that kinda thing, though I really hope I haven't had syphilis or another scary disease and not known it."

Lenore kisses him on the cheek. "I'm glad we're in agreement. We can make an appointment for next week, if they have any openings. They say a guy who wants to get a girl in bed before marriage doesn't respect her, but it's pretty damn respectful in my eyes if you care so much about wanting me to avoid getting in trouble and making sure you don't have a disease. I'm glad I'm your girl."

Allen kisses her on the eyelids. "You must really like me if you wanna be together in that way. Don't worry, I don't think you're a disreputable girl for wanting to do that with a guy you only like."

"I don't just like you, Allen," Lenore says, holding his hands. "I love you."

He smiles at her. "You love me?"

"I love you," she repeats. "You've already told me you love me a million times, and now I'm finally telling you. You're the only guy I want to kiss or touch me for the rest of my life."

He squeezes her hands. "You've just made me the happiest guy in the world all over again. I waited a long time to hear you say that to me."

"And I waited a long time to tell you. You did say you wanted it to be special for me and not just something I had to say back."

Allen hugs her. "You're such a sweet girl, Lenore. I'm the luckiest guy in the world to have found you and to have the honor of being your fellow."

***

Adicia, Justine, and Ernestine and her friends come to visit on Halloween, Sunday, arriving while Allen is buying extra Halloween candy for the neighborhood children. The girls admire how nicely Allen and Lenore have decorated—fake cobwebs, dangling spiders and bats, a Halloween tree, rubber skeletons, green and black streamers; banners depicting ghosts, witches, skeletons, Vampyres, and scarecrows; several jack-o-lanterns; and a display of gourds on the coffeetable. Even the van Niftriks didn't decorate so nicely, and they're hosting a Halloween party for their adult friends while Betsy and some of her friends from eighth grade are at a party in a Greenwich Village brownstone. Ernestine and her friends understand they couldn't be invited because Betsy and her parents don't want to get them in trouble for squatting or living without parents.

"Are you sick again, Lenore?" Justine asks worriedly when she sees Lenore opening the medicine cabinet and taking out a package of pills. "Sit down and relax if you don't feel well."

"I'm not sick, sweetie. These are special pills for grownup girls."

Girl gives her the side-eye. "Just what kind of pills are you taking?"

"They control my menstrual period," Lenore says vaguely. "Though I haven't used them long enough for that to start happening."

"So you can take pills that make you stop having it?" Girl asks wistfully.

"I could, if I wanted to. You're a little too young for these pills. Most girls using 'em don't use 'em for that reason."

Ernestine gets a closer look at them. "Those look like the pills Gemma had, the pills you take when you don't wanna have a baby."

"Are they really those new-fangled birth control pills?" Girl gasps. "You and Allen are having sexual intercourse?"

"Not yet. I got them to be prepared. He was sweet enough to go into the room with me when the female physician saw me. We're only at second base."

"What does baseball have to do with a grownup relationship?" Adicia asks.

"Second base is when you let a guy touch your breasts and you touch his chest," Ernestine supplies. "Third base is when you go south of the border, and a home run is going all the way."

"Why would any girl in her right mind want a guy to touch private parts of her body?" Baby asks. "You older people do a lot of goofy stuff."

"If you think that's goofy, just wait'll you find out how babies are made," Girl says. "Don't worry, I won't tell you till you're older."

"It feels like heaven when you're with someone you love," Lenore says.

"Does this mean we're gonna hear wedding bells by next year?" Adicia asks. "Only respectable people do that before marriage if they're really serious about each other and want to get married. If I had a boyfriend, and I was older, I'd only let him do that stuff to me if I knew we'd be getting married."

"I'm glad you're not letting so-called decent society dictate to you when to be intimate," Girl says. "If you really love a person, the feeling is mutual, and you take precautions to avoid a scandal, why shouldn't you do what feels natural? It's not like it's gonna be more special after marriage. It's special 'cause you were with a special person and you waited awhile before doing those special things together, not 'cause you waited to be Mr. and Mrs. and to have wedding rings."

"Are you really going to be a Troy?" Justine asks. "You'd be a nice Mrs. Troy, not like our mother."

"I've never thought about myself as anything other than a

Hartlein," Lenore admits. "Even if it is the name of the man who was so horrid to me, it's my name too. I have no family history with the name Troy."

"I don't think Allen would like that answer," Ernestine says. "He's kinda old-fashioned when it comes to guy-girl stuff. The guy is supposed to be the one who works hard to bring in money for his family, and if they make enough money from just him, the wife shouldn't have to work too. I don't think we've ever known a couple with different last names. Since he's the only decent Troy brother, he's the only branch of our family tree that could pass our name on."

"I dare you to write out your name as Lenore Eve Troy and see if you don't like it," Adicia says. "I'd change my name if I got married, just to not have the Troy name anymore. It reminds me of my parents and the bad life they gave me."

"I hear him coming down the hall," Boy says. "You'd better quit your girly talk. I don't know what I did to deserve to be the only guy among a bunch of girls."

"Girls will really like you when you're older," Ernestine promises. "Allen said girls would flock to him like flies to honey when they found out he's got six sisters. You've got three sisters, plus me, Julie, Adicia, Justine, and Betsy. Guys who grow up surrounded by girls usually understand what makes us tick more than guys who only had brothers or only one or two sisters."

Lenore opens a box of brownie mix and pulls out the mixing bowl and whisk. "Justine, you can be my big helper and get the eggs, milk, and Crisco."

"Can Infant and I lick the bowl, whisk, and wooden spoon?"

"Of course you may." Lenore smiles down at them.

Adicia stands back when her brother returns and hugs Lenore around her waist from behind, kissing her on both sides of her neck. She tries to put the image of Allen touching Lenore's breasts out of her head, but just can't do it. Even if Ernestine, Lenore, and Girl are right about that kind of stuff making sense and seeming beautiful at the right age, with the right person, it still seems gross. All she can think about as Allen and Lenore hand out Halloween candy is that when they're alone together, they take off some of their clothes and touch one another's bodies. It's bad enough when she walks in on or overhears their parents doing that. She was feeling like more of a big girl since starting sixth grade, her final year of elementary school, but now she feels almost as young as Justine and Infant. Although perhaps the special nursery magic that made the Velveteen Rabbit real also applies to children and magically makes them into grownups when they're old enough, the same way the Rabbit is different from an ordinary toy who hasn't been loved.

***

A few days later, when Allen and Lenore are making out on his bed, Lenore starts pulling off her skirt and stockings, then tries to reach over for Allen's belt.

"What are you doing?" he asks. "You're not ready to go all the way, are you?"

"Not now. I wanna go to third base. My whole body is on fire at the thought of you touching me there."

"You didn't even let me ask you for permission like a gentleman!"

"Oh, please, Allen. Normal guys aren't thinking of how to be perfect gentlemen when they're going this far with a girl. Now shut up and touch me there." She pulls off his belt. "You can let me touch you there too if you want."

"That's not a good idea. If you do, I probably wouldn't be able to go to bed without a cold shower. It's not fair to get a guy all excited like that and not be able to satisfy himself."

"What do you think we're doing now? We're making out without going all the way."

"It's different for guys."

"Okay, fine, have it your way, but I want you to round third base with me right now. Are you a man or are you a mouse?"

"You're sure you want me to do this?"

"I'm asking you, aren't I?" She grabs his hand and leads it over to between her thighs. "Let's see if you can remember somea those techniques from that Indian book."

"I hope I don't mess up," he says as he tentatively starts moving his finger up and down.

Lenore gasps. "That feels really good. You can continue whatever it is you're doing."

Allen tries to remember some of the things he read about in *The Kama Sutra*, and hopes he's doing something right. He hears Lenore breathing very fast and making strange noises, and sees her writhing back and forth. Hopefully none of the neighbors can hear her through the walls.

Lenore feels a deep pressure building up inside as her body jerks around spasmodically. Whatever Allen is doing feels so good she isn't embarrassed at the involuntarily loud noises she's making and the heavy breathing accompanying them. When it feels as though she can't handle any more of the intense tension building up, she lets out a scream and jerks her legs around before falling back onto the bed, her heart beating very fast.

"What was that?" she manages to gasp. "That felt like nothing I ever experienced before."

"That was called an orgasm. Most women don't get them that intensely their first time. I never thought it could come from something that wasn't intercourse."

"I sure hope that wasn't a one-off fluke," she gasps. "I'd like to try that again soon."

"If that was only the first time, I can't wait to see what happens the second time. I never thought I was that good at pleasuring a woman."

"You're good, believe me." Lenore runs her hand over his hair. "Can I sleep in your bed tonight?"

"You just asked if we could share a bed?"

"Not in that way. I know you won't do anything funny. Come on, I want to spend the night in your bed. I don't like going back to my lonely room when my handsome boyfriend is right here to cuddle with all night long."

Allen stands up. "Sure, I guess. I'll get a pair of pajamas for you."

"Why do I have to wear pajamas? Can't I sleep like this?"

He stares at her in disbelief. "Won't you get cold? It's November."

"There are enough extra blankets. Now lie down beside me and warm me up."

"Well, I'm wearing pajamas. No one slept in the nude at my home growing up. I'd still be seeing a shrink if I'd seen my parents or siblings naked. It was bad enough we often walked in on our folks doing it, but they were always covered by a sheet."

Lenore takes in his body as he undresses and pulls on a pair of white pajamas with thick indigo vertical stripes. Allen tries to do it as quickly as possible so she won't be looking at him for an extended period.

"You've got a nice body," she says when he crawls into bed next to her. "You're not six feet tall or a muscle man, but you're in nice shape."

"You've got a beautiful body yourself. I hope I'm the only guy you ever want to share it with."

"I hope you are too. Sweet dreams, my sweet prince."

***

The next evening, when they're making out as usual on Allen's bed, Lenore reaches for his belt like she did the previous evening. Every time he tries to pry her hand away, she grabs his belt again even harder.

"I really want you. I've been crazy about you for three years. I want to be with you completely, the way a grownup woman is with a grownup man."

He pauses and looks her in the eyes. "Are you sure about this? You do realize we'd be crossing the point of no return. You can't go back to just holding hands or making out after you've gone all the way."

"I don't want to either. I'm old enough to be with you, and I have those pills so you can't get me in trouble."

Allen looks at her longingly. "I'm not a pure innocent virgin, but I never had much more than a simplistic coupling before. It was only physical. I don't wanna mess up the first time I make love to a woman, and I hope I don't hurt you."

"I'm not a physical virgin, in case you'd forgotten. I won't bleed unless you're really rough, which I hope you won't be. Come on, you've been wanting me for three years. I want to lie skin to skin with you and feel your heart beating against mine, to be your grownup lover instead of just a girlfriend."

"You have to be sure about wanting to do this. That's not something you can undo. I don't want you waking up in the morning and regretting going all the way after only four months. I won't go around telling people, but we'd know what we did. It really can make you closer to a person, change your relationship and make it more complex. Are you prepared to feel such an intimate bond to me and not be able to undo it?"

"I'm not a child anymore. I know my own mind and heart, and I'm begging you to become my grownup lover, the only man I ever want to have such intimate access to me. I don't mind being bonded to you in that way for the rest of my life." Lenore draws him close to her and kisses him more deeply than usual, slithering her tongue inside his mouth.

Allen undoes his belt and struggles to unbutton his pants as he climbs on top of Lenore. She reaches down and helps him with pulling them off, tossing them onto the floor, then raises her hips so he can unzip her skirt and pull down her stockings. Lenore gasps her approval as he explores her body with his hands, mouth, and tongue. She breathes hard and fast as she feels his tongue between her legs. When he climbs on top of her again, she arches her hips up and opens her legs for him, feeling him entering her slowly so he won't hurt her or make her uncomfortable. Once inside of her, he moves slowly and gently as she digs her hands into the back of his shoulders, every so often leaning down to kiss her neck, mouth, or face.

"I love you," he whispers when he finishes up and exits her.

Lenore puts her arms around him and rests her head on his chest, feeling his heart beating against her ear. "Oh, Allen, that was incredible."

He strokes her face and hair. "Are you okay? Did I do okay? I hope I didn't mess up my first time with the only girl I've ever loved."

"You were great," she reassures him. "It was very romantic."

"You feel different?"

"I can't really put it into words, but I do feel different. Like I just changed from a little kid to a member of the grownup club. Now I know what this big secret mystery of adult life is all about."

"I still love you and respect you. I think I love you even more now."

"I feel like the luckiest girl in the world. I never dreamt when I met you that you'd be my grownup lover someday."

He crooks his arms tightly around her. "I never wanna do that with anyone else ever again."

"That suits me fine," she purrs as she drifts off to sleep.

In the morning, Allen has to wake up before Lenore to get ready for work. He watches her peacefully sleeping as he pulls on fresh clothes, and kisses her on the forehead before he goes into the kitchen to get cereal and an orange. Before he leaves, he writes a note and leaves it on her pillow.

Lenore wakes up at 8:30 and is very disappointed she wasn't able to wake up with Allen the morning after. She pulls the covers around her for warmth as she reaches for the note.

My beautiful Lenore,

Sorry I couldn't wake up with you, but you know I have to be at work at a certain time, and I didn't want to wake my Sleeping Beauty. Don't worry, I still respect you the morning after. I hope you don't regret anything either. I'm looking forward to doing that again tonight so long as you want to. Can't wait to see you again.

I love you forever,

Allen

Lenore smiles as she gets out of bed and goes to her room to get dressed. She feels different from head to toe, as though a great, invisible change has taken place within her. When she goes out to her classes during the afternoon, she wonders if anyone notices the change about her, the added spring in her step, the invisible glow she feels she's projecting. She can barely concentrate on what her teachers are talking about. All she can think about is what happened last night. Her body tingles at the memory.

Allen comes home from work at 6:30, carrying a large bouquet of pink, purple, and blue Michaelmas daisies in one hand and a heart-shaped box of chocolates in the other. Lenore's eyes light up at the sight of him as she rushes to hug him. He kisses her on the ear as she takes the flowers to a vase.

"You're gorgeous," he breathes in awe. "I don't take much stock in religion, but God made no mistakes whatsoever when he made you."

"I'm glad to know you think I look good," she says, smiling shyly.

"So you don't regret what happened I hope? 'Cause if you do, I'll step back and respect that you changed your mind."

Lenore hugs him again. "I love you more than ever, my sweet. Why don't you sit down, and I'll take stuffed peppers and mutton outta the oven in a few minutes."

Allen takes a seat, staring at Lenore as she bends over the oven and opens the door to take out supper. As soon as she sets it on the table, he pulls her onto his lap and kisses her, his hands traveling under her blouse.

"As soon as we finish eating, I want you back in my room immediately. In fact, let's not call it my room anymore. It's our room. We'll use your old room as an office, or a guest room for the girls. God, I can't wait to make love to you all night long. I couldn't stop thinking about it all day at work today."

"I couldn't stop thinking about it at school today either."

"Damn, I'm glad you're my woman."

As soon as they finish eating, Allen picks Lenore up and carries her into his room, throwing her onto the bed and pulling off her clothes as frantically as he can without ripping them. After he throws his own clothes on the floor, he climbs into bed and lustily takes Lenore in his arms, rising to his desire for her five times before heading off to get a drink of water. When he returns to bed, he lies there catching his breath for a little while, then pulls Lenore on top of him and couples with her four more times in that position. After making love twice in the spoon position, he rolls over and rests his head on Lenore's breasts, and falls asleep to her stroking his thick brown hair.

The next morning, Lenore awakes to another love note on the pillow. She smiles as she reads it, then goes for breakfast. Before heading out to her classes, she moves some of her clothes into Allen's closet and chest of drawers. All day she feels as though she's walking on cloud nine. By now she's convinced the other adults around her can tell something is somehow different about her, that she's been initiated into the secret world of womanhood, that she now knows all the mysterious secrets that come with sexual awakening. A part of her is sad Allen wasn't a virgin for her, but she's the first one he's ever made love to instead of just having a roll in the hay with, and all his prior experience has taught him how best to please a woman and minimize her pain and discomfort.

That evening when he comes home from work, Allen is a little later than usual. He looks like he has something special on his mind as he comes in the door carrying a paper bag. Lenore watches him rush into his room and close the door. She wonders if there's a present in the bag, and he's hiding it for later.

As soon as they're done eating beef barley stew and stuffed tomatoes, Allen rushes into the bedroom again, beckoning to Lenore. She notices he looks nervous as he undresses, and hopes he hasn't changed his mind already. In the back of her mind, she can't help but feel a nagging sense of doubt that someone so handsome, experienced, and financially established, at least in a working-class sense, couldn't possibly want to be with her in the long term. He could have any girl he wanted. Maybe he'll love her for just a little while and lose interest, particularly since she already gave herself to him in the most intimate way possible after not even four and a half months of going steady.

After coupling with her five times, Allen turns the nightstand lamp on. "Lenore, I have to talk to you about something."

Lenore's heart sinks into her stomach at those words. She starts bracing herself for the worst.

"I hope from the bottom of my heart you don't think I disrespect you or love you any less. I'd never want you to think I'm the kinda guy who'd have his roll in the hay with a girl and lose interest in her. My interest in you was always about a lot more than that. I'd never want you to think I only wanted to do my thing with you and throw you away and disrespect you like that. I loved you from the first time I saw you. I had a funny feeling in my gut that you were special, and it was so hard to refrain from telling you how I felt 'cause you were so young. I haven't lost any respect for you the way a lot of guys do when they sleep with a girl outside of marriage."

"Allen, are you crying?" Lenore asks.

"I hope you don't think I'm acting unmanly. I swear I've only cried once before in my life since I was a little boy, when you were unconscious. I'm only crying because I love you so much. I've never been in love with anyone ever before in all my life. I can't imagine ever loving any other girl. I want you to be my woman for as long as I'm breathing, as long as the rivers flow to the sea, as long as the wind blows, as long as the rain falls. I want to grow old with you, to have a new generation of Troys with you, to have grandkids together someday, maybe great-grandkids if we're blessed to live so long, to go through both happiness and sadness at your side, and when the day comes, to spend eternity next to you six feet underground. I want to make you a respectable woman, not sit by and watch as you continue to shack up with me and people who don't know anything about us make judgmental comments. I want everyone to know about and approve of our love. I hope you feel the same way about me."

"Of course I love you too, babykins. Why do you want to tell me all this now, though? I thought you wanted to tell me something bad."

"I need to talk to you about this now. I just can't wait any longer." Allen reaches under his pillow and pulls out a small box. "What I'm trying to say is that I'm asking you if you'll marry me and be my respectable wife."

Lenore takes the box and opens it. An emerald ring with two small accent diamonds is inside. "Oh, Allen!" she gasps. "Of course I'll marry you!"

"I hope you don't think less of me 'cause I didn't ask you right away after the first time. I'd never want you to think I only wanted you for that and that I intended to disrespect you by sleeping with you but not marrying you." He takes the ring out of the box and slides it onto her left hand. "I measured your ring finger with a tape measure when you were asleep, and told your measurements to the jeweler so he could figure out your size. I hope you don't mind it's not a diamond solitaire, but the dark green matches your beautiful eyes, and a guy like me can't afford an expensive diamond on a platinum band."

"I'd barely care if you gave me a ring from a crane game! It's the most beautiful engagement ring I could've asked for!"

Allen kisses her on the cheek. "I'm the luckiest guy in the world to be marrying the girl of my dreams. I can't wait to make you a respectable woman in front of God and all my sisters. We can ask the Episcopal priest in Yorkville to officiate. I can't think of any clergyman who'd be a better choice. Justine will be our flower girl, Emeline can be your maid of honor, Giovanni could be the ring-bearer, and the rest of my sisters can be bridesmaids. Ernestine's friends can be there too. Maybe they can be additional bridesmaids, and Boy can be a junior groomsman. Boy, it's gonna feel like forever till you're my lawfully wedded wife and don't have to pretend to be Mrs. Troy anymore. You'll be a nice Mrs. Troy, not like my mother, who doesn't deserve that title. One day we'll have a bunch of little Troys too. How about three? Not too many and not too few."

"One thing at a time," Lenore laughs. "We haven't even picked a wedding date. You can't plan a wedding overnight."

"Most married people I know were only engaged for a couple of months. If you don't mind waiting a little longer, we can have a nice spring or summer wedding. I don't want a winter wedding."

"We can have a July wedding, on the fourth anniversary of the day we met."

"That sounds perfect. Boy, I still can't believe what a lucky guy I am to be marrying the most beautiful girl in the world. I don't take much stock in superstitious talk about predestination and Fate, but something tells me we were meant to meet at that place and at that moment. Emeline quoted a line a couple of times, from a book by Voltaire, something about everything being joined up for a reason."

"'All events are linked together in this best of all possible worlds.' We studied that book in one of my classes. It's called *Candide*."

"I'm so glad you're my woman," he repeats as he wraps his arms around her.

Lenore isn't religious, but as she drifts off to sleep, she feels some force greater than herself must've meant for her to meet Allen. Only in this best and worst of all possible cities could a boy from the Lower East Side and a girl from Greenpoint meet in the West Village and find a special new life together.

Chapter 30: Blackout

Adicia and Justine are eating corndogs and waiting for their parents to get home from work late on the afternoon of November 9, Tuesday, when suddenly the lights go out. At first they assume their parents didn't pay the utility bills, but then they hear people elsewhere in the building exclaiming that their power went out. They rush to the window and look out into the street, and see block after block of buildings no longer lit up, and traffic lights no longer working. When Adicia picks up the phone, there's no signal noise.

"What do you think happened?" Justine asks. "I thought there are only blackouts when it's really hot, or when there's a storm."

"Maybe the power went out in the neighborhood. It'll probably be back on before long."

"Can we go to Mrs. Doyle while we're waiting? I'm scared to be alone in the dark."

Adicia finds a flashlight and takes Justine in her other hand. They peek out their front door and walk across the hall, hoping they won't trip on anything in the dark. They're not worried about Tommy, on the second floor with the Gómez boys.

Justine knocks on the door. "Mrs. Doyle, can we stay with you till we get the lights back?"

Mrs. Doyle opens the door and squints down at them. "Of course, you dear sweet girls. You can look after Caroline for me while I finish lighting candles. Matthew is taking a nap."

Adicia pulls fifteen-month-old Caroline onto her lap as they watch Mrs. Doyle go around lighting a variety of candles. She and Justine wonder what Lucine and Emeline are doing now, and if they have a blackout where they are too.

"I hope my little girl is indoors and won't suffer too much in this blackout," Mrs. Doyle says as she lights the last candle.

Adicia looks at her strangely. "Isn't your first daughter dead?"

"Oh, no. At least, not that I know of. When I've said I lost her, I meant I lost her to my ex-husband, not that she died of an accident or a childhood disease. Women unfortunately don't have a lot of rights, and keeping children after a divorce is one of them."

"You couldn't keep your own little girl after you left a very bad man?" Justine asks. "That's very sad."

"That's why Mr. Doyle and I live here even though we can afford a better neighborhood like the Upper West Side or Yorkville. I was here when I was married before, and I have a lingering hope that maybe, just maybe, I'll somehow find my daughter if I keep living in Hell's Kitchen. I have no idea if my ex-husband moved after our divorce, but he didn't make enough money to move anywhere but another run-down neighborhood. He didn't have a respectable job like Mr. Doyle."

"I'm sorry you had to lose your daughter," Adicia says. "Bad people like my parents deserved to lose my sisters when they moved away, but nice parents like you don't deserve to lose their kids."

"What are we gonna do about supper?" Justine asks. "If the blackout lasts longer than a few minutes, we won't have power for cooking."

"The stove will work," Mrs. Doyle says. "It's gas-powered. I hope the perishables in the refrigerator and freezer don't spoil or melt. Mr. Doyle works very hard to make money for our groceries."

"Can we help you with supper?" Adicia asks. "We're good helpers. We always help our big brother Allen and his fiancée Lenore."

"Just sit back and enjoy being little girls for awhile. When you're in my home, you don't have to assume any grownup responsibilities."

"We saw Allen and Lenore this weekend," Justine says as Mrs. Doyle pulls a big stockpot of chicken and dumpling soup out of the refrigerator. "He gave her a beautiful engagement ring. It's a green rock with two little diamonds on the side."

"It's a lot prettier than the one our oldest sister Gemma got from her beastly ex-husband," Adicia says. "That ring was boring. Gemma threw it into the street when she made a big scene at supper and told everyone she'd divorced him."

"Would you like to see mine?" Mrs. Doyle twists her engagement ring off and hands it to them after she puts on one of the gas burners.

Adicia and Justine come close to the candlelight and examine it. It's a silver band with an oval-cut, slightly blue diamond, two small pearls on either side. They can make out an inscription on the inside, "From BID to SMB, 5-15-59."

"You can get rings inscribed?" Adicia asks. "Allen didn't have Lenore's ring inscribed. Is it very expensive to do that?"

"I didn't ask Mr. Doyle how much it cost. It's just our initials and the date we got engaged. He was counting on me saying yes, since he put the exact date he proposed on it."

"Can I ask what your initials stand for? When I was younger, I used to think all married ladies had the name Mrs. I know it's not polite to call grownups by their first names, but I'd like to know just because."

"Mr. Doyle's name is Benjamin Isaac, and my name is Suzanne Mary. The B stands for Bowstead, my maiden name. I took back my old name after I was divorced."

"That name sounds familiar. I think I heard it somewhere before, but I can't remember where."

"Suzanne is a pretty name!" Justine says. "It has more personality than Susan. There are a bunch of Susans in my first grade class, but no Suzannes."

"It's not an uncommon name for women my age, though I've heard it more on girls of your generation. You two have names you'll probably never have to worry about sharing."

"Most of the girls I've known have been named Debbie, Linda, Barbara, Susan, Sharon, Karen, Kathy, Carol, Diane, or Nancy," Adicia says. "Those are the names I've heard over and over again. I don't think anyone else would ever name their daughter Adicia, since I'm named for the Greek goddess of injustice."

"Can we eat our supper on the floor?" Justine asks. "It's easier to eat on the floor when there are no lights."

"Sure, that'll be fun," Mrs. Doyle says. "We'll have a little picnic on the rug."

When the soup finishes heating up, Mrs. Doyle ladles it into four bowls and sticks spoons into them. She pulls trays out of the closet and puts each bowl on a tray. Caroline eats leftover mashed potatoes Mrs. Doyle puts on top of a metal tray, using her hands and getting them on her face.

"You're a nice mother," Justine says. "I wish our mother was as nice as you. She'd never let us eat on the floor or with trays."

"Our mother couldn't even feed us our own bottles," Adicia says. "She only gave them to Tommy after she got Sarah to be our nanny."

"Is there dessert too? We only have dessert on very special occasions."

"I made a chocolate cake with chocolate icing the other day," Mrs. Doyle says. "You girls are welcome to have some of it."

Matthew stands up when someone knocks on the door. "Can I get it? I hope it's Daddy coming home from work, so he can join us in our picnic."

"Go ahead, darling."

When Matthew opens the door, they see Tommy standing there in the darkness. Adicia and Justine hope he's not about to crash their nice time.

"I'm going to a Spanish restaurant with the Gómezes. They'll have lanterns and candles. I guess Mommy and Daddy won't be home for awhile 'cause everything's broken and so dark, so it's okay for me to have supper with them. But if they do come home during the blackout, they'll know where I went."

"Have fun," Adicia says. "I know we don't like each other, but I won't tell our parents you went out to eat with your Puerto Rican friends if they ask what you did about supper tonight."

Tommy runs back down the hall and jumps down several steps at a time, not bothering to thank her for promising not to squeal on him. Adicia and Justine are sorry he doesn't trip and fall.

***

All the power at the bakery suddenly shut off a little before 5:30, and a couple of lanterns from a utility closet were brought out for the customers brave enough to stop by. As soon as the bakery closed down at 6:00, Allen rushed home through eerily blackened streets, not a single light to be seen. Only a full Moon in a perfect cloudless sky lit the way back home.

Lenore is on the fire escape looking up at the beautiful full Moon when she hears Allen unlocking their door. She turns around and watches him feeling his way around over to her, glad he's home safe and sound and that she'll no longer be trapped alone in the dark.

"I couldn't get home a moment sooner," he says as he hugs her. "I hope you weren't too scared all alone with no power."

"I'm always happiest when you're here, my darling." She nuzzles her face against his neck. "I hope you don't mind having a cold supper."

Allen looks at her more closely. "You're not wearing a coat? If you catch a chill, you might get sick all over again. You have to be extra-careful after what happened last winter."

"I'm fine. It's not like there's a raging blizzard."

Allen puts his jacket over her. "You have a habit of not dressing properly for the weather. That's the third time I've had to give up a coat to you."

She rolls her eyes. "I'm not made of glass. I can handle standing outside for a little while without a jacket."

"You have no idea what it did to me when I found you lying unconscious in the snow. I'll never forget that image. It's even worse now that I know it was my fault you were out there in the first place. I never would've told you I was in love with another girl I was afraid to ask out if I'd known you had a mutual crush on me all along."

"I often cried myself to sleep after you told me that. I could barely stand to be around you. You sure had me fooled. I thought your sisters and Ernestine's friends were imagining things when they told me you had a thing for me, and I always told them you'd never go for me since I was so inexperienced and a lot younger. I was really heartbroken."

Allen hugs her again, tighter this time. "I hate the thought of doing anything that'd make my sweet Lenore cry or break your heart."

Lenore walks back inside and squints her way over to the kitchen. "Do you want turkey, ham, bologna, or salami? After we have sandwiches and cake, we can warm each other up the old-fashioned way."

"How about we go out for supper? We can find a diner with gas stoves and candlelight, and have a nice romantic meal. Besides, I wanna show my woman off to as many people as I can. You have to put on your jacket before we go anywhere."

"Are you sure they'll be open with the power outage?"

"There are always people who wanna go to restaurants. Besides, I'm sure lots of other people must have the same idea, since they can't see and don't have power to cook either."

Lenore hands Allen his jacket and goes to the closet for hers. "Maybe it will be romantic. It's not every day you get to go on a date in the middle of the week."

They go down the fire escape so the full Moon can light the way, instead of feeling along walls while going down the stairs inside. It's very surreal to walk past block after block of darkened buildings and see broken traffic lights in the city that never sleeps. Perhaps this was what it was like to walk through Manhattan a century ago, before electricity powered everything and everyone relied so much on it for everything. Allen remembers how there was only a sliver of the Moon in the sky the night Adicia, Justine, and Giovanni went from Tompkins Square Park to the Bowery Mission. They probably would've given anything to have had their way lit by a big full Moon in a cloudless sky.

"Did I ever tell you I would've still loved you if you'd been paralyzed?" Allen asks as they round a corner near a diner with light coming from it.

"You don't mean that. Your older brother's a useless cripple, and your family all washed their hands of him since his accident."

"I would've still taken you home with me if you'd been crippled. I'd be pushing you in a wheelchair right now if God forbid you'd been paralyzed. Would you still love me if I were a cripple or had another handicap or disfigurement?"

"I never thought about that. Don't tempt Fate like that. If you keep talking like that, you might get run over by a car that doesn't see you, and I'd be so sad if I had to watch you dying or being maimed." Lenore holds his hand a little tighter.

Allen holds the door of the diner for her. When they walk inside, they see a number of other people in the candlelight, with several gas stoves and wood-burning fireplaces working in the background. Someone has put a transistor radio on a table in the middle of the diner and turned it up.

"Table for two?" a waiter asks.

"Yes, please," Allen says. "Can we have a table with extra candles? I want to see my fiancée's engagement ring sparkling in the candlelight."

"You're engaged?" a woman at a nearby table asks. "How soon is your wedding?"

"July twenty-ninth of next year. It's the fourth anniversary of the day we met," Allen says proudly, pulling off Lenore's left glove. "Show everyone your ring, Lenore."

"That's a long engagement," a man says. "Most people I know are married within three or four months of getting engaged."

"We got engaged under a week ago," Lenore says in embarrassment as Allen holds up her left hand. "We don't wanna have a wedding during the coldest time of year. I can wait for a nice time of year and a special day."

The waiter leads them to a booth in the corner, with six candles on the table, and hands them menus. "It'll be on the house, our gift to you for your engagement."

Lenore wants to protest, but Allen is so overcome with pride at showing her off and letting everyone know about their engagement, she doesn't have the heart to disappoint him. She remembers how overprotective of her he is since her illness, and so orders a turkey pot pie, steak fries, and clam chowder. When their orders come, Allen insists she have some of his double burger with mushrooms, onions, lettuce, and tomatoes, potato skins with melted cheese and bacon bits, and butternut squash soup. She hopes no one can see her eating from his spoon and taking bites out of his hamburger. At least he wants his woman to have a healthy appetite, she tells herself in resignation, instead of looking down on her for not eating like a bird and keeping herself skinny like a lot of other girls do.

By the time they place their orders for dessert, they've found out from the transistor radio that this blackout is more than just a neighborhood power outage. Almost the entire Eastern Seaboard is bathed in darkness—New York City and much of Upstate; Ontario, Canada, including the capital city of Toronto; Maine; and New England. They wonder how the girls are doing, and Allen secretly hopes his parents are among the people caught in elevators or subway tunnels and unable to come home tonight. It would serve them right to spend a night in the dark and cold, surrounded by strangers, many of them probably the very people they preach against so much just because they have some money and live in nice neighborhoods. For good measure, he hopes that mean-spirited busybody Mrs. Rossi is stuck along with them. Mr. Doyle and Mr. van Niftrik must also probably be trapped in a subway tunnel or darkened workplace, but sometimes the innocent have to suffer along with the guilty.

"Have some of my chocolate ice-cream float," he insists as Lenore nibbles at a banana split.

"Allen, you're embarrassing me!" she whispers. "These nice people are gonna think I'm a pig who can't control her appetite!"

"My older sister's ex-husband's family were guilty of that, but not me. They forced all this food on her when she was ready to pop twenty times over. I'd never make you eat when you felt sick. I'm just letting you take some bites of my food." He leans over to her and whispers in her ear. "Besides, I'm sure you'll burn off some of these calories when we get home tonight with my help, if you know what I mean. I can't wait to get to bed with you and generate our own electricity and heat."

Lenore is a hundred shades of red as she takes a few sips from Allen's straw.

***

Ernestine is fumbling for matches or a flashlight when she feels as though she's wet herself. Hoping against hope it's not what she dreads it is, and at this worst of all possible times, she dashes out to the fire escape and looks around for people on nearby fire escapes or down on the street. When the coast is clear, she pulls down her skirt and underwear. In the bright light of the full Moon, she sees what looks like a colored stain and lets out an angry shout.

Girl comes running out onto the fire escape after her. "Ernestine, what in the world are you doing with the bottom half of your clothes down where everyone could see you? Even I ain't so into the mystical and unexplained I believe people go nuts with a full Moon."

"Look at this," Ernestine whispers in mortification. "I'm having my first menses. Damn, I wish I could stay on this fire escape all night and bleed onto it. No one would know what I was doing."

Girl puts her arm around her. "I know it stinks. Pull your clothes back up and we'll go to Mrs. van Niftrik. She helped me when I got mine."

"Can't I spend all night sitting on the toilet?" Ernestine begs in mortification. "I don't like the idea of anyone else knowing."

"What if someone else needed to use it? They'd wonder what you was doing in there so long. Boy would be embarrassed beyond belief if he was told you was in there all night 'cause you were menstruating. I don't envy him, the only guy in a household full of girls."

"I can sit on a bucket, and switch buckets if I fill one up all the way."

"Even I think that's gross. Come on, Mrs. van Niftrik was a girl once. She knows how to handle this. I keep the cloth sanitary napkins in a purple laundry bag in the bathroom closet. Yours are in a smaller blue laundry bag within the big laundry bag, 'cause it ain't healthy to share something as personal as that. We'll take 'em over to Mrs. van Niftrik and let her do the rest."

Ernestine feels herself blushing in the dark as Girl leads her over to the bathroom and pulls out the blue laundry bag, then takes her by the hand and slowly makes her way across the hall. The other four assume they're going to borrow a flashlight and don't question why they're leaving.

"We're glad to see you, girls." Mrs. van Niftrik smiles at them when she opens the door. "We were just wondering how you all were making out with the power outage. You can all come over and keep us company if you want. Mr. van Niftrik isn't home yet. I assume he's trapped in the subway with all those other poor people."

"Ernestine needs your help," Girl says. "She just started to menstruate."

Ernestine hangs her head in shame.

"There's nothing to be embarrassed about, dear," Mrs. van Niftrik tries to reassure her. "All normal girls have that happen at about your age. It's a normal part of growing up, and it means everything is working just as it should. It's inconvenient, and you don't always feel your best during this time, but just think, this is your body's way of preparing for having a baby when you're a grownup."

"But normal girls don't have babies as teenagers anymore," Ernestine protests as Mrs. van Niftrik ushers them inside. "Why couldn't our bodies evolve to do that when we're eighteen or twenty-one instead of twelve or thirteen? I don't want all those years of menstruation when I'm not old enough to get married or have a baby. My ten-greats-grandma got married and had her first kid at my age!"

"I'm not looking forward to my first one either," Betsy admits. "That filmstrip we saw in sixth grade made me even more confused and scared about what's gonna happen, and so did that silly booklet. Why am I supposed to look forward to something so annoying and cherish it as a magical, special part of becoming a young lady? Those dumb booklets were written by people who think all girls in junior high wear makeup and go on dates. I'm not allowed to wear makeup till I'm sixteen, and I can't go on a date till I'm in high school."

"Well, complaining about it won't make it go away, will it?" Mrs. van Niftrik asks. "I'll help fix Ernestine up, and we'll all have roasted marshmallows and chocolate bars."

***

Mrs. Doyle let Adicia and Justine sleep in her bed when their parents didn't come home. At about 10:00, she went to the second floor to check with the Gómezes that Tommy was spending the night with them, then came back to take care of the girls. Adicia and Justine both had wonderful dreams their parents were trapped in a darkened subway tunnel surrounded by strangers from the nice part of town, and the cops came after them for using drugs and arrested them.

"They somehow managed to put a paper together," Mrs. Doyle says as she fetches the November 10 edition of *The New York Times* while the children eat fruit and dry cereal for breakfast. "Only ten pages, but I'm surprised they managed to put out anything with all the power out."

Adicia, Justine, and Matthew look at the picture on the front page in amazement. The famous city skyline is shown with every single light out, giving it a very eerie appearance, as though life ceased to exist, leaving only buildings behind.

"Do you think we'll have to go to school today?" Justine asks.

They hear angry footsteps in the hall and Mrs. Troy's angry muttering. The power must be back on.

"Would you believe the nerve of this city's pathetic so-called law enforcement?" Mrs. Troy demands, bursting into the Doyles' apartment without knocking. "While I was at work yesterday, my parole officer and a cop paid me a surprise visit and said since I hadn't paid back any of that money I embezzled, they'd start garnishing my paychecks till the debt is cleared! I'll be working till I die to pay back five thousand dollars!"

"You stole five thousand bucks?" Matthew asks.

"It was mostly to pay for my second daughter's wedding that never happened. I ain't a selfish woman who embezzled it all for myself."

"So, I guess this means the power came back on?" Justine asks.

"I was trapped in Times Square all night long without any drugs or alcohol to help get me through it! The couple of cigarettes I was given by a woman next to me barely did anything to keep my nerves down! As if being told I can't keep any of my rightful money for myself wasn't bad enough for one day! At this rate, I might as well quit working altogether and stay at home doing jobs under the table, so the bank don't steal my money."

"That was their money you stole," Adicia says. "You have to pay them back."

"I suppose Tommy's on the second floor with his spic friends. I hope he enjoyed his night with them, 'cause that sure as hell ain't never happening again. I don't approve of the races mixing."

"Where's Dad?"

"Hopefully his subway will come rolling in here any minute now. I wish he'd take a job closer to home, but no, he has to keep that stupid old job of his back in the old neighborhood. He's had that job for what, fifteen or twenty years?"

"You act like it's a bad thing to work the same job for a long time," Justine says.

"Look at me. Have I ever worked a job for even six months?"

"That's not something to be proud of," Adicia says.

"Well, I am proud of it. One day you'll stop trying to get above your raising and realize our kind don't do things the way rich people do. Why don't you finish getting ready for school so I can relax and smoke cocaine before I have to head back out to work all over again."

Adicia and Justine go into the Doyles' bedroom to change into the fresh pairs of clothes they brought over after supper last night, take their schoolbags, and head down with Matthew to wait for the school bus. Tommy is waiting with the Gómezes, not a care in the world. Nothing surprises Adicia about her mother anymore, but she'd thought being stuck in the subway of Times Square all night, surrounded by strangers, without any lights or heat, would've moved even her hardened heart a little. Probably a lot of people in this huge metropolis felt more connected to one another after being without power for that long, but not Mrs. Troy. It was just another annoying inconvenience, not a chance to step back and appreciate what's really important. She probably didn't look at the full Moon in the cloudless sky as a beautiful miracle, providing a source of light and hope to the darkened city that had shut down. It's her mother's loss for being so disconnected from human emotions, but Adicia can't help feeling it's not fair to have been saddled with her for a mother.

Chapter 31: A New Year Full of Hope

"You are not," Julie insists. "You are not going to call the radio station with the van Niftriks' phone and ask them to play a Beatles' song with your name in it. The disc jockey would either think you were joking or wonder where your parents are and try to get them arrested for not giving you a proper name."

It's the first day of 1966, a Saturday, and Adicia, Justine, Ernestine and her friends, and Betsy are sitting around in Betsy's apartment, having snacks, and playing records while Mr. and Mrs. van Niftrik are out visiting friends for the New Year's celebration. Girl has been beside herself with excitement since they all got their own copies of *Rubber Soul* for Christmas and found a song called "Girl" on side two, sung by John, her favorite Beatle.

"It's my name, ain't it? I'm proud of my name. It might not be my name forever, since I'll be a woman eventually, and it's silly for a woman to go by Girl, but it's my name now. Why can't I ask that my special song be played on the radio just for me, as a cool treat for the New Year?"

"I like the song, but it's not exactly about the nicest girl in the world," Ernestine says. "The girl in the song is really mean to him."

"Why don't you lie and say your name's Michelle, if you want the disc jockey to play a Beatles' song with a girl's name in it?" Julie asks.

Girl laughs. "How many Michelles have you known? It might be more common in France, but I don't think I've ever heard it on a girl here. If it does get more common, you can bet it'll be onea those names that gets really popular all of a sudden and is old hat in another generation or two. Take your mother's name. Didn't you say it was Susan? That name's so popular among girls our age, you can't throw a stick without hitting five of 'em."

"My mommy's name was Suzanne."

"I like that name," Justine says. "Our next door neighbor Mrs. Doyle told us her real name is Suzanne. It has more personality than Susan, even if it sounds almost the same."

"You got your neighbor to tell you her real name?" Baby asks. "I thought it was supposed to be rude to ask a grownup her real name."

"We were looking at her engagement ring in the candlelight during the blackout, and it was inscribed on the inside with her and her husband's initials and the date they got engaged," Adicia says. "So we asked what they stood for."

"What are your parents' real names, Betsy?" Julie asks. "I guess grownups really do have their own names they use when they're with other grownups. In some places, all grownups call each other Mr. and Mrs. even when there are no kids around, but I don't think we live in a place like that."

"My mom's name is Gloria Ruth, and my dad's Arthur Lawrence. My mom's maiden name was Reinders. That's a Dutch name too."

"Is your real name Betsy?" Infant asks. "I mean, is it short for Elizabeth?"

"Just Betsy. My parents liked how it sounded on its own. Not all nicknames work by themselves or sound grownup when you get older. Did you ever think of what name you might like when you get older and need a true name?"

"I never thought about that. I'm only going on seven. I won't need a grownup name for a long time."

"I think I can get away with being called Baby forever," Baby says. "It sounds like a respectful nickname. Your mother said there's a French name that sounds like Baby, a name a couple of actresses from the olden days had."

"Bebe," Girl supplies as she inches closer to the phone. "One of the women at the squat said there's an actress named Bebe Daniels, who she really liked. She got the Presidential Medal of Freedom from President Truman for her war efforts. I assume it's a nickname, since it means 'baby' in French." She raises the receiver from the hook.

"You're *not* really doing it," Ernestine protests.

"I have the number memorized from how many times they announce it on the air for people who wanna make requests," Girl brags as she begins dialing.

"What if Betsy's parents get mad at an extra charge on their phone bill?" Boy asks.

"I'm so glad we don't need to talk to an operator and ask to be connected anymore when we place phonecalls," Girl says as she waits for the disc jockey to pick up. "No more middlewoman."

The other children sit back in suspense as they hear someone responding on the other end of the line. She surely can't be so stupid as to publicly admit on the air that her name is actually Girl, and thus invite a lot of questions.

"Hi. My name's Colleen Ryan, and I'm calling to request my new favorite Beatles' song, 'Girl.' I like it so much 'cause it's sung by John, my favorite, and my name means 'Girl' in English. I like to pretend he's singing to me when I hear it, even though the girl in the song isn't so nice."

"Your wish is my command, Miss Ryan," the disc jockey tells her.

Girl smiles at them after she hangs up. "See? I told yous guys I could pull it off. You just have to know how to say the right things, use proper English, make up a convincing story."

"Where'd you dig up the name Colleen?" Julie asks. "Does it really mean 'girl'?"

"Yup. No one in Ireland would use it, of course, but Irish-Americans who don't know jack about our language or heritage don't balk at using it."

"Maybe you should pick an Irish name when you have to get a legit name," Adicia suggests as the disc jockey starts to announce the request on the air. "It's nice to have a name that shows off where your ancestors came from."

Girl sits back with her eyes closed dreamily as the radio plays "Girl." Julie, Ernestine, Betsy, and Adicia like the song too, but wonder why in the world she'd enjoy having her name in it so much when the lyrics describe a girl who makes her boyfriend feel so poorly and uses guilt to keep him around every time he tries to break up. None of them would dare treat a man who loved them so meanly.

"We might see Emeline and Lucine this summer," Ernestine announces after the song is over. "They're supposed to come to Allen and Lenore's wedding."

"I hope they come!" Justine says. "They must both be grownups by now."

"Lucine will be twenty this month, and Emeline's seventeen and a half. Emeline will be outta school by the time we hopefully see her again."

"Maybe this means we can see Giovanni again too, since he was adopted by the minister Allen wants to do the wedding!" Adicia says. "He let Lucine and Emeline go to his special school uptown."

"They're not getting married in the Church of St. Luke in the

Fields?" Betsy asks. "Why go uptown to a church and reverend they don't know?"

"They've done a lot for Lucine and Emeline, and adopted our baby nephew Giovanni. Allen couldn't imagine anyone else doing the honors," Ernestine says. "If we didn't go to such a cool school, I'd wanna go to that place too. I'm probably not the boarding school type, and I'd never wanna wear a uniform or have to go to church once a week."

"Church isn't too bad. Maybe it's different when you grow up going every week instead of hopping from church to church for just the two big holidays. We go to a Dutch Reformed church."

"Emeline respects Jesus as a wise, kind-hearted teacher and spiritual leader, and has a general belief in God, but isn't too into Christianity in general after all the bad things done in its name over history. She's more interested in religions from India and the Orient."

"Do we have anything we could talk about with them anymore?" Adicia asks. "They've been away for so long, and now they have friends their own ages."

"I'm sure we'll have lots to catch up on. Emeline likes The Beatles, so we can talk about them with her. I wonder what her favorite songs are. She only told us her favorite is George, and didn't tell us if she had any favorite songs or records."

"Is he really?" Betsy asks. "I think he's the least-popular one among the girls at our junior high. Your sister isn't afraid to be different and like the underdog."

"You can meet her too," Justine says. "We'll invite you as our guest to the wedding. Emeline's so smart and knows so much about everything. She's known how to read since she was three, knows a couple of other languages, reads nonstop, and wants to be a librarian when she grows up."

"Librarians are supposed to wear glasses, wear their hair in buns, and be old maids who knit in their spare time and have twenty cats. That's how they always show them in movies and television."

"Emeline's pretty!" Adicia says. "She doesn't wear glasses or wear her hair like an old lady, and she can't knit. She's got chestnut-brown hair with russet streaks and brown eyes like me, Ernestine, and Lucine. The only way she's like that image of a librarian is that she's always reading, and she's quiet when she's not around our family."

"No wonder he's her favorite," Julie says. "I guess people who are shy and quiet feel pulled to others of their kind."

"Emeline always talked to us lots," Ernestine says. "She taught us so much from her books, and always read to us. It's just that she's not too talkative when she's with other people. She knows they wouldn't be interested in hearing about a writer she's mad about, a story from Greek mythology, or what an Indian god taught."

"Emeline's gonna be the maid of honor," Adicia says. "She gets to stand up at the altar with them when they make their vows. Justine will be the flower girl, so she'll walk in front of them and sprinkle petals while they're walking up the aisle. Me, Ernestine, Lucine, Julie, and the Ryan girls will be the bridesmaids. Boy's a little too old to be the ring-bearer."

"You can sure say that again. I'll be twelve by their wedding. No guy my age wants to be a ring-bearer."

"How about little Giovanni?" Ernestine asks. "He'll only be five. Just the right age."

"What a great idea!" Girl says.

"We'll go to a nice bridal shop uptown to look for our dresses," Adicia says. "Maybe it can be the same shop we went to for Gemma's wedding and Lucine's cancelled wedding."

"This time we can get pretty dresses we want to wear," Justine says. "Last time we had to choose stuff we didn't like 'cause we knew we'd never wear it."

"We can get dresses in our favorite colors like we did when Gemma was married," Ernestine says. "Red for me, dark blue for Adicia, green for Emeline, purple for Lucine, and pink for you."

"I still have the flower girl dress I wore at Gemma's wedding," Adicia says. "I saved my pretty dress from the fire. Emeline saved her dress too."

"So did I, but we all deserve nice, pretty, new dresses. I'd hate to wear hand-me-downs on such a special occasion."

"They're probably haunted and cursed," Girl says. "It's like wearing your mother's wedding dress if her marriage ended badly or she lost her husband really young."

"What's their processional music?" Betsy asks. "I don't want to use 'Here Comes the Bride' when I get married. I'd like classical music, to make a really special entrance, and something soft and pretty for my bridal party's processional."

"Lenore likes a song from local folk singers she listened to when she was sick," Adicia says. "She says the record was so soft and pretty. She's not a religious Catholic, but she recognized it as part of the Latin Mass. The words mean 'Blessèd is the one who comes in the name of the Lord.' The singers had Jewish names, I think. Kinda funny Jewish guys would sing a song from a Christian service."

"'*Benedictus qui venit in nomine Domini,*'" Girl supplies. "They're the same fellows who have the current number one song in the charts, 'The Sound of Silence.' Me, I'm still a Beatles girl, but I love folk stuff."

"Do you think your parents would have the record, Betsy?" Julie asks. "Lenore played it to us when we visited last time, but I don't think it was popular. The version of the song that's a hit now is a lot slower on that record. Your parents like stuff that isn't always so popular, so they of all people might own a copy."

"Nope, they're more into classical music, and I like the pop stuff. We're not really into that folk stuff coming from Greenwich Village."

"That's a strange name for a song," Baby says. "How can silence have a sound?"

"I think it's supposed to be a metaphor," Ernestine says. "It's giving a characteristic or description to an abstract concept."

"It still doesn't make a lick of sense to me. Maybe I'd understand it if I went to school."

Justine reaches into the big bowl of popcorn on the coffeetable. "I hope 1966 will be our best year ever."

"We thought '63 would be the best ever, and then the Wicked Witch of the West came storming over and ruined our Christmas," Adicia says. "I don't want to jinx anything by thinking this brand new year will be the best ever when it's only just begun."

"Lenore's gonna become our sister! How could that not make this the best year for us ever?"

"It's a new year," Ernestine says. "A blank slate. So far we don't know if it'll be great or awful. Real life isn't perfect anyway."

"I don't think anything could make our new year as bad as other years. The worst has already happened. I think 1962 was our worst year ever. I wish our worst year didn't have to be the first year I can remember."

"That year started out awful and got great, and went to Hell all over again on Christmas Eve," Adicia says. "But all years have their good and bad spots. This year will be great for Allen and Lenore, but it might not be as great for us."

"Do you think they'll have a baby right away after they're married?" Infant asks. "Ain't that why you get married, to have babies?"

"Oh, believe me, they could have a baby if they wanted, but they're doing the respectable thing by not having an accident outside of marriage and when they're this young," Girl says. "Remember, Lenore is taking those pills?"

"I came into their apartment in December and called for them, but they wouldn't answer me," Ernestine says. "Their door was closed, and I could hear Lenore screaming. I knew better than to think Allen was beating her up, since he'd probably kill anyone who laid a hand on her, and boy, did they turn red when they came outta their room and saw me. I know how you have relations, at least in a basic sense, but I never knew it makes people scream and make funny noises. Lenore gave me a talk about how when I'm older, and with a guy I really love, I'll understand. It still seems bizarre."

"You're not the only one," Betsy says. "I don't get how a guy putting his private parts in a woman's private parts is supposed to show affection or love."

"*That's* how you make a baby?" Baby asks. "I never want to do that ever!"

"Neither do I," Adicia says. "If I get married, he can kiss me and hug me, but he can't do that."

"You can marry another girl," Ernestine suggests.

"That's weird. Why would I want to marry another girl when everyone marries guys? Is there a part of the world they do that in?"

"Can we get back to playing records?" Boy asks. "Damn, I wish I had another guy around to talk to about guy subjects instead of hearing this girly talk all the time."

Betsy hurries to get more records from the cabinet to add to the stack.

"Can you believe today makes it two years since we moved here?" Girl asks.

"Seems like a longer time ago," Ernestine says. "I'm glad no one kicked us out yet."

"It's been a bit over three years since Justine and I have been stuck in Hell's Kitchen," Adicia reflects.

"I hope we get to stay here for another four and a half years, till I graduate high school, and that you and Justine are able to find your way outta that literal hellhole," Ernestine proclaims as she raises a glass of ginger ale. "Here's to 1966 being a year that's more good than bad."

"I need to know if you'll agree to marry us, and if so, if you'll be available on July twenty-ninth, Friday, to perform the ceremony," Allen says as he takes a cup of tea from Mrs. Murphy. "You and your wife have done so much for my sisters and nephew, so I thought it was only fitting you do our ceremony."

"We don't want to lie to you," Lenore says. "I was baptized Catholic, but I'm not religious, and never went to church much. Do you perform interfaith marriages? Allen doesn't know what denomination his parents had him baptized, but he's not very religious either. We go to an Episcopal church in Greenwich Village when we do go to church. We like your denomination."

"I think you'd run into more problems if you were trying to get married by a Catholic priest," Father Murphy admits. "Do you plan to have your children baptized?"

"I guess so," Allen says. "Though it'd be a mockery of religion to baptize 'em and never take 'em to church, except for the holidays and every so often during the year."

"We don't intend to raise atheists, if that's what you're asking. If you don't want to perform our ceremony since we're not Episcopalians and not sure what to do about future kids' religious upbringing, we can find a Unitarian minister."

"We won't hear of a justice of the peace ceremony. My beautiful Lenore deserves only the nicest wedding we can afford. If you want to officiate, we'd like to ask if Giovanni can be our ring-bearer."

Giovanni is playing with a wooden train set on the carpet. His ears perk up at the sound of his name. "That's awfully nice of you to invite me to be in your wedding party, Mister."

"Giovanni, this isn't just any young man who wants your father to officiate at his wedding," Mrs. Murphy says. "You were too young to remember him, but this is your uncle Allen. When he was eighteen, he was very brave and saved you, and your aunts Adicia and Justine, from a fire."

"I couldn't get those images outta my head for weeks. There were pieces of flaming rafters coming down when I came back into the burning building. We got out of there only moments before the entire apartment was completely engulfed in flames."

"So you saved my life?" Giovanni asks. "That was awfully nice of you."

"Your uncle's a hero," Lenore says. "It'd mean a lot to him if you were our little ring-bearer."

"Because of you, there's a me," Giovanni says in awe. "Can I be in his wedding, Mommy and Daddy?"

"You sure can," Father Murphy says. "You're as good as practicing Episcopalians if that's the denomination you go to. I'm not so strict and old-fashioned I demand all prospective brides and grooms be weekly churchgoers."

"So you'll perform a ceremony between a Catholic and a Protestant?" Allen asks.

"I've done a few ceremonies where the Catholic partner was non-practicing. I'm an Episcopal priest, not a Catholic priest."

"How do you feel about performing weddings for couples who've cohabited outside of marriage? We were regular roommates for a long time before we were romantically involved, but now we're living together as a couple who's married in all but name."

"People have always cohabited through history, even if there are laws against it. I'm a progressive man, so I don't look down on it as long as you're not anti-marriage and intend to get married sooner than later. Did you know marriage wasn't a sacrament of the Catholic Church till 1215? In Biblical times, cohabitation automatically made a couple married. Besides, I'd be doing you a favor by performing your marriage and validating your relationship in the eyes of everyone. I don't like the idea of any young couple being persecuted or having to live in secret just because they're violating laws that are a holdover from the days of the Puritans. Isn't it a shame how some people insist on trying to force their view of morality on everyone, even total strangers?"

"So I assume you also won't balk at performing a marriage for people who've been intimate outside of marriage?"

Lenore hides her face, mortified Allen is revealing their private business to someone she doesn't know, someone who'll hopefully perform their marriage.

"Why are you embarrassed?" Allen squeezes her hand. "I'm not ashamed of our love. This guy's our friend, not our enemy."

"Allen's parents think I'm a whore because we met at the bus stop. They refuse to believe we were just roommates and friends for the longest time, and that he respected me too much to approach me about his feelings since I was three years younger."

"It's probably scandalous for a clergyman to say such a thing, but more people than so-called decent society would like to admit have relations before marriage. Christ himself said there's nothing higher than love, so how could I as a man of God condemn and judge a nice young couple for loving one another? So long as one isn't promiscuous and ideally only has premarital relations with one's future spouse, what's there to be offended by? You're doing the right thing by legitimizing your relationship in the eyes of everyone instead of indefinitely cohabiting."

Mrs. Murphy kneels by Giovanni. "Sweetheart, your uncle Allen's older sister Gemma was your first mommy. Would you like to meet her if she comes to the wedding?"

"The lady who let yous guys be my parents? That was really nice of her to give me a nicer life with you."

"Your birth mother looks just like you," Allen says. "I haven't seen her in almost four years, but I'll never forget what she looks like. You get your blonde hair and green eyes from her."

"Your girlfriend has green eyes too." Giovanni points. "I like having green eyes."

"Lenore's eyes are a lot darker than yours. You have a light shade of green."

"So we're settled on you performing our wedding?" Lenore asks.

"Yes, I'll be very pleased to officiate at the wedding of the brave young man who saved my little boy's life," Father Murphy agrees. "I'll book it for Friday evening, July twenty-ninth, and make sure not to schedule any other commitments for that day. I won't burden you by asking for a deposit now. As the day gets closer, I'll discuss my fee with you."

"Thank you very much." Allen shakes Father Murphy's hand. "I'll keep in touch with you."

"Is it okay if we use non-traditional music for our processional?" Lenore asks. "I fell in love with a really pretty song called 'Benedictus.' I'd really like to use it for our bridal party. We haven't selected a song for our own entrance, though."

"Use whatever special songs and music you like. We're not funda-mentalists. All sorts of music can glorify God and celebrate the human spirit. For our dress code, we insist on skirts that go at least to the knee, sleeves that cover at least the shoulder, and necklines that don't plunge."

"I'll make the pillow for the rings from the leftover fabric from my dress," Lenore says. "Giovanni, I'm sure your parents will find you a nice little suit. You'll be the escort for your aunt Justine, the flower girl, when our bridal party walks back down the aisle after the ceremony. Do you think you can do it?"

"I can't wait to be in a real wedding!" Giovanni proclaims. "You're the best aunt and uncle ever!"

***

Lenore has made an appointment at Upper East Side Beautiful Brides for April 16, Saturday, the weekend after Easter. Though Adicia and Justine are as upset as always about not getting Easter baskets and being made fun of in church because of their clothes, they're very ex-cited about the rare chance to go uptown and get pretty dresses. They met Lenore and Ernestine and her friends at the subway station in the Meatpacking District, not wanting to risk the subway in Hell's Kitchen. Even after living there for over three years, they don't like walking in certain areas, though they blend in with their ragged clothes and often unkempt appearance. They don't know how nice, refined people like Mr. and Mrs. Doyle can bear to live there for so many years.

On the subway ride uptown, Adicia and Justine chatter on about how Tommy got a huge Easter basket full of treats and presents Mrs. Troy bought with money she took from Mr. Troy. Though all her pay-checks are garnished, she couldn't let a holiday go by without spoiling Tommy. Now, instead of heat and hot water, Tommy has a brand new blue bicycle, another toy robot for his collection, several pounds of chocolates, candied fruit slices, roasted nuts, candybars, Tinkertoys, rubber balls, and ten new Matchbox cars. Mr. Troy hemmed and hawed about it, but ultimately threw up his hands and let his wife get away with it as always.

"Do we have to pay Allen back?" Julie asks as they get off on the Upper East Side and start making their way to the bridal shop. "I mean, when we're old enough to make that kinda money."

"You don't owe us a penny, sweetheart," Lenore says. "They're our gift to you. You can save it in tissue paper, and if you have a little girl someday, she can wear it when she goes to a wedding."

"But we're not your real family," Baby says.

"You're our extended family now. I wonder if the owner will recognize the girls. She gave Mrs. Troy an earful when she called trying to get her money back."

"Do you think we should make up names if anyone asks?" Girl asks. "I was thinking of applying for a library card, but I realized they'd never give one to a minor living on her own, and they'd never accept my name as it is. I never thought about that kinda stuff when I was younger."

"I don't know if I could ever think of you as anything other than Girl. It just fits who you are."

"There's the shop!" Adicia points. "I hope their dresses are as nice as always. Don't worry, we won't choose very expensive things."

"Where are you gonna store your dress, Lenore?" Ernestine asks. "The idea of bad luck is bunk, but even I think it's unlucky if your groom sees your dress before the wedding."

"Why don't you keep it at your place?" Lenore suggests. "Maybe the van Niftriks could store it to keep it extra-safe."

"I hope Betsy doesn't feel too insulted she won't be in the bridal party," Julie says.

"We can't have too many bridesmaids, since we're not royalty, and usually bridesmaids are close friends or relatives. I'm sure she'll love coming to the wedding and wearing a nice dress."

Adicia opens the door and stops in her tracks as she's starting to walk into the lobby. Emeline is in one of the chairs, reading *The Ramayana*, and next to her is a young woman who looks like Lucine, reading one of the magazines put out by the proprietor.

"Emeline, is that really you?" she gasps, overcome with joy.

Emeline looks up and puts her book down. "Of course it's me, my darling little sister! Allen told us to come here today, and we decided to arrive ahead of yous guys so we could surprise you!" She wraps Adicia tightly in her arms. "Look how much you've grown!"

"You look like a woman, Lucine," Ernestine says in admiration. "I can't believe you're really twenty."

Lucine hugs Ernestine, Adicia, and Justine in turn. "And I can't believe you all got so big!"

"I'm seven," Justine says proudly. "Adicia's eleven and Ernestine's fourteen. In case you care, Tommy's ten."

"We have another surprise for you, though you might not like it as much as seeing us. Guess who else is here."

"Sarah?" Adicia asks hopefully.

"Sorry to say, neither of us knows where she is. But we do have another sister." Lucine motions to Gemma coming out from the powder room. "Gemma was invited to the wedding, though she won't be in the bridal party."

Adicia looks at their oldest sister uncertainly. "You look a lot better than you did the last time I saw you."

"Thank you. Being married to Francesco added at least ten years to my appearance, but now I look closer to my age."

"You're twenty-four now?" Ernestine asks, subtracting 1942 from 1966 in her head. "Wow. That's a grownup's age."

"And you're a teenager now. I can't say I imagined you with a bustline or being this tall."

"We need some introductions," Emeline says. "Gemma, Lucine, this is Julie Spirnak, the little girl who moved across the hall from us back in our old place. Lucine met her once, but I don't think you recognize her. She'll be twelve next month. These are Ernestine's other friends she lives with, the Ryans. Girl's fourteen, Boy will be twelve in June, Baby's going on nine, and Infant's going on seven. And of course, the beautiful young lady is Lenore Hartlein, Allen's future bride. She'll be nineteen in June."

"You really have no names?" Gemma asks the Ryans. "Even if your parents never properly named you, couldn't you adopt your own names? Once you get to a certain age, those names start to seem derogatory. Boy is often used as an anti-Negro insult."

"I'll take my own name when I go to college," Girl says. "I think I'd like to be called Deirdre. Its possible meaning is 'woman,' and it's one of the Irish names normal people in this country can spell and pronounce. I'm proud of my heritage, but not so much I'd wanna adopt a name that ain't pronounced like it's spelled."

Lenore wanders over to the racks of wedding dresses and starts going through them. She's very overwhelmed at how many choices there are, and how almost none are non-white or non-ivory.

"Oh, you don't have to pick your own dresses," Lucine says. "An associate will pick some she thinks will suit you, and you try 'em on in the changing room. Welcome to our family, by the way. I would've greeted you right away, but I hadn't seen my little sisters in four years and needed to catch up with them first of all."

"Do you think I should let them know I need a gown that's not white?" Lenore whispers. "I don't want to misrepresent myself on the most important day of my life."

Lucine smiles. "Not that I want the mental image of my own brother, but how long did it take him to get you there? He never waited long with any of his prior girls."

"A little over four months after we started going steady. He proposed soon after and apologized for waiting a few days to ask me to marry him. He didn't want to disrespect me by continuing to live with me and have that kind of relationship outside of marriage without making it legit. I was the one who initiated it the first time we made love."

"I've never seen Allen so nuts over a girl," Ernestine says. "You should see how many presents he's bought her—a whole miniature zoo of stuffed animals, flowers every week, chocolates, perfume, jewelry, and for Christmas a silver fox fur coat. For Easter, he got her a basket of chocolate-covered fruit, a special left-handed fountain pen, and an emerald necklace. He gave her an emerald bracelet for her last birthday, and an emerald engagement ring. All she had to do was show up at the bus stop, and a strange magical force turned him into this lovesick slave."

"He asked her permission to kiss her, hold her hand, and put his arm around her for the first time," Adicia adds.

"Wow," Gemma says. "Our brother really shaped up into a gentleman and a decent member of society."

Mrs. Marsenko comes out of the changing room area with a departing bride and her mother. She looks at the girls in astonishment.

"Your mother was the cocaine addict who married off her oldest daughter to a grotesque Italian brute and tried to marry her second daughter off to another man of ill repute! Whose turn is it to get married against her will this time?"

"I'm divorced," Gemma says proudly. "I'm a senior at Hofstra University, and after I graduate, I'm gonna open my own business."

"I thought Hofstra was a college," Adicia says.

"It was, but it got university status while I was a freshman."

"I used a fire to fake my death on the eve of my planned wedding," Lucine says. "I hear my mother called you in a real tizzy the day after, tryna get back the money she spent on the destroyed dresses, with no receipt. I'm a sophomore at Hunter."

"It's for her." Emeline points to Lenore. "This lucky girl's marrying our one nice brother in July. Our mother isn't here. Don't worry, this is a wedding everyone wants."

"Do you have any dresses that aren't white?" Lenore asks.

Mrs. Marsenko smiles. "You can wear whatever color you want. God knows, you wouldn't be the first nonvirginal bride in modern history to wear white or ivory. It's a myth that white advertises virginity. Some people might believe it does, but it's not the true origin of the custom. You can go back to the dressing room, and I'll have an associate bring you four or five dresses."

While Lenore goes back to the dressing area, the younger girls start pulling dresses off the racks. Baby is drawn to a yellow taffeta dress, Infant favors a light blue chiffon dress, and Justine picks out a pink silk dress, while the others have a harder time making up their minds. Adicia pulls out three dark blue dresses and sets them on a chair, while Julie pulls out four dresses of all different colors, Ernestine picks out three red dresses, and Girl stands back mystified at how to go about selecting a formal dress.

"There are three free dressing rooms," an associate tells them. "You can ring the bell in your room if you need any help with changing."

Adicia and Ernestine go off to one dressing room, Justine and Infant take the second, and Baby and Julie take the third. Girl continues to stand and stare at the dresses in confusion, while Lucine and Emeline take their time to look through the choices in their favorite colors before selecting a couple of gowns to try on.

"May I help you, young lady?" Mrs. Marsenko asks Girl.

"I'm supposed to be one of the bridesmaids, but I've never worn a fancy dress in my life. I don't know what colors, fabrics, or styles look good on me."

"Why don't you select a few dresses you think look nice. Your friends, my associates, and I will help you decide what looks best on you."

Boy sits on the floor uncomfortably, wishing he didn't have to give up a Saturday to go to a bridal shop with a bunch of girls. Even the magazines in the lobby are all geared towards the female of the species, not boys or men. He begins twiddling his thumbs for lack of anything more stimulating to do.

"Can we help you, young man?" Mrs. Marsenko asks. "At least you're not tearing up the store the way those girls' brat of a little brother did. I don't think I'll ever forget that family, particularly not their mother. What's your name?"

"David." It's the first name that comes to mind. "David Ryan."

"How old are you?"

"I'll be twelve in June. This girl stuff is really boring. Don't you have anything that can keep me busy while they try on their dresses?"

"Have you got any pocket money?" Gemma asks. "There's a movie house not far from here. Why don't you run along and watch something while we're occupied? I used to have a boy, and I bet he'd be bored as hell to have to tag along to something like this. He's gonna be five in June. The minister performing the wedding and his wife are my birth son's parents now."

Boy looks expectantly at his older sister.

"Sure, go ahead," Girl says. "I wish I could join you."

The other girls come out modeling their dresses and critique how they look on one another. Ernestine is mortified the first dress shows her bra straps, Emeline hates how she can never find a dress that fits both her small shoulders and large bustline, and Adicia's first dress tugs across her chest.

"How can I have gained that much weight when we're almost on a starvation diet under Mother's lousy cooking skills and poor food selection? I've never been overweight!"

Lucine looks down at her and smiles. "You're only three months away from twelve. I think you're sprouting a bust."

Adicia feels her chest. "That can't be! I'm only in sixth grade, and I'm one of the youngest girls in my class! I won't be twelve till the summer!"

"I'm not twelve till next month, and I'm starting to grow one too," Julie consoles her. "It's not so bad. Let's see who gets more of a bustline sooner, and who gets a bra first."

Adicia forgets about her embarrassing problem when Lenore

comes out in the first gown, one of the attendants holding the train so she doesn't trip. Everyone clusters around her and exclaims over how beautiful she looks.

"You look like a bride in that," Emeline says. "Anything else would just be a dress that happens to be for a bride. You look like you're wearing the wedding dress made for you and you only."

"It's not too plain and not too fancy," Ernestine says.

"It's not too revealing and not too modest," Adicia says. "I don't like dresses that go right up to the collarbone."

"I still have three more dresses to try on!" Lenore protests. "You might like the others even more."

"And it's ivory," Girl says. "You were afraid that color wouldn't be appropriate since you're not a pure little maiden. Don't let so-called decent society dictate to you what color wedding dress to wear. More brides than they'd like to think ain't virginal."

"Shall we try on the other dresses we picked out?" Ernestine asks. "We don't have all day to play dress-up and decide on our bridesmaid dresses."

Girl pulls out a couple of random dresses she thinks are about her size and follows the rest of them back to the changing area. Everyone else is very excited at getting to try on a bunch of fancy dresses, since they so rarely experience a luxury like this, but she's so used to being on the tomboy side and only wearing practical clothes, she doesn't think of this as something fun or special. If she had her way, she'd make her own dress from a bolt of silk or satin instead of going to a bridal salon and trying on four or five dresses.

By the end of their appointment, they've found a green satin gown with black lace trim for Emeline, a lavender silk gown with cream-colored lace trim for Lucine, a red organza gown with a white sash for Ernestine, a plum-colored rayon gown with a pink sash for Julie, and a dark blue chiffon gown with a black sash for Adicia. Justine, Infant, and Baby liked their dresses so much they didn't want to try on any others. Girl eventually settled on a turquoise chiffon dress, after deciding it had the most eye-catching color of any of the dresses in the store.

"You looked best in the first dress you tried on," Emeline tells Lenore as the other girls are having their purchases wrapped and put in boxes. "The second dress showed a little too much skin, the third had far too much beading and was distracting, and the one you've got on is a bad color for you. Even if you want a non-white dress, ice-blue doesn't go well with your emerald-colored eyes, and it makes your skin look washed-out."

"You looked like a princess from the Middle Ages or the Renaissance in the first one!" Ernestine says. "Those other dresses aren't as classic or timeless. When your grandkids look at your wedding pictures someday, they'll know what decade you got married in. You don't wanna look back and wonder what you were thinking to wear a style that dates itself, do you?"

"I hated the Chantilly lace dress I had to wear at my wedding," Gemma says. "When I have a second marriage someday, I sure won't wear something so trendy."

"How much money is this setting Allen back?" Baby asks, putting her elbows on the checkout counter. "I don't wanna think he's spending all his paychecks to buy us dresses we'll probably never wear again."

"He's got enough money in the bank," Lenore reassures her. "He pays forty a month for rent, maybe twenty for utilities, and usually under fifty for our monthly food bill. He makes ninety dollars a week, three hundred sixty a month. He repaid the Bowery Mission people their three hundred dollar loan awhile ago. I think he'll be able to afford this."

"But we're buying ten dresses, one of 'em a bridal gown!" Infant says. "That stuff ain't cheap."

"That first wedding dress you all liked so much is one hundred," Mrs. Marsenko informs them as an associate starts ringing up the purchases. "The other dresses are between twenty and thirty each."

"Wow, that's an awful lot of dough," Baby says.

"Have we decided on the wedding dress, or will you need to come back to look at more?"

"Wear the first one!" Adicia insists. "Take this blue one off, try the first one on again, and see if you like it more."

"I'll handle paying." Emeline takes Lenore's pocketbook off her arm. "Just try on the first one again and see how you feel the second time."

Lenore follows an associate back to the dressing room while Emeline counts out the cash Allen put into Lenore's pocketbook. Almost his entire monthly salary is there. Emeline marvels at how he's moved up in his station sufficiently enough to be able to spend so much money on wedding clothes. In the old days, he would've spent that kind of money on drugs, clothes, shoes, alcohol, or cigarettes.

"It's wasteful we can't wear these dresses to any other events," Ernestine says. "We're not uptown girls who go to parties and society functions every week. It's like throwing money away, just so we can look nice on one day."

"Oh, I'm sure you'll be able to wear them at four other events this spring," Lucine says. "We've got four graduations coming up, and you always wear nice clothes at a graduation ceremony and party."

"Four?" Adicia asks. "There's my graduation from elementary school and Ernestine's graduation from junior high. Who else is graduating?"

"I'm graduating high school!" Emeline reminds them. "You're all invited to the ceremony and my party in Yorkville in June."

"And you can all come down to Hempstead in May for my college graduation," Gemma says. "I'll be the first person in our family to graduate from not only high school, but college too. Wish I'd been able to graduate two years ago, but the past is what it is. My friends and I are going out to supper at a nice restaurant that day, and if you want, you can go down to onea the beaches on the island."

"A real beach?" Justine asks. "With warm sand, pretty shells, lighthouses, and pretty blue waves?"

"I can't wait to go to the beach!" Adicia says. "You're a neat big sister. You got a lot nicer since we last saw you."

Lenore comes back out in the first dress, this time with a veil over her hair and white leather shoes with a slight thick heel. Everyone stops to stare at her in awe.

"You look like even more of a bride!" Adicia says. "Please get this dress! Allen will fall in love with you all over again when he sees you!"

"Who's walking you down the aisle, by the way?" Lucine asks. "I suppose Father Murphy will escort me when I get married someday, in addition to performing my ceremony."

"Do I have to be escorted by someone?" Lenore asks. "I see it as Allen and I giving ourselves to each other, since we don't have decent parents to give us in marriage to each other."

"Are you or aren't you gonna buy this gorgeous dress?" Emeline asks. "You look like a Medieval princess, like Ernestine said. Allen will feel like the luckiest guy in the world to be marrying such a beautiful bride."

"Please get this one!" Justine begs.

"Even I think it's beautiful, and I don't ordinarily get into alla that girly stuff," Girl says.

"All you need is a bouquet, and you'll look like the perfect bride," Julie says.

"Allen won't be satisfied with anything but the best for his beautiful bride," Adicia says. "All you have to do is change back into your clothes, pay for the dress, and let Mr. and Mrs. van Niftrik store it so Allen won't see it till your wedding day."

"We can pick up my brother and go out to eat, if you've got any money left," Girl says. "I kinda wish I was a girly girl right now, since I'd love to play dress-up and look like a princess for one special day."

Lenore looks around at the girls, then turns around to look at herself in the mirror for the umpteenth time. "It is a really beautiful dress. I suppose I deserve a gorgeous wedding dress like this after what I've been through. Okay, it's the one. I'll get this dress."

Emeline pulls out five twenty-dollar bills from Lenore's pocketbook as she goes back with the attendant to change into her street clothes. The younger girls are all smiles as they take their boxed dresses and wait in the lobby.

"Do you think I'll be lucky enough to bag a nice guy of my own someday and wear a pretty dress like Lenore's?" Adicia asks. "Allen can't be the only nice guy in the world."

"You're a pretty girl," Emeline says. "I'm sure any nice boy would love to be your fellow when you're old enough. Even if you have to wait awhile, there's no shame in being a dark horse. You'll just find your fellow later than most girls, when no one expects it."

"What's a dark horse?"

"Like an underdog. The one no one expects to win the race, the one everyone underestimates. All us Troys are like that. No one ever expected us to come up in society and do as well as we have."

"So it's like someone who sneaks up on the other horses and wins at the last minute?"

"Yes, the one no one pays much attention to 'cause they think he's of no account. It's good we're such dark horses, since we'll get an even better last laugh on the people who made fun of us all these years. They won't see it coming when we make good."

Chapter 33: Four Graduations and a Wedding

"We're really riding over the Brooklyn Bridge!" Adicia says happily as she looks through the window at the beautiful blue waters of the East River. "I used to daydream I could walk across it when we went to the East River Park and saw the Brooklyn Bridge and the Williamsburg Bridge."

"We're taking a real train after we get off the bus in Long Island," Allen promises her. "I don't think you've ever ridden on a train, have you?"

"This is gonna be the best weekend ever!" Justine says.

For Gemma's college graduation weekend in mid-May, her younger sisters and one competent brother have made plans to come down and celebrate with their prodigal oldest sibling. In addition to the celebratory supper at the restaurant with Gemma and her friends, they're also staying at a hotel on a beach. Mrs. Troy was too drugged out to comprehend when Adicia and Justine asked her if they could spend a weekend with Allen, and Mr. Troy cared less his final two daughters wanted to go away for one weekend.

"Are we gonna squat at the hotel?" Baby asks.

"We're staying in three rooms I'm paying for. Lenore and I are in one room, Emeline, Lucine, Adicia, and Justine are in the second, and the rest of yous are in the third. You can fight over who gets which bed and who sleeps on the sofa bed when we get there."

"What are our sign-in names again?" Infant asks. "I don't wanna mess up and let people know our parents didn't give us real names."

"Deirdre, David, Fiona, and Aoife," Girl says.

"How come you gave me the hardest name to spell? It sounds like Eva with an F, but it has a funny spelling."

"I'll write the name for you. I wanted our names to match, and I wanted Irish names I liked but that aren't too common. Don't worry, we ain't the only ones on this trip using fake names."

Lenore looks at the borrowed wedding ring on her finger and hopes no one suspects she and Allen are pretending to be married again. She hates to lie, though most decent hotels would never rent to an unmarried couple. Lenore Troy she'll have to be for the duration of this weekend.

"Did you all bring your bathing suits?" Julie asks. "Mrs. van Niftrik took us shopping for them."

"Lenore took Justine and me to Macy's," Adicia says. "Mine is pretty blue with yellow flowers, and Justine's is pink with blue flowers."

"Might the future Mrs. Troy be wearing a two-piece bathing suit?" Allen whispers to Lenore.

Lenore blushes. "It's a one-piece green swimsuit with a skirt attached, so it doesn't show too much of my body."

"You really didn't hafta take us with you," Girl says. "Folks from our social class don't come by that kinda dough overnight. You'll have to work overtime to get back the money you're spending on this and your wedding."

"It's my treat," Allen insists. "When you grow up poor and come into a little bit of money, you wanna indulge yourself from time to time. I still have enough set aside for the basics."

When the bus stops in Long Island, Adicia, Justine, and Ernestine pick up their schoolbags, and Ernestine's friends pick up their pillowcases. Allen and Lenore have actual suitcases. Adicia wonders if she'll ever be able to pack her things in a suitcase, or if she'll own enough things to fit in a normal-sized suitcase.

"It's a real train!" Justine shouts when they walk up to the train station. "Just like in the old pictures I've seen in my schoolbooks!"

"It's a modern train," Allen says. "Those pictures you've seen were probably old-fashioned steam locomotives. Trains have come a long way since then."

"1966 really is our best year ever!" Adicia declares as the train comes into view. "The only way it could get better would be if Justine and I moved back with you and Lenore!"

"Can I give you and Lenore my seashells?" Justine asks. "Knowing Tommy, he'd smash them and laugh in my face if he found them."

"Of course you can, sweetie," Lenore says. "We can search for shells together."

"There are also a lot of pretty rocks on the seashore," Ernestine says. "Some people have a hobby of collecting rocks."

"Can we take back any little animal friends, like hermit crabs, fish, or seahorses?" Baby asks. "I'd like a pet."

"It's not very nice to take strange animals away from their homes and families," Girl says. "How would you like it if you were a hermit crab and a child on vacation kidnapped you?"

"Maybe someday we'll have a pet," Ernestine says.

Adicia excitedly scrambles aboard the train after all the passengers stopping here have debarked. After she, her sisters, and their friends put their luggage in the baggage compartment above their seats, they start wandering the aisles of each car and exploring their new surroundings.

"You might wanna keep seated," Allen calls. "Hempstead isn't too far from here. It's not like we're going all the way out to the Hamptons."

"Who are the Hamptons?" Baby asks.

"They're not people," Girl says. "The Hamptons are a bunch of villages on the east end of Long Island. A lot of rich people have beach homes there."

"You mean we're not allowed to wander around the train?" Infant asks sadly. "When will we get to take another train ride?"

"You're not forbidden to walk around, but I think they like people, particularly kids, to stay seated," Allen says. "Besides, with the train stopping so soon, we don't wanna get separated from each other."

They reluctantly take their seats and try to compensate by people-watching and looking through the windows. Long Island's a lot prettier than Manhattan. The streets aren't crowded with high-rise buildings, and the residents aren't forced to be crammed on top of one another. People here also live in houses and have their own yards, where they can grow flowers and fruit trees.

"Do you think someday we'll have our own houses?" Adicia asks as the train pulls into Hempstead.

"You bet," Lenore says. "I want my kids to grow up with a yard to play in and a real house that's all their own, not an apartment you have to share with a bunch of neighbors and pay to live in every month."

"I'd like a mansion if I ever get enough money," Justine says. "It'd have twenty bedrooms, so we all could live there together."

"How are we getting to our hotel?" Girl asks. "I don't think this city has a beach."

"You'll see," Lenore says.

The depot is full of people, but Adicia manages to spot Emeline, Lucine, and Gemma in the crowd. She and Justine run over to them, tugging the others with them. Gemma has a bouffant hairstyle and a skirt showing her knees, while Lucine and Emeline wear sundresses going to their mid-calves, their hair long, loose, and natural as always. Adicia thinks it looks like Gemma's got a beehive on top of her hair, and can't understand why this is such a popular hairstyle. Ernestine and Girl meanwhile think it's very daring for her to show her knees, and wonder if they can start wearing skirts like that. They've heard women used to be arrested for showing so much skin, and feel very lucky they're growing up now instead of fifty or a hundred years ago.

"We're parked a short ways away from here," Lucine says. "Come with us. Gemma will take Allen, Lenore, Adicia, and Justine, I'll take Ernestine, Julie, Girl, and Baby, and Emeline will take Boy and Infant."

"You know how to drive?" Ernestine asks. "When did that happen?"

"When you live on the island, you need to know how to drive," Gemma says. "Lucine got driving lessons her freshman year at Hunter, and got her license on her nineteenth birthday. Emeline didn't learn to drive yet, so she's taking a taxi."

"You own cars?" Boy asks.

"They're rentals," Lucine says. "I wanted to learn to drive while I was young enough to learn it well, and have that skill before I move outta the city."

"We'll be going in real cars?" Baby asks. "I've never ridden in a car before!"

"I rode in a police car once," Adicia says. "Emeline, Tommy, Justine, Allen, and our mother were there too. A cop took us to see Carlos in the hospital after his accident. I got to wear a seatbelt, since I sat in the front."

"These cars have seatbelts in the front seats too," Lucine says. "You can put your luggage in the trunks."

They all take in the fresh air as they go to the parking lot. It's a pity they'll only be here over a weekend and have to get back to reality in Manhattan, but it's nice to get away for a little while. Adicia tells herself that if she ever gets enough money, she'll always take a summer vacation to a beach, and stay for longer than just one weekend. Justine, Baby, and Infant meanwhile are so overcome with excitement at the thought of staying at the seashore, they don't care they don't have any beach toys to play with. It's enough to go in the water and feel the sand between their toes.

Lucine's rental is a blue Volkswagen Beetle, and Gemma's is a yellow Chrysler. Boy and Infant don't care they'll only be riding in a taxi, since a car is a car. They try to remember their false names as they get into the cab with Emeline. Infant is overcome with fear at remembering how to spell her new name. The average person will assume she's saying Eva with a lisp, but she'll never be able to remember that funny Irish spelling Girl showed her. It doesn't make any sense to have three vowels in a row.

"I'm David," Boy tells the taxi driver. "That's my sister Aoife. We have two other sisters, but they're going to our hotel in other cars."

"Pretty name." The driver smiles back at her. "I think you're the first blonde Eva I've ever met. All the Evas I've known had dark hair."

"I'm Irish. It's the Irish form of Eva," Infant says. "At least, I'm part Irish. I don't know enough about our family history to know if we're Irish on both sides all the way back."

"I'm not surprised. It seems like about half the population of Manhattan is of Irish ancestry. I have an Irish great-grandmother on my mother's side myself. Your older friend said she's half-French and half-Belgian."

"Our last name's Ryan," Boy says. "Our mother had an Irish name too."

The girls in the other cars wave at them as they pull out of the lot. Justine stands up in the backseat and waves her rabbit's paw at them too.

"That's my best friend Justine," Infant says. "Someone at a mission in my old neighborhood gave her that bunny at Easter when she was thirteen months old. It's been her friend ever since. It's just like in a story Emeline told us once, about a little boy who gets a stuffed rabbit for Christmas and loves it so much it eventually turns into a real rabbit."

"*The Velveteen Rabbit*," Emeline provides. "Isn't that a beautiful story? When someone loves you enough, even if you're run-down and shabby-looking, it doesn't matter what anyone else thinks of you. You're beautiful and real to the people who love you."

Gemma's car is the first to arrive at the hotel. Adicia and Justine scramble out and gaze at the seashore, only a short distance from the hotel. They impatiently wait for Allen and Lenore to get their luggage and go into the main office to check in, so eager are they to put on their swimsuits and head down to the beach to swim, bask in the sun, and feel the warm sand underfoot.

"Three of these girls are my sisters," Allen says as he signs his name to the hotel register. "The older two girls are also my sisters, but they've already checked in. Two of my younger sisters are staying with them, and our other sister will be in a room with her friends."

When it comes time for Infant to sign her false name, she just writes Eva. As it is, Eva and Aoife sound almost exactly alike, only Eva looks more American and has a much easier to remember spelling. Girl hopes it doesn't stick out like too much of a sore thumb among their other assumed names of Deirdre, David, and Fiona, the way Carlos's name always stuck out among the other eight names of his siblings. She tries to console herself with the thought that it doesn't mismatch as badly as a name like Persephone or Ursuline.

Lenore starts to sign her last name as Hartlein, then remembers she and Allen are supposed to be married. She crosses it out and writes Troy in the space above her blacked-out surname.

"Not married long, are you?" the proprietor's wife asks.

"Yes, this is my bride." Allen smiles, putting his arm around Lenore. "I don't think she's used to her new name yet."

"Don't worry about that," the proprietor's wife says kindly. "Most women take awhile to get used to writing their new name and thinking of themselves by that name. I could never understand the girls who immediately transition to a new name, as though that were always their name. It took me a good six months before I started thinking of myself as Mrs. Jackson and not thinking people were calling my mother-in-law when I heard that name."

The girls run into their assigned rooms and throw their luggage on the beds, barely caring this is only a 3-star hotel, not a 5-star affair like the Waldorf. After changing into their swimsuits, they rush down to the beach and find a space big enough for their towels, saving space for Lucine, Emeline, Allen, Lenore, and Boy. By the time the other members of their party join them, they're all down by the water's edge. Justine and Infant are filling an ice bucket with shells and small rocks, Ernestine and Girl are taking a walk down the beach, Adicia and Julie are up to their necks in the water, and Baby is taking a walk along the large rocks jutting into the ocean.

"Can we stay here all weekend?" Justine begs. "I never wanna go back to Hell's Kitchen after this!"

"You know what would happen if we tried that," Allen says. "You don't want that witch to ruin your summer vacation like she ruined our Christmas."

Adicia floats on her back as Julie doggy-paddles around. Even the sun and the sky seem healthier here. Julie's never been swimming, and Adicia's only ever swum at public baths like the Hamilton Fish Park Pool, never in the wide open ocean before. Everyone looks really happy, free of the often surly looks they see in New York City. Mrs. Troy would no doubt hit the roof if she found out Allen took her daughters here, but the odds are very small that hateful, evil, vindictive, spiteful woman will ever find out what they're doing this weekend. She's probably drinking or using drugs at the moment. Besides, Adicia and Justine will have to go back into Hell's Kitchen soon enough, so they need to savor every last minute of this nice break from reality.

***

That night, while Allen takes a walk on the beach as the tide comes in, the girls think they hear Lenore screaming. Emeline abruptly stops reading a book to Adicia and Justine, and Ernestine and Girl stop laughing about the unattractive people they saw on the beach. Adicia, Ernestine, and Emeline knock on her door, but she doesn't seem to hear them. Ernestine tries to turn the knob, but the door is locked, and when Emeline calls her name, there's no response.

"I didn't hear anyone coming down the hall and breaking in," Adicia muses. "Do you think someone broke in through the window?"

"You and Ernestine run down to the beach and get Allen," Emeline orders. "He's got the key."

"Should we ask the hotel manager for help? What if there's a bad guy in there with a gun?"

"This isn't Manhattan. I doubt someone here would have a gun."

Adicia and Ernestine hold hands and take off towards the beach, shoeless and pajama-clad. They barely feel sharp pebbles under their feet as they run towards the shore. When they get to the beach, they try to dig their toes into the sand as hard as they can to avoid falling into the tide and being swept out to sea. The tide is splashing up to their knees when they finally catch sight of Allen in the dark.

"We need you to come back to our hotel," Ernestine says. "We think someone broke into your hotel room, and Lenore won't answer us and the door is locked."

"What?"

"We heard her screaming at someone to stop hurting her," Adicia says. "I hope he doesn't have a gun. He might shoot you, and we'd lose our only good brother and our family name would be lost."

"I'll kill him. I don't care if I go to jail. I'll dismember him if he's killed her."

The girls trail behind him as he races back towards the hotel. By the time they get back to their floor, Julie, Girl, Lucine, and Justine are outside the door with Emeline. Allen pushes through them to open the door, a mad look in his eyes.

"Can we turn on the lights, or will that make the burglar mad?" Justine whispers.

Allen flips on the light switch and sees no one else in the room. The girls feel very stupid when they see Lenore thrashing around in bed, her eyes closed, not another soul to be seen. Allen looks under the bed and in the kitchen and bathroom, and finds no one.

"She's just having a bad dream," he says in relief. "Adicia, fill up the ice bucket with cold water and get a washcloth."

Adicia obeys her brother as he sits on the bed and gently shakes Lenore awake. When Lenore opens her eyes, she picks up an ashtray on the nightstand and raises it towards Allen's head. He ducks, and it lands across the room.

"What are you doing, sweetheart? It's me. You were just having a nightmare. The girls thought someone broke into our room and was hurting you."

Adicia runs over with the ice bucket full of cold water and dips a washcloth in it, holding it over Lenore's head. Julie and Ernestine sit on the foot of the bed.

"What were you dreaming about?" Ernestine asks.

Lenore reaches over for Allen and feels his arm and face to make sure he's really her belovèd and not the attacker in her nightmare. "I dreamt my father found us and broke into our room when you were out. He was touching me and doing his other depraved things."

"I sometimes dream about my daddy hurting me too," Julie says. "Don't feel bad and think you're the only one who still has nightmares about that."

"He'll never find you," Allen promises Lenore. "If ever he does, I'll kill him. I swear to God, I'll kill your father if I ever meet him, and

I'll dismember him too. A gun would be too good for that thing. I'd use my bare hands."

"Do you want something to eat?" Adicia asks. "Maybe you can stand on the balcony for fresh air to make you feel better."

"I think I'll be fine after my heartrate goes down. I'm sorry I scared all of you so much." She strokes Allen's hair. "I couldn't forgive myself if I'd hit you with that ashtray. I thought you were my father, so I wanted to defend myself."

Ernestine goes to the small refrigerator and pulls out some of the food Allen and Lenore brought. "I hope you feel better by tomorrow. We're going to Gemma's college graduation and a supper at a nice restaurant. She and her friends booked an entire room, and we've got our own table."

"You'll have some food, and you'll get back to sleep," Allen says. "Girls, I think you all can go back to your rooms. I can take care of her from here."

Adicia is very glad Lenore was only having a nightmare, but is also very jealous as she trudges back to her room. All Lenore had to do was show up at the bus stop and Allen was instantly head over heels in love with her. Adicia can only hope when she's old enough, the mere sight of her will likewise make a guy just as devoted and protective towards her.

***

This has been a very monumental spring for Adicia. She'll never forget her weekend in Long Island, watching Gemma graduate from Hofstra in a cap and gown, and going to a fancy restaurant afterwards, with a private room all their own. Seeing Gemma be the first person in their family to graduate college is a big source of pride and inspiration, though Gemma was always last on her list of favorite sisters. In early June, they went up to Yorkville to watch Emeline graduating high school. She took her place as the fourth person in the family to graduate high school. Emeline graduated fifteenth in her class of one hundred, and received awards for her talent, skill, and promise in writing, history, English, German, and Latin. Afterwards they went out to eat at a modest restaurant, and all the restaurant patrons came up to her in her cap and gown to congratulate her and wish her well. Adicia is sad Emeline won't be staying in the city when she goes away to college in the fall, but Emeline's personality isn't the best match for life in the big city. Emeline will study history and German Studies at Vassar College in Poughkeepsie, about an hour and a half north. After that, she's going to graduate school for her degree in library studies.

In mid-June, Ernestine and Betsy graduated from their junior high in Greenwich Village. Mr. and Mrs. Troy cared less their sixth-born child was having a graduation ceremony or that Ernestine was the only one in the eighth grade class without parents in attendance. At least that enabled Lucine and Emeline to attend and meet the van Niftriks. The day after the evening ceremony, Mr. and Mrs. van Niftrik took them all out to lunch in Chelsea. They even bought Ernestine a graduation present, a coral bracelet to match her red bridesmaid dress.

Now it's Adicia's turn to have a graduation ceremony. After two and a half years at the Hell's Kitchen elementary school, she's graduating sixth grade. True to form, Mr. and Mrs. Troy care less and haven't shown up. Adicia is wearing her bridesmaid dress so she can look pretty, not caring if anyone asks where someone who lives in such a crummy neighborhood was able to get such a nice dress. Some of the other girls are also wearing nicer dresses than usual. Their parents must care about their children and making them look nice for special occasions, instead of taking delight in being poor and trying to force the next generation to stay down in the gutter with them.

"I useta think the Lower East Side was the pits," Lucine says as they take their seats. "This neighborhood gives it a run for its money."

"I don't understand why any self-respecting neighborhood would want the word Hell in its name," Allen says.

"I don't feel safe here," Lenore says. "I wanna go back home as soon as this is over."

"There are gang fights on a regular basis," Emeline says. "I don't know why the Doyles wanna stay here when they can afford to live somewhere better."

"Adicia said they only stay 'cause that's where Mrs. Doyle lived when she was married before, and she hopes she might find her long-lost daughter if she stays put," Ernestine says. "If her ex-husband were that much of a jerk, I wouldn't be surprised if he took their kid and moved to South America."

"I hated it when I lived here." Julie wrinkles her nose. "I wish I could graduate with Adicia, but my daddy didn't let me go to school, and no one would let me enroll in school when I don't have parents and we're squatting."

"Mrs. Doyle sends her regards," Justine says. "She had to take Caroline to the doctor, so she had to miss Adicia's ceremony."

Adicia smiles out at her friends and family as her class takes their places on the stage. The first part of the program is a boring speech from the principal about how they're going on to junior high, the next level of their education, and growing up in the fall. Most of the kids and parents in attendance probably think the speech is a joke. A lot of them will probably drop out of school, join the local gangs, end up in jail, and/or work dead-end, low-wage jobs like Mr. and Mrs. Troy and Carlos. The principal probably knows it too, but doesn't want to offend anybody by stating the obvious. The next part of the program is a short awards ceremony. The students being given awards for their high marks in math, science, English, history, French, art, music, writing, shop, and home economics might be the ones who go on to college someday, or they might fall into the influence of the less than savory local elements.

Adicia patiently waits until the principal gets toward the end of the alphabet to hear her name called, and gets up to take her diploma and shake hands with him and the art teacher helping with distributing diplomas. Never having been publicly acknowledged or announced before, she gets up with a big surge of pride when the principal pronounces the name Adicia Éloïse Troy. She walks proudly, her head held high, from her folding chair to the principal and the art teacher, remembering to shake with the right and take with the left. Emeline taught her the handshake was invented by fellow southpaw Julius Caesar, and done with the right hand so he could conceal his weapon in his stronger hand. That makes it a lot easier to remember which hand to shake with. As she heads back to her seat, she waves at her friends and family and smiles.

"Our little sister isn't really a little girl anymore," Lucine says proudly.

"This means I'm alone at this school now," Justine says. "Matthew will be here, but he's not the same as our own family."

"I think you'll be alright," Emeline tries to soothe her. "I know it's really scary to be all by yourself at a school, but you can't be dependent on your sisters your whole life. I hope it makes you strong, brave, and able to rely on yourself."

"Justine will be in second grade in the fall," Allen says. "I think she's got enough time to get used to being the only member of our family at a school."

"I hope so," Justine says miserably.

After the ceremony concludes, Adicia finds her friends and family and shows them her diploma. She points with delight to the proper diacritical marks in her middle name, which most people spell as Eloise, a spelling that would be pronounced El-WAZ and not Ey-lo-EEZ in French.

"Let's get outta here," Lenore says. "We'll take you to lunch in Chelsea. Do you want the same place we had Ernestine and Betsy's lunch at?"

"Sure," Adicia agrees. "Can we go there to celebrate again when you get your scores from your high school equivalency diploma test?"

"Of course we'll go there again when our beautiful Lenore gets her GED," Allen says, swinging his arm around his fiancée.

"I hope 1966 never ends!" Adicia says as they make their way out of the school. "There are already at least twenty reasons this is our best year ever!"

***

All the members of the wedding party are scheduled to gather at Father Murphy's church in Midtown the afternoon before the wedding for a rehearsal. Mr. and Mrs. Troy are too lost in their world of drugs and alcohol to get suspicious about why Adicia and Justine have gone away so many weekends this summer, which is just as well, Adicia thinks as she and Justine settle into the guest room in the Murphys' apartment.

"I hope Mother doesn't crash the wedding," Justine says.

"She's probably relieved Allen's making a respectable woman of Lenore and that she won't have to hear talk about how her one competent older son is living in sin with a girl he met at the bus stop," Adicia says.

"I hope so. She'd be mad as a wet hen if she crashed the wedding and saw Lucine and Emeline. She'd probably have a fit to see Gemma and Giovanni too."

"Girls, are you ready to go?" Mrs. Murphy calls. "You'll go with me and Giovanni in a cab. Your clothes are fine. You don't need to wear your bridesmaid gowns when it's just a rehearsal."

"We can't wait to rehearse!" Justine says.

Adicia and Justine follow Mrs. Murphy and Giovanni, remembering to smile at the elevator operator and the doorman. On the taxi ride over to the church, Mrs. Murphy tells Giovanni about how Adicia took him and Justine to safety at the Bowery Mission after the fire. Giovanni thinks it's very exciting how he was taken from the park to the mission at night while concealed in Adicia's schoolbag, and that only a sliver of the Moon lit their way as they walked through rough neighborhoods. He tells them he thinks his birth grandparents are bad people, but his birth aunts and uncle are awesome.

Lucine hands them wedding programs when they arrive. "Allen and Lenore wanted yous guys to look these over and make sure they're good to go. If there are any changes you'd like, let them know, and they can do last-minute reprintings."

Adicia and Justine look over the programs, made with thick cream-colored pieces of paper, tied with light pink ribbons on the outer seams, and typeset with indigo ink in an ornate typeface.

Welcome to the celebration of marriage between

Lenore Eve Hartlein

and

Allen Théodore Troy

Episcopal Church of Christ Our Friend and Savior

Midtown, Manhattan, New York City,

Father Warren Ambrose Murphy, Officiant

Friday, July 29, 1966, 4:00 p.m.

Prelude: "Water Music," George Frideric Handel

Processional: "Benedictus," Simon and Garfunkel

Bride's Entrance: "And I Love Her," The Beatles

Opening Prayer by Father Murphy

Bible Reading: Ecclesiastes 4:9-12, read by Lucine Camille Troy

Reading from Plato's Symposium, by Emeline Rosalie Troy

Irish Wedding Blessing, read by Deirdre Ryan

Marriage Ceremony
Exchange of Vows
Blessing and Exchange of Rings
Pronouncement of Marriage
Recessional: "Ebb Tide," The Righteous Brothers
Bridal Party:
Maid of Honor:
Emeline Rosalie Troy, Groom's Sister and Bride's Best Friend
Bridesmaids:
Lucine Camille Troy, Groom's Sister
Ernestine Zénobie Troy, Groom's Sister
Adicia Éloïse Troy, Groom's Sister
Julie Claire Spirnak, Family Friend
Deirdre Ryan, Family Friend
Fiona "Baby" Ryan, Family Friend
Eva (Aoife) Ryan, Family Friend
Flower Girl, Justine Anastasie Troy, Groom's Sister
Best Man, John "Jack" William Watson, Groom's Co-Worker
Groomsmen:
David Ryan, Family Friend
Douglas James Cason, Groom's Co-Worker
Steven Alexander Schubert, Groom's Co-Worker
Ring-Bearer, Giovanni Edoardo Murphy, Groom's Nephew
Thank you for sharing the celebration of our love!

"Very pretty," Adicia says approvingly. "I'll preserve my copy forever and look at it when I wanna relive this happy memory."

"You know you can't do that," Emeline says. "If Mother, Dad, or Tommy found it, they'd know Lucine is alive and well, and that you've seen me too. I don't want yous guys to get in trouble. Mother would also flip out if she saw onea the songs is by Jewish musicians and from the Latin Mass. That's a double heart attack. She has such disgusting racist, anti-Jewish, anti-Catholic attitudes."

"I'm sure Allen will keep copies for you and Justine," Lucine says.

Lenore comes over to them. "Are we ready to start rehearsing? We'll probably go through it a few times today before going out to supper."

"Supper!" Adicia says excitedly. "Can we eat uptown?"

"We sure can, sweetie. You and the other girls in the bridal party are gonna get little gifts during supper."

Adicia hugs her around the neck. "You're gonna be the best sister-in-law ever! I'm so glad Justine and I decided to talk to you when we saw you in our bus stop!"

***

Adicia and Justine wake up very nervous on Friday morning, hoping they remember everything they practiced thrice yesterday. They're going to line up with Ernestine first, then Adicia, Julie, Girl, Baby, and Infant, with Lucine last, since she's oldest. Then Emeline will walk down the aisle. They have to walk about twenty feet apart, slowly, turning and smiling instead of walking at a normal pace or looking straight ahead. Giovanni will go next, holding the rings on the pillow. Justine will go just before Lenore and slowly sprinkle the peach rose petals on the carpet. Then everyone will rise and turn to look at the beautiful bride making her grand entrance, and after Lenore reaches the altar, the ceremony will begin.

After having breakfast, bathing, and watching television, they take their clothes and go with the Murphys in a taxi to the church. While they wait for everyone else to arrive, they have a light lunch in the social hall and go over who's going to do what one last time. They also meet the photographer Allen hired. The church pianist, who usually plays the music himself instead of broadcasting it over records on the church sound system, goes over when to put down and release the needle on the four records they're going to use.

"Isn't it nice to be a girl?" Adicia asks as they change into their dresses. "The guys don't get to wear pretty dresses and have their hair done all special. All they're doing is putting on suits."

"We get our own special entrance too," Justine says. "The guys only enter by a side door and don't get their own special march up the aisle."

Ernestine, Lucine, and Emeline start doing their makeup after they put on their dresses. Adicia looks at them wistfully, wishing she were old enough to wear makeup, while Girl cares less to put any on in spite of being fourteen.

"Why are you putting on makeup, Lenore?" Baby asks. "Allen likes you just the way you already look, with no makeup."

"Makeup shows up better in pictures, and it's fun to wear it on special occasions. I'm not anti-makeup, just that I was never that interested in caking it all over my face to try to look prettier."

"Can I wear a little too, just this once?" Adicia begs as Lenore puts on green eyeshadow. "I don't wanna look like a little kid in the photos when I'm twelve."

"You can take the stuff I'm supposed to wear," Girl says.

"You have to put on makeup, Girl," Ernestine pleads. "How can a teenage bridesmaid not wear any?"

"I cracked about wanting to wear a girly dress. I ain't cracking about the makeup."

"Just this once?" Julie asks. "I'd like to wear makeup too."

Adicia fiddles with the lapis lazuli bracelet she got as her bridesmaid gift. "We don't have to look like girls of ill repute if we wear a little makeup. I am going into junior high in the fall."

"Okay, I'll help you," Lucine says. "I have blue eyeshadow for Adicia and a pale plum shade for Julie, to match your dresses. You can wear a little lipstick too."

"Your hair is pretty, Lenore," Baby says. "I've never seen you wearing it up before. It looks a lot nicer than that horrible beehive thing Gemma wears her hair up in."

"Don't say that to Gemma's face," Lucine warns. "I think the beehive thing is heinous too, but I won't tell her. She's always been about the latest fashions, and won't change her mind if someone tells her her hair or clothes look stupid."

"I feel like a clown," Girl complains when Emeline comes over and starts putting lipstick on her. "I'll never wear this junk again after today."

"I'm not really into makeup myself, but it's nice to play dress-up once in awhile," Emeline says.

Twenty minutes later, Infant goes to the door and peeks out toward the hall. She sees the guests starting to arrive, Gemma and the van Niftriks among them. When it looks as though everyone is in the church and seated, the cheerful, trilling strains of Handel's "Water Music" start to fill the air.

"It must be time to line up!" Ernestine says nervously. "Does everyone remember her place?"

"Take your bouquets," Lucine reminds them. "It doesn't matter which one, since they're all identical except Lenore's."

Adicia grabs her small bouquet of baby's breath, irises, and gladioluses and rushes to take her place second in the line. There's a brief moment after "Water Music" ends, and Ernestine starts slowly walking up the aisle as they hear the starting notes of "Benedictus." When Adicia hears the first few syllables of the word *Benedictus* starting, she begins her walk, remembering to make eye contact and smile. Julie starts her processional at *qui*, Girl starts up at *in nomine*, Baby begins at the first repetition of *in nomine*, Infant begins at the second repetition, Lucine begins midway through the second repetition, and Emeline makes her entrance at the third *in nomine Domini*. Giovanni goes up at the final *in nomine*, and Justine makes her entrance at the last line, one final *in nomine Domini*. Adicia smiles at them when they're all at the altar, not only happy to be a bridesmaid at her belovèd big brother's wedding but also to have been escorted down the aisle by such a beautiful, angelic-sounding song that didn't make her afraid or nervous. A part of her almost wishes her mother would know about Allen and Lenore's choice of music, since it wouldn't be a bad thing if such a miserable woman and disgrace to motherhood really did have a double heart attack at the thought of her own offspring selecting a song from the Latin Mass and sung by two Jewish musicians.

Everyone stands and turns when Lenore's processional song starts. Allen falls in love with Lenore all over again when he sees her carrying a bouquet of wildflowers, wearing makeup for the first time since he's known her, a long lacy veil, her hair in a soft updo, faux diamond barrettes, and wearing the ivory velvet gown with chiffon sleeves, which makes her look like a Medieval or Renaissance princess. He doesn't care if the entire congregation and the wedding party see him tearing up in public.

Lenore smiles at him, hands her bouquet to Emeline, and joins her hands in his when she reaches the altar. She and the bridal party exchange smiles before turning their attention to Father Murphy as he delivers the opening benediction.

"Dearly belovèd, we have gathered here today in the presence of God to bless and witness the joining together of this man and this woman in holy matrimony. The bond and covenant of marriage was established by God in creation, and our Lord Jesus Christ adorned this manner of life by his presence and first miracle at a wedding in Cana of Galilee. It signifies to us the mystery of the union between Christ and his Church, and holy scripture commends it to be honored among all people.

"The union of husband and wife in heart, body, and mind is intended by God for their mutual joy; for the help and comfort given one another in prosperity and adversity; and, when it is God's will, for the procreation of children and their nurture in the knowledge and love of the Lord. Therefore, marriage is not to be entered into unadvisedly or lightly, but reverently, deliberately, and in accordance with the purposes for which it was instituted by God.

"Into this holy union Allen Théodore Troy and Lenore Eve Hartlein now come to be joined. As they have no parents to represent them and give them away, they are giving themselves to one another in marriage. If any of you can show just cause why they may not lawfully be married, speak now; or forever hold your peace.

"Our Father, love has been your richest and greatest gift to the world. Love between a man and woman which matures into marriage is one of your most beautiful types of loves. Today we celebrate that love. May your blessing be on this wedding service. Protect, guide, and bless Allen Théodore Troy and Lenore Eve Hartlein in their marriage. Surround them and us with your love now and always. In the name of Jesus Christ, amen."

Lucine walks up to the podium, setting her bouquet next to the large Bible as she opens to the bookmarked page with Ecclesiastes 4:9-12. Turning to face her family and friends, she begins reading with poise. "'Two are better than one because they have a good return for their labor. For if either of them falls, the one will lift up his companion. But woe to the one who falls when there is not another to lift him up. Furthermore, if two lie down together, they keep warm, but how can one be warm alone? And if one can overpower him who is alone, two can resist him. A cord of three strands is not quickly torn apart.'"

Emeline gets up next and reads four paragraphs from Plato's Symposium. Her reading talks about how the mysterious and unknown power of love originated in humankind's original nature, when people had two sets of arms and legs and two faces looking in different directions, and there were three biological sexes. Eventually Zeus divided the humans in half, but each person so desired his or her other half, they came together again in a mutual embrace, longing to become one again. Thus, ever since, people have been looking for their other halves and desiring to spend their lives as one instead of two.

Girl is the last reader before the marriage ceremony itself. She puts her bouquet on the podium and reaches down for the paper where Mrs. van Niftrik typed the Irish wedding blessing she dictated. "May the road rise to meet you. May the wind be always at your backs. May the sun shine warm upon your faces, the rains fall soft upon the fields. May the light of friendship guide your paths together. May the laughter of children grace the halls of your home. May the joy of living for one another trip a smile from your lips, a twinkle from your eyes. And when eternity beckons, at the end of a life heaped high with love, may the good Lord embrace you with the arms that have nurtured you the whole length of your joy-filled days. May the gracious God hold you both in the palm of his hands. And, today, may the spirit of love find a dwelling place in your hearts. Amen."

Father Murphy conducts a prayer service, vaguely familiar to Adicia from the times she's gone to Episcopal churches. She and Justine went over the words of the Our Father before the ceremony, so they won't have to mouth the words and reveal themselves as non-practicing Christians. It's a welcome relief there's no Communion on weekdays, so she and the other non-practicing bridesmaids don't have to choose between embarrassing themselves by not moving from their positions, or misrepresenting themselves. Father Murphy would probably let them take Communion because of how progressive he is, coupled with the fact that non-Catholic Communion doesn't require baptism in that particular church or regular visits to Confession, but Adicia isn't comfortable at the thought of doing something she knows she shouldn't do.

Allen and Lenore join hands again and face Father Murphy when the requisite religious portion of the ceremony is over and the vows begin.

"Allen Théodore Troy, will you have this woman to be your wedded wife, to live together after God's ordinance in the holy estate of matrimony? Will you love her, comfort her, honor and keep her, in sickness and in health, and forsaking all others keep yourself only unto her as long as you both shall live?"

"I sure will." Allen smiles.

"Will you repeat after me, or have you memorized your vows?"

"I've got this one." Allen turns to Lenore. "In the name of God, I, Allen Théodore Troy, take you, Lenore Eve Hartlein, to be my wife, to have and to hold from this day forward, for better, for worse, for richer, for poorer, in sickness and health, to love and to cherish, until we are parted by death. This is my solemn vow."

"Lenore Eve Hartlein, will you have this man to be your wedded husband, to live together after God's ordinance in the holy estate of matrimony? Will you love him, comfort him, honor and keep him, in sickness and in health, and forsaking all others keep yourself only unto him as long as you both shall live?"

"Yes, I will."

"Have you also memorized your vows?"

She nods. "In the name of God, I, Lenore Eve Hartlein, take you, Allen Théodore Troy, to be my husband, to have and to hold from this day forward, for better, for worse, for richer, for poorer, in sickness and health, to love and to cherish, until we are parted by death. This is my solemn vow."

Father Murphy reaches down for the pillow with the rings. Giovanni smiles a big smile at his father and uncle as Father Murphy holds the pillow aloft and blesses them.

"Bless, O Lord, these rings to be a sign of the vows by which this man and this woman have bound themselves to each other; through Jesus Christ our Lord. Amen."

Allen puts the smaller gold band on Lenore's ring finger, his hands trembling, and recites, "Lenore Eve Hartlein, I give you this ring as a symbol of my vow, and with all that I am, and all that I have, I honor you, in the name of God."

Lenore picks up the larger ring and carefully slips it onto Allen's ring finger, reciting, "Allen Théodore Troy, I give you this ring as a symbol of my vow, and with all that I am, and all that I have, I honor you, in the name of God."

They join hands again as Father Murphy pronounces the final benediction. "Now that Allen Théodore Troy and Lenore Eve Hartlein have given themselves to each other by solemn vows, with the joining of hands, and the giving and receiving of rings, I pronounce they are husband and wife, in the name of the Father, the Son, and the Holy Ghost. Those whom God has joined together, let no one put asunder. You may seal your marriage with a kiss."

After Allen and Lenore have exchanged their first kiss as a married couple, Father Murphy entreats everyone to go in peace, and the recessional song, "Ebb Tide," starts. Allen and Lenore go down the aisle first, followed by Emeline with the best man Jack, Lucine with the groomsman Douglas, Ernestine and Adicia with the groomsman Steven, Girl and Julie with Boy, Baby walking alone, and Giovanni with Justine and Infant. After the bridal party has exited the sanctuary, they stand outside in a receiving line for awhile, and Emeline and Jack are called inside to sign the marriage certificate as witnesses. Allen, Lenore, and Father Murphy sign it next.

"I'm so glad you're officially in our family now," Emeline gushes.

"I'm happy to be a member of your family too." Lenore smiles.

"You need directions to the reception?" Allen asks.

"We remember," Emeline assures him. "It's only a few blocks west."

"We can't wait to see you all there." Lenore gazes up at Allen. "I hope you like the supper menu and our dessert buffet, and the songs we asked the disc jockey to play."

"You did a great job with that Plato reading," Allen says. "I wouldn't have known about it if you hadn't suggested it. I was surprised two of the three original races were men who preferred men and women who preferred women."

"They were a lot more open about that kinda stuff in ancient Greece," Emeline says. "In the meantime, we need to start making our way to the reception!"

***

When everyone has arrived at the social hall, they're required to line up for one final processional. The disc jockey explains they'll be announced as they enter the main hall, going in the same order as the first processional. The most exciting part will be when Allen and Lenore enter at the end, when everyone will stand up and hear them announced as husband and wife for the very first time in public. Adicia hopes someday she'll get a nice wedding like this too and be publicly announced as the respectable, belovèd wife and new bride of a handsome man who takes care of her and loves her just the way she is.

After they've put their modest gifts on the designated table, they line up in the hallway and walk in as the disc jockey announces each of them and what their role in the bridal party was. This time they don't have to walk formally or wait a little while between each. The guests in the social hall applaud as they enter, and Betsy waves at them. Father and Mrs. Murphy are also in the processional this time. Gemma smiles at Giovanni, and he smiles back and waves at her, fascinated at how much his birth mother resembles him, with the same light green eyes and light blonde hair. She meanwhile is very pleased to see he looks exactly the same, and that his features didn't turn darker to resemble that brute Francesco as he aged. Only in America could a blonde-haired, green-eyed kid have an Italian first and middle name paired with an Irish last name. She has to concede that's more realistically American than a so-called all-American name like Bobby or Johnny.

Everyone stands up when Allen and Lenore appear at the doorway. Justine, Infant, Baby, and Giovanni stand on their chairs to get a better view of them as they come in, arm in arm, smiling and waving at everyone. Allen specifically requested the disc jockey announce them as their names, not Mr. and Mrs. Allen Troy, since he considers Lenore her own person, not a passive extension of himself. The girls are very proud of him for being so forward-thinking and enlightened. He might not be modern and radical enough to consider the idea of Lenore remaining a Hartlein, but his attitude is a step forward.

"Thank you all so much for coming to our wedding, celebrating this happy event, and sharing in our love!" Allen tells them after they've been announced. "Lenore, how does it feel to be a Troy?"

"This has been such a beautiful, special day! I'm not entirely sure if I dreamt the whole thing, or if I dreamt the past four years!"

"This is no dream, Mrs. Troy." Allen sweeps her into his arms as their first song, Buddy Holly's "True Love Ways," starts playing.

Though she's a tad jealous, Adicia is happy to see them looking so very, very happy. It hardly seems like only four years have gone by since they met Lenore and she immediately became part of their family. It also seems like it's been more than thirteen months since Allen and

Lenore became more than friends.

Midway through the dancing, there's a break for supper. The menu consists of salmon, roasted potatoes, something called mushroom risotto, and stuffed tomatoes. The girls are very impressed there are servers to whom they can dictate how much they want, instead of having to accept whatever portions are brought out to them. They even get to go up for seconds on the grape soda pop.

Several people get up to make toasts during supper. Adicia's favorite toast is Emeline's, since she talks about how today not only makes it four years since Allen and Lenore met, but also four years since she, Adicia, and Justine met Lenore. Their story is proof that real, true love waits and will still be there after the initial infatuation if it's meant to be. Real, lasting love, relationships, and friendships can sometimes be found in the least likely of places, and all events really are linked together in this best of all possible worlds. If they hadn't gone to the park that day, spent all day there, and decided to wait a little while in the bus stop due to the heavy rain, had taken the subway or a taxi instead, or not talked to Lenore, they never would be here now. Adicia smiles at Emeline when she sits back down, proud not only of her beautiful toast but also of how good she was at both of her public speaking occasions today. Emeline can speak very well among strangers when she wants to, though she has to put up with the sticking label of "the quiet one," the one many people don't expect much from since she's so serious and bookish. Maybe someday Adicia will prove people wrong about herself too, show them she's not just another poor girl but someone who can make good in society and leave her shabby origins behind.

There's another dancing portion of the reception, and at the conclusion, Lenore calls all the unmarried ladies onto the dance floor so she can toss her bouquet. Adicia, her sisters, Betsy, Julie, the Ryan girls, and some of the young female guests scamper onto the floor and try to get into the best places to catch it. Infant, Justine, and Baby stand on their tiptoes. Lenore turns around and flings the bouquet of wildflowers behind her.

"It's Lucine!" Ernestine shouts. "Lucine, you caught the bouquet!"

Lucine lowers her left hand, not having initially processed that she was the one who caught it. She breaks into a huge smile and starts hugging her sisters and their friends.

"You are twenty," Emeline teases. "Only a year older than Lenore. Maybe in another year or two, we'll catch your bouquet."

"I'm only going into my junior year of college!" Lucine laughs. "I don't wanna get serious with a guy till I'm out of school!"

"You never know," Gemma says. "I'd peg you as getting married before I remarry."

"We can talk more about this over the dessert buffet," Lenore says. "Wait'll yous guys see the cake."

The photographer takes a picture of Allen and Lenore cutting the three-layer cake together. It has white frosting, purple and peach roses, strawberry jelly filling, and marble cake. Other desserts on the buffet table include baklava, raspberry torte, chocolate chip cookies, key lime pie, chocolate rugelach, and several choices of cheesecake. Adicia is glad they live in Manhattan, where they have so many nice bakeries to choose from, including ethnic bakeries, as much as she otherwise hates living in this crowded cesspool of a town.

"Your brother sure knows how to put on a nice wedding," Betsy says as they leave the social hall at the conclusion of the evening. "I wonder if he and Lenore will put on such a nice party when they have a kid."

"They haven't been married for a whole day," Ernestine protests. "They probably don't want a kid this soon."

"They don't have to worry about a scandal anymore," Girl points out. "Not that I like the idea of immediately having a kid after marriage, but they might change their minds. We'll have to wait and see."

"Are there plans for a honeymoon?" Betsy asks.

"If they have one, it won't be right away," Ernestine says. "They spent a pretty penny on today. Working-class people don't come by that kinda dough easily. Maybe they'll take another modest trip to Long Island while the weather's still warm."

Everyone stands back as Allen and Lenore get into a taxi with a "Just Married" sign in the back. The adult groomsmen put the wedding gifts into the trunk. As the taxi starts driving, they wave out the backseat window. *It must be nice to be a newlywed*, Adicia thinks.

***

When the taxi stops in front of their apartment, Allen gets out first and pulls Lenore out by her hands. He opens the trunk and pulls out the gifts, mostly placed into bags to make for easier carrying. After he hands the driver his fare and a tip, he puts his arm around Lenore and goes to unlock the front door. He makes several trips to bring all the gifts up to the apartment, then takes Lenore by the hand. As soon as the elevator gets to the fifth floor, he picks her up and carries her to 515.

"I can walk, darling. I'm not unconscious anymore."

"I wouldn't dream of not carrying my bride over the threshold of our home. Let me do my husbandly duty."

"But it's not a brand-new home. I've lived here for four years!"

"Not as my wife." He unlocks the door and steps inside, still carrying Lenore. "How does it feel to come here as husband and wife for the first time?"

"I love being your wife. And I love being a Troy."

"Just the answer I wanted to hear." He sets her down in their room. "You need any help getting outta your dress?"

"You can unhook the back."

He obligingly unhooks her dress, then peels off his suit and hangs it up in the closet. After Lenore hangs her dress up, Allen turns to her with a smile.

"Is the new Mrs. Troy up for consummating our marriage?"

"Take me, I'm all yours." She pulls him down onto the bed with her.

"I'm the luckiest guy in the world," he says as he runs his hands along her body. "Could you have imagined when we met four years ago tonight, we'd be husband and wife four years to the day? I knew I'd just met my future wife, but I don't think you knew right away."

"I had a special feeling about you too, even if I didn't think anything would ever come of it. I'm glad I'm here with you now as your bride."

"Now, always, and forever."

Chapter 34: Changing Lives

"All those religious nuts are making a big deal outta nothing," Ernestine says as she and Betsy wait for the school bus on their first day of high school. "But then again, I'm not a practicing Christian, and John has always been my favorite."

"Yeah, those people burning and smashing their Beatles' records are nuts. My reverend hasn't said anything on the subject. Shouldn't Christian clergymen focus on real issues like world hunger, the war in Vietnam, and civil rights, not what a musician says in an interview?"

"I can't believe it's still going on. He made those comments in March, and no one in England gave a damn when that interview was published. People in America can be really messed up about so-called morality. I'm glad I live here, but we're so backwards compared to Europe. There are so many holdovers from the Puritans' era it's silly."

"Shouldn't these people, if they're that concerned and upset, look into why modern rock groups are more popular than Jesus? If I were a minister and heard that kinda statement, I'd make my church or denomination more appealing to young people instead of throwing a hissy fit and calling for censorship and record-burning."

"My old nanny Sarah told us about how the Nazis burnt books by people they didn't like, years before they started killing and imprisoning people they didn't like. She quoted us a line from one of her favorite poets, Heinrich Heine, 'Wherever they burn books they will, in the end, burn people.' Maybe it's easier for people to look the other way and not bother, 'cause they think someone else will step in and do the right thing for them."

"I'm glad we're not in the South. The anti-Beatle stuff is the worst down there."

Ernestine grins. "Speaking of popular music, I heard a song on the radio the other day that reminded me of Allen and Lenore. You'd never believe this. It's like the song was written just for them. It's about a couple who meets at a bus stop and eventually marries. I'm gonna buy a copy and give it to them as a joke gift."

Betsy giggles. "I love your sense of humor. It's one of the reasons I like being your friend."

As Ernestine and Betsy get into the school bus pulling up at the curb, Adicia rides on the bus taking her to her new junior high school, not a single friend or relative aboard. Justine, Tommy, and Matthew are still in elementary school, while she has no choice but to get used to a new school in a building that looked frightening when she went there with the other graduating sixth graders for an orientation visit. It's old, run-down, and gloomy, and projects a bad energy. She hopes she can fade into the woodwork instead of becoming a target for mean girls and bullies. She's heard the kids in junior high are meaner than in elementary school, because they're older and bolder, no longer as inclined to behave or listen to teachers when reprimanded. At least if Julie went to school, she might have a friend, though Julie lives in the district served by the schools of Greenwich Village.

When she arrives, some of the children are fighting in the schoolyard, and others are smoking. Adicia hardly believes children her age are smoking. Even Gemma, Carlos, and Allen didn't take up smoking till they were out of junior high. A number of the girls are wearing clothes that look a little too grownup, like the knee-baring skirts Gemma wears. Some of them are kissing boys too, which is just scandalous. Adicia still thinks the idea of making out, let alone having full intimacy, is gross. She hopes no boy approaches her for a date.

Adicia succeeds in finding her homeroom without getting lost or asking for directions, and finds a seat near the teacher. The bad kids always sit in the back of the room and the bus, unless there's an assigned seating chart. The kids filtering into the room, which doubles as their first period French class, seem to be a mix of good kids and rough elements. In spite of her mother's racist attitudes, she thinks some of the white kids look a lot worse than the Puerto Ricans and Negroes.

The teacher looks very young, probably about Gemma's age. *This must be her first teaching job*, Adicia thinks. She introduces herself as Charlotte Petersen and says she'll be twenty-five at the end of the month. The children are to call her Mademoiselle Petersen. She looks sweet-faced and friendly, but Adicia is afraid to raise her hand when she asks if anyone knows any French already. She doesn't want to get labeled a teacher's pet on the first day of school by revealing she's half-French, her father sometimes speaks French when he's mad, and her older sisters have taught her a little. When Mlle. Petersen passes around a sheet of paper so they can write their names next to the French name they want to use in class, Adicia automatically chooses Éloïse, glad she's at the front of the class and can get first dibs on her middle name.

Her second through fourth period classes are English, math, and history. The kids in those classes also seem a mix of roughs and good kids, and the teachers are really young. Adicia wonders if most teachers only work here because they want their first job and are too innocent to believe kids could be so bad. *There's probably a high quitting rate,* she thinks as she tries to find an empty table at lunch.

"Would you like to eat with me? I don't have no one to sit with either."

Adicia looks to her right. A pretty girl with a blue dress, red leather shoes, braids, and a Barbie lunchbox is smiling at her.

"Sure." Adicia smiles back. "What's your name? I'm Adicia Troy."

"I'm Marjani Washington. Are you in seventh grade too?"

"Yes, it's my first day." Adicia is a little jealous of Marjani's relatively new lunchbox, while she's had the same plain metal lunchbox since 1960. None of the Troy children except Tommy ever merited a lunchbox with toys, cartoons, or movie or television characters. "You said your name's Marjorie?"

"Marjani. It's Swahili for 'coral.' My parents wanted to give me a nice Black name instead of something that didn't reflect our heritage." Marjani sits at the end of a table where a couple of other outcasts are sitting alone or in small groups.

"A what name? You mean a Negro name?"

"We don't use that word in our home anymore. My parents think it's offensive these days, after all those struggles we went through to get equal rights. I know you didn't mean no harm, though. It's not like darky or coon."

"My mother uses those words, but my sisters told me those are very bad words. She hates how my little brother has friends who aren't all white, but she doesn't forbid him to play with them, so long as he doesn't take them home. What kind of apartment do you live in? We live in an old tenement with three rooms, a bedroom, kitchen, and living room."

Marjani puts down her thermos. "Are you serious? Ain't that against the law?"

"It's fairly new, not onea the ones that got all that bad attention in the old days. We used to live in a much bigger tenement on the Lower East Side, with a kitchen, a bathroom, a living room, three bedrooms, and one tiny room we used as another bedroom. It was only so big 'cause it used to belong to the landlord's family. We lost that place in a big fire in June '62."

"Gee, my family lives in a nice, modern apartment with three bedrooms. The building itself ain't so nice, but at least it was built within the last twenty years. How many brothers and sisters do you have?"

"I'm the seventh of nine. I have four older sisters, two older brothers, a younger sister, and a younger brother. Only three of us are left at home. My older sister Ernestine starts high school today, but she's lucky and lives with friends in the Meatpacking District. She goes to school in Greenwich Village. I visit her a lot."

"That's a lot of kids. My sister Subira's fifteen and my brother Zuberi's nine. How old are your siblings?"

"Gemma's twenty-four, Carlos, who's been crippled for four years, is twenty-three, Allen's twenty-two, Lucine's twenty, Emeline's eighteen, Ernestine's fourteen, I'm twelve, Tommy's ten, and Justine's seven. We also just got an awesome sister-in-law, Lenore, who's nineteen. She's married to Allen. Me, Emeline, and Justine used to live with them, and Ernestine and her friends lived in the basement, till our mean mother ruined our Christmas four years ago. She got all mad 'cause she assumed they were living in sin. She also thought Lenore was a girl of ill repute 'cause we met her at a bus stop. My mother is crazy. By the way, I like your braids. If I had longer hair, I'd wanna wear mine in braids."

"They're called cornrows. It's a traditional African hairstyle, though mosta the Black girls and women I know straighten their hair to look white. Your mother sounds awful. What kinda Scrooge ruins Christmas for her own children? And who automatically assumes every girl at a bus stop is an immoral woman and not just waiting for a bus?"

"Yeah, she's kinda nuts. She's also a cocaine addict and a drunk. I can't wait till I can get away from her."

Marjani pulls her schedule out of her schoolbag. "What are your classes for the rest of the day? Maybe we have a class together."

Adicia gets out her schedule. "Biology, art, home ec, and typing."

"I've got art sixth and home ec seventh too. Are your teachers Miss Elliott and Mrs. McKenna?"

"They are. I guess I'll see you again later today."

"If you want, you can come over to my place after school sometime. Unlike your mother, my parents don't care if I bring over friends who ain't the same race as us. What's your ancestry, by the way? I know there's a city called Troy upstate, but I don't know the origin of the name itself."

"I'm French on my dad's side and Belgian on my mother's side. My first name is Greek, after the goddess of injustice. My mother thought it was an injustice to be given a fifth daughter."

"What a horrible, horrible woman. The name Adicia is pretty, but who deliberately gives a kid a name with a negative meaning?"

"If you ever meet my mother, you'll find out just how nuts she is. Not that I'd wish meeting her on anybody."

"Well, I'm sure you'll like my family. They're nice to people, don't use drugs or drink, and don't think it's awful there are more girls than boys in our family."

Adicia hates having to go to this depressing junior high and suffer through two years with a lot of unsavory elements, but it might be a little more bearable with a new friend. She doesn't care what color Marjani's skin is. All that matters is she's a nice person who likes her. Mrs. Troy can hem and haw about it all she wants, but Adicia will take Marjani up on her offer to come over to her place. That miserable woman certainly hasn't done anything to prevent Adicia and Justine from regularly visiting Allen and Lenore or Ernestine and her friends.

***

The first weekend in October, the girls arrive at Allen and Lenore's apartment for their first visit since school began. They're very eager to hear all about the honeymoon Allen and Lenore took to Oyster Bay in Long Island the first weekend of September.

"Come sit down," Lenore says, looking a little pale. "I haven't been feeling so well lately, but I'm well enough to show you our pictures and tell you all about our trip."

"You're not feeling well?" Justine asks. "I don't want you to get sick again. You can lie down on the sofa bed and we can sit around you as you show us the pictures."

"Did you catch something in Long Island?" Girl asks. "Maybe you drank bad water or had fish with worms in it."

"Does Allen know you don't feel well?" Ernestine asks. "I can't imagine he would've gone off to work had he known his bride didn't feel well. You know how overprotective he is."

"Enough about me," Lenore says. "Why don't you girls tell me about your lives first?"

"I'm here too," Boy reminds them. "I hate being lumped together with all these girls."

"Betsy turned us on to a really groovy new television show," Ernestine says. "It's called *The Monkees*, and it airs on Monday nights. Me, Julie, and Girl go over to the van Niftriks' place to watch it. We even got Baby into watching it. She thinks they're cute, and can't wait till we buy their album."

"Baby's having her first celebrity crush?" Lenore asks. "She was just a little girl when I met her!"

"I'm nine now," Baby says. "I was five when I met you."

"Girl and I both like Peter best," Ernestine says. "It's like we share a brain. It's the same way with how John is our favorite Beatle; we came to that choice by ourselves, without knowing the other had made it."

"I like Davy best," Julie says. "I think he's the cutest."

"That's the same reason you picked Paul as your favorite Beatle," Girl says. "I think they're all cute too, but you should have a more solid reason for picking your favorite member of a group besides how cute he happens to be."

"I don't think I have a favorite," Baby says. "I just think all four of 'em are cute."

"I wish I could watch that show," Adicia says. "My new friend Marjani's parents would probably let me come over to watch it, since they have a television, but I don't wanna walk alone after dark in Hell's Kitchen."

"What kinda name is that?" Lenore asks. "Is she foreign?"

"She's a Negro, but she and her family don't use that word. They call themselves Black. That's the new progressive word used by Negroes who are into their culture and equal rights. She, her mother, and her older sister wear their hair in something called cornrows. They're tight little braids, braided right against their heads instead of loose like Betsy's braids. They wear pretty colored beads in their braids. Their names are from a language called Swahili, which is used in some Western African countries. Her name means 'coral,' and her sister Subira's name means 'patience.' Their brother Zuberi's name means 'strong.' I don't know if their parents have African names. They're just Mr. and

Mrs. Washington to me."

"They live in the tenement?" Boy asks. "I don't remember you mentioning there was a Negro family there, though I know your mom hates the Puerto Ricans."

"They live about fifteen minutes away. I've visited them a couple of times."

"Wow," Ernestine says. "How is Mother handling that?"

"I don't think she knows. All she knows is I sometimes go to visit a new friend with a name that sounds a little funny. Even if she knew, she'd probably grudgingly accept it like she accepts how Tommy has Puerto Rican friends. So long as we don't bring our non-white friends home, she's okay."

"Oh, Lenore, I got you and Allen a present," Ernestine laughs. "It's a single by a British group. I thought of yous guys when I heard it, since it's about a couple who meets the same way you met."

"Someone made a song about a couple meeting at a bus stop?" Lenore asks in amusement. "Does the boy's mother also accuse him of soliciting a hooker? I don't know what kind of bus stops that woman has been hanging around if she's so convinced the only reason to be there is to buy drugs or pick up girls of ill repute."

"I think she's smoked too much cocaine," Adicia says.

"Excuse me for a moment. I think I'm gonna be sick again."

"Let me help you," Ernestine says. "If you need to throw up, I can hold your hair back for you. You've got so much of it."

Lenore bolts into the bathroom and runs the water so they don't have to hear her throwing up. Girl and Ernestine rush into the kitchen to make chicken noodle soup, while Adicia puts crackers on a plate and pours a glass of ginger ale.

"Are you gonna be okay?" Infant asks when Lenore comes out of the bathroom. "Why don't you sit down, and we'll bring you food as soon as it's done being made."

"Do you think it's a stomach bug?" Julie asks. "I hope you're not contagious."

"I've been feeling really tired in the middle of the day, besides starting to vomit lately. At least I've never thrown up when Allen's home. I've been having weird dreams too."

Girl looks at her with a slight grin. "Not that I was ever around her that much, but I was five when my mother was pregnant with Baby and seven when she had Infant. She got tired in the middle of the day and threw up a bunch. She said morning sickness was the wrong name for it, since she didn't only get sick in the mornings. Do you think it's possible?"

"I'd better not be. That's the last thing we need, after we spent a pretty penny on our wedding and just had a five-day honeymoon. I'm not even working, though I did get my GED over the summer."

"When did you last menstruate?" Ernestine asks. "For all anyone knows, maybe it really is a stomach bug, but you are newlyweds. I've heard stories of newlyweds getting careless with their birth control, since they no longer have to worry about scandal."

"August. But it's normal sometimes to skip. It's only the first of October."

"When in August?" Girl asks. "Can you remember?"

"Probably earlier in August. I forgot my birth control pills when we went on our honeymoon—"

"What! How could you forget them, particularly when you don't want a kid right away? Were you thinking with newlywed brain?"

"I keep them in the medicine cabinet, not my purse. It slipped my mind to check the medicine cabinet for anything we needed to take. This was during the last active week of that pill package, and then came the week where you're supposed to have your menses. I just thought it was a little late in arriving."

"Honeymoon babies are so romantic. They're like wedding night babies, a special reminder of how in love newlyweds are."

"Have you taken any pills since you came home?" Julie asks.

"No. I don't know, maybe a part of me did wanna have a baby and make us a family of three. It's not abnormal to wanna have a baby by your new husband and make your family complete, is it?"

"I hope you are!" Justine says. "Then we can have a little niece or nephew to play with. We can keep this one, not like how we had to say goodbye to Giovanni for such a long time."

"Can I be an aunt too?" Baby asks.

"I ain't doing nothing too important next week," Girl says. "I'll go with you if you can make an appointment to that progressive place where you got the pills. If you are, I know just the way you can break the news to Allen. Have a note sent to the bakery, asking him to frost a cake congratulating a couple on expecting a baby. You'll show up later to claim your order, and when he checks your order number against the cake in the box, he'll know you're having a baby."

"That's so clever!" Julie says. "We'll all be so happy for you if you really are having a baby!"

"I hope Allen won't be mad if I am. I didn't tell him about forgetting my pills on our honeymoon or how I've been feeling sick and haven't menstruated in over a month. He didn't want a kid this soon after we were married. He might feel I tricked him into fatherhood."

"Has he ever been mad at you?" Adicia asks. "I wish I have a boyfriend and husband just like my brother when I'm old enough. Allen worships the ground you walk on and would do anything to please you and make you happy. I bet he'd be over the moon to find out you might be having a baby."

"I wouldn't recommend you go to a traditional doctor when it comes time to get the kid outta you," Ernestine says. "Allen would lose it if he wasn't allowed to be with you when you give birth and saw bruises and rubbed-off skin on your wrists and around your ankles. Gemma was tied down to a table and left lying in her own waste for hours while her doctor went out to supper and saw a movie. She can't remember giving birth. She also hated how she had to go to a male doctor."

"Maybe we can find onea them old-fashioned doctors who comes to your home to deliver your baby here in the Village," Girl suggests. "We all know how Bohemian and progressive this neighborhood is."

"First things first," Lenore says. "We have to find out if it's true before doing anything else."

"We promise we'll keep mum till we know for sure," Adicia says. "Boy, this is exciting news if it really is true! It'll make this year our best ever, from start to finish!"

***

Two and a half weeks later, a typewritten note is given to Allen at work. It's strange to get an order delivered in this way instead of over the phone or in person, but he looks at it to see what it's about.

Dear Mr. Troy,

You've frosted some of our cakes before, and I really enjoyed your craftsmanship. I'm writing to you because my husband and I are expecting our first baby in June, and I haven't broken the news to him yet. I'd like you to frost a cake for us, with the words "Congratulations on your coming arrival!" The cake should be chocolate, with white frosting, orange lettering, and raspberry jam filling. I'll come in later today to pick it up. Thank you in advance for doing this.

Thinking nothing of it, Allen goes to the refrigerator and pulls out eggs, butter, and milk, and starts measuring ingredients into bowls.

Meanwhile, Lenore is visiting Girl and Mrs. van Niftrik, while the rest of Girl's party are off performing odd jobs on the streets of Greenwich Village to earn enough money to buy groceries for the week, and hopefully finish putting enough money in their kitty to indulge in a couple of records. All the older girls want to buy *The Monkees*; Girl and Ernestine want to buy *Parsley, Sage, Rosemary, and Thyme*; Boy wants to buy a couple of his favorite songs on the radio; and Julie wants to buy *Both Sides of Herman's Hermits*. They were set back a bit when Girl bought the double Bob Dylan album *Blonde on Blonde* during the summer, so they're working on saving their money back up again. They barely had enough money left in their music fund to buy The Beatles' newest album, *Revolver*, which came out in August. Girl feels very strongly that folk music is the music of the people, their people. As much as she enjoys the more pop-oriented acts, it's better to give money to folk rockers telling it like it is and sharing in their struggle.

"Don't make the mistake of buying all new things," Mrs. van Niftrik says. "The only modern things you need are a crib and stroller. You can even cut out the cost of a crib by having the baby sleep in your bed. Betsy slept with us till she was two, back when we lived in Tribeca. My family and friends all thought I was kind of daffy, but you'll be right there when the baby cries in the middle of the night, instead of having to get up and go to another room. I fed Betsy the old-fashioned way too, so all I had to do was give her my breast and go back to sleep while she nursed. But then again, Arthur and I have always been progressive, not afraid to do things a little differently or hold differing opinions. My parents bought us a stroller, though sometimes I carted Betsy around in a kind of homemade sling, the way Indians carried their babies."

"Did you have Betsy at home too?" Girl asks. "You're my kinda mother. If I have a kid someday, I'll do the exact same things. I don't care what the stuffy establishment thinks of me. They're the ones who are nuts, convincing people over the last fifty or a hundred years that the natural way of doing things for most of human history is dangerous, bad for kids, and deserves to be laughed at."

"Oh, even I wasn't that radical. I don't think I would've known where to find a midwife, and I wasn't sure anyone still did that. I had a rotten experience in the hospital, though. I wouldn't recommend doing that if I could avoid it, knowing what I know about your past. Ernestine's oldest sister's experience sounds scarily like my own. I can't remember giving birth to Betsy."

"If it happened in early September, we have about seven and a half months to prepare. Just tell us what we need to get, and we'll make it or hustle up money to buy it. I'll start by making diapers from old clothes and rags."

"I think Arthur and I are the only people you know with the disposable income to afford a stroller. We'll buy you a nice one. Don't even think of refusing. It's our gift."

"I wouldn't buy or make any clothes in stereotypical boy or girl colors. I ain't never liked the color pink, and Boy's never been particularly drawn to blue neither. I wish more people would let kids be kids, instead of making them adhere to a particular set of interests, thoughts, actions, and physical looks. Do you have a feeling about what it is?"

"It doesn't matter to me. But I hope Allen takes it well if it turns out to be a girl. He'll have yet another girl for his harem."

"Allen takes being surrounded by girls a lot better than my brother. His older brother went the opposite direction instead of having the same kinda respect for women. Does anyone know how that loser at life is doing, by the way? Last I heard, he was back with his senses and in a rehab program for learning to function on his own with paralysis. I wouldn't wanna be his caretaker if I was a nurse. I was shocked but not really sorry when I found out he'd become crippled."

"The word from Adicia is that he can do simple things on his own, though he's probably a long way from being considered for living on his own. The cops, their old landlord, and the people whose cars he stole from filed charges against him a long time ago, so the statute of limitations wouldn't expire. They might go to court within the next year, since he's now mentally fit to stand trial."

"I'll make you a list of necessary baby supplies," Mrs. van Niftrik says. "It's always more practical and economical to receive donations from friends and relatives who've already had babies, or to scour thrift stores for bargains. A baby won't care if it's dressed in used clothes or the latest designs, and they outgrow them so fast. You'll need lots of clothes."

"My sisters-in-law grew up wearing hand-me-downs."

"There's a big difference between hand-me-downs so old they're turning into rags and gently-used hand-me-downs. You'll probably want a pacifier too, and a playpen is always nice."

"You'll need a highchair," Girl says. "I can sew bibs. I enjoy making clothes and other fabric things, even if I ain't got no sewing machine and hafta do 'em all by hand."

"In the meantime, Allen still doesn't know," Lenore says. "What time should I pick up that cake? I hope he takes it well instead of thinking I tricked him into fatherhood."

"This baby isn't illegitimate," Mrs. van Niftrik says. "It's the most normal and natural thing in the world for a husband and wife to have a baby. And it's better to start early instead of putting it off too long, till you're thirty or older."

"You're going to rock his world," Girl says.

***

Allen is a little surprised to see Lenore coming into the bakery at 5:30. He always brings home the leftovers at the end of the day, and often gets complementary baked goods for working there, so it's not like she needs to buy anything. Maybe she wants to watch him working, or misses him so much she couldn't help stopping in for a quick hello and a stolen cuddle.

"How are you doing, sweetheart? Is there a reason for your visit?"

"I came to pick up an order I placed earlier today." She hands him her order ticket. "We're going to enjoy it for dessert tonight."

"You didn't hafta do that. You make such nice baked goods, and we're always getting free stuff besides."

"It's already done. Be a good boy and go fetch the order, and I'll pay for it."

Allen goes to get the box whose number on the receipt matches the number on the order ticket. When he returns to the front of the bakery, he sets it on the counter and opens the box to make sure it's the right order.

"There's been a mistake. The order numbers must've gotten mixed up somehow. This is a cake I frosted for a couple who's having a baby."

"I know," Lenore says.

"Did you just understand what I said?" he asks in confusion. "This can't be the same cake you ordered, since it's for a couple having a kid. I'll have to take you back so you can look at the other cakes and see if you can pick out the right one."

"Allen, I am well aware of what the inscription says. There's no mistake. That's the cake I ordered."

"What are you talking about? You must be thinking with newly-wed brain. I'll go back and check the other orders that haven't been picked up yet."

Lenore takes a seat and waits for Allen to check the other boxes waiting for pickup in the back. Five contain various types of cookies, four contain jellyrolls, three contain doughnuts, six contain pies, and two contain brownies. He looks in the refrigerators, and only finds a couple of wedding cakes.

"I'm afraid your order never got filled. I can't find any other cakes that could be what you wanted. Why don't you tell me what kind of cake you had in mind, and I'll make it right now. It'll be warm from the oven when I come home."

Lenore goes over to the counter and points to the cake. "That's our cake. Marble cake, raspberry filling, white frosting, orange lettering that says 'Congratulations on your coming arrival!' Exactly what I ordered."

Allen looks at the cake and back at Lenore several times before a slight smile appears on his face. "Are you…?"

She nods.

He rushes over to her. "Are you sure?"

"I forgot my birth control pills on our honeymoon, and I didn't think anything of it since that was my last active week. Then I started getting sick and tired a lot during the day, and my menses never showed up. About a week and a half ago I had it confirmed by my doctor. I'm sorry if this is far too soon and was a mistake."

Allen hugs her. "Are you kidding? This is fantastic news! Not only did I finally marry my dream girl, we also got our own little honeymoon baby! Boy, am I excited to meet our baby!" He kisses her on the cheek. "Sit right down, and I'll bring you somea the three-day-old cookies and stuff I'm supposed to take home today. You're eating for two now."

"I'm supposed to eat healthy foods, not sugary things!"

"I can't believe I'm gonna be a father next year. If it happened on our honeymoon, it might be born on my birthday. Can you try to have it on my birthday? That would be the best birthday present ever!"

Lenore is helpless to protest when he brings her a box filled with chocolate chip cookies, thumbprint cookies, cinnamon rolls, strawberry rugelach, vanilla cupcakes with strawberry frosting, and date bars. He looks at her adoringly as another customer comes in and he starts filling up a box with apricot danishes, éclairs, and butterscotch brownies.

"That's my wife," he brags to the middle-aged housewife awaiting her order. "We got married in July. Just now I found out we're having a baby. See the cake she had me decorate as a way to break the news? Boy, if we have a girl, I hope she gets her mother's beautiful emerald-green eyes. Of course, a boy wouldn't be so bad either, but given how I have six sisters and four unofficial sisters, I'll probably get another girl for my harem."

Lenore looks down in embarrassment and tries to continue eating as many of the baked goods as she can without stuffing herself or spoiling her appetite. Her embarrassment increases when Allen relays the news to all the other customers who come in during the remainder of the business day. It comes as a welcome relief when the bakery closes for the day and Allen comes over to her, carrying the cake.

"Ready to walk home, Mrs. Troy? Don't even think about making supper tonight. I'll make it for you. You'd better believe I'm gonna spoil you even more from now on. I want you to stay as healthy as you can so we have the cutest, healthiest baby possible. After what happened to my older sister, I wouldn't hear of you going to a hospital to have the baby. I don't want you being tied down to a bed, left all alone, and unable to hold the baby right away or remember anything. We'll find someone who makes housecalls and have it the old-fashioned way. Just think, our very own honeymoon baby. That kid is gonna be so loved and spoilt."

"Don't get too ahead of yourself. I'm not past the first three months yet."

"Everything will go fine. We're gonna be a family of three, the way it was intended. It's been just us for long enough. This weekend, we'll have the girls over and have a celebration. Can I name it if it's a boy? You can name it if it's a girl."

"As long as you don't want a mimeographed copy of yourself. I'm not a fan of Juniors and Roman numerals. Let the kid have his own name."

"I think that's stupid too. We're not having a prince."

The manager comes over to them before they can leave. "I couldn't help but hear the news. Here, take this double chocolate cake as a present."

"You don't have to give away your food!" Lenore protests.

"Your husband's a hard worker, Mrs. Troy, and I wouldn't dream of not giving a special treat to any of my long-time workers when he's going to become a first-time father. Take it and have a great evening."

Lenore walks out into the evening with Allen, a part of her feeling as though the past four years are either a dream or a dream come true. She's come a long way from Greenpoint, and the modern-day Manhattan fairytale she stepped into keeps getting better.

"No fair, Allen," Adicia protests. "It's my turn to feel Lenore's baby moving. You get your turn all the time. It won't hurt you to take a little break now and then."

"It's not just Lenore's baby," he says as he reluctantly takes his hands away from Lenore's protruding midsection. "It's my baby too."

It's now March 1967, and Lenore is six months pregnant. Since it's been so long since their respective mothers were pregnant, the Troy and Ryan girls are fascinated by how Lenore's body has been expanding and how they can now feel movement. Adicia feels bad for Lenore because her ankles are swelling up and she's getting stretch marks, but Lenore tries to cheer her up by saying stretch marks usually fade away in due time, and Allen massages her ankles every night. Ernestine and Girl meanwhile are envious Lenore gets out of menstruating.

Right now they're waiting for a prospective midwife to arrive. Lenore found one by word of mouth, since it's very dangerous to advertise oneself even in an alternative publication in a progressive, free-thinking neighborhood. Girl is pontificating about how ridiculous it is that hospitals are now supposed to be the norm, whereas until very recently, people went there to die or because they were poor. Her speech is interrupted when the midwife arrives, carrying a photo album under her right arm.

"Pleased to meet you, Mr. and Mrs. Troy." She shakes their hands. "I'm Veronica Zoravkov, and I hope I can be your midwife. I'll give you a chance to discuss what you'd like out of your birth experience, your expectations, and your contingency plans, but first introduce me to everybody. Are all these girls going to be present at the birth?"

"I ain't no girl!" Boy protests. "Just 'cause I'm the only guy in a group of girls don't mean my maleness don't count!"

"These are my younger sisters, Ernestine, Adicia, and Justine," Allen indicates. "Those are my sisters' friends, Julie and the Ryans. Their parents called them Girl, Boy, Baby, and Infant, though they finally decided on real names last year."

"Deirdre," Girl reminds him. "My brother is David, Baby is Fiona, and Infant is Aoife, or Eva."

"Are you a Miss or a Mrs.?" Adicia asks.

"Just call me Veronica. We're all friends here. I probably won't answer if you call me Mrs. Zoravkov, since only people who don't personally know me address me by my title instead of my first name."

"Is that a Russian name?" Julie asks.

"Bulgarian. My maiden name was Bulgarian too. I wanted to marry another Bulgarian-American to keep my heritage alive instead of diluting it, since I'm so proud of where I come from."

"Where's Bulgaria?" Infant asks. "Is it very far away?"

"It's on the Black Sea," Ernestine says. "It's in Southeastern Europe, in an area called the Balkans. It borders Romania, Greece, and Yugoslavia."

"What's in your picture book?" Justine asks. "Can we look at it?"

"They're pictures of past clients and their babies. If your brother and sister-in-law choose me and everything goes well, their pictures will be in here too. It's meant to reassure my prospective clients that normal people just like them have had their babies with a midwife, and that everything turns out alright in the majority of cases. If the baby's breech, or any other complications arise, we'll have to take you to the hospital."

"What's a breech?" Baby asks.

"It's when the baby is facing the wrong way," Girl explains. "Babies are supposed to be born head-first, but sometimes they come out with their feet or rear end facing first."

While Allen and Lenore chat with Veronica, the girls look at the pictures in the album. A number of times they express surprise that the newly-born babies are rather unattractive instead of cute, cuddly, and cleaned-up. The parents look like normal people, just as Veronica said. They don't look like oddballs, but rather people they might pass in the street and not assume any anti-establishment thoughts about.

Allen looks over at them questioningly when there hasn't been a peep out of them for more than several minutes. Adicia, Ernestine, and Justine in particular are bent over one page, looking intently at one photograph.

"What's so interesting?" he asks. "Something we should be alarmed about?"

"Sarah!" Adicia shouts. "It's Sarah! She's in a picture!"

"You'll have to tell me more details," Veronica says. "I've delivered more than a few Sarahs, though most of them didn't pronounce it with a long A."

"Sarah Katz, our nanny till our mean mother fired her! I know it's our Sarah. Even her tattoo is the same as our Sarah's."

Ernestine brings the book over to show Allen, and his jaw drops when he too recognizes the face of the woman who helped to raise him since he was three years old. Since he wasn't as close to her as his sisters, he wouldn't know if the tattoo bears the exact same numbers, but he does see a number tattooed on her left forearm.

"Yes, her name is Sarah with a long A, and her last name is still Katz. I think she's the only woman I've ever delivered who had a different last name from her husband. She was the only member of her family who survived the war, and she didn't want her name to be lost. She was one of the oldest first-time mothers I've ever worked with. I delivered her son Fritz when she was thirty-eight. She's expecting another child now, and wants me to deliver her again."

"Sarah finally found a husband and had her own baby!" Justine says happily.

"She chose me because of what happened to your biggest sister when she gave birth. I don't blame her for being afraid such an experience might bring back vivid memories of her ordeal during the war. So many doctors and nurses treat laboring women like they have no rights or emotions. The things I've seen as a labor and delivery nurse are just horrific. It's so ironic how it was women who fought hardest for twilight sleep delivery, not doctors themselves. Now it's doctors who promote it, and women often don't think to question it."

"Gemma's stories were really scary," Adicia says. "I don't want that to happen to our Lenore."

Lenore squeezes Allen's hand. "I hope there isn't a serious problem that requires us going to the hospital. I had a really bad, ongoing experience with a horrible doctor when I was growing up, and being drugged unconscious would make it even worse."

"Before I go, I'll feel for the baby's position. Even if it's breech now, babies shift position. I always do everything I can to assure the mother has a safe and event-free delivery, the way Nature intended."

"Pardon me," Girl says. "I'd like to know more about this twilight drug. I'm very interested in how the establishment exploits people, and in how many modern doctors don't have the best interests of women and the poor at heart. Me and my three younger siblings was all born unassisted at home, and we're all healthy and normal."

"I'm curious too," Ernestine says. "I might be sorry I asked, but I want to know what exactly happened to Gemma."

"How old are you?" Veronica asks.

"We'll be fifteen next month," Ernestine says. "My birthday's April eleventh and Girl's is the eighth. Adicia and Julie are going on thirteen, Baby's going on ten, Justine just turned eight, and Infant's going on eight. We're used to seeing and hearing things people from the other half of society think are indecent and inappropriate for kids."

"Sure, I'll tell you. Ernestine, right? And…Dara?"

"Just call me Girl, but if you want, you can call me Deirdre. It's a Celtic name that possibly means 'woman.' I've got no idea how much Irish blood I have, but both my parents had Irish surnames, and they never talked about family histories from places like Germany, Sweden, or Italy. As far as I'm concerned, I'm all Irish. I'm like you being proud of being Bulgarian. Anyway, I don't mind being called Girl. There's a Beatles' song with my name in it, and it's sung by John, my favorite. He's Ernestine's favorite Beatle too. I like how smart he is, that he ain't afraid to speak his mind, and that he writes about real stuff instead of just the typical lovey-dovey stuff. He's part Irish too, since Lennon is an Irish surname. We Irish are the best."

Veronica smiles at her. "You're certainly a very interesting and intelligent young lady. You could probably charm a cat."

"Can this lesson wait?" Allen asks. "I don't want to think about my beautiful Lenore having a complicated delivery or even God forbid losing the baby because of something that happened to her when she was sick. I almost lost her two years ago, and going through that again would destroy me." He puts his hand on Lenore's pregnancy bulge protectively. "She's kicking. Since I'm almost totally surrounded by girls, we both think it's probably yet another girl for my harem."

"I'm sure your wife will do fine. The human body is very resilient. Given the chance, the body wants to heal. I'd never guess she had a health scare so recently, since she looks like a normal, healthy young woman."

"If there's an emergency, would I be able to be there with Lenore?" Allen still has his hand on the pregnancy bulge. "I'd never give my consent for a freaky drug cocktail like that or to have her strapped down to a delivery bed."

"The only husbands I saw who were admitted to delivery rooms were the husbands of women with a lot of money, or doctors whose wives were patients. You'd have to wait in the so-called Stork Club. The average husband has no idea what's happening to his wife, and she can't tell him anything, since she has no memory of it. Twilight sleep isn't the wonder drug it was lauded as. It only takes away memory, not pain. Women go crazy under its effects, hence why they're tethered to the bed."

Allen turns his face towards Lenore's bulge. "That's not happening to you, Baby. You're gonna be born where it's safe and where your mommy can move around and remember everything. We'll hold you as soon as you're born, and you'll go to sleep, eat, and take a bath in the safety of your own home. Can you try to be born on my birthday, princess? I can't wait to hear the name your mommy said she selected for you."

"Oh, boy, Allen, if only our folks could see you now," Ernestine laughs. "Mother in particular would grouse about how you've turned into a first-rate pansy."

"She hasn't shut up about how you're with Lenore, even after you made her a respectable woman," Adicia says. "Lenore will always be the girl you met at the bus stop, and there's no convincing her we were there for a normal reason. I don't know what the big deal is about meeting your future wife at a bus stop. There was even a song about that last fall. She acts like we were at a cocaine den or like the only reason anyone would be in a bus stop would be to buy drugs or pick up girls of ill repute."

"Our mother is nuts," Allen tells Veronica. "She's not welcome here ever. She'll never know her grandchildren. Anyway, can we get back to discussing the birth experience?"

"I wasn't planning to go there anyway if I have a kid someday, but now I'm doubly-convinced to stay the hell away from there," Girl says. "Women, the poor, and the working-class get such a bum deal in this country."

"If you helped our Sarah have her baby and are gonna help her have another baby, we trust you to help our Lenore," Adicia says.

"Just so long as everything goes according to plan," Lenore says. "I'm a little scared of how painful it might be."

"Gemma read a book by a doctor who advocated fear-free birth,"

Ernestine says. "His name was Grant or Graham, I think."

"Dr. Grantly Dick-Read," Veronica says. "I'll be glad to give you a list of books before I go."

"Everything will be just fine." Allen rubs the bulge. "It's my husbandly duty to take care of you and protect you. I'll make sure you're as comfortable as you can be and that you won't need to go to one of those scary hospitals and be forced to take drugs."

"We'll play soft, soothing music so you feel relaxed," Girl promises. "I've got lots of folk rock, so you can take your pick. Mr. and Mrs. van Niftrik would probably lend you somea their classical records too."

"I hope you're right," Lenore says.

"You'll have the nicest birth experience possible," Allen says. "I can't wait for our little family of two to become a family of three."

***

Allen's birthday falls on a Tuesday this year. Lenore has been planning to bake a double chocolate cake, but her plans change when she wakes with a stabbing pain shortly after he's left for work. She almost wishes she weren't so terrified of doctors and hospitals, and that hospitals offered a drug other than a mixture of morphine and scopolamine to laboring mothers. Ernestine, Adicia, and Justine are in school until mid-afternoon, and Ernestine's friends are off doing their odd jobs and musical and dance performances now that the weather's nice. Since Veronica said it's not necessary for a midwife to be there for the entire labor, only when it comes closer to the actual estimated delivery time, Lenore doesn't want to trouble her by calling her up so early. Hoping the pain will calm down a little while she's waiting, but still wanting company, she reaches for the phone and calls Emeline. Her first year at Vassar just ended, and she's subletting an off-campus apartment for the summer.

"Emeline, it's Lenore. Do you have a way to get down here as soon as you can? I'm pretty sure my labor started, but it's too soon to call my midwife. I don't wanna disturb Allen at work, but I don't want to be alone the entire day either."

"You're really in labor? I guess the baby did listen to Allen and decide to get born on his birthday. Are you in very much pain?"

"It feels like the baby's scraping against my back, though my water hasn't broken, and I don't see any blood or feel the need to push. It's just a very big pain. Can you please hurry?"

"I've got Greyhound and train schedules around somewhere, and I'm pretty sure they both make stops somewhere in Greenwich Village. If the stop isn't within walking distance of your place, I'll find a bus the rest of the way. I'll bring records. There's a really groovy Indian song on The Beatles' newest album that might take your mind to another place and make you forget the pain."

"That would be nice. Bring whatever music you think will relax me and calm me down. Please hurry so I don't have to be alone longer than necessary."

Emeline arrives three hours later, at 11:00, and comes in through the front door, which is always propped open in the mornings and afternoons to let the mailman and other deliverymen in. She also finds the door to 515 propped open with a wooden wedge. Lenore is lying on the sofa bed, watching television and clutching the latest addition to her miniature zoo, a light green stuffed parakeet.

"I'm so glad you came." Lenore looks at her with sad eyes. "I don't feel her pushing against my back so badly on my side."

Emeline puts down her records and pulls some other things out of a large hand-woven bag. "I brought you food, if you feel you can keep anything down. I told my employer at the school library I'd have to take today and possibly tomorrow off because my sister-in-law's having a baby, and she was okay with it. My Vassar friends think it's far-out you're having your baby at home. Mosta my close friends are into the hippie ideas and lifestyle, so they don't see anything wrong with it. We've attended anti-war rallies together and learnt about things like astrology, meditation, Eastern and Indian religions, and Yoga. By the way, I brought a stopwatch, so we'll know the exact time your baby gets born. I want to have a full astrological chart made for her."

Lenore notices Emeline's hair is much longer than it's ever been. It looks as though she hasn't had a haircut since she went away to Vassar last August, when her hair fell to about her shoulder blades. It now reaches almost to her waist, and there are real flowers woven into a crown of sorts. She's also wearing leather sandals, a long string of green beads, a billowing red skirt with little jingle bells reaching almost to the floor, and a loose-fitting blue-green paisley blouse. If Lenore didn't know any better, she'd think Emeline had been studying in San Francisco and not Poughkeepsie for the past year.

"I also picked up the newspaper for you. It was lying outside your door. I thought of my old nanny Sarah when I saw the front page. How sad that her people aren't allowed to live in peace in their own homeland they fought so hard to get, only a generation after the Nazis tried to kill them all. I hope Israel wins the war that was just started against it. Here, let me make you a little something to eat, and we can watch television. Have you heard of granola? My hippie friends at Vassar turned me on to it. It's cereal made of toasted oats, with nuts and dried fruit, and honey or molasses to hold the oats together in little clusters. I brought cans of coconut milk from a local ethnic grocery. I'm trying as hard as I can to go vegetarian and wean myself away from dairy products as well."

"Is that healthy?" Lenore clutches the stuffed parakeet harder as she feels another contraction. "What do you eat if you don't eat meat or dairy?"

"Fruits, vegetables, rice, noodles, pasta, something called tofu, a grain called quinoa, nuts, seeds, and various types of meat substitutes made from soybeans. When you grow up poor, you're thankful for any food put in fronta you, but now that I have a choice, and am really tuning in to important issues I always cared about but didn't have the proper chance to pursue, I can pick my own meals. It's unhealthy how Americans eat so much meat. Humans are the only species that drinks the milk of another species, or that drinks milk period past weaning. I never had a chance to think about those things when I was too busy worrying about where the next meal would come from. The Indians apologized to the game they killed, since they respected it was another life. They felt the need to explain they needed their life source to survive. Today, people don't give a damn half the time where their food comes from. Now I know why religious Jews wait certain periods between meat and dairy products, since the Biblical prohibition against boiling a kid in its mother's milk is much deeper than what the text says." Emeline brings a bowl of granola swimming in coconut milk to Lenore. "Are you at all able to sit up?"

Lenore struggles to pull herself into a sitting position and props pillows behind her before taking the bowl. "Are you still studying history and German, and planning to go to graduate school to become a librarian after this?"

"Nothing's changed. In my heart, I'd love to move to San Francisco or live on a commune, but that won't earn me a living or let me do anything with my lifelong passion for reading, history, and languages. What would I do if I switched my major to something like philosophy or asked permission to design my own major, become a professor or write arcane articles published in journals most people don't read? I don't have the personality to be a professor. I'd be happiest working in a library, museum, or archive." Emeline puts her hands on the bulge. "I can feel her moving, though not violently."

"That's because she's doing most of her movement along my back! She must've moved around recently. I hope she doesn't turn out breech. I don't wanna end up in the hospital, particularly not after what the midwife told us. I don't wanna be tied down and unable to remember anything, and I'd be scared outta my mind if I had to do that all alone."

"Would you like me to call Allen? He'd come rushing home if he knew you were in labor, even if the actual delivery time isn't for awhile."

"You can't do that," Lenore begs between bites. "His co-workers and manager assume we're doing it in the hospital. Our midwife could get arrested if people find out she's assisting births at home, even though she's a former nurse and not a maverick with no medical knowledge or birthing experience. We might live in the Village, but Allen works for a normal bakery, not a folk music club or coffeeshop. His co-workers and manager would think we're nuts. They'd also wonder why he wants to wait in the Stork Club instead of working through the day and getting the call I had the baby."

Emeline gets up to light jasmine and strawberry incense. "Do you have a preference for music?"

"What did you bring?"

"I have some duplicate records with yous guys, so I only brought the ones I know you don't already have. I got the newest Monkees' album, *Headquarters*; a self-titled album by a new Los Angeles band called The Doors; *Surrealistic Pillow*, by a psychedelic San Francisco Group called Jefferson Airplane; *There's a Kind of Hush All Over the World*, by Herman's Hermits, which I really like, though I'm quite a bit older than their typical fan; and *Evolution*, a new album from the British band The Hollies, the group who sang 'Bus Stop.' Oh, and of course, The Beatles' newest album, *Sgt. Pepper's Lonely Hearts Club Band*, with that groovy Indian song I told you about. George sings it, so of course it's my favorite. Wait'll you hear the far-out Indian instruments. I some-times smoke pot when I listen to these albums, though I haven't brought a lot with me." Emeline drops the revelation that she's been smoking marijuana as casually as though she's telling Lenore about a new book she's reading.

"Wait, what?" Lenore forgets about her labor pains in her shock. "*You* of all people have been smoking marijuana?! When the hell did that start happening?"

Emeline giggles. "All hippies do it. It's not like I've been doing LSD, though I am curious. I know what you're probably thinking, but I'm not overusing it. Now I know why pot was Allen's favorite drug. It mellows you out and opens your mind. A lot of music sounds even trippier." Emeline flips through Allen and Lenore's record collection in a simple cardboard box. "Like this album, *Parsley, Sage, Rosemary, and Thyme*. I love this record. You haven't heard 'Scarborough Fair' proper-ly till you've heard it while you're high on marijuana. It sounds even trippier."

"But how can you keep up your grades and pay attention to your studies if you're using drugs? You were so proud of Allen when he quit drugs cold turkey!"

"I don't overuse it. I only use it to relax and open up my mind. Did you know the opposition to this harmless substance began in large part because it was originally brought here by Mexican migrant work-ers and popularized by Negro—I mean, Black—jazz musicians? God forbid the nice white kids imitate the so-called inferior races."

"Let's hear that Indian song." Lenore's mind reels at how her best friend and sister-in-law has turned into a bona fide hippie.

"Ooh, good choice." Emeline puts the record on the turntable. "It's the first song on side two, and what an opener it is. I can't explain how I felt the first time I heard it. It was far-out enough to see The Beatles with facial hair and to hear them making psychedelic noises, but George's song opened up my mind and soul to this new, mysteri-ous, strange world I hadn't known about. It was like the invisible door to another world opened up. I'd been interested in Indian religions since I was eleven or twelve, but this song brought it all home for me. I knew he was my favorite for a deeper reason besides just feeling a pro-tective, mothering instinct towards him 'cause he's the baby of the band."

"Did you smoke marijuana before you came here?" Lenore asks as Emeline sets the needle on the groove.

"Why would I already be smoking first thing in the morning? I'm not a drug addict who needs her fix as soon as she wakes up. By the way, the song is called 'Within You Without You.' Mosta my friends said it's their least-favorite song, but it's my favorite hands-down. Some people just don't appreciate what the song is tryna say, or don't get anything with non-Western music."

Lenore tries to relax on the sofa bed as Emeline rubs her back, periodically gets up to turn and change the records on the turntable, and gets her light things to eat and drink. At 3:30, when side one of *Evolution* is playing and Emeline is telling Lenore about how this band has been popular in their native Britain for a couple of years already in spite of only recently becoming known in America, the phone rings.

"Is that you, Allen?" Emeline asks.

"No, it's Ernestine, calling from Betsy's place," Ernestine stammers, shocked at hearing Emeline's voice. "How come you're visiting, Emeline? Allen and Lenore never told us you'd be coming!"

"I didn't know I'd be coming either. Lenore called me to tell me she was in labor, and she wanted me to come down to keep her company till it was closer to the time she'd need to call her midwife."

"What!" Ernestine gasps in happy surprise. "She's seriously in labor as we speak? That's pretty far-out that she went into labor on Allen's birthday, just like he was hoping!"

"Lenore's in labor?" Julie asks in the background. "Can we come over to help her and watch the baby being born?"

"Is it okay if we come over? I just got home from school a little while ago. I'll call Adicia and Justine if it's cool with Lenore for all of us to be there."

"Allen and Lenore are really gonna have their baby on Allen's birthday?" Betsy asks. "That is pretty groovy!"

Emeline covers the phone. "Lenore, is it okay if the girls come over? They'd really like to see the baby being born."

"I don't know. My midwife said first labors usually last a long time. What if I'm still in labor in the middle of the night?" She doubles up in pain and slides off of the sofa bed, getting on her hands and knees to crawl around. "I don't know when I'll be ready to push."

"They'd love to be here, since they all love you so much."

"I don't want them to see me in pain." Lenore starts panting like a dog in heat. "We'll wait for Allen to get home, and then we can call my midwife."

"I think we should let your midwife know. Even if she comes too early, it's better than coming too late."

"All the important phone numbers are on the refrigerator. Her name's Veronica Zoravkov. The older girls can come over if they'd like, so long as they're home by a reasonable hour."

Emeline turns back to the phone. "Lenore says you older girls can come over. She's worried she might scare you or upset you because you've never seen her in so much pain before."

"What's her definition of older?" Ernestine asks. "Me, Girl, and Julie?"

"I can't dump Baby and Infant on Mrs. van Niftrik for that long," Girl says. "I know she'd watch them, but it ain't right to take advantage of a person like that. They're all coming along. That includes you too, Boy."

"I saw Infant being born," Baby says. "I was only two and can't remember it, but it couldn't have been that scary or traumatic. No one ever told me I was scared."

"You took it like a pro." Girl smiles at her. "You were really cute when Infant came out of our mother. You went around the squat telling everyone you were a big sister. I still remember your happy little face."

"Well, we'd better go out to catch the next subway," Julie says. "Would you like to come too, Betsy?"

"Too many cooks spoil the broth. But I can't wait to hear what it is and to come see the baby when it's okay to have visitors."

After Ernestine phones Adicia and Justine, they start out for the subway station. At 4:30, they arrive on Allen and Lenore's block and go up the fire escape, since the front door is no longer propped open. Emeline rushes to let them in.

"Emeline, you look so different!" Adicia gives her a big hug.

"Whoa." Girl stands back. "You look like onea them flower children out in San Francisco. What's that smell?"

"I've been burning jasmine and strawberry incense all afternoon."

Lenore squats on a birthing stool Veronica brought over, alternating heavy breathing with screaming. Justine, Baby, and Infant look at her with scared eyes, while Boy just looks uncomfortable.

"Is Lenore going to be okay, Mrs. Midwife?" Justine asks. "She won't have to go to the hospital, will she?"

"Your sister-in-law's having back labor, which means the baby's head is facing against her back instead of towards the front. It's not breech, so we probably won't need to transfer her to the hospital. The pain from back labor usually lessens if she's crouching or on her hands and knees. The standard flat on your back position doctors insist on is the absolute worst position to have a baby in, particularly if it's in a non-standard position like this. The baby also feels a little on the large side, so that adds to her discomfort."

"Can't you get it out of me right now?" Lenore begs in desperation. "Take a knife and cut her out!"

"I can't perform Caesarean deliveries," Veronica says patiently. "There's no medical need for you to have one right now. Believe me, I'll immediately let you know if we need to take you to the hospital for complications."

Adicia rushes over and puts her hands and head on the bulge. She smiles up at Lenore, hoping to cheer her up.

"You're just as cute and sweet as you were when I met you." Lenore smiles weakly. "I can't believe you'll be thirteen next month. You don't look almost thirteen. Julie's only two months your senior, and she looks more thirteen than you."

"I'm almost ready for my first bra!" Julie says proudly.

"I did not need to know that," Boy says darkly.

"I've got breast buds too, but mine aren't as prominent as Julie's," Adicia says. "I haven't had my first menses yet either. I think Julie will beat me to it, not that I'm looking forward to that."

"Does Allen know you're in labor?" Girl asks. "He doesn't seem the type to go off to work like everything's normal when his belovèd wife is having their firstborn child. I thought he wanted to be here."

"I didn't wanna disturb him at work, and we could all get in trouble if his co-workers or manager found out we're not at the hospital."

"Are you serious?" Ernestine asks. "He'll probably be even more worried when he comes home and sees what's going on!"

"Mrs. Zoravkov, is it safe for Lenore to smoke pot to ease her pain?" Emeline asks. "I have a couple of joints in my purse, and I'd gladly give them all to her if it'd make her feel better."

"What! That's even more shocking, *you* of all people using drugs of any sort! Even if you became a hippie, you coulda kept it to the life philosophy, music, and clothes, not started smoking the green stuff! Our parents, Carlos, and Allen had really bad experiences with drugs! We were all so proud of Allen when he went straight cold turkey!"

"Today's a new day. I smoke in moderation, and I haven't tried any LSD yet. I'd never dream of sampling the harder stuff like cocaine, heroin, or meth. It relaxes me and opens my mind to a whole new hidden world of possibilities."

"You should've heard her waxing on about how groovy she thinks George's Indian song on the new Beatles' album is, and how much better it sounds when she's high," Lenore pants. "She said it was like an invisible door to another world opened up in her mind and heart."

"You like *that* song?" Julie asks. "I know he's your favorite, but come on! Who wants to listen to those weird Indian instruments and a five-minute song about philosophy?"

"I've always been different from the others. I'm not about to start being just like everyone else now that I'm a legal adult and away at college. Being a hippie is about being different from the so-called norm. I always knew there was a special reason I liked him best, not just 'cause I felt a mothering, protective instinct towards him as the youngest. I've also been interested in Indian philosophy and religion for a long time."

"If that's what happens to you when you go away to college, sign me up next!" Girl says. "I'd love to meet a group of like-minded people who are proud of being different from the others and ain't afraid to flaunt it in public."

"My friends and I go to anti-war protests too. I'll be sick to my stomach if this country starts another draft and makes our Allen go. He's just the right age, and this isn't a morally justified war like the last one. Hell, it was immoral our country stayed neutral and isolationist as long as it did. Our Sarah might've been saved from the awful things she went through if we'd gotten involved sooner, and she might have all her family alive today. Hopefully the war won't last another five years and threaten Boy too."

"You're fab gear," Girl says in awe. "You ain't even out in California, where all this hippie stuff's centered."

Lenore eases down off the birthing stool and lets out another scream. "Can't someone get her out of me before my insides are all ripped apart? I don't know if I'll be able to do this again, or even have physical intimacy, if it hurts this much!"

"Every labor's different," Veronica tries to tell her. "Your next baby might not give you back labor or be as big."

"I'm not even twenty yet!" Lenore gasps. "I'm too young to do this!"

"I've delivered girls younger than you, and they did fine. Girls your age also usually get their figures back quicker than older mothers. Just think, you're getting this out of the way sooner than later. I felt so bad for that woman, Sarah, who said your mother-in-law forbade her from doing anything outside of taking care of her own children for her. She didn't want to be a first-time mother at thirty-eight and to have her second child at forty. She's due any day now for that second child."

"Where does Sarah live?" Justine asks.

"The Upper West Side. She and her husband are planning to move out of the city, though. Can't say I blame them, after she has such bad memories of living here. At least she's not in that cesspool of a neighborhood you used to live in. Why would your parents be proud of living in such a poor, run-down neighborhood for over a hundred years?"

"Our section of the old neighborhood has been renamed," Emeline says. "The nicer part of the neighborhood decided to break away from the Lower East Side and declare themselves the East Village. They didn't want the stigma of being part of a historically immigrant, poor, and working-class neighborhood, so they're remodeling themselves as an eastern version of Greenwich Village."

"I don't care what they call themselves nowadays," Ernestine says. "I'm never going back there. That place was depressing, though at least it wasn't as skid-row as The Bowery."

Lenore curls up in the fetal position. "Can I cut her out of me myself?"

"She'll come out the way Nature intended soon enough," Veronica says. "If you'd like, you can get in the bathtub and let the water help with pain relief. Just don't let the water get too hot, and don't stay in too long."

When Allen turns his key in the lock at 6:30, he's greeted by ear-shattering screams and sees Lenore crawling around on the floor and arching her back. The scent of the incense also hits him sharply. Barely noticing Emeline is there and looking like a flower child, he hurries over to Lenore.

"How long has she been in labor?" he demands of Veronica. "Why wasn't I called immediately?"

"She woke up in labor and called Emeline, the hippie, to keep her company and help her till she felt it was closer to the time to call for me. Your other sisters, their friends, and that boy came over shortly after I did. Your wife has just hit transition and is having hard back labor."

Lenore lies on her side and puts her head on Allen's lap. "Are you mad at me 'cause I didn't call you? I didn't wanna disturb you or get us in trouble if your colleagues found out I'm having this baby at home."

"You could've let me know." He strokes her hair. "I wouldn't have told anyone we're breaking the law by not doing it in a hospital."

"She's in so much pain she's been begging for a Caesarean," Veronica says. "She asked if she could perform the procedure on herself."

"We're staying far away from the hospital, remember? You don't wanna have surgery and not be able to hold my hand. You wouldn't even get to see the baby for a couple of days."

"I saw the photos you took of Lenore during her pregnancy," Girl says. "They're very beautiful. Not just that Lenore is beautiful, but the way you took the pictures was also beautiful. You used light and shadow very well, and posed her well. I get the sense these pictures were taken by someone who loves her very much. I'd get that feeling even if you were strangers. I can't wait to see what you do with photos of the baby."

"Emeline smokes pot!" Adicia says.

Allen barely registers this news and continues stroking Lenore's hair and rubbing her back. "You're gonna get through this just fine. Your maiden name, Hartlein, means 'brave little one,' and that's just what you are. You've already been so strong and brave so many times before. You're strong enough to handle all this pain and get through it without unnecessary surgery."

"Can't you reach in there and pull her around to face the proper way, so she won't scrape against my back anymore?" Lenore gasps.

"That's just the way the baby wants to come out," Veronica says. "The last time I checked you, she was facing in the opposite direction. Babies rotate."

"Can't you get forceps and yank her out?"

"Not unless you want to risk hemorrhaging to death. It's not like the baby's stuck. She's just not ready to come out yet."

"Can we spend the night?" Adicia asks. "I don't wanna walk with Justine after dark in our neighborhood."

"Sure, I'll think of an excuse to tell Mother," Allen says. "I'm not about to send yous out into Hell's Kitchen by yourselves after dark."

While Allen's on the phone, Girl looks through the six records Emeline brought over. The variety of bands is an odd combination, but overall it's a nice sampling of Emeline's musical taste.

"You've got groovy taste in music," she says admiringly. "I knew you was into The Beatles, but not that you like The Monkees too. We all love them here. Who's your favorite?"

"I like Peter best. He seems like an interesting person in interviews, not like the dummy he plays on television."

"Ernestine and I like him best too. Julie prefers Davy 'cause she thinks he's the cutest. That's the same reason Paul is her favorite Beatle. Baby's favorite is Micky. Though I'm kinda surprised someone your age and of your leanings would own a Herman's Hermits record. Julie likes them 'cause she thinks Peter Noone is cute. I think he's cute too, but have a substantial reason for liking a band or having a favorite bandmember!"

"Their songs are cute and catchy, even if they are being marketed as clean-cut boys next door. I'm allowed to like a couple of bands more geared towards mass popularity instead of only liking bands that do more serious, mature songs. Besides, they're a real band, even if mosta their younger fans are only into them 'cause they're cute and have catchy songs. The Monkees started out as a bunch of actors playing a band, but they still make good music. Have you bought their new record yet? They've written a lot more songs than usual, and played mosta the instruments."

Allen hangs up the phone. "Adicia and Justine can spend the night, and our parents won't find out Lenore gave birth at home. I called home and no one answered, and when I called the Doyles, Mrs. Doyle said Carlos is going to trial and our folks are staying in a hotel with him so they don't look bad. Mrs. Doyle said you can stay with her. Tommy's staying with his Puerto Rican friends, which is probably making Mother wet herself in fear."

"Mrs. Doyle's a great mother," Adicia says. "I wish she was my mother and we could stay with her forever."

"We love her kids," Justine says. "Matthew will be seven next month, and Caroline will be three in August. If she ever finds her little girl from her first marriage, she could be a new friend for Adicia, since her first daughter was only born two months before her."

"She could be my friend too," Julie says. "I'd be her age exactly."

Lenore screams and arches her back again. Allen runs back to her as she rocks back and forth in a squatting position.

"She's still in transition," Veronica says. "Very soon we'll see if it might be time to start pushing."

"You can do this," Emeline tells Lenore. "This is how women did it for thousands of years. Just think, maybe your next labor won't be this painful."

Girl goes to get the door when she hears knocking, looking through the peephole first to make sure it's a friendly face. To her relief, it's a woman dressed much like Emeline, with a pink crocheted beret and a paisley dress.

"I'm sorry, but I couldn't help but hear Mrs. Troy screaming. I wondered if she needs help getting to the hospital."

"We're doing this at home. There's no way in hell she wants to be pumped full of drugs and have her memories erased, or be tied to a table."

"Oh, really? That's far-out. Can't say I blame her for wanting to go the natural route. I'm not married, but I might want to try that when it's my time. Don't worry, I won't tell anyone it was born at home. Most people in this neighborhood have open minds instead of feeding into the systematic brainwashing of the establishment. Just let me know if you need anything. My name's Yvette Simon, and I live in 505. Good luck."

Baby, Justine, and Infant are supposed to go to bed by 9:30, and they protest when that time comes and goes and Lenore is still breathing heavily, screaming, crawling around, rocking back and forth, and curling up on her side. They figure they won't be able to fall asleep, since she's making so much noise. Allen reluctantly agrees with them and tells them to lie down quietly on Lenore's old bed, with the lights dimmed.

"She's still in transition," Veronica reports. "Hopefully soon she'll feel the need to start pushing."

"I don't care anymore how she gets out of me! Just get her out of me and get her to stop scraping against my back!"

"I don't like seeing you in so much pain." Adicia puts her arm around Lenore and rests her head in the crook of her neck.

"I'm sorry I ruined your birthday, Allen," Lenore says weakly. "This wasn't what you wanted to come home to. We weren't able to do anything special."

"My birthday isn't ruined." He rests his head on the opposite crook of her neck. "If this kid gets born before the end of the day, it'll be the best birthday ever."

"Mrs. Zoravkov, should I heat up some blankets in the oven so they can be ready when Lenore has the baby?" Emeline asks, taking a puff on a joint.

"I told you to call me Veronica, and yes, it might be a good idea to put some blankets in. Remember to wrap them in foil so they don't burn, and keep an eye on them in case we have to take them out if the baby hasn't come yet."

"I might be a hippie, but I can't shake years of training to call my elders Mr., Miss, and Mrs. It seems rude to call my elders by their first names, unless I got to know them as friends and equals first." Emeline picks up some blankets and heads for the kitchen.

Lenore gets onto her hands and knees again and gasps loudly. Allen notices her face of agony bears a striking resemblance to her face of ecstasy. It's strange there should be such a close similarity between expressions of such opposite feelings.

"Just do what your body tells you," Veronica says. "If you don't feel the physical urge to push, don't do it."

Emeline has to take the blankets out of the oven several times, because Lenore doesn't feel the urge to push. It's 10:15 when she finally starts pushing, and at 11:00, she lets out her loudest scream all day.

"It's crowning," Veronica says. "That means it's almost over. After the baby comes out, all we have left to do is wait to deliver the afterbirth."

"Why don't you welcome your baby to the world with the same angelic song we walked down the aisle to in the bridal party processional?" Emeline asks. "'Benedictus,' *'Benedictus qui venit in nomine Domini,'* 'Blessèd is the one who comes in the name of God.'"

"Can you please let me take it from here?" Allen begs Veronica as Emeline pulls *Wednesday Morning, 3 A.M.* out of the record box and sets the needle down on the fifth groove on side one. "I wanna catch the baby."

"What!" Lenore shouts. "You're not trained to do that!"

"No one *needs* to catch a baby if everything's normal," Girl interjects. "When my mother had Baby, it was almost like she laid an egg. It was that simple and peaceful."

"Don't I wish I'd had such an easy and pain-free labor!" Lenore gasps as she arches her back.

"Put your hands on the head," Veronica tells Allen. "Gently. Don't squeeze the head or let go. Hopefully just a few more pushes, and you'll become a father for your twenty-third birthday present."

Lenore breathes heavily and pushes as hard as she feels able to. The next thing she knows, she doesn't feel any more pain, and Allen is smiling a lovestruck grin at her and cradling a newborn in his arms.

"Well, what do you know," he laughs, staring down at the baby. "I really did get yet another girl for my harem."

"Give me my baby!"

"I love you more than ever," Allen declares adoringly as he gently hands over the baby. "You went through all that pain to bring our first-born child into this world. I don't think I coulda handled it like such a pro. I bet you're glad you didn't crack and get a Caesarean."

"Whoa," Emeline says as the next song starts up. "This song is like a Buddhist koan. What does the sound of silence sound like?"

"Emeline, did you smoke too much weed?"

"No, I'm just tripping you out, man. Come on, let's take family pictures."

Veronica takes a few pictures of Allen and Lenore with the baby, and then a group picture of everyone, with both Allen's camera and her camera. After the pictures are taken, she delivers the placenta, which most of the girls think looks disgusting. Girl tells them that in some cultures, women eat or bury the placenta. When the umbilical cord stops pulsating, Veronica lets Allen cut it with the one pair of left-handed scissors she has, and then the baby is weighed.

"Ten pounds even," she informs them.

"Wow, that's one big baby," Adicia says. "No wonder you were in so much pain."

"Your sister-in-law's a real champ," Veronica says. "In spite of the big size and back labor, there isn't any tearing that needs to be repaired."

"What's her name?" Justine asks as the baby starts suckling on Lenore's breast. "I wanna find out the name before I go to bed."

"Irene Lily Troy," Lenore says proudly. "Irene means 'peace,' and lilies are a symbol of purity."

"What a beautiful name," Allen says. "A beautiful name for a beautiful girl."

"It's time for everyone to go to bed," Emeline says. "By the way, her time of birth was 11:31 and fourteen seconds. I'll have a full astrological chart drawn up for her soon."

"Always the ones you least suspect," Allen says, still shocked over Emeline's transformation into a pot-smoking flower child.

"Well, you know what they say about the quiet ones!" she laughs.

"Oh, I made you a present." Girl pulls something out of her bag, "I embroidered it on a piece of linen and put it in a frame."

Allen looks at it while Lenore falls asleep as Irene nurses. Girl has stitched an Irish baby blessing and shamrocks in emerald-green thread matching Lenore's eyes.

May all the blessings of our Lord touch your life today.
May he send his little angels to protect you on your way.
Such a miraculous gift, sent from above.
Someone so precious to cherish and love.
May sunshine and moonbeams dance over your head
As you quietly slumber in your bed.
May good luck be with you wherever you go
And your blessings outnumber the shamrocks that grow.
—Deirdre Ryan, 6-6-1967

"I stitched in the date today while Lenore was in labor. It's the least I could do after you've been so great to my family."

"That was very nice of you." Allen smiles, casting another glance over at Irene and Lenore.

"*Benedictus qui venit in nomine Domini,*" Emeline whispers in Irene's ear before everyone else heads off to sleep. "Welcome to our imperfect yet beautiful world, Miss Irene."

Chapter 36: Carlos Goes on Trial

While Mrs. Troy cares less about not working for an extended period of time, particularly since this means her paychecks won't be garnished, Mr. Troy is livid his degenerate firstborn son's long-awaited trial requires so much time off from work. He's proudly reported to that box-making factory for almost a quarter of a century, and was happy minimum wage was raised to $1.40 an hour this year. His long work record means nothing when he has to take off more than a couple of days. He doesn't want to think about what'll happen if he loses his job, in spite of explaining to the boss why he has to miss such a long period of time. The tenement rents for $20, with utilities about the same, but they can't afford that if he's not working and Mrs. Troy isn't able to keep any of her money. He hopes selling drugs on the side will pull in enough money in the meantime.

Mrs. Troy meanwhile is fuming about having to be away from Tommy for so long, and the fact that he'll be staying with the Gómezes. She cares less about her daughters going to school, but Prince Tommy is different and special. She wants him to go to school, and is looking forward to having a nice celebration for her pet child when he graduates high school in 1974. That, and the fact that she doesn't want to get a reputation as any more of a bad mother if any of her children are reported for truancy.

"Can I have some meth?" Carlos whines as his mother wheels him into their hotel room after the first day of the trial. "I was dying for drugs all day. I miss being able to get legally high. Them drugs they gave me for pain relief all that time in the hospital was the best ever."

"Get your own damn drugs," Mr. Troy snaps. "You think I'm gonna risk getting busted myself by bringing drugs into the courtroom or this hotel? As it is, I'm the only one of us without any criminal record and who works honestly at his job!"

"No fair," Carlos whines. "I can't quit cold turkey."

"You think I enjoy this any more than you do?" Mrs. Troy demands. "Do you, young man? It was bad enough when I was without any fix in prison!"

"Who the hell are you calling 'young man,' you stupid old woman? I'm twenty-four, in case you'd forgotten. 'Young man' is something you call a misbehaving little boy, not a grownup man!"

"'Old woman'?" Mrs. Troy yells, lighting a cigarette. "Just how the hell old do you think I am, you insolent punk?"

"Forty-four. That's pretty ancient."

"I'm forty-four too." Mr. Troy picks up *Le Monde*, trying to tune his oldest son and wife out.

"Oh, that's okay. Men are allowed to get old. Women get ugly and useless after thirty. You're a dried-up old prune, Mother. I don't even think you was attractive when you was young. You've always looked like you rolled outta a garbage dumpster."

Mr. Troy chuckles. "True enough, son. Dolores was never a looker even when she was a teenager. Thank God our daughters got their looks from my superior French side of the family."

Carlos looks expectantly at his parents. "So who's helping me with bathing, dressing and undressing, and getting into bed tonight?"

"Neither of us," they say in one voice.

"Hey, that ain't fair. I ain't the same guy I was before this junk happened to me. I wish I didn't have to go through the humiliation of my parents seeing me naked and helping me do basic tasks. It ain't my fault I got crippled. We should really be taking Mighty Mike's Mechanics to court for how I got injured at work."

"You learnt your poor work habits from your wretched mother, my boy. Unlike her and you, I ain't never used drugs or drank at *my* job. You save that stuff for home or on the weekends. Do you remember how you got crippled?"

"Yeah, the car jack wasn't fastened tight enough, and it came crashing down on my spine! I'll never be a man again. Not only can't I walk or feel my legs, but I can't sexually perform either, even for myself. I'll never have a little Carlos, Jr. or Carlotta to carry on my fine bloodline. At least you people got nine kids before Mother's doctor closed down the baby factory for her."

"You were high, you dummy. It was your own stupid fault that car jack wasn't fastened tightly enough. And like hell I wanted to know anything about the state of my own son's unmentionables."

"Hey, one of you is gonna be seeing those unmentionables a lot over the course of this trial, like it or not, since I ain't got no nurse to assist me. Now someone help me get a sponge bath."

"Don't look at me, Antoine," Mrs. Troy snaps. "It is most improper for a lady to look at or touch her grown son's taboo body parts."

"You ain't never been no lady, Dolores. Now get cracking, woman. I ain't no homosexual to wanna look at or touch a naked man, even if he is my own son. You know you'd be running to do this if it was your belovèd Prince Thomas who was a cripple."

Mrs. Troy curses her life as she takes his clothes off, helps Carlos with his sponge bath, helps him into pajamas, and finally helps him out of the wheelchair and into the hotel bed.

***

"I don't miss our parents a bit," Adicia says as Mrs. van Niftrik puts a bowl of strawberries and cream on the table. "Justine and I go to Mrs. Doyle when we come home from school, and she treats us better than our mother ever did. Mr. Doyle doesn't mind having us around when he gets home from work. I love helping with Matthew and Caroline. I wish our parents would be down on the Lower East Side at stupid Carlos's trial forever."

"Are they in the current Lower East Side, or the so-called East Village?" Ernestine asks. "I don't get why the residents wanted to secede from the rest of the neighborhood and call themselves the East Village. Are we so dirty they didn't wanna be associated with our kind?"

"I don't care where they are or what it's called," Justine says. "I'm just happy they're gone."

Though Lenore is perfectly capable of being up and about, Veronica told her to rest for a few weeks and not to go out with Irene more than absolutely necessary. Mrs. van Niftrik is one of the volunteers who signed up to come by and bring them meals.

"I'm shocked you delivered a ten-pound baby with no pain medication or transfer to the hospital," Mrs. van Niftrik says as she pours Lenore a glass of elderberry juice. "If Betsy had been that big, my doctor probably would've ordered a Caesarean."

"No tearing or stitches either," Girl says.

"If you'd been seeing a traditional doctor, you would've had some idea you were having such a large baby. They always X-ray to check for size and position. I refused it, since I didn't think X-rays are safe for a developing baby, but my doctor thought I was a bit odd. He also told my friends it was safe to smoke during pregnancy, to help them keep their weight down. If I were to have another child at my age, I'd never go back to such a foolish doctor. I'd try to find a midwife."

"Do you want another baby, Mrs. van Niftrik?" Infant asks sweetly. "I bet Betsy would love a little brother or sister. I wish I had one, though I like being the baby of the family."

"I had Betsy when I was twenty-two, and she's fifteen now. That's a little old to decide you want another child unless you've regularly been having kids all along."

"I like being an only child," Betsy says. "That would be freaky if I got a sibling at my age, particularly knowing how babies are made."

"Speaking of, they still didn't show me that filmstrip about growing up and menstruating," Adicia says. "All my older sisters saw filmstrips about it when they were in sixth grade, and I'm going into eighth grade. I was looking forward to making fun of the silly booklet too."

"Well, you've already witnessed your little niece being born." Allen smiles at her across the table. "I'd wager that's more of an education than any silly filmstrip they can drag in. I saw the boys' equivalent of those films at your age, and they were just as silly and creepy. I had to watch one where the coach was commenting on the guys' bodies. Talk about inappropriate behavior!"

"No way!" Ernestine laughs. "At least you didn't have to see a Disney cartoon about menstruation like Lucine."

"Disney made a cartoon about *that*?" Betsy asks. "Learn something new every day."

"So, do you think that waste of life Carlos will go away for a short sentence like your equally wasteful mom, or will they throw the book at him and lock him up in the slammer for a couple of years at least?" Girl heaps strawberries on her plate.

"It all depends on the jury," Ernestine says. "They might feel sorry for him 'cause he's a cripple, or he might lie and pretend he's repented. But if the judge feels he deserves a stiffer sentence, he can override the jury. Not that Carlos can do much harm to society or himself, since he's confined to a wheelchair, can't live on his own, and is paralyzed from the waist down."

"Oh, I hate when criminals pretend they repented or found God. It's a separate issue from how our criminal justice system is stacked against the poor. Hell, it wasn't until last year cops was required to tell suspects their rights before arresting them."

"I read about that too. I wonder if they told Carlos about his rights before they finally placed him under arrest and sent him to trial."

"I hope none of us have to testify," Adicia says. "I don't wanna go on the witness stand and talk about old days. Plus school is still in session for a little while longer."

Lenore puts an orange paisley smock over herself to nurse Irene. Boy pointedly looks away, though no one can see anything.

"Would you prefer she use bottles and spend money Allen doesn't have on formula?" Ernestine asks. "I didn't know until recently that anyone in America still did that. I assumed only really poor women had to nurse. I didn't know anything about nurses giving shots to dry up the milk or a public campaign to convince people feeding the way Nature intended is dirty and low-class."

"She looks so beautiful when she's being nursed by her mommy," Allen says. "I've taken photos of Lenore nursing Irene. I don't care if anyone thinks it's indecent."

"Yeah, *David*, it's just a mammal baby being fed the way mammal mommies were designed to feed their young," Girl says. "How come you picked the name David? If I was a guy and someone asked my name when I didn't have a real one, I'd say John. David wouldn't be the first guy name that came into my mind."

"King David. He was a warrior and got all the girls."

"Carlos won't get any girls ever again, even if he wants to," Ernestine snickers. "Since he was paralyzed below the waist, everything stopped working there."

"Does that mean he can't go to the bathroom?" Baby asks. "Wouldn't he explode from holding it all in for five years?"

"No, his excretory system works fine, but he can't feel anything below the waist, and that means he can't have a baby," Girl says. "The nerve endings don't work anymore. Boy, he must be right humiliated to have his parents helping him relieve himself, bathe himself, and dress himself. That task probably fell to your mother. From what I know about your dad, he seems like he's got half a lick of sense, even if he don't act like it mosta the time."

***

Carlos feels like he's been in prison for the last five years, but the judge and jury won't count that as time already served. He's facing thirty counts of petty theft, one count of arson, one count each for using, possessing, and selling drugs, and, most damning of all, twenty counts of murder. Mr. and Mrs. Troy are beside themselves with horror at how their reputations will be shot no matter what.

"Instead of taking me to court, they should be taking the landlord, the architect, the electrician, or the city of New York to court!" Carlos bleats in the hotel room after the first week of the trial has concluded. "Our old neighborhood's famous for tenements, most of 'em overcrowded, dirty, and fire hazards! Who hasn't stuffed a penny in the socket of a fuse box?"

"Feel lucky you got your caretakers to pay your bail," Mr. Troy sneers as he reads *Le Monde*. "Would you rather be rotting in jail instead of in this hotel with us?"

"I don't think you'll face any jail time for the petty theft," Mrs. Troy says. "Mosta the stuff you stole from the cars was found in your locker at work."

"I didn't know till just recently they was charging me with twenty murders! The fire was an accident! Sure I stole, sold and used drugs, broke into cars and houses, and beat people up, but I never murdered nobody or went around setting fires!"

"You didn't just put a penny in the fuse socket," Mr. Troy lectures. "You spilled stolen gasoline and threw a match on the ground. Are you that dumb, or was you permanently high in them days? Who knows, maybe your head was squeezed by forceps. Your mother was put to sleep for all her births, so it could've happened when she was unaware of it."

"I'm itching to take the witness stand. I'll set them all straight. Who could send a cripple to prison? Ain't I suffered enough? Who'd be my caretaker in prison?"

"You wouldn't be the first cripple to go to prison. They'll tell you all about how things will be different for you as a disabled prisoner, although I wouldn't give a damn if they just dumped you in there in your wheelchair and left you to fend for yourself for the rest of your sorry days."

"It ain't very fatherly to wish such harm on your firstborn son."

"You was a mistake! You think I wanted to be saddled with nine children, almost ten, all of 'em mistakes, and to be forced into marriage and fatherhood at only eighteen? At least you'll never marry or reproduce in your state, though it'd be Divine justice if you had to suffer the way I've suffered and know what it feels like to have to support so many unplanned kids. At least only three of 'em are left at home.

Hell, if I'd had my way, you woulda had a proper French name like mosta the resta your siblings. Dolores can't claim to hate spics so much when she gave her own firstborn son a spic name."

"It's a Portuguese name too, and I don't hate the Portuguese," Mrs. Troy says. "And so what if it is a spic name? Just 'cause I liked the name don't mean I like the culture that goes along with it."

Carlos reaches for a cigarette and flops out of his wheelchair. Both of his parents ignore him on the floor and laugh at his efforts to pull himself back up using only his arms and hands. Mr. Troy adds insult to injury by kicking away the lighter and pack of cigarettes. Carlos starts pulling himself along the floor with his hands, undeterred.

"He looks like a crippled caterpillar, Antoine!" Mrs. Troy laughs.

"What kind of sadists are yous guys? Wasn't I always a good oldest son, turning over a lot of my money to you, sharing my drugs, and behaving well?"

"Here, read the paper to keep yourself amused." Mr. Troy throws down *The New York Times*. "Oh, look, it opened right to the birth announcements. That must be salt in your wounds, since you won't never marry, reproduce, or have intercourse ever again."

Carlos's eyes latch onto the name of his old nanny. "Well, whaddaya know? That might be our old servant who just had a baby. A woman named Sarah Katz and a husband named Henry Rosen had a girl on June 7, Nessa Tzipora Rosenkatz. Do you think it's the same girl?"

Mrs. Troy grabs the paper. "Whoever that is, she's a lunatic, keeping her maiden name after what I hope is a respectable marriage to the child's father, and combining both of their last names into one for the child. If that really is the same Sarah Katz who useta work for us, I had no idea she was that insane."

"That girl would be pretty old for having babies by now," Mr. Troy says. "She'd be forty."

"Well, ain't this just as swell." Mrs. Troy's eyes drift farther down the page. "Allen and his bus stop whore just had a baby too, Irene Lily Troy. Nice to know I was informed my secondborn grandchild came into the world."

"I wonder if they're using the proper French pronunciation, Ee-REHN. They'd also need an accent grave over the first E."

"The kid's only a quarter French, you dumb frog. Even if they did intend to use the French form of Irene, only a handful of people in this country would know the correct pronunciation. It's as silly as how you gave that traitor Lucine the middle name Camille and huffily corrected anyone who pronounced it Ca-MEEL instead of Ca-MEEY. Talk about pretentious."

"So, wait, Allen's married?" Carlos asks.

"He got married last July," Mrs. Troy says testily. "At least he ain't living in sin no more. He coulda been arrested for living in sin and having intercourse with a minor."

"What about what I'm facing?" Carlos pleads, starting to inch along the floor again. "I don't wanna be locked up in the slammer for an arson I didn't do on purpose and twenty murders I didn't directly commit!"

"I already washed my hands of you when your mother was in prison," Mr. Troy says. "I had you made a ward of the state. I only came back here 'cause it'd look bad if you went to trial alone. Reputation's very important even to people like us. We don't want anyone thinking we don't care about our kids and that we threw you to the wolves when you was facing jail time. I really don't care what happens to you, you fool. It's about me and your mother, not you."

***

During July, Lucine comes to visit her newborn niece and bring baby gifts. She's highly amused to learn Carlos is finally on trial and that the word through the grapevine is their parents are only staying with him through the trial because they're afraid of looking bad if they're no-shows.

"*Twenty* murders?" she repeats as she's holding Irene. "I never knew they published a list of victims."

"It wasn't in the paper, but the cops must've compiled a list," Allen says. "You and Julie are listed as unaccounted for."

"What kinda murder charges are they exactly?" Girl asks. "I'd assume involuntary manslaughter, since the arson wasn't premeditated."

"It's first-degree arson, since people died. The charges for petty theft and drugs are misdemeanors. I think they'll try to get him a lighter sentence with a criminally negligent, involuntary manslaughter charge stemming from the unintended arson."

"Mother cares less about her work record, since she's had a couple hundred jobs over the last twenty-some years, but Dad is said to be fuming about having to miss so much work," Ernestine says. "Why do they legally need to be at the trial? Unless they're testifying, they're not required to be there for each and every single day."

"He'll be in a mental prison for the rest of his life, but I hope they throw him in a real prison forever too," Lucine says. "You can't get off scot-free after you've burnt down a ten-floor building with about two hundred people. I don't care he didn't set the fire on purpose. Normal people don't stick pennies in sockets and throw lit matches on the same floor they spilled gasoline on. Anyone in his right mind understands that's a serious fire hazard."

"Will we see the list of people who died in the fire?" Adicia asks. "We mighta known some of 'em besides that horrible Mr. Spirnak."

"I'm sure there'll be a story in the paper eventually. Boy, I'd love to be a fly on the wall of the hotel where Carlos and our parents are staying. This must be the most hands-on parenting they've done in years. Dad seems to have a kernel of sense sometimes, so I assume Mother was forced to shoulder the dirty work like sponge baths and dressing him."

"Are there any plans for a baptism and welcoming ceremony?" Ernestine asks.

"I don't wanna look like a hypocrite for baptizing our kids when we aren't regular churchgoers and weren't raised religious, but we did get married in a church. She deserves some sorta identity." Allen takes something that looks like a handbag out of a box. "Mrs. van Niftrik made this for us, in addition to buying us the stroller. It's a homemade baby carrier, like how Indians used to carry the papoose. They used one for Betsy when she was a baby."

"Betsy stopped wearing braids," Girl announces. "I was shocked when we came over to see her last night and her hair was hanging loose. It was all curly from being wound in braids so long."

"It must be hot as Hell during summer to wear loose hair that long," Ernestine says. "She's got brown hair like us, so it must feel even hotter."

"She was wearing a long calico skirt with a crazy pattern, an orange paisley blouse, and leather sandals just like Emeline's. All she needs are flowers in her hair and she'll look like a hippie."

"I'm not getting into that look," Lucine says. "I don't know if anyone would hire me as a social worker if I showed up looking like a flower child. I've gone to a couple of anti-war protests and bought a couple of the popular records, but that's about it for me. I still can't get over you having Irene at home. What if something had gone wrong?"

"Lenore took the pain like a pro," Allen says proudly. "She made it without drugs, stitches, or forceps. It didn't even cross our minds that this was a hippie thing to do. We did it 'cause of Lenore's bad experiences with doctors and hospitals, and plus the midwife scared the hell outta us by telling us about that weird drug cocktail Gemma got."

"Her hair is so dark. Maybe she'll take after Lenore. If you have a boy next time, he might take after you."

"We might not have a boy. Our family seems to run to girls."

"There are still three brothers in our family," Adicia reminds him. "I hope you and Lenore have a little boy someday."

"So, what's going on with Mother and Dad's tenement?" Lucine asks. "If they're gonna be away for this long, will they wanna pay rent if they're not there? I wonder if their stuff will get repossessed."

"Dad hates it, but he's holding it open by kicking in rent so no one moves in and leaves them homeless," Allen says. "Carlos's state-appointed lawyer is paying for their hotel. It's not the Waldorf, but it's not crawling with roaches and rats either."

"How is he getting the money when he's had to take off from work for this trial, or don't I want to know?"

"The usual way they get money in scrapes. Selling drugs and stealing."

"Boy, isn't that irony. Carlos's charges include selling, using, and possessing drugs, and Dad goes doing the exact same things during that very trial. When do they think they'll have a verdict?"

"They're hoping to wrap everything up within the next six months, maybe sooner. Mother's already showing signs of a nervous breakdown from having to deal with Carlos all the time."

"I know all about nervous breakdowns," Adicia says. "My French teacher had one. She was out of school for about seven months and finally came back when the year was almost over. The kids in class were so bad and disrespectful. There was one bully in particular, Bernard, who was mean to everyone. One time he ripped the flag off the wall, kicked it around like a ball, and threw it out the window."

"Was he punished?" Girl asks. "I have mixed feelings about what the flag stands for and how it's held up like no other country's flag, like how we're the only place in the world that makes schoolchildren recite a daily pledge to it, but even I'm disgusted to hear about that."

"No punishment whatsoever. I heard he was suspended or expelled at the end of the year. I hope he never comes back. He's a really bad bully who thinks other people don't have feelings and that they deserve to be beaten up or made fun of for being different or not meeting his approval."

"That's how people like Carlos start out," Lucine says. "Teachers and parents think it's harmless stuff, and it continues until the kids are too big and out of control to have their behavior nipped in the bud. They need people to intervene while things are still manageable."

"There were lots of jerks in seventh grade. One boy, Richard, acted like he belonged in the loonybin, though he could also be halfway normal and decent. Once our science teacher said there was something in the room that was annoying a lot of people today, and when he raised his hand to volunteer the answer, he said, 'Your face.' He got in trouble for that. There was also another bully named Logan. He was hardly the best person to be a bully, since he looked like a real egghead, the type of person who usually gets bullied himself. What a jerk. I hope I don't have any classes with him next year."

"His name was Logan?" Girl asks. "I've never heard that name."

"Maybe it's his mother's maiden name," Lucine suggests. "Though it's awfully pretentious."

"You should never believe that nonsense about how boys only bully you if they secretly like you. There are nicer ways to show affection, and if that's the only way he can think of to give his crush attention without confessing his feelings, he ain't mature enough to have a girlfriend or go on dates."

"Boys in junior high are sadists. Junior high girls are plenty catty and mean too."

"At least I only have another year left," Adicia says. "I'm looking forward to high school, so I can blend in easier."

"There are bullies and cliques there too, though sometimes you can avoid becoming a target. Usually by the time you get to high school, the smarter kids are grouped together in most of the same classes, though there's no guarantee there won't be any bullies among the kids from nicer families or in the honors track."

"Carlos is a big bully," Justine says. "I hope someone bullies him in jail."

"It'll probably happen. There's always a pecking order in jail. If he's lucky, he'll find someone to do his bidding for him, or someone to protect him and add him to his gang."

***

"Will you raise your right hand and swear to tell the truth, the whole truth, nothing but the truth, so help you God?"

"Yup," Carlos says.

It's the second week in September, and the prosecution has decided to put Carlos on the stand. The defense declined to use him as a witness, citing his alleged diminished mental capacity and the fact that he's already been through enough trauma, but the prosecution lawyer thinks he's either crazy like a fox or so genuinely stupid he'll be putty in their hands.

"Will you please state your name?"

"Carlos Ghislain Troy."

"Now, Mr. Troy, at the time of your accident, July 3, 1962, you were working at Mighty Mike's Mechanics on Twelfth Street, correct?"

"It was the second job I had in my life," he says proudly. "I was a car repairman and mechanic."

"What did this job entail?"

"I fixed cars and performed basic maintenance services."

"Did you ever take anything out of the cars you were entrusted with?"

"All the time. That's onea the reasons I wanted the job after I was fired from my first job. I knew rich people would take their cars in, and I'd help myself to their belongings. They either wouldn't miss 'em or would just buy new stuff. Hell, my own mother right there told me she hoped I'd steal from the cars the same way I useta help myself to cereal when I worked in a cereal factory."

Mrs. Troy hangs her head in her hands.

"So you're basically admitting to stealing from your customers and pleading guilty to the thirty counts of petty theft you're facing?"

"All poor people steal. We deserve nice stuff, and rich snobs deserve to be put in their place. Besides, I was told they found mosta the stuff in my work locker. That problem is solved and the charges should be waived."

"That's not up to you, Mr. Troy. That's up to the judge and jury.

Now here's another question for you. Can you remember when you started using or selling drugs?"

"I was fourteen, maybe? I think I waited till I started high school to join my parents in the wonderful world of drugs. We useta have a whole stockpile before the fire."

Now Mr. Troy hangs his head in his hands.

"Did you start selling them at the same time you began using them?"

"I want to say yes. I sold and used all kinds of drugs you can imagine, though my favorite was meth. Speaking of, I'm dying for some meth right now. Can anyone oblige me?"

Mrs. Troy wishes she could run out of the courtroom.

"Mr. Troy, are you aware you're incriminating yourself by your testimony? You do have Fifth Amendment rights to refuse to answer any of these questions."

"You asked if I'd tell the whole truth, and I agreed. I ain't got nothing to hide. I'm proud of my roots and what I've done."

"Fine. Now that we've quickly established you did steal from your customers at the car shop and that you're a drug user and pusher, let's move on to the most serious charges you're facing. Do you remember what you were doing on the late afternoon of June 27, 1962, Wednesday?"

"Using meth, probably. Is that supposed to be the day our old tenement burnt down?"

"Yes it is. Does that jog your memory, now that you know what exactly I'm asking about?"

"That was the day I got my job at Mighty Mike's Mechanics. On my way home, I siphoned off some gas from a fancy car for my buddy Nick and his wife Louise, onea the few families I knew with their own automobile. Nick and his wife lived on the fourth floor. Nick told me their electricity got shut off 'cause they didn't paid their utility bill, and asked if I'd please go into the basement to try to fix it by fiddling with the fuse box. I gladly obliged. The cheapskate landlord had taken out the penny I'd put into the socket last time I worked with the fuse, so I stuck another in. It was really dark, so I lit a match to see. After I was done fiddling with the fuse, I threw the match on the ground. It musta come in contact with somea the gasoline I'd accidentally spilled when I set the canister down. So as you can see, this fire was a total accident. I did not maliciously set a fire or intend to kill nobody."

"Sir, are you aware of what putting a penny into a socket or fuse breaker can do?"

"I guess it could cause a fire hazard, but that ain't no reason to never do it. Tons of people get in cars every day, and they ain't avoiding 'em for fear of dying in accidents."

"Are you aware of how flammable gasoline is, and even more so when it comes into direct contact with a flame such as a match?"

Carlos waves his hand dismissively. "Those were complete accidents. It was pretty funny when we looked out our door and saw a fire at the bottom of the steps. It was onea them 'Did little old me do that?' moments."

"You find it funny you caused a massive gasoline and electrical fire that completely consumed a ten-floor building where roughly two hundred people lived, claimed twenty lives, and left everyone homeless?"

"Of course that part wasn't funny! It's like how you laugh when someone falls on a banana peel. It ain't funny for him, but it's funny to watch since it ain't you, and 'cause people getting hurt are funny."

Mr. and Mrs. Troy's mouths are hanging open in shock. They'll have no reputation left if anyone reads about this in the papers or hears about it through the grapevine.

"Sir, are you aware of how quickly a gasoline fire spreads, and that when combined with a concurrent electrical fire, the end results will be disastrous?"

"You act like I did this on purpose! I hated losing everything I owned and being made homeless, though at least we was able to move right into a new place."

"Did you make any efforts to report this to the police, or let the firemen know how it had started?"

"Why in the hell would I incriminate myself like that? Accidents happen. That don't mean all harmless accidents need to be treated like criminal matters."

"Now I'm going to read you a list of names, and you can tell me if you recognize any of them or know how these names relate to one another. Angela Barbieri, Maria Delmonico, Edward Gallagher, Hannah Gallagher, Stanley Houlihan, Jane Johnson, Lisa Jones, Nathan Jones, Timothy Jones, Adela Levine, Charles Levine, Peter MacIntosh, Georgia McIntyre, Philip McNulty, Alexander Nankin, Vera O'Loughlin, Richard Rogers, Randolph Spirnak, Jerry Teitelbaum, and Sharon Zoltanovsky."

"My mother was friends with a Mrs. Nankin on onea the lower floors, but I don't remember if I personally knew that family. The only name on that list that rings a bell is Spirnak, who moved across the hall from us that May. He had a daughter Julie who'd just turned eight. Spirnak sold drugs as his full-time job. My parents and I became somea his best clients. There was no Mrs. Spirnak, since they'd divorced a couple of years prior. That bitch tried to tell the cops and lawyers he was doing degenerate things to their daughter, but we all know how women make stuff up when they're desperate for attention or tryna get people to take their side. The girl, Julie, disappeared not that long after they moved in, and I have no idea where she went. Why, are these people the ones charging me for accidentally burning down the building?"

"No, they can't do anything now, because they're all dead. Most of them were found dead when the firemen arrived too late to save the building or anyone inside, and Mrs. O'Loughlin, Mr. MacIntosh, and Miss Lisa Jones, who was only nine years old, died shortly thereafter in the hospital of their injuries. Do you feel any remorse, now that you've learnt the names attached to the people who died in the fire you started?"

"Why should I feel bad for something I didn't do on purpose? I ain't a pansy like my brother Allen, who was pathetic enough to quit all drugs, alcohol, and cigarettes, and who don't mind being surrounded by more girls than guys."

The prosecuting attorney smirks and turns to the defense. "Mr. Hoffman, would you like to cross-examine this hapless witness?"

Carlos's lawyer feels like throwing his hands up. "No, that's fine. I don't think my client will be able to get out of the hole he's just dug for himself no matter what I ask him."

Mrs. Troy looks like she wants to murder Carlos as he wheels himself off the witness stand. Mr. Troy has to suppress the urge to reach out and smack his firstborn son upside the head. Just about the only thing a poor family can claim to be proud of is its name, and now they probably don't have any name left after Carlos has cavalierly admitted in court to using and selling drugs, stealing at work, and starting a fire.

***

"We finally saw it!" Adicia cheerily announces when she and the other girls are visiting Allen, Irene, and Lenore the first weekend in October. "They took the boys into one room and kept us girls in the other, and showed us a color filmstrip called *Girl to Woman*. They even named the parts of the body they didn't name in the films and booklets Lucine, Emeline, and Ernestine got."

"Your class got a *color* filmstrip?" Ernestine asks jealously. "Betsy and I got a black and white one, and we're only two years older than you."

"Would you like to step out for awhile, Allen?" Lenore asks. "This girl talk is probably gonna embarrass you."

"I'm stepping out right now," Boy announces, not waiting to be asked.

"They even had a Negro—I mean, Black—girl in the opening scene, where a bunch of girls were chatting at a party and talking about stuff like body changes and boys. The film told us about sweating, menstruation, body hair, and how our bodies develop."

"I'm dying to see what kinda booklet you got to go along with it," Ernestine says. "They're always so much fun to make fun of."

Adicia pulls it out. "It's from Modess, and called 'How Shall I Tell My Daughter?' Like Mother cares about telling any of us anything about growing up. I still haven't needed to open the big box of Modess napkins she dumped in the bathroom six months ago."

"Does it by any chance use the words 'dainty' and 'daintiness'?" Girl asks. "Ain't nothing dainty about that time of the month, and ain't nothing dainty about us poor and working-class girls."

"It does, but there's no calendar attached, and no instructions on how to use a belt."

"I hate those damn belts," Lenore says. "You'd think they would've thought up something more practical by now."

"Ernestine and I don't use belts," Girl says. "We use handmade napkins and throw 'em in the regular wash after we soak 'em in a bucket of water with baking soda. They snap right on, no need to worry about keeping a belt up and around your waist all day long, and making sure the napkin stays attached to both hooks."

"Do you miss not menstruating, Lenore, now that you've had Irene?" Ernestine asks.

"Postpartum bleeding is worse than the worst menstrual period," Lenore says. "I slept on top of an old absorbent blanket just in case I bled through my pajamas at night."

"You mean you get non-menstrual bleeding after you give birth?" Girl asks. "That must really stink."

"I bled for a couple of weeks. Veronica joked it's like getting all the menses you missed rolled up into one."

"I'm glad I'm not a woman," Allen admits. "I don't think I could deal with the half of what you ladies have to go through."

"Yeah, guys get off so easy," Girl says. "That ain't fair."

"Maybe that means we're capable of handling more pain and annoyance than guys," Ernestine suggests. "We're really special if we're strong enough to deal with stuff like birth, menstruation, and pregnancy. We wouldn't be given more than we can handle."

Lenore eases Irene under her blouse to nurse her, not worrying about covering up since Boy left. "We decided we wanted to have her baptized at Father Murphy's church, though we go to St. Luke in the Fields. He agreed to do it, for the same reason he agreed to do our wedding."

"So yous guys are becoming nominal Episcopalians?" Girl asks. "If I was to choose a Christian denomination, I'd go Unitarian. Not that I'd voluntarily pick Christianity. I'm more interested in the original religion of Ireland, when women ruled and were worshipped."

"They're not a bad little denomination," Allen says. "I think we'll do fine raising her to go to church more often than we did."

"I think I'm a Catholic," Julie says. "My last name's Czechoslovakian, and there aren't many Protestants there. I think my mommy was Catholic too."

"Speaking of religion, do you think Carlos has a prison chaplain assigned to him?" Ernestine asks. "I wonder if he'll pretend to find God in jail so they'll let him out sooner."

"That man is beyond redemption," Allen says. "He's not evil or deliberately malicious, but he's so stupid and clueless. He just doesn't get it, even when it's explained he's done something thoughtless or harmful."

"I hope he falls out of his wheelchair in prison and no one helps him back up," Justine says. "He almost killed us."

"I'm sure he'll be punished to the fullest extent of the law for what he's done. It's already so long overdue."

"Will he get the death penalty?" Adicia asks.

"No, he's just facing a lengthy jail sentence. He didn't do anything that legally merits death."

"I'm not looking forward to our parents coming home," Justine says. "I wish they'd go to prison along with Carlos."

"It's in the hands of the judge and jury. All we can do is hope they sentence him as much as he deserves."

***

Mr. and Mrs. Troy stand up as the judge enters the courtroom the day before Thanksgiving. Carlos is confident the jury will be easy on him since he's a paralytic and didn't start the fire on purpose.

The judge takes his seat and turns to the jury, addressing the jury foreman. "Have you reached your decision, Mr. Coleman?"

"Yes we have."

"Will you please stand—" the judge starts to say to Carlos, before remembering this part of the sentencing rubric doesn't apply to a paralytic. "Pardon me. Just turn and look at the jury and pay attention." He gives Mrs. Troy a sharp look for her hysterical peals of laughter. "Mrs. Troy, this is a very serious criminal matter. If you cannot stop laughing, I'll have you removed from the courtroom."

"New York State Supreme Court of New York City, County of New York, in the matter of the State of New York versus Carlos Ghislain Troy, Case Number SD089433, we the jury in the above entitled action find the defendant, Carlos Ghislain Troy, guilty of petit larceny, in violation of Penal Code Section 155.25, a misdemeanor, upon customers of Mighty Mike's Mechanics, as charged in Count One of the information.

"New York State Supreme Court, County of New York, in the matter of the State of New York versus Carlos Ghislain Troy, Case Number SD089433, we the jury in the above entitled action find the defendant, Carlos Ghislain Troy, guilty of grand larceny in the fourth degree, in violation of Penal Code Section 155.30, a misdemeanor, upon customers of Mighty Mike's Mechanics, as charged in Count Two of the information.

"New York State Supreme Court, County of New York, in the matter of the State of New York versus Carlos Ghislain Troy, Case Number SD089433, we the jury in the above entitled action find the defendant, Carlos Ghislain Troy, guilty of criminal possession of a controlled substance in the seventh degree, in violation of the Penal Code Section 220.03, a misdemeanor, as charged in Count Three of the information.

"New York State Supreme Court, County of New York, in the matter of the State of New York versus Carlos Ghislain Troy, Case Number SD089433, we the jury in the above entitled action find the defendant, Carlos Ghislain Troy, guilty of criminal sale of a controlled substance in the fifth degree, in violation of Penal Code Section 220.31, a misdemeanor, as charged in Count Four of the information.

"New York State Supreme Court, County of New York, in the matter of the State of New York versus Carlos Ghislain Troy, Case Number SD089433, we the jury in the above entitled action find the defendant, Carlos Ghislain Troy, guilty of first-degree arson, in violation of Penal Code Section 150.20, a felony, upon the defendant's former residence, as charged in Count Five of the information.

"New York State Supreme Court, County of New York, in the matter of the State of New York versus Carlos Ghislain Troy, Case Number SD089433, we the jury in the above entitled action find the defendant, Carlos Ghislain Troy, guilty of criminally negligent homicide in violation of the Penal Code Section 125.10, a felony, upon Angela Sophia Castelli Barbieri, a person, a human being, as charged in Count Six of the information...."

Carlos sits in shock and his parents hold onto the chairs in front of them to prevent fainting from shock as the jury foreman continues reading off the guilty verdicts for all the people who died in the fire. He's found guilty of all twenty counts of criminally negligent homicide.

"Ladies and gentlemen of the jury, is this your verdict, so say you one, so say you all?"

The jury responds in the affirmative.

"I'm not appealing this one," Carlos's lawyer mutters. "Have fun in jail."

Mrs. Troy throws an exaggerated faint and screams when someone comes to wheel Carlos off to a holding cell, where he'll stay till the judge determines his sentence. Mr. Troy gets out of the courtroom as soon as court is adjourned, not waiting around for his wife.

"What is my son gonna do as a crippled prisoner?" Mrs. Troy demands. "He needs a caretaker for all the basic things!"

"I'm sure Carlos won't be the first paralytic cripple there," the lawyer says. "They'll find a way to deal with him in his state."

"Can we stay in the hotel till the sentence is announced?"

"Sure, if you can pony up enough money to stay there for about three more months. I'm done with you people."

***

While Adicia and Justine are in the middle of Thanksgiving supper with the Doyles the next day, Mr. and Mrs. Troy come storming in. Mrs. Troy is dragging a screaming, pouting Tommy by the hand.

"You girls are coming back with us, now that Carlos's trial is over," Mrs. Troy says. "Your father just unlocked our place, and it had a very bad smell from no one living there or cleaning it in almost six months. I picked turkey lunchmeat up at the butcher's, and there are canned vegetables that won't go bad, so we can have our own Thanksgiving meal. Tommy is taking it very hard after leaving the Thanksgiving meal he was having with the spics. You shoulda seen the spic food they was serving in addition to traditional American turkey and stuffing. Black beans, rice, flat cornbread, pig feet, and oxtail stew. Repulsive."

"That's all you're having for Thanksgiving, turkey breast and canned vegetables?" Matthew asks. "That's not a good holiday meal."

"How did you get the money to afford even that if Dad hasn't worked since early June?" Adicia asks.

"Selling drugs, of course," Mrs. Troy says. "That was our lifeline during this whole stupid mess with Carlos."

"Thank God my boss said I can come back to work right after the holiday," Mr. Troy says. "He knows I've been a good, loyal worker for over twenty years and that sometimes things happen that are outta our control. Unlike certain other people we might think of, I have a solid record of work at the same place, and don't have a work record plagued by absenteeism, tardiness, stealing, drinking and using drugs on the job, loafing, or constantly quitting and being fired. How many jobs have you ever had again, Dolores, three hundred?"

"I lost count after awhile."

"Why are you proud of being a crummy worker and having hundreds of jobs?" Matthew asks.

"She can't answer, 'cause she knows she's a failure at life." Mr. Troy goes back across the hall, gagging as he re-enters their tenement.

"Does anyone have Lysol or perfume to drive this horrible stench away?"

"Just open the window, Antoine," Mrs. Troy snaps. "That'll air the place out."

"Can I have some of your yummy turkey, Mrs. Doyle?" Tommy asks.

"She ain't your mother. We're gonna have a real Thanksgiving supper that aligns with our class origins. Poor people don't eat roasted turkeys, stuffing, mashed potatoes, fresh roasted vegetables, candied yams with marshmallows, cranberry sauce, and stuffed mushrooms. Let's go, the three of yous."

"Can we wrap some of the extra food up and bring it home?" Justine asks.

"Of course not. You've gotten spoilt the past six months you was eating uppity food like this. It's time to get back to reality and start eating normal poor people's food again."

Adicia and Justine cast sad looks back at Mrs. Doyle as they follow their mother and Tommy across the hall.

***

February 26, 1968, Monday, Mr. and Mrs. Troy go back downtown to hear what kind of sentence the judge and jury cooked up for Carlos. Mrs. Troy partly covers her eyes with her hands, overcome with shame and embarrassment. This is the kind of thing a family's reputation never recovers from, no matter where they might relocate. It'll be in the papers, and total strangers will hear about this great family shame through the grapevine. Mrs. Troy feels lucky her picture won't be in the paper, so total strangers won't recognize her.

Carlos's hands are in shackles when he's wheeled into the courtroom, so he won't get any ideas and start wheeling himself out onto the street. This just adds insult to injury, since only a complete lunatic would think he could do anything if he made a break. He has no money, no weapons, no plans with friends on the outside, no temporary haven, no change of clothes, no way to get out of the handcuffs, and no use of his legs.

Mrs. Troy rolls her eyes as the judge recites the same rubric for each part of the sentencing, as though they all need to hear the name of the court, the county, the case number and name, and Carlos's name repeated anew for each charge he's been convicted of. Midway through his reading, the judge stops and looks out at her.

"Mrs. Troy, do I see you rolling your eyes at me? Unless you have a neurological defect or are currently high on drugs like your son was when he committed all these crimes, I'd wager you're showing disrespect for me, the court, and the criminal procedure. If you don't stop, I'll have you removed for contempt of court. Is that clear?"

Mrs. Troy nods, if only because she wants to hear exactly how long Carlos is going away for.

"So what exactly does that mean for me?" Carlos asks when the judge finishes reading the sentence. "How long do I get locked up for?"

"Math wasn't your strong suit, obviously. You're getting three months for the petit larceny, three months for the grand larceny, a year for possessing drugs, a year for selling drugs, five years for first-degree arson, and twenty-five years to life for each of the twenty criminally negligent homicides. That adds up to five hundred seven years and six months. You're never getting out of jail unless someone invents a drug that lets people live hundreds of years. Understood?"

"Yeah, but I don't like it."

"No one asked you if you liked it. Jail is a punishment, not a reward. It's not supposed to be something felons enjoy."

"But I'm a cripple! I can't even feel my legs!"

"That's your own fault, you drug addict. Had you been straight and fastened that car jack properly, you wouldn't be spending the rest of your life in a wheelchair, now would you? Your sentence will begin next week, as soon as you're transferred to federal jail Upstate."

Carlos casts begging glances at his parents, but they walk right past him as court is adjourned. A police officer comes to wheel him back to the holding cell, not exchanging a word with him. At this point, Carlos wishes he'd never regained his senses, since he wouldn't be aware of being paralyzed and wouldn't be headed off to prison as a convicted felon and murderer. Now he's in jail twice over for the rest of his life, in both a physical and mental prison.

Chapter 37: The Year the World Went Up in Flames

"I just don't understand why we're still over there, or why we went there in the first place," Betsy says as she tosses her long loose hair behind her. "What did the Vietnamese ever do to us?"

"The same reason our government has usually decided to butt into other countries' affairs when it don't concern them," Girl says. "Most wars we've gotten involved in ain't been morally justified like the Civil War, the Second World War, or the American Revolution. Our leaders was tryna impose their own definition of proper government or morality on people with different cultural, social, historical, and political worldviews. That, and Americans for the past fifty years have been brainwashed to believe Socialism and Communism are evil and hafta be stopped. God forbid someone see sense or justice in an economic, political, and philosophical system that ain't capitalism. So many Americans don't understand dictators like Stalin don't represent real Communism or Socialism. He was a totalitarian in a place whose experiment in Communism never got past the dictatorship of the proletariat stage."

"I'm kinda glad you don't go to school, much as I love you," Ernestine says. "You'd probably be expelled for spouting off such radical views, no matter how correct you might be."

"I just can't get that image outta my head." Baby hugs her knees to her chest. "If the South Vietnamese are supposed to be our friends, why did one of them shoot a prisoner in the head? I'm still having nightmares about that since I saw it on the news in February."

"Well, we're having an election for a new president in November," Betsy says hopefully. "It's too bad high school kids can't vote. My parents plan to vote for President Kennedy's brother Robert, if he makes it to the election and wins all the primaries."

"Girl and I aren't looking forward to our sixteenth birthdays," Ernestine says. "How can we be happy about a milestone birthday when so many serious things are happening in the world?"

"I don't see sixteen as a milestone year. Seems just like any other year to me. I'm not interested in wearing makeup, and there's no one special I'd like to date, though my parents said I'm old enough for both now. Maybe it's a bigger deal in places where teenagers are allowed to drive at that age. I don't know many people with cars. Everyone walks, bicycles, or takes public transportation."

"In the old days, sixteen was seen as ripe for the picking," Girl says. "You know the saying, 'Sweet sixteen and never been kissed.' As though a girl's virginity, childbearing, and marriageability should be dictated and decided by men, or anyone other than herself. We don't live in a country or era when normal girls marry or have kids at sixteen. The lifespan's so much longer than it was a couple hundred years ago, so we don't need to get married off and start having kids almost as soon as we're fertile."

"Do you think I'll get my first menstrual period soon?" Julie asks. "Since I did just get my first bra. It still feels strange wearing it."

"I hate wearing them. They're barely better than corsets and Chinese foot-binding, if you ask me. There ain't a medical or scientific reason to wear one. I'm more comfortable when I ain't wearing one."

"You're probably not long in coming for that," Betsy says. "Me, Girl, and Ernestine all got ours at thirteen, and you'll be fourteen next month. Thirteen is the average age when girls nowadays start."

Mrs. van Niftrik comes running into the apartment, not bothering to knock or announce herself. "Girls, come very quickly. I don't have time to explain."

"Are we late for supper?" Betsy asks as she gets up. "I'm sorry if I lost track of the time."

"Supper won't be for awhile. It's something else," her mother says as they go across the hall.

Mr. van Niftrik stands like a statue in front of the television. He doesn't say a word as the others file into the apartment and gather around him. The regular 7:00 programming on CBS has been interrupted for a news program with anchorman Walter Cronkite discussing the life and Civil Rights contributions of Dr. Martin Luther King, Jr., who was shot in Memphis a little after 6:00 and recently pronounced dead. Shortly thereafter, there's a broadcasting of statements by President Johnson and Vice President Humphrey, coupled with footage of a speech Dr. King delivered yesterday, which now seems eerily prophetic because it acknowledges the fact that he might not live a long life. They all stand and stare, unable to move or speak until there's a break in the programming.

"I smell something burning," Infant announces.

Mrs. van Niftrik rushes to the stove and pulls out a casserole dish whose bottom layer is starting to turn black, as she discovers when she puts a spoon into it. She, Mr. van Niftrik, and Betsy are too shocked by the news to complain about their supper being partly burnt.

"Why do people kill each other?" Baby asks as Girl goes across the hall to fetch extra food. "Why would someone be mean and kill someone who was all about peace?"

"Someone taught him to hate somewhere along the line," Ernestine says. "People aren't born hating other people for having a different skin color, religion, ethnic background, or having a physical disfigurement. And some people think killing someone who was a leader for peace and harmony in the world and between the races will kill the entire movement. This isn't the Middle Ages. People who want change in the world will never let themselves be forced underground for hundreds of years out of fear."

"This is not going to be a good year," Mr. van Niftrik says, shaking his head. "I could be wrong, but if the first few months of this year are any indication, things will only get worse, not get better."

***

Mr. van Niftrik was right, Ernestine thinks as they make their way to St. Patrick's Cathedral in Midtown on June 7, Friday, to view the body of presidential candidate Robert F. Kennedy. Following Dr. King's assassination, there were riots in many cities around the country, and in other news, there have been bloody revolts in Paris led by students and professors of the Sorbonne, a student-led occupation of some of the buildings of Columbia University, and an attempted assassination of pop artist Andy Warhol. None of them wants to know if anything worse will happen this year, what with over six months left.

Adicia notices Ernestine and Girl exchanging a strange look, the kind of look Allen used to give Lenore before he finally told her how he felt about her. Julie, Justine, Baby, and Betsy notice it too, but shrug it off as best friends in shock and exchanging a look of solidarity, sympathy, and love.

"What a rotten birthday I had yesterday," Allen says as the cathedral slowly comes into view. "To think that last year on my birthday, I was celebrating becoming a father to this cute little pumpkin." He leans down to kiss Irene's head.

"Some people look at us kinda strangely 'cause we alternate the stroller and the homemade slings Mrs. van Niftrik made for us," Lenore says. "Today people have other things on their minds than staring at the quasi-hippie daddy carrying his baby in a sling instead of pushing her in a stroller."

"That's a mighty long line to get inside," Infant says. "What if I have to go to the bathroom while we're waiting?"

"Do I have to look at him?" Baby asks. "I wanna pay my respects, but I'm scared to see a dead person."

"What if he's missing part of his head?" Justine asks. "I heard he was shot in his head and neck, and I don't wanna see bloody wounds and holes in his head and neck."

"Morticians can do amazing things," Mr. van Niftrik says. "If you don't want to look, no one will make you. You can stand off to the side. Your presence counts as paying your respects, even if you don't look."

"Do you think there'll be a wax dummy in case someone crazy enough tries to steal the body?" Emeline asks, adjusting her crown of daisies. "When Rudolph Valentino died, the funeral director put a wax body on display so deranged fans couldn't steal it. Senator Kennedy was just as popular, even if it wasn't as a sex symbol. I wonder if someone will be crazy enough to do that."

"There are probably gonna be police patrolling this area like crazy," Allen says. "Speaking of, I hope you don't have any pot on you in case we have to be frisked."

"I left my pot in Poughkeepsie. I told you I only use it to relax and open my mind. I'm not an addict. I haven't dropped any acid, in spite of mosta my hippie friends having tried it at least once. Can't say I'm not tempted."

"Mother cares less Senator Kennedy was killed," Adicia says. "She was happy when Dr. King was killed. I don't know why she's such a racist and so apathetic to what's happening in the world."

"At least she won't be up here and risk seeing me," Lucine says. "I barely had any time to be happy about graduating college before this happened."

"Are you gonna get your first social worker job over the summer?"

"I wish. I have to do two years in the master's program before anyone will hire me. You're not qualified if you only have a bachelor's degree."

"Oh, goody. You're still gonna be somewhere in the city for two more years." Justine smiles up at her and squeezes her hands.

"Is there a bathroom in the church?" Julie whispers to Mrs. van Niftrik. "I really need to go there."

"Can you hold it for much longer? You'll lose your place in the line if you step out, and I don't think they'd let you back in even with everyone holding your spot. They also probably wouldn't let you budge ahead into the church just for the bathroom, since it's so crowded."

"I don't know if I can wait so much longer," she whispers desperately. "I think I'm starting my first menstrual period."

"Why do you think you have it?" Girl whispers. "I don't have any supplies on me, and none of us has a jacket or sweater for you to tie over your backside."

"I feel like I wet myself, though I wouldn't do that at my age without being aware of it. If it's true, I'm gonna be bleeding all over my clothes by the time we go past the coffin, and everyone will stare at me."

"Don't worry, even if you are, I can get the stain out," Mrs. van Niftrik promises. "It might feel like it when you're caught unprepared, but you're really not leaking a gallon of blood a minute."

"I might have something." Emeline pulls a forest green shawl out of her hand-woven bag. "Do you know how to tie it around your waist so it looks like a skirt?"

Julie flashes her a smile and ties it on top of her knee-length green paisley skirt, trying to look as casual as possible. She hopes it lasts until they get home, whenever that is, and Mrs. van Niftrik can help her in place of her missing mother.

After what feels like a very long wait, they finally approach the head of the line leading into the cathedral and follow the people in front of them towards the coffin where Senator Kennedy is lying in state. Justine, Infant, and Baby give him quick looks before looking away, glad he wasn't put on display with visible gunshot wounds. The line is so long, they don't have much time to stop, reflect, and look at him.

Adicia, while very sorry the potential next president of the United States was assassinated, can't help but feel a tiny bit jealous of him for having so many people who thought enough of him to turn out in droves for his wake, many of whom will probably show up tomorrow for the funeral as well. Most of the people paying regards are total strangers. She wonders if anyone outside her own small circle would care that much if she passed on or took sick.

"Who are we gonna vote for now?" Girl asks as they file out of the cathedral and back onto the street.

"I don't like Vice President Humphrey or Senator Gene Mc-Carthy enough to vote for either," Mrs. van Niftrik says. "Arthur and I have always preferred candidates a little outside the establishment of the party, and whose ideas we support. We're as far left as Democrats go before being considered Socialists."

"I hope it's another Democrat. I ain't never liked Republicans. I've read about how progressive they was in the early days of their party, and then I see how modern Republicans act and think nothing like Abraham Lincoln or Teddy Roosevelt. The original Republicans are probably throwing up in their graves over what happened to their party. Richard Nixon in particular gives me a bad feeling. He projects a sinister energy. I probably sound nuts, but I've always been able to sense invisible fields of energy coming from people and things, like if someone has bad light or a positive energy force."

"You're not nuts," Emeline says. "At least, I don't think you're nuts. My hippie friends and I have experimented with feeling and seeing one another's energy fields. It's pretty intense to reach out and feel invisible energy around a person after you do specific exercises to charge up. I was disappointed I wasn't onea the ones who could see the auras."

"Is the world gonna come to an end?" Baby asks as they walk towards the subway station. "While I was playing my tambourine and dancing in the streets yesterday, I heard a crazy guy ranting about how all the bad stuff happening recently means the world's gonna end soon."

"The world won't end for another five billion years," Girl asserts. "That's when the Sun's gonna become a red giant and not be able to support life on Earth anymore. People have always been predicting the end of the world and thinking things will never get any worse. It's sick how religious fanatics actually look forward to their believed end of the world. If you ask me, I don't think Revelations, the last book of the Bible, is meant to be interpreted as a bunch of prophecies for the end of the world. It's more of a warning about what could happen if people don't shape up their act, or Saint John writing about his own times or fears for the future. Just because it might seem like the end of the world for people inclined to believe in that bunk doesn't mean Revelations, Nostradamus, or what have you should be applied to it and held up as so-called prophecies coming true. The best prophecies are open-ended, not definitive."

"What's a red giant?" Justine asks as they step onto a subway going towards the Meatpacking District.

"It's part of the lifecycle of a star," Ernestine says. "We learnt a bit about astronomy in my earth science class this year. I hated that class, though I enjoyed learning about stars. When a star gets hot enough, after a very, very, very, very long time of being alive, it turns into a red giant. Our Sun will explode and get way too hot for life to be supported on the planet. Earth, if it survives the red giant phase and isn't pulled into the Sun's newly-expanded orbit, will become too cold to support life, without any light. It'll become a planetary nebula and then a white dwarf. It could also become a black dwarf. Eventually it might turn into a real black hole."

"Like in science fiction stories?" Boy asks. "That's groovy. I wish I went to school so I could learn about far-out stuff like that."

"None of us will be alive when that happens. It's over ten billion years in the future."

"Can't scientists find a way to stop that from happening?" Baby asks, having forgotten about her fears the world will end this year. "I don't want our entire planet erased and swallowed into the Sun as though nothing ever happened here. Our entire existence would be in vain if we left no record behind and everything we ever did as a human race was erased without a trace."

"Probably," Girl says as they watch their stop getting closer. "I'm sure people that far in the future will have much more advanced science. Besides, self-preservation is onea the strongest human instincts."

Baby is still mulling over it when they get off at their stop and wave goodbye to the others. She sits on her mattress and thinks about how awful it'll be if the entire history of the human race on this planet were to be wiped out as though it had never been. She barely notices Julie going over to the van Niftriks' apartment. When Julie comes back after about twenty minutes, Baby likewise hardly notices Julie's excited announcement she has in fact started her first menstrual period, nor Boy's exasperated groaning about how he didn't have to know that.

"Do you think I'm a square for worrying so much about something that won't happen for billions of years?" Baby asks as Julie puts *The Birds, the Bees, and The Monkees* onto the turntable, a record she got as her fourteenth birthday present from Mr. and Mrs. van Niftrik last month. "I'm only eleven and should be worried about more important stuff."

"We're living through a scary, intense time," Girl says. "It's normal to be nervous. We won't be around to know what happens in the far distant future, but I did read a short story by Isaac Asimov awhile ago, 'The Last Question.' He's a famous science fiction writer. The story is about a machine called the Multivac, and how all through future human history, it keeps getting asked the question 'How can the process of entropy be reversed?' The Multivac doesn't know the answer, but it keeps tryna figure it out, even after the last person is gone, and time and space no longer exist. Finally, one day, the Multivac's descendant figures it out, though there are no longer any people around to hear the answer. The machine reverses the process of entropy and starts the universe and its evolution all over again. It's just like onea the lines early in the Bible, 'And AC said, "LET THERE BE LIGHT!" And there was light—' So I believe humankind will find a way to stop the destruction of our world, even if the very processes of human and stellar evolution have to start all over again."

"You're smart. I wish I could be as smart and read as much as you. You remember so much of what you read and learn, and you ain't never been to school."

"When you wanna learn, you find a way. With any luck, I'll be able to go to college same as Ernestine and Betsy. I'll knock them away with my admissions essay, and I'll get a GED just like Lenore. You don't gotta go to a formal school to be smart enough for college."

"Do you have to go away?" Infant asks. "Or could we go with you?"

"We'll figure something out. Whatever happens, our little family will survive, just like this big wide world of ours will survive these hardships."

***

The world has continued going to Hell in a handbasket with the brutal crushing by Soviet troops of the Prague Spring, the Czechoslovakian people's sadly short-lived experience of freedom and openness.

Not long afterwards, police violently beat peaceful protestors at the Democratic National Convention in Chicago without any provocation. The van Niftriks have gone away to Long Island for two weeks, and Julie, Boy, Baby, and Infant have gone to see Allen, Lenore, and Irene for a break from the nightly news, so Ernestine and Girl have the place all to themselves.

"People in power can be such jerks," Girl proclaims as she drops the new Simon and Garfunkel album *Bookends*, which she got as a birthday present from Mr. and Mrs. van Niftrik, onto the turntable. "I'm glad I have you to cling to with everything crazy going on lately."

Ernestine touches the record cover. "This picture reminds me of us. So many times we're like one person with two heads, thinking with the same brain, joined at the hip. We think the same thing before the other person shares it, like how we both decided John was our favorite Beatle, and that Peter was our favorite Monkee."

"We're soulmates, I believe. There are many types of soulmates— lifelong best friends, romantic lovers, collaborative partners who write songs together or co-star in a lot of movies or plays. Remember how Emeline read that thing from Plato at Allen and Lenore's wedding, about how there was once three races of human beings till Zeus split them all in half? Maybe we're descended from the race that once consisted of two women." Girl smiles at her, giving her the kind of look several other people have seen them exchanging recently. "Will you be my friend forever, just like it says in 'Old Friends,' even until we're seventy?"

"Of course I will. Call me crazy, but I useta assume I'd get a boyfriend and eventually marry when I was older, just like everyone else, but lately I've been feeling I don't need a guy. All I want is you. You're not just my best friend, but the soulmate I wanna be with throughout life. I hope you don't think that makes me mentally ill. I didn't plan to start feeling that odd way about you. I told my second grade teacher that if most boys are so stupid they wouldn't wanna marry a girl who wants to keep her last name, maybe I'd hafta marry another girl, but I never dreamt I'd start having those kinds of feelings about my best friend."

"Speak of the Devil. I've been thinking much the same things about you, but I didn't have the guts to tell you. I always assumed I'd get a husband once I was old enough, not that I'd start to get a crush on my very best friend."

They look at one another awkwardly and nervously for a couple of very long minutes, not entirely sure what to do or say next.

Girl finally breaks the silence. "I don't think anyone will suspect anything funny if we go on a date. No one thinks anything when girls go out socially or live together."

"What exactly do you do on a date? I know what you can do, but how is it different to go out to eat or the movies as friends versus a date?"

"We have better things to do with our time than go on dates. You're going back to school soon, and I have to do what I can to help with getting money. How would it be if this was just our special little secret at first? Ours is the love that dare not speak its name."

Propelled by adrenaline, her heart racing, Girl walks over to Ernestine as "Old Friends" is playing, puts her shaking arms around her, and kisses her. Ernestine smiles a nervous smile at her and kisses her back. Barely aware of what they're doing, they walk over to their mattress and start making out as "Bookends," the last track on side one, starts. Ernestine involuntarily gasps when she feels Girl's hand under her blouse. *So this is why Lenore said it felt so good to kiss, touch, and be touched when you're with someone you really care about,* she thinks as the needle automatically lifts off the last groove when neither of them gets up to flip it over.

"Oh, Girl," she breathes.

"Deirdre. My name is Deirdre to you from now on. It ain't my legal name yet, but it'll be the special name between the two of us before I go official with it."

Ernestine kisses her. "Deirdre. I'll never call you Girl again. You're my grownup lover Deirdre now."

***

"Can I ask you a kinda personal question, Lenore?" Girl asks the second week of September. "Ernestine wanted to ask this too, but she's at school now, and would feel strange asking the woman who's married to her brother."

"How personal is this question?" Lenore asks as she finishes nursing Irene and puts her in her highchair.

"Well, I was kinda wondering if you could tell me what an orgasm feels like, since I think I mighta had one, but I ain't sure if that's what it really was."

Lenore starts choking on her chicken salad. "What! I didn't even know you had a boyfriend! Where did you meet this guy, and how long has it been going on? I never pegged you as the type to start getting that serious with a guy you don't know very well!"

"I don't have a boyfriend," she says honestly. "I was kinda fooling around with this person a bunch of times the last two weeks, and wanted to know if it feels the way I thought it might."

"What was this, a one-night stand? A guy you just met and immediately started making out with? You haven't gone all the way yet, have you?"

"That depends on what you define as all the way."

"Always the ones you least suspect. I know there are other ways to get ecstasy besides intercourse, but doesn't everyone view intercourse as going all the way?"

"I can't have intercourse with this person. It's physically impossible."

"Not physically possible? Is this guy defective below the belt, or is there something wrong with you?"

"You have to promise not to tell. You're a real swell person who doesn't go around squealing other people's secrets, and you're pretty open-minded. You lived with Allen and had relations with him before marriage, so you know there ain't only one socially-sanctioned way to love a person."

"Does anyone else know you have a boyfriend, or a guy you're fooling around with?"

"You have to promise no matter what I tell you, you won't turn me in to the authorities or think I'm mentally ill. This is very confidential, classified information I'm about to share with you."

"Well, the longer you drag out not telling me, the worse I'm gonna assume it is. What exactly is the story between you and this guy, whoever he is?"

"That's just it. It's not a guy. It's another girl."

Lenore starts choking on her food again.

"Well, I'm sure you knew such a thing existed. There are a bunch of bars and clubs for adults who prefer their own kind right here in the Village, in case you were unaware."

"You found another girl who wants to be your girlfriend? When, how, and where did this happen? Would I happen to know this other girl?"

"You also have to promise not to tell anyone that bit of information either. It's Ernestine."

Lenore begins choking for the third time.

"Neither of us planned or expected it. You know how sometimes you can be just really good friends, and one day you realize your relationship's heading towards more than friendship, or that a romantic relationship is the next logical step. The best relationships start out as friendship, since you have that history of seeing and relating to each other as more than just someone to fool around with. You and Allen was just friends for three years even though you both secretly wanted more."

"Were you drinking or on drugs when this happened?"

"No, perfectly sober. We were listening to *Bookends* and talking about how we hoped we'd also be friends even when we're seventy, just like it says in onea the songs. We both started confessing about how we've kinda fallen for each other, and then I made the first move. One thing sorta led to the other, and we went to third base that night. We can't go to traditional home base since we're both girls. How does it feel when you reach climax? I feel all warm and fuzzy, have a tingly feeling, and make involuntary noises. Not that either of us expects the other to be a grade A lover, since we're sixteen-year-old virgins. Do you think we should still be considered virgins if we only ever make love to another woman? We're doing something sexual, even if there's no penetration."

Lenore struggles to compose herself and come up with somewhat of a coherent answer, in spite of her massive shock at the things Girl is telling her. "You don't experience a sense of ecstasy the same way every time, though once you learn your usual reactions, you have a good sense of if you're having it. Sometimes you laugh hysterically, scream, breathe heavily, thrash your body around, make involuntary noises, and even cry. You kinda feel a deep sense of pressure building up, and then it gets released. Believe me, you can tell when you're letting that build-up of tension out. Usually, if you're just getting a tingly feeling, it's only an early stage of getting turned on."

"Oh, so I probably have experienced it. I'm glad I can ask you about this stuff. You certainly can't read about it in decent books or magazines, though there ain't no more Comstock Act to prevent the distribution of educational materials. I'll pass that along to Ernestine. Would you consider us virgins? We've done things that probably got us off, though we'll never be able to have actual intercourse."

"Allen always considered me a pure virgin. I wasn't a virgin by the standard, traditional, physical definition, but I never voluntarily did that. Allen knew those things were done to me against my will, and that when I first made love with him, it was my first real time. He's the only man I've ever done anything with, and he didn't think I was used merchandise or a fallen woman. I had my first orgasm with him through manual sex, not intercourse, which we did for the first time the night before we first had intercourse. That was definitely real to me, not something I'd dismiss as practice or meaningless just 'cause it wasn't intercourse. If you don't consider yourself a virgin anymore, either physically or emotionally, I guess you're not. I felt so different the day after our first time. It was like a great, invisible change had taken place within me, like I'd been inducted into the secret, mysterious world of the grownups and now shared the same secret knowledge of sex they did."

"That's a nice way of putting it. Hey, at least we won't have to worry about birth control pills or rubbers. May I have something to eat?"

Lenore points to the refrigerator. "We've got egg salad, stuffed tomatoes, and lunchmeat."

Girl helps herself to a salami sandwich and a stuffed tomato. "So, what did you think of the protests against the Miss America Pageant on Saturday? I say more power to the protestors."

"Whatever I think is irrelevant, since I'm just a housewife and mother. Not that I plan to do this forever, just until all our eventual kids are old enough for school. Allen likes the idea of going out to work while I'm at home taking care of Irene, doing housework, and cooking him supper. He likes having a Mrs. Troy too, though he thinks it's sexist for me to be called Mrs. Allen Troy, like I'm his possession and not my own person. Mrs. Woman's Name traditionally is only for divorcées or widows, but those conventions originated in an era when women couldn't vote and literally were their husbands' and fathers' property."

"You ain't a typical housewife. You're certainly not June Cleaver or Donna Reed. You're more like a hippie housewife, even if you didn't get as deep into it as Emeline. You know what they say about those quiet ones. The protest was long overdue. There was already a protest in July against *The New York Times* for its sexist Help Wanted ads, and there was a ruling that said it's against the Civil Rights Act to put separate ads for men and women. What does having indoor versus outdoor plumbing have to do with your qualifications for a job? They'd better obey the ruling and change the Help Wanted ads soon. Even the progressive *Village Voice* puts the ads in different categories, which is inexcusable."

"Allen complained about that too. He thought somea the jobs under 'Help Wanted—Female' sounded more interesting than the jobs meant only for guys. I don't think he'd agree with the idea of entering Irene in any beauty pageants, though he knows she's a beautiful little girl."

"It's revolting how they announce the measurements of the contestants and how the applicants have to fill out a questionnaire detailing their ancestry to prove they're a hundred percent white. I wouldn't care if I found out I had Negro, Indian, or Oriental blood. I consider myself Irish-American because that's what I know I am. It don't matter what an obscure, long-distant ancestor mighta been or done. I also don't like the title Miss. I know it's my proper title since I'm sixteen and unmarried, but if you're past the age of eighteen, it's silly to use Miss. It ain't accurate to go by Mrs. if you ain't married, but Miss is childish. I wish they had a title for women that didn't denote their marital status and presumed age, the way men have the default title Mr."

"I never really thought about that. I suppose you're right. Maybe someday someone will come up with a title for women between girlhood and marriage, women who are older but not married, or women who are married but haven't changed their names. The other languages I know of don't have an in-between title for women either. You're either a Miss or a Mrs., but that isn't accurate in today's world."

"I wish I could throw my bra into a garbage can. It's too bad they were forbidden from burning the symbols of our enslavement. I hate wearing a bra, and I'll never wear makeup if I can help it. Don't get me started on high heels and bikinis. I'm glad you and Allen ain't intending to teach Irene her only ambitions in life should be marriage and motherhood, and that she's somehow dangerous and unwomanly if she wants to go to college and have a career. I'm glad so many women are finally waking up and realizing we have a voice, that we don't gotta smile, keep sweet, be pretty, and let men make all our decisions for us."

Lenore smiles at her. "Since you trusted me with your secret, I'll trust you with my own secret. I'm already thinking of having another baby. I haven't told Allen yet, but I think I'll save it for the end of the year. It'll put them about two years apart in age. I can't imagine he'd be averse to the idea of having a second child."

"I bet he won't!" Girl grins. "It's a scary world to bring a new baby into, but what better way to fight back, help in creating a more positive future, and celebrate creation over killing?"

***

Throughout the autumn, more tumultuous events have included a violent crushing of a student-led protest in Mexico City, an ongoing teachers' strike in the city, and the Summer Olympics, held in October this year. Thirty-two nations boycotted the games due to South Africa's participation, and during the course of the games, two Black athletes who won medals in the 200-meter dash gave a Black Power salute while the national anthem played at their medal ceremony. Now perhaps the most significant news of the year is unfolding, as Ernestine and her friends are gathered around the van Niftriks' television on election night, November 5. Ultimately, Mr. and Mrs. van Niftrik, Allen, Lenore, Mr. and Mrs. Doyle, and Lucine threw their support behind George McGovern. He didn't win the nomination in Chicago, so they were forced to vote for Hubert Humphrey as the lesser of two evils.

"I don't think that racist George Wallace stands a snowball's chance in Hell of winning." Ernestine gives a secret look to Girl. "Not that third-party candidates stand much of a chance of winning in this rigged two-party system."

"It better not be that clown Nixon," Girl says. "He has a negative aura. I don't like him, besides the fact that he's a Republican."

"He just might," Betsy says in disgust. "His campaign was all about bringing law and order back to America, and that appealed to people who must be sick and tired of all the riots and protests of the past couple of years, never mind that there was a subtle hint of racism about that 'law and order' mantra."

"He doesn't like Chief Justice Warren," Mrs. van Niftrik says. "I don't know why so many people are so deathly afraid of progressive policies, like separation of church and state, civil rights, and civil liberties. Arthur and I are very proud members of the ACLU, since we were seventeen. We're cringing at the thought of Nixon getting elected and appointing conservative, reactionary Supreme Court justices."

Throughout the night, as election returns continue coming in, the results are too close to call. The popular vote seems like a dead heat, though Nixon is leading in the Electoral College. Girl rants about how the Electoral College is an unfair system that ought to be abolished, while Mr. van Niftrik makes strawberry crêpes with powdered sugar and maple syrup.

"I wish they had elections on weekends," Betsy says. "Then I could stay up all night to wait for all the returns to come in and the election to be declared. It's not as exciting to be told in the morning who won. I want to stay till all the votes are tabulated and witness the historic calling of an election right when it happens."

"You'll be away at college when we have our next election," Mrs. van Niftrik says. "You'll still be a year away from being old enough to vote, but you'll be old enough by then to stay up all night and wait for all the returns to come in."

Betsy has to go to bed at 11:00, and Girl, Ernestine, Boy, and Julie feel it's only polite to go across the hall to their own quarters at that point. Infant and Baby have already fallen asleep and have to be gently nudged awake for the short trip across the hall. Ernestine and Girl can hardly sleep at all, so nervous about who's going to win the election. Every time they awaken during the night, they're newly disappointed it's still dark outside and that none of the three networks will be back on the air. By the time morning finally breaks, they're exhausted from hardly having slept a wink.

Ernestine throws on some clothes and gobbles down a piece of stale toast with leftover bacon, while Girl munches on dry cereal. As soon as they're finished eating, they go back across the hall. Betsy is perched on a high stool by the kitchen counter, eating scrambled eggs and drinking orange juice, while the television is on.

"Disgusting," Mr. van Niftrik says as he shuts his briefcase. "That damn fool Nixon won. At least Humphrey won our state."

"The key states were Ohio, California, and Illinois," Mrs. van Niftrik says. "Wallace only carried a couple of states in the Deep

South, to absolutely no one's surprise."

"That's not fair," Girl protests. "Nixon supports the war. If he wants to continue it for four more years, that means my brother could be drafted when he turns eighteen. And he likes anti-progress policies."

"The majority spoke, or at least the majority of the people who cared enough to vote," Betsy says. "Now we have to wait four years for another election. I wish we had the option of overthrowing elected leaders who don't do a good job or whose policies are bad for the people."

"I hate Republicans. They're bad for the poor, the working-class, women, and minorities. People don't vote for them 'cause they want change. They vote for them 'cause they wanna preserve the good old boys' status quo and are scared 'cause they think the underclasses and repressed groups like women and Negroes are acting uppity by demanding more rights and protesting against things that need protesting."

"It's not fair we'll only be twenty at the next election and not old enough to vote him out," Ernestine says. "Why are our boys old enough to die at eighteen, but neither guys or girls can vote for three more years?"

"I bet Nixon wouldn't have been elected if they'd let eighteen-year-olds vote," Betsy says. "There would've been a huge landslide for Humphrey."

"It could always be worse," Mrs. van Niftrik says. "We get to vote every four years, instead of having a monarch or dictator for life. And there are more radical people than Nixon. We'll have to grin and bear it, the same way we slowly made it through eight years of Eisenhower. At least Eisenhower was a great general, in spite of being a lousy president. He did give a great Farewell Address, warning us against the dangers of the military-industrial complex. Maybe Nixon will surprise us like that too."

***

New Year's Eve is a Tuesday this year. The final day of the year can't come a moment too soon, Allen and Lenore think as they watch the big aluminum ball dropping in Times Square on CBS. Irene is sound asleep on the sofa bed as her parents bid good riddance to 1968 and welcome in 1969. Allen and Lenore envy her for being too young to remember or be aware of what a tumultuous year she's just lived through. She only cares about being fed and clothed, paid attention to, bathed, having her diaper changed, and having interesting things to play with. Only later, when she's older, will she understand what it meant to live through those days, the same way Allen didn't understand till he was older what it meant to have been born on D-Day. For all she's aware of, this was a perfectly normal, safe, predictable year, not the year the world went up in flames.

"I have something I've been meaning to talk to you about, Allen," Lenore says after they've relocated to their room.

He pulls off his clothes and throws them in the hamper. "Should I be worried?"

"I hope not. It's just that I've been thinking a lot about trying for a second child—that is, if you want a second child this soon."

He sits on the bed and pulls her onto his lap. "Are you serious? You'd wanna bring another child into this crazy world? Can't we wait a little while, until things simmer down a bit?"

"That's the whole point. Creation is the opposite of killing. Not only that, it's older than the act of killing. What better way to celebrate life than to create a new one? It's our way of protesting all the bad things in the world, saying we're better than that, that we're not afraid to carry on and create life in the face of death."

He sits and thinks about it. "I know you're right, but it's scary to think about. I was born during a war, and Irene was born during two wars, the Vietnam War and the Six-Day War. When does it end?"

"It'll end when everyone decides they love life more than death. World peace is probably a long way off, but we can't stop everything while we wait for the impossible. Besides, two years between siblings is the perfect age difference."

"Irene would love a little sister." Allen already presumes their second child will be yet another girl in his life. "I never wanted an only child. You're a really good mommy, Lenore. Having two kids would make you even better, and it's best to have all your kids when you're young."

"So what's your answer? You can think about it for as long as you want to. I'll keep using my diaphragm till you're ready to have another baby." Lenore makes a face at it as she pulls the nightstand drawer open. "I miss birth control pills, but I can't take them when I'm nursing."

"Get rid of that damn thing. You won't be needing it for awhile. Are you ready to try getting lucky tonight, Mrs. Troy?"

Lenore pushes the drawer shut and crawls over to Allen. "I love you."

"Enough talk," he says, pulling her on top of him. "We've got a new life to work on creating. Let me help you outta your clothes."

During their three couplings that night, Lenore feels she's got the best husband in the world. After everything Allen has already done for her, now he's also her partner in defiance against the culture of death and violence that reigned this past year.

Chapter 38: The Sacrifice of Adicia

"Mother's been in a worse mood than usual lately," Adicia says when she, her sisters, and their friends are visiting Allen and Lenore the weekend before St. Patrick's Day 1969. "She's been ranting about how she might get thrown back in prison if she doesn't pay off the remainder of the five thousand bucks she embezzled by August."

"How much has she paid back?" Ernestine gives Girl one of their secret looks. "I didn't know she was given a deadline."

"She didn't pay back a single penny for the first three years she was outta jail. She got visited by a cop right before that big blackout, and was told all her paychecks would be garnished till it was paid back, since she wasn't doing it on her own. When was the blackout, November '65?"

"November ninth," Julie remembers. "That was a pretty scary night, though we had a really pretty full Moon in a cloudless sky to make us not feel so scared and alone. I knew my mommy, wherever she is now, was looking up at that same Moon. It makes me a little less sad to know we're looking at the same Moon, even if we haven't been together since I was four and a half."

Twenty-one-month-old Irene toddles around the living room as Lenore sets a plate of homemade chocolate chip cookies on the coffeetable. Adicia and Ernestine smile at their niece, remembering fondly when Justine was that small and just learning how to talk. It's really swell to have a little person in their family again and the chance to have that experience of watching a baby grow up and become her own person. Justine is just as smitten with her niece, never having had that experience since she's the baby of the family. She experienced it a little bit with Caroline, but it wasn't the same as watching a family member grow up.

"Allen and I have important news," Lenore says as she sits down. "Do you want to tell them, or should I?"

"Go ahead and tell them, sweetheart." Allen smiles at her adoringly.

Lenore looks out at the girls. "Our family is growing again. Allen and I are expecting our second child. It's due in October."

"Oh, boy!" Adicia says. "Can we watch it be born again?"

"Do you think it's another girl?" Baby asks.

"Are you using the same midwife?" Girl asks.

"Are you doing it at home again?" Ernestine asks.

"Will Emeline come down again to help you when you give birth?" Justine asks.

"Do you have any names picked out?" Infant asks.

"One question at a time," Lenore tells them patiently. "We're having another home delivery, and using Veronica Zoravkov again. I don't know if you can come down again and watch, since babies don't come on a predictable schedule. I'd like to have Emeline here, but since it's due in the middle of her semester, she won't be able to come unless it happens on a weekend."

"Lenore hasn't thought about names yet," Allen says. "Since our family runs to girls, I half-expect a new addition to my harem instead of a little boy. If it's another girl, Lenore will get to name her again. You'll have to wait till it's born to find out the name, and so will I."

"Does this mean you can't nurse Irene anymore, since you're pregnant?" Girl asks.

"Oh, no, I'm still able to nurse her. Your milk doesn't dry up just 'cause you're expecting, if you've regularly been nursing," Lenore explains.

"It's really far-out you've nursed Irene for this long," Ernestine says. "I don't think any of us got bottles past a year and a half, if that."

"Some women around the world nurse till their kids are four or five," Girl says. "Of course, those women don't live in cultures where breasts are sexualized instead of recognized as a source of life-giving food for babies and young children. I hate how women are objectified in this sick culture of ours."

"I hope Mother never sees Irene or your future baby," Adicia says. "She's such a horrible mother; I can only imagine what a rotten grandma she'd be. She wasn't very grandmotherly to Giovanni when we had him."

"She's in trouble with the law again," Justine says. "She's got five months left to pay back everything she embezzled, or she's going back to jail. They said enough time has gone by and that it's time to step it up."

"She's had almost seven years to pay that dough back, and she didn't obey any of her parole conditions," Ernestine says. "I have no idea how much money they've garnished from her paltry paychecks since they finally got wise to her little game."

"She didn't work for the six months Carlos was on trial," Adicia says.

"So the worst that could happen is she goes back to jail," Girl says. "Good riddance. At least your dad makes money. He's a crummy parent too, but he seems to have some functioning brain cells."

"How do you not obey your parole conditions and think the courts won't notice?" Julie asks. "Is she that much of a drug addict?"

"She thought the city has enough problems with murders, robberies, and major drug crimes that they wouldn't bother keeping up with a petty criminal whose only convicted crime was embezzlement," Ernestine says. "Part of her release conditions included finding and keeping steady employment, getting off drugs, and making an effort to be a mother to her children."

"Don't tell me her way of coming up with the remaining money is more embezzlement," Girl says. "That's like robbing Peter to pay Paul."

"She's always sold drugs on the side," Adicia says. "Minimum wage is under a buck and a half, and she works six days a week, ten or twelve hours a day, with holidays off. That's probably enough to have paid about half of it back by now, if she'd been steadily working all that time. What has she been doing that they're threatening her with sending her back to jail for not paying enough back?"

"Dad makes minimum wage. Mother doesn't always take jobs that pay that much," Ernestine says. "And she's always quitting or getting fired. She's never steadily worked a job in her whole working life, unlike Dad, who's so proud of his long record at the box-making factory. He cares when minimum wage is raised, and he's never gotten drunk or high on the job. He has a very good work record and ethic, even if he is a crummy parent."

"They wanna make an example of her," Girl says. "Governor Rockefeller is so tough on crime. Sure she ain't a murderer, but she did embezzle a lot of money. Cops, judges, and politicians usually hate the poor. They know she can't pay it back at the same rate a wealthier person could, so they're punishing her. Not that I care if that crazy woman spends the rest of her life rotting in jail, but it's how the system works."

"I almost wish she'd go back to jail. Dad barely pays attention to us, Tommy is less annoying when Mother isn't around to spoil him off his rocker, and we could go back to spending more time with Mrs. Doyle," Adicia says. "She's been more of a mother to us than our own mother has ever been."

"She sounds like a swell lady," Baby says. "I wish I could have a real mother or substitute mother. Mrs. van Niftrik is great, but it ain't the same as having a real mother or mother substitute right there at home all the time. She's Betsy's mother, not ours."

"I wish I could visit yous guys, but I hated Hell's Kitchen when I lived there," Julie says. "You told me Mrs. Doyle always makes milk and cookies for you. My mommy used to do that too. She'd make milk and cookies for me and all the other neighborhood kids. She made really yummy cookies. My favorites were chocolate chip, chocolate peanut butter, and butterscotch chip. She also made really yummy brownies and bar cookies."

"Maybe sometime I can ask her to make extras for you," Adicia says.

"In the meantime, you can enjoy Lenore's cookies," Allen says. "If we ever leave the city, I'm thinking of opening our own bakery. Lenore can help me run the business and sell her delicious baked goods. I might've worked at a bakery for so many years, but her baked goods taste better than mine."

"You'd actually leave us?" Justine asks sadly.

"There are no plans to leave yet, but we wanna move Upstate eventually. The city's no place to raise kids. Don't worry, you've still got us for now. I don't know what might happen to you if I left too early and you only had our rotten parents for help and support."

***

Adicia finally got her first bra in December, the same month she started shaving, though she hasn't gotten her first menstrual period yet at going on fifteen. She's very self-conscious to be one of the smallest girls in ninth grade, made even worse by the fact that she looks young for her age in addition to having a small bustline. In comparison, her friend Marjani already has a prominent bustline and has been menstruating since twelve and a half. Boys don't look at Adicia the way they look at the other high school girls, who wear miniskirts, makeup, nailpolish, perfume, and high heels. Emeline, at just turned twenty-one, has never kissed a boy or gone on a date, in spite of being surrounded by hippies who are into free love, but it's Emeline's choice not to do such personal things with any old person. Adicia doesn't even get any offers to go out on a date.

"The worst part is my own mother is looking at my body lately and commenting on it," she tells Marjani as they sit on Marjani's bed after school the first week of June. "She's making comments about it, like comparing me to a horse or a piece of meat in how I'm developing, how big my breasts are, how long my legs are, and how wide my hips are. I hope she's not already thinking of trading me off to a gross much-older husband."

"That's really weird for a mother to say that stuff about her own daughter. It's hard enough to be a teenage girl without having extra criticism and pressure from your own mother."

"I don't think I'd wanna wear miniskirts and high heels even if I had longer legs and wider hips. I'd feel self-conscious, like all the guys were looking at my body and not me. Maybe I'm just too modest and old-fashioned."

"You don't wanna look like those girls. I'm sure mosta 'em are dressing like that only to get the attention of boys, not to show off their bodies 'cause they're proud of how good they look and so liberated they feel comfortable in their own skins. Like Dr. King said, there will one day be a world where we're judged by the content of our character, not by our skin color, our sex, how developed our bodies are, or what we wear. People should be people, not stereotypes."

"I don't know if I'll ever have a boyfriend when I'm old enough, or even a baby if I get married. I'll be fifteen next month and have never menstruated. That's pretty old to not have done it."

"It'll come when it's good and ready, I'm sure. It's not like you're eighteen. Then it'd be pretty odd to never have had it. Remember that filmstrip we saw in eighth grade? It said it's normal for girls to mature at different rates. Some girls look like miniature women at ten years old, while others are only starting to get more mature bodies at our age. I have a cousin in The Bronx who didn't need a bra till she was fifteen, and she made up for lost time by sprouting huge breasts."

"My friend Julie was a slow developer too, but she's got bigger breasts than me, and she's been menstruating for a whole year. I look younger than my stupid thirteen-year-old little brother Tommy. I'm supposed to be his older sister, not his little sister."

"I'd feel murderous if Zuberi was the type of little brother you describe Tommy as. I get that your mom was happy to finally have a boy again after so many girls, if she thinks boys are better than girls, but her spoiling of him is almost comical. He's either gonna grow up to be the smuggest, most entitled brat ever, or he's gonna get beat up by guys who are bigger and stronger than he is if he wanders into the wrong part of town or tries his spoilt prince song and dance on people who don't think he's hot stuff just for existing and being a boy."

"His latest thing is so annoying. Some British rock group put out a double album last month that just so happens to be called *Tommy*, and now he's going on about how he has a whole double album named after himself. As though they even know that little parasite exists. My mother's encouraging him. It might be a bit more tolerable if he didn't have such a bratty voice. It's like she taught him how to talk in such an annoying voice from the time he first began uttering words as a baby."

"How again did Tommy end up a spoilt, entitled little prince, and your mom and dad didn't spoil their two older sons off their rockers?"

"Carlos and Allen were just extra money sources to them. They weren't born after five girls, four of us in a row. My mom was more upset over losing onea her additional sources of income when Carlos got paralyzed than she was over him becoming a cripple. She and my dad only stayed with him for his trial 'cause they thought it'd look bad if they didn't go. It's all about them, not their own children. Real parents are supposed to love their kids more than anything."

"Does Prince Tommy know the title character in that double album is blind, deaf, and dumb? I don't think he'd be that happy about sharing the same name if he knew that key bit of information."

"My sister Ernestine has that album. She played it for me last time I came over. The Who, that's the name of the band. They've been popular in England for about four years, but they didn't catch on here till more recently. They played at that music festival in Monterey in '67. The title character later gets his senses back and becomes a messiah figure, but he reverts to his former state when he sees his followers haven't gotten his message. Ernestine said the message is supposed to be about people who have all their senses but who are blind, deaf, and dumb in their souls. I'll have to take her word for it, since I don't listen to music for such deep, serious meanings."

"Sounds just like your parents and that spoilt little brother of yours. It reminds me of the line 'There are none so blind as those who will not see.' You know you're better than those people."

"The story on the album gets weirder, though. I musta been too dumb to get this on my own, but Ernestine told me the fictional Tommy isn't really missing all those senses. He shut down after he saw his parents murder his mother's lover. He can see his reflection in the mirror. After really awful events, some people are unable to speak, see, or hear. Our friend Girl used a fancy word for it. Psycho-something."

"Like a hypochondriac? That's someone who's always convinced he's dying or there's something wrong with him, though he's perfectly healthy. I have an uncle in Queens like that."

"Psychosomatic, that was the word. Tommy's a psychosomatic mute. There was a really disturbing book my sister Emeline read a few years ago that also featured a psychosomatic mute. It was called *The Painted Bird*. I vividly remember the stuff she told me about it. The people in that book make my parents almost look like saints. Maybe they got part of the idea for their album from this book."

"Emeline sounds really groovy. She's read about so much stuff and remembers most of it, and she's open to just about everything, even if it's from a different culture or religion. She'll make an awesome librarian someday. Me, I'd like to go to college too, though not Vassar. Maybe the same school Subira's going to in the fall. Howard University in Washington, D.C. It's a historically Black college, which my family likes. Not that we can't get a great education at a place like Radcliffe or Smith, but it's nice to have the opportunity to be in a majority. It's the same deal with primarily Jewish or Catholic colleges. It's not about only wanting to associate with my own kind, but I'd feel more comfortable in an educational setting where I could be sure I wasn't being held down by white teachers who have nothing in common with where I come from."

"I wish I came from a special group like you. I'm just a run of the mill American who's half-French and half-Belgian. Nobody cares about that, not like they care about Irish- or Italian-Americans, Indians, Chinese-Americans, or Black people. I'm not even a special religion like Catholic or Jewish. I'm just some type of Protestant."

"You're Huguenot on your dad's side. That's pretty cool to have in your ancestry. The people who admit you to colleges might like to hear about that in the essay you have to write. It's never too early to start thinking about college, my parents say. Education is one of the tools my people need to use to empower ourselves and get ahead."

"I don't know if my parents will let me graduate high school."

"They can't force you to drop out. You could live with your brother Allen if they tried that stunt on you. They're nuts regardless for thinking a girl in this day and age is supposed to drop outta school and marry an older guy her parents picked for her, and never make a living to support her family. What use would I be to a future husband if I didn't have an education and a job? Sure I might do the housewife thing when my future kids are little, but no self-respecting Black man should be interested in a woman who wants to do jack all day while he's the only one working. What if, God forbid, my future husband died young or became too disabled to work like your brother Carlos? I'd need an education and job skills to support the family in his stead."

"I know you're right, but my parents are the ones who need to hear it."

"Your parents are willfully blind, deaf, and dumb if they're ignoring all the social and cultural upheavals that've been taking place over this decade. They're the biggest idiots I've ever heard of. I'm going to laugh when you tell me someday about how they've been left all alone because all their kids deserted them and they couldn't get in touch with modern realities."

***

Mrs. Troy is wringing her hands and pacing back and forth on a hot day in mid-August when she sees Adicia coming in. Her eyes light up, and she smiles at her hated penultimate daughter. Adicia gets a very bad feeling in her stomach and already dreads coming home from a visit to Marjani.

"I know how much you like book learning, Adicia. How would you like to graduate high school instead of dropping out to get married at sixteen the way your father and I was planning?"

"You and Dad would let me finish school instead of making me marry an old guy and drop out? What's the catch?"

"You're developing a pretty pair of breasts and promising womanly hips. I'm sure any man would love to be the first to touch them."

Adicia wants to vomit, but continues engaging her mother, afraid of what might happen if she runs out. "How come you're so interested in my body? Isn't it a little strange for a mother to comment on her teenage daughter's body?'"

"Your father used to always comment on the size of your brothers' male organs when they was in diapers." Mrs. Troy ignores Adicia's disgusted look and blazes on. "I'm as baffled as anyone by this sudden, unexpected deadline my parole officer threw at me. Must be wanting to make an example of me to show New Yorkers crime don't pay, though I sure as hell didn't commit no murders, arson, or larceny like Carlos."

"Maybe he's also upset you didn't pay back anything in the first three years you were outta prison."

"How should I have known he'd catch up to me eventually! This city's a teeming cesspool of crime and degeneracy, particularly around Times Square. God knows, there shoulda been plenty of murders and other real crimes for the so-called justice system to concern 'emselves with instead of a petty thief."

"So what does being allowed to finish high school have to do with you having to pay back the resta the money or go back to jail?"

"There's a man I met while buying cocaine the other day. We got to swapping stories about our lives while waiting on a ridiculously long line to get to the dealer, and I told him I've got three kids still at home, one of 'em a girl who just turned fifteen last month. His eyes lit up when I told him you've got a promising womanly body and you're an untouched virgin, unlike a lot of other girls your age these days. He loves being a virgin's first lay, and he's got plenty of money from his own drug-dealing operations. He could easily give us the remaining money if you sleep with him. Think about it. I only have about two more weeks left before I'm sent back to jail. You could save our family's whole reputation if you make this sacrifice for us. Remember, you get to graduate high school, and your father and I will make sure to select a nicer husband for you. That man we married Gemma to was an idiot, I realize now. You'll get a man who's much better-looking, with better manners, and who don't live with his parents at pushing forty."

Adicia is ready to vomit, and wishes she could report this to the police. Instead she hears herself asking, "Isn't what you're suggesting prostitution? We could all get in trouble if the cops find out you made me sleep with a man for money. You'd be charged as an accessory to prostitution."

"It ain't a crime if you don't get caught. We all know Carlos's dealings in the world of drugs went much deeper than what the jury convicted him of, but since they couldn't prove it, they gave him a seventh-degree charge for possessing drugs and a fifth-degree charge for selling drugs. Governor Rockefeller woulda thrown the book at us had he known about the drug stash we useta have."

Adicia's mind is racing. She wishes Sarah were there to protect her from this disgrace to motherhood. If Sarah had been her real mother, she never would've sent off her fifteen-year-old daughter to be raped by a grown man, a drug-user, in exchange for money to avoid being sent to jail and as a precondition for being allowed to graduate high school. Mrs. Troy probably doesn't realize the irony of committing a crime to avoid another jail term. Lucine would've protected her too, but she's off on Cape Cod with some of her fellow Hunter students. Emeline likewise can be no help either, since she and some of her hippie friends are at the three-day music festival at Woodstock. No one will be able to get in touch with her until she gets home. She knows without question the Doyles, the van Niftriks, and Allen and Lenore would stand up for her and try to protect her, but they're not her guardians. No one can do anything to protect Adicia from this revolting excuse of a mother she was given. Even if Allen and Lenore tried to seek legal custody of her and Justine, Mrs. Troy would doubtless find a way to prevent it, the same way she destroyed their Christmas and forced them to leave Allen and Lenore.

"Well? I'll never forget it if you do this great favor for me. You don't want your mother to go to jail, do you? I know you wanna complete high school and not hafta get married at sixteen."

Adicia is terrified out of her mind. "What if he gives me a venereal disease or gets me in trouble?"

"I was thinking the exact same thing. I ain't as dumb as you think I am. Your father and I ain't got the money to pay for a doctor to perform an abortion under the table, or to send you off to Europe to have the procedure performed legally and properly in a hospital. Nor do we have the money to treat a venereal disease. Plus, we can't afford such a scandal so soon after the Carlos mess. You'd have no marriage prospects if you was known as a fallen woman."

"Won't I have bad marriage prospects anyway if I'm not a virgin?"

"Well, we won't be marrying you to a young man, so get that silly idea outta your head. It'll be another older guy, like we chose for Gemma and Lucine. Maybe a widower or divorced man, so he won't care as much about not getting a pure wedding-night virgin. Besides, you're doing this to save your family's reputation, not running around with boys like an unbridled slut."

"You want me to sacrifice my virginity so you won't go to jail?"

"You'll get to graduate high school and get a handsome husband with a good job in return when it comes your time for marriage. Don't worry, he'll use rubbers so he won't get you in trouble." Mrs. Troy looks very impatient. "Well, what's your answer? Yes means you want to save your family from disgrace and your mother from jail. No means you're a selfish, silly girl who wants to get above her raising and cares more about herself than her family. Once my paychecks are no longer being garnished, we'll have more money. I'm thinking about moving back to the Lower East Side once we get enough money saved up. I've had it with the gang fights in this neighborhood."

"Does Dad know about this?"

"I'm sure he'll agree with what we did once he finds out. Besides, that dumb frog can't do nothing about it after it's already done. He ain't a pansy like Allen turned into. A poor man has little else besides his good name, and he won't have any good name if his wife goes to prison for the second time, in addition to his oldest son serving life in prison."

Adicia desperately wishes she could jump out of the window and start running to Allen and Lenore, never looking back, but she feels herself mutely nodding. Everything else her mother says after that is one big blur. All she comprehends in her terror-stricken state is that she's going to meet this man on 50th Street at midnight and get into his old blue van. He'll give her a plain brown paper bag containing the remaining three thousand dollars Mrs. Troy owes after he violates her, and will drop her back off in front of the tenement by 6:00 in the morning. If she dares to tell anybody, the whole deal is off. Adicia may tell people after the fact only at her own discretion, but if she values her reputation, she wouldn't dare tell anyone.

Justine stirs awake that night when she feels Adicia getting out of bed. She watches her sister pulling her pajamas off and putting on day clothes. Adicia won't tell her anything except to go back to sleep. In the dark, Justine sees their mother, sitting at the kitchen table smoking cocaine, smiling a creepy smile at Adicia. This must mean Adicia isn't running away, but whatever is going on, it can't be good.

***

Adicia stumbles into the tenement at 5:00 in the morning and throws the bag of cash on the kitchen table. Mrs. Troy, who's getting ready for her job *du jour* at a fabric store in the Garment District, ignores her daughter's tears and continues getting her clothes on. Her only reaction is to open the bag and count out the money after she finishes getting dressed.

"Wonderful. I might notta completed high school, but I know basic math. Thirty hundred-dollar bills equal three thousand bucks." She pulls an extra fifty-dollar bill out of a small envelope. "Oh, how nice. Ethan included a personal note. 'This is for being such a good virgin lay.' You did the right thing by turning over the extra cash to me instead of selfishly keeping it all for yourself. Your work here is done now. Let me figure out how to explain suddenly having three thousand dollars in cash right on the eve of my deadline. Remember, you've earned yourself a high school diploma and a handsome husband with a good job."

Mr. Troy shuts off the alarm clock and heads to the bathroom to shave. When he comes back out to get dressed, he sees his wife putting rubber bands around small piles of cash, while Adicia audibly sobs in bed.

"Where the hell did this cash come from, Dolores? I better not be about to find out you embezzled all over again to avoid another stay in the clink."

"This seventh-born child of ours ain't so worthless, Antoine. I arranged with a new friend of mine for her to sacrifice her virginity in exchange for saving our family's reputation and keeping me from prison. Our deal was that she could finish high school and get a handsome husband with a good job when she's eighteen. Wasn't that mistake Adicia a good, obedient daughter for once in her life?"

Mr. Troy snaps wide awake in spite of the early hour and spits on the floor. "What the hell have you gone and done behind my back, you stupid cow? What if this unknown drug buddy of yours gave her a venereal disease or knocked her up? Those are equal stains on our family's good name, even worse than someone going to prison for a little while for a minor crime!"

"We worked that all out, you dumb frog. He used rubbers to prevent a scandal. Didn't he, Adicia?"

"Yes," she says, her voice muffled by the pillow her face is buried in.

"You see? Adicia herself raised this concern when we was hammering out our little agreement yesterday. She ain't stupid. She knows as well as anyone that a girl will lose her reputation if she becomes pregnant outta wedlock. Besides, we ain't got the kinda money to pay for an abortion, either here or abroad. We don't even have money to waste on antibiotics for a venereal disease. Ain't you proud of us for finding a quick, easy solution to this legal mess I found myself in?"

"The hell I ain't! How the hell are we gonna find this handsome potential husband with a good job if she's no longer a virgin? No man wants an unvirginal bride! We're gonna have such a hard time finding a husband to take her off of our hands now, thanks to you!"

"I told her we'd look among older widowers and divorced men. Someone like that will be less likely to care he's getting damaged merchandise."

"How do you intend to explain to the police and the lawyer how you came into possession of the exact sum of money you have to pay back, only two weeks before the deadline? I bet you anything they think it's drug money."

"Oh, take it easy. I'll find an explanation that don't sound fishy."

"You have risked bringing even more disgrace into this family at a time when it's the last thing we want. Adicia I can excuse for her role in it, since it's her job to obey her parents and do whatever they tell her. You, as her mother and a grownup, shoulda known better than to risk exposing her to all matter of shame and disgrace. What if he'd murdered her instead of only having relations with her? What if he hadn't brought her back to the apartment, but had taken her into white slavery? What if somea his buddies had shown up and had their way with her too, and not bothered to use rubbers? You've got a lot of explaining to do, Dolores, not only to me, your husband of twenty-eight years, but also to your children, the law enforcement officials, your parole officer, and the criminal justice system. Good luck on cooking up explanations that don't make it sound like you aided and abetted an act of prostitution. One crime does not excuse another."

"Ain't a crime if no one gets caught." Mrs. Troy shrugs, utterly unfazed by her husband's tirade. "You'd better to hell not be going to report us to the cops. That would ruin our family's name. As far as we know, I came into a windfall of money from jobs I worked under the table, and I worked hard at saving up all this money. Do I look like I could be an accessory to prostitution? No jury would convict a forty-six-year-old mother of nine, with her firstborn son a cripple and in jail for life."

"I'd convict you in a heartbeat if I was on that jury. Have you looked in the mirror lately, you foolish woman? You've always looked like you just rolled outta a garbage dumpster. You've done a lot of hard living that makes you look a good twenty years older. You ain't a middle-class or rich lady who could get away with appealing to people's sympathy for a mother. Besides, we've only got three children left at home."

Mrs. Troy rolls her eyes. "What's done is done. Now it's time for me to head off to the subway station so I won't be late to work. Thanks again for saving me, Adicia."

Mr. Troy is fuming as he gets dressed and rushes out to catch his subway, hoping the fight didn't make him late for his belovèd job. He totally ignores his sobbing daughter and Tommy's whining for breakfast. The only thing he can think about is how much he wishes he'd never gotten his girlfriend in trouble when they were eighteen and been forced into marrying her and being stuck with her for the rest of his life.

As soon as their father has gone and Tommy has gotten the hint and gone down to the Gómezes for breakfast after dressing, Adicia drags herself out of bed and throws her clothes in the garbage can. Justine trails after her, very worried about what's happened to her, and not having entirely understood what their parents were fighting about loudly enough to wake her up.

"Do you need onea those Modess pads?" Justine asks when she sees her leaving a trail of blood. "You bled on the bed too."

"I'm afraid I'm not finally having my first menses. I'm bleeding for a different reason." Adicia grabs the box and takes the white belt Mrs. Troy bought for her three years ago, still sealed in its original packaging. "I'll figure out how to use this somehow. It'll stop up the bleeding till it goes away."

"Why are you crying so much? What happened to you last night?

Are you dying of cancer?"

"Justine, you know I love you, but right now I want you to please go away. I'll deal with this on my own."

Justine grabs a handful of leftover bacon from the refrigerator and a slice of bread, gobbling them down on her way across the hall. Adicia is relieved when the door shuts, but not for long. Less than ten minutes later, the door opens again and Justine comes skipping back with Mrs. Doyle. She doesn't look either of them in the eyes as they come over to the bed.

"What did your mother do to you?" Mrs. Doyle asks in concern. "Justine says your parents got in a fight about something before they left for work, and it was about something your mother made you do to keep her from going back to jail." She looks at the now-opened box of Modess pads and the packaging for the belt, which Adicia threw on the floor. "If it's what I suspect it might be, it explains why you need that when you claim you're not bleeding from your first menses. I was sick to my stomach when a similar thing happened to my daughter from my first marriage. I couldn't save her from her perverted father, but I hope I can do something to save you from whatever it is that happened to you."

"What does prostitution mean?" Justine asks.

"If it'll get you all off my back, my mother gave me little choice but to give up my virginity to a stranger she met while waiting on line for drugs the other day. He had enough money to pay off the rest of what she embezzled. She woulda gone back to jail at the end of the month if she didn't cough up the rest of the dough. She promised I could graduate high school and get a handsome husband with a good job if I sacrificed myself to save our family's reputation. What else could I have done?"

Mrs. Doyle's mouth hangs open. "A normal mother's instinct is to protect her children, not willingly send them out to be abused! My first daughter would be your age now, and I never would've left her behind after my divorce if I hadn't been legally kept from her! What kind of mother uses the right to finish school and have a decent husband in a forced marriage as leverage against her teenage daughter?"

"What's done is done. I don't wanna stay here. Can I please use your phone to call the van Niftriks so they can tell Ernestine I'm on my way? Our phone got shut off 'cause our parents didn't pay the bill this month."

"Of course you can, sweetheart." Mrs. Doyle hugs her. "I'll make you eggs Benedict with lox and Hollandaise sauce on English muffins. Go over and lie down in my bed, and I'll bring your breakfast to you on a tray."

"You're a swell lady, Mrs. Doyle. I wish you were my mother instead of that evil witch who bore me. You're the next-best thing to my old nanny Sarah."

***

Mrs. van Niftrik comes into Ernestine and her friends' apartment. "I just got a call from Adicia. She sounded hysterical and in tears. What I could make out is that she's on her way over here, and she really wants to see you, Girl, and Julie."

"She's coming to see us instead of Allen and Lenore? She knows we can always go down there after she arrives, and we can all discuss whatever it is together."

"She didn't say much else beyond that she really wanted to see you and your mother did something horrible to her. Your neighbor Mrs. Doyle is taking her to the subway station so she doesn't have to walk there alone, but she'll be arriving here alone. I can't imagine what that vile woman did this time. I haven't heard of many more worst unfit mothers than her."

"I wonder if this has anything to do with how Mrs. Troy was about to go back to prison if she didn't pay back the resta that money," Girl says. "Maybe she forced her to do drug running for her to scare up the money."

"She also asked if Infant could leave and stay in my apartment. Something about not wanting her to hear what happened to her."

"I'm ten," Infant protests. "I'm not a baby anymore."

Girl gives her baby sister the kind of look she rarely does, telling her in as many words to listen to the grownups and leave until they're done with their adult business. Very disappointed, Infant picks up some of her toys and goes across the hall. Mrs. van Niftrik follows her, promising they'll watch something interesting on television and make cookies.

While they wait for Adicia to arrive, Ernestine and Girl discuss the recent riots at the Stonewall Inn in Greenwich Village and what it might mean for the future of the homosexual community. By now Julie has been told about the secret between them, and though she thinks it's a little strange, she doesn't think it's a big deal and hasn't told anyone. Neither of them likes any of the terms they've heard applied to people who love the same sex—homosexual, homophile, gay, lesbian. As far as they're concerned, they're best friends who happened to fall in love. They'd always been interested in boys prior, and just felt their secret relationship is the natural next step of their close relationship. As Girl has often said, people should be people, not stereotypes or labels.

Baby gets the door for Adicia when she knocks at 11:00. She stands back in fear at the sight of her. Her entire face is swollen and red from crying almost nonstop for hours, she hasn't brushed her hair, and she just threw on the first clothes she found, not caring the blouse and skirt don't match at all. Her shoes also aren't appropriate summer shoes.

"What happened?" Ernestine asks in fear.

Adicia goes over to the first mattress she sees, Julie's bed, and lies down. "Could we please shut out the lights? I don't want any light coming in."

Boy pulls the curtains shut.

"What exactly did your mother do to you?" Baby asks.

Adicia bursts into tears again. "I didn't wanna do it, but I had no choice. My mother said I could graduate high school and not have to drop out and marry a gross older guy at sixteen if I saved her from the slammer. Our family would lose even more of its reputation if I didn't do it. My dad was furious when he found out, but he wasn't furious because of what was done to me. It was all about their family reputation, how our mother would explain getting three thousand bucks on the eve of her payback deadline, and how hard it'd be to find me a husband now that I'm damaged merchandise."

"'Damaged merchandise'? I've heard that term before, but I don't know what it means."

"It means my mother made me sacrifice my virginity in exchange for three thousand dollars to keep her from going back to jail, and to ensure I'd get to graduate high school and have a handsome husband with a good job when I'm old enough. I can still see those images and feel that stabbing pain."

Ernestine screams, which brings Mrs. van Niftrik and Infant running. Girl whispers in Mrs. van Niftrik's ear, and Mrs. van Niftrik turns gray.

"What happened?" Infant asks. "Is Adicia gonna be alright?"

"Her mother did something very evil to her," Mrs. van Niftrik tries to explain. "She used her to do something against the law to save herself from going back to prison, something normal mothers who love their children would never dream of doing."

"Is Betsy here?" Adicia asks. "Can she come over too?"

"Betsy's doing back to school shopping uptown with a couple of friends. They're spending the day there and coming back around four. I'm sure she'll want to see you and make sure you're okay after she gets back."

Julie lies next to Adicia and puts her arms around her in the spoon position. "I couldn't get those images and feelings outta my head for ages either after my daddy used to hurt me. Sometimes I still have nightmares about it."

"Now I know how you musta felt," Adicia says. "I'm wearing a sanitary napkin and using that stupid belt, though I'm not bleeding from menstruation."

Mrs. van Niftrik takes Infant by the hand and leads her back across the hall before the conversation becomes any more adult. Infant protests and sends sad looks back at Adicia on her way out.

"Is that all there is to it?" she asks, her face muffled in the pillow. "It didn't feel good at all, not like I was told it's supposed to feel. A cold piece of flesh ripping into you and stabbing at you like a thousand knives, a thirty-five-year-old guy smelling of drugs, alcohol, and garlic forcibly kissing you, his huge, calloused hands poking and probing you. I don't think I can ever do that willingly with a guy. I felt like I was being kicked in the stomach as he stabbed at me with that part of his body. I don't know if I'll ever stop bleeding."

"What the hell kind of crazy woman is your mother?" Girl asks in shock. "I already knew she was crazy from the one time I had the misfortune of meeting her, but now I know she's even crazier. Risking her daughter's reputation just so she can get outta serving the time for something that was her own damn fault? Holding your wish to finish school above your head and promising you a cute husband who earns decent money if you'll take part in an act of prostitution?"

"They won't treat you like a slut if you go to Planned Parenthood," Ernestine says. "I hope he didn't destroy your life by giving you a venereal disease or knocking you up."

"He used rubbers. Mother insisted on it so he wouldn't get me involved in a scandal. We can't afford to pay for an abortion, either an illegal one here or a legal one in Europe, and she doesn't wanna waste any money on drugs to treat a disease either." Adicia lays her head in the pillow and continues sobbing.

Girl tiptoes over to her, sits on the edge of the mattress, and rubs her shoulders. "How about some nice, soft music to help you relax and make you feel better? It don't erase the vile crime your mother perpetrated against you, but it couldn't hurt."

Ernestine pulls a couple of records out of the crates. "I'll play you *Parsley, Sage, Rosemary, and Thyme, Rubber Soul,* and 'Underture' from *Tommy.* Do you have any other musical suggestions, Deirdre?"

Adicia is too submerged in shock and grief to ask why Ernestine has been calling Girl Deirdre for the past year. She wonders what the secret between them is, why they exchange so many funny looks, but doesn't care to find out their secret now of all possible times.

"Folk rock is so soft and soothing. How about Bob Dylan?" Girl asks as she continues rubbing Adicia's shoulders and pushing her hair out of her face.

"No! He has a terrible voice!"

Girl laughs. "Well, I think he'd be the first to acknowledge he'll never win any beauty pageants and that he ain't got the most mellifluous voice out there. It ain't so much about his voice, but the content of his songs. That's why I like the folk stuff so much. It's about real stuff, not boy loves girl lovey-dovey stuff any fool could write or sing."

"I'm sorry. I know he's onea your favorites."

"Don't apologize for anything. You've been through enough. If you don't wanna listen to Dylan, we won't make you. Unlike your mother, we respect what people want and don't force unwanted things on them."

Adicia relaxes onto the mattress and closes her eyes as Ernestine drops the first record onto the turntable. "I like this record. It makes me feel safe and comfortable. Say, can I talk to Lenore on the van Niftriks' phone later?"

"You can do whatever you want, sweetheart," Ernestine promises, hating their mother for having been forced into the role of substitute mother to someone who's only two years and three months her junior.

"In fact, I'll call her now."

Allen is looking through the recent photos he took of Lenore, now in her seventh month of pregnancy, when the phone rings. He hears a distraught Ernestine on the other end and can barely make out a word she's babbling.

"Calm down. I can't help you if I can't understand what you're saying."

"Adicia wants to talk to Lenore. She's very upset over something Mother made her do last night."

"I'm afraid Lenore stepped out for a bit to buy groceries. How urgent is this matter? You know any of you can always talk to me about something important."

"We know, but right now Adicia really needs to talk to Lenore and not you. You wouldn't understand what she wants to talk about."

"Is this girl stuff?"

"Sort of, and sort of not. It's just that Lenore's been through pretty much the same thing Adicia just went through, and she'll be able to personally understand and emphasize."

Allen drops the photos on the floor. "Am I about to hear something that'll make me wanna murder our parents?"

"Probably. Mother used Adicia to avoid going back to jail. She coerced her into sacrificing her virginity in exchange for the remaining three thousand bucks. As you can imagine, she's really broken up about it. Mother promised she could graduate high school and get a better husband than Gemma if she did this."

"I'll kill him. I'll be right over there to get more answers, and then I'll murder the guy who disgraced our little sister."

Ernestine starts to protest, but finds the deafening sound of silence on the other end of the line. Allen has already hung up. She hopes he's not about to do something rash.

Adicia sleeps intermittently as the first record plays, as Julie continues holding her and lying beside her, and Baby watches over her protectively. Girl helps her drink a glass of warm milk brought over by Mrs. van Niftrik, while Ernestine lies on the foot of the mattress and Boy stalks back and forth, muttering about how rotten Mrs. Troy is.

"That song always gives me chills," Girl says as the needle lifts off of side two after "Seven o'Clock News/Silent Night" has finished. "How sad that it's just as eerily pertinent almost three years on. Only now Nixon's the president, and he and many others still think anti-war protestors are the greatest thing working against America today."

"The Monkees' song 'Zor and Zam' always gives me chills too," Ernestine says. "Why can't people grow up and realize war is a waste of time and life? Maybe someday they really will give a war and no one will come."

Girl gets up to change records, pulls *Rubber Soul* out of the paper sleeve, and plops it onto the turntable. In the middle of "Think for Yourself," the door swings open and Allen comes charging in. Ernestine hides her face, hoping he hasn't already done anything he'll regret.

"You didn't bring Lenore?" Adicia asks sadly. "All I wanted was to talk to her on the phone. I didn't need to see you in person."

"She's out with Irene buying groceries, so I came in her place." He sits on the mattress, and Girl automatically gets up. "What the hell kinda mother gets onea her drug buddies to rape her fifteen-year-old daughter in exchange for money and avoiding jail time? She has no maternal instincts whatsoever!"

Adicia sits up and puts her arms around her brother, sobbing against his chest. Allen hugs her back, the first time he's ever hugged any of his sisters. He can't entirely shake his social conditioning about manly versus unmanly behavior, but he's hardly acting like a pansy by comforting someone he loves. He hugs her as tightly as he knows how, to make up for all the years he never did it. Seeing how she only comes up to the middle of his chest makes him painfully aware of how small she is for her age, how much she resembles a little ragdoll even at fifteen. She's not even five feet tall.

"I'm not really sure I believe God exists, but onea the things that makes me think he might exist is that I got the best big brother in the world. Out of all the families in the world, we were chosen for each other."

"You're not *really* gonna kill this guy, are you, Allen?" Ernestine asks. "I don't think Lenore would wanna stay married to a guy with blood on his hands."

"Going to jail for murder is the last thing I want when my second child is gonna come into the world in only two months. Maybe we can contact the cops and have them handle it legally."

"No!" Adicia protests. "That would ruin my reputation! Even if they believed me and didn't think I was a lying slut or poor trash desperate for attention, I'd still have to go through a trial and have my virtue and reputation questioned by his attorneys. Mother would also be mighty mad at me. She might rescind her promise of letting me finish school."

"You know this is the truth, as sexist and classist as it is," Girl says. "Cops and lawyers operate from the assumption that the woman is lying and tryna ruin the guy's reputation, or that she's a slut. It's the whole reason why Julie didn't stay with her mother after her parents divorced, why Lenore ran away instead of pressing charges against her father, and why Mrs. Doyle wasn't able to keep her daughter after her divorce."

"I'm a fallen woman. No decent boy will ever wanna date me, even if I did wanna do that when I'm older. I wanted it to be really special, when I was old enough and with someone I really wanted to marry or was celebrating my wedding night with. I'm ruined merchandise. Mother says she'll look among older widowers and divorced guys so she can find me a husband who won't mind a nonvirginal bride so much."

"Look at me," Allen says. "Lenore wasn't a physical virgin, but I always considered her a pure, sweet, unsullied virgin, because her heart was in one piece. No decent man who's worth marrying will judge you or refuse to be with you because of things done to you against your will. The first time I made love with her was as much her first time as it would've been had she never been raped. Understand?"

"Most guys don't think that way."

"The right guy will think that way, even if you don't meet him right away. The right person is always worth waiting for."

"Yeah, don't let patriarchal society dictate to you what constitutes real virginity," Girl says. "Ernestine and I don't consider ourselves virgins anymore, though we've never had intercourse, since we've gone all the way in the way two girls—" Her voice trails off as she remembers her audience and that only Julie knew about their secret.

Allen stares at them. "Well, that's the second big shock of my day. My seventeen-year-old sister and her best friend are lesbians."

"What's a lesbian?" Baby asks.

"That's not important right now," Ernestine says. "Adicia is our focus now."

"How long has it been going on?" Allen demands. "I know such a thing exists, but I never expected it to happen within my own family!"

"Late August of last year," Girl admits. "I told Lenore about two weeks later, and she's kept our secret. Julie was told a little while ago too, and she's also kept mum. Now all you other people know too."

"My own wife knew and kept that secret from me for almost a year?"

"Don't be mad at Lenore," Ernestine begs. "It shows what a good person she is for keeping confidential secrets and not squealing."

"I guess so," he mutters, too in shock to know how to react.

"You have to keep my secret too, Allen," Adicia begs. "The cops and lawyers must never know. What Mother made me do was an act of prostitution. It'd ruin my reputation if word got around, and I already feel horrible enough at what I was coerced into doing."

"What's his name? At least tell me that much."

"Ethan Pitskowski. He lives on 55th Street. He's thirty-five and has greasy brown hair and beady little light blue eyes. He's about six feet tall."

"That's all the information I need. Don't worry. I'll take care of this rapist, and he'll never mess with you again or feel a need to get drawn into Mother's criminal schemes. Maybe I'm too old-fashioned about some things, but I don't think it's too old-fashioned to wanna teach a lesson to someone who violated my little sister. He's lucky I'm not gonna murder him and dump the body in the Hudson River."

***

Ethan is shutting off the lights in his brownstone, paid for with his drug money, when he hears a window opening and footsteps approaching that night. He wishes he lived in an apartment so other people could hear him screaming when he sees someone carrying a big knife approaching him.

"Are you or are you not Ethan Pitskowski, age thirty-five, who met my worthless mother Dolores Troy several days ago while waiting to buy drugs?"

"Yes I am. What's your deal with me? I've never laid eyes on you before."

"And are you the same Ethan Pitskowski who made a deal with my mother to provide the three thousand bucks she had to cough up by the end of the month or go back to jail, a deal that involved taking the virginity of my fifteen-year-old sister Adicia?"

"She was a great virgin lay. I love deflowering virgins. I gave the girl fifty extra dollars for being such a good virgin lay."

"That 'great virgin lay' of yours is my little sister, who looks more like a twelve-year-old than a fifteen-year-old, who hasn't even gotten her first menstrual period yet or kissed a boy! You and my equally degenerate, heartless, soulless mother had no right to do something so vile to her and leave her so shell-shocked and disgraced! How many other young girls have you destroyed the innocence of in exchange for money?"

"I've lost count. They're only girls. No one cares about them. They know they can't tell the cops, since they'd always take my side. Why do you care so much about this personal matter? She's only your sister, not your daughter or wife."

"Oh, believe me, I'd kill you if you'd raped my wife or our daughter." Allen pushes him towards the davenport. "Take your clothes off and have a seat."

Ethan stares at him in disbelief. "Are you some kind of pervert?"

"You'll find out soon enough what I'm gonna do to you, you worthless excuse for life."

Ethan hesitates, then takes a look at the knife and starts taking off his clothes. Allen paces over to him and starts carving something in his chest. Ethan screams in pain.

"What the hell are you doing to me? Are you mentally ill?"

"No, but everyone will know just how mentally ill you are every time they see you without a shirt. It says 'I rape little girls and use and sell drugs.' That sums you up nicely, doesn't it?"

"If you're gonna do this to me, why did you make me take off my pants? Do you intend to carve things on my legs too?"

"You'll see after I'm done putting this warning on your chest."

Ethan feels faint from the blood loss, which Allen keeps cleaning off with pillows and slipcovers from the davenport. Just when it seems Allen is finally done mutilating him, Ethan feels an intense, sharp pain.

"What the hell are you doing to me now? Get that knife away from there!"

"Did my sweet little sister have a choice when you were raping her in your van last night? Why the hell should I give you a choice?" He continues cutting.

"Are you castrating me?"

"Smart guy. Now everyone will know why you lost those organs when they see the message on your chest. Come to think of it, why don't I take everything off? You certainly don't deserve to keep any of it after the vile thing you did to my sister."

Ethan screams, desperately wishing someone from the street below or in one of the houses next door can hear him.

"Scream all you want. Now you know how terrified my little sister was last night. You'll never rape anyone else again after I'm done with you. You also won't tell the cops if you know what's good for you. Who's gonna believe you?"

"You're evil!"

"You think *I'm* the evil one? I'm the one who cares enough about his family to seek revenge on their behalf, not the one who goes around raping little girls and engaging in acts of prostitution. You got involved with the wrong family if you expected to get off scot-free yet again."

Ethan slumps to the floor screaming as Allen departs, staring at his amputated male organs lying on the floor in a pool of blood. Allen slams the front door and sticks the knife into a plastic bag, which he throws into the large shopping bag he brought. He's still seething with hatred at his mother and Ethan as he gets on the next subway home, but at least now this creep knows some of the fear and terror Adicia felt last night. That seems more of a fitting punishment than going to prison.

About a week after Adicia's innocence was taken from her, she and Justine walk into the Doyles' apartment in the afternoon and find Mrs. Doyle packing a suitcase. Boxes and other suitcases are all over the floor.

"Are you leaving?" Justine asks. "I hope you're not going away because of what our mother did to Adicia last week."

"You're the best neighbor ever!" Adicia adds. "You're more motherly to us than our mother ever has been!"

"We're moving Upstate," Matthew says from the table, where he's eating homemade cinnamon toast.

"I'll go to kindergarten in a nice school!" Caroline says proudly. "Mommy doesn't want me to start school in this awful neighborhood."

"When were you planning to tell us?" Adicia asks.

"I'm sorry," Mrs. Doyle says. "Mr. Doyle and I were thinking about this for a long time. Your parents are horrible people, but that wasn't the reason we wanted to move. My husband makes enough money for us to afford a nicer uptown neighborhood or move out of the city entirely. I only stayed in this blasted neighborhood so long because this is where I lived during my first marriage. I kept clinging to the hope that if I stayed here, I might somehow run into my little girl. Now I know I'll never find her again. I found out my ex-husband died in a fire in June '62. He lived on Avenue A, according to the P.I. My daughter was never found among the bodies, and there have been no reports of her since. She was only eight."

"That's awful!" Justine says. "It was scary enough when Adicia and I thought we were gonna die when our tenement burnt down."

"Our tenement also burnt down in June '62," Adicia says. "We also lived on Avenue A. Do you think it's possible your ex-husband was onea our neighbors and we didn't know it?"

"Well, isn't that something. Your old place and my ex-husband's last residence probably were one and the same. Imagine that."

"So Carlos is in prison for causing the accidental death of a guy who deserved to die. It's too bad you get sent to jail even if you kill a bad guy."

"When are you moving, and to what city?" Justine asks.

"Mr. Doyle and I want to move before the school year starts, so Matthew and Caroline won't have to transfer midway through the year. I'm also expecting again, and we want our third child to be born and grow up in a much nicer place."

"Oh, how exciting! Are you hoping for a boy or a girl?"

"We'll find out in March. I'll send pictures to Allen. If I sent them here, your parents might throw the letter away or rip it up. I'm thinking of doing it the way your sister-in-law Lenore did. I hated being treated like an impersonal cog on an assembly line the three prior times I gave birth, fighting with nurses not to get the shot drying up my milk, and how I can't remember giving birth to any of my children." Mrs. Doyle rushes to pick up her ringing phone.

"I'll get to watch my baby brother or sister being born," Matthew says proudly. "I'm hoping for a brother."

"I want a little sister," Caroline insists.

"Maybe you'll both get what you want if your mommy has twins, one of each," Justine says.

"That would be really nifty!" Matthew says. "I'd get one, and Caroline would get one."

"We liked the midwife Lenore used," Adicia says. "She's the first grownup we ever met who told us to call her by her first name instead of Mrs. She used to be a nurse, but she moved to delivering babies at home. We can ask Lenore for her number if your mother wants to use her too, if she travels out of the city for her clients."

Mrs. Doyle hangs up the phone and goes back to the children. "That was the moving contractor. He wants me to come over to discuss the terms of our agreement so there won't be any surprises for either of us when we load up the moving truck next week. Would you dear girls mind helping me pack more stuff while I'm gone? There's so much to do, and the more we pack up now, the better."

"You'd let us see your personal stuff?" Justine asks.

"You're helping me pack with my permission, not snooping. You can start with my bureau. It's mostly clothes, but there are a few other things, like satchels of potpourri and jewelry. You should find all the boxes labeled with what goes in which. If you get hungry, you can help yourselves to butterscotch chip cookies and graham crackers."

"Sure, we'll help you," Adicia agrees.

After Mrs. Doyle has gone, taking Matthew and Caroline with her,

Adicia and Justine pull open the top drawer of the old mahogany bureau. They try not to look too closely at Mrs. Doyle's bras, stockings, and underwear as they take the clothes out and carefully put them into the suitcase where she's already started putting her clothes. They make sure to leave spares, so she'll still have clothes to wear over the next week.

Justine opens a trunk for the clothes in the second drawer, where Mrs. Doyle keeps her blouses, dresses, and skirts. As Adicia takes out a stack of folded blouses, an envelope falls out, and several pieces of paper fall on the floor.

"Are we allowed to look at that to put it back in the envelope, or should we leave it there till Mrs. Doyle comes back?" Justine asks. "She might think we were snooping if she finds out we saw her papers."

"She gave us permission, remember? Besides, these things happen. We won't read them. It's none of our business what she might have in her personal papers." Adicia leans down to pick up the papers and gasps.

"What's wrong?"

Adicia takes the papers over to Mrs. Doyle's bed and sits down, looking at them again and again. Justine sits next to her and looks over her shoulder.

"This is a birth certificate for someone born May 10, 1954, in the borough of Manhattan, filed May 13 of that same year, to parents named Randolph James Spirnak and Suzanne Mary Bowstead. The birth certificate is for Julie Claire Spirnak. This has to be *our* Julie's birth certificate."

"Are you serious?"

"And this. This is a newspaper clipping from May 20, 1954, from the birth announcements section, saying a Mr. and Mrs. Randolph J. Spirnak of Hell's Kitchen had a daughter named Julie Claire Spirnak on May 10, 1954."

Justine takes the documents and looks them over. "Are you thinking what I'm thinking?"

"Mrs. Doyle is Julie's mother. Why else would she have these papers? All these other papers and documents have Julie's name on them too." Adicia looks into the envelope to see if she missed anything, and several pictures fall out. The little girl in the pictures looks like a smaller version of how Julie looked when she met her in 1962.

"Julie's mother's name was Suzanne too, but it's not an uncommon name for women her age. Her maiden name was Bowstead too."

"I thought I'd heard that name somewhere before. Do you think I heard it that time we asked Julie what her mother's maiden name was?"

"Maybe it was where we heard it before. We saw the list of people who died in the fire. Julie's father's name was Randolph too. I don't think it's a coincidence all three of these names just happen to be shared by two different families."

Adicia starts thinking back over the past seven years she's known Mrs. Doyle and Julie. "Are we that stupid? Why couldn't we put two and two together a long time ago? Mrs. Doyle said part of Caroline's name is another form of her first daughter's name, and Caroline's middle name is Julia. Julie was born on May 10, 1954, and her parents also divorced when her mother discovered her father was abusing her. She used to live in Hell's Kitchen. Her mother used to always make milk, cookies, and brownies for the neighborhood kids. And now we know Mrs. Doyle's first husband was living in our old building at the same time as the fire."

"Have you ever told Mrs. Doyle we have a friend named Julie?"

"Yes, but not her last name. It's a kinda popular, common name, even if it's not as overused as Deborah or Barbara. Mrs. Doyle probably assumed I have a friend who happens to share her name with her first daughter."

"What are we gonna do about this? Should we tell Mrs. Doyle our suspicions? If Julie really is her daughter, it's not right to keep them apart any longer, but Julie's been with Ernestine and the Ryans for seven years. That's tearing up their little family. And if the Doyles are moving Upstate, we'd lose Julie as our friend. Being a penpal isn't the same as visiting her in person regularly."

"I don't wanna lose Julie either, but it's not right to keep this a secret. It was one thing when we didn't know any better, but it's cruel to let Mrs. Doyle move out of the city thinking her firstborn daughter died in a fire seven years ago."

Mrs. Doyle and her children return an hour later, by which time Adicia and Justine have packed most of the clothes and about half the books. The envelope is in the middle of the table while the girls drink milk and eat graham crackers. At first, Mrs. Doyle doesn't notice the

envelope, but rather how beaten-down Adicia looks after what happened last week. She wishes she were able to take both the girls with
her.

"Mrs. Doyle, why do you have my friend Julie's birth certificate?"
Adicia asks.

Mrs. Doyle looks at them strangely. "What?"

"We're sorry, we didn't mean to pry, but when we were taking your
clothes out of the bureau, that envelope fell out, and the papers fell out
too. When I picked them up, I saw the name of onea my best friends.
Your daughter has the exact same birthdate as my friend Julie
Spirnak."

"How can that be? My daughter was presumed dead seven years
ago."

"Our friend Julie Spirnak lives with our sister Ernestine and our
friends the Ryans. Julie and her father moved across the hall from us in
May '62, but I didn't get to meet her right away, since her dad always
kept her locked up. One day I saw her in the hall playing jacks, and we
got to know each other. I was scared to go into her apartment 'cause
there were all these strange, scary noises, her dad sold drugs, and he
looked really scary. He came out into the hall and dragged her back
inside, and Carlos followed them to buy drugs. I heard all these really
scary, strange noises again, and Allen decided to buy drugs after the
door opened again, so he could stall for time while I took Julie to The
Bowery. She's been with Ernestine and the Ryans ever since."

"Her mother's name is Suzanne too," Justine jumps in. "Her
mother used to always give milk and cookies to the local kids, and her
parents were divorced. Her mother was also forbidden to keep her, and
the cops took her deranged dad's side even though he was abusing
her."

"I knew I'd heard your maiden name somewhere before, and now
I think it was when we asked Julie what her mother's maiden name
was. Bowstead isn't a very common surname, I don't think."

"Julie's birthday is also May 10, 1954, and her middle name is
Claire."

"Are you serious?" Mrs. Doyle has had to sit down to prevent
fainting.

"Mommy, are you crying?" Caroline asks. "Mommies and daddies
aren't supposed to cry. It means something is very bad."

"Please don't hate us," Adicia pleads. "We were really stupid to not put two and two together from all the clues out in the open all this time. We're not very good detectives if it took this long to figure it out."

"I'm not a bit mad at you. God knows, you've had bigger things going on in your lives than playing detectives."

"Are you still gonna leave the city if our Julie really is the same as your Julie?" Justine asks. "We don't wanna lose our friend."

"I have to see her with my own two eyes before I can be sure your friend is one and the same as my missing daughter. When can we see her?"

"Probably now," Adicia says. "They usually run around doing odd jobs during the day, but usually at least one of 'em is at home."

"What does your friend look like? Like the little girl in the pictures you saw?"

"She has blue-gray eyes and hair that's either dark blonde or light brown, I can't decide which. It's sorta wavy. She's my same size, at least in terms of her body type. She's taller than me, but she has a small, petite frame."

"Does this mean I have a big sister?" Caroline asks.

"We'll find out very soon, my darling." Mrs. Doyle stands up. "We're going to the subway. If what you say is true, we'll be coming back with six people."

***

Baby and Infant are having a tea party when they hear footsteps in the hall. Justine announces herself and swings the door open.

"Would you like to join our tea party?" Infant asks. "We wanted to have a little party so we wouldn't be too lonely or bored."

"Where is everyone today?" Justine asks.

"Boy's walking dogs, Ernestine has an interview at a record store in Greenwich Village, Girl's parked on a street corner selling crocheted slippers and shrug shawls, and Julie's washing windshields," Baby says. "I guess you're Mrs. Doyle, Matthew, and Caroline."

"Yes, we are," Mrs. Doyle says. "What's your name? You're a very pretty young girl. Brown hair and brown eyes are my favorite features, even if most people think blonde hair and blue eyes are the best."

"Hey, Justine and I have blonde hair and blue eyes," Infant protests.

"I'm Baby Ryan, and that's my little sister Infant. I'm twelve, and she's ten. Our brother Boy's fifteen, and our sister Girl's seventeen."

"Those are really your given names?"

"Girl decided she wanted to be called Deirdre when she's ready to go to college and get grownup jobs, and Ernestine calls her that now, but since we have no birth certificates, those are our names for now. Our parents called us what we were, and since they got two more girls after the first one, they called me Baby and the third one Infant."

"My name on the wedding program for Allen and Lenore was Aoife, which most people will confuse with Eva. I don't know why she gave me the only name that can't be spelled or pronounced properly outside of Ireland."

"My name was Fiona. Our brother was David."

"Well, it might be a cute nickname for your family, but a twelve-year-old is a little too grownup to go by Baby," Mrs. Doyle says. "Fiona Ryan is a lovely Irish name."

"Are you Irish-American too?"

"No, Doyle's only my married name. My maiden name was Bow-stead, which is English."

"Bowstead? Ain't that Julie's mother's maiden name?"

"That's why she came over," Adicia says. "We think she *is* Julie's mother. Today I found Julie's birth certificate, birth announcement, and a bunch of other documents about her. There were so many clues right under our noses for a long time, but we musta been too dumb to put two and two together sooner. Mrs. Doyle told us this afternoon her ex-husband died in the same fire we had. How many other tenements on Avenue A burnt down in June '62 and included a casualty named Randolph Spirnak?"

"Are you serious?" Infant asks. "Your next door neighbor coulda been Julie's mom and no one ever suspected it all these years?"

"We'll find out very soon if it's one big crazy coincidence or if it's the honest truth. Is Julie supposed to be out all day washing wind-shields?"

"She'll probably come back around suppertime, maybe six or so."

"If your friend is my daughter, she'll never have to wash another windshield ever again," Mrs. Doyle says. "Do you have any idea which blocks she's canvassing?"

"Canvassing?" Baby asks.

"Making the rounds of," Adicia explains.

"Oh. I think today she was going down Seventh Avenue and its vicinity. Do you want me to run out and try to find her?"

"It's a safe neighborhood," Infant adds.

"Don't feel like you have to find her," Mrs. Doyle says. "I don't want you running up and down trying to find her all day. I can always call my husband and let him know what's going on, and stay here in the meantime. Why don't I make you supper, and it'll be on the table by the time the others are due back?"

"Wow, you're really groovy," Baby says. "We haven't known many adults who were so nice."

"Would you like to listen to some of our music?" Infant asks. "I'm sure Girl won't mind if we play somea her records while she's gone."

"If you want grownup music, we have classical records Ernestine sometimes finds in the free bin of the record store. Girl's into folk rock mostly. Sometimes I wish she wasn't such a folkie. Not everything in life has to be so serious. These are important issues to fight for, but some-times you just need to relax and have fun."

Infant goes to get a pitcher of raspberry iced tea from the refriger-ator. "So what does this mean if you really are Julie's mom? Will she have to leave us?"

"I'm moving Upstate next week, and if your friend is my daughter from my first marriage, I couldn't bear to leave her behind. Maybe she'd choose to stay here, but I couldn't stand knowing my Divinely-returned firstborn child wasn't with me in the final few years of her childhood. I've already missed almost eleven years of her life."

***

Ernestine, Girl, Julie, and Boy come back at 6:15. Girl comes first, carrying a pail filled with coins and bills. Boy comes in next, toting his bucket full of change and bills. Ernestine and Julie come in together, carrying Julie's bucket of money.

"I see we have the pleasure of company," Girl says.

"These are Mrs. Doyle and her kids Matthew and Caroline," Adi-cia says. "Matthew's nine and Caroline's five."

"Mrs. Doyle made us supper," Justine adds. "Spinach and potato casserole. It should be ready any minute."

Julie stares at Mrs. Doyle, letting go of the bucket. "Mommy?"

Mrs. Doyle nods, tears welling up in her eyes.

"Well, ain't that something," Girl says in wonder as Julie runs into Mrs. Doyle's arms. "How did yous figure it out?"

"We'll tell you the whole story around the table," Adicia promises.

"I don't have to go back and live in Hell's Kitchen again, do I?" Julie asks, clinging to her mother.

"No, you won't, sweetheart. We're moving Upstate next week, where they have nice schools, houses that are spaced apart, yards, trees, flowers, and fresh air. Would you like to go to school next month?"

"I've never gone to school ever," Julie says sadly. "I'd be a sophomore in high school next month."

"And you will be! I'm sure you grew up to be a smart girl and won't have any problem passing placement tests. At most, you might only be a year or two behind. And guess what else. You're going to have a baby brother or sister in March."

"Oh, wow! I love helping with babies and little kids! Do I get to help with Matthew and Caroline too? I can't believe I have a little brother and sister and one more on the way!"

"Of course you can help. Now tell me the one thing you'd really like most, and I'll grant your wish. Anything at all, sweetheart, and I'll get it for you as a present."

"Can I get my ears pierced?"

Mrs. Doyle laughs. "That's an easy request to grant. You can come with me to Macy's and pick out earrings. Maybe your friends can pierce your ears, since I'm afraid I don't know how."

"I can do it," Girl volunteers.

"So does this mean I need to change my name to Doyle?" Julie asks. "I'm used to thinking of myself as a Spirnak."

"And does this mean Julie will be leaving us?" Ernestine asks. "We've been our own little family for seven years."

"I want to live in a real house with a backyard and see trees and grass instead of nothing but buildings when I look out the window. And I want to go to school and get to be a big sister."

Justine pulls the casserole out of the oven when the timer goes off.

"Everything's already arranged," Mrs. Doyle says. "The only unplanned thing was that I never expected to find you. I found out your father died in that fire, and that you were never found among the bodies or heard from again afterwards. Our plan is to stay in a three-bedroom apartment for six months or so while your stepfather looks for a house in Plattsburgh. We're in the process of packing up, so maybe you'd like to stay with your friends for one more week to say goodbye to them. Would you like to stay here a little longer, or do you want to come home with me tonight?"

"I'd love to go back with you right now, but I don't like living in tenements. Do you mind if I don't come back to live with you till you're ready to move?"

"If that's what you want, that's what I want. Though we probably will need to get your custody ironed out before we go."

"Sure any judge will give you back custody," Girl says. "Your loathsome ex-husband is dead, and you have a stable living situation."

"Where's Plattsburgh?" Baby asks. "Is that near Yonkers, just above the city?"

"It's a lot farther away," Mrs. Doyle says. "It's up near Canada, near the border with Vermont, right on Lake Champlain. There will be lots of fun things to do there during the warmer months. It's a very historic city, with a lot of reminders of its French origins."

"Hey, that's not fair. That's too far away to come and visit," Infant says.

"We won't be staying in this city forever either," Girl says. "Maybe we'll end up within a reasonable distance of Julie."

"Can we eat now?" Justine asks. "I'm hungry."

"Yeah, let's eat," Ernestine says. "I'm really eager to learn the story of how you came to find out Mrs. Doyle is Julie's mother."

***

The day before Julie and the Doyles are set to move to Plattsburgh, the van Niftriks host a going-away party in a private room at a French restaurant on the Upper East Side. Julie sits beaming between her mother and Caroline, her new amethyst earrings dangling from her earlobes and sparkling in the light.

"How much money would you like me and my husband to give you?" Mrs. Doyle asks Betsy's parents. "You've helped to take care of Julie for over five and a half years. The least we could do is to give you money to show our appreciation."

"Save your money," Mr. van Niftrik insists. "We never expected money in return for doing the right thing."

"You need all your money when you're going to be moving, buying a house, and having a new baby," Mrs. van Niftrik agrees.

"How about you, Allen?" Mr. Doyle asks. "You and Lenore helped with taking care of my stepdaughter for seven years. Tell us how much money you want in return, and we'll give it to you."

"We don't wanna take your money away from you," Lenore says, resting her hands on her pregnancy bulge. "It's always nice to have extra money, but we don't deserve extra cash for doing what decent people are supposed to do."

"We insist," Mrs. Doyle says. "Adicia says it was Allen's idea to go into my ex-husband's apartment and stall him for time so Julie could be smuggled away from him. How about twenty-five dollars?"

"We're not taking your money," Allen says.

"We're not leaving this city without giving you money in appreciation for your efforts," Mr. Doyle says. "You and Lenore get twenty-five, and Mr. and Mrs. van Niftrik get twenty-five. Don't try to refuse. We won't hear of letting your good deeds go unrewarded."

"If you insist," Allen says reluctantly, watching Irene feeding herself French onion soup to make sure she doesn't spill. He's quite pleased his firstborn has turned out to be a fellow southpaw.

"How much money do you make, Mr. Doyle?" Infant asks.

Girl sends her a look. "It ain't polite to ask people what they make."

"I'm an assistant manager at an ad agency," Mr. Doyle says. "Once we get to Plattsburgh, I'll be working for another ad agency. We create advertising slogans, approve artwork, and come up with good marketing campaigns to sell products. Our income level makes us middle-class, in spite of where we live."

"I can't wait to leave the city when I'm older," Ernestine says. "I'm jealous of yous guys."

"I'm sure you'll find a way to get out of New York," Mrs. Doyle says. "Good things always come to those who wait, even if the miracle or change of fortune isn't always immediately forthcoming."

"You're taking this much better than before," Emeline marvels. "You barely seem to be in labor."

"She's not having back labor this time, and she knows more about what to expect," Veronica says. "I told you all labors are different."

It's October 18, Saturday, and Lenore has been in labor since Friday night. This time, she barely feels any pain, and calmly walks around and moves rhythmically. She periodically goes into the kitchen for light food.

"Last year I finally got to read *Narcissus and Goldmund*, by Hermann Hesse," Emeline says. "It was just as good as Sarah told me. There's a moment when Goldmund sees a woman giving birth in a barn. He makes the surprising connection between this woman's face at her moment of great agony and the way a woman's face looks at the moment of sexual ecstasy. He never before thought there could be such a close similarity between pain and pleasure, and it became onea his artistic goals to put that into the dream Madonna he hoped to create."

"You had to wait till it was translated to read it?" Adicia asks. "Aren't you studying German as onea your majors?"

"Knowing how to read, write, and talk fluently in a language isn't quite the same as being able to read an entire book written in it. Sometimes I still need a dictionary, don't grasp a particular nuance, or find it hard to concentrate after too much time forcing myself to think in a foreign language. I'm rather annoyed a bunch of my hippie buddies, and hippies in general, are so into Hermann Hesse. He was onea my favorite writers a long time before he became so hip among the countercultural crowd. My love of him isn't a phase or something I'm only interested in 'cause it's so hip at the moment. Real literature is timeless, and I'll still read his books over and over again after he's no longer so insanely popular. He won the Nobel Prize a good twenty-three years ago, and he wrote his books from 1904 to 1943. The masses are only now rediscovering how groovy he was."

"Do you think I'd like his books?"

"You can always try a few and see if you like 'em. A lot of his books prominently feature friendships, the search for enlightenment, and what it's like to be different from the others." Emeline gets up to light more lavender and orange incense. "If I didn't know any better, Lenore, I'd think you timed your second birth on purpose for a weekend so I could come down and be your labor support person again."

"Are you gonna go to Vassar for your graduate studies too?" Ernestine asks. "Girl and I were thinking of applying there, since that's the first school Betsy wants. She has a legacy from her mother. Mr. and Mrs. van Niftrik also met when Mrs. van Niftrik was at Vassar."

"Vassar doesn't have a graduate program, unfortunately. But good luck to all three of yous. It's a wonderful school."

"How could Betsy's parents have met there?" Adicia asks. "Isn't Vassar a girls' college?"

"Not anymore. They started admitting guys this fall. Her dad musta been at Adelphi and been on the campus for some reason."

"It's too bad the school's going co-ed," Girl says. "I liked the idea of going to an all-girl school and being surrounded by others of my own kind, instead of having to put up with guys hogging the teacher's attention or getting better grades just 'cause they've got outdoor plumbing."

"How do you intend to get there? You don't go to school, and don't even have a birth certificate."

"I figure I can pass a GED test and write a good application essay. The van Niftriks are letting us borrow their typewriter after Betsy finishes writing her essay. They said they'd pay the application fee for us as well."

"We'll have to go to the department of health to get birth certificates," Baby says. "We also have to get social security cards. We'll have to stand on line for a few hours and get our names officially recorded. I like being called Baby. I don't wanna be called Fiona."

"Don't you need some form of ID to get a birth certificate?" Emeline asks.

"What are they gonna do, deport us for being illegal residents?" Girl asks. "Normal people understand these things happen. They'll just have four more people from the underclass to have to deal with."

"So, is Allen coming home from work early today?" Adicia asks. "He'd hate to miss the new baby being born."

"If I get close enough, I'll call him at work and tell him to come," Lenore says. "Emeline, what did you bring for music?"

Emeline pulls a small stack of records out of her bag and holds them up. "*Instant Replay* and *The Monkees Present*, which unfortunately were made without Peter; *Cloud Nine*, by The Temptations; *Abbey Road*, The Beatles' newest; the *Hair* soundtrack; and *On the Threshold of a Dream*, by The Moody Blues."

"*Instant Replay* is my favorite of the two albums The Monkees put out this year," Ernestine says.

"Marjani has that Temptations album," Adicia says. "She has lots of the Motown stuff, but even if we had a record player and I could afford to buy records, Mother would smash 'em 'cause they're made by Black singers. The title track's about growing up poor like we did."

"Does Mother have any idea you have a Black friend?" Emeline asks.

"She has no idea. She just thinks I have a friend with a kinda funny name. Mr. and Mrs. Washington don't care when I come over, since I'm their sister in struggle. We're equally exploited by capitalism and the establishment, no matter what color our skin is."

"That's what I say," Girl agrees.

"Is Mother still in trouble with the law, by the way?" Emeline asks.

"They looked at her kinda funny when she showed up with exactly three thousand dollars in cash so close to her deadline, but they bought her explanation of working jobs under the table and saving up money. I still feel dirty and ruined after what she made me do, but I can't keep dwelling on it if I wanna get over it," Adicia says.

Emeline puts her arm around her. "You're not dirty or ruined. You were forced into doing something awful, but your heart and soul are still pure and beautiful. You're as much of a virgin as I am, even if your sexual innocence is gone."

"Do your friends know you're still a virgin?" Lenore asks.

"I don't go around telling everyone, but they know I'm not into free love. I got a couple of offers from random strangers at Woodstock in August, but I declined. I'll be onea the rare people to graduate from college as a virgin in this day and age, but I haven't found a guy I wanna marry. I don't think you need to be married to live together or be intimate, but I think you oughta know this is heading towards marriage and not just be getting your jollies off any old person. I don't feel like a freak for being twenty-one and never having gone on a date or kissed a guy. Why waste special firsts like that on a guy I don't love and who doesn't love me? I'm probably the most old-fashioned, hypocritical hippie you'll ever meet, but I think it's really sweet and special to marry the first and only person you do anything with. When I find my future husband, I won't be comparing him to how well other guys kissed or made love, and I won't have shared myself so intimately and vulnerably with someone who just walked away after we did something so personal."

Adicia bursts into tears.

"Oh, I'm sorry, sweetie." Emeline hugs her very tightly.

"If this were a just world, Mother and that guy would be awaiting trial, not walking around freely."

"Didn't Allen do the next-best thing to him?" Lenore eases herself down next to Adicia and rubs her back. "That worthless little bastard probably had a good twenty years taken off his life after Allen paid him that visit and put the fear of God into him."

"Why couldn't Allen have killed him?"

"Do you really wanna risk him going to jail and leaving me, Irene, and the new baby by ourselves? Besides, he'll never be able to do that with any girl ever again. Allen castrated him and carved that message into his chest, so everyone will know what he's all about when he has to appear shirtless."

"He didn't just castrate him," Girl smirks. "He gave him a penectomy too."

"A what?" Baby asks.

"A removal of the main male organ. That's even worse than what happened to Carlos. Carlos still physically has his male parts, though he can't feel or use them."

"I'm gonna hafta do that with the guy they make me marry when I'm eighteen," Adicia sniffles. "I don't care how handsome he is or how good his job is; he's gonna be a lot older, and he probably won't love me."

"You have a choice," Emeline says. "You don't hafta marry anybody you don't want to. You owe it to Justine to get away from these people and take her with you. You don't want Justine to be led to the slaughter like you and Gemma, do you?"

"I'd do almost anything to protect her."

"Then you can do whatever it takes to leave that den of sin and save her before she's much older. She's the only one of us who still has a chance to have any years of her childhood saved."

Justine and Infant are at Washington Square Park with Boy. Boy didn't want to be present at another birth, and Lenore and Emeline felt it best for Justine and Infant to be away until it comes closer to the actual birth because of Adicia's still emotionally fragile state. Lenore gave Boy enough money to buy hotdogs, ice-cream, popcorn, or any other food they'd like from the vendors, and told him to bring the girls back before the Sun starts setting.

"How's Julie doing?" Emeline asks as she massages Lenore's shoulders during a contraction. "I can't believe how far north they moved. They're practically in Canada."

"She did really well on her school placement exams," Ernestine says. "She tested up to her age level on English, history, and home ec. Science and math she wasn't so advanced on, but they put her in a normal tenth grade geometry class and told her to come in for extra help if she needs any. She's in a biology class with students from all grades, and not doing so bad so far. She's also taking basic art, first-year Latin, and regular phys ed."

"Just goes to show someone who's entirely self-taught or home-taught can be just as smart as anyone who's formally taught in a school," Girl says. "I bet I can pass a GED test easily and get into college next fall."

"I think the most amazing thing is she immediately recognized her mother," Emeline says. "She didn't have to hear about the evidence you found or all the clues too numerous to all be coincidences. She was a girl who knew her mother even after eleven years of separation."

"I wish our mother were that nice and motherly," Adicia says. "I'm not hoping for a nice mother-in-law at this point."

"You can always make up for it by being the best mother to your kids," Lenore says. "You already have good examples in Sarah, Mrs. Doyle, Mrs. van Niftrik, Mrs. Washington, and Mrs. Murphy."

"I never had the guts to say this to her, but I always wondered why Julie referred to her mother as 'Mommy,' even as a teenager. Girls our age aren't supposed to call our mothers 'Mommy.'"

"She was four and a half the last time she saw her," Ernestine says. "Probably in her mind, she still thought of her as her mommy."

Irene wakes up from a nap and trots out to the living room, trailing her stuffed panda behind her. "Mommy, is the baby born yet?"

"Not yet, baby. You can put your head on my stomach and feel her moving if you'd like."

"You're not at transition yet," Veronica says.

"Is it true second labors are faster than first ones?"

"Many times, but not always. You're handling this one like a pro."

When Allen gets home from work at 6:30, Lenore is entering transition and having very strong contractions. Emeline rubs her back and shoulders as incense burns and the *Hair* soundtrack plays, while Boy is in the kitchen, trying his best to avoid having anything to do with Lenore's labor and making fish sticks and French fries for Justine and Infant. Adicia, Girl, Baby, and Ernestine are on the davenport, watching television and eating TV dinners of macaroni and cheese, chicken breasts, corn, and apple cobbler.

"Hi, Daddy!" Irene bounces over to Allen and jumps up into his arms.

Adicia looks on very jealously at her brother holding his twenty-eight-month-old daughter, kissing her on the cheek, and tossing her up in the air. Irene knows her father as a good guy, someone who loves her, takes care of her, spoils her, and protects her. He was the first person who held her when she came into the world, immediately bonding to her. She's never been a burden or someone to be ignored, insulted, or hated.

"Your wife is holding up like a champ," Veronica says. "You might be holding your second child in a few more hours."

"You hear that, Irene? You're gonna get a little sister before the night is up."

"What if it's a boy?" Emeline asks.

"I don't mind another girl. What's one more girl in our female-dominated family? Lenore thinks it's another girl too."

"Would you like some of our supper, Allen?" Justine calls. "We're having fish sticks and French fries."

"No, I think I'll heat up something more substantial than that. Emeline, have you eaten yet?"

"I'll make rice with vegetables and a Middle Eastern salad in a little bit. Don't worry, I brought my own food so I won't steal yours."

Allen winces after Emeline makes her supper and puts the bowls on bamboo placemats on the floor, with chrysanthemum tea. After being raised on meat and potatoes, he can't fathom anyone willingly adopting a diet devoid of meat, fish, and most dairy products. Emeline used to wolf down lamb, beef, chicken, turkey, salmon, tuna, cheese, milk, bacon, pork, and ham, but now she eats like an Indian yogi.

"Do you have anemia yet?"

"Did you know that prior to the modern era, Americans ate a lot less meat and dairy products? No one was convinced they were gonna die 'cause they had more varied diets and didn't eat an almost nonstop diet of meat. Humans are also the only species to drink milk past weaning, let alone to drink the milk of another species. I do like goat cheese, though."

Lenore crawls onto the nest of pillows Emeline set up for her. "I feel her coming out of me!"

"Are you sure?" Allen asks. "It didn't take you such a short time before!"

"Come over here and help me!"

Allen goes over and sets Irene on the floor as Lenore arches her back and starts pushing. Irene stares at the rush of water spilling out of her mother's body and drenching her father's arms.

"Can I catch the baby again?" he begs Veronica.

"I feel her head coming out!"

Irene watches in amazement as a baby emerges from her mother, right into her father's arms.

"Come say hello to your new sister, princess," Allen says, not attempting to hide his tears.

"Another girl?" Lenore asks.

Allen puts the baby on her chest, the umbilical cord still attached. "We sure know how to make beautiful kids, don't we?"

"She's beautiful!"

"She's messy," Irene says.

"You'll look even prettier when you get cleaned up, won't you?" Lenore asks the baby.

"You looked like this too when you were born," Allen tells Irene.

"I think she likes you." Lenore smiles when she sees the baby gripping Irene's finger in her tiny hand. "You're going to be a good big sister, aren't you?"

"Why is there a snake on her?"

"That's called the umbilical cord," Veronica explains. "It's what connects the baby to the mother before birth. She gets her food, blood, and oxygen through it. In a little while, your mother will deliver something called the placenta, the organ the cord is attached to at the other end, and we'll be able to cut it off."

"What's her name?" Adicia asks.

"Amelia Katherine Troy," Lenore announces.

"That's a pretty name!" Ernestine says. "And it goes so well with Irene Lily!"

"You'll never understand how much you can love another person till you've had your own baby. My hope for my children is that they grow up in a much happier and more peaceful world than the one we live in now."

***

"Guess what, I passed my GED," Girl says as they come bounding into Allen and Lenore's apartment the first weekend in December. "Ernestine and Betsy both got 1300 on their SATs. All combined, we were able to send off early decision applications to Vassar last month, right before the deadline. Now all I gotta do is get myself a birth certificate and social security card. I said my parents lost both on my application and that I'll send along my social security number as soon as I can procure copies."

"That's nice," Lenore says lifelessly.

"I wish I were in college," Allen says, just as lifelessly. "I always wanted to go to some type of college program, but I musta waited too long."

"Oh, it's never too late to get a higher education," Ernestine says encouragingly. "Maybe when your girls are older, you can go to school while Lenore works."

"Who knows, maybe they'll excuse me 'cause I've got three dependents, even if I'm not in college," Allen says softly.

"What are you talking about?" Girl demands. "Is it what I suspect it is?"

"If only I was a year older, I wouldn't be worried sick about this. My lottery number's one hundred ten. That's not a good number to have. It's too low. They could call me in to fight in that neverending, pointless bloodbath in Vietnam, and I don't wanna die young, leave Lenore an even younger widow, leave two half-orphans, and have you girls losing me."

"One hundred ten?" Ernestine gasps.

"It was the number they randomly assigned to all guys born on

June sixth between 1944 and 1950. I knew there'd be trouble if Nixon was elected. How can they reinstate a draft for such an unpopular war? It's not morally justified or a war we're winning!"

"They might not call your number," Boy says. "I don't know if they plan to call each and every single number."

"You turn eighteen in 1972," Girl reminds him. "If the war's still going on then, you might be at risk too. Maybe we shouldn't get you a birth certificate if this is what it might mean, yet another guy from the underclass to use as potential cannon fodder."

"I'll go to college to avoid it. I was planning to go anyway, but now I wanna go even more."

"You'd better go," Allen says. "I'm probably the closest to a brother you'll ever have, and I'm ordering you to go to college when you're old enough. I might be able to get outta this by saying I have a job, a wife, and two young kids, but you're just a poor boy, the kind they love to throw in front of cannons."

"Yeah, guys with connections, money, real jobs, and college educations can get outta it," Girl says. "Getting an education is your only chance to stay safe."

"One thing I know is I can't leave the country to avoid it. I'm not about to desert yous guys, particularly not so soon after what my mother did to Adicia."

"Can we not talk about this?" Baby begs. "It's too upsetting."

"We should think about other things to take our minds off it," Lenore says sadly. "There's a cranberry walnut bread I made last night, and you girls can have it for a snack. I'll make orange blossom tea." She hands Amelia to Allen.

"Who wrote your recommendation letters?" Allen asks as Lenore sets the table.

"My boss at my new job at the record shop, Mrs. van Niftrik, and my history teacher," Ernestine says. "Betsy used her English teacher, the advisor of her after school philosophy club, and her Latin teacher."

"I hope they're cool with my not having an SAT score," Girl says. "Someone with a GED ain't in a position to take that test."

"Deirdre's essay was about how she grew up poor and had to raise not only herself, but three younger siblings. It also talked about how she's lived in a number of different places, none of 'em guaranteed, like that subway tunnel and the big hole in the road."

"Betsy wrote about how going to school in Greenwich Village and having such progressive parents taught her how to respect and accept all kinds of different people, not merely to tolerate differences, and that there's more than one correct way to live your life. Ernestine wrote about how she left home at a young age and how we've been our own little family, raising ourselves, and even though she came from such rotten stock, she turned out the exact opposite of her diseased parents."

"Who wrote your recommendation letters?" Lenore asks.

"Mrs. van Niftrik, this nice lady who runs a boutique I sometimes work at, and the advisor of onea the social action programs I participate in from St. Luke in the Fields. I might be undocumented, but people in the community know who I am."

"We're going down to get our birth certificates next week," Infant says proudly. "Girl wants an outlandish Greek middle name."

"Apollonia. It sounds groovy. It's the feminine form of Apollo, who was a pretty neat god. He was the god of light, prophecy, sun, medicine, art, music, wisdom, law, and beauty."

"Are you really ready to switch over to real names?" Allen asks.

"It'll be strange at first, but I'm too old to still answer to Infant," Infant says. "Plus it's pretty degrading to not have a proper name."

"Do you think we'll get in trouble for being undocumented so long?" Baby asks.

"They can't do nothing about it after the fact," Girl says. "We ain't the first people to never get birth certificates."

"What's Lenore gonna do for a job if you go to war? Will you use daycare or a babysitter, or can she take Irene and Amelia to work with her?"

"They mighta given me a low draft number, but they'll haul me there over my dead body. I got outta being drafted since President Johnson started it in '65, and I hope I'm just as lucky now that there's a damn lottery for it. I almost wanna burn my draft card, but I can't risk going to prison."

"You can't go," Lenore says. "Tell them you have a wife and two small children, and a steady job that can't let you go."

"I can do one better. I can enroll in the Borough of Manhattan Community College for the winter semester. Mosta their degree programs are business-related, and if we open our own bakery after we leave town, it'd be nice to have a background in what it takes. A guy like me could never get accepted at or afford a fancy school like Columbia or NYU, but a degree from a two-year school is better than no degree at all. It's such a blessing this city's public colleges rarely charge tuition."

"You'd really go to college?" Justine asks.

"I'll do whatever it takes to take care of my family. I'd probably have to take a lot of night and weekend classes, and Lenore would be alone more often, but if that's what it takes to save my hide from Uncle Sam, so be it."

***

"We're here to get birth certificates and social security cards," Girl tells the man behind the desk at the health department. "None of us ever got 'em."

Infant smiles up at him, hoping to charm him and make him more amenable to their cause after he finds out just why they don't have those documents.

"Are you sure you don't have those documents? What have your parents said about it? They might know where they are even if you don't."

"Please don't patronize us." Girl smiles at him sarcastically. "Why the hell would we waste a trip down here and waiting three hours on line if we weren't a million percent sure we never had birth certificates or social security cards? We might be young, but we're not stupid. In fact, we're probably more adult for our ages than the middle-class and rich kids who've been shielded from unpleasant truths their whole lives and not been made to grow up and fend for themselves from an early age."

He looks at her dismissively. "Okay then. Do you know which hospital or hospitals you were born in, so we can request copies of the records from them?"

"We weren't born in hospitals."

He stares at them for a good long while before finding his tongue again. "What were your parents, hippies who didn't trust the system?"

"Our parents were rather ahead of the hippie movement. They had their own reasons for having unassisted homebirths. To save you another needless question, no, we didn't have a midwife or any other birth assistant present who'd have documentation of our births."

He gapes at them again. "So what does this mean, the four of you have been undocumented residents your entire lives?"

"Sort of. That's why we need proper documents, particularly since I'm going to college next fall. I passed my GED with flying colors and applied to Vassar. Don't give me that dismissive, mocking look. Just 'cause I grew up poor and fending for myself doesn't mean I'm not intelligent, smart, and capable of handling the work at a prestigious college."

"We don't even have proper names," Boy says. "Our parents just called us Girl, Boy, Baby, and Infant. Girl's been going by Deirdre for awhile, but it's not consistent yet."

"Don't ask where our parents are, 'cause we don't know," Baby says. "They disappeared when Girl was seven, shortly after Infant was born. They left us in the care of a community of like-minded people. But we do have a last name. We're the Ryans."

"Excuse me for a moment." The man gets up from behind the desk and goes off into another section of the building.

"Wow, we sure rocked his world," Girl laughs. "He's clearly middle-class or upper-class if he's this surprised to find out people like us exist. God forbid you not be born in a hospital or raised with your parents in a so-called traditional family in a nice part of town."

Twenty minutes later, he returns with a woman in a dark gray business jacket and skirt. She beckons to them to step aside so the line can keep moving.

"My name is Miss Cecilia Skoloda, and I'm here to help you. I was told you lack birth certificates and social security numbers because your parents never registered your births. Would you like to come into my office downstairs?"

"Do you have lollipops or candy on your desk?" Infant asks.

"Yes, for a pretty little girl like you, I sure do. Follow me."

"Nothing personal, but you look a little on the old side to still go by Miss," Girl says. "I wish they had an in-between title for women too old to be a Miss, but who aren't a Mrs. either." She's making a special effort to use proper English so the officials here won't take them less seriously.

"I'm thirty-three," she says as they follow her into her office and she shuts the door. "You're probably right. Even if I were to get married, it's silly for a professional woman to be called Mrs. I think of a Mrs. as a teacher, society matron, or housewife, not a woman with a career. I have friends who were doctors before they were married, but they're called Mrs. instead of Dr. by people who don't know them very well. It's insulting to their professional achievements."

"You're my kinda woman," Girl says in admiration.

"Now on to why you came here. Some of my co-workers have certain attitudes against people like you, but I'm not one of them. Sometimes it happens a birth goes unregistered, and it's not done with deliberate criminal or political intent. I suppose you don't have any legal guardians either."

"Our parents knew they couldn't register our births with only the names Girl, Boy, Baby, and Infant, born at home or not. They couldn't even be bothered to give us dime a dozen names like Mary, John, Elizabeth, and Margaret."

"We can choose whatever names we want when we get registered?" Baby asks.

"Within reason," Miss Skoloda says. "Have you already got names in mind?"

"Our surname is Ryan," Girl says. "I've been going by Deirdre in official situations for awhile, and my best friend has been calling me that for the last year. I want my middle name to be Apollonia. Would you like me to spell those out for you?"

"No, I know how to spell both those names. I'm familiar with the plays 'Deirdre' by William Butler Yeats and 'Deirdre of the Sorrows' by J.M. Synge. And since my family's Catholic, I know of Saint Apollonia." She picks up a pen and begins writing on a legal pad.

"I know you have to put the names of your parents on your birth certificate. Our mother's birth name was Mulrennan, M-u-l-r-e-double n-a-n. Her first and middle names were Teresa Kathleen. That's Teresa with no H, and Kathleen with a K."

Infant stares at her. "How did you know that?"

"I was seven the last time I saw her. I was more than old enough to remember our parents, and I knew a few things about them, like their names. Our dad's name was Floyd Everett Ryan. I don't think I ever got their birthdates, though."

"That's fine," Miss Skoloda says. "We don't care about parents' birthdates. Do you happen to know your birthdates?"

"They told me I was born on April 8, 1952, and I believed 'em. Some people who were around them at that time and still living with us when I was old enough to remember told me the same date. Boy was born June 13, 1954; Baby was born May 19, 1957; and Infant was born April 20, 1959. My little sisters were born in The Bowery, my brother was born in Chinatown, and I was born on the Lower East Side. I think the part of the neighborhood I was born in might be part of the East Village nowadays. I'd have to see a map. I know it was on East Tenth Street."

"We don't put neighborhoods on birth certificates, but we do need to know you were all born in Manhattan. This is probably a long shot, but is there any way you know the whereabouts of anyone who witnessed your births and could attest to that in writing?"

"I remember names of people who lived with us, but I've not seen or heard from any of 'em since our commune in The Bowery was raided by the cops in late August '62. We've been on our own since then, with my best friend and a friend of ours who recently moved Upstate with her long-lost mother. We also have really swell neighbors with a daughter my age."

"Girl wants to go to Vassar next fall, and we'd like to go with her," Baby says. "We know you can't live with family in the dorms, but they could let her live off-campus in an apartment if we were legally in her custody. Can you make her our guardian even though she's underage?"

"Your sister isn't eighteen quite yet, so she can't become your guardian unless she becomes legally emancipated. I don't think the courts would put up much of a fight about that, since your parents have been MIA for ten and a half years and probably won't ever come back to claim you."

"If they need proof I'm financially self-sufficient, I can tell them I work at a boutique in Greenwich Village. We do all sorts of odd jobs and perform for money, but I'm old enough now to work legit jobs for an official paycheck." Girl reaches over to Miss Skoloda's desk for a candybar.

"Can we get all this stuff worked out by the time Girl goes to college?" Baby asks. "Assuming Vassar accepts her."

"I got a great GED score. Some people smugly assume you can't be that smart or intelligent if you do all your learning in the home."

"We'll have to file a number of different petitions and documents," Miss Skoloda says. "Legal emancipation, legal guardianship, birth certificates, and social security cards. Since your births were never registered, you won't have to go through the additional paperwork and fees for name changes."

Girl turns to her siblings. "Are you okay with the names you've been using in official situations, or would you like to select new ones?"

"I'm David," Boy says. "It was the first name that came to mind when I was asked my name once. King David was a heroic warrior and got all the women. Can my middle name be Edgar? I always thought that was a pretty groovy name."

"David Edgar Ryan it is," Miss Skoloda says, continuing to write everything down. "How about the second girl?"

"Do I look like a Fiona?" Baby asks uncertainly. "It's a nice Irish name, but I don't look Irish with my dark brown hair and eyes."

"Not all Irish have freckles, red hair, and pale eyes," Girl scoffs. "Those are stereotypes. Our ancestral homeland was invaded so many times and had a bunch of shipwrecks, so Irish people look all sorts of ways. There's no one way to look properly Irish. Boy and I have brown hair and eyes too, though our hair isn't as dark as yours. If Fiona's the name you want to keep for your own, then I say you look every inch a Fiona."

Baby looks to Girl for guidance. "I'm not as good with names as you are. What sounds like a good middle name for Fiona?"

"How about Fiona Líobhan Ryan? Líobhan means 'beautiful woman' or 'the beauty of women' in Irish."

"Now both of those names I think I will need spelled out," Miss Skoloda says.

Girl writes them down and lets Baby look. "If you think the middle name has a non-intuitive pronunciation, just wait'll you hear the first name Infant's taking."

"Do I have to use that weird Irish spelling?" Infant asks. "Everyone will spell and say it as Eva."

"Her name's Aoife, A-o-i-f-e. Kinda like Eva with an F sound. It's easy to remember once you see it enough. You don't wanna see somea the even stranger spellings that have no resemblance to their pronunciations under the rules of English."

"What would you suggest for my middle name?"

"Saoirse means 'freedom' in Irish. That's a pretty name, though you'll hate the spelling. Once you learn the basic rules of Irish pronunciation, it's not hard to figure out how to pronounce stuff."

Infant does a double-take when Girl writes the name. "How am I gonna remember that one?"

"You know how Aoife's spelled. This name also has the a-o-i cluster, and you know from how Aoife is pronounced that it makes the sound of the letter E. The second S is said SH. Perfectly simple once you know the rules. SEER-sha."

"If you say so."

"I wouldn't suggest it if I didn't think it'd fit you. Would you really rather be one of several score of Debbies, Barbaras, Sharons, Lindas, Dianes, Judies, Donnas, and Karens? It's so annoying when people pick a name just 'cause it's safe and popular, not 'cause they want their kid to be an individual and have a more uncommon name."

"Aoife Saoirse it is."

"Do you have a phone where you live?" Miss Skoloda asks. "I'll need to keep in touch with you about these matters. The birth certificates and social security cards come first, then the legal emancipation for Deirdre, and finally the legal guardianship issue."

"Our neighbors across the hall have a phone," Boy says. "Since I'm going on the books as existing, does this mean I have to register for the draft when I'm eighteen?"

"That's a whole other issue, and I'm not the best person to deal with it. Although we should all be hopeful we'll be out of there by the time you're eighteen."

"Maybe I can get outta it by telling them the truth and saying I'm a pacifist."

"Well, for now all you need to worry about is having your existence registered. You can write your phone number and address here, and I'll get back to you within a couple of weeks."

"You're a really swell lady for helping us," Baby says. "Most grownups outside our own community haven't been so nice to us."

As they walk out into the street and towards the subway station, Girl feels a sense of pride at having made this first step of becoming an official part of society. She'll never be part of high society, but to be respectably working-class like Allen and Lenore is good enough. Even lower-middle-class might not be so bad. Because of her origins, she'll always be keenly aware of the social injustice in the world, but maybe now she'll be in more of a position to advocate for changes. If she were to stay poor and a squatter her whole life, she'd be no better than Mr.

and Mrs. Troy with their insistence it's morally wrong to get above one's raising. Normal people want to do better than what they were raised with, not continue to wallow in that way of life even when better opportunities present themselves. And whatever the future might hold, she'll meet it as Deirdre Apollonia Ryan, under her own name and identity, not the anonymous identity of Girl Ryan, who could've been any girl from the poor side of the tracks, ignored and dismissed by the rest of society.

"I have a pleasant surprise for everyone," Mrs. Troy announces at supper a week before Christmas. "Next week at this very time, we'll be back home to celebrate Christmas."

"But we are home," Tommy says in confusion. "How are we not home?"

"Back in the old neighborhood. I've been thinking about this and wanting this for a long time. In fact, I already called the moving men and used somea the money from your father's paychecks to make the deposit. Like hell we're abandoning the nice things we got from Gemma and Francesco. I like having a phone, bed linens, towels, a bureau, and real beds."

"This is a surprise, but not a pleasant one," Mr. Troy says irately. "Did you never think to consult me when you was making these plans with moving men? Don't tell me you used somea my money for rent too."

"Of course I did, Antoine. We'll be right back on Essex Street, so it'll be even more like coming home. It's a family apartment on the second floor of a building that useta be a matzah factory, back when the neighborhood had more Yids. The bottom floor is now a kosher bakery, but they're letting us have the top floor for thirty dollars a month. There are three bedrooms, a living room, a bathroom, and a kitchen. It was a cake deal, so I seized at it."

"Isn't that part of the East Village nowadays?" Adicia asks.

"Thank God, no. We'll be right back where we was before, just south of the border of that uppity part of the neighborhood that got uppity ideas and seceded from the rest of us. It's close to where Essex Street turns into Avenue A, about the same distance from Tompkins Square Park as we was before. Just think, Adicia, you'll finish high school at the same school as your oldest siblings."

"Not fair!" Tommy protests. "I was looking forward to graduating junior high with my friends in June and starting high school with 'em in the fall!"

"Just think, sweetheart, you'll be the most popular boy at your new school 'cause you're new. And you'll have extra street credibility with 'em, since that's your hometown."

"I don't care about street credibility! I wanna stay with my friends!"

"What the hell does this little milksop need with street credibility, Dolores?" Mr. Troy asks. "You've raised him to be a pampered mama's boy, not an urchin on the streets. At least you didn't make him into Little Lord Fauntleroy, since he'd be guaranteed regular beatings at school and on the streets."

"We'll finally be back in an area that ain't been taken over by Puerto Ricans and coons," Mrs. Troy crashes on, ignoring everyone's negative reactions. "Back with our own kind. Just in time for a new decade."

"I don't wear the pants in this family." Mr. Troy throws a chicken bone on the floor. "If only my friends and co-workers knew how much my evil wife goes behind my back and walks all over me. I rue the day we got in the backseat of that stolen car and created Gemma. Then I never woulda had to marry you and be trapped as your husband for the resta my life."

"Why do we have to move?" Tommy asks.

"If your father went and relocated to this literal hellhole while I was jailed, why can't I decide to move without consulting him? I hated Two Bridges, but I didn't wanna move to this piece of junk neighborhood in exchange! Seven years here has been seven years too many for me."

"Why do you wanna do this in the middle of the school year?"

"Just think, Antoine, you won't gotta commute to your job no more. That's thirty extra cents a day we can use to buy more drugs or set aside for utility bills."

"This tenement is a piece of junk, but it's my home! I've been livin' here since I was six!"

"Just think, your own bedroom for the very first time. You are getting a bit old to still sleep with your parents."

"No kidding," Mr. Troy says.

"How could we go wrong moving back to the place our ancestors called home for over a hundred years? It's like how elephants always go home even when they've been away for years."

"Elephants go home to die!" Tommy shouts. "They don't just move back to the old neighborhood outta the blue!"

"Yes, we will all die in the old neighborhood. Born there, raised there, and going to die there. Just the way it's been in this family for over a century."

Adicia has been looking forward to going over to Marjani's home to share in the Washingtons' celebration of Kwanzaa, a new holiday observed by people very passionate about their African heritage and creating their own identity instead of trying to curry favor with the white establishment by copying them. She says nothing about this to her parents, of course, since in all likelihood they've never heard of Kwanzaa, and her mother in particular will be furious to find out she has a Black friend. Mrs. Troy would be even more stunned to learn Adicia's best friend is from a Black pride family, the kind of girl who wears her hair in cornrows instead of straightening it, wants to go to Howard University, and has African food like black-eyed bean pancakes and stewed mangoes in her lunchbox.

"If Tommy takes this move like a man and don't complain about it no more, he'll get extra presents next week," Mrs. Troy promises.

"Ain't your current job as a cleaning lady?" Mr. Troy asks. "I didn't know cleaning ladies made enough money to buy their thirteen-year-old spoilt rotten mama's boy sons double the Christmas presents."

"You know as well as I do the money to pay for 'em will be coming from your paychecks. Who wants to start packing tomorrow?"

"Can I get G.I. Joes, a new robot for my collection, Colorforms, and a View-Master?" Tommy asks.

"I'd buy you the Brooklyn Bridge if you asked for it, my pet."

Part of Adicia wishes the war will still be going on when Tommy turns eighteen so he might be drafted, if he wants a G.I. Joe so badly. She can't see Tommy becoming a family man, a breadwinner, and a student at a two-year college like Allen. The thought of having toy soldiers in the tenement makes her sick, even knowing G.I. Joes have been modified lately to include aquanauts, astronauts, and adventurers instead of soldiers.

"Can I get a TV for Christmas too?" Tommy asks excitedly, seemingly having forgotten his upset at being forced to switch schools.

Mr. Troy glares at Mrs. Troy when she starts to open her mouth in a big smile. "Don't even try that, Dolores. If you wanna get this spoilt brat a TV, you're on your own."

"Aw, come on, Dad, everyone has a TV nowadays. I'd get to watch Saturday morning cartoons, movies, and funny shows. Plus when something important happens in the news, I'd be able to see it happening live 'steada having to hear about it at school afterwards. These dumb girls watch TV all the time when they go over to see Allen and his wife. They got to see the Moon landing this summer, and I didn't. That wasn't fair."

"Only uppity people wanna keep up with the nightly news," Mrs. Troy scoffs. "Decent poor people care more about where their next meal is coming from and how to earn money, not what rich boy astronauts did or what's happening in government. So long as the news don't affect us, I don't give a damn about any of it."

"You didn't care we put a man on the Moon?" Justine asks.

"Like I said. I care more about what's for supper or how to get money."

"But I could watch cartoons, movies, and shows?" Tommy asks.

"You ain't watching any of it on my dime," Mr. Troy asserts. "If I see a television set being brought into this home as onea this little brat's Christmas presents, it's being returned to the store and you ain't getting no sex for a month. Is that understood, woman?"

"You stink, Dad!"

"Your enabling mother can't pay for a TV on her own dime, and she knows that. If you want a TV that badly, she can take a job that pays more than peanuts, or you can get a job delivering papers and save up the money for it. I'm tired of being taken to the cleaners so she can buy you expensive presents. I never had fancy toys growing up, and I didn't complain. You woulda hated growing up a hundred years ago, before TV, radio, record players, and mass-produced toys."

"Well, like it or not, Antoine, we're moving back home within the week," Mrs. Troy says. "Before you all know it, it'll feel like we've always been back home and like the past seven years was just a bad dream."

***

"Why is your mother pulling you outta school in the middle of the year?" Marjani asks several days later as she and Adicia are walking down 49th Street after school. "And who gives her family only a week to prepare for moving?"

"She's a disgrace to motherhood. What she did to me in August shows that more than ever. I don't know why she likes our old neighborhood so much. This neighborhood's pretty awful too, but it's not like we're going back to something nicer. The old place is known for overcrowding and poverty just like this place has become known for gang fights."

"At least you'll be living on top of a bakery. The bakers might feel sorry for you and Justine and let yous eat leftover food."

"We'll be in the new neighborhood borders. Before, we were just inside what they call the East Village nowadays, up near Tompkins Square Park, a little after Essex Street turns into Avenue A."

"I'm surprised they still have family apartments above stores. That's so old-fashioned."

"Must be why my mother thought it was a deal not to be missed. She's been frothing at the bit to leave this neighborhood for ages, but I never thought she'd do it. Tommy's her pet, so I'm shocked she's making him leave his school when his junior high graduation's in six months."

"If my parents moved, they'd wait till I'm done with high school, and not when Zuberi's in the middle of a school year. Why is she so sentimental towards the Lower East Side? You had pretty bad final memories of it."

"My family on both sides lived there for over a hundred years. She thinks we're supposed to follow in our ancestors' footsteps and be born there, grow up there, raise families there, and die there. We'd be getting above our raising if we dared move uptown or outta the city. What was good enough for our ancestors should be good enough for us."

"If my family had followed that stupid logic, we'd still be working crummy jobs and letting the white man walk all over us. Your dad wouldn't have a labor union if his ancestors had just accepted the status quo."

Adicia stops in her tracks when she sees her mother approaching them. Marjani has never met Mrs. Troy, but recognizes her from Adicia's description of a woman with light brown hair full of split ends and rats' nests, leathery skin from too much smoking, and who looks like she just rolled out of a garbage dumpster. Her ubiquitous cocaine pipe is also in her hand.

"Mother, I thought you still had work now."

"I quit that job," Mrs. Troy says in a surly voice, taking a hit on the pipe. "I told the boss man I was moving, so I couldn't go such a big distance to work no more. I'll find a new job, same as I always have. Jobs are like men and buses; a new one always comes along every fifteen minutes."

"My parents both work in different neighborhoods," Marjani says. "Your husband commutes too. It's just another neighborhood, not another city or state."

"Adicia, who is this darky you're walking with? It's bad enough Tommy's best friends are spics."

"This is my friend Marjani Washington. She lives in the neighborhood. And she prefers the term Black, not Negro, darky, or any of the other words you like to use."

"Bully for her. I'll call 'em whatever the hell I wanna call 'em. We had freedom of speech in this country last time I checked."

"Mother, you've worked many jobs in different neighborhoods."

"They was all in the same area. When we lived downtown, I took jobs in other downtown neighborhoods, and while we've been midtown, I've worked jobs in midtown neighborhoods. That don't answer my question of what you're doing with a darky."

"We made friends the first day of junior high. We've never cared what the other's skin color is. We're people, not stereotypes or labels. Like Dr. King said, we should all be judged by the content of our character, not skin color."

"Thank God we're leaving this neighborhood by Christmas. Otherwise I might wanna punish you for having a darky friend for this long and never telling me what she was. I thought you just had a friend with a kinda funny name. Why is her hair in them funny braids? Is that a hairstyle from the darkest wilds of Africa?"

"They're called cornrows," Marjani says, trying to ignore Mrs. Troy's racist epithets. "It's a West African traditional hairstyle. Many girls and women in the Black pride movement style their hair like this."

"Oh, great, you went and made yourself a friend from that domestic terrorist organization the Black Panthers. All the self-respecting darky women I've known have straightened their hair."

"My family ain't involved with the Black Panthers. We agree with some of their beliefs, but we'd never advocate violence to achieve respect and equality. Education and empowerment are the key, not preaching hatred and violence. Adicia is my sister in struggle, since capitalism and the establishment keep us down equally. Only rich white Protestant men with money and the socially-approved political leanings have historically counted for much of anything in this country.

You've been used and exploited by the system too, Mrs. Troy. Why else are you a drug addict, a drunk, the mother of nine children, and trapped in dead-end, low-paying jobs and crummy neighborhoods? If you'd been given the same opportunities as a man from a family with money, you mighta only had three or four kids, been a respectable housewife, and moved to a decent job available to women after your kids was all in school, not turned to drugs and drink for escape from reality, and lived uptown by now, maybe even in a real house."

"I don't got time for this political rant. Adicia, you know what time to come home for supper by. Thank God we're moving back to the Lower East Side. The worst we've gotta worry about there are the leftover Yids from the neighborhood's glory days and maybe some Chinks spilling over from nearby Chinatown."

Marjani stares at Mrs. Troy as she continues walking on, unable to believe so much stupidity, obliviousness, hatred, and hypocrisy can exist in the same person. The fact that she's a terrible mother makes her even more irredeemable.

"At least I only have two and a half more years left with her. I wish I could figure out a way to save Justine along with myself. I can't bear the thought of her suffering alone."

"You'll find a way somehow. People always find a way when they're faced with a choice between sink or swim."

"I hope you're right."

"Self-preservation and protecting your family line are the two strongest human instincts. You'd be amazed at the crazy stuff some people have done to save themselves, or save their family or friends when they knew they was gonna die."

"I'd protect Justine no matter what. I'd have to be in pretty desperate straits to abandon her and tell her to save herself while I escaped."

"Then you're gonna do fine when you move back to your old neighborhood. Your sister's counting on you to leave your crazy family far behind and to save her along with you. It might not happen tomorrow, but it'll happen."

"She was always our real-life baby doll, when she was little. We always said she was our baby, no matter how old she'd get. A lot of the things we went through were all for the younger sisters. Now I'm the oldest sister left, and I have no choice but to stick my neck out for her.

She's the only one of us left who still has a chance to enjoy something of a childhood."

"Trust in yourself. When the time is right and a situation presents itself, things meant to happen, happen."

***

Christmas Day, Thursday, Adicia and Justine stand in their new apartment looking down on the street below. The Troys moved in last night, with a lot of people stopping to stare at them for moving on Christmas Eve. When Mrs. Troy snapped at them to mind their own business, they instinctively kept away and made a mental note to avoid these new neighbors. For Christmas Eve services, they wandered the streets and walked into the first church they found, which happened to be Presbyterian. Not much has been unpacked, but Tommy got all his Christmas presents in the morning. True to Tommy's wishes and Mrs. Troy's promise, he got another new robot, G.I. Joes, Matchbox cars, three kinds of Colorforms, a View-Master with ten different slideshows, enough candy to rot his teeth a hundred times over, oranges, roasted nuts, pajamas with cars on them, fuzzy dragon slippers, a basketball, a Yankees baseball cap, and a new neon green schoolbag. Mrs. Troy also bought him his own mattress. Mr. Troy is so relieved to finally have Tommy out of their bedroom, he barely cares the money to pay for it came out of his paychecks as always.

"We've been through a lot since we've been outta this neighborhood," Adicia says as they watch customers coming around to the front door of the bakery. "It's hard to imagine so many turbulent things can happen in such a short span of time."

"I hope the new decade's a lot calmer," Justine agrees. "I can't wait for the Seventies."

"Why the hell is that bakery open today?" Mrs. Troy asks as she takes a hit on her pipe. "And why are they getting any customers?"

"This is a historically Jewish neighborhood, Mother," Adicia reminds her. "To them, it's just another day."

"Well, they should shape up like proper, decent Americans and respect that most Americans, even if they ain't Christians, observe Christmas! I've worked with Yids who put up Christmas trees and gave their kids presents."

"I thought onea the best things about our country was that it's home to so many different types of people," Tommy says as he plays with his alien Colorforms. "We have freedom of religion and speech, and don't have to follow a state religion or set of customs."

"It's called a melting pot for a reason. Lots of different people come here, and they come outta the pot reborn as Americans. They came to the wrong country if they expected to hold onto their native languages, customs, and foreign religions."

"I've never known any self-respecting Jews who put up Christmas trees and got presents," Adicia says. "You musta known people who weren't that religious and didn't care about passing on their heritage to their kids. Sarah was Reform, and even she didn't believe in doing that."

"Oh, nonsense. I've come to Tommy's Christmas pageants, and I always see some Yid names in the programs, like Moses Silverberg or Rachel Cohen. Them kids didn't balk at singing Christmas music."

"Sharing in someone else's holiday celebration and appreciating beautiful music from another faith tradition isn't the same as actively celebrating a holiday yourself." Adicia leaves out the fact that the processional music at Allen and Lenore's wedding was from the Latin Mass and sung by two Jewish guys, though she'd love for her spiteful mother to have a double heart attack and never bother them again.

"Can I go to the East River Park and go sledding?" Tommy asks. By now even he's embarrassed by his mother's racism and stupidity, and is cringing at her awful grammar.

"You don't have a sled, sweetheart," Mrs. Troy says. "Would you like to take money from your father's wallet and see if any non-Christian stores are open so you can buy yourself a sled?"

"Don't say nothing more, Dolores, 'cause that sure as hell ain't happening," Mr. Troy barks. "He can pick a lid offa a garbage can and use that as his sled, the way all our other kids did, the way I went sledding. If he thinks it's not as fun as using a real sled, he can start working odd jobs they'll accept an eighth grader for and save up money."

"It's not so bad," Adicia tells Tommy. "A garbage can lid is better than sitting on top of a hill and sliding down by yourself."

"You stink, Dad," Tommy glowers as he pulls on his coat, hat, mittens, and boots.

"You're lucky I don't wallop you across the mouth for that kinda sass, young man. In my day, you never got away with saying such things to your elders."

"You touch a hair on the head of this boy and I'll beat you back," Mrs. Troy threatens.

"Can Justine and I go downstairs to look around at the bakery?" Adicia asks. "We won't steal anything."

"That's your racket if you wanna get acquainted with the new neighbors." Mrs. Troy inhales deeply on her pipe.

Adicia takes Justine by the hand and leads her downstairs just in time to see the owners putting a "Closed for Lunch" sign on the front door. They smile at the couple and their departing employees.

"We're sorry, but we've just closed for lunch. You can take a number so we can take your order first after we come back in forty minutes," the woman says kindly.

"Oh, no, we haven't come to buy anything. We moved upstairs last night, and we wanted to introduce ourselves. I don't think our parents or spoilt brother Tommy will ever care to meet yous guys, but we do. I'm Adicia Troy and I'm fifteen, and this is my baby sister Justine. She's ten."

"We used to live in this neighborhood, but we were gone for seven and a half years," Justine says. "We lived on Avenue A, not too far up from where the street name changes from Essex Street. Where do you live?"

"We live on Eldridge Street, a couple of blocks to the west of here," the man says. "We're Mr. and Mrs. Straussler."

"Would you like tea?" Mrs. Straussler asks. "You look like you could use something warm to drink. Those clothes can't be very good protection against the cold."

"I hope you don't mind we're not Jewish," Justine says. "Are we allowed to live on top of your bakery if we're Protestants?"

"Of course you are, you dear little girl. Sit down and I'll make you tea. Why aren't you spending today with your parents and brother? All the Christians I've ever known celebrate Christmas as a big, special family day."

"Our parents never get us Christmas presents," Adicia says. "Even when we were little, we never believed in Santa either. Only my little brother gets presents. He's thirteen. The only time we got presents was in '62, when we lived with our big brother for a few months. Our mother stormed over on Christmas Eve, shortly after she got outta jail for embezzling, and forced me, Justine, and one of our other sisters to go to her new tenement in Hell's Kitchen. Our brother, another sister, and our friends gave us their gifts before we left. Ever since, they've been scared to ship us presents, for fear our mother wouldn't give 'em to us or would sell 'em for drugs."

"Are you kidding?" Mr. Straussler gasps. "What kind of parents have you been cursed with? And just how many kids are there in your family? If I was counting correctly, there are at least six of yous!"

"Nine, six girls and three boys."

"Mr. Straussler and I only have three children," Mrs. Straussler says. "We had the first when I was twenty-one and the last when I was twenty-seven. I can't imagine having nine, or having school-aged children in my early fifties."

"Our parents aren't quite that old," Justine says. "They're forty-six, though our mother looks a good twenty years older except for not having gray hair yet."

"Have you lived in this neighborhood very long?" Adicia asks as Mrs. Straussler brings over a tray with tea and sets it on the little table near their chairs. "My mother thinks it's our Divine right to move back here and never leave just 'cause we've been here for over a hundred years on both sides of the family."

"Both of our parents came here when they were children," Mr. Straussler says. "That was in the 1890s. Has your family really been in America for over a century? That's pretty impressive."

"Our mother's people came over from Belgium in the late 1840s, and our dad's people were Huguenots who came here in the 1680s. I don't know when our dad's people came to this city, but they've been here at least as long as our mother's people. As groovy as it is to know I'm a fourteenth-generation American on one branch of my family tree, and that my family lived here before there was an America, I'm not treated the same as someone from a family with money and connections. My long American roots don't mean jack since I'm just a poor girl."

"Would you like some of our leftovers?" Mrs. Straussler asks. "We always give some of our overstock that's three days old and over to charity groups like the Bowery Mission or beggars who come to us on the Sabbath, but you could use some too."

"Oh, no, keep your food for people who need it more than us."

"Do you have any leftover challah?" Justine asks. "That bread is yummy. I remember eating it when we had our German-Jewish nanny Sarah. Our mother fired her shortly before we left the old neighborhood, for a really mean reason."

"Sarah was barely paid anything. She was little more than a slave, but she was more of a mother to us than our own mother could ever be."

"We have a few extra rolls not too stale to be given away," Mrs. Straussler says. "Honey with sesame seeds, challah with raisins, or challah with chocolate chips?"

"Can we have the one with chocolate chips?" Justine begs. "We don't have desserts very often."

"Our brother Allen works in a bakery too," Adicia says. "He's thinking about opening his own with his wife Lenore if they move Upstate. He's hoping to enroll in a two-year college so he can learn business management and get a student deferment in case he's drafted. His lottery number's only one hundred ten, so we're really scared."

"Our middle child is a boy," Mr. Straussler says. "Thankfully, he was born in '42, so he's just too old to be a victim of that draft. Though sadly, we do have nephews and cousins who've been forced to go over there. I proudly fought in the last war, but I don't think this one in Vietnam is at all justified. I can't understand what they ever did to us that was so awful it made such a long, bloody war necessary."

"It's swell you're a veteran. Our dad didn't serve, and the other kids at school made fun of us for that a lot. All their dads, uncles, and older brothers served in the Second World War. He did show up to take his tests, but they refused to take him when he failed all the medical and psychological tests for using drugs and drinking."

"Would you like cookies too?" Mrs. Straussler offers. "Our leftovers include apricot danish, orange, green, blue, and pink thumbprint cookies, chocolate and strawberry rugelach, and chocolate macaroons."

"You can't give all of them to us! That's taking it away from people who need food even more."

"You're not getting any Christmas presents from your parents. Think of this as a Christmas present from us, and a welcome back to the old neighborhood."

"What other kinds of things do you make here?" Justine asks, transfixed by the platter of cookies Mrs. Straussler is holding before them.

"Cinnamon buns, babka, cinnamon raisin bread, chocolate bread, pies, cakes, tortes, rolls, doughnuts, cookies, pastries, almond horns, maple rolls, sticky buns, hamantaschen at Purim, fruit rings, chocolate chip bread, pecan rings, cheesecakes, meltaways, jelly rolls, that sort of thing."

"Your bakery's awesome!"

"You're welcome to come by any time you'd like, and we'll give you some of our leftovers. We live on the second floor of a yellow walkup on Eldridge, if you'd ever like to stop by and talk. It's about three blocks south of the intersection between Eldridge and Houston Streets."

That night, when Adicia and Justine are back home, they think about how lucky they are to have left Hell's Kitchen behind and to have moved upstairs from a bakery run by such a nice couple. Christmas miracles have never existed in the Troy household, but this is pretty close to one. As they look up at the stars, Adicia remembers how Emeline once gave her a synopsis of *The Divine Comedy*, telling her Dante had to sink to the lowest, saddest point possible before he could slowly begin rising up to happier, more hopeful, and more beautiful places and ultimately emerge a better person. She also thinks about what Emeline told her about the similarity between agony and ecstasy, two emotions that don't seem at first glance to be such conjoined twins. Nothing can exist without its opposite, for otherwise how would anyone know what one versus the other felt like?

The twinkling of the stars in the night sky gives her hope that perhaps the Seventies will be a much better decade than the one that only has one week left. Emeline said each of the three sections of *The Divine Comedy* ends with the word "stars," a sweet, beautiful symbol of hope in the face of uncertainty and fear. Dante and Virgil see stars when they climb out of the Fourth Ring of the Ninth Circle of Hell, just like Adicia and Justine are now looking up at the same beautiful stars after they've left Hell's Kitchen to begin what they hope will be their ascent through Purgatory and Paradise.

Part IV: The Velveteen Ragdoll

(January 1972–July 1973)

Two shall be born the whole wide world apart...
And bend each wandering step to this one end,
That one day, out of darkness, they shall meet
And read life's meaning in each other's eyes.
(First intertitle of *Moran of the Lady Letty*, 1922)

"It doesn't happen all at once," said the Skin Horse. "You become. It takes a long time. That's why it doesn't happen often to people who break easily, or have sharp edges, or who have to be carefully kept. Generally, by the time you are Real, most of your hair has been loved off, and your eyes drop out and you get loose in the joints and very shabby. But these things don't matter at all, because once you are Real you can't be ugly, except to people who don't understand."
(*The Velveteen Rabbit*, Margery Williams)

Chapter 42: Introducing the Carsons

"Oh, look, we're getting new neighbors." Justine stops at the intersection between Houston and Essex Streets as she and Adicia are walking home from school shortly after the winter break has ended.

"They're in the nice part of the neighborhood," Adicia says jealously. "They must have money if they can live in the East Village and not our neck of the woods."

Justine gapes even more when moving men, clad in heavy winter coats, get out of a truck and van, unlock the moving truck, and start moving furniture and boxes into a six-story limestone townhouse on Avenue A, shortly after the switch from Essex Street to the part of the street now located in the East Village. From where they're standing, it looks like it's only a few buildings down from where they used to live, back before the East Village existed and the entire eastern section of downtown above the Financial District and Two Bridges was the Lower East Side. Hoping to get a closer look at the new neighbors who have enough money to afford a house in a nice neighborhood, the girls cross the street as soon as the light changes.

"Hello there. I guess you're watching my family moving into our new house," a strange but friendly voice says.

Adicia and Justine look up at a boy with slightly wavy, dark brown hair and deep brown eyes, standing about a foot taller than Adicia. Adicia thinks he's kind of cute, and wonders why a boy who must come from money is talking to girls who so obviously belong to the lower class.

"Oh, yes. We're somea your new neighbors. We live about another block south of here, right before Essex turns into Avenue A," Adicia says. "Right on the intersection with Houston."

"HOUSE-ton? My parents and I were pronouncing the name of that street like the city in Texas all day when we were trying to get directions. The native Manhattanites must've been laughing at us behind our backs."

"You're not from the city?" Justine asks. "Where are you moving from?"

"We're from Syracuse. My dad decided to quit his job, since he and my mother have been unhappy with the way the area's been heading lately. They found work in the Financial District, not too far from here, and thought the East Village sounded like a lovely neighborhood."

"We used to live in the East Village too, back when it was part of the Lower East Side," Adicia says. "That nice neighborhood your parents liked so much didn't exist till the last decade. The residents in the northern part of the neighborhood decided they were better than us and made an eastern version of Greenwich Village."

"Really? This was all the same neighborhood less than ten years ago?"

"Many of us still think of it as part of the Lower East Side," Justine says. "Lots of older people, particularly the Jewish people in our neighborhood, don't recognize the so-called East Village."

The boy smiles at them. "I'm sorry. I just realized I didn't introduce myself. My name's Ricky Carson."

"Glad to meet you," Adicia says. "I'm Adicia Troy, and this is my baby sister Justine. Is Ricky short for Richard or Eric?"

"Neither. Would you like another guess?"

Adicia thinks for a minute. "Frederick? Broderick?"

"You're still wrong. My real name is Warrick. It was my mother's maiden name. You can imagine why I go by Ricky."

"Warrick?" Justine asks. "What an awful name!"

"So your name is Alicia?" Ricky asks Adicia. "You don't look Spanish."

"Adicia. It's the Latinized form of Adikia, who was a Greek goddess. I've never met anyone else with my name."

"Pretty name. It's certainly nicer than Warrick."

"Are you gonna be going to high school with me? I'm a senior."

"You're a high school senior? I thought you were all of thirteen or fourteen! You've certainly kept your age well. By the time you're thirty, it'll be a good thing to look a lot younger."

"I'm only four foot ten. I'm probably the shortest girl in the senior class, besides being onea the youngest. My birthday isn't till July."

"Wow, you're only two years younger than me. I'm nineteen."

"So you're a college boy?" Justine asks. "Were you going to school in Syracuse, or are you switching to a school here?"

"I'm a college sophomore. I was going to Syracuse University, but my parents made me move with them and enrolled me in Columbia. They said I can't live on campus since we're so close by. That's money they could be spending on other things they need more. Say, what school are you going to in the fall?"

"My parents don't approve of higher education," Adicia says. "You don't wanna know what I had to do to secure being allowed to graduate high school. My older siblings attended college because they left home, but I can't run away and leave my sister behind."

A woman wearing an ocelot fur coat, very sharp, severe red lipstick and dark blue eyeshadow, gray hose, red stilettos, and a ridiculous hat with fake birds, playing cards, cigarettes, and holly berries affixed to it marches up to them. "Warrick Grover Carson, what in the hell are you doing talking to these ragged street urchins? You've been raised better than to even deign to associate with such trash!"

"Mother, these are the Troy girls, some of our new neighbors." Ricky sends them an apologetic look. "They live in the Lower East Side, just a short distance from here."

Mrs. Carson looks at the block behind them. "Ugh. I didn't realize we had moved so close to the ghetto. Don't tell me these girls are Jewish too."

"We're Protestants, not that it matters," Justine says, not willing to let this strange woman's insults stand. "For your information, your new-fangled East Village *was* part of the Lower East Side until five or so years ago. We useta live in its boundaries. Why are you calling my family's neighborhood for over a century a ghetto? It's come a long way since the days of overcrowding and tenements."

Mrs. Carson looks down at Justine with disgust. "Apparently they don't teach poor ghetto trash kids to be seen and not heard, nor do they teach you to watch your mouth around your elders and superiors. My Warrick knows better than to talk back to his elders. Go home to your ghetto, you pieces of trash."

"If you wanna be so mean to us when we don't even know yous guys, we're not sending a welcoming gift," Adicia states.

"Is that how they talk here?" Mr. Carson asks. "'Yous guys'? It sounds like something a hick from the Ozarks might say, in the same underclass league as 'y'all'!"

Mr. Carson is wearing a red derby with a peacock feather, a mauve mink coat, orange leather boots, and black pants that look like silk or satin. Adicia and Justine want to burst out laughing at how ridiculously Ricky's parents are dressed.

"They seem like swell girls," Ricky says. "Is it okay if they come over for supper or tea sometime? They only live a very short walk from here."

"These girls are no good, Warrick," Mrs. Carson repeats icily. "They're poor trash. Just look at how they're dressed and where they live. I won't have you associating with their ilk. Is that understood?"

"I'm nineteen, Mother. You might be able to control whom I associate with in the house, but not whom I choose to talk to when I'm on my own."

"Our neighborhood isn't so bad," Adicia says, barely able to believe she's defending it. "I lived in Hell's Kitchen for seven years before I came back home, and the Lower East Side's a paradise in comparison."

"Oh, how lovely. They're also former residents of that gangland Hell's Kitchen. Warrick, your father and I will stop paying your college tuition if you're caught associating with these ghetto girls or any other people, boy or girl, Negro, white, Oriental, or Spanish, Jew or Gentile, young or old, from *that* neighborhood. Understood?"

She and Mr. Carson disappear into the house, casting nasty looks back at Adicia and Justine on their way in. Ricky looks at them sympathetically.

"I don't share the attitudes of my parents about the classes mixing. I'll talk to whomever I want to, whenever I want to." He looks intently at Adicia. "Now that I know you're seventeen and not a kid in junior high, I can ask if you'd like to meet me sometime for a bite to eat."

"Are you asking Adicia out on a date?" Justine blurts out, not letting Adicia answer first.

"It is kinda forward to ask out a girl I've just met, but it's worth a shot, right? That is, if you don't already have a fellow."

"I'm just a poor girl." Adicia is very taken aback at how this rich boy she barely knows is already asking her out. "Not even working-class or lower-middle-class. I'll meet you as friends, but nothing more. People from such different social classes don't have anything in common, and most people don't approve of us mixing."

"Why don't I meet you at Tompkins Square Library after school sometime this week? Classes at Columbia won't start till a bit later in the month. You might not be the richest girl in town and really short for your age, but you're awfully pretty."

"You really think so?" Adicia hopes she isn't blushing. "Usually people say I look like a little ragdoll."

"In that case, you're the prettiest little ragdoll I've ever seen." Ricky starts walking up the steps to his new house. "I hope I see you again at the library, Adicia. It was nice meeting you too, Justine."

Adicia tries to laugh it off as they cross the street back into the boundaries of their neighborhood. It's so ridiculous, a rich, cute stranger who just moved into town asking her of all people out on a date. Even the fellow poor and working-class boys at school don't ask her out. Ricky would probably laugh if he knew she's never been on a date and hasn't even gotten her first menstrual period yet, at seventeen and a half. If he knew she's not a physical virgin, he'd probably immediately lose all interest in her.

"What, you don't like him?" Justine demands. "He's so cute, and he seems so nice!"

"He does seem nice, and he is really cute. But I don't know him. How can you like someone you've barely met? He doesn't know me. All he knows is he thinks I'm pretty. I don't wanna go out with a boy whose only basis for asking me out is I'm pretty. I want him to respect I have a brain too, and to like me for me, for what's inside and not just what's outside."

"Plus he's two years older than you. An older boy likes you."

"He's not that much older. Two years of difference at our ages isn't that big of a deal."

"Well, I think it's a big deal. An older boy is an older boy. Usually older boys don't bother with girls your age unless they really like them. He could easily ask out a college girl, but he decided he liked a high school senior instead."

Adicia looks back up the street before they start up the fire escape to their apartment. "A rich boy and a poor girl might be able to be friends, but they could never be more. I'll meet him as friends and nothing more."

"What if you start liking him as more than a friend?"

"I can't let myself like any guy as more than friends after what happened with that Pitskowski creep. I don't even want a guy touching me, even if he's the world's nicest guy. Now I know how Lenore felt when we met her. You can't get those images and feelings outta your head."

"Remember how Girl—I mean, Deirdre—always useta talk about auras, those invisible energy fields put out by people and things? I had a very good feeling about Ricky. He's not onea the bad guys. He's onea the rich people we can trust, not onea the ones who secretly pretends to be our friend but laughs at us or sabotages us behind our backs. Maybe he's our ticket outta this place. At least, he could be your ticket out."

"Guys don't want a girl who's not a virgin. I can't believe I still haven't menstruated yet at seventeen and a half. And I'm so short. That's not a woman, that's a little girl playing at being a woman."

"I don't know. Don't be so eager to rule out anything. Either this is the beginning of a beautiful friendship, or it's a guy you've got nothing in common with. I don't think you ever meet anybody by accident. Remember that line Emeline used to quote a lot, from Voltaire?"

"'All events are linked together in this best of all possible worlds.'"

"I think that was the best chance meeting we've ever had."

Chapter 43: "Don't Get Above Your Raising"

Adicia is at a table at the Tompkins Square Library with Justine a few days later, reading the latest issue of *Seventeen* and daydreaming they have enough money to buy the pretty clothes, when Ricky comes into the library and joins their table without asking.

"Hello," Adicia says in a quiet voice. "You still remember us?"

"You're Adicia, and that's Justine. The Troy girls. You remember me, right?"

"Warrick Grover Carson, Ricky for short."

"Is Grover after Grover Cleveland?" Justine asks. "You're too old to be named after the Muppet on *Sesame Street*. Our brother's daughters watch that show, and we spend a lot of time with them on the weekends and during summer vacation. Our parents don't have a TV."

"No, it's just another family name. I hate having three surnames in a row. Why couldn't I have been just another Joe, Mike, or Pete?"

"I never wished I had a more common name," Adicia says. "Mosta the girls I've known have only had about twenty names between 'em. My sisters and I used to refer to some of them as the Debbies, the Lindas, and the Susans."

"Are you an only child?" Justine asks. "We have seven other siblings."

"Nine kids! That's a different extreme from me being an only child. Are you the youngest?"

"I'm the seventh and Justine's the baby," Adicia says. "We have a brother, Tommy, in between us, who's gonna be sixteen next month. We're the last ones left at home. Besides us, the only one left in the city is our big brother Allen. He wanted me to try applying to colleges, but our parents would never let me, and I don't know if I woulda passed the math section if I'd taken the SAT."

"You didn't take an SAT? Aren't all seniors required to take it? My parents made me take it as a junior, and when I didn't do as well as they wanted, they made me take it twice more."

"My parents don't wanna throw their money away on something like that. I'm not allowed to go to college, though my older sisters went."

"How did your sisters get to go to college but you can't?"

"They ran away. I might've done that a long time ago, but I can't leave Justine all by herself. I'd just about die for her."

"Our oldest sister Gemma went to Hofstra, our second sister Lucine went to Hunter, our next sister Emeline went to Vassar and is now at the University at Albany, and our sister Ernestine's at Vassar," Justine says. "Allen just graduated the Borough of Manhattan Community College with an associate's degree in business management. He really needed an additional draft deferment."

"Oh, that would scare me so much if I faced being drafted. My parents are confident I'll get out of it 'cause I'm a full-time student and we've got money. I feel bad for those boys who don't have the connections to avoid Vietnam. The draft, and the military in general, preys on poor and working-class boys. Maybe I'm a limousine liberal, but it's what I really believe. I'll never have the first-hand experience you do, but at least I can be your ally."

"What are you studying at college?" Adicia asks.

"Political science and art history. My parents want me to be a professor, if I won't be a doctor or lawyer."

"I don't know what I'd study if I went to college. I kinda like what my sister-in-law Lenore does, taking care of her kids while my brother goes to work. She used to write press releases for an art gallery. If they move Upstate, they'll open a bakery. We live on top of a bakery now. You can come and visit if you'd like. It's run by an older German-Jewish couple named the Strausslers. They're first-generation Americans."

Ricky looks over at the magazine. "I've seen a lot of girls reading that magazine. Is it any good?"

"We'll never be able to afford the clothes, and we never go to the movies or on dates, but it's nice to daydream. We've listened to popular music, but we don't have our own records or record player. Our oldest sister Gemma used to subscribe. I can't believe they still advertise china, silverware, wedding dresses, and engagement rings so many years later, even if some girls still marry really young."

"Adicia's getting married as soon as she's eighteen," Justine says.

"You are? I thought you didn't have a boyfriend."

"My parents will pick the guy. They don't believe in girls getting educated. What was good enough for them should be good enough for me. He'll probably be at least twenty years older. At least they promised me a handsome husband with a good job for making a big sacrifice when I was fifteen."

"That's not a nice fate. You're not helpless, are you? Once you're eighteen, they can't do anything legally to keep you or to force you to get married. That's also pretty young to be married, unless you have to get married because of a baby."

"I'll try to think of ways to escape as the date gets closer. I wish there were a way to take Justine with me."

"You haven't heard the half of how terrible our parents are," Justine says.

Adicia looks up and sees a familiar form bending over the magazine rack. She grimaces when the woman pulls herself back up and looks in their direction.

"Who's that?" Justine asks. "What did we do to her?"

"Do you remember that busybody Mrs. Rossi? That's the same woman, only a lot fatter."

Mrs. Rossi swaggers over to their table. "Hello, girls. Who's the young man?"

"He's a new neighbor," Adicia says. "Do you live around here now?"

"I've been in Little Italy since the fire, and I currently work in the Meatpacking District. Do your parents know you have a boyfriend, Adicia?"

"He's not a boyfriend. We just met him a few days ago."

"You should know better than to get too friendly with boys, knowing your parents are gonna find a husband for you this summer. Besides, even if you wanna have your teenage fun with boys before it's time to buckle down and become a married woman and a mother, no decent boy wants to date damaged merchandise. I'm sure your mother will be most interested to learn of this."

"How is Adicia damaged merchandise?" Justine asks.

"Oh, stop playing stupid. You know as well as anyone what she did to keep your mother from returning to the slammer. You're lucky, Adicia, that your parents will find you an older widower or divorced man, someone who won't care he ain't getting a pure, untouched virgin for a bride."

Adicia hides her face in the magazine as Mrs. Rossi shuffles up to the circulation desk with her magazines.

"What was she talking about?" Ricky asks in confusion. "Your mother's been in prison and almost went back to prison at some point? And she said you're not a virgin?"

"It's nothing," Adicia says in a small voice, her voice cracking. "Just troubled water under the bridge."

"Please don't remind her of it." Justine puts her arm around Adicia protectively. "Adicia feels awful enough she agreed to go through with that."

"Go through with *what?*"

"That's not something we wanna tell someone we barely know. All you need to know is our brother tracked this guy down and put the fear of God into him. He's not in jail or dead, but Allen did the next-best thing. He probably had a good twenty years taken off his life that night."

"That's okay if you don't want to discuss such a personal matter with someone you only met a few days ago, but I hope eventually you'll like and trust me enough to clue me in. If you're really not a virgin, I don't think that's a character flaw or a sin, however it happened."

"Thank you," Adicia says lifelessly. "You won't go around telling people, will you?"

"I'm not like that. I was never one of those guys who thinks boys will be boys but a girl is a fallen woman if she does that, even if it was done to her and not something she chose to do. Your secret's safe with me."

"That's really nice of you," Justine says. "I like you already."

"I'm glad you like me. I hope Adicia likes me too."

"I'm taking a wait and see approach to that," Adicia says.

***

Mrs. Troy is puffing away at her cocaine pipe when the girls come home at 6:00. Tommy is dribbling his basketball, uncaring the customers at the Strausslers' bakery are very annoyed at all the noise he's making.

"My friend Luigina stopped me in the street when I was on my way home from my new job and told me she saw you at the library with a strange boy. Even if you told her the truth that he ain't a boyfriend you're running around with like a wanton slut, I'd like to know just who the hell he is."

"Adicia has a boyfriend?" Tommy asks. "Wonders never cease."

"He's not a boyfriend," Adicia says. "We just met him a few days ago, when he moved up the street with his parents. He did ask me out, but I said I just wanted to get to know him as a friend.”

“You were right to turn him down. Like hell I’d let you date anyone. Your role in life is to go straight from our home to your future husband’s home. Either this fall or this summer, you’re gonna become a married woman, and to an older man, not a fresh-faced boy your age. Is he at least a fellow poor boy?”

“His parents are rich,” Justine says. “They don’t like him talking to us, but he’s old enough to do his own thing and not listen to their classist ideas.”

“You’re dreaming if you think a rich boy who lives in that uppity part of the neighborhood wants to be your friend or boyfriend. The classes ain’t supposed to mix. Don’t get above your raising, Adicia. Even if he’s crazy enough to be sincere about wanting to be friends with you, he’s gonna give you ideas, like maybe you oughta go to college, postpone marriage and motherhood, work a real career, move outta the neighborhood, live in a real house, only have two or three kids, drive a car, dress in minks and silks, marry for love. Your fate is to follow in my footsteps and the footsteps of all our foremothers. You’ll work a series of menial jobs, live in the same neighborhood, pop out nine or ten kids, live in crummy apartments and tenements, have a husband who might not love you but who brings in the bacon. Do you understand your responsibilities and obligations as a poor girl from a poor family?”

“Do you have any candidates in mind for my future husband?”

“Not yet, but your father and I will send out the bloodhounds if we have to. Your wedding will be our crowning triumph, a chance to say that finally we got a kid who didn’t get above her raising, who accepted her socially-dictated role in life. Your wedding will finally shut up all my critics.”

“Do I hafta get married at eighteen too?” Tommy asks nervously. “I’m not interested in girls like that yet. The girls in my classes are all either whores or prudes.”

“You’re a boy. Boys don’t gotta get married as young as girls. They have the right to experience life a little before being tied down forever. Maybe when you’re thirty I’ll start looking.”

“Being a boy rocks!”

“What if I can’t have kids?” Adicia asks. “He might reject me as a wife, and you'd be embarrassed all over again. You know I've never menstruated."

"You're small for your age. Girls like you sometimes start a lot later than their friends. If it ain't started by your eighteenth birthday, we'll have you inspected to make sure you're quality merchandise. You have a very promising womanly body in spite of your shortness. Any man would be a fool to turn that package down just 'cause there might be a delay with childbearing. Tommy, wouldn't you love to marry a woman who looks like a child? That's most men's dream come true."

"That's gross. Why would I wanna date or marry a woman 'cause she looks like a little kid? Only perverts and deviants are attracted to little kids."

"Adicia, how old is this fellow Luigina caught you with?"

"Nineteen."

"So even if he was from our class and a marriage candidate we approved of, he wouldn't be nearly old enough for you. He's a teenager. Teenage boys don't make enough money to support a wife and kids. I know. I got married when your father and I was eighteen. Teenage boys ain't even got enough experience to be good lovers. We'll find you a much-older man who's been around the block enough times to know how to please a woman."

"I'm not interested in Ricky in that way, Mother."

"The best thing you can do is to ignore any further attempts on his part at friendship. Most of all, don't let yourself develop any feelings for him. It'll be worse when it comes time to get married, since your husband wouldn't be the man in your heart. Remember, only trouble comes from the classes mixing."

***

That Sunday, while Justine visits Lenore and the girls, Adicia and Ricky have lunch at an outdoor café in the West Village. Adicia is confident in her decision to only make friends with Ricky, nothing more, and figures having an ally on the block can't hurt. He might come in handy if she needs to run away to avoid being traded off like a piece of meat by her parents.

After their sandwich plates are cleared, a waiter brings dessert menus. Adicia looks over it long and hard before finally deciding on a blueberry turnover with powdered sugar and whipped cream.

"You must not have dessert too often," Ricky says after the waiter takes their orders.

"We have a lot of it when we visit our brother, but not at home. I've only rarely gone to a real restaurant."

He smiles at her. "In that case, I'd be happy to take you out every weekend. It's not right for anyone to grow up not knowing what it's like to eat out or have fancy desserts."

Adicia looks around and then at the ground. "I'm used to it. I just like having a chance to do it when I can. Don't feel obligated to keep taking me out. Remember, this isn't a date."

Ten minutes later, the waiter returns with their desserts. Adicia sees Ricky moving his fork to the left side of his plate just like she's doing. Across the table, Ricky smiles at her when he sees what she's doing.

Adicia laughs. "Don't tell me the universe put yet another lefty in my circle. That makes thirteen of us."

"My kindergarten teacher tied weights to my hand, but that only lasted one day. My parents threatened to sue the school and get a private tutor for me if she didn't leave me alone. I've never known a female lefty before. So you know a lot of others?"

"Me, my sisters Emeline, Ernestine, and Justine, my brother Allen, my sister-in-law Lenore, my nieces Irene and Amelia, our four friends the Ryans, and now you. My dad was born one, but he gave in to teachers tryna switch him."

"Now I like you even more, knowing you're one of my own."

Out of the corner of her eye, Adicia thinks she sees her brother. Her suspicions are confirmed when he approaches their table.

"What a surprise to see you, Da—" Allen stops mid-word when he realizes she's sitting with a stranger. "That's not David!"

"Why would I be out with David? He lives in Poughkeepsie."

"Who's David, a former boyfriend?" Ricky asks.

"He's a really good friend of mine. We grew up together and knew each other since we were seven. He's my sister Ernestine's best friend's brother."

Allen looks at his sister and her companion in shock. "Adicia, are you on a date?"

"No! This is Ricky, who moved up the street recently. I'm just getting to know him as friends."

"Well, in my experience, if a girl wants to get to know a guy as only friends, they don't go out to eat. What are your intentions towards my sister?"

"To be honest, I really would like to go on a date with her, but she insists she only wants to be friends and that a poor girl and rich boy shouldn't get mixed up."

Allen stares at him even more intently. "You're a rich boy? What in the hell are you doing with my little sister? Don't you know she comes from an entirely different world than you? A rich boy and a poor girl could never have anything in common. You could have any rich girl you wanted. Why raise my sister's hopes and let her believe she could be the wife or girlfriend of a rich man? Even just being friends is cruel to her. She's getting a glimpse of a world she knows will never be hers. At the end of the day, she'll still be coming home to a poor neighborhood and our crummy parents, not a lavish mansion on the Upper West Side, servants, a chauffeured limo, caviar for breakfast, designer clothes, and boarding school." He looks over to his sister. "And you, Adicia. What's so wrong about a boy like David Ryan? He's one of us, and practically family. He'd be a much better match for you than this rich boy. Don't tell me he's a limousine liberal who thinks he knows and understands the struggles of the working man so much better than we do. These people can bleat and protest all they want about the exploitation of the poor and working-class, but at the end of the day, they'll be going home to their cushy neighborhoods, far away from the grim realities we grew up facing."

"I don't live on the Upper West Side. My parents and I live in the East Village. We just moved from Syracuse earlier this week. We were such out-of-towners, we didn't know we were mispronouncing Houston Street when we asked for directions our first day here. How were we supposed to know it's not pronounced like the city in Texas?"

"That's even better. A pampered rich kid who didn't grow up in the city, who knows absolutely nothing of what we've lived through. He was raised in an exclusive suburb of Syracuse, far away from the poverty, crime, and violence of the city. Do you know your precious, so-called East Village used to be a part of *our* old neighborhood till about six years ago? Your little mansion's only a stone's throw away from the city's historic ghetto region."

"We don't live in a mansion. We live in a townhouse."

"Makes no difference. Most New Yorkers don't have the luxury of living in houses. Even a lot of rich people live in apartments. What makes your family so much better than the rest of us that you deserve your own entire house all to yourselves? People Upstate live in houses. Us city folk live in apartments."

"My parents don't like poor or working-class people. They didn't want to share living space with anyone who might not be from money, so they picked a downtown neighborhood that sounded upscale."

"Oh, and I suppose you're gonna tell me how much you love the lower classes and support us in our struggle, when you've been shielded from harsh realities of life by your parents your entire life. By the time all of us were ten years old, we knew about stuff most rich kids don't know exist till they're adults! Growing up poor makes you a lot more grown-up and mature for your age. I became the man of the house when I was eighteen and had my little sisters living with me for a time, whereas you'll still be sheltered by your rich parents at eighteen, not made to work and rent your own place."

"I'm not Adicia's age. I'm nineteen."

"Isn't this great. Not only are you a rich boy from out of area, but you're also too old for her. She's not even eighteen! My wife is three years my junior, and I didn't do or say anything about it till she was eighteen!"

"Please, Allen," Adicia begs. "You're causing a scene. The difference between seventeen and nineteen isn't a big deal."

"Do you know my sister has never had any romantic attention from a boy her entire life? You're diseased if you plan to get her hopes up and leave for a rich girl. Adicia, I'd like you to come home with me. I was on my way to buy groceries, and boy, am I glad I decided to run that errand. The rich boy can pay for whatever you ordered. Money grows on trees for him."

"I haven't finished eating."

"We'll get the waiter to wrap it up for you, and then you're coming with me. I'm sure Lenore will also wanna have a talk with you about how you're best off if you stick to your own kind."

"You're not being fair. You sound like Mother and Dad with their 'Don't get above your raising' speeches."

"I have no problem with you doing better than the awful way they raised us. You're supposed to want to do better than your parents. What I do have a problem with is the idea of a rich boy thinking he can seduce my little sister as a charity project. There are plenty of nice boys in the neighborhood, I'm sure, who'd love to date a pretty girl like you and make you a respectable wife. I'd gladly approve of any of those boys for a potential boyfriend or husband. This guy isn't it."

Adicia seethes as she walks back with Allen after a waiter wraps up her dessert. When Ricky waves goodbye, Allen takes her by the hand that isn't holding the takeout package and steers her down the street, taking a longer walk to the grocer so they don't have to walk in front of the café.

After Allen purchases a loaf of bread, eggs, milk, cheese, mushrooms, and two pounds of beef, he turns to Adicia and smilingly asks if she'd like any candy or chocolate to make her feel better. Too angry at him to speak, she silently shakes her head.

"Why the long face?" Lenore asks when they come through the door of 515.

"Adicia's a little upset 'cause I had to crash a date she was on. She'll forgive me before long, when she realizes I acted in her own best interest."

"It was not a date," Adicia says. "Can't a boy and a girl just be friends?"

"Wait, Adicia was on a date?" Lenore asks. "Where did she get a boyfriend?"

"Ricky's a swell guy," Justine says. "I really like him."

Allen turns to look at their baby sister. "You know this guy too?"

"Yeah, we met him when he and his awful parents moved up the street. We haven't known him very long, but already I think he's a really nice guy."

"I know he likes me, but I only want to get to know him as a friend," Adicia says. "He might come in handy when I need a place to go so I don't have to marry whatever guy Mother and Dad force on me after I graduate."

"You always have a place here," Allen says. "All you have to do is come here, and Lenore and I will protect you. Justine can join you, if you're worried about leaving her behind. I'll get custody of yous guys before Mother can do what she did last time. I'd do anything to protect you and take care of you. It's my job as your big brother and the only real man in your life."

"Does he know you only want to get to know him as a friend?" Lenore asks.

"I've told him that. If he's a gentleman, he'll respect that and not try to push for more." Adicia opens the takeout box and starts eating the pastry with her hands.

"You see?" Allen asks. "I'm perfectly fine with you eating with your hands. Rich boys like Ricky think it's a scandal if you don't eat everything with a fork and knife. I've heard some rich people even eat watermelon, bacon, fried chicken, and bananas with a fork."

"His name is Richard?" Lenore asks. "You had an awful bully named Richard in Hell's Kitchen. I would've thought you developed a bad association with that name. Plus it's the name of that ogre Nixon."

"His full name is Warrick. It was his mother's maiden name."

"What a perfect rich boy name, Warrick," Allen says. "Only rich people give their kids surnames as first names. That kinda name would sound ridiculous on a boy of our class."

"Some rich people are our friends. They really mean it when they say they care about us, and they're in a better position than we are to do something about helping us. A guy who comes from money can get elected to government and make laws that help us get outta poverty, like raising minimum wage, giving free birth control to women who already have too many kids, and improving schools in run-down neighborhoods so more kids will graduate and wanna go to college."

"And what is this Warrick fellow doing to make any of that happen?"

"He's just a college boy. He was going to Syracuse University, but his parents forced him to move with them and enrolled him at Columbia. He'll be starting there soon, when the winter break ends. He's studying political science and art history."

"Oh, just like all the other pampered college kids from money who've been staging all those anti-war protests and claiming they care so much about the common man. They only get to do that 'cause their parents had the money to send them to college! While they've been busy protesting the draft, I was fighting to stay safe 'cause I don't have the kinda money to get an automatic deferment! Even the school I got the student deferment from was a two-year school, not a school for rich kids like Columbia, Yale, or Harvard! The boy is your classic limousine liberal."

"What's a limousine liberal?" Justine asks. "I've heard the term before, but I never understood what it meant."

"A rich person who bleats about how much he loves the common man and champions our causes, like better wages and nicer schools, but goes back to his mansion in his limo at the end of the day, far away from the reality we live through. He does nothing to achieve those things. He's all talk and no action. Going to a bunch of student protests doesn't mean jack if you're not taking the next step and campaigning for change too."

"But Ricky really does wanna be friends with me and Justine," Adicia says. "Even if he is a so-called limousine liberal, what's the harm in that? He supports us instead of pretending we don't exist or being mean to us."

"Does your Ricky have a job, or is he supported by his parents while he plays at Columbia?"

"He has a trust fund he got access to when he turned eighteen. He tries to be responsible and practical about what he spends the money on now that it's his for the taking."

"How can you hate him so much when you don't know him?" Justine asks. "What did he do to you that was so awful?"

"Rich people have nothing in common with us," Allen says. "Our life experiences are worlds apart. He can never relate to the half of what Adicia's gone through. Think of the consequences of a potential relationship or God forbid marriage. You'd never be accepted by his family and friends 'cause you're not rich or even upper-middle-class, and he'd never be accepted in our poor and working-class world. You'd both become pariahs. I didn't marry above or beneath me. Lenore comes from a poor family just like ours. She knows very well about the kinda stuff I went through growing up, and was forced to grow up really fast too. Tell me, Adicia, don't you feel more like thirty or forty than seventeen?"

"Yes, but it doesn't change the fact that I'm a teenager. It's nice to be able to do normal teenage stuff from time to time."

"Even if I were to give this Ricky character the benefit of the doubt that he really does wanna be your friend and that his intentions are sincere, you have no business meeting with him if you only want friendship and he wants to be your boyfriend. The worst thing you can do to someone who has feelings for you is lead him on. I'd be just as upset if you were the one who liked him and he was leading you on to expect more in the future."

"I've told him I only wanna be friends. I'm not dumb. If he wants more, he's dreaming."

"Feelings for a person don't die overnight. When you really like a person, you don't just stop liking her 'cause there's no forthcoming relationship. Lenore and I liked each other for three years before we did anything about it. And it killed me inside to be so close to the girl I loved but unable to do anything about it for so long. Every time you meet with him as just friends, he'll see that as a reason to get his hopes up that you might really be starting to like him as a boyfriend. This can only end badly."

"Oh, come on, Allen, let her enjoy the attentions of a boy who likes her," Lenore jumps in. "If he's legit, he'll get the message soon that Adicia only wants friendship and stop tryna pursue it. He won't be the first guy who's ever had a romantic disappointment. He can move on to a girl who wants to be his girlfriend and continue just getting to know Adicia as a friend. Is he handsome?"

"He's pretty cute," Adicia admits. "Beautiful deep brown eyes and dark brown wavy hair. He's about a foot taller than me, though most guys are. He's nineteen."

Lenore smiles at her. "How exciting! An older guy likes you! I wish Allen hadn't insisted on being such a damn gentleman and waiting till I was eighteen to tell me he loved me. There's not much difference between seventeen and nineteen."

"She's not even eighteen," Allen says, unable to believe his wife and both of his sisters are against him.

"It's not like he's forty or she's twelve. It's usually better if a girl gets a boyfriend or husband who's a little older than her. An older man can take care of you and support you and your future family better than a guy who's your age."

"Most of the guys in my senior class are pretty immature, not guys I wanna date or even be friends with," Adicia agrees. "And I just discovered today he's a fellow southpaw."

"No way!" Justine says. "That makes thirteen of us!"

"What's his full name?" Lenore asks.

"Warrick Grover Carson," Adicia says. "Poor guy got three surnames in a row."

"Carson is an English surname, isn't it?" Allen asks.

"Are you tryna tell me I can't even be friends with someone from a different ancestry? What about the Ryans? You were just suggesting David is a perfect match for me!"

"British-Americans haven't had as much of a bum deal as other immigrants. Even his ancestors probably weren't poor."

"You wanted her to go out with David?" Lenore asks in amusement. "He's practically her brother! They've known each other since age seven!"

"I noticed he's kinda cute in the last pictures from Ernestine, but if he or Adicia ever liked each other, they kept it top secret," Justine says.

"*You* think he's cute?" Allen demands. "You'll only be thirteen in March!"

"So? I can't start noticing boys at my age?"

"He's five years older than you!"

"I hope you don't act this crazy and overprotective when Irene and Amelia are old enough to start noticing boys and getting date offers," Lenore says.

Adicia gets up to go to the bathroom, a nagging cramp in the bottom of her stomach. She assumes her stomach is all in knots from the argument and having her meeting with Ricky crashed so rudely, but she freezes when she sees a bloodstain. *This is only about four or five years overdue,* she thinks as she creeps up to the bathroom door and looks around. When she sees Allen in the kitchen, preparing an early supper for the girls, she leans out and quietly calls for Lenore.

"What is it, sweetie? Are you getting sick?"

"I need your help," she whispers in mortification, hoping Allen stays put in the kitchen.

"If you have a stomachache…" Lenore's voice trails off when she sees the bloodstain.

"Do you have any safety pins or something that can hold a napkin in place till I get home and can put on a belt?"

"Oh, sweetie, you're finally a real woman! I was starting to think this day would never come!" Lenore hugs her. "Now you can make babies!"

"Not till I'm married, I hope."

"This is onea the things that separates girls from women. I'm so glad I was here when you finally had this rite of passage. It's like pregnancy, birth, and your first consensual sex. Now you know what the big mysterious secret is all about. Seventeen is on the late end to get your first menses, but better late than never, right?"

"Are you crying, Lenore?"

"I've known you since you were eight years old. Watching you and your sisters grow up has been a really special thing for me. You were a little girl when I met you, and now you're a full woman."

"Please don't tell Allen."

"He doesn't hafta know. Particularly not after what a beast he was to you today. In the meantime, you can borrow some of my napkins. Wait'll you see what kind they are."

"Those look like ordinary sanitary napkins to me," Adicia scoffs when Lenore pulls a box from under the sink.

"Just wait'll you take one out of the box. These are really special."

Adicia looks at it closely on both sides. "What's so special about it? Are these somea those flushable ones?"

"You don't need a belt to wear these!" Lenore whispers happily. "They have adhesive strips on the back!"

"No way! They finally invented something you can just stick on without pins or a belt?"

"You can take the whole box if you'd like, since I won't need 'em again until the fall." Lenore gently strokes her midsection.

"You're the best sister-in-law ever. You're the best thing we ever found at a bus stop."

"Nothing in this world ever happens by chance. Just like it was destiny I met you and Allen at that bus stop, it might very well be destiny you met that cute older rich boy. Time will only tell just why you met him when you met him."

Chapter 44: Allen and Lenore's Difficult Decision

On a Sunday towards the end of January, Allen, Lenore, and their girls go ice-skating at the Lasker Rink at Central Park. Their skate rentals are cheaper than the Wollman Rink. Amelia thinks she's a big kid because they were able to find a pair of ice-skates to fit her little two-year-old feet, though she feels a little safer when she glides around the rink as someone holds her.

Irene is the spitting image of Lenore, with emerald-green eyes and raven hair, and Amelia looks like Allen, with brown eyes and slightly wavy brown hair. Lenore wonders what their coming third child will look like. If it's a third girl, maybe she'll have green eyes and brown hair instead of taking so totally after one parent. If it's a boy, she hopes he looks like Allen. He deserves to have a child in his own image after he's been so surrounded by girls and women his entire life. As of now, Lenore has known she's pregnant for about six weeks, which probably would put the conception date sometime in early December. If Allen knew, he might not let her go ice-skating, for fear she might miscarry if she falls. Sometimes his overprotectiveness is more annoying than sweet, particularly considering her health scare was seven years ago.

"Daddy, I'm hungry," Irene announces. "Can we take a break and get something from a vendor?"

"Anything for one of my beautiful princesses," he says. "Do you have a preference?"

"I like hot chocolate with crème Chantilly, though no one makes it better than Mommy. Do they sell hotdogs and hamburgers in the winter?"

"Irene Lily Troy, your father isn't made of money," Lenore chides her gently. "The proper response is to tell him you'd like to eat and drink whatever's available, not request things he might not be able to afford or find."

"It's not a big deal." Allen pats Irene on the head. "It's not like she demanded I find her caviar and filet mignon."

"What's that?" Irene asks.

"Caviar is fish eggs, and filet mignon is an expensive kind of steak. Rich people eat that stuff."

"Ew, that's gross. Who wants to eat fish eggs?"

"People like your aunt Adicia's new rich friend Ricky and his parents, that's who."

"Oh, Allen, lay off her," Lenore pleads. "Her friend seems honorable so far. You know from our own experience a person can take a totally different path from one's parents and not just blindly follow family history."

"You don't even know Ricky," Irene agrees. "Why do you hate someone you only met once? You decided right away he was no good for Aunt Adicia."

"That boy has got a hell of a lot of proving to do before I'll accept he's a decent friend for her, but I'm not gonna have that argument in front of you and Amelia. I'll go find hot chocolate and whatever hot food I can. Why don't you wait for me on a bench?"

"There are so many benches here, you'll have to see us over to one first so you don't get lost or can't find us when you get back," Lenore says. "I know how you get if you think I disappeared after what happened seven years ago."

"What happened to you seven years ago, Mommy?" Irene asks after they've sat down on a bench and Allen has gone off to find refreshments.

"I got very sick," Lenore says vaguely, not wanting her four-and-a-half-year-old to be upset at too many details. "I fell down in the snow and went to sleep for two weeks. Your daddy wasn't my boyfriend yet, but he loved me very much and went to look for me. He gave me his coat, gloves, and hat, carried me home, and got me to the hospital. Ever since then, he's been very scared I might get sick again if I don't eat enough or if I get too cold. When you're a grownup, I hope you have a husband who wants to protect you just as much, though not as fanatically as your daddy."

"Why did you sleep for two weeks?" Amelia asks.

"I got really cold from being out in the falling snow and freezing weather with no winter clothes. I also had a very high fever. That'll never happen to either of you, since you always wear warm clothes in the winter. Your mommy wasn't thinking straight when she ran away from your daddy that night. The only good thing that came of that ordeal was that it showed me just how very much he loved me, if he would take care of me so tenderly and nurse me back to health over so many months, when he didn't have any obligation to do anything for me. He paid my entire hospital bill and pretended to the doctors and nurses we were married, so they'd treat me nicely."

"How come you had to pretend to be married?" Irene asks.

"A lot of people think bad things about a man and a woman who live together without being married, even if they're just roommates. People assume some very silly things. By the time you're old enough to be married, you'll probably be able to live with your husbands before marriage without many people blinking an eye or judging you. I hope you appreciate all the good things you'll have growing up, things girls couldn't dream of when I was growing up."

"Hello, Lenore."

Lenore turns to look at the man who just sat next to them and blanches, immediately pulling her daughters closer to her.

"How come you're shaking, Mommy?" Irene asks. "Your heart is beating so loud I can hear it."

"So you've gone and had yourself a couple of brats since you ran away from Greenpoint. Are these your only kids, or do you have some older ones where they came from? What are you now, twenty-five?"

"Twenty-four," she says nervously. "These are my only children."

"I always took such good care to send you off to the doctor every week to check for pregnancy and venereal diseases. I guess once you took off on your own, you wasn't so careful anymore about avoiding scandal. Do both these brats have the same father? Do you even know who the father is?"

"These are my husband's children! I've been married for five and a half years and have known my husband for nine and a half years. If he knew you found me and are sitting here talking to me, he'd want to kill you for what you did to me."

"You found a man willing to marry a fallen woman? He musta been desperate for a wife and to get laid if he'd voluntarily pick a girl who wasn't a virgin."

"My husband is a perfectly respectable working-class man who works hard to take care of his family, and would do anything for us. Believe it or not, Father, he always considered me a virgin because I never willingly did that. My husband is the only man I've ever done anything with. What you forced on me doesn't count, since I didn't want it. What are you doing out of Brooklyn?" Lenore looks around to see if Allen's coming back, but can't make him out in the crowds.

"Can't a man visit Central Park to go skating just because he wants to? This husband of yours ain't here now. He probably won't miss you if you come back to Brooklyn with me. These brats can come with you. They're almost old enough to be broken in, don't you think?"

"You will *never* touch my daughters!" Lenore screams, picking Amelia up and dragging Irene by the hand, running into the crowd as fast as she can on ice-skates.

"Where are we going, Mommy?" Irene asks, struggling to keep up with her mother's ferocious speed. "Was that man your daddy?"

"He's a very bad man," Lenore says breathlessly, trying to picture how to get out of the park and to 34th Street, where they can go into Macy's and hide until she thinks it's safe to come out.

"How's Daddy gonna find us? He's gonna go crazy if he finds us missing."

"I'll worry about that later."

Instead of running towards the 110th Street entrance, Lenore winds up going farther into the park and running aimlessly among the crowds. She hopes there aren't any pickpockets and that she doesn't drop Amelia or let go of Irene. She barely cares if they leave wearing their ice-skates and are punished for stealing. All she can think about is how to get far, far away from her degenerate father.

"Mommy, look out, we're on ice!" Irene shouts as they approach Pilgrim Hill.

Lenore skids on the patch of ice and slides down the hill as sledders try their best to steer out of her way. She holds onto Amelia tightly so she doesn't go flying, letting go of Irene's hand. Irene sits down and pushes herself down the hill.

"Are you okay, Mommy?"

"My right foot hurts. I hope it's not broken."

"Where were you trying to go?"

"I was thinking about Macy's on 34th Street. It's not that far from the park. Amelia, does anything hurt?"

"I'm scared," Amelia whimpers. "I want Daddy."

"I'm scared to try to get up. If I broke my foot, standing up will put too much weight on it and make it worse." Lenore gently sets Amelia down and brings her hands to her midsection. "Oh, God, I hope I didn't lose the baby."

"You're having a baby, Mommy?" Irene asks excitedly. "Why didn't you tell us?"

"It was supposed to be a surprise for your daddy. Your aunts knew about it, but I wanted to wait a little while before I let your daddy know. I was hoping it'd be a boy, so your daddy could finally get his son."

Irene huddles close to her mother and sister as they try to stay out of the way of the sledders. No one offers them any assistance during the two hours they're waiting for a friendly cop to show up, or to catch sight of Allen. Lenore's first thought when they finally see Allen coming over the horizon is that she hopes he won't be too mad at her for running away without telling him.

"What happened to you? I was about ready to give up searching the park and start checking out hospitals."

"Mommy hurt her right foot," Irene reports. "She's afraid she might've lost her new baby when she fell down the hill."

"Baby? Lenore, are you pregnant?"

She nods, bursting into tears. "Please don't be angry at me, Allen. I love you more than anyone in this world besides our girls."

He kneels on the snow and hugs her tightly. "How long have you known?"

"About six weeks. It probably happened in early December or late November. I wanted to wait for a special time to tell you, and not let you in on the secret right away, since you knew so soon with the girls. Please don't be mad at me for not telling you or for running away."

"Is our food still hot?" Irene asks when she sees the paper bag in her father's hands. "Did you get us hot chocolate?"

"You can eat it on the subway back home. Cold food and warm hot cocoa aren't as important as finding you."

"A very bad man sat on our bench and said horrible things to Mommy. She yelled at him and ran away with us."

"Who was he? Why didn't you find a cop and report him for threatening you? I could've taken care of the creep myself if you'd waited long enough for me to come back."

"He was my father," Lenore says in a voice barely above a whisper.

"Mommy's daddy called me and Amelia brats a few times," Irene adds.

"Take me away from here, Allen. You can help me walk back to the locker room so I can put my boots back on, we'll give back our skates, and then we'll get the hell outta here forever. I don't want him to find me again."

"That monster found you after all these years? Leave him to me. If he shows up again, I'll murder him. That excuse for life isn't worth the air he breathes. He's not gonna get away with this."

"You never want to come back to Central Park, Mommy?" Irene asks sadly.

"I never want to come back to New York City again ever. This city is a black hole of doom and despair in most places outside our little safe haven in the Village. Your daddy and I will take you to a nice, safe place Upstate, where you can breathe fresh air, live in a house, and go to a nice school."

"Leave the city?" Allen asks. "On such short notice, and a lot sooner than we'd been thinking about?"

"I'm not staying in the same city as my degenerate father and leaving myself open to being found again. It's your husbandly duty to protect me, and your fatherly duty to protect the girls. Are you a man or a mouse?"

"I don't wanna leave Adicia and Justine all by themselves, without a single friend or ally left."

"I don't wanna leave them behind either, but Adicia will be eighteen in July. We have to trust she'll find a way to escape your diseased parents and take Justine with her. Then we can all be together again, maybe in the city where Lucine lives."

"I'd do anything for my family. Still, I have to give at least two weeks notice at the bakery and start looking for a job in that city. We can't move away overnight. First things first, though. We're gonna turn our skates in, and I'll take you home. I've kept you safe from your father for nine and a half years, and I'm not about to let you down now."

***

Adicia and Justine file into Allen and Lenore's apartment the first weekend of February, carrying handmade get well cards and a bouquet of camellias they got for 75% off at a friendly florist's shop on Orchard Street. The florist knows them as nice neighborhood girls with rotten parents, and felt sorry for them when they told him their pregnant sister-in-law recently sprained her ankle very badly. He told them to take the flowers at the reduced rate as a gesture of kindness and goodwill, and not to feel they owe him any money. They also have apple melt-away, cinnamon babka, and cherry danish from the Strausslers.

"Are you still pregnant?" Justine asks worriedly.

"Veronica found a healthy heartbeat." Allen pats Lenore's abdomen. "He's still safely baking inside of his mommy."

"Amelia and I want a little brother this time," Irene says. "But another sister would be nice too."

"The flowers are beautiful," Lenore says. "They're the same kind you got me when I was in the hospital."

"Are you gonna be in that ankle brace a long time?" Adicia asks.

"The doctor said maybe two months. I can't wait for it to heal, not only so I can start walking again, but also so we can get outta here."

"You're leaving the Village?" Justine asks. "But it's so nice here! Did your landlord raise your rent too high?"

"Lenore and I made a decision," Allen starts nervously. "As soon as her ankle heals, we're moving Upstate. We're hoping to move to the same city Lucine moved to."

"Why are you leaving us? You're all we have left."

"Don't you have to sign a year-long lease when you rent a place?" Adicia asks. "You've still got till early July."

"I'll put an ad in *The Village Voice*. Probably some college kids from NYU will jump at the chance to rent a two-bedroom apartment in such a nice neighborhood. I wish I could get another loan from the Bowery people so we'll have extra cash to put into our bakery. I'm also gonna start a photography business on the side, maybe sell some of my own photographs."

"But why *now*?" Justine pleads. "Can't you wait till Adicia graduates and take both of us with you? We can all move together."

"I've been having nightmares ever since that day at the park," Lenore says. "I'm so terrified he'll find me again, I've had the girls sleeping in our bed and fanatically checking to make sure all the doors and windows are locked. Even if I hadn't sprained my ankle, I wouldn't wanna leave the apartment for fear he'll find me and kidnap me and the girls."

"Who is this guy you're afraid of?" Adicia asks. "Did he attack you at the park, and that's why you hurt your ankle?"

"I fell down Pilgrim Hill when I was running away from him on my ice-skates. He kept referring to the girls as brats, couldn't believe I found a respectable husband after what he did to me, and said I could take the girls with me when I went home to Brooklyn so he could break them in. The thought of that sick man doing to my innocent girls what he did to me makes me sick. I've had nightmares where he broke into the apartment, came into our bed, and started molesting them."

"Your *father*? How did he find you?"

"What was he doing out of Brooklyn?" Justine asks.

"Who knows?" Allen asks. "Better yet, who cares? All that matters is he's seen Lenore and the girls, and knows they live in this borough. We've got legal rights, and the cops would take our side if that sick excuse for life broke in here or grabbed them on the street, but getting justice after the fact isn't much comfort. If she'd miscarried when she slid down the hill, I'd be even angrier at him."

"Our parents never found out where Lucine and Emeline went, though they were in the city for years," Adicia says.

"Even if that was just a one-time thing and he just happened to see her, that's one time too many. We wanted to leave the city anyway. Come on, don't you agree this isn't a very nice place to live? Everyone who can afford to move does. Who wants to live in a city with such a high crime rate?"

"But you live in onea the nice neighborhoods. The secret is knowing where to walk, and at what time. When the Ryans lived in The Bowery, Fiona and Aoife weren't allowed out except to use the outhouse. Deirdre didn't want them wandering around such a skid-row area. When Justine and I lived in Hell's Kitchen, we knew which blocks to avoid at what times. If you see someone being mugged or beaten up, you just turn around and run in the other direction, or duck behind a garbage can. We knew what areas the gangs usually fought in and never ventured there."

"I never want Irene and Amelia to have to learn that. No child should have to learn how to adapt to living in a city with a high crime rate or a neighborhood full of gang violence. I want my kids to have a childhood, not be forced to become miniature grownups before they're ten years old."

"We're going to live in a house soon," Irene says excitedly. "We'll have a yard in the front and the back of the house, clean air, pretty trees and flowers, our own car, and maybe a dog or a cat."

"I want a bunny," Amelia says.

"But how will we know how to find you?" Justine asks. "We don't know the addresses for Lucine, Emeline, Ernestine, or the Ryans either, and we can't write to Julie and expect a letter back, since Mother might get mad if she saw we have a penpal."

"You can always go to Mr. and Mrs. van Niftrik," Lenore says. "As far as anyone knows, your parents don't know or care about them."

"Lucine and her husband said we could stay with them for a little bit till we find our own place," Allen says. "They live in a nice city a reasonable driving distance from Saratoga. When you join us, we can go to see the horses racing in the summer."

"I don't wanna see racing horses," Justine pouts. "I only want our family to be back together like it was ten years ago."

"Don't worry. We'll be back together before you know it. In the meantime, you've still got us for a little while longer."

"You can help us with packing," Lenore says. "Would you like to do that?"

"No, but I guess we don't have a choice," Justine says.

"Don't you want Lenore to be safe from her father?" Allen asks. "Maybe the baby will come when you're with us. She's not due till about September, so if you come after Adicia graduates, you'll be able to witness the birth of all three of our kids."

"We can suck it up for a little while longer," Adicia reluctantly admits. "I just wish it were already June, so we could start this new life together as one family."

***

March 30, Thursday, Allen and Lenore stand looking at the last nine and a half years packed up in boxes being loaded into a waiting moving truck. The furniture has already been loaded. Allen asked the landlord, and he gave his permission to take the furniture that came with the apartment. It's not meant as a partly-furnished apartment, though the prior renters left some of their furniture. All they have to do is clean it reasonably well, secure subletters until the lease runs out in July, lock up, and hand the keys over to the subletters.

"Are we really taking a big bus to Hudson Falls?" Irene asks. "I can't wait to watch all the pretty scenery going by."

"It's called a Greyhound bus," Lenore says, her voice catching.

"Don't cry, Mommy. We're going to have a big adventure with moving. I bet it's pretty in Hudson Falls."

Lenore does one last walk-through as the girls sit in the hall, watching the movers coming in and out of the elevator with the boxes. She limps as she walks through the five rooms and looks into all the closets. Allen winces each time he sees her limping, positive she never would've sprained her ankle had he been there when her father showed up. He would've protected her and the girls, and they'd never have felt compelled to run away. As if it weren't bad enough he still feels guilty about what happened seven years ago.

"Please don't cry, babykins," he begs, putting his arms around her. "By tomorrow at this time, we'll be in Lucine and Zachary's house, starting our new lives in Hudson Falls. We'll make new memories in a new house."

"Our girls were born in this apartment. Amelia was conceived here. This was the safe place I came to when I ran away from Brooklyn. We celebrated birthdays and holidays here. You nursed me back to health here. We first told each other 'I love you' here. Our first kiss was here. We first made love here. This was our home for almost a decade. After we leave and lock up, we'll never see it again. It'll be as if we never lived here, all our memories gone."

"Our memories aren't going anywhere. We'll just have to remember them in a different way. We had a really good run here, but it's time to pack up and move on. Remember why we're doing this."

"Our new house Upstate won't be as special as our first home. If these walls could only talk, they'd have such stories to tell."

"And just imagine what stories our new house is gonna tell someday. Hopefully we'll live there even longer. That's where the girls are gonna grow up and where our third little Troy's gonna be born. With any luck, Adicia and Justine will join us before the end of the year. We'll make the new house a home full of love, happiness, and memories, just like we did here."

"All things have to come to an end sometime," Lenore admits sadly, picking up her suitcase.

When they get on the bus at 4:00, Irene takes a seat by the window and holds up her stuffed panda so it can watch the Village disappearing behind them. For a moment, Allen flashes back to Adicia's eighth birthday, July 11, 1962, the day she, Emeline, and Justine came to live with him. Justine was only a year younger than Irene, and she held her stuffed white rabbit up to the window so it could see the city going by too. When Allen took his three sisters out of Two Bridges and to his new apartment in a friendly area, he was only eighteen, suffering the effects of quitting drugs, cigarettes, and alcohol cold turkey, and just starting his first legit job after graduating high school. As he leaves the city, he's twenty-seven, a married man, with two children and a third on the way. So much has happened to all of them in the intervening years. As Allen watches the friendly Bohemian neighborhood of his early adult years vanishing in the distance, his greatest hope is that the next new beginning in his life will be at least as fortuitous as the new beginning that's now an ending.

Chapter 45: Bartered Like a Piece of Meat

"Isn't this park great?" Justine asks. "Now that the weather's getting nicer, we'll be able to show you all the groovy places in the neighborhood."

"This park has beautiful elms," Ricky admits.

"Justine and I hid out among the elms with our baby nephew Giovanni after our old place burnt down," Adicia says. "When night fell, we walked to the Bowery Mission. I wish I could take shelter among the elms and stay there safely till my eighteenth birthday passes, so my parents can't make me marry someone I don't want to."

"Have they found someone?" Ricky gives the side-eye to a group of Hare Krishnas setting up under the elms.

"Those people are basically harmless," Adicia whispers. "My sister Emeline's very into Hinduism, the Krishna sect in particular. Krishna's just another name for God for her. The story of Krishna appeals to her more than Christianity. She said it's more personal and taught her how to relate to God as more than a stern old man in the sky. It's more about what the story represents than whether there were an actual man named Krishna, or if he did everything as the story records."

"Emeline's the hippie, right?"

"She was interested in a lot of hippie ideas and beliefs before there was a hippie scene. She was ahead of the curve. Her favorite Beatle was George, and it's hardly a secret he got really into Hinduism too. Not that she'd care how popular or trendy Eastern religions are. She was reading about them since she was eleven or twelve."

"Don't worry, she doesn't shave her head, dress all in orange, and chant 'Hare Krishna' and bang a tambourine in public," Justine says. "She just likes the philosophy and stories."

"She said Vishnu only took on a human avatar, and earlier animal avatars, when the balance of evil overwhelmed that of good in the world. I wish he'd take on another avatar and help save me from my parents. Just look what they made me get." Adicia pulls something out of her pocket and hands it to Ricky.

"Is this your driver's license?"

"It's a State ID for non-drivers. I'll never get a chance to learn how to drive or even afford a car."

"You look pretty in the picture. You look pretty even when you look like you've lost your best friend. Why the long face?"

"I need an additional form of ID besides my birth certificate when my parents drag me over with my future husband to get the marriage license. They wanted to get this detail taken care of now, instead of scrambling around at the last minute."

"They're not bluffing when they say they'll get Adicia a husband and make her get married by the fall," Justine says.

"I don't intend to go through with any forced marriage, but I have to play along just like Gemma and Lucine, so they won't suspect anything funny."

"I'd be glad to help you if you want it," Ricky volunteers. "You're a really nice girl, and you shouldn't be traded away to an older guy like a sack of potatoes in this day and age. Even if you don't want to be my girlfriend, I'll do whatever I can to protect you."

"You're a nice rich person," Justine says. "I know you wanna be our friend 'cause you like us and you're a nice guy, not 'cause you think we're a pathetic charity project or you want the adventure of having friends from the wrong side of the tracks."

Ricky looks at the ID again. "What does the E stand for? I never asked your middle name, did I?"

"Éloïse. My dad's all French, so he insisted all nine of us get at least one French name. You should hear the way Lucine's middle name is pronounced in French. It looks like the English name Camille, but it's pronounced kinda like Ca-MEE-yeh. Names like Genevieve and Henri have pronunciations that sound just as silly and pretentious in English. There's an accent aigu over the E and an umlaut over the I. My dad says no one would pronounce the name properly in French if there were no accent marks, though the average person in this country won't see the name without accents and want to pronounce it El-WAZ."

"It's a pretty name, however it looks in French. Aren't there a couple of children's books about an Eloise?"

"Emeline read them to us when we were younger. Eloise lives on the top floor of the Plaza Hotel. I wish we had that kinda money to afford living in a hotel, and the penthouse suite no less."

"Can we see your ID?" Justine asks. "I don't think I've ever seen an ID where the person was smiling."

Ricky reaches into his inner front jacket pocket for his wallet. "I learnt a few tricks since living in the city. Pickpockets can't steal your money if it's hidden." He pulls out his driver's license, and another card falls out with it.

"Very clever," Adicia says. "We've known that trick our whole lives, but you don't expect a rich guy to figure that one out."

"My parents have both been pickpocketed since we've been here. My dad musta looked like an easy target, since he was wearing a full tweed business suit on a weekend, at five in the afternoon. He got on the wrong subway and ended up in Chinatown. My mother was taking a walk and ended up in The Bowery. She was wearing one of her trademark ridiculous hats, five hundred-dollar high heels, and a blue Russian sable fur coat that must've cost at least several thousand dollars."

"Her hats are dumb," Justine agrees. "They look like they were assembled by a blind drunk. Who thinks cigarettes, fake birds, holly berries, and playing cards look good on the same hat?"

"You haven't seen her worst one. It has polished, rounded, colored pieces of glass, miniature violins and flutes, little ceramic cupcakes, and jingle bells. Most women don't wear hats anymore. It makes her look even more out of touch than she already is."

"Your birthday's only four days after mine," Adicia says. "You didn't tell me you had a July birthday too." She notices the other card that fell out and leans over to pick it up. "What is *this*? I've never seen a card like this before."

"That's my draft card. All guys have to register for Selective Service when they turn eighteen, though most of us never go. I had half a mind to burn mine at one of the anti-war protests at Syracuse University, but my parents threatened to cut me off if I tried anything like that."

"Aren't guys born in 1952 being sent to Vietnam this year? What's your lottery number? Our brother Allen was one hundred ten, but he managed to avoid it 'cause he had a job, three dependents, and was a community college student."

"Eighty-eight."

The girls look at him in disbelief and horror. They can't believe he's so calm about having such a low number, even lower than Allen's.

"Don't worry about me. I have an automatic deferment as a full-time college student, and my parents have connections and money to keep me safe. Besides, they've been withdrawing troops lately. They'd have to be desperate to pick me. I'm no soldier. I'd rather make friends with the Vietnamese than kill them sight unseen. I'm a pacifist."

"That's still an awful number to have!" Adicia says.

"Would you miss me if they were stupid and desperate enough to take me?"

"You're the only real friend I have left since Allen and Lenore moved away. I see my friend Marjani sometimes, but not nearly as often as when I lived in the same neighborhood. Of course I'd miss you."

"Well, I'm glad to know you like me, even if it's not as a potential boyfriend. Being a friend of convenience is better than not being a friend at all."

Adicia hands him back his draft card and driver's license. "You're a nice guy, Ricky. Don't think I only wanna be your friend 'cause you happen to live up the street and I have no friends left in the neighborhood. I'd wanna be your pal even if all my sisters and friends lived nearby."

"Do you have a girlfriend yet?" Justine asks. "You're not a bad-looking guy. I bet you're popular with the ladies."

"Some dates here and there, but none of them as pretty, nice, or sweet as your sister."

Adicia looks down and blushes.

"You've got it made if you go steady with Ricky, Adicia," Justine tries to tempt her. "He'd be your golden ticket outta poverty, and Mother and Dad couldn't force you to marry whomever they pick if you were already married."

"My folks know I've got a crush on her. They won't let me bring her around the house or go out with her 'cause they say she's no good," he says forlornly. "They'd get really upset if they knew I'm meeting with you as just pals. I probably can't blame them for their classist attitudes, since they're living what they know. They've never seen anyone who was rich associating with, let alone dating, a poor or working-class person."

"They're like Mrs. Chatterton in the Five Little Peppers series," Adicia says. "It's been so long since we read those books with Emeline. I don't know why they still stick out in my head so much. She's a really disagreeable cousin of the Peppers' rich benefactor who moves into their house in the second book. She's horrified at how everyone around her has warmly accepted the Peppers into their social circle and good graces in spite of how they started out poor as church mice and had to always fight to keep the wolf from the door."

"Is that the series where they always gas on and on about how great it was to be poor?" Justine asks.

"Yeah, I hated that part too. If only I had a dollar for every time they oversentimentalize their 'little brown house days,' I'd be rich myself by now. Why have they all conveniently forgotten how horrible it was to be so desperately poor? Ernestine and I both hated Phronsie too."

"I vaguely remember those books from when I was a boy," Ricky says. "They really have sentimental feelings towards their poor days?"

"I get that they were happy and had each other in spite of being poor, but it grates on my nerves. And it's just too stupid and convenient how their mother's long-lost rich cousin just happens to be the son-in-law of their benefactor. I think Emeline liked those books more for the historical value than quality writing."

"There's nothing wrong with a happy ending. Sometimes they happen in real life too. You told me that story about how you met the guy who turned out to be a millionaire in a famous band, and how he gave you ten dollars for washing his windshield. Sometimes real life hands you a deus ex machina ending that could only be described as a modern miracle."

***

When Adicia, Justine, and Tommy come home from school one day in the middle of May, a strange man is in the living room with Mrs. Troy. Adicia is sick to her stomach and instantly knows this must be the man who's been chosen as her husband. He looks almost sixty, projects a very bad aura, smells bad, and certainly isn't as cute as Ricky. Adicia might not be interested in Ricky as a boyfriend, but she likes him as a friend, and he really likes her and would treat her well if she were his wife or girlfriend.

"Well, Adicia, I found him. Your father approves of him too. After how nuts he went when he found out about what we did to keep me from prison, I made sure to consult him this time. He's met your new fiancé a few times and thinks he's a good future son-in-law. While we're waiting for you to graduate and turn eighteen, we can pick a wedding date and start making wedding plans and buying clothes."

"My name's Seth Oswaldtwistle, and I'm your future husband." He smiles a partly toothless grin at Adicia. "I run a pharmacy and grocery store in Chelsea. That's where I live too. You'll be living with my elderly mother and my five kids from my first marriage. They're thirty-five, thirty-two, twenty-nine, twenty-seven, and twenty-four. We each get our own floor of the townhouse, though my mother will be with us. My kids are all married and have their own kids. They don't expect you to play stepmother to them at their ages."

"Are you divorced or a widower?" Tommy asks.

"I'm a widower. There was a tragic accident with my first wife when she had an internal hemorrhage after I beat her a little too hard one night."

Justine squeezes Adicia's hand. "Why did you beat your wife? Did you go to jail for it?"

"A little jail time's no skin off my back. The judge and jury realized it was an accident, and only gave me fifteen years. I was drunk, and she spent ten minutes too many out on what was supposed to be a fifteen-minute run to the store. After I got outta prison, I spent the last nine years turning over a new leaf and starting my own successful business."

"How old are you?" Adicia asks.

"I'll be fifty-eight next month. Wow, I'm getting a really pretty young bride. It's too bad you ain't a virgin, but your mother explained about that bit of business. It's not like you're the town whore who went out and fornicated with scores of men for kicks and giggles."

"What was your last name again?"

"Oswaldtwistle. You'll get used to spelling, saying, and remembering it before long." Seth devours her with his eyes. "I always like to inspect the merchandise before I buy it. Open your mouth."

"Whatever for?"

"Oh, stop being so willful and do what your future husband says!" Mrs. Troy snaps irritably. "He wants to inspect you to make sure you ain't defective!"

Adicia is very tempted to snap her jaws down and bite Seth's fingers as he inspects her teeth. Mrs. Troy casually fills up her cocaine pipe and starts puffing away as Seth runs his leathered hands over Adicia's entire body, poking, pinching, and squeezing her, and finally forcing a violent kiss on her. Tommy doesn't leap in to object to his sister being treated like a horse up for auction either. Only Justine stands in shock and anger at what's happening.

"Mrs. Troy, can I take the car for a test drive later on?"

"By all means do. Adicia ain't a virgin no more, so it ain't like she's disgracing herself by having intercourse before marriage. Her name is dirt. Oh, but make sure to use rubbers. Even if she's already a fallen woman, I don't want a scandal with an out of wedlock pregnancy. I don't believe in speeding weddings up just 'cause someone couldn't do what must be done to prevent accidents."

"I sell plenty of 'em at the pharmacy. I'll help myself to some when the time comes. I hope she's still nice and tight after having another man before me."

Adicia runs to the bathroom to throw up. As she sits there with Justine holding her hair back, she thinks this must be exactly how Gemma felt. Gemma's wishes and feelings were violated and disregarded too. All the adults considered it annoying how she refused to take this lying down and didn't want her parents to decide for her she'd get married at only eighteen, to a grotesque man old enough to be her father. Adicia knows she's rather passive, unlike her older sisters, but she's had to stay so long and passively go along with whatever their parents have made her do so she can continue protecting Justine. She knows she'll never marry Seth, but her time is running out on finding a solution that involves not only escape but also saving Justine.

***

While Mr. and Mrs. Troy are at work on a Saturday several weeks later, and Tommy is at soccer practice, Adicia and Justine watch from the window as Mr. and Mrs. Carson get into their car. Their first thought after daydreaming about how nice it must be to have one's own car is that maybe they'll get to see the inside of Ricky's house if his parents are gone long enough. The last time they were inside a real house was when they went to Francesco's parents' house ten years ago. This is a fair size bigger, and looks much nicer from the outside too. Not wasting a moment, they join hands and go down the steps through the bakery, which is closed for the Sabbath. Adicia carries the keys, since the bakery door automatically locks behind them.

"They have a real fancy door-knocker," Justine breathes in wonder as Adicia raises the handle around the ornate golden lion in her left hand and gives it a few bangs on the heavy oak door. "I wonder if they have servants too, or if they make you take your shoes off when you come inside."

Ricky pulls the door open and smiles at them when he sees who his guests are. "Come right in! What brings you by on this pleasant Saturday?"

"We saw your parents driving away, and thought if they were out long enough, we'd get a chance to tour your house." Adicia idly notices what a cute smile he has.

"They went to the Hamptons for the weekend. They just bought a house out there and wanted to start enjoying it now that summer's here. Don't worry about them coming back early by surprise and ganging up on us for associating with each other. Our maid and cook won't be coming over today either. I prefer to cook and clean for myself instead of making other people do it for me."

Justine almost trips over something when they're walking down the front hallway. Ricky leans over to push the strange object out of the way.

"Are those stone dragons?" Adicia asks.

"Gargoyles. We used to have them in our garden in Syracuse. Some local pranksters kept stealing them, and finally my dad got tired of walking up and down nearby streets to find them and just moved them inside permanently. I didn't know there'd be thieves and pranksters in a nice neighborhood like this."

"What's a gargoyle?" Justine asks.

"They're carved grotesque figures that traditionally spewed water through their mouths. Nowadays they don't have to have water spouts."

"My intended future husband is a big gargoyle," Adicia says as they walk downstairs into the garden level kitchen and Ricky opens the refrigerator.

"He's forty years older than Adicia," Justine says. "He spent fifteen years in prison for beating his first wife to death when he was drunk and upset she was ten minutes too long at the store. He's got five grown kids who all live with him, on different floors with their own families. I did the math in my head, and he killed his wife when the youngest kid was just a baby."

"He was inspecting me like a horse at auction," Adicia remembers, shuddering. "I wanted to bite him when he was poking around at my teeth. After he was done pawing all over me, he kissed me against my will. I can't decide which forced kiss was worse, his or the ones from that guy I was forced to meet to keep my mother out of prison. I was promised a handsome husband with a good job if I slept with that guy when I was fifteen. This guy Seth does have a good job, but he's not young, and he's not what I'd consider good-looking. I couldn't expect them to pick me someone like you, since a fallen woman only has so many options." Without thinking about what she's doing, Adicia reaches across the table and takes Ricky's hand.

"Are you serious? They expect you to marry an ex-convict who beat his first wife to death?"

"If I can't find a way to get outta this in time, I'll have no choice. I don't wanna marry a guy who'd beat me. Gemma's ex-husband beat her and did all sorts of other bad stuff, like cheating on her, raping her, drinking, and making her do humiliating stuff like clipping his toenails, bathing him, and trimming his nose hair."

"If you were my girl, I'd never beat you. I'd do something every day to make you feel special."

"I wish I did like you in that way, Ricky. But a marriage of convenience is still a marriage of convenience, even if both people like each other. That's the one thing I can't do to escape from this awful situation. You deserve a girl who likes you back, and I wanna marry a guy I love, not someone I only like or have to grow to love like in an arranged marriage."

"Well, we have to figure out some way to get outta this mess," Justine says. "Mother said she'd like a September wedding date."

"What exactly did she make you do when you were fifteen? And why was she in prison?"

"Our mother embezzled five thousand bucks from a bank she worked at," Adicia begins. "The majority was for Lucine's wedding that never happened. She could never afford a nice wedding on her own, and there were no in-laws footing the bill. Somea the money she used for other things, like presents for Tommy. Her boss was on to her, and on my eighth birthday, she was followed home by an undercover cop who arrested her in front of us. She sat in jail for a month awaiting trial, while Emeline, Justine, and I lived with Allen. No one paid her bail. After her trial, she served four months. She got out in December and thought the case was closed, since she had no intentions of paying back the money or following any of the other terms of her release."

"She just waltzed out of jail and expected no one would ever follow up on her case? Is she that much of a drug addict?"

"She came home the morning after the big blackout in November '65 in a really foul mood. A cop paid her a visit at work and said all her paychecks would be garnished, since she'd made no effort to pay the money back on her own. She thought there were enough robberies and murders in the city for the cops to be kept busy and forget all about her."

"How were you brought into this sordid mess?"

"In March '69, she was informed that unless she paid back the remaining three thousand bucks by the end of August, she'd go back to prison. We think it was to try to make an example of her, to prove Governor Rockefeller's tough on crime. It was also probably because she's poor, and poor people often have no choice but to go to prison 'cause they can't come up with legal fees or powerful friends to help them stay outta trouble. One day when she was waiting on line to buy drugs, she met a thirty-five-year-old creep named Ethan Pitskowski. He was most interested when she told him about her virgin teenage daughter, and said he'd give her the three thousand bucks if I gave up my virginity. All a poor girl has in this world is her good name, and my name is dirt because I was dishonored. He agreed to use rubbers so he wouldn't cause a scandal by giving me a disease or knocking me up. Allen went after him that night, cut off all his male organs, and carved a message in his chest, about how he rapes little girls and uses and sells drugs. It doesn't change what I did. My arm was twisted. I had little choice but to go along with it." She hangs her head. "He gave me an extra fifty bucks for being such a good virgin lay, but I handed that over to my mother. I didn't want that tainted money for myself."

Ricky squeezes her hand. "Why you? Why you?"

"My mother knows I'm an easy target. I don't know how to be a real grownup, no matter how much I was forced to grow up early. I've had to go along with what my parents wanted so I don't rock the boat or stand out too much. I'm too passive. Things happen to me. I never made things happen for myself. I have no idea how I'm gonna run away after graduation or get along on my own. My older sisters got outta poverty by their smarts and motivation, but I always had a silly idea I'd be rescued by a modern knight on a white horse. I'm not dumb, but I don't know if I'm smart enough to go to college. I've never had to take care of a household by myself. I'm little more than the next-youngest sister. You must think I'm so pathetic. Not only am I a fallen woman, damaged merchandise, but I'm also more like a little kid playing at being grownup. As if it wasn't already bad enough I look like a little kid too. I look like a living ragdoll."

"I don't care about any of that," Ricky tries to tell her. "You have a really refreshing natural prettiness, no matter how petite you are. Most girls your age nowadays aren't so sweet and humble. I don't think any of the girls I know would want to hang out with their seventh grade kid sister all the time, shun makeup and fashionable clothes, or talk about books, philosophy, or world events. A lot of them are only interested in talking about themselves, or how things in the world affect them. You can't be very selfish or superficial when you grow up thankful for everything you get."

"I never had a boyfriend or a single date before my mother forced me into that situation. My first experiences with being kissed, touched by a man, and having sexual relations were through force, not something I did willingly with a nice guy like you. This Seth fellow asked my mother if he could sleep with me before the wedding to take me for a test drive, and she agreed so long as he uses rubbers. She has no mothering instincts at all. If my old nanny Sarah were my mother, she would've done everything to protect me from the advances of older men, not willingly sent me out to be raped by drug dealers in exchange for money to keep her from prison. She'd let me go to college and find a guy I loved to marry, not make me marry a creep pushing sixty."

"Part of the deal was that Adicia would get to graduate high school and not get married till she was eighteen if she slept with that Ethan fellow," Justine says. "She wanted so badly to graduate high school and not have to get married at only sixteen."

"She used that as a bribe against you?" Ricky asks. "My mother may be cold and unfeeling, but at least she has maternal feelings towards me! Who forces her daughter to sleep with a grown man in exchange for finishing school and not entering a forced child marriage?"

"Can I have something to eat?" Adicia asks. "Talking about this upsets me. I only have till September to figure out an escape, and it stresses me out having to dredge up the past in addition to thinking about how to get outta here in time."

"Can we take a tour of your house after we eat?" Justine asks.

"Of course," Ricky says.

"You're a nice guy," Adicia says. "I'm glad you're our neighbor and that you don't think I'm trash because of what happened."

"You've got a really sweet heart. I like and accept you just as you are. Just the way you are now."

"You really do? I never thought anyone from the outside world would ever like me, let alone like me for me."

"Well, I'm telling you I do like you just the way you are. Though I've only known you since January, I feel really connected to you. I promise I'll try to help you. It's not conditional upon you being my girlfriend. Besides, you're a fellow lefty. There aren't that many of us, so we have to stick together and help each other out."

"I don't know if I believe in God, but I think you must be my guardian angel. Not many poor girls get a rich friend to help them out."

"Ricky likes you just like the Boy loves the Velveteen Rabbit just like he is," Justine says. "It's a really special thing when you're Real, since that means someone accepts you just the way you are, no matter what you look like or what you've been through."

Adicia's heart races as she remembers the scene near the end of *The Velveteen Rabbit*, when the Rabbit is lying in the pile of toys and bedding waiting to be burnt, a tear falling from his eye. She hopes she too is able to be rescued in time, the same way the Rabbit was turned into a real rabbit before he was thrown into the bonfire.

Chapter 46: Adicia's Only Hope Left

Mrs. Marsenko blanches when she sees Mrs. Troy entering the bridal shop with Adicia and Justine following her. This time a strange elderly woman is with them, along with two older women who look somewhere in their thirties. Mrs. Marsenko has a very bad feeling about this, never having forgotten Mrs. Troy or her unhappy daughters. Unlike when the sisters and their friends came here for Lenore's wedding, there are no smiles or happy chatter this time. *This must be another forced wedding*, she thinks unhappily as she comes forward to greet them.

"I'm Mrs. Dolores Troy, and these—"

"Save your breath, Mrs. Troy. You think I've once forgotten you since I met you twelve years ago? Which daughter are you forcing to get married this time?"

"How nice you remember me! Most shopkeepers forget me or pretend they don't know me, even if I'm a regular. This time it's for Adicia, the brunette. We need a wedding dress for her, bridesmaid dresses for her fiancé's daughters, and a maid of honor gown for my daughter Justine. Unfortunately, Adicia's fiancé's daughters-in-law was unable to make this appointment. They prefer to work rather than plan a wedding. What nerve."

"So it looks like all your other daughters deserted you. Can't say I blame 'em for running away from your sick schemes to marry them all off like cattle before they're even twenty."

"I don't have time for this self-righteous rant. Just help us with finding dresses, will you? We came here for wedding clothes, not value judgments on how I choose to live my life and raise my remaining daughters."

"She won't be wearing white, ivory, or cream, no colors like that, since she's a fallen woman," Seth's mother announces loudly. "Steer her right towards the dresses for brides who ain't virgins."

"My favorite color is dark blue," Adicia says softly, knowing in the back of her mind she'll never wear any wedding dress her mother purchases here.

"Nonsense. Dark blue looks hideous on even a non-virgin bride," Mrs. Oswaldtwistle rambles on. "How about a nice pale shade of pink, blue, yellow, or green? Pastels look nice. It tells everyone you ain't a pure virgin, but it ain't loud and obnoxious like a dark blue dress."

"It's just an old wives' tale that white stands for virginity." Mrs. Marsenko feels horrible for how this old woman is talking to Adicia, who looks even more innocent and fragile than ever before. "More brides than you'd like to believe aren't virgins, and they still wear white or ivory."

"My daughter ain't gonna be onea them brides pretending to the world she's a pure virgin," Mrs. Troy says. "Come on, we're paying you to find us dresses, not stand around and lecture us."

"Do they make bridal dresses of any color her size?" Seth's older daughter, Jody, laughs. "Or do you have to find dresses in the children's section and tailor them to fit someone with breasts?"

"Don't pick on my sister 'cause she's short and small for her age." Justine puts her arm around Adicia. "She's a lot prettier than you'll ever be."

"You're lucky your parents found my dad to take you offa their hands," the younger daughter, Joan, says. "Most respectable men, even older ones like my dad, don't wanna marry girls who ain't virgins."

"Come with me," Mrs. Marsenko says. "One of my associates will find you some dresses."

Justine takes her time looking through the dresses on the racks, knowing she'll never wear this dress. It won't matter how unflattering or unfashionable it is. The Oswaldtwistle women and their grand-mother continue making disparaging comments about Adicia as they look for their dresses, not bothering to keep it to stage whispers. Mrs. Troy joins in, leaving Justine blushing and angry.

"What happened since I last saw you?" Mrs. Marsenko whispers as they wait for an associate to come back with a few non-white dress-es. "You can tell me. Unlike those cackling hens out there, I don't dis-parage people who are already down, nor do I spread such stories around."

"My mother used me to save herself from going back to jail 'cause she hadn't paid back enough of the money she embezzled. She made me sacrifice my virginity in exchange for three thousand bucks and the chance to graduate high school. She said I'd get a handsome husband with a good job, but I wasn't expecting a fifty-eight-year-old man who was in prison for fifteen years for beating his first wife to death."

Mrs. Marsenko sits on the bench next to her and puts her arm around her. "Do you intend to go through with this forced marriage? If you're eighteen, she can't legally force you to do anything."

"I just graduated high school, but I won't be eighteen for a few more days. A slightly older guy who lives up the street has promised he'll try to help me. The idea of us marrying has been floated a few times, but I don't want that. He really likes me, but I only see him as a friend. He might be rich, cute, and nice, but I don't want him to be stuck married to someone who doesn't see him the way a wife's supposed to see a husband. I don't wanna marry a guy I don't love in that way either."

"There are worse things in this world than marriages of convenience where the parties at least like each other. Some of my clients are Orthodox Jewish girls having arranged marriages, and they talk about how they're a very good match with their intendeds, not about how they feel butterflies in their stomachs and are so overwhelmed by feelings of passion they can't think straight. Marrying only for love isn't always the best predictor of staying married or in love. At least you like this young man, unlike that brute your mother wants you to marry. Sometimes the truest and most lasting love bonds come when you grow instead of fall in love."

"Well, whatever happens, I only have till September to decide. I've never had to make such a big decision before, and I'm terrified."

An associate comes back with four dresses—a pastel blue satin gown with beading on the bodice, a pink silk number with yellow lace trimming, a pale orange organza gown with a white sash, and a light green chiffon gown with a pearl neckline. Adicia doesn't like any of them, but she obediently tries them on and parades around in front of the critical eyes of her mother, Seth's mother, and Seth's daughters, passively enduring their scathing critiques of her body and how each dress looks on her. She wishes she could punch them every time they say something about how the dress is hanging off her because she's so petite. She's sick to her stomach every time her mother snaps at Justine for speaking up to defend her against these shrill Harpies. Adicia wishes she'd been given the same gift of speech Justine possesses, able to speak up and defend herself more often. Emeline was right when she said once you've been saddled with the label "the quiet one," people tend to underestimate you and take advantage of you because they don't think you can defend yourself or prove yourself of much accord.

She hopes she can prove them all wrong soon, when she'll have to make her decision about escape. Whatever she does, it'll be the first real bold, decisive act of her life, the first time she acts instead of passively being acted on.

***

"We found Adicia's dress," Mrs. Troy says during supper that evening, one of her usual horrible meals, melted processed orange cheese on top of shredded bologna and hamburger meat. "It's orange organza."

"Ew, orange for a wedding gown." Tommy wrinkles his nose.

"Adicia ain't a virgin. She can't wear white."

"Can we see this wedding gown?" Mr. Troy asks. "I wish you'd make me heartier meals, woman. Have you entirely forgotten how to cook meat?"

"This is meat. Might not be a rack of lamb, beef roast, or duck confit, but it's meat. The dress had to remain behind for extra tailoring. It ain't my fault Adicia's so puny. I come from a line of women who are all at least five feet tall."

"Will I have a job at Seth's pharmacy?" Adicia asks.

"Of course not. He brings in enough money to support both of yous. Unlike your father, Seth don't work for minimum wage. Only women whose husbands work lousy jobs need to bother with working."

"But it'll be boring to sit around all day doing nothing."

"Your work is to raise kids, and lots of 'em. You'll also get to run errands and meet with other young wives and mothers. It's as respectable as a girl of our class can get. With any luck, he'll impregnate you right away, so we can expect a baby next summer. Don't you dare complain about seeing a male doctor and giving birth put to sleep. Gemma didn't know her place when she complained about that."

"But I don't want a strange man to be my doctor, and I don't want a drug cocktail that makes me forget everything that happened. I've heard some hospitals don't automatically give women drugs anymore, and some even let the husbands in if they produce a certificate saying they took a class in childbirth."

"What lunatics. Seth will decide for you what hospital and doctor you have, and if he wants you to see a man, you'll just have to forget your stupid, silly ideas about modesty. If he wants you drugged to the hilt and if he don't wanna be there, that's his decision too. Decent men don't want nothing to do with the dirty process of birthing babies."

"Allen caught both of his daughters."

"Your brother and his wife are lunatics too. Imagine a modern woman voluntarily choosing to give birth with no drugs whatsoever and not doing it in the safety of a hospital with a trained doctor. I heard a rumor your sister-in-law was pregnant when they moved. If so, I hope she dies in childbirth."

"That's a really mean thing to say," Justine says. "Lenore's onea the nicest people we know."

"She's nothing but a bus stop whore who got lucky. I hope they don't do nothing disgraceful Upstate that would reflect poorly on me."

Seth enters the apartment through the fire escape door. Adicia almost chokes on her food.

"What a nice surprise, my future son-in-law," Mrs. Troy says warmly. "Would you like to sit down and join us?"

"Naw, I just came over to let you know I chose tonight to take my new car for a test drive. Is it okay if she meets me in my van at nine o'clock on Avenue B? I'm in the neighborhood on business, and I thought I'd kill two birds with one stone."

"By all means do. This willful child needs breaking in. She'll need to get over her uppity fantasy about marrying a guy who ain't poor or working-class. Only nitwits marry for love. Can you believe a rich boy up the street was interested in dating her? I'd never let any of my kids get above their raising so badly. But remember, take precautions so we don't have no scandal a few months before the wedding."

Adicia has completely lost her appetite. She picks at her food after Seth departs, and when Mrs. Troy says if she doesn't want to finish it, she can give it to Tommy, Adicia pushes her plate over, uncaring her stomach isn't very full and that normally she'd never let her spoilt little brother take food away from her. Tommy cheers and wolfs down the remaining food on the plate after moving the fork from left to right. Even at sixteen, he has barely any empathy for anyone other than himself, his overindulgent mother, or his select close friends. He hasn't grown up a bit. Out of the nine Troy children, only he and Gemma weren't forced into miniature grownups at a very young age. Although at least Gemma grew up better late than never. Adicia very much doubts Tommy will ever do the same.

Mrs. Troy lights up some meth at 8:30, while Mr. Troy drinks two six-packs of beer he bought with his last paycheck. She gives Adicia a sharp glance when she sees her on the davenport reading.

"You'd better start walking there now, you dumb cow. Seth will be very angry if you're late, and you don't want him to beat you like he beat his first wife, do you? This will make him like you more. You might start to like him more too. You might not ever love him, but marriage ain't supposed to be about love. Once you start enjoying intercourse, it gets better. That's the only good thing left of my own marriage. It feels damn good, even if you don't love the guy. Remember, even if you don't like it, pretend to so you don't hurt his feelings."

Justine watches sadly as Adicia gets up in resignation and starts going down the fire escape to meet Seth. Ricky's right. Adicia is too innocent, dear, and sweet to deserve this. None of their other four sisters would've caved to their mother's unmotherly demands and gone out to be raped by sinister grown men, but because Adicia is too timid to stand out or rock the boat, and because she's committed herself to staying there to protect Justine at any costs, she's being emotionally manipulated yet again. Justine hopes this is the last time Adicia rolls over and obeys, since there are only two months left before the alleged wedding.

***

Adicia stumbles into the apartment at midnight, her clothes rumpled and her hair hanging in her face. Mr. Troy is passed out drunk on the kitchen floor, and Mrs. Troy is wandering around down Avenue C in her meth haze. Justine springs up out of bed when she hears Adicia coming in.

"What happened?"

"The same disgusting thing that happened before. Let me tell you, it hurts like hell. Don't believe that bunk about how it's so magical and special. Imagine being kicked in the stomach by a battering ram hundreds of times, and a cold, hard, thick, rubber-wrapped hunk of flesh forcing its way into the most narrow orifice on your body. All while someone reeking of beer is kissing you, forcing his tongue in your mouth, and putting his hands all over your body. I'll never do that with a guy I like in the future. Whoever thought up sex musta been a man, 'cause I can't see how any woman in her right mind would find it remotely fun or enjoyable. Maybe I should become a lesbian like Ernestine and Deirdre."

"We have to get outta here. Both of us. Tonight. You can't stay and be forced into marrying this creep, and I can't stay without you. Do we have enough money for a cab? We could get on a bus at Penn Station and ride all the way outta the city, or outta the state entirely."

"We can't both disappear at once. That'd look too suspicious." Adicia pulls her suitcase and schoolbag out from under their bed and turns on the light. "I'm gonna pack everything I own, and I'll go to Ricky's house for the night. His parents went to the Hamptons for an entire week, and won't be coming home anytime soon."

"How will I know how to find you if you don't know where you're going?"

"Listen, Justine, I don't want the additional risk of taking you with me when I'm so unsure myself of what to do. When I'm settled into a new place, I'll send for you. One lone girl is bad enough, but two of them would be an even bigger target for criminals. Save yourself and run away after I do. I'm no longer able to protect you when I need protecting myself right now. How about you go to the van Niftriks or the Washingtons. I'll get in touch with them when I get to wherever I end up going."

"It's not fair you're leaving me."

"Would you rather everyone think we ran away together and search for both of us? If we run away separately, we don't risk being found together and having to be hauled back kicking and screaming. I'm begging you, wait just a little bit more and save yourself when a week or two has gone by. You have to be the brave one now, the same way I had to step up as the oldest sister after Emeline left."

"I don't know how to be an only sister. What if they get mad at me and think I know something about where you went?"

"I can't believe I'm saying this, but at least you have Tommy as a buffer between you and our parents. He might be a huge brat, but he's not evil. He won't hurt you. The most he can do is ignore you or call you names. Let him enjoy being the oldest child for a little bit. When you escape, he'll be the only child left. That's what Mother always wanted, for Tommy to be her only kid."

"Are you sure you're gonna be safe on your own out there?"

"I have no choice left. By this time next year, we'll hopefully all be back together again. Doesn't that sound like a nice dream?"

"I don't wanna dream a dream alone. We always dreamt our

dreams together."

"Remember what Sarah told us the last time we saw her? When people are meant to be together, they find their way back to each other, even if they've been separated by years or miles." Adicia shuts her suitcase, puts her schoolbag over her shoulders, and hugs Justine very tightly. "Be good and try not to rock the boat so much. You have a big mouth like Ernestine and Deirdre, and that can get you in trouble."

"I'll be strong for you," Justine promises tearfully.

"Remember, this'll be a distant nightmare someday, troubled water under the bridge," Adicia tells her before she shuts the fire escape door and leaves the building for the last time.

***

Ricky stumbles out of bed at 12:30 when he hears the doorbell ringing repeatedly. He thinks it's either his parents, back home because they forgot something, or a merry prankster, until he opens the door and sees Adicia. She looks like even more of a lost soul than ever.

"What's going on?"

"I'm so sorry to wake you at this hour, but I had to run away right now. I cannot stay in that place anymore. I hate to leave Justine, but I have no more options. Please help me like you promised so many times."

"Sure, come on in. You can sleep in my mother's bed, and in the morning we'll figure out what we're gonna do."

"Your mother's bed?" Adicia asks as he groggily leads her upstairs to Mr. and Mrs. Carson's room. "Don't your parents share a bed? I saw just one bed when I was over before."

"They pushed their beds together that time. They're so old-fashioned, they sleep in twin beds and push them together when they want to have marital relations. Would you like me to get you something to eat or drink?"

"I'm not in any mood to eat or drink after what just happened. Seth decided to take his new car for a test drive before buying it. I feel more like vomiting than eating."

"Your parents have no souls," Ricky says angrily. "Or are they from the Medieval school of thought that says girls have no rights and their feelings don't count? What do they think you are, chattel to be passed from owner to owner?"

"That pretty much sums them up." Adicia sets her suitcase and schoolbag down. "Thank you so much for letting me stay here, and thanks in advance for helping me devise a plan of escape. Most rich people don't give the time of day to us, let alone wanna be our pals."

"Don't worry, I won't let your parents or that Seth fellow find you here. I won't open the door to anyone except the mailman, and I won't tell anyone I let an unrelated girl spend the night alone with me. You don't need any more black marks on your reputation."

Adicia shuts the door, dumps her clothes under the bed, not sure she'll ever want to wear them again after tonight, puts on her pajamas, turns off the light, and gets in bed. She pulls a stuffed koala out of her schoolbag, which Allen bought her after the horrific experience with Ethan. She wishes she had her big brother or one of her big sisters here to hug, but for now, the koala will have to suffice.

When morning light breaks, Ricky goes into the kitchen to put together breakfast for Adicia. He puts bacon in a frying pan with Crisco, pours orange juice, peels an orange, and cracks three eggs into another frying pan with Crisco. At 9:00, he walks into his parents' room and presents her with the food on a tray.

"Good morning, Sleeping Beauty. Did you sleep well?"

Adicia notices Ricky looks even cuter with his hair tousled. "You didn't have to make me breakfast. I know how to make my own."

"I have an obligation to serve my guest and let you have all the best things. After you're done eating, you can take a bath and call me when you're ready to discuss options for getting out of here. Do you think your parents or Seth suspect you went here?"

"I hope not. Justine would never squeal on me, and all my parents know is you live up the street. Tommy cares less either way."

"We should keep watch from the windows to make sure they're not on the street. What are their work hours?"

"My dad usually works till about six or seven, unless he's picking up extra shifts. Unless my mother chooses today to quit yet another job, or is fired today, she'll be at a hat shop in Tribeca till five."

"Then we're set. You have plenty of time to decide where you're going and get out of here."

As she eats breakfast and soaks in the tub, hoping to scrub every last molecule of Seth's off her body, Adicia thinks about where to go. She could always go to the Bowery Mission, though that would only be a temporary haven. She'd have to leave eventually and find another place. Perhaps she could go to the van Niftriks, but that too would only be a temporary solution. The Washingtons would let her stay for a little while too, but she doesn't want to go back into Hell's Kitchen for any reason. The Murphys are another option, but she doesn't remember their address, nor does she remember the exact address of their church. She knows the Doyles' address, but she's not sure she has enough money for a bus or train ticket that far north. It's also very far away from Lucine, Allen, and Lenore. The Strausslers would let her in too, but they live only a few blocks over from her parents, which runs too high a risk of discovery.

Adicia sits down with Ricky at 12:30 and goes over all her options. With no more information to go on about the whereabouts of Lucine, Allen, and Lenore than that they live near Saratoga, it's pointless to buy a ticket for a random city and start poking about from town to town to try to find them. With not much money in her pockets and only the belongings in her suitcase and schoolbag, most of which are ragged clothes, Adicia starts feeling resigned to becoming a run of the mill runaway, perhaps taking up squatting. Justine will almost certainly never find her that way, but she holds onto what Sarah said, that when people are meant to be together, they'll eventually find their way back to one another, no matter how long it takes.

Ricky thinks she's too much of an easy target to become a random runaway, taking refuge in places like subway tunnels and abandoned buildings with other street people. Ernestine and the Ryans had street smarts, and the Ryans had the additional advantage of living that way their entire lives. Adicia has never had to survive on her own wits and look for places to live. It's possible she could take up squatting in the basement of Allen and Lenore's old apartment, but there's no saying if the same sympathetic coal deliveryman still works there, or if there's a new deliveryman who wouldn't be so sympathetic to someone he discovers squatting.

Adicia finally decides she'll get on the subway and go to the end of the line. Uptown, there won't be as many rough elements. Ricky counts out money from his wallet to cover a few nights in a nice hotel, where she can stay while she looks up the Murphys in the phonebook. She hopes if she asks nicely and the right way, they'll let her stay there for at least one night. They know where Lucine lives, and she can get in touch with Lucine from there. She'll also be far from her family and

Seth's family that far uptown, no danger of running into any of them.

"So we're all settled?" Ricky asks at 3:30. "You know where to go and what to do from here?"

She nods. "Thanks for being such a great friend. Most people I've known aren't so nice."

"Will I ever see you again?" he asks as she puts her schoolbag on backwards, so it doesn't get cut off by a thief.

"You never know. I won't forget you anytime soon."

Ricky opens the door for her and hands her her suitcase. "You probably don't feel comfortable letting me hug you goodbye."

"I wish you could. Will a handshake do?"

Ricky takes her small hand and shakes it. "Goodbye, Adicia. I won't forget you anytime soon either. Maybe in another life we could've been more than friends."

He watches her going down the steps and up Avenue A, until he can't see her anymore. Hopeful she'll get to the next subway station without being molested, he goes into the living room to watch TV.

After Adicia has just passed Tompkins Square Park, hoping she looks the picture of confidence and normalcy, she spies her mother out of the corner of her eye, coming down East 9th Street and towards the intersection with Avenue A. Full of terror, but knowing her mother hasn't seen her, she turns around and begins running as fast as she can back to Ricky's house. If Mrs. Troy sees her, her plans are shot, and she can't dash into the park and hide out among the elms like she did when she was seven. Adicia doesn't care at this point what her mother's doing out of work at this hour, since it's such a common event for Mrs. Troy to quit or be fired.

Tearing back down the street at record speed, and sweating from the hot July weather and the extra baggage, she reaches Ricky's house in under fifteen minutes, dashes back up the front steps, and frantically rings the bell, all while hoping her mother is still far behind her and hasn't seen her.

"What's wrong?" Ricky asks as she pushes past him into the house and slams the door. "Did you forget something?"

"Lock all the doors and windows, and draw all the blinds. My mother's coming down the street right now. If she sees me with my baggage, she'll know I'm running away."

Ricky goes to look out the window while Adicia sits on the floor, below window level so her mother won't have any reason to get any glimpse of her. About five minutes later, he sees a woman who matches the description Adicia and Justine have given their mother.

"Is your mother about fifty, with ratty light brown hair with no gray streaks, a surly look in her eyes, hardened skin, about five foot five, and with a green and brown pipe in her hand?"

"She's forty-nine, and yes, that is definitely her."

Ricky watches Mrs. Troy continue on down the street and crossing the intersection between Houston and Avenue A/Essex Street. Adicia crawls over and peeks through the blinds to watch her mother disappearing into the apartment. Her one consolation is that neither of her parents have ever used corporal punishment. They're emotionally, mentally, and psychologically abusive and neglectful, but they've never hit any of their nine children. Justine will hopefully be able to withstand the storm that'll be unleashed once they realize Adicia's missing.

"How come you ran back here, by the way?" Ricky asks as he shuts the blinds.

"You saw my mother! I was right out in the open and had nowhere to go but back! I wasn't about to risk darting into the park and having her see me before I found my way over to the elms to hide."

"You graduated high school with a B plus average, so you're not stupid. And you grew up in this area. You know how all the streets connect and what goes where. You could've hightailed it down a nearby intersecting street instead of coming directly back here."

"When you're panicking like that, you don't exactly have the kinda time to stop and think about that. Why, are you upset to see me? Are you waiting for a girlfriend to come over?"

"I haven't had a date in awhile. You're still the only girl I like. I think you came back here 'cause we were meant to be more than friends for just six months before parting ways. Even if you didn't think about it like that, I think there's a higher reason you ran back here. It wasn't time for us to say goodbye."

"What are you implying? That I have a crush on you? I'm sorry to break it to you, but I still only like you as a friend."

"But you like me, right?"

"Yeah, you've been such a good friend. If you'd like to keep in touch with me after I leave, I know your address."

"I hate Columbia and this city. The university isn't a good fit for me. I liked Syracuse University, but my parents made me move with them. I'm like you, afraid to rock the boat and stand up to my parents. I don't care if they stop paying my tuition or kick me out, since I'm almost twenty and have my own bank account. The only nice thing about this city is you. I'm not cut out to live in a big city. I've also had it up to here with my parents' racist, classist attitudes. They'd probably pick me a wife who comes from a lot of money, instead of letting me choose my own. I'd much rather spend the rest of my life with a nice, sweet, humble girl like you than a rich snob who can't say 'please' or 'thank you,' and who thinks it's acceptable to be rude to people who are different from her. Would you let me join you in running away? I've got the money for a moving van, and we can be out of here before my parents come back. I'll withdraw from Columbia too. I don't care that ends my student deferment if they call number eighty-eight. At the rate the troop withdrawal has been going, they might not call anyone else. What do you say?"

"Running away together? Isn't that something only boyfriends and girlfriends do? I might be just a poor girl, but I still care about what remains of my reputation. Strangers might not know I'm not a physical virgin, but they'd note I'm traveling with a guy I'm not related to, and without a chaperone. People talk about that."

"You're too good of a person to subject to that. The only respectable way we could travel together would be if we were married. Adicia, will you marry me and be my sweet little wifey?"

Adicia bursts out laughing. "Are you serious? Even if I did love you back, I'm not eighteen! I need parental permission, and I can't let my parents know anything about my whereabouts!"

"Look, I know you don't love me the way a wife's supposed to love a husband, but you care about me as a friend. The concept of marrying for love is a relatively recent idea when you consider how long human history is. People a few hundred years ago would've laughed at the thought of marrying only for love and physical attraction, not because they were a good match and cared about each other as more than dating partners. I'll never lay a hand on you unless you tell me you want it. We'll sleep in different bedrooms."

"Mrs. Marsenko at the bridal salon told me the exact same thing the other day, that it's not the worst thing in the world to marry someone you only like if you're otherwise a good match. She said the strongest, longest-lasting, most serious love bonds sometimes come from growing instead of falling in love. This is my only hope left, Ricky. I couldn't even handle it when I saw my mother. Someone with real skills for surviving on her own wouldn't have come racing back here like a little coward. Though I hate the idea of marrying someone I don't love, and of you being stuck as the husband of someone who doesn't love you back and doesn't sleep in your bed or want to do anything physical with you."

"This doesn't have to last forever. If you don't like it, you can divorce me after a respectable period, when we've gotten settled down in a new city. I'll pay you a good alimony and remain your friend. But on the other hand, maybe you'll grow to love me the way a wife loves a husband. I hope you're able to grow to love me. I don't love you in that way either. Being in love with someone isn't the same kind of love that can only come after you've been together for a long time and been through both bad and good times together. I'd never force you to get married if you think it's best not to, but I'm making you a pretty respectable offer. I don't expect anything in return."

"I'll have to think about it. Marriage is a big deal, even if it's just for convenience."

"You have to decide sooner than later. We can't hide out here forever. Your parents will notice you missing before long, and they'll probably come here first if they find out it's where I live. And you need to wait twenty-four hours to use a marriage license. But whatever you decide, I'm dropping all the fall classes I registered for. I'm done with that school and this city." Ricky points to the calendar. "Today's July ninth. Your birthday's the eleventh. You won't need parental permission anymore then."

Adicia sits in shock, barely able to process what Ricky's asking her, as she listens to him on the phone with the Columbia registrar. Not only is Ricky dropping all his classes for the fall semester of his junior year, but he's also completely withdrawing from the university. Mr. and Mrs. Carson will hit the roof once they find out what he's done.

As soon as he's done throwing his parents' tuition money down the drain, Ricky goes to the basement for boxes. He begins collecting his belongings and putting them into the boxes, and puts things like clothes into his suitcases. Adicia watches television as he packs, not quite sure exactly what's happening.

"I'll call the moving company and ask them to come here in two days. They'll move all the boxes and my furniture into the truck. I'll drive it myself. I hope you brought your birth certificate and State ID, so we can have a quick, easy time of it at the county clerk's office."

"I've got them both. I can't believe you're really running away. You've got it made, and you're throwing it all away. At least I need to get out of here."

"This isn't the life I want to lead for myself. Money doesn't mean anything if I'm not happy with it. I have about five million dollars in my bank account, since I don't spend money like a drunken sailor. We can use some of it to buy a house. We might not be a traditional husband and wife, but I'd take care of you financially like a husband's supposed to take care of his wife."

"Carson is an easier name to spell, say, and remember than Oswald-whatever. It'd be harder for my parents to find me if I had a different name. No one could force me to come back home if I were your wife."

"I'll be a good husband, Adicia. I might not be the exact husband you dreamt of, but it's better to marry someone you like, who likes you, and who'll take good care of you than wait around for a mythical knight in shining armor on a white horse who might never show up."

"Wouldn't you resent me after awhile, since your needs as a man won't be met? I guess you can have affairs with other women for that."

Ricky pats her shoulder. "Even if it is a marriage of convenience, I'd never cheat on my wife. And my feelings for you are still strong. I hope you grow to love me the way a wife loves a husband, and that someday you'll love me back and feel comfortable enough with physical contact to consummate our marriage. Maybe someday, if this all works out, we'll have a couple of baby Carsons. You'd be such a good mommy, Adicia. You'd give your kids the kind of love and attention you never got from your mother."

"I had a mother. Her name was Sarah Katz. I might've lost her when I was seven, but I never forgot her. Everything I remember about how to be a real mother, I learnt from her." She hides her face in her hands.

"Hey, don't cry. Maybe you'll meet her again someday. She told you when people are meant to be together, they find their way back to each other."

"I hope you're right."

"I'll make you supper in the meantime. Would you like stuffed roasted duck, pork loins, or turtle soup?"

"Duck, please. I can't believe your parents eat turtles. I didn't know anyone ate them anymore."

Ricky calls the moving company before getting the duck out of the refrigerator and putting it in the oven. Adicia is impressed he knows how to cook. It's one thing that Allen knows how to cook and bake well, but he didn't grow up wealthy and having all his needs taken care of. Adicia puts that as another mark in favor of entering into a marriage of convenience with Ricky.

***

July 11, Tuesday, is the day the movers are scheduled to arrive and load everything up. They told Ricky they wouldn't arrive till 1:00, so Ricky and Adicia are able to eat breakfast in peace instead of worrying they might come in at any moment.

"Happy birthday, my pretty little ragdoll," Ricky says. "When I went out yesterday, I got you a present."

"You didn't have to do that," Adicia tries to protest as he hands her a small wrapped box. "You've already put yourself out enough for me."

"If you don't like it, I can return it to the store."

Adicia's eyes widen when she finds a dark blue velvet ring box and pops it open to see a deep blue sapphire with two small diamonds on each side, set on a white gold band. "Ricky, this must've cost you a fortune!"

"A gentleman never tells a lady how much he spent on her, but I can tell you it was one of the more modestly-priced rings. Dark blue is your favorite color, and it matches your beautiful lapis lazuli bracelet."

"Is this intended as an engagement ring?"

"I'll ask you again, just to make sure of your answer before we get out of here. Adicia Éloïse Troy, will you marry me and become my darling wife, and promise you'll grow to love me the way a wife loves a husband?"

"I thought about it over the last two days, and I believe I'll agree to your proposition. It's an unlikely match and not the usual modern reason for getting married, but I think you'll be a good husband. Besides, I'd much rather marry a cute boy who's only two years my senior instead of a gargoyle forty years my senior."

He squeezes her hand, then slips the ring onto her left hand. "A perfect fit. I told them you're very petite and have very small hands. They showed me their selection in size four. You're so tiny. Now we know what size to get your wedding band in."

"I can't believe I'm gonna be marrying you. You coulda knocked me over with a feather if you'd told me, back in January, that in only six months I'd marry the cute rich boy who just moved up the street."

"I couldn't have guessed I'd be marrying you either. Most people don't leap from unrequited love and only friends to spouses that quickly."

Adicia picks her fork back up and shovels scrambled eggs into her mouth. She blushes as she washes it down with orange juice. "Even if we only do a quick ceremony at a courthouse with a judge, what are we gonna do at the end? Are you allowed to not kiss the bride? What if we tell them we don't wanna do something so personal with an audience?"

"If they don't buy that excuse, I'll be as quick as I can. It's not so bad if you do it with someone you like. I've done it with maybe five girls. Just so you know, I didn't like them nearly as much as I like you."

"So I'm the first girl you've been in love with?"

"I guess so."

"Well, if I eventually grow to love you, you'll be the first guy I loved too. I'll be a good wife, even if I won't sleep with you for a long time."

"You never know. Neither of us could've guessed six months ago we'd rush into a marriage of convenience and run away together. Maybe you'll feel ready to be with me completely sooner than we think too."

Adicia goes back to her scrambled eggs. "Whatever happens, I'm really grateful you're doing so much to help me. I can't thank you enough for this."

"I won't let you down. I'll be the best husband I can be, even if I'm only a few days shy of twenty. I know this is your only hope left, but I won't take advantage of your situation. To me, you're a pretty girl I'm lucky enough to be marrying. I don't care you're a runaway or from a poor family."

Adicia sees the image of the crying Velveteen Rabbit on the

garbage heap again, only this time that scene is followed by the Rabbit turning into a real rabbit and hopping around with the other living, breathing rabbits. Ricky's love for her, unrequited as it may be, has finally made her Real, just as the Boy's love for the Rabbit made him Real.

Chapter 47: Adicia's New Identity

Adicia is a little bit nervous when she and Ricky are called to the next available desk after reaching the head of the line at the county clerk's office. She hopes they have enough proper identification documents and aren't sent on a wild goose chase to get further proof of identification or residency. It was bad enough they had to go to Planned Parenthood for a premarital blood test and that Ricky had to pay an expedited fee so they could get their results instantly. At least they found a female doctor, and Adicia avoided a full physical examination.

"Happy birthday, Miss Troy," the woman at the desk says when she sees Adicia's State ID and birth certificate. "You couldn't wait a minute longer to marry your boyfriend, could you?"

"I'm glad to be eighteen."

The form they have to fill out asks for their names, birthdates, places of birth, occupations, the names and birthplaces of their parents, addresses, and if they have any aliases or prior marriages. Adicia knows both of her parents were born in Manhattan, but Ricky has to think a little while before putting down Rochester as his mother's birthplace and Elmira for his father. Adicia stifles a giggle when she looks over and sees Ricky's parents' names, Willoughby Aristotle Carson and Georgiana Christiana-Helen Chantelle Whitestone Warrick Carson. The name Warrick Grover doesn't seem quite so silly and pretentious anymore.

"What do you put for occupation if you don't have a job?" Adicia asks. "My fiancé's a student, and I just graduated high school."

"I just withdrew from Columbia and amn't sure where I'll transfer," Ricky admits. "I might want to work for a little while before going back to school."

"Student is fine. Your fiancée can put that she's a housewife in the meantime, unless she's going to college in the fall." The woman glances at their forms. "You have very good handwriting for being left-handed, Miss Troy."

"I have a friend who taught me how to hold the pen properly, how to position my arm and the paper, and how to form the letters."

"Maybe you can teach me that too," Ricky says. "It's never too late to learn better handwriting."

"How about our address?" Adicia asks after they've filled every-thing else out. "We don't have a permanent address."

"We're sort of in between addresses at the moment," Ricky con-fesses. "To tell you the truth, one of the reasons we're getting married this quickly and so young is because her parents were trying to force her to marry a gargoyle forty years her senior. We're running away from them. Don't worry, I have a lot of family money in my bank ac-count to take care of her. We're not stupid kids getting married with no money in our pockets."

The woman looks at them very sympathetically. "Thank God your girlfriend just turned eighteen. When you marry the person you love, it's always better than an arranged marriage. She's a very pretty young lady. I hope you take good care of her. If you have any friends or rela-tives in the city, you can use their address. It won't be the first time someone's had to use an address he didn't really live at, since he wasn't settled into his own place yet."

"Mr. and Mrs. van Niftrik," Adicia says. "They're the parents of a friend of mine who's at Vassar."

"They can forward any documents we send, or you can go to their place to pick your mail up," the woman says as Adicia writes the van Niftriks' address. "We'll process your documents, and call you when your marriage license is ready. You need to wait a minimum of twenty-four hours before you can get married."

Ricky takes Adicia's hand as they go over to a bench to wait, try-ing to give the impression of a happy young couple. While they're sit-ting on the bench, Adicia notices she doesn't even come up to his shoulder. She always did want a tall man, though just about any guy of average height seems a lot taller than she is. The fact that Ricky is so much taller makes her feel physically protected, the way she might if she had a huge Great Dane or Irish Wolfhound. She doesn't flinch when he puts his arm around her. Deep in the back of her mind, she wonders what it would feel like to kiss him or have some sort of sexual intimacy, even if it's not intercourse. She knows from what Ernestine and Deirdre have chosen to share that one need not have intercourse to have a satisfying, complete sexual experience. Unlike Ethan and Seth, Ricky makes her feel safe and has a very comforting aura.

"Where did you go that was out of the country?" she whispers. "You used a passport for one of your IDs, but I don't think you ever told me you went abroad."

"I went to Europe with my parents when I was younger, and I went to Italy, England, Ireland, France, and Spain on a grand tour of Europe after I graduated high school. All rich parents send their kids on the grand tour, though I would've preferred a place like India, Brazil, Mexico, or Egypt. Everyone goes to Europe, but not everyone chooses to visit places that aren't such popular or common tourist attractions. I would've loved to see the beautiful, ancient Buddhist statues in Thailand and Cambodia too, but we all know what's going on in that region now. There was a protest against the invasion of Cambodia my senior year of high school, and my parents were livid when they found out I attended it. They thought I'd get shot like those four poor kids in Ohio, and they also thought it was a stain on the family reputation that I'd get involved in so-called radical politics."

"Your parents are really outta touch with modern life. I'm glad I won't have to deal with them as parents-in-law."

After a brief wait, Ricky and Adicia are called back up to get their marriage license. They're given instructions to have it signed by the officiant and two witnesses who are at least eighteen, and to have the officiant send it to the bureau of vital records as soon as possible. Adicia for once is glad she's so poor, so young, and not a man, since the only things she'll need to change her name on are the State ID and her social security card. She has no passport, driver's license, loans, bank accounts, tax forms at a job, mortgage, insurance, medical records, checkbook, savings accounts, credit cards, or voter registration. Once they get to their new city, she'll go to the DMV and have her ID changed, and she'll have to go to the social security office to have her card changed. She hopes she has all the paperwork in order by November so she can register for the presidential election in time. Adicia is very excited eighteen-year-olds are allowed to vote now, and is looking forward to helping to vote Nixon out of office.

"Where are we going to stay while we're waiting?" Ricky asks. "Should we check into a hotel with different rooms?"

"Why don't we see if my friend Betsy's parents will let us stay overnight? They live in the Meatpacking District, in a building that useta be some sorta factory. Their apartment is one wide-open space except for the bathroom and closets. They put up wooden panels to separate their bedrooms and the big space they use for the kitchen and living room. We could ask them if they'd be our witnesses. Once you hop back into the moving van, I'll give you the directions."

"Meatpacking District?" Ricky asks nervously. "So I suppose that neighborhood is famous for slaughterhouses?"

"It's a district, so it's quite a bit smaller than a regular neighborhood. It's located partly inside my brother Allen's old neighborhood, the West Village, which itself is part of Greenwich Village. A bunch of neighborhoods here are all intertwined. It's a pretty safe neighborhood, since it's between Chelsea and the Village."

"I can't keep all these neighborhoods straight. I only knew about maybe seven Manhattan neighborhoods before I moved here. I've had to nod along when someone mentions a neighborhood I've never heard of, so I won't give myself away as even more of a greenhorn. At least you corrected me on how to pronounce Houston Street my first day here."

"Well, we'll both be greenhorns soon. I'll miss this town, since I grew up here and it's so familiar, but I also won't miss it, 'cause I haven't had the easiest life here. It's not nice to live in a place where you have to worry about a high crime rate."

Once they're back on the street, they have to walk about five blocks to the moving van. Ricky has to pull Adicia up into the passenger seat, since it's such a big step up. She doesn't bother to fasten the safety belt, though Ricky immediately puts on his. Adicia doesn't see the point in hindering the joy of the ride with that constricting belt. At her height, the belt doesn't fit. Those things seem to have been designed with adults of normal stature in mind, not girls with tiny bone structure and a height below five feet. Adicia wishes she were at least two inches taller, just to say she's five feet tall. It's so childish to say she's four feet ten inches tall. Children, not newly-legal adults, measure their height in four feet plus inches over. It's also embarrassing to know her ring size is only a four. Even that's a child's size. She doesn't even weigh one hundred pounds. She wonders if she'll have to buy her wedding dress in the children's section.

"New York City drivers are crazy," Ricky comments as he has to abruptly backtrack into the spot where they're parallel-parked, to avoid being hit by someone speeding down the road and laying on the horn. "Do they all think they're immune from causing an accident?"

"Big city drivers are always reckless. They run stop signs and red lights, speed through lights changing from yellow to red, don't watch for pedestrians, break the speed limit, use their horns all the time, usually honk at people who are driving safely and obeying the road rules, make illegal turns, park illegally, go when they don't have right of way, turn into a lane of oncoming traffic with right of way, all sorts of crazy stunts. I've seen people stop and make U-turns right in the middle of a lane of traffic. One time I saw someone get outta his car at a red light and go somewhere to do something. By the time he got back to his car, the light had changed and everyone was honking."

"Maybe that's another reason so many people here take public transportation. They don't want to be run over or have their vehicles wrecked by all these crazy drivers."

Adicia admires the sapphire ring on her left hand as Ricky drives according to the directions she gives him. Since she has such tiny fingers, the stone looks even bigger, which isn't such a bad thing. This definitely cost more money than the lapis lazuli bracelet she got as her bridesmaid gift, and even more money than the charm bracelet she got with the leftover money from that memorable day she washed the kind stranger's windshield and got ten whole dollars. A tiny part of Adicia wonders if Lenore will be jealous, since the emerald jewelry Allen has given her probably cost under $100, if that, each. This ring looks like it cost at least $300.

"So you really like it?" he asks as they pull up to the last light before the van Niftriks' building. "I thought maybe you'd be offended 'cause the main stone isn't a diamond. Some girls don't think it's a real engagement ring unless it only has diamonds."

"I like pretty colors, and dark blue is my favorite. Diamonds are kinda boring, since they have no color, and everyone gets them. This ring reflects my personality and what I like. You didn't get it just 'cause an ad campaign told you to get it. And all-diamond rings are very expensive. That's money you could be spending on a house, a car, or groceries."

He smiles over at her as the light changes and he starts driving again. "I bet I couldn't find many rich or middle-class girls who shared that attitude. You poor and working-class girls are so much more humble and real, genuinely thankful for anything you get instead of demanding it be one certain way, exactly like everyone else."

"It shows you care about me as a person. Why would I reject or insult a gift from the heart if it's all you could afford or what you specially selected 'cause you thought I'd really like it? Any girl who'd reject a beautiful ring like this 'cause it wasn't expensive enough or didn't have platinum or diamonds is really selfish. I wouldn't care if you'd gotten me something even more modestly priced if it was all you could afford or if you knew it'd appeal to me more than something costing hundreds or thousands of dollars."

Ricky brakes as he pulls into a large enough vacant spot on the street in front of the indicated former factory. "You're such a good person."

"You don't need to praise me for doing what I'm supposed to do. Decent people are supposed to be thankful for what they have and not demand extra things." Adicia opens her door and lets Ricky help her down the big step.

"I hope I'm not annoying you by telling you how swell you are. It's just that I'm not used to someone who's so sweet, humble, pure, and good, just like I'm sure you're not used to an upper-class person who's so friendly with people who aren't from his social class." Ricky goes to unlock the back of the truck to pull out their suitcases. "What floor are they on again?"

"The fourth floor. You'll know which apartment is theirs. The one Ernestine and her friends lived in is all boarded-up. You'll only see the hair-thin door frame if you look really, really closely and carefully. That's onea the reasons they got away with squatting here for six and a half years."

Adicia looks around to make sure no one's following them and that no one who knows her family or Seth's family is lurking about. Satisfied the coast is clear, she takes Ricky's hand, her suitcase in her other hand, and starts towards the front door.

"Do we have to ring for the doorman, or can we just walk in?"

"Most people in this district don't have doormen. I've never lived in a building with a doorman. Only time I ever experienced one was when Justine and I stayed with the Murphys in Yorkville. They even had an elevator operator. Boy, I hope Justine's holding up well. I hate the thought of her fending for herself with only our parents and Tommy." Adicia turns the knob and steps inside. "I haven't been here since August of 1970, but I remember it like the back of my hand. It's hard to believe I haven't come by in so long. There were so many memories in this place."

"That's a huge elevator," Ricky marvels.

"This place useta be a factory. They must've used it for transporting huge bales of grain or lots of dead cows from floor to floor."

Adicia knocks on the door after the short ride up to the fourth floor. The van Niftriks go away on vacation during the summer, so she's not entirely sure anyone will be at home during this particular week. After about half a minute, she finally hears approaching footsteps.

"Adicia! We didn't know you were coming to visit!" Betsy says. "Who's this, your boyfriend? I never knew you'd gotten yourself a fellow!"

Betsy is dressed in an ankle-length pink dress with white flowers and a lace-trimmed neckline, turquoise beads hanging down to her waist, a lot of golden and silver bangle bracelets on both wrists, a mood ring on her right hand, and open-toed white plastic sandals. Her long brown hair hangs loose, with a crown of daisies. She wears no makeup except for an image of two fish painted on her right cheek.

"It's not permanent," she says when she notices Adicia staring at it. "I just had it done in the Village. A woman was painting astrological signs on people for a buck. I'm Pisces, the fish chained to each other for all of eternity, no matter how hard they try to swim away. You're Cancer, the crab. We're both water signs."

"This is Ricky Carson, my fiancé. We're getting married at the courthouse tomorrow. We know this is a really huge imposition and favor to ask, but is it okay to stay here overnight while we're waiting for our marriage license to become valid? You can come to our ceremony if you want, since we do need witnesses. I would've gone up to Marjani's place, but I didn't wanna leave our moving van with all our stuff in Hell's Kitchen overnight. Someone would probably break into it."

"You're *engaged*?" Betsy shouts excitedly. "Of course I'll come to your wedding! Are yous guys eloping?"

"I guess we are."

Betsy leads them inside. "Mom, Dad, is it okay for Adicia and her boyfriend to stay here overnight? They're getting married tomorrow at the courthouse and need somewhere to stay till their marriage license becomes valid. They're eloping."

Mrs. van Niftrik rushes over to them. "How nice to see you again,

Adicia! Of course you and your young man can stay here. We have a guest bed, and we can put up a spare wooden panel to give you privacy."

"Just one guest bed?" Adicia blushes. "One of us will have to sleep on the sofa bed."

"You're not sleeping together yet?" Betsy asks. "I thought all couples nowadays took the car for a test drive before getting married. If I had a serious boyfriend, I'd try him out beforehand, and my parents would be cool with that. Is it because of what happened with that Ethan punk? But surely if you're enough recovered from that rotten thing to get married, you'd be okay with doing that by now."

"This is not a love match, at least not for me," Adicia admits as she sits on the davenport. "It's a marriage of convenience, kinda like an arranged marriage. We're both running away, Ricky from his snobby, out of touch, rich parents, and me from my own parents, who were forcing me to marry a grotesque creature forty years older than me. This prize they picked for me was in prison for fifteen years for beating his first wife to death."

"We won't be consummating our marriage right away," Ricky agrees. "I hope Adicia grows to love me over time, just like my feelings of being in love with her will change into a more mature love after enough time passes."

"You're marrying someone you don't love?" Betsy asks. "And you're okay with this decision? Gee, I didn't think anyone still had arranged marriages outside of really religious people. Even if you're compatible in other ways, what's going to keep you married if you're not in love?"

"I like him as a friend," Adicia says. "Part of me really wishes I could've had a husband I fell madly in love with and felt butterflies in my stomach for, the kind of love at first sight Allen and Lenore had, but maybe it's true a strong bond of love can come from growing instead of falling in love."

"You can tell us more about this over supper," Mrs. van Niftrik says. "I'll make it early tonight. I suppose you're right on some level. Many hasty marriages and painful divorces could be avoided if people didn't only think with their hearts. Being blindly, passionately in love today doesn't mean you'll get along and be able to run a household and live together in the long run, after the fireworks die down and it's time to attend to more serious, grownup matters like raising kids, paying bills, and dealing with medical emergencies."

"Today's Adicia's eighteenth birthday, by the way," Ricky says.

"So it is," Betsy says when she looks at the calendar and sees the date is July 11. "Why don't you and me go out to celebrate tomorrow before your wedding? Mom, can we go to Macy's to get Adicia wedding presents?"

"I'll gladly go with you," Mrs. van Niftrik says. "I have a pretty good idea of what kinds of things you need to set up your first household. Just tell me what you want, and I'll try to buy it for you. I'll help you with picking out a nice dress too."

"If this convenience marriage works out and we both love each other in another year or two, it'd be really swell if we could get our vows renewed in a real ceremony, with all our friends and decent family," Ricky says. "But don't worry, we don't intend to ask for wedding presents all over again if we make it long enough to merit a renewal ceremony."

"Can I use your phone to invite Marjani to come with us?" Adicia asks.

"Of course you may," Mrs. van Niftrik says. "You shouldn't have an entirely impersonal elopement ceremony. Afterwards, we can take you out to eat."

"By the way, do you know where Lucine, Allen, and Lenore are?"

"Hudson Falls," Betsy says. "It's a bit south of Lake George and a bit northeast of Saratoga. Since Julie's going to Skidmore in the fall, she won't be too far away. Emeline lives there too. I can give you the address after supper."

"Thank you so much for putting yourselves out for us," Adicia says.

"It's nothing doing," Mrs. van Niftrik says. "It's just the right thing to do for a friend. Now come into the kitchen and tell me what you'd like for supper, and you can tell us all about what led you to this elopement."

***

Wednesday after breakfast, Adicia, Betsy, and Mrs. van Niftrik set out for Macy's, looking around every step of the way toward the subway for signs of that spiteful busybody Mrs. Rossi. Adicia has no idea where she works, but it's in this neighborhood, and that's reason enough to worry. Unlike Mrs. Troy, Mrs. Rossi has a decent work history and isn't known for suddenly quitting jobs or getting fired and then waltzing down the streets unexpectedly.

When they meet Marjani on 34th Street, she's wearing a multicolored polyester blouse, blue open-toed leather sandals, very dark indigo bell-bottom jeans, and white, purple, and light blue beads in her cornrows. A hobo bag is slung over her right shoulder. Adicia is a little taken aback Marjani is wearing pants. She doubts she'd have the nerve to pull off wearing pants. It just seems right that girls wear skirts and dresses while guys wear pants. She also feels more protected when she wears something that covers at least part of her legs and doesn't outline her body. Emeline has told her much the same thing, that she feels like she's being seen as a person, not a sex object, when she wears a skirt or dress with a properly modest hemline. The only pairs of pants Emeline owns are very loose, baggy pants that look more like a skirt and don't outline her crotch.

"Let me see your ring," Marjani says.

Adicia shyly holds up her left hand.

"Maybe one day when I have a career, I'll be able to buy myself jewelry like that. I ain't like you. I wanna buy my own jewelry and not depend on a man to give me expensive presents. It'll be nice if my future husband buys me jewelry, but I don't expect him to drop serious cash on it if I'm equally capable of buying it. I don't know if I want an engagement ring, or at least not one a guy buys for me. I'd rather buy my own, so I don't have that symbol of being bought and owned by a man."

"I'm a disappointment to the women's liberation movement," Adicia says as they walk into Macy's. "Modern girls aren't supposed to get married fresh outta high school or rely on guys to rescue them from bad situations. Modern girls don't automatically change their last names either."

"You ran away from your parents and didn't just roll over and let them sell you like chattel to that ex-convict," Betsy says. "That's pretty enlightened to me."

"Your parents are morally messed up if they see nothing wrong with tryna force you to marry an ex-convict," Marjani says. "My parents would be beside themselves with horror if they found out I was dating or planning to marry a guy who'd been in prison for killing his first wife. Your mother left a really bad taste in my mouth."

"He's old enough to be your grandpa! That's so gross. I don't even wanna go out with guys who are five years older. Ricky's the perfect age for you, not too old or too young. Two years is the perfect age difference when you're eighteen."

"Have you heard of the half plus seven rule? You divide your age in half and add seven to determine who's too old or young for you to go out with. I ain't good at doing math in my head, but I don't need to do any math to figure out that Seth guy doesn't fall within the half plus seven rule at all for someone who's just turned eighteen."

Adicia's eyes sparkle when they enter the kitchen department. So many times, she and her sisters window-shopped here and dreamt of owning the beautiful tableware and cookware. Now, for the first time in her life, she's going to get some of these beautiful things as wedding presents. She doesn't want to take advantage of Mrs. van Niftrik's generosity, but she also doesn't want to pass up the chance of a lifetime and skimp out on getting everything she really wants.

"What would you recommend? How much tableware and cookware do we really need if it's just the two of us and hopefully Justine as soon as humanly possible?"

"If you're having your family as guests, you'll need more than just three table settings. You can buy two nice dinnerware sets for eight or ten, since you have such a large family, including the Ryans. For just the two of you, Justine, and maybe a future child, you can get a couple of dinnerware sets for four. You can do the same with the silverware. When we get to the cookware section, I can advise you on what you absolutely need, and what you can function without. Later, when your household's more established and you have more disposable income, you can indulge in things that aren't so necessary but are still nice to have for special occasions or specialty foods."

"How are we gonna carry all this stuff? We only have eight arms among the four of us, and they don't have shopping carts or baskets."

"You can bring the things up to the cash register and have them held till we're ready to check out. We'll have them delivered to the apartment, and from there we can put them into your moving truck."

While they're looking through the china sets and Mrs. van Niftrik patiently explains what is and isn't essential in a dinnerware set, an associate who looks to be in her upper forties, with a very snobbish look, approaches them. Adicia thinks she's going to ask if she can help them, but instead she utters a question worthy of Mrs. Troy.

"Ladies, is this girl in bell-bottoms bothering you?"

"I'm with them." Marjani glares at her.

"You mean she's not following you around?"

"Boy, are you a racist. Do you know it's 1972 now? Black and white people can be friends now, you know." Marjani looks at her name tag. "We won't be checking out at your register, Florence."

"What an idiot," Betsy says after she disappears in a huff.

"At least she didn't accuse me of shoplifting."

"That happened to us a lot too," Adicia says. "When my sisters and I went into stores, clerks would follow us around, like they thought poor girls in ragged clothes could only be there to steal."

"It takes awhile for some people to get used to new ideas," Mrs. van Niftrik says. "Change is scary."

"Marjani, would you sign my marriage certificate as onea the witnesses? My parents and Ricky's parents would all have heart attacks if they found out a Black girl signed as a witness to a marriage none of 'em approve of."

"I'd do anything to stick it to your mother. She deserves all the blots on her reputation she can get. That woman ain't mother or woman of the year."

Adicia ends up selecting two white and blue china dinnerware sets for ten, four informal dinnerware sets for four, in blue, yellow, red, and lilac, two sets of silverware for ten, three pots and three pans, four casserole dishes, salt and pepper shakers, twenty drinking glasses, a gravy boat, two white serving platters, one wide, deep serving dish, a teakettle, a toaster, two wooden spoons, a set of knives, a spatula, and a cookie sheet. She's very glad Ricky gave her permission to use some of the money he withdrew from the bank before they left home, since this is a very large order for Mrs. van Niftrik to shoulder on her own. The cashier nods when they tell her to ship the purchases to the address given. This cashier doesn't have any rude remarks about what Marjani's doing with them, nor does she look at her funny.

"Now we can look at jewelry!" Betsy says. "How much money do you have left from that cute fiancé of yours? I'd wanna marry a guy for convenience too if he were a real-live millionaire."

"He told me his ring size is ten and to get a plain gold band," Adicia says. "There's five hundred bucks left."

"Wow, you really landed your golden ticket outta poverty," Marjani says. "My ticket outta the working-class world is Howard University, and yours is marrying a millionaire. We'll both have happy endings, even if our methods are different."

"He has five million bucks in his bank account. That's not much, considering his parents have a lot more money. All that money will be gone eventually, since he's not going into a profession that rakes in the big bucks or marrying another millionaire."

"It's still way more dough than you ever thought you'd see in your lifetime! Maybe for Christmas he'll use somea that dough to buy you a mink coat and a Rolls-Royce."

Adicia looks at the selection of wedding rings for awhile, just taking in all the sparkling gold, diamonds, and silver, before telling the woman behind the counter she'd like to see a traditional gold band in a man's size ten. The associate obliges and hands the ring to her after unlocking the glass counter.

"It'll do. Guys don't care as much as girls about getting a pretty wedding ring. That's all he wanted, a plain gold band."

"Would you like it engraved on the inside?" the associate asks.

"Not now. Maybe later, if we have a bigger ceremony and vow renewal down the road. We're getting married at the courthouse today and don't have time for a big affair with lots of people."

"What about your ring? Do you want a plain gold band too, or something with a little decoration?"

"What about this ring?" Adicia points. "The one with little flowers in the middle."

The associate pulls out a white gold band with three flowers across the center, one silver, one gold, and the third rose-plated gold, with little diamonds in the center of each. "These are Hawaiian plumerias. It's a popular motif with customers who want something a little different."

"It's really pretty. I'd love to get this one. Do you make it in a size four?"

"I don't believe we carry rings that small, but we can have it resized for you while you wait. Can you come back in an hour?"

"Yes, we still need to look for a dress. Should we pay for the rings now?"

"No, you can take care of everything here when you get back."

They head over to the clothing department, looking in both petites and juniors. Adicia immediately vetoes all the leftover prom dresses on the clearance rack, finding them too fancy and formal. A lot of them have hemlines a bit too high for her, since she doesn't like showing her knees or anything above them. Others she rejects because the fabrics aren't her style. She'd never wear polyester on her wedding day, even if it is just a quick courthouse ceremony. It's tricky to find something she likes that isn't too fancy or too informal. The dress she wears on her wedding should be at least a little special, even if it's not several hundred dollars and from an upscale bridal salon like Mrs. Marsenko's.

After almost an hour, Adicia finally finds a dark blue cotton dress with sleeves covering the shoulders and a mid-calf hemline. The neckline goes to the collarbone and is embroidered with pale blue lace. It's meant as a sundress for younger girls, not eloping eighteen-year-olds, but it'll do. She always thought she'd be surrounded by friends and decent family on her wedding day, wearing a beautiful lace gown with a veil and a train, carrying a beautiful bouquet of roses, marrying a man she loves, and celebrating with a nice supper and party afterwards, but she knows all too well her life has always been more like a Grimms' fairytale than a Disney fairytale. Even the handsome prince she's been given isn't a love match, and he's not taking her to a castle in a fairytale kingdom after the wedding. This can't be Ricky's dream wedding day either. Though he might be marrying the girl he's in love with, she doesn't love him back. Still, it's a nicer prospect than being forced to marry Seth.

***

Late in the afternoon, their party of six arrives at the courthouse downtown. Instead of making a grand entrance to a beautiful song like "Benedictus," she and Ricky just enter the appropriate room when their number is called, Marjani and the van Niftriks following them. Adicia is almost humiliated at how impersonal this is, being treated like cogs on an assembly line instead of unique individuals celebrating their marriage. Ricky hands the marriage license to the judge and puts the box with the rings on his desk.

"Is it okay if you Xerox us a copy after it's signed, so we can use it as temporary proof of our marriage till the official one comes in the mail?" he asks.

"I can do that." The judge sets the license on the desk. "How long have you known each other?"

"Six months."

"And you're only eighteen and nineteen?"

"I'll be twenty in three days."

"It's nice to see a couple who's not wasting time by just dating for a couple of years. I miss the days when most people married by their early twenties, within six months to a year of meeting. All these radical young people nowadays want to shack up with people they don't intend to marry."

"Is it okay if we don't kiss at the end of the ceremony?" Adicia asks, blushing. "I'm too shy to do something so personal with an audience."

"Well, that's certainly a request I've never had before."

"My bride is very shy and old-fashioned." Ricky puts his arm around Adicia. "She believes in saving personal stuff for private, keeping it only between the two of us."

"I had a Jewish nanny when I was a little girl, Sarah, and she told me and my sisters about the traditional Jewish wedding once. The bride and groom go to a room alone after the ceremony and kiss or touch there. They don't do something so personal and intimate in front of everyone, since that cheapens intimacy. It's more special when it's something only the two of you share instead of displaying it for everyone and letting them be privy to such personal moments. I usually look away when I see people kissing or groping each other in public."

"You really are an old-fashioned bride. Not at all like those crazy women's libbers who think marriage is slavery and sleeping around is liberating. I'll be glad to perform your marriage."

"Can we take pictures?" Betsy asks.

"Sure, go ahead." The judge picks up the license to remind himself of their names. "Warrick Grover Carson and Adicia Éloïse Troy?"

"My fiancé goes by Ricky," Adicia says. "I thought it was short for Richard or Eric when I met him."

"Wasn't Adicia the Greek goddess of injustice?"

"My mother thought it was an injustice to have a fifth daughter, particularly since I was the fourth of four girls in a row."

The judge shakes his head. "Very well then. Let's begin. We are gathered here today to celebrate the marriage of Adicia Éloïse Troy and Warrick Grover Carson. Marriage is a covenant between a man and a woman to love and support one another for all their days, for better or for worse, till only death can part them. If anyone here has just reason for why they should not be joined in matrimony, speak now or forever hold your peace."

Betsy takes a picture of them standing by the desk.

"Adicia, will you take Warrick to be your lawfully-wedded husband, to love, comfort, honor, and protect him, for richer or poorer, in sickness and in health, for better or for worse, and forsaking all others be faithful to him till death do you part?"

"I will," Adicia says, though she feels horribly guilty for how she's been reduced to marrying a man she doesn't love and entering into such a serious bond as matrimony. Then again, she doesn't have to feel romantic or sexual love for Ricky to be true to the words of her vows.

"Warrick, will you take Adicia to be your lawfully-wedded wife, to love, comfort, honor, and protect her, for richer or poorer, in sickness and in health, for better or for worse, and forsaking all others be faithful to her till death do you part?"

"Yes, I will."

After they repeat the vows after the judge, they're asked to repeat the ring vows, "This ring I give you, as a symbol of my vow, as a token and pledge of our love, with all that I am and all that I have." Adicia's hands are shaking as she puts the ring on Ricky's finger, hoping she doesn't drop it and that it doesn't get stuck on his finger. Her throat tightens as Ricky puts the pretty plumeria ring on her finger, knowing there can be no backing out of this agreement. For better or for worse, this boy from up the street, whom she's only known for six months, is now joined to her legally. They'll have to live together as husband and wife after they leave the courthouse. She hopes there's truth in the words that say arranged marriages are often better than contemporary Western love matches, since they're based on something more than fleeting physical attraction and lust.

"By your consent, both written and spoken, through the exchange of rings, and by the power invested in me by the State of New York, I now pronounce you man and wife. Ladies and gentleman, I now present to you Mr. and Mrs. Warrick Grover Carson."

Adicia is numb as she shakes hands with the judge and Marjani and the van Niftriks hug her. The judge, Marjani, and Mr. van Niftrik sign the license, and then Adicia and Ricky sign. While the judge Xeroxes it, Betsy takes pictures of the newlyweds, and Mrs. van Niftrik takes pictures of Adicia with Betsy and Marjani. When the judge comes back, he obliges them and takes a picture of everyone together.

"Congratulations," he says as they file out of the room.

As Betsy takes another picture of the newlyweds on the courthouse steps, Adicia feels like she's just been robbed of her dream wedding day. These are not the wedding pictures of a happy couple she wanted to display in beautiful frames on the mantelpiece or wall. These are pictures of a couple of nervous misfit kids who have no idea what they're doing, who haven't even known one another for a whole year, who've been joined together in the most serious commitment possible. She doesn't have a bouquet to toss, and none of her family are here. Allen will probably hit the roof when he finds out Adicia married Ricky, the guy he dislikes so much. But she'll have to think about all those things tomorrow. Right now she has bigger fish to fry than the long-term implications of this impulsive convenience marriage she's just entered into.

Chapter 48: Leaving New York City

After the brief courthouse nuptials, Mr. and Mrs. van Niftrik took Ricky, Adicia, Betsy, and Marjani to supper at the restaurant in Chelsea they've had celebratory meals at before. Marjani went home on the subway and the van Niftriks went home in a taxi. Ricky decided he'd like to take the subway once before they leave, only having taken cabs since he's been in the city, so he and Adicia are taking a short walk from the restaurant to the nearest subway station.

"It must be around the new Hebrew month." Adicia points at the tiny sliver of the Moon visible in the sky. "Sarah told us the new Jewish month always starts with the new Moon, and there's a full Moon in the middle. There was a tiny sliver of the Moon in the sky that night I took Justine and Giovanni to the Bowery Mission after the fire, so it must've been either the end or the beginning of a new Hebrew month."

"I had a nanny when I was little too, but my parents paid her, and she wasn't so nice as you describe your Sarah. I don't think my nanny liked kids. She had none of her own and had no wish to."

"Sarah has two kids now, Fritz and Nessa. Nessa was born only one day after Irene."

"So there you are, you ungrateful whore."

Adicia freezes in her tracks when she sees Seth standing in front of them. It completely slipped her mind the Oswaldtwistles live in Chelsea and that she should've done a better job of looking around before doing anything in this neighborhood.

"Your parents noticed you missing on Monday evening, and your brother and sister said they had no idea where you were. I guess you were lying to your mother when you said you weren't going around with that rich boy up the street. Was I not good enough in bed for you that you'd run away to a boy who probably ain't been with a woman to know how to screw her? I've half a mind to beat you black and blue like I often had to do to teach my first wife a lesson." He clamps his hands around her upper arms.

"Seth, you're hurting me."

"My wife is not going anywhere with you," Ricky says. "Even you must know it's not right to lay your hands on another man's wife."

"How the hell could she be your wife? Mr. and Mrs. Troy

promised her to me! She only ran away a few days ago! How the hell could you already have married her on such short notice?"

"We could and we did. Adicia is my legally-wedded wife now. We got married this afternoon."

"Oh, so I can still take her back to her parents' home. I assume your pretend marriage ain't had time to be consummated, so it can be annulled in time for our promised marriage in September. What does someone so young know about being married? Her parents had a reason they wanted her to marry someone forty years her senior!"

"I'm not going with you, Seth. I'm staying with my husband. I'm eighteen now and no longer legally under my parents' jurisdiction. And I asked you to let go of me. You're gonna leave bruises in my arms or cut my skin open."

A foul smile appears on Seth's face. "If you refuse to do your duty and return with me, I can wait a few more years for that pretty little sister of yours to be old enough to marry. I always did want a blonde, and I'll bet she's nice and tight."

"No!" Adicia screams. "If you touch a hair on Justine's head, I'll kill you! She's my baby!"

"Well, if you choose to stay with this man-child you've married and don't come home to the Lower East Side, you can't really do anything about keeping that girl from me, can you? What's more important, protecting yourself or your sister?"

Adicia desperately wishes she'd never left Justine alone, but there's no way she or Ricky can go back there and smuggle her out without their parents finding them out. Ever since March 1959, when Justine was born, Adicia loved her and knew she'd always protect her and look out for her. Now, at the vulnerable age of thirteen, Justine is languishing alone with only Tommy left as a buffer between her and their parents. The few days they've been apart feel like an eternity.

Ricky jumps into the street when he sees a police car driving by, jumping up and down and waving his hands. Adicia told him Chelsea is one of the nicer neighborhoods in Manhattan, so he hopes the cop is nice to them and doesn't automatically assume they're up to no good.

The cop pulls over to the side of the road and gets out of the car. "Do you need my help, young man?"

"This man is threatening my wife! Her parents were trying to force her to marry him in September, but she decided to marry me as soon as she turned eighteen. What girl in her right mind wants to marry a guy her parents picked for her, someone forty years her senior, who's been in jail for fifteen years for killing his first wife?"

"I don't believe their story that they're married," Seth says. "This willful child ran away from home a few days ago, and already they had time to get a marriage license, have the premarital bloodwork, and have the marriage ceremony?"

Ricky pulls the marriage license out of his pocket. "We had the judge make us a copy till the real one comes in the mail, since we didn't want any trouble with people thinking we're shacking up."

The cop shines his flashlight onto it. "This is a legit, legal document of marriage, Sir. If you don't take your hands off Mrs. Carson, I'll have you run in for attempted kidnapping and assault."

"It's not a valid marriage!" Seth protests, still holding onto Adicia. "She's gonna be Mrs. Oswaldtwistle in September! These fool kids ain't consummated their marriage, so it can still be annulled and she can come home to her parents! Or else I'll wait a few years and marry her little sister instead when she turns sixteen."

"How could we have had time to consummate our marriage when we just got married late in the afternoon?" Ricky asks.

"Valid point," the cop agrees. "If I have to ask you again to let go of this newlywed bride, I'll run you in. Since you've already had a stretch in prison, you wouldn't be any stranger to the inside of a prison cell."

Adicia barely has any feeling left in her arms when Seth finally lets go of her. Ricky rushes over to support her when she looks like she's about to start slumping onto the ground.

"Where are you two going?" the cop asks as Seth skulks away, glaring in their direction.

"We were headed towards the subway," Ricky says. "We're staying with a friend and her parents. After we get back, we're going to collect our things and drive to Hudson Falls, where Adicia's older siblings have relocated."

"You're not from New York, are you?"

"I'm a native New Yorker. I was born and raised in Syracuse, and moved to the city in January."

"No, I meant not from the city. You have no New York accent."

"I'm a native Manhattanite," Adicia says, finally finding her voice.

"I've lived in the Lower East Side, Two Bridges, the Village, and Hell's Kitchen. My friends live in the Meatpacking District. I've gone there enough times to know which subway to get on."

"*That's* what a New York accent sounds like," the cop tells Ricky. "You haven't lived here long enough to pick one up. Would yous guys like a ride? I wouldn't recommend getting on the subway at this hour, particularly not after what just happened with that ex-convict. You'll definitely be safer if you're taken home with a police escort. Personally, I advise yous guys to get out of the city as soon as you can. That brute looks like the kind of guy who won't take no for an answer."

"Oh, we'd love a ride in your car, Officer! But I don't wanna take you away from your beat if you had something important to do here."

"It's all part of my job. Hop in the back, and I'll drive there."

Ricky helps Adicia into the backseat, where she slumps against him. He feels her violently shaking when he puts his arm around her, and her heart is still beating very loudly. Still terrified of what just happened and what might happen to Justine, she begins giving directions to the cop.

"I think there are gonna be bruises on my arms in a day or two," she whimpers like a lost child. "At least he didn't break my arms or cause any bleeding."

"Well, it's over now. You're in the safest place possible," Ricky tries to reassure her. "I'm sorry I didn't try to fight him off you, but I was scared of getting more than a few bruises or scrapes. The guy's been in jail for fifteen years for beating his first wife to death."

"He gave her an internal hemorrhage. She was ten minutes too late for him when she went out to a store when their youngest kid was a baby. I wonder if any of the customers at that supposedly successful pharmacy and grocery store of his know it's run by an ex-convict."

"It's usually a bad idea to try to take on criminals and people threatening you," the cop agrees. "You should do what you can to stay calm and protect yourself until the cops arrive. A lot of times the bad guys turn it around and say you were the one assaulting them."

"That happened at my junior high a lot. A friend of mine was ganged up on by a bunch of bad kids after lunch one day, and she was the one suspended 'cause she fought back. Nonea the kids who attacked her were punished. There were lots of bad kids who should've been arrested or taken to juvenile hall. I bet a few of 'em will be in adult jail soon."

"They didn't punish bad behavior that didn't involve beating other kids up, so why should the teachers or administrators have bothered with consequences for the really serious stuff?" Ricky asks. "That story about Bernard you told me made me sick. This little hoodlum tore the flag from their homeroom and first period class off the wall, kicked it around, and threw it out the window. He never got a punishment for that. That was during the seven months they had a long-term substitute 'cause their French teacher had a nervous breakdown from all the bad kids."

"This city does have a lot of rotten elements," the cop agrees. "You look like nice kids. A big city like this is no place for a couple of innocent-faced kids who haven't been sucked down into depravity. If I were that Bernard's father, teacher, or juvenile officer, I would've given him a beating for being so disrespectful towards the flag. I didn't get wounded in Okinawa in '45 for some punk kid a generation later to turn around and desecrate the symbol of freedom I fought for."

"Is there any way you or another officer can go to my parents' place on Essex Street and take my little sister out of there?" Adicia begs. "He threatened my thirteen-year-old baby sister and said he'd marry her instead of me if I didn't go with him. I'm hoping against hope our sixteen-year-old brother Tommy does the brotherly thing for once in his life and looks after her while I'm gone. I told her to wait awhile and then join me. I won't be able to sleep till I see my baby sister again."

"I'm not a fan of underage runaways, but in cases like yours, that's probably the best course of action. Once you reach your new city, you can file for legal guardianship. I'll ask someone to place a call to her tomorrow so she won't have to wait around for that guy to show up. Do you have a contact number?"

"We live on top of a kosher bakery run by Adara and Nathan Straussler. They know me and Justine and what our parents are about. I have an extra business card of theirs." She reaches into her purse and fumbles around to find it. "You can keep it. They have really delicious food. I'm Protestant, so I know you don't hafta be Jewish to enjoy stuff from a kosher bakery. But maybe I'm biased since I had a Jewish nanny."

The cop pulls up in front of the van Niftriks' apartment. "Here you go. Is that moving truck yours?"

"Yes it is. We'll go up, get our suitcases, say goodbye, and be out of here. It's about two hundred five miles away, about three and a half hours if we don't make any stops. My husband rented the moving truck for a maximum of five days, and will turn it over at the local branch of that company after we find an apartment or house."

"Good luck to both of you. My name's Officer Brankovic, by the way."

"Thank you for helping us," Adicia says as she gets out of the car. "I'm sorry about your war wounds. Being shot must hurt a lot."

"Adicia's dad wasn't in the war," Ricky says. "He flunked all his medical and psychological tests 'cause he was such a drunk and drug addict."

"I got them for a good cause, and scars make the body more interesting," Officer Brankovic says. "I have a more unique story to tell about myself, and we're never given more than we can handle."

Adicia still has to be supported by Ricky as they go into the building and take the elevator up to the fourth floor. She collapses onto the davenport almost as soon as Betsy lets them inside.

"Why are you so pale?" Mrs. van Niftrik asks. "Did something happen on the subway?"

"We got a ride back in a police car," Ricky says. "We had a little run-in with that Seth fellow before we got to the subway station."

"He left marks on my arms. I bet I'll have bruises. If we find Allen when we go to Hudson Falls, he's gonna wanna do the same thing to Seth he did to Ethan."

Ricky tells them what happened while he collects their suitcases and makes sure they have everything they brought. The van Niftriks think Seth should've been arrested, even if just for twenty-four hours, but at least Officer Brankovic got his name and found out where he works. There might be consequences for an ex-convict running his own business and not letting his customers know just whom they're doing business with. And he did promise to get Justine out of that foul environment before Seth can have his way with her or Mr. and Mrs. Troy can barter her off like a piece of meat too.

"Be careful," Betsy says when she walks them to the door. "New York drivers are crazy enough, but you should also be extra careful when you're driving late at night. Do you know how to get there from here?"

"We've got a map," Ricky says. "And we have the address you gave us for Lucine and Zachary, though we'll need a city map once we get there. We'll stay at a hotel, maybe a furnished apartment, till we find a decent house for sale."

"I'll come up to visit you over winter vacation. Poughkeepsie isn't too far from where you're going. Ernestine and the Ryans will come with me, of course."

"Thank you for everything you've ever done for me and my family," Adicia says. "It's been so nice to have sympathetic grownups in my life, and to have friends outside of my sisters."

"We'll tell Justine you're safe if she comes to see us," Mrs. van Niftrik promises.

Adicia picks up her suitcase and schoolbag and follows after Ricky, finally up to walking on her own without being partially supported. Betsy and her parents go to the window and wave at them when they appear on the street below. After Ricky unlocks the back of the truck and they put their remaining baggage inside, Adicia waits for him by the passenger side door to be helped up into the truck. She feels little emotion as Ricky turns the headlights on and pulls out of the parking spot. Like her siblings have often said, the only people who enjoy living in Manhattan have money, and the only people who think it's so glamorous, romantic, and exciting to live here are either rich or not from the area. Adicia only looks through the window from time to time to watch landmarks and familiar places going by in the dark. She's leaving the past behind and going forward to her future, whatever it may hold.

***

Ricky and Adicia roll into Hudson Falls at 2:30 in the morning, after stopping at one rest station so Ricky could get coffee to prevent falling asleep at the wheel. There weren't very many people on the roads once they got out of Manhattan, so there weren't many delays with traffic. The hardest part was figuring out how to get into Hudson Falls once they got off the highway and had to navigate their way around a city again. Adicia is already asleep when Ricky parks in the lot of a respectable-looking hotel and goes inside to inquire about lodgings for at least two nights and one day. Once he's secured a room on the second floor, Ricky goes back out and brings the luggage up to the room, then goes back for Adicia. She barely stirs when he opens the door and lifts her out like an oversized ragdoll.

Adicia flutters her eyes open when they're getting off the elevator and walking down the hall to their room. "Where am I?"

"We're safe. We got to Hudson Falls, and you fell asleep during the drive. We're going to stay in this hotel for maybe two days, till we find somewhere more permanent. I'll put you in the bed, and I can sleep on the sofa. You can go back to sleep, and I'll tuck you in."

"You really wanted to carry me over the threshold, didn't you?" she asks before drifting back to sleep.

Ricky sets Adicia on the bed and pulls the covers over her, taking the stuffed koala out of her schoolbag and tucking it in next to her, then goes into the bathroom to change into pajamas and falls asleep on the pull-out sofa. This isn't the wedding night he always imagined, but even if it were a mutual love match, he's too tired to do anything. The most important thing is they're over two hundred miles away from Manhattan, in a small town where probably no one will be able to find them or suspect they've gone to. Their parents and Seth are far away and can't force them to do anything anymore. The only missing piece of the puzzle is Justine, but hopefully she'll be able to find her way up to them soon.

Adicia wakes up at 9:00 and finds breakfast pastries, a peeled orange, and two strawberry Pop-Tarts on the bedside table, on one of the lilac plates she bought the other day. Ricky is on the sofa, looking through real estate and rental guides.

"Oh, you're finally up. I don't blame you for sleeping so long after what happened to you yesterday. I walked around the nearby streets and bought stuff we don't need to cook. Our housing pickings might be slim, but this is where most of your family lives. I hope we find something soon, since we have to turn this truck in by Saturday or pay a fine for overtime."

"Did you see any for-rent signs?"

"You deserve a real house. Imagine having your own backyard and front yard, with room to grow a garden and trees. Maybe we can get a puppy or kitten to keep you company while I'm at work. You don't mind if I have to commute, do you? I also picked up stuff for lunch, by the way. Do you mind dried fruit, cashews, crackers with peanut butter, sunflower seeds, and granola bars?"

Adicia stares at the plumeria ring on her hand. "Did we actually get married yesterday?"

"Believe it or not, we're now man and wife. If the arrangement doesn't work out, we don't have to stay married, but we'd better make the most of it now that it's happened. Maybe we won't be able to stand each other for more than a couple of months, but maybe it'll bring us closer together and make us grow into the kind of love a married couple's supposed to have. I'm sorry I couldn't give you a nicer wedding, even if you don't love me."

"We did what we had to do. You've been a good husband so far. If I had to marry someone I didn't love, I couldn't have asked for a nicer guy."

"I hope your brother doesn't kill me. He really didn't like me."

"He'll have to accept it. I'm sure he'd agree we did what we had to do to get out of there safely. He'd much rather prefer to see me safe and taken care of than in a dangerous situation. I'm a bit embarrassed I need a man to take care of me when it's 1972, but not all women can be street smart and self-sufficient. I kinda like the old-fashioned sweetness of a guy taking care of me."

"There's nothing wrong with being old-fashioned. I always wanted a girl who'd take care of me, someone I could look forward to coming home to, even if I don't want a June Cleaver or Donna Reed. Men and women are different, even if I think women should have equal rights. There's something comforting about the idea of a sweet little wifey cooking for me and cheering me up after a bad day at work, and kids do best when they have one parent at home with them when they're young. It could be the guy who stays home, but I don't know of any guys who stay home with the baby and do all the housework while the woman works."

Adicia looks at the koala. "I'm probably one of the few newlywed brides who slept with a stuffed animal and not her new groom on her wedding night."

"I'll have to buy you your own bed. You deserve a queen-sized bed. It's better if yours is the bigger bed. If you decide you want to be together as a real husband and wife, I'll join you in the queen, and we'll give my double to Justine."

"What are we doing about money? Your bank account has a ton of dough in it, but it's not wise to exist on savings and not bring any additional money in regularly. And you have to transfer all your money from the old bank to a new local bank."

"We'll have a joint account. What's mine is yours, and you deserve to buy nice things even if you don't have a job. I'm not interested in going back to school at this point. I'll defer my last two years till we get more settled. We also need a car. I don't know if this town has a bus system, but it's always best to have your own car and not rely on public transportation. What kind of car would you like?"

"I think VW Beetles are cute."

"Then that's what we'll try to look for. We can rent a car in the meantime. I could easily plunk down enough money for a fancy car like a Ferrari or Aston Martin, but I don't care for a silly status symbol like that. We shouldn't do anything to stand out just 'cause we've got some money. My parents look so out of touch 'cause they dress like rich snobs from fifty years ago, even when they're in normal work or social settings."

"Will you teach me how to drive?"

"If I'm working, I can only teach you on weekends. Hey, how'd you like to learn to ride a horse too? I bet they have horse farms around here. You'd be such a cute little equestrian, and you're just the right size to be a jockey. If you like it, I'll buy you your own horse, and you can store him at a stable. My mother had a horse growing up, but since she didn't live on a farm or have enough land to keep horses, it was boarded at a stable, and she'd come by every couple of days to ride it."

"My own horse? That would be really nifty! I like the kinds with spots on them, and I also think Arabian horses are beautiful."

"We'll have to get stuff to decorate our house. Posters, tapestries, statues, artwork, that kinda thing. Do you have any favorite artists or musicians?"

"I never had the kinda time to develop an interest in any special bands or artists, though I like plenty of 'em. I never even had a favorite Beatle, since I had more important things to worry about."

"Fair enough. I always was partial to Albrecht Dürer, Egon Schiele, Paul Klee, Pablo Picasso, and Salvador Dalí. I enjoy so-called conventional, traditional art too, but the modern schools of art, and artists who don't always paint inside the lines, so to speak, have always appealed to me more."

"You'll have to tell me more about those artists. I'm only familiar with Picasso and Dalí, and the only thing of Dürer's I'd recognize is *Praying Hands*."

"I'd love to tell you all about my favorite artists. Onea my majors was art history, so I know a lot about art and artists. I brought along my old portfolios from my high school art classes, sketchbooks, and some of the little drawings I've made over the years, if you'd like to look at them."

After Adicia finishes eating, she gets out of bed and has a look at the real estate catalogue. Her favorite is a two-story house with two and a half bathrooms, four bedrooms, a living room and kitchen with large dimensions, a basement and attic, ten closets, including four walk-ins, a dining room, and three additional rooms, which can be used as a study or office, a library, and a playroom for potential future children. The back veranda is almost the entire length of the house. She cares less about a dining room, since she's grown up eating in the kitchen and associates eating in a dining room with rich people. All the rooms and the lavish dimensions are a dizzying dream come true after the small Manhattan tenements and apartments she's used to. After consulting a map, they figure out this house is about a twenty-minute walk away.

Ricky uses the phone in the room to call the real estate agent, and gets a 2:00 appointment. Wanting to make his bride happy, Ricky doesn't bother calling the real estate agents for any of the other houses, nor does he bother calling apartment landlords or people offering summer sublets. He has to agree all the other houses pale in comparison to the one she's fallen in love with. Before they eat lunch, they use the phonebook to look up a department store selling mattresses and bedding. They'll also need a phone. Ricky already has a radio and record player, but he doesn't have his own television set. Adicia is giddy with delight over the thought of having a real television in her own house. This is a dream come true, a rags to riches story as unbelievable as that of the Five Little Peppers. The only thing that would make her joy complete is her non-annoying version of Phronsie, Justine, joining them.

***

"You really want this house, Mr. Carson?" the real estate agent asks after he's given Ricky and Adicia a tour. "It's only your first viewing, and you haven't looked at any other houses in the area!"

"I never lived in a house growing up," Adicia says wistfully. "This is my dream come true, to live in a house, and one this big."

"Does it have any other potential bidders or buyers?" Ricky asks.

"It's been on the market for two years. A lot of people toured it and liked it, but they either changed their minds or couldn't afford it. It is a very nice house, I agree."

"How soon can I sign the contract and give you the money?"

The agent looks at him closely. "How old are you again, Mr. Carson?"

"I'll be twenty on Saturday. My bride just turned eighteen on Tuesday."

"So I assume this would be your first home? Most young couples rent or purchase something much more modest for a first home. What do you need with all that space?"

"My baby sister's coming to join us soon, and we'll need a guest room, since I have a big family. Plus there might be kids someday," Adicia says.

"Do you and Mrs. Carson have the kind of money for this house?" The agent again addresses Ricky instead of Adicia. "You do realize the asking price is fifty thousand dollars."

"I'll write you a check for that amount right now if it'll mean we can start moving in by Friday."

"What are you, independently wealthy?"

"I have a sum of money that's nothing to sneeze at in my bank account. I got access to my trust fund when I turned eighteen, and have been spending very frugally till now. Now that I'm married, I need to dip into it for bigger purchases."

"Are your parents going to be co-signing this contract with you? Will you need a loan?"

"We've got enough to afford it and not go into the poorhouse, to say the least. Can we complete the sale by tomorrow? I have to give back the moving truck by then, or I'll have to pay a fee for overtime. Who wants to start married life in a hotel?"

The agent looks at him in slack-jawed disbelief. "I'll have the paperwork for you later today, and you can write a check for the entire amount."

"Do I sign the contract too?" Adicia asks. "I am going to be the co-owner."

"Ladies don't co-own anything. Your husband will have the house entirely in his name, the same way he's entirely paying for it. All ladies need permission to use their husband's bank accounts, open credit cards, and sign loans. Don't tell me you're one of those crazy libbers."

"My wife is going to be the legal co-owner of the house," Ricky says forcefully. "We're creating a joint bank account, so she does have my so-called permission to use my money and sign contracts with me. Women aren't dumb children who can't function without men. You don't have to be a radical feminist to want equal rights between men and women."

"Have it your way," the man mutters. "You have my business card. Meet me at my office at five, and you can sign the contract and pay me. Boy, you kids today are too radical for me."

While they're waiting, Adicia and Ricky take a walk around the neighborhood, looking into shop windows and admiring the houses. Adicia wonders if any of the houses belong to Lucine, Allen and Lenore, or Emeline, or if they live beyond walking distance. As it is, they're going to have to drive to the real estate agent's office in the moving truck because it's too far to walk. After they return to the hotel, Adicia practices writing her new name on the hotel notepad. She's always found it rather pretentious to drop one's middle name and use one's birth surname in the middle slot. She likes her middle name and doesn't want to give it up. Adopting the official name Adicia Éloïse Troy Carson also sounds rather pretentious and silly. Adicia Éloïse Carson doesn't sound quite right, but she supposes Lenore probably felt strange about going from Miss Lenore Eve Hartlein to Mrs. Lenore Eve Troy. She wonders if Lucine is now Lucine Camille Martel, or if she decided to hyphenate.

They arrive at the real estate agent's office at 5:00 and sign the papers, Adicia still feeling strange about turning over her identity as a Troy in favor of a surname she has no history with. She'll have to ask Lenore how it felt to go from a Hartlein to a Troy, and how long it took to get used to having that strange new identity.

"Here are the keys to the house, Mr. Carson," the agent says, not looking at Adicia. "You can start moving in immediately, as you requested. Boy, I never met any couple this eager to buy the first and only house they saw, to pay in full right away, and to move in as soon as the ink was dry."

"Thank you for letting us buy this house on such short notice,"

Ricky says. "You have no idea how much this means to us."

The agent looks glad to be rid of them as he sees them out of the office. Adicia is glad to be rid of him too, the way he always addressed Ricky even if she were the one speaking. It's news to her women need permission to sign loans and contracts, open credit cards, and take money out from the bank, but she vaguely remembers Francesco saying so-called respectable women need their husbands' permission to get birth control, and how scandalized he was Gemma got birth control pills without his knowledge or permission. Then again, where she's from, no one gets credit cards or has any reason to have loans or buy expensive things like cars and houses.

"How do you like the house, Mrs. Carson?" Ricky asks as the moving men transport the boxes and other baggage into the various rooms of the house.

"It's my dream house! Can my room be the one upstairs with the window looking out on the backyard? There's a beautiful magnolia tree out there."

"I wonder if anyone lives next door. It looks kept-up, but there's no car in the driveway."

"Maybe they went away on summer vacation. Lake George isn't too far north. Can we take a vacation there? Maybe we can have a honeymoon at the lake."

"Come on, you deserve a nicer honeymoon than a lake. How about a real beach on the ocean, like Cape Cod, Maine, or Rhode Island?"

"Could we take Justine with us?"

"Of course. Justine deserves a nice vacation too."

"This is the best thing that's ever happened to me! I can't believe I'm not really dreaming and that any moment I'm gonna wake up still on the Lower East Side, living above the Strausslers' bakery."

After all the furniture, boxes, suitcases, and other things are inside, Ricky pays the movers and motions to Adicia to follow him so they can return the truck. He already used the hotel phone to arrange for a rental car at the drop-off location. Adicia thinks the rental, a maroon Oldsmobile, looks like a big old boat, with a huge square hood, and definitely not as cute as the VW Beetle, but it'll have to suffice until Ricky buys their own car. She hopes they can buy a car as quickly as they bought the house.

Their first stop after the drop-off and pick-up is the department store, where Adicia tries out what feels like a dazzling array of queen-size mattresses to see which one she'd most like to sleep on. Adicia has never slept on a queen before, and can barely believe she'll be sleeping on such a luxuriously large mattress tonight and every night thereafter. She's very tempted to jump on all the beds too, but she knows such behavior is considered undesirable in someone her age. She selects a dark blue bedding set, two fluffy down pillows, and a double wedding ring quilt.

Ricky pays an expedited fee to have the mattress and box spring shipped immediately. Adicia is still unable to believe a poor girl from the Lower East Side and Hell's Kitchen is now married to a cute millionaire. Like the Five Little Peppers, she'll never forget her origins, but it does feel good to have her own deus ex machina happy ending and to come into so much money.

Chapter 49: The Flight of Justine

While Justine reads the latest issue of *Ms.*, Tommy rolls around on the new roller-skates Mrs. Troy bought him for completing his sophomore year with a B average, and Mr. and Mrs. Troy are at work on Friday afternoon, the fire escape door opens and Seth comes in. Tommy doesn't acknowledge him, and Justine buries her face in the magazine, hoping he won't bother her.

"You told your parents you had no idea where Adicia disappeared to. Well, guess who I found on Wednesday night when I was walking home from work! You're gonna start talking to me, or I'll have to beat the answers outta you brats. Where is that ungrateful whore, who helped her run away, and how long has she been in cahoots with that fresh-faced rich boy up the street? And did either of yous know she's now Mrs. Carson and no longer Miss Troy?"

"I barely talk to my sisters. Why would I have any idea?" Tommy skates over to the kitchen and pulls the refrigerator open for a snack.

"You mean you never eavesdrop or read their diaries?"

"Adicia and I never kept diaries," Justine says. "Tommy might be annoying, but he doesn't eavesdrop. He has better things to do."

"She became very agitated when I suggested I'll marry you if she don't come back home, after I wait a few years for you to reach the minimum legal marriage age. If she cares so much about protecting you, she never woulda left you here. That wench can't very well do anything to keep me away from you if she ain't here, can she?"

Justine's stomach turns to ice. "I'm glad Adicia got away from you. She deserves a happy ending and a nice husband. You'll have to find another woman who wants to marry an ex-convict who beat his first wife to death."

"If she don't show her face and come back home after coming to her senses and having her silly play marriage annulled, you'd be a good enough second choice. Would you like to come live with me while we wait for you to be sixteen? I always did want a pretty blonde, and I bet you're nice and tight 'cause you're presumably still a virgin."

"Leave my little sister alone," Tommy says. "That's a really disgusting, perverted thing you're suggesting. If Adicia ran off and married that guy up the street, that's her business. She's eighteen now and can't be forced back here. What are you, a pedophile?"

"Where'd an overgrown mama's boy like you learn a big, fancy word like that? I didn't know they taught about such unmentionable things in school nowadays."

"I didn't learn about it in school. I've heard talk among other guys in the hallways and the locker room. By the way, it's really creepy how you came in without knocking or calling ahead. That's called trespassing, and it's against the law."

"Decent people should always expect company at any moment, unless they're hiding something. Where's your hospitality?"

"A man's home is his castle—"

"You're a sixteen-year-old little pipsqueak! You ain't the man of this house! And knowing how much your father despises you for being your mother's pet, I'm sure he'd be furious to hear you pretending to be the man of this house."

"Tommy's a lot of things, but he's not a pipsqueak anymore," Justine says. "His voice changed awhile ago. I don't know what definition of pipsqueak you're using."

Seth looks with horror at Justine's magazine. "So you're onea them libbers. I miss the days when all women knew their place and didn't step outta line tryna demand equal or extra rights. When I was born, women couldn't vote, smoke in public, show their legs, or get birth control devices without their husband's permission. Women were content to be wives and mothers, and didn't want higher education or careers. If you become my second wife, I'd never let you work or go to college."

"I'm only going into eighth grade. I have no desire to become anyone's wife. I don't even have a boyfriend."

"Can you please leave our apartment?" Tommy asks. "I don't like you."

"I don't like you neither, you overgrown brat! And it ain't your house! Your parents rent this place! You don't pay a penny for anything on it, unless I am very much mistaken and you have a job!"

"My mother buys me everything I want. I don't need a job."

"Oh, and I suppose your plan is to marry a rich girl, just like Adicia married a rich boy, so you'll never have to worry about working like people in the real world. What girl or woman would have you?"

"Tommy isn't that bad-looking," Justine says. "His entitled personality makes him seem less attractive, but if I weren't his sister, I might see where he could be called kinda cute."

Justine can barely believe she's coming to the defense of Tommy of all people, but it's stalling Seth for time, and Tommy did come to her defense first. Maybe, for once in his life, Tommy is acting with a semblance of decency and maturity because he's the oldest child left, and has no choice but to step up and grow up a little bit better late than never.

"Do you know the address or phone number of that rich boy who stole her away from me? What are the addresses and numbers of their friends?"

"I'd never give that up to you, and if Ricky married her, he's no longer at his old address and number," Justine asserts. "We should have you arrested for entering our place without permission, and for threatening us."

"You're just a couple of stupid teenagers! If you don't start giving up any names and contact information of people your disobedient sister might've gone to, I'll have to beat it outta you."

"I'll tell my mother you hit me, and she'll have you thrown in prison," Tommy says. "Do you really wanna go back to jail?"

"Our parents never hit us even when they're mad or they're outta their minds on drugs or alcohol," Justine says. "Only cavemen hit kids."

"All proper parents spank their children, and all proper men beat their wives! Since neither of yous are talking, I'm gonna have to get my answers the hard way. Which one of you wants to go first?"

The door on the other side of the apartment opens, and Mr. Straussler comes in as Seth is trying to pin Tommy down on the davenport, dodging the kicks aimed at his face and Justine's kicks from behind.

"Who the hell are you, and what are you doing to these children?"

"I'm Seth Oswaldtwistle, Adicia's fiancé, and I'm here to get answers from these twerps one way or another about where in the hell she and that boy husband of hers disappeared to! If we can't find her even if they do cough up explanations and clues, I'm taking Justine to my house and breaking her in. When she turns sixteen, I'll make her my wife. They both deserve a good beating for holding out on me when I know they must know something, and that sneaky fiancée of mine deserves an even bigger beating for running away and marrying someone else behind all our backs!"

Tommy lands a very hard kick to Seth's head, even more painful than a normal kick to the head because of the roller-skate.

"You little bastard, you're gonna pay for that! I don't give a damn what your enabling mother does to me if I beat you black and blue!"

"Sir, I have to ask you to leave this home. If you don't, I'll call the police and have you arrested for attempted assault, breaking and entering, and disturbing the peace. I run a bakery downstairs, and my customers don't wanna hear this uproar. You'd also be interested to know that just before I came up here, I received a call from the police, saying you were threatening to kidnap this young lady and forcibly marry her, and if I'd help with taking her out of this poisonous living situation. It also might interest you to know I have a gun and I'm not afraid to use it."

"My mother will hear all about this when she comes home from work!" Tommy shouts indignantly as Seth releases him. "Nobody gets away with messing with her pet child!"

Justine runs over to Mr. Straussler and stands next to him as Seth slowly stands back up and walks over to the fire escape door, walking down the steps as slow as molasses in January. Tommy skates over to the door and makes obscene gestures at Seth.

"Do you really have a gun?" Justine asks.

"Mrs. Straussler and I both know how to fire a gun, and so do all three of our kids. After what happened to my people in Europe thirty years ago, I figured better safe than sorry in case anything like that ever happens over here. I want to be able to fight back instead of being led like a lamb to the slaughter."

"Can you teach me how to use a gun?" Tommy asks.

"Your mother would probably grant you permission to go with me to a shooting range and pay for your lessons. I'm talking about a handgun, not a rifle or shotgun for hunting or shooting at clay discs."

"That would be awesome! All my friends would be jealous of me 'cause I know how to fire a gun!"

"In the meantime, we have to get Justine out of here. The bakery's about to close for lunch break, but Mrs. Straussler and I always stay there to keep an eye on things and catch up with book-keeping. I heard an awful story from the police officer who called, about what that man did to your sister on Wednesday night. We don't wanna take any chances he'll do the same to you, or try to go back after her again. How long will it take you to pack your things?"

"I mostly only own clothes," Justine says. "I have my schoolbag and the suitcase our parents got me when we moved here."

"Your parents don't come home on lunch break, do they?"

"Our dad works farther down south, really close to the borders with the Financial District, and our mother's new job is in a candy shop run out of someone's home in Two Bridges. She's probably gonna be fired as quickly as last time, 'cause she was bragging about how she's helping herself to as much chocolate as she can when the owners and other employees aren't looking."

"Tommy, do you know how to get to Eldridge Street? It's only five blocks west of here. Orchard Street is midway between our block and your block. You'll know you're halfway there when you see the street with all the old tenements. I'll give Justine our key. We'll be home a little earlier today, since the Sabbath begins tonight."

"You want me to take Justine to your place? Can't she walk there herself if it's so close by?"

"It's the brotherly thing to do, isn't it? Even if you never were the closest of siblings, it's nice to escort your little sister somewhere instead of making her walk alone."

Justine goes into her bedroom and starts putting all her clothing into her suitcase, then tucks in her few other possessions, such as the rabbit fur muff Allen got her for what would've been her first real Christmas, the tea cozy Lenore crocheted for her, and the rose quartz bracelet she got as her flower girl gift. She tucks her library magazines and books into her schoolbag. Most thirteen-year-olds have a lot more belongings, but her life is what it is, she thinks with sad resignation. She hopes soon she'll own a lot more things besides clothing and small trinkets.

Justine comes out with her suitcase in her left hand, her schoolbag backwards, and her twelve-year-old stuffed white rabbit, worn a bit thin and threadbare, under her right arm. Mr. Straussler thinks she looks like the picture of innocence, with her blonde hair, blue eyes, petite frame, albeit not as tiny as Adicia's, and the stuffed animal that's been her companion and friend since she was thirteen months old. He doesn't know of any other thirteen-year-olds who'd openly carry a stuffed animal around with them or admit they still sleep with one.

"We have a television, radio, and record player, though you might not like our records. They're mostly classical and ragtime instead of modern rock and pop. You can also read any of our books or magazines you'd like. We'll come home around six, and we'll keep you with us till Saturday. Do you have a place to go to after that?"

"I'll try Mr. and Mrs. van Niftrik in the Meatpacking District, and if they don't know anything, I'll try Adicia's friend Marjani in Hell's Kitchen."

"Then it's settled. Tommy, take your little sister to my apartment and make sure she gets inside. I assume you know how to find your way back here from there. You just go west along Houston Street and turn south onto Eldridge."

Tommy takes off his roller-skates and puts on blue sandals Mrs. Troy bought him when he complained all the other boys at the Hamilton Fish Park Pool had more fashionable footwear. After Mr. Straussler returns to the bakery, Tommy goes down the fire escape with Justine. Justine is very surprised when he reaches over and takes her hand.

"I can do the big brother thing once in my life. Allen must be a lot better at the big brother thing than me, since he's so much older and has a ton more experience doing it, but even I know you're supposed to hold your little sister's hand when you go somewhere with her."

"You're not so bad when you put your mind towards acting decent, Tommy. I wish you'd act like this more often, instead of acting like an overgrown, spoilt little boy and letting Mother continue to treat you like her helpless little boy. You'll be eighteen in two years. I don't think Dad will wanna keep you at home while Mother continues to spoil you off your rocker and doesn't let you learn how to be a grownup."

"I've got it made if I write a college essay about growing up poor and with drug addicts and drunks for parents. They might give me a free scholarship. I love how Mommy buys me all the nice things I want, but my friends might start making fun of me if I continue living off her once I'm a legal adult. Even I know grownup guys aren't supposed to live at home and let their mothers unquestioningly do everything for them."

"That was a really nice kick you gave Seth. I bet he'll remember you for a long time. You mighta given him a goose bump with that roller-skate, or made him bleed inside his head.”

“I’m telling Mommy about what he did when she comes home. I hope she has him arrested for what he tried to do to me. I might be her special pet, but I never thought she was perfect. She has a really crummy work ethic, she’s a racist, antisemitic, and anti-Catholic, and I never got why she wanted to marry all you girls off as soon as you became legal, to guys who were way older. Guys who wanna marry or fool around with girls twenty or forty years younger are gross. I can see a forty-year-old woman and a sixty-year-old man, but if the younger person’s only a teenager, that’s totally gross. At least she doesn’t wanna marry me off as soon as I’m eighteen, since I’m a boy.”

“You won’t do so bad for yourself once you’re the only kid left at home. Even if Mother wants you there indefinitely, Dad for sure will wanna kick you out almost as soon as you’re no longer his legal responsibility. Like Seth said, Dad hates you ’cause you’re Mother’s little darling. Maybe you wouldn’t have grown up treated like such a little prince if there’d been less girls, and our only other brothers hadn’t been so much older than you.”

“I’m looking forward to finally being an only child. Being on the bottom of a huge heap of kids stinks. I wouldn’t wish being the eighth of nine on anyone. If I ever take a woman, I only want a couple of kids.”

They turn onto Eldridge Street and walk about three blocks to the Straysslers’ yellow walk-up. Justine opens the door and goes up to the second floor. Tommy watches her unlocking the door and going into the living room, taking in what a nice place the Straysslers have. It may be only a one-bedroom apartment, but it’s clean and well-lit, and has an inviting atmosphere. All the places he’s lived in have had very bad, negative energies, with the possible exception of their brief stay in Two Bridges. In spite of all Francesco’s repulsive qualities, he cared enough to select a nice apartment instead of deliberately choosing the worst, cheapest place possible, and Gemma cleaned it and kept it looking like an inviting home.

“Have a nice life with Adicia and her new husband after you get outta here. Maybe we’ll run into each other again sometime.”

“Maybe. Thanks for stepping up and being somewhat of a decent big brother the past few days.”

Justine goes to the window after she puts her schoolbag and suitcase down, and she and her old rabbit watch Tommy turning back around and going home. Her parents will hit the roof to find she's gone missing too, but Mrs. Troy will be quickly distracted when Tommy tells her about what happened with Seth. Given her ferocious over-protectiveness of Prince Tommy, Mrs. Troy might press charges against Seth for trying to assault her golden baby boy, and he'll leave them all alone forever. Just as all of them long predicted, Mr. and Mrs. Troy will be left all alone. It took a long time to get here, but the best revenge never happens overnight.

***

Justine enjoyed a marvelous Friday night dinner with Mr. and Mrs. Straussler, and took the subway to the Village Temple on East 12th Street on Saturday morning. In spite of the neighborhood's Jewish history, there are currently no Reform synagogues there. Justine doesn't have much memory of going to this synagogue years ago, so she had no idea what to expect, but she had a nice time. Everyone was so nice, and didn't care she was a visiting Protestant. Afterwards, Justine and several other guests had a wonderful lunch, and Mr. and Mrs. Straussler took a walk with her around the neighborhood, pointing out some of the old landmarks. Justine found it a little sad so many of these old stores, synagogues, and buildings are abandoned or little more than historical relics of the days when the neighborhood was full of poor immigrants crammed on top of one another. She's glad those days are largely in the past, but a neighborhood or city shouldn't let its history languish in disrepair. She wonders if some of her ancestors lived in the squalid old tenements lining Orchard Street, the street that seems to have the most old tenements still standing.

After the end of the Sabbath, the Strausslers called for a taxi and gave the driver directions to the van Niftriks' apartment. Justine held her rabbit on her lap as the cab zipped through the darkened streets of downtown Manhattan and headed up towards the area between downtown and midtown. When the taxi reached its destination, Justine got out and paid him with the money Mr. Straussler gave her. Now she's waiting for someone to get the door at the van Niftriks' apartment.

"Justine?" Betsy asks. "Come right in, and we'll tell you everything we know."

Justine sits on the davenport, letting Mr. van Niftrik take her things to the guest bed. "I have no idea what happened to Adicia, only that a cop called the Strausslers' bakery yesterday and told them to take care of me till I could go to some of our friends who might know more about where she went. That Seth fellow came into our home and threatened me and Tommy, but Tommy kicked him in the head with a roller-skate when he was tryna pin him down on the davenport and give him a spanking or something. Mr. Straussler threatened to shoot him."

"What the hell was that creature doing inside your home? And why did he wanna give a sixteen-year-old boy a spanking? Does he prefer men and underage boys in addition to teenage girls?"

"It was really creepy. I wouldn't be surprised if he were a pederast as well. He said he'd hafta beat answers outta us, and didn't believe neither of us knew anything about where Adicia went. I hope he never finds us. Boy, he's taking this really hard. Francesco and Jacob never went after us to try to find Gemma and Lucine after they went AWOL. I'm glad Ricky took Adicia far away from this brute. I don't want Seth to beat my best sister to death or rape her again. Ricky is to us what Jasper was to the Five Little Peppers, a goodwill emissary from the other side of the tracks appearing at just the right time to take us outta poverty forever. Only Ricky isn't the little brother of our mother's long-lost rich cousin's wife."

"He's pretty cute. I'd be very tempted to marry a guy I didn't love for convenience if he were a cute millionaire."

"I wouldn't care if he were an ogre so long as he were nice to Adicia and had what it took to take care of her and get her outta this city."

"He seemed like a very nice young man," Mrs. van Niftrik says. "He'll be a good husband to Adicia and a good brother-in-law to you. Though I'm afraid we haven't heard from them since Wednesday night, when they set out for Hudson Falls after their run-in with Seth. Don't worry, they came home in a police car after Ricky flagged down a passing cop. Your poor sister thought she'd have bruises on her arms from how long and hard he held onto her."

"Seth hurt her again?" Justine asks in horror.

"They ran into Seth on their way to the Chelsea subway. He grabbed her arms and wouldn't let go until the cop ordered him twice to stop. The poor thing could barely walk afterwards, she was so dazed and scared out of her mind. At least he probably won't think to look for them where they went. Thank God your neighbor came up in time to prevent that brute from beating you or your brother."

"He held Tommy down on the davenport?" Mr. van Niftrik asks. "Doesn't he know you and Adicia have never exactly been close chums with that boy? What did he think would happen when your mother found out what he did to her pet child? Even if Adicia were still here, that marriage would probably be called off after that!"

"I didn't know Tommy could kick that hard. I hope Seth suffered permanent brain damage from getting kicked so hard in the head by a roller-skate."

Betsy pulls a state map off the bookshelf along the back wall. "This is where they went." She opens the map and puts it over their laps. "Hudson Falls, about three and a half hours north. A little south of Lake George and a bit northeast of Saratoga, the city where all the horses race in the summer. The closest big cities are Glens Falls and Queensbury. I don't know if they have Greyhound or train service. You could get a bus to Glens Falls or Queensbury and call for a cab."

"Would you like to stay here till Adicia contacts us?" Mr. van Niftrik asks. "We'd never give you up to your parents if they found out where you are."

"I need to get as far away from them as I can. I hate to go back to Hell's Kitchen, but maybe Adicia told Marjani something."

"She helped us pick out kitchen stuff, wedding rings, and a decent wedding dress at Macy's," Betsy says. "She also signed the marriage license as onea the witnesses. My dad was the other. Boy, your mom would have a quintuple heart attack if she found out a Black girl was onea the witnesses on a marriage she won't approve of."

"As soon as our film develops, we'll send you the wedding pictures," Mrs. van Niftrik says. "Maybe someday she'll have a marriage renewal, and you could be her maid of honor."

"It was such a casual wedding, Marjani wore bell-bottoms and a polyester shirt. If there's a vow renewal, no one can get away with such informal clothes."

"Do you remember how to get to Marjani's place from here?" Mr. van Niftrik asks. "Would you like one of us to walk you to the subway or the bus stop in the morning?"

"I can manage it. I hope you don't think I'm being rude by wanting to leave so soon, but I don't wanna stay close to my parents. There's gonna be more trouble tomorrow, when Mr. and Mrs. Carson come back from their week in the Hamptons and find Ricky gone, along with all his stuff."

"He withdrew from Columbia," Betsy says. "His folks are gonna blow a fuse when they find that out. There might be a letter waiting in the mail by the time they get back, like an apology it didn't work out there, or saying they have his transcript on file in case he's transferring to another school. He wasn't sure if he'd go back to college right away. He thought maybe he'd work for a little while."

"Ricky withdrew?" Justine asks in shock. "But his lottery number is eighty-eight, and he has no more student deferment should they call that number!"

"Eighty-eight?" Betsy gasps. "I never knew about that! That's way too low to go walking around with a target on his back! As soon as you find them, you and Adicia have got to convince him to enroll back in school, even if it's just a two-year school! Adicia will be terrified out of her mind at losing him!"

"There's no guarantee they'd use him if they called eighty-eight," Mrs. van Niftrik tries to soothe them. "Maybe he's not physically fit enough, they'll think he's not all right in the brain for what he just did, or they'll have filled their quota of other eighty-eights."

"Mom, you saw Ricky! He's not Mr. Bodybuilder, but he's not a stick figure either! He's not the type of guy they'd reject for being out of shape or too skinny!"

"They're withdrawing a lot of troops," Mr. van Niftrik says. "I wouldn't be surprised if they scrapped the draft altogether soon. Besides, how much hardship does that girl have to go through? It couldn't be possible that after all she's already been through, she'd immediately have her happy ending snatched away from her so prematurely."

"I hope you're right. If only Ricky was her age or a year older instead of two years older. They're calling all the guys born in '52 this year. Ernestine, Deirdre, and I are so glad we're girls."

"This talk is scaring me," Justine says. "Can we talk about nicer things?"

"I'm doing something very productive tomorrow." Betsy grins. "I decided to go over to that bully's pharmacy and grocery store and put up flyers all over the neighborhood and near the store, saying it's run by an ex-convict who spent fifteen years in prison for beating his first wife to death when he was drunk. I hope he's put outta business forever."

"What if someone catches you and hurts you, or if Seth himself discovers you?"

"I'm doing a public service. My dad said he'd Xerox a bunch of flyers at his work. I'll take care of the rest at the library. I can add in a bit about how he tried to beat up you and Tommy, and that he might be a pederast."

"Isn't that libel?"

"Okay, maybe I can leave that last bit out, but all the rest stands. This jerk isn't gonna get away with what he did to Adicia and you. One way or another, he's gonna pay for the vile things he's done. Good people always get a reward eventually, just like Adicia did, and bad people always get what's coming to them in the end."

***

On Sunday afternoon, while Betsy and her parents go through with the potentially risky plan to paper Chelsea with flyers warning residents and patrons about what Seth is really all about, Justine takes a cab up to Marjani's apartment. Mr. and Mrs. van Niftrik thought it'd be too risky for a thirteen-year-old girl to take the bus or subway to such a tough neighborhood all by herself, so they called a cab and gave her enough money for fare and a tip. As she looks through the back windows, she has to agree that was a better idea. A lot of the people walking by don't look like people she'd want to run into alone. It's hard to believe, looking back two and a half years later, that she and Adicia survived relatively unscathed during their seven years in Hell's Kitchen.

"Is this your building, Miss?" the driver asks.

"Yup," Justine says when she sees the Washingtons' building, one of the relatively nicer buildings in the area.

After she pulls the fare and tip out of her pocket, she gets out and walks up the front stairs as quickly as she can, to minimize any time on the street. She goes up to the third floor, skipping as many steps as she can under the weight of her suitcase and schoolbag, and looks around nervously before ringing the bell.

A teenage boy with an Afro, whom she guesses must be Zuberi, answers the door. "Are you selling something? If you're a Jehovah's Witness or Mormon, I'll have you know we're members of the African Methodist Episcopal Church and consider Mormonism and Jehovah's

Witnesses cults."

"No, I'm Justine, your sister Marjani's friend Adicia's little sister. Marjani went to my sister's wedding on Wednesday, and I thought Adicia mighta called her."

"Oh, sure. Come on in."

"Zuberi, do you have to give that speech to every unfamiliar person who comes to the door?" Mrs. Washington nags. "It's embarrassing. You assume every stranger's a salesperson or missionary."

"I like your hair," Justine says. "I don't think I ever met you before. You're pretty cute."

Zuberi smiles at her. "Thanks. You're onea the few white chicks who hasn't been afraid to tell me she thinks I'm good-looking. I like colorblind people."

"Zuberi!" Mrs. Washington chides from the kitchen. "How many times do your father and I have to tell you not to call women 'chicks'?"

"But everyone does it, Mom."

"A lot of white people call us niggers, darkies, and coons, but that don't make that right neither."

"But that's different. Chick is a neutral word for me, not a slur against women."

Mrs. Washington rolls her eyes. "Come sit down at the table, Justine. Marjani and her older sister Subira just went downstairs to visit friends, but they'll probably be back within the hour. Would you like something to eat in the meantime?"

"I don't wanna impose on you more than I have to, or steal your food. I had enough at breakfast to tide me over till I get on the road again."

"Nonsense. All guests to this home get to eat at our table. Have you ever had African food?"

"What kind of African food? There are so many countries in Africa. I don't think they'd all have the same kinda foods."

"We usually eat Western African and Ethiopian food, though we sometimes have Eastern and Southern African food. We're not such connoisseurs of North African food. As delicious as it is, that's not traditional Black food. It's more Arab."

"I'll have whatever you're serving. I'll try something new."

While Zuberi rants about Nixon and the Vietnam War, Mrs. Washington makes a fruit salad with apricots, mangoes, peaches, oranges, and apples, black-eyed bean pancakes, and a stew with potatoes, tomatoes, peppers, and chicken. Justine's mouth waters when she sees all the food being set before her. She still isn't used to having enough to eat at every meal or being served actual food instead of a fly by the seat of one's pants recipe like melted processed cheese mixed with hamburger meat and canned vegetables, or chicken breasts wrapped in bacon and cooked in ketchup and orange slices.

Marjani and Subira come back while Justine is rapaciously shoveling stew and black-eyed bean pancakes into her mouth. She guiltily puts her utensils down, embarrassed to be seen feeding herself like a pig by her hosts.

"You can go back to eating," Marjani says. "We know all about the starvation rations your pitiful parents make yous guys eat. Boy, your sister's gonna eat like a queen from now on, since she married that cute rich boy. I wonder if they're having caviar and stuffed sea urchins, or similar rich people food, for lunch right now."

"I'm Subira." Marjani's older sister extends her hand. "I don't think I ever met you. I'm twenty-one and an incoming senior at Howard University in Washington, D.C. Marjani's going there as a freshwoman in the fall."

"What kinda stupid word is freshwoman?" Zuberi scoffs as he flips through *The Village Voice*. "I'm all for women's lib, but not for making up stupid words just so you don't hafta use a masculine root."

"I ain't a man, or at least I wasn't last time I checked," Marjani says. "Why should I be called a freshman when I'm clearly a woman? I'm glad that finally women are waking up and questioning all this so-called default masculine, androcentric language. There's no logical need to use a diminutive feminine suffix or prefix neither unless it's absolutely necessary, like priest versus priestess or lion versus lioness."

"A very excellent point," Subira says.

"So, Justine, you must wanna know where Adicia went. She called me from her new house earlier this morning. Did you go to see Betsy and her parents already?"

"I just got a taxi from their place after spending the night there. I was with Mr. and Mrs. Straussler over most of Friday and Saturday after Seth broke into our home, threatened me and Tommy, and tried to beat us."

"What! That evil degenerate came into your home and did that?

Why don't he learn to pick on people his own size?"

"With any luck, Tommy did him some permanent damage when he kicked him in the head with a roller-skate. Seth was tryna pin him down on the davenport to spank him or beat him, and while Tommy was struggling, he managed to land a really good kick. Mr. Straussler came upstairs while this was going on and managed to make Seth leave. The cops called him at the bakery and asked him to get me out of that place."

"I hope he's arrested," Subira says.

"Right now, Betsy and her parents are papering Chelsea with flyers broadcasting what Seth is really all about. They're hoping to put him outta business. I can't imagine any sane person would wanna continue patronizing his store if they knew it was run by a convicted murderer. At least Carlos wasn't aware he was starting a fire or that twenty people died."

Marjani goes to the phone for Adicia's contact information. "Adicia's in Hudson Falls. There's a city called Glens Falls just to the west of it, maybe a couple of miles away. She suggested you could get a Greyhound or train up there and find a taxi into Hudson Falls. They got a phone hooked up in their new house on Friday, only one day after they bought it, and they bought a car yesterday. Her husband's onea the good rich guys. He's using his money for practical purchases, not flinging it around on stupid stuff like parties and sports cars. It must be nice to have that much money. When you've got a lot of dough, it talks. They'd probably still be hanging around in a hotel or cheap apartment if he didn't have so much money stored away."

"Zuberi, you'll walk with Justine to the bus station," Mrs. Washington orders. "It's not safe for a girl her age to walk alone, particularly not when she's carrying luggage. It makes her look like even more of an open target. Justine, how much money do you think you'll need to cover the trip?"

"Oh, no, I can't take your money away from you," she tries to protest.

"How much cash do you have?" Subira asks.

"Three bucks, I think. They might offer a discount 'cause I'm only thirteen."

"You're going to take ten extra dollars just in case, and don't bother trying to pay us back. It's yours to keep. Zuberi, you'll stay with Justine till she gets on that bus and the bus pulls out of the station. Justine, you're gonna call us once you get there. You should call Betsy's parents too, and the Strausslers." Mrs. Washington goes into her room for her purse.

"I can take you over to Penn Station and get you on a train," Zuberi suggests. "Sometimes it's harder to find a bus that leaves past this time on a Sunday."

"I hope I don't get lost," Justine says. "What if I have to change trains and get on the wrong one?"

"Zuberi can ask someone to sit with you," Mrs. Washington says. "They have a service like that for younger people traveling alone on an aeroplane."

"Do you really think they're gonna do anything a fifteen-year-old kid with an Afro tells them?" Zuberi asks. "They might think I'm kidnapping her. I don't think it's right, but that's what a lot of people think when they see a Black guy with a white girl."

"I don't care what they think when they see you as my escort," Justine says. "All I want is to get on a train or bus somewhere, anywhere, that'll take me to Adicia. She must be worried outta her mind about me."

"The judge didn't flinch when I signed as onea the witnesses," Marjani says. "Your cowardly thinking holds us back from complete equality with the white man. Change never happened 'cause people just sat down and accepted the status quo."

"We don't live in the South," Subira says. "I don't think they're gonna do to you what they did to Emmett Till. This is New York City, not Alabama or Mississippi."

"My pampered sixteen-year-old brother could kick an intruder in the head with a roller-skate," Justine says. "You can do your part in looking out for me by taking me to a train or bus station."

Zuberi puts down the paper in resignation. "Guess I'm outnumbered by all you chicks. I'll do it."

"Zuberi, what have I told you!" Mrs. Washington shouts. "Women are people, not 'chicks'!"

Zuberi rolls his eyes.

***

Justine is exhausted by the time her taxi approaches the end of the cul-de-sac where Ricky and Adicia live. Zuberi found a train leaving

Penn Station at 5:00 and, true to his word, escorted her onto it and waited by the window till it started pulling out of the station. The train reached Glens Falls at about 8:30, from whence she boarded a cab a short distance away. She handed the driver the address and settled down in the back, fighting off the urge to fall asleep.

"Which house do your sister and brother-in-law live in?" the driver asks. "The last one on the cul-de-sac, or the second-last?"

"The next-to-last one, I was told. Wow, that's a mighty impressive house."

"We're here. I'll get your luggage out of the trunk."

Justine turns on the overhead light to count out the cab fare and figures in another dollar for a tip. After she hands over the money, she picks up her suitcase, puts on her schoolbag, and tucks her rabbit under her arm. Her heart pounding, she approaches the front door of the house she was told was the address.

Adicia looks up from the Glens Falls newspaper when she hears the bell ringing at that late hour. "Do you think that's a prankster? No one knows who we are yet to pay us a call, and if the neighbors are back from their vacation, they sure picked a bad hour to welcome us to the neighborhood."

Ricky gets up to answer the door. "Well, isn't this a great surprise. Adicia, come take a look at who the cat dragged in."

Adicia shrieks and flies towards Justine, pulling her into her arms, kissing her on the cheek, and holding her very tightly. Justine hugs her back, finally breathing the sigh of relief she's been holding in for a week.

"That *bastard* is never going to touch a hair on your head! You've been my baby since you were born, and he'll have to kill me before I'll ever let him touch you or even look at you! Tell me you got away without any molestation by him, 'cause if he dared to come anywhere near my sweet baby sister, I'll go back there now and murder him!"

From the look in her eyes, Ricky knows she's serious. He wouldn't have suspected such a ferocious mama tiger lay inside of his tiny little bride, but then again, he knows what they say about those quiet ones.

"I think Mother will press charges against him after what he did on Friday. He came into the apartment, threatened me and Tommy, and said he'd beat answers outta us if we didn't talk. While he was tryna pin Tommy down to the davenport for a beating, Mr. Straussler came to the rescue. I bet Mother's raising the roof after finding out what happened to her pet child. Tommy was wearing his new roller-skates when this happened, so the kick he landed on Seth's head was even more painful than a normal kick to the head."

"He came into the apartment when your parents were out and threatened you?" Ricky asks. "Thank God you got out of there!"

"Tommy held my hand when he walked me over to the Strauss-lers' apartment after that incident. He's slowly starting to get it as he gets older. He's no longer quite as selfish and bratty as he was when he was younger. Slow progress is still progress. He said he wants to go to college. That'll make eight outta nine kids who got above their raising and left our parents behind in the dust."

"I'll never leave you ever again," Adicia sobs. "No one will ever take you away from me. We're going to start a beautiful new life here, and after we finish unpacking and get all settled in, we'll find Lucine. She'll be able to tell us where Allen and Lenore are, and where Eme-line lives. Isn't that a beautiful dream come true, all of us together again in the same place?"

"Can I go to sleep now? I'm so tired."

"You can go right up to the big bedroom on the upper floor, with a window overlooking a magnolia tree. That's my room. The bed is queen, so there's enough room for both of us. Do you want me to tuck you in or make you tea?"

"I'll be fine. Tomorrow I'll tell yous guys more about what hap-pened to me since Friday."

"I love you," Adicia calls as Justine wearily trudges upstairs with her rabbit. "Always and forever, even into the next lifetime."

"I love you too," Justine says as she's halfway up the stairs. "You're the best big sister I coulda asked for."

Chapter 50: Ricky's Parents Make Trouble

First thing Monday morning, Adicia and Justine made long-distance calls to the Strausslers, the van Niftriks, and the Washingtons to let them know Justine arrived in Hudson Falls safe and sound. Justine feels like she's a princess and Adicia is a queen as Ricky takes her on a tour around the house. This house positively feels like a mansion after what she's used to. The fact that there's a cute dark red Super Beetle in the driveway makes it seem like even more of a fairytale come true.

"What would you like me to buy you, Justine?" Ricky asks. "Adicia's still trying to decide what she most wants as a wedding present. I don't count the house, the car, or her mattress as wedding gifts. Those aren't personal gifts like jewelry or a puppy."

"Wasn't your birthday recently? Golly, I'm embarrassed I didn't bring any present with me, after how much you've stuck your neck out for botha us without having to."

"I turned twenty on the fifteenth, Saturday, the day before you came here. You don't have to get me anything. Adicia being so happy is present enough for me."

"Can I have my own bike with pretty pink streamers on the handlebars?"

Ricky smiles. "Sure you can, kiddo. You can get a bike and Adicia can get driving lessons."

Downstairs, Adicia gets up to peer through the peephole to see who's ringing the bell. She almost stops breathing when she sees Ricky's parents looking very bemused.

"Ricky, I think you might wanna come down here and deal with our visitors!"

"What are they, missionaries?" he calls downstairs.

"You'll see in just a moment."

The Carsons ring the bell again, louder this time. Ricky goes downstairs with Justine and opens the door. He almost faints when he sees his parents.

Mrs. Carson doesn't wait for an invitation and just marches in, depositing a pile of mail on the coffeetable. "Do you know what a ruckus Mr. and Mrs. Troy have been raising since your poor trash bride ran away from home the day we left for the Hamptons? Now we come to find out not only have you run away yourself, but you took this no-good poor trash with you, married her and brought her into our formerly flawless family, and withdrew from Columbia!”

“Mrs. Troy is pressing charges against your underclass wife's ex-fiancé for breaking and entering and attempting to assault your brother-in-law!” Mr. Carson rants. “What did your mother and I ever do to deserve being caught up in this sordid underworld drama? And long-time friends of your underclass wife decided to go and paper an entire neighborhood so they can drive this ex-convict out of business! Are you on drugs that you would act so crazy and get involved with street trash like this?”

“Please don't talk to my wife like that,” Ricky says. “You might think she's no good, but she's the dearest, sweetest, kindest, most humble person I've ever known.”

“Was this a shotgun marriage?” Mrs. Carson demands. “How long were you sneaking around with this urchin and disgracing her outside the bonds of proper matrimony? You were taught that if you did that outside of marriage, to give her the money to go to Europe for an abortion or to use a prophylactic!”

“Adicia's not pregnant. It's impossible, since our marriage is unconsummated. I've never even kissed her.”

“Are you nuts?” Mr. Carson demands. “Who goes to so much trouble to run away and marry a girl in record time, only to have a non-physical relationship? Are you homosexual, son? Are you using her as a cover? We have more than enough money to pay for psychotherapy to cure you of this illness.”

“How did you find us?” Adicia asks.

“We called the moving company and asked for any records they might have of renting a truck to Warrick within the last week, and we found out where it was dropped off. We drove up here and started inquiring around at car rental places and car dealerships to see if you might've done business with them, and they provided your address. Very simple. Maybe your parents don't give a damn when one of their countless children goes missing, but my wife and I do give a damn when our only child disappears.”

“You wouldn't dare tell the Troys where we are,” Ricky says.

“I wouldn't touch Mrs. Troy with a hundred-foot pole, and Mr. Troy, while marginally more intelligent than his wife, still isn't a person

I'd willingly associate with. Since this ridiculous marriage is uncon-summated, you can follow us home and forget this ever happened. You've got your little bit of youthful rebellion out of your system, and now it's time to return to reality. We'll have the marriage annulled im-mediately."

"You can't force two legal adults to have their marriage annulled. I made a vow to honor, comfort, protect, and love Adicia till death do us part, no matter what the circumstances. She made that vow to me too. I take our marriage seriously, even if it is starting out as a marriage of convenience. I know she doesn't love me back, but she likes me as a friend, and we're a very good match. Maybe this'll be a failed experi-ment, but maybe she'll grow to love me like a wife loves a husband."

"Is this girl living here too?" Mrs. Carson asks. "You sure know how to surround yourself with trash, Warrick."

"Don't you dare call my baby sister trash!" Adicia shouts, protec-tively putting her arms around Justine from behind. "She's a much bet-ter person than you'll ever be!"

"Your brother Thomas sounds like a savage. When your fiancé, a man of your own proper class, broke into your home, he should've done the civilized thing and called the police. Instead he got into an altercation with him and kicked him in the head. At sixteen, he should be far too old to pull childish stunts like that. He must've watched too many low-budget movies to think that was a good idea. And he was wearing roller-skates. That could've caused a cerebral hemorrhage, which could lead to death. Do you like the thought that two of your three brothers would be murderers?"

"Tommy was defending me and our home the only way he knew how!" Justine shouts. "Give him some credit for what was probably the first somewhat mature, brotherly act of his life!"

"How long do you intend to fake your way through this pretend marriage?" Mr. Carson asks. "Or do you intend to satisfy your natural urges on the side with other women? You already threw all sense of propriety out the window, so why not travel and live with this ragamuf-fin without marrying her? I don't think many people care too much nowadays about couples living in sin."

"But I care," Ricky says. "And Adicia cares. All a poor girl has is her good name, and I didn't want to make her good name into trash by disrespecting her by traveling and living with her without marrying her."

"We've heard through the grapevine this childish-looking pretend wife of yours isn't a virgin. She engaged in an act of prostitution to save her mother from going back to prison, and just before she ran away, she lay down with her ex-fiancé. Even if she decides she wants to be your normal wife someday, you'd be getting damaged merchandise. You don't want to be the third man to get a piece of her. You need an unblemished, virgin bride, with the factory seal fresh on her."

"My wife was raped by both of those excuses for men! It might not be the so-called traditional scenario where a masked stranger pulls a girl into an alleyway or the back of his car and holds her there at knifepoint, but she was coerced both times! Do you really think such a sweet-hearted girl would voluntarily choose to have her first sexual experience with a thirty-five-year-old drug dealer when she's all of fifteen, or to do anything with a repulsive ex-convict forty years her senior?"

"Only bad girls and fallen women give in that easily. Well-bred ladies always safeguard their reputations and virginity, even if it means death. If she didn't fight to preserve her purity and virtue, she's a whore. If you ever sleep with her, you'll always feel inadequate and robbed because you weren't the first man to have her."

"My sister is a great person," Justine says. "How dare you slander her character and filter her good name! If I were you, Mrs. Carson, I wouldn't be the first to throw stones at anyone. Just lookit that dumb hat you're wearing. Who mixes up tiny lightbulbs, Russian nesting dolls, parrot feathers, and jumping jacks on the same hat?"

"Shut up, you insolent child. Apparently no one ever taught you not to talk back to your elders or betters."

"If you talk to either my wife or my sister-in-law so disrespectfully again, I'm going to throw you out of our house right away," Ricky says. "In fact, I've half a mind to throw both of you out right now. You can't say anything nice or constructive."

"Why are you here?" Adicia asks. "This is our home. We don't want you in it. Your son made a choice to marry me, and he's been a very good husband in the six days we've been married. He's done more to take care of me and protect me than a lot of husbands do in six years."

Mr. Carson grabs Adicia's hand and examines her rings. "Sapphire and diamonds, with a white gold band, and gold and silver with diamonds. I'm scandalized you spent so much money on jewelry for this whore, Warrick. Knowing girls of her ilk, she'll lose both, or damage them beyond repair. Fine jewelry wasn't meant for common street girls. It was designed only to grace the perfect hands of upper-class ladies."

Mrs. Carson bursts out laughing. "What kind of childish wedding ring is that? Three little flowers with diamonds in the center? How old are you, little girl, twelve? You certainly don't look eighteen."

"You're living in a dreamworld if you think you're going to stay married to Warrick and live happily ever after. He's coming with us, and will be re-enrolled at Columbia. If this house is already paid for in full, you and that urchin sister of yours can have fun making it into a pigsty by yourselves. Thank God my son didn't consummate the marriage, since it would ruin his good name if he were tied to a street girl forever by a child. Warrick, we're going to wait for you to pack up your things and join us. You're going to leave these two ragamuffins behind and forget this past week ever happened. Miss Troy, I hope you had your fun pretending to be married and getting a taste of the moneyed world, a world you don't deserve, while it lasted."

"Where did you buy the wedding ring?" Mrs. Carson is still examining it. "Certainly not at a proper store like DeBeers, where they sell only quality rings."

"Mother, please take your hands off my wife," Ricky orders. "They're plumeria flowers from Hawaii. Adicia wanted this ring more than any other. It's what made her happy. A plain gold band wouldn't reflect her specialness. Her wedding ring is cute and not like every other ring."

"We got it at Macy's," Adicia says in a small voice.

"Why are you being so mean to my sister?" Justine demands. "She never did anything bad to you. She's the best big sister I ever coulda asked for. Adicia would give me the Moon if I asked for it, 'cause that's the kinda big sister she is. And Ricky's the best brother-in-law ever."

"Oh, nonsense," Mrs. Carson scoffs. "Poor trash like you don't have feelings. You're like rats or fleas. Warrick, I won't ask again for you to collect your things and come with us. Leave the house and everything else to the ragged poor girls."

"You wouldn't dare choose Miss Troy and her pathetic sister over your own parents, the family wealth, and your reputation, would you?"

"Please show my wife the proper respect due to her and use the correct title. Adicia is Mrs. Carson now, no longer Miss Troy."

The senior Mrs. Carson laughs. "Do you really think a slum-dwelling piece of trash and street whore like that deserves or knows what to do with the title Mrs. Warrick Grover Carson?"

Ricky goes over to the door, pulls it open, and points outside. "Get out of my house. I'm done with yous guys forever. Never try to contact me again. You oughta be ashamed of yourselves for the cruel, appalling way you've spoken to my beautiful bride and her darling baby sister. It's nice to know you think a girl who's been raped twice is a whore. If Adicia and I have kids eventually, you'll never know them. Get out of our house before I call the cops."

"You're starting to talk like them!" Mr. Carson says. "Before we moved from Syracuse and you started hanging around with social undesirables, you never had the term 'yous guys' in your vocabulary!"

"Get out of my house," Adicia orders. "Ricky is my husband now, no longer your little boy you get to boss around and control. We've chosen this life for ourselves, whether you like it or not. We don't need your blessings or approval."

"You heard my wife," Ricky says. "Go back to the city and leave us alone forever. You took a trip up here for nothing."

"Don't let the door hit yous on the way out!" Justine catcalls as they turn around and storm out.

Adicia goes over to the front windows to watch them getting in their extravagant luxury sports car and backing out of the driveway. She hopes they get into an accident after how they spoke to her and Justine.

"They know where we live," Justine says. "What if our parents pry it outta them? This was supposed to be a happy ending for me and Adicia, not just another chapter in a neverending Grimms' fairytale!"

"We have to do something to get legal custody of you," Ricky says. "I don't think any judge in his right mind would deny that motion. If lawyers or social workers interviewed your folks, they'd quickly find out just how terrible and unfit they are. If they investigated your home, they'd find all the drugs. Of course, that might mean Tommy would be taken away from your mother, and she'd be furious if she lost him."

"If Justine's gonna live with us, we need to become her guardians," Adicia says. "We won't be able to enroll her in school, make medical decisions, or do anything important otherwise."

"Well, we can't do everything at once. The most important things were to secure a house, get a car, hook up a phone, and find Justine. Now we can slow down a little and focus on something like shopping for more furniture and finding work. I might be only twenty, but a man should work to support his family no matter how young he is. How about you and Justine go grocery shopping while I look through the classifieds and call a bunch of places for interviews?"

"How are we gonna go grocery shopping if I can't drive?"

"What if your parents come back?" Justine asks. "I don't think they're gonna take losing you that easily. What rotten, rotten parents we have."

"I won't let them in again, believe me," Ricky says. "I'll contact a lawyer if I have to so we can get an order keeping them away from us. They have no hearts or souls if that's how they see fit to talk to you. I can't believe you just stood there and let all their insults and accusations stand."

"I'm used to being verbally abused," Adicia says. "Crying and screaming only make it worse. You learn early on to either make yourself as invisible as possible when dealing with poisonous jerks like that, or to just stand there and take it until the person is done carrying on and abusing you."

Ricky stands behind her and rubs her shoulders. "You don't have to put up with such awful treatment from anyone anymore. I know you'll never be able to forget the rotten life you came from, but as long as this convenience marriage lasts, I'll take really good care of you and treat you like my queen. I might not be the toughest guy or the most experienced with women, but I'm not so out of touch I don't know basic things about defending my woman and how to treat a lady properly."

Adicia smiles over her shoulder at him. "I couldn't have imagined such a good match would come from such an entirely different world. Maybe this is how marriages started in the really old days, when husband and wife were still getting to know each other after the wedding, not entirely sure they'd ever become a successful married couple and grow to love each other."

"Can we go grocery shopping together?" Justine asks. "It won't take that long, since there are only three of us to feed. Then we can look at classifieds. Maybe tomorrow we can go furniture shopping. Can we have a puppy or kitten?"

"A beautiful bird with exotic, bright feathers would be nice too. We never had any pets growing up, and since we won't be having a baby for probably a long time, a cute little animal would be a nice substitute. A pet would keep us company while you're at work."

"Sounds like a plan," Ricky says.

***

Adicia and Justine don't know which is more awesome, having unlimited money to buy whatever food they want, or shopping in an actual supermarket. They've always had to get their food at smaller grocers' stores, not full supermarkets, and they've often had to go to different stores to get produce, fish, and meat. Now everything is all together under one roof, and they get a whole shopping cart to push instead of shopping bags and baskets. Justine hopes they can go shopping for better clothes afterwards.

"I don't think there's much difference between the really expensive gourmet brands and the generic store stuff," Ricky says. "Food is usually food. Don't worry that I have the same exclusive tastes as my parents. I can live without gourmet crackers with pumpkin seeds and baked-in goat cheese, fruit from South America or India, and artisan bread with exotic spices."

"Still, I don't wanna eat like a poor person or get the cheapest stuff possible," Adicia says. "Getting only generic store brands, discount dented cans, and stuff that's one day away from the garbage marks you as poor."

"Is caviar really as yummy as it's said to be?" Justine asks.

"I had some on a bagel with tomato and smoked salmon a few times," Ricky says. "My parents couldn't believe I bought bagels. They said they were beneath us, and that I was sullying caviar's reputation by mixing it up with lower-class food like bagels."

"Your parents are awful," Adicia says. "How can you live in the city and never have bagels?"

"They thought I was nuts to drink egg cream too."

"Egg creams are awesome," Justine says. "If we find some here, can we get them?"

"So long as they're not the only beverages you get. We need healthy drinks too, like orange juice, grape juice, milk, and water."

"Allen didn't let us only eat junk food either," Adicia reminds her. "He made sure we ate healthy, substantial stuff, just like he made us go to bed at a reasonable hour. Living with someone who's not a parent doesn't mean all rules fly out the window."

"Oh, I don't expect Ricky to spoil us, but it's nice to have treats." Justine picks up apples and starts examining them for defects.

A pregnant woman comes up pushing a half-full cart and stops opposite them to look at oranges. While she's looking for the freshest specimens, she begins looking at them curiously.

"Adicia and Justine?"

They look back at her and break into huge smiles when they recognize Lucine. She pushes her cart around and hugs both of them very tightly.

"What are you doing here? How did you find out this is where I am? Who are you staying with? None of us knew you were on your way up!"

"You look like a real grownup," Justine says, still holding onto Lucine. "We knew you lived in Hudson Falls, but we didn't expect to see you here."

"Are you really having a baby?" Adicia asks. "Can I touch it?"

"It's due in October. I'm only due one month after Lenore. Go ahead and touch it. She's been moving around a lot this afternoon and will probably kick for her aunts."

"Are you having it at home like Lenore?" Justine asks as she and Adicia feel Lucine's baby making fluttery kicks.

"Oh, God no. I'm not that brave. The hospital will let my husband Zachary come in with me if we show them the certificate that says we've taken a Bradley childbirth class. I won't have drugs, but I wanna be in a hospital in case anything goes wrong."

"It's swell they don't automatically give you that spooky twilight cocktail anymore and bar your husband from being with you," Adicia says. "I bet you'd try to fight back if anyone tried to tie you to a bed like they did to Gemma."

"You don't mess with a girl from the Lower East Side. I'd land a well-placed kick to the doctor or nurse's head if anyone dared try to tie me down or wrap gauze around my head so I couldn't see."

"I bet you would," Justine says. "You shoulda seen the great kick Tommy gave to the ogre our parents were tryna force Adicia to marry."

"What? Our parents found Adicia another of their prizes to marry? Don't tell me that's what you're doing up here, to run away from that fate."

"We're safe," Adicia reassures her. "He's right mad I ran away, but he's in a lot of trouble now and probably won't come up here, nor will he come anywhere near Tommy and our parents for a long time. Mother's pressing charges for how he tried to assault Tommy on Friday afternoon. My friend Betsy and her parents put up flyers all over Chelsea, letting everyone know the owner of their successful pharmacy and grocery store is an ex-convict who was in jail for fifteen years for beating his first wife to death."

"He left bruises on Adicia's arms from how he grabbed her and wouldn't let go when he found her on Wednesday night," Justine says. "A nice cop came to her rescue and drove her back to the van Niftriks' place."

Lucine hugs Adicia again. "Thank God you're far away from New York and that menace! We'll take good care of you here and won't let anyone hurt you. Unfortunately, I'm afraid you can't visit me today, since Zachary and I are leaving for Lake George. I came to pick up groceries for the fridge at the cottage we're renting, and to eat on the road. Allen, Lenore, and their girls are up at Lake George, but our vacations weren't able to coincide. They'll be back in a few days, on Thursday night, I think." Lucine looks over at Ricky curiously. "Are you with my sisters? Girls, who's your new friend?"

"This is my husband Ricky Carson," Adicia says nervously.

"What! You got *married*? When did this happen, and how long have you known this guy?" Lucine takes Adicia's left hand. "Nice rings. My wedding ring's just a plain ol' gold band, and my engagement ring's a heart-shaped garnet, my birthstone, with tiny diamonds around it."

"Adicia and I met in January," Ricky starts to explain. "I lived up the street from her. This is a marriage of convenience so we could get away from our parents and not cause a scandal by traveling and living together outside of marriage. I'm in love with her, but it's not mutual."

"You married a man you don't love, sweetie? Were you that desperate to escape?"

"He's been a great husband so far. Just think of it as an arranged marriage. If it works out, I'll grow to love him like a real husband over enough time. Isn't this better than me being all alone, with no one to protect me?"

"This isn't *Fiddler on the Roof!* Modern people pick their own spouses for love! They don't get matched up with people, strangers, they don't love in a romantic way."

"The marriage isn't consummated," Adicia whispers. "We sleep in different rooms."

"Is this by any chance the guy Allen was ranting about, the guy he saw you having a date with? The rich boy, the limousine liberal?"

"Maybe he is a limousine liberal, but his intentions are honorable. Aren't you happy I found someone to love me and take care of me, no matter how unexpected and unconventional the circumstances?"

Lucine looks at Ricky. "The most important thing is that Adicia is happy, though I can't imagine how any modern woman would choose what's essentially an arranged marriage. You'd better take good care of my little sister, or our older brother will let you have it."

"Can we go to Gemma's antique store with you when you come back from vacation?" Justine asks, hoping to change the subject.

"Gemma's on her honeymoon. She finally remarried about a month ago, in a very small, low-key ceremony. She invited the Murphys, and Giovanni, who's eleven now, was really excited to see his birth mother again. He looks just like Gemma, it's like she spit him out herself and there was no genetic input from that ogre Francesco. Her husband's named Tyrone Duffy. He's five years younger than her."

"Isn't Tyrone a county in Ireland?" Ricky asks.

"His mother named him after Tyrone Power, a very famous, handsome actor in the Forties and Fifties. I believe the name did originate because of the Irish county."

"Are you Mrs. Martel now?" Justine asks.

"I'm Ms. Troy-Martel. Gemma became Ms. Duffy-Troy. When you're a professional woman, it's harder to surrender your established identity."

"I hope you don't think Adicia's a slap in the face to women's liberation. She's gonna legally change her name to Carson."

Lucine shrugs. "It's not what I'd choose for myself, but there'd be no balance in the world if there were no old-fashioned girls left. Not all of us modern women wanna go out in the workforce."

"Can you please not tell Allen about me being married?" Adicia asks. "I don't want him to cut his vacation short and rush back here, or have the rest of his vacation ruined when he finds out Ricky married me. I'll find a way to break it to him gradually when he comes home."

"Sure, whatever you want. I'm just glad both of yous are safe."

Adicia has a new spring in her step as they push their cart next to Lucine's. Even if Lucine and her husband are heading out of town today for their summer vacation, they've found one of the missing members of their family. With any luck, the run-in with Ricky's parents was just a bump in the road, and the other missing pieces of the puzzle will start coming together as her well-deserved happy ending continues unfolding and turning into a glorious new beginning.

Chapter 51: The Worst That Could Happen

On Tuesday, while Ricky is out interviewing at a couple of jobs in Glens Falls, Adicia goes through the mail. Most is junk mail, but a couple are from people and groups welcoming them to the neighborhood. Ricky gave her permission to sort through the mail his parents brought over, so she goes over to that pile next. She rips up the junk mail and tosses it in the trash, then moves on to the letters that look more official. One is the letter from Columbia, which Mr. and Mrs. Carson already opened, telling him they're sorry he's withdrawn and that his transcript will be kept on file. The second official-looking letter has been forwarded from Syracuse, and has a bunch of serious-looking stamps and seals.

"Justine, what do you think this group wants with Ricky that they'd go to the trouble of forwarding this instead of accepting he's no longer at that address?"

Justine looks over her shoulder. "That's from the Selective Service! I bet you anything it's Ricky's draft notice!"

"You can't be serious. They're withdrawing a bunch of troops on a regular basis. They couldn't possibly still be calling anybody."

"Well, open it and see if you're right. Maybe they're declaring the draft is over and everyone can stop worrying."

Adicia opens it with shaking fingers and pulls out the letter. She begins screaming hysterically, over and over again, as she sees the official letterhead and seal of the Selective Service System. Ricky was ordered to report for inspection several months ago, and is probably in trouble as a suspected draft-dodger because he hasn't known about this to show up. With any luck, they'll reject him at the recruiting station and accept his explanation about why he couldn't show up when he was supposed to.

"They can't take him away from us," she says numbly, holding Justine. "What have we done that was so rotten we don't deserve to live happily ever after? How long are we gonna continue walking around in this nightmarish Grimms' fairytale? Why can't we have a quick, easy, permanent happy ending like the Five Little Peppers?"

"We've never had anything handed to us on a silver platter. Why should we expect a deus ex machina ending and to never have troubles again? Look on the bright side. It's only asking him to report for physical examination, not to be inducted into the service. They could always flunk him out like they did with Dad."

"Ricky doesn't drink or use drugs, and he's as healthy as can be! Plus he's no longer a student! If they choose him and he goes over there, what if he dies? He'd die without ever enjoying his wife the way a husband's supposed to. I'm pretty sure he's a virgin. A lot of guys going to war hate the thought of dying virgins, so they do it with a hooker or their girlfriend before going away, to have that experience once in their life just in case."

Justine looks into her eyes. "You'd actually consider doing that? If it's a false alarm, that's really mean to Ricky to lead him on like that. If they reject him, he'd already know what it feels like. He might want to do it again, and you'd have to refuse him 'cause you don't love him."

"They don't induct guys the very day they show up for inspection, even if they're accepted into the service. Maybe this is just a test, one final hardship before our beautiful happy ending, like in onea the Hindu stories Emeline told us about the Pandava brothers. At the end of their lives, they were walking to the other world, and all the younger brothers and their wife were falling dead. The oldest brother kept on walking and refused to part from a dog following him. The gods asked him why he kept this dog when he hadn't cared about his own brothers and wife dying. He said it was their time to go, but he could still show kindness to this dear little dog. Then he was shown a vision of his brothers and their wife tied up and being tortured in Hell, with their enemy cousins the Kauravas in Paradise. The big brother, Yudhisthira, said he wanted to join his brothers and their wife, even if it was in Hell. Then it was revealed the dog was his father, the sun god, and it was just one last test to prove how good and righteous he was. The Pandavas and their wife Draupadi were rewarded with Paradise after long, righteous lives. It's gotta be something like that for us too, Justine."

"If it is, I hope that doesn't mean we're about to die!"

"Of course not. We're too young to die. Maybe they'll let him go when he tells them he's a newlywed. Sarah said the traditional Jewish custom in ancient Israel was to let a newlywed stay at home with his bride for the first year of marriage. The authorities recognized it's not right to rip a guy away from his bride and force the bride to spend the first year of their marriage alone and lonely."

"They have no hearts or souls if they'd take a newlywed away from his bride. Even if you're not consummating the marriage, you're still newlyweds and deserve to get to know each other more. You're still learning how to be husband and wife, and you'd hafta start all over again if they take him."

"They don't care about people's feelings. All they care about is meeting their quota and getting more of our boys in front of cannons. What if they capture him, make him a POW, and torture him? He doesn't deserve that."

"Jumping to conclusions is gonna make it worse. Wait till Ricky gets back, and he can do what he has to do to not get in trouble. With any luck, it's just a formality and he can get back to us as soon as they decide not to use him."

"I hate war," Adicia whimpers. "I wish they'd give a war someday and no one would come, like in that Monkees' song, 'Zor and Zam.' I don't get why they're continuing this war when it's so unpopular and it's murdered so many innocent boys. Why did we even go over there?"

"People in this country are afraid of Socialism and Communism, like Deirdre said. They wanna force their political system on everyone, even if capitalism doesn't work in other cultures. Capitalism screwed us over big time, so I don't think it makes a lick of sense anywhere."

"I shoulda known all this was too good to be true. Poor, ragged girls from the bad side of town never get cute millionaire husbands and live happily ever after. There was a catch to this happy ending all along, I just didn't wanna think about it. Maybe I'd be better-off marrying a fellow poor boy like David."

Justine goes to make Adicia tea and light lunch. Adicia refuses to get back up and sit on a chair or the new davenport, just sits slumped over on the floor for the rest of the afternoon, barely responding to anything Justine says. Adicia has never been entirely sure God exists, but now she's more agnostic than ever. At best, there might be a God who's half-good and half-evil, like the god Abraxas discussed in the Hermann Hesse novel *Demian*. That would be the perfect explanation for why she was taken out of poverty by Ricky and got such a swell big brother like Allen, but also had to go through so much pain and suffering in her short life. Emeline's devotion to Krishna is also starting to sound very appealing, since Vishnu only took on his avatars when the balance of evil overwhelmed that of good, and he needed to come to Earth to help good people in danger. Vishnu's next avatar will come at the end of the current Hindu age of Kali Yuga, and fight one final battle between good and evil. Now would be as good of a time as any to end this horrific age of Kali Yuga and bring peace, safety, love, and understanding to the world.

When Ricky comes through the door at 3:00, Adicia leaps up and throws her arms around him. She's never hugged him before, but now's as good a time as any to do it.

"What's wrong? Did my parents come back? Come on, I hate it when you cry."

Justine hands him the draft notice. "This came for you in the pile of mail your folks brought over. It was forwarded from your old Syracuse address."

Ricky takes it with one hand while keeping his other arm tightly around Adicia. "Oh, boy, this was the last thing I expected."

"They probably think you're a draft-dodger and are looking for you, since you never knew about this to show up when you were called!" Adicia wails.

"Can you call them or go to the nearest station and explain what happened, so they won't be any madder at you?" Justine asks.

"They're taking you away from me. I don't wanna lose you so soon. I don't know how to exist on my own and run a household all by myself."

"I'm sure they won't take me. I'm not built like a soldier. I'm an intellectual and artist, not a fighter or athletic guy. I'd rather go to an art museum or talk about world literature than fire a rifle at total strangers."

"I don't know what I'd do without you. You've already done more for me in the last week than a lot of husbands do in a lifetime. I could never have made it outta New York and gotten settled here so quickly and safely if it weren't for you."

"They might release me when I say I've got two dependents. Surely they're not that desperate to put any old guys into uniform that they'd take a newlywed and college-educated intellectual."

"You're not in college anymore! You withdrew so we could run away!"

"You have to take care of this as soon as you can," Justine begs.

"This is the worst possible time for this to happen, and it's not being made any better by just talking about it."

"Can you look in the phonebook now? I want this resolved as soon as possible."

"I have no choice. I hope their office is still open, so I can have this all taken care of by tonight."

***

Wednesday makes it a week since the hasty marriage at the courthouse. Instead of celebrating their week-anniversary, Ricky and Adicia are on pins and needles waiting for the mail to come. The people at the recruiting station accepted Ricky's explanation for why he was so late in reporting for examination, and said they'd immediately mail out their decision so no more time would be wasted. Adicia wonders if this might be Divine revenge for how she ran away from home and tried to avoid her fate.

Justine goes to get the mail when it arrives after what feels like an eternity. Ricky grabs the letter from Selective Service, one of only two pieces of mail, and opens it with shaking hands. Adicia hides her face.

"Well, this definitely isn't the news I wanted to get on our week-anniversary. Tomorrow at six-thirty in the morning, I'm supposed to report for induction to the Air Force, and they'll take me right to basic training. I'd better start packing what I need. This was too good to be true. Normal people don't get a happy ending handed to them with no hitches or snags."

"Haven't I suffered enough?" Adicia wails. "What did I do that was so bad I deserve to get punished like this?"

"Maybe they'll pull out all the remaining troops by the time I'm done with basic, or I won't be in combat for very long before the war ends. At least, that's what I hope. You'll stay here waiting for me, won't you? Knowing I have a sweet little wifey to come home to and write letters to will make it seem not so horrible."

"What choice do I have? I'm not gonna ask for an annulment or run around with other guys while you're over there risking your life. That's just mean, and adding salt to your wounds. You don't deserve to be left or cheated on during your darkest moments."

Ricky looks at her sadly. "You're such a sweet girl. I wish we'd met in another era, so we'd be able to set up our household and start married life in peace and normalcy."

"Let me stay with you tonight. You don't deserve to sleep all alone during your last night. Will you let me comfort you with my presence?"

Justine's eyebrows shoot up.

"Let's not think about that right now. I don't think I'll get any sleep anyway. Why don't we do something fun today to take our minds off of what's happening tomorrow? How does a restaurant sound, or a museum, or a trip to Lake George?"

"Do you think we could drive around to see if there are any county fairs nearby?" Adicia asks. "I've read about them, but I've never been to one. Big city living is good for some things, but you also miss out on stuff like county fairs. Sometimes they have rides at county fairs. I've never been on an amusement park ride."

"That'd be really fun, if we can find one!" Justine says.

"My parents never liked that kinda stuff, and thought it was like looking at the bottom of a garbage can. I, however, always enjoyed amusement parks and county fairs. This might very well be the last nice thing I ever do in this lifetime." Ricky goes to get the car keys.

Adicia slides into the passenger seat, and Justine gets into the backseat. With only a roadmap for guidance, they ride around Warren County until they find a big open space with a fairgrounds set up. Adicia and Justine look around at their surroundings with wide eyes after Ricky parks on the grass, and they start walking towards the ticket booth. Being in so much wide-open space is dizzying after they've grown up in the exact opposite of wide-open space. They can barely believe how much fresh air they're breathing and how much grass they have to walk on. They're very tempted to kick off their sandals and walk around barefoot.

"Limousine liberal or not, you're a man of the people now," Adicia says. "Rich people never go to carnivals like this."

"I don't know what I wanna do first!" Justine exclaims. "What ride do you recommend?"

"Can we get something to eat first? I'd like a hamburger, a corn-dog, cotton candy, ice-cream with lots of toppings, elephant ears, and chili."

"I want funnel cake, ice-cream, cotton candy, a chili dog, popcorn, shishkebab, and sausage with peppers."

"And lemonade. No pulp. We hate pulp."

"Do you think you're tall enough to go on all the rides?" Ricky teases her.

"I think the minimum height is four feet. I'm not that short. Justine's still shorter than I am for the time being."

"I'm four foot eight," Justine says. "Only two more inches and I'll be your same height. Cheer up, you might still grow a little. Onea the girls in my class asked a question about average heights, when we had that silly filmstrip about growing up, and the teacher said it's not uncommon for a girl to continue growing for two more years after her first period. You just started in January, so there's a chance you might hit five feet by the time you're nineteen."

Adicia blushes furiously, looking away from Ricky.

"You mean that didn't happen until the month I met you? Wow, that's really late. I thought most modern girls started around thirteen."

"I was a very late bloomer. I didn't need to wear a bra till I was fourteen. It's no wonder you assumed I was only in junior high when you met me."

"You'll keep your age very well, I bet. You won't mind being taken for much younger when you're thirty or forty."

"You don't look your age either," Adicia says as they walk towards the line of concession stands. "I always liked men with soft, boyish faces like yours, with non-threatening facial features, though all the magazines tell us we're supposed to prefer guys with more traditionally masculine features like an angular jaw. I feel safer with guys who look youthful."

"Well, I'm glad to know you think I'm attractive, even if you're not in love with me. If I make it home alive and you eventually start to love me in that way, we'd probably make a really good-looking kid."

"You might have more girls than guys," Justine says. "I hope you don't mind our family runs to girls."

"Let's not think that far ahead," Adicia says. "We're not here to talk about such serious stuff."

After they buy their food, they navigate their way to a free picnic table while trying their best not to drop or spill the trays. Adicia and Justine freely gobble it down, for once not embarrassed to be seen eating rapaciously. Some of the people around them look like they might come from the underclass themselves, and probably pay little regard to conventional table manners too. Adicia knows that over time, they'll start to eat at a normal pace, and not want to eat so much with their hands. After being hungry, one doesn't adjust to normal portions and a leisurely dining pace overnight. Sarah had to relearn how to not gobble her food, use a knife, fork, and spoon, and stop hoarding whatever she couldn't finish.

Ricky thinks the carnival games are a waste of money, since they're so stacked against winning easily on the first few tries, but he's interested in the arts and crafts booths. While Adicia and Justine admire handmade artisan jewelry, aprons made from a gorgeous array of printed fabrics, wind chimes, and crocheted potholders, bags, shawls, and slippers, Ricky browses through the paintings, murals, tapestries, and prints. He eventually comes back to them with three paintings and two Dürer prints.

"Why do you like such a depressing, dark picture?" Justine asks when he unrolls *The Four Horsemen of the Apocalypse*.

"Real life isn't pretty, as we all know. I like how Albrecht Dürer reached into the dark places of the soul many people wouldn't want to admit they have. This is one of a series of fifteen woodcuts about the Apocalypse. He's one of my favorite artists. Have you ever heard the story behind his most famous drawing, *Praying Hands*? For all I know, it's an urban myth, but it's a really beautiful story that reminds me of your family. He and his brother Albert both wanted to go to art school, but they had a very poor family with a lot of kids, so they flipped a coin to decide who'd go first. Albrecht won and went to study art, while Albert went to work to pay for it. When Albrecht came home and said it was time to switch, Albert showed him his hands and said he could no longer become an artist because of how ruined his hands had become, no longer able to hold a paintbrush or woodcutting tool. And thus this woodcut was born, Albrecht painting Albert's praying hands. It represents the sacrifice siblings make for one another when they love each other very much, just like so many of your siblings made sacrifices so you could get out of that cesspool."

"That's a really nice story. Is it okay if we buy jewelry?"

"You can go ahead and buy whatever you want. I brought enough cash for plenty of purchases. After I've barely spent much money my whole life, it's nice to splurge while I still have a chance."

Adicia selects a lapis lazuli necklace, a turquoise bracelet, an onyx necklace, and malachite earrings. Justine picks out a rose quartz necklace, a long necklace with amethyst beads supposed to be worn doubled over, a citrine bracelet, and jasper earrings. Now that they have earrings, they can finally get their ears pierced. Adicia also selects a bright red apron with a swirly black design, a potholder made from the same fabric, a large dark blue bag with pink and white flowers crocheted on it, a pair of black ballet slippers with butterflies embroidered on them, and a pretty pair of wind chimes to hang from the back veranda. She feels like a kid in a candy store, and hopes Ricky doesn't think she's spending too much of his money.

After browsing the produce tables, Justine buys several jars of honey made with various types of berries, and Adicia picks out fresh berries in little boxes. By now they have so many things, they have to go back to the car and throw them into the trunk, making sure to put the honey and berries in the shade so they don't cook to death in the July heat.

Following their trip to the car, they return to the concession booths to get elephant ears, funnel cake, popcorn, cotton candy, and icecream. Adicia and Justine are overwhelmed by how many desserts they're allowed to eat. They haven't had so many desserts at once since Allen and Lenore's wedding six years ago. Carnival food might not be as refined as the baklava, cheesecake, wedding cake, and other goodies at the dessert buffet, but dessert is dessert, and they can't afford to be picky after growing up in a home where dessert was extremely rare.

"Can we have our pictures taken in the photo booth?" Justine asks as she stuffs a sugary strand of pink cotton candy into her mouth. "We've never had our own pictures. The older ones had group school pictures, but Sarah took them with her when our mother fired her. It was the only thing she had to remember them by. We're in Allen and Lenore's wedding pictures too, and the pictures they took when Irene and Amelia were born, but nothing we've had to keep for our own."

"You can get anything you'd like. Who wants to go first?"

"Let Justine have her picture taken alone first," Adicia urges. "She's the youngest. Then I can go in with her, and we can all have our pictures taken together."

"Can three people fit in a photo booth picture?" Ricky questions as Justine scampers into the booth with enough change.

"It might be a tight squeeze, but we can probably do it."

After Justine and Adicia have both had their pictures taken alone, they go in together, and then Ricky goes in for a group picture. Justine insists Adicia and Ricky stay for one more picture, and goes outside to wait.

"Are you almost done?" a man asks. "I thought there was a limit on turns."

"My sister and her husband got married a week ago, and tomorrow he's being drafted into the military to go to Vietnam. This may be all we have to remember him by."

The man looks very flustered and apologetic. "That's not right to rip a newlywed husband away from his bride. At least in the last war, most men joined voluntarily and weren't forced. How old's your sister?"

"She turned eighteen the day before they got married, and my brother-in-law turned twenty on Saturday."

"That's a shame. Their lives should just be beginning, not ending."

When they come out of the photo booth, the man turns to them and offers his hand. "I was told you're newlyweds and that you're being inducted tomorrow. I wish you luck and hope you'll be able to have a reunion after they're done with you or the war, whichever comes first."

"Thank you," Ricky says. "This isn't exactly how I pictured married life starting."

The man's wife turns to Adicia. "I trust you're going to make the most of your last night you'll have with your husband for a long time. The memory of your last night will keep both of you warm when you're far apart," she whispers.

"I'll try my best." Adicia blushes.

During the remaining sunlight, they go on the rides. This fair has a Ferris wheel, a small carousel, bumper cars, a Tilt-A-Whirl, Scramblers, a haunted house, Flying Swings, a funhouse, a Whip, and a Round-Up. Ricky can hardly believe the Troys never went to Coney Island and that this is their first time with amusement park rides. Adicia and Justine have to inform him the Coney Island he's thinking of exists only in memories, since Luna Park closed in 1946, before either of them were born, and Steeplechase Park closed in 1964. Like many people who aren't native New Yorkers, he has an idealized, romanticized view of all things New York City, a view that doesn't match with reality for many residents.

As stars start to appear in the sky, they get on the Ferris wheel, which goes fifty feet up. Justine sits at the far end of their car and lets the newlyweds sit close to one another on the other end, knowing this is their last night together for a long time, possibly ever.

"We didn't always get a good view of the stars, since we had so much light, factory soot, and tall buildings blocking them," Adicia says as she snuggles up against Ricky. "We had a beautiful view of the stars the night of the blackout in November '65, when we had that perfect full Moon in the cloudless sky."

"If I come home, we can buy a telescope so we can look at stars out on the back veranda. Did you ever take astronomy?"

"We studied a little about it, but we didn't have a full class. I know the names of a few of the stars and constellations. A lot of times when I see stars, I think of Dante. Emeline told me each section of *The Divine Comedy* ends with the word 'stars,' and that they serve as a beautiful symbol of hope for Dante during his incredible, otherworldly journey. Maybe someday I'll read it."

"I feel like we're trapped in our own *Divine Comedy*," Justine says. "It's like God put *The Divine Comedy* in a blender with a bunch of Grimms' fairytales to produce our lives. Only we haven't begun the Paradise part of the story yet. I thought we had, but it was just a false start."

"Things always get worse before they get better," Ricky says.

"Do you think this is a test to see if I deserve a happy ending?" Adicia asks. "One final test to see if I'm worthy of a nice life and a good husband, and then everything will be smooth sailing."

"I hope so," he says glumly. "Whatever happens, you're well taken care of with the house, a car, and our joint bank account with more than enough money to cover at least a year of living expenses. No one's gonna evict you, and you're not homeless, penniless, or stuck without transportation. Maybe your sister can give you driving lessons after I'm gone."

"At least you won't hafta face the music with Allen when he comes back from vacation." Adicia tries desperately to look on what little bright side there is. "I don't think he'll take it very well to find out you married me, and that I married you for convenience and not outta love."

After the ride stops, they wander around the fairgrounds for a little longer, taking in the beautiful stars in the night sky and breathing in the crisp, fresh air. As they're passing around the outer perimeter of the fairgrounds on their way back towards the parking area, Justine spies a tunnel of love and insists Adicia and Ricky go in it as one last ride of the night, saying she'll take the keys and go back to the car to wait for them.

"Isn't that a ride where people are supposed to make out?" Adicia asks nervously.

"It can just be a nice private ride in the dark," Justine says. "Come on, you'll probably regret not taking the ride when you have to part tomorrow."

"It can't hurt," Ricky says. "One more ride and then we drive home."

Adicia holds onto his arm as they walk into the darkened tunnel and take their seats in a swan-shaped boat. They're probably the only young couple taking the ride who aren't kissing or making out, and they're definitely the only couple who aren't mutually in love. With a bittersweet feeling in her heart, she snuggles up against him and wonders if she really should offer herself to him tonight, so he won't die a virgin or have no physical memories of her to keep from going insane when they're apart.

"If anything happens to me, will you still remember me?"

"I'll never forget you. You're the only person from the outside world who ever loved me unconditionally."

"Will you write me letters every day and send me care packages and pictures?"

"Of course. I really care about you. I'll stay right where I am waiting for you, and won't move away or run around on you. Even if I don't have those sorts of feelings for you, I'm an old-fashioned girl, and I take marriage vows very seriously. They're not just a suggestion. You're supposed to stay loyal to your spouse and stay together even if you're sick, poor, or in hard times."

"You're the nicest girl I could've asked to be thrown together with." He strokes her hair. "You have really soft hair. It's like petting a kitten."

"Can I touch your hair too?"

"Go ahead."

Adicia reaches up and runs her hands through his dark brown wavy hair. "I like your hair. I always liked dark hair and eyes the best."

"If the worst happens to me, I'll never forget you, Adicia. I'll think of you as I lie dying or wounded, and what a swell girl you are. You're not the type of girl to send her soldier husband a Dear John letter. But don't worry, if the worst happens, I won't expect you to wear widow's weeds for the rest of your life. You're too young to have to be loyal to my memory forever, particularly considering you never loved me in that way."

"I might not love you, but I think I have a crush on you. You won't go off with a Vietnamese hooker over there, will you?"

"I wouldn't know what to do if I had a hooker. I've never been with a woman in that way, I'm afraid."

"Would you like to be with me in that way before you have to leave? I don't want you to die a virgin, or have no memory of that when you're over there scared and alone. It might help you get through the conscription easier."

"That's a really sweet thing to offer, but I think I can get through it without that. If I've never done that, I don't know what I'm missing. And it wasn't that long ago you had that experience with Seth."

"Maybe it's a bad idea. If I don't like it, I'll let you know, and we'll spend the rest of the night in different beds. But you are my husband, however unconventional the circumstances, and it might be nice to have you in that way while I still have a chance. I promise you I don't have any venereal diseases, since both of the others took precautions to avoid a scandal."

"I promised I'd never lay a hand on you unless you came to me and told me you wanted it. I didn't expect you'd ask for that till you loved me back."

Adicia inches away from him. "Fine, if you're not interested, you don't hafta accept my offer. I was just suggesting something I thought you might want while you still have the chance. I wasn't gonna force you to do anything."

He reaches over for her hand. "Hey, don't be like that. I'd do anything to make you happy while I'm still here with you. I just know what happened with those two jerks, and I need to make sure you're offering this for the right reasons. I'll still be your husband even if I go away without consummating the marriage."

She nods, looking ahead at the darkened water sadly. "Why does this water hafta be so calm when we're swimming frantically against a mass of troubled waters that doesn't seem like it'll ever abate? And why did God, if he exists, have to punish me by showing me a glimpse of a happy ending and giving me a cute husband if I can't have either until I've been through yet another tribulation? Other couples thrown together in arranged marriages sleep together when they're not in love. I guess I don't deserve even that one consolation when you're about to go away. I thought you loved me unconditionally, just the way I am. Who knows, maybe you're not man enough to wanna do it. You rich intellectuals and limousine liberals really are all talk and no game when it comes to doing something you profess to care about so much."

This last comment seizes his attention. "Is that what you think of me? I'll show you who's a man and not a mouse."

Adicia feels butterflies in her stomach as Ricky takes her chin under his hand and gently kisses her. When he sees the awestruck smile on her face in the dark and that she's not pulling away, he does it again for longer. He only separates himself from her when he sees the exit tunnel approaching, not wanting to get caught by the ride operator or anyone still walking around.

"How was that for someone you thought was a mouse and not a man?" he whispers as they walk back to the car.

"That was really nice," she says giddily. "Now I know why they say it feels so good and special when you're with someone you really like, and not something someone forces on you."

"So I take it your offer to make a man of me is still open?"

"Most definitely."

***

When they get home at 10:00, Adicia asks Justine to sleep in Ricky's bedroom just for tonight, so she and Ricky can spend their last night together in the big queen bed. Justine hopes her sister knows what she's doing as she trots down the hall with her pajamas and her stuffed rabbit.

"I hope you don't think I'm a baby because I'm so nervous," Adicia says as she slowly takes her clothes off and folds them up on a chair. "Did you wanna do this part?"

"I'd probably be even more nervous about doing this for the first time if I had to fumble at buttons in the dark. Don't worry, I don't think you're a baby. You've never done this before either, even if you had things done to you."

Adicia crawls under the covers and looks off to the side until Ricky gets in, not wanting to see anything. She notices his heart beating almost as loudly as hers as he starts to kiss her and tentatively get acquainted with her body. Slowly she starts to explore his body too, hoping she's touching him like a woman is supposed to touch a man when they're in bed together. She's slightly embarrassed when an involuntary noise escapes from her, hoping Justine can't hear anything or that she's already asleep. It would be too embarrassing if there were a repeat of the scene Ernestine once described, coming over to visit Allen and Lenore and hearing them going at it really loudly behind a locked door, no idea they had a visitor until they came out.

"I guess I'm not too bad for someone who has no idea what he's doing," he says. "Are you still okay?"

"So far."

After several hours of just kissing, necking, and petting, during which time she's grown to feel more comfortable with the thought of physical intimacy, Adicia feels him starting to climb on top of her. She looks up at him and sees he looks just as nervous as she is.

"You still wanna go all the way, or is this enough for you?"

"I'll tell you if it hurts too much or brings on a flashback."

"I hope I don't crush you since you're so much smaller than I am. I'll try not to hurt you that way either."

"I'm not made of glass," she says as she feels him very slowly penetrating her.

"You still feeling okay?"

"Yes, that doesn't hurt. It feels strange, but it doesn't hurt."

"This does feel strange," he agrees as he settles on top of her. "You want me to finish, or is this all you're comfortable with?"

"You look really scared." Adicia wraps her arms around him. "I thought guys weren't supposed to be scared of this."

"I just don't wanna mess up or hurt you."

"You're doing just fine. We might as well finish what we started, don't you think?"

He moves slowly, partly because he's not entirely sure what he's supposed to do, and partly because he doesn't want to hurt Adicia or make her have any flashbacks to Ethan or Seth. They exchange nervous smiles afterwards, not entirely sure what to do or say next.

"I love you," Ricky finally says, putting his arms around her waist.

"That was really nice. Thank you for showing me how nice and beautiful this can be. I never thought I'd wanna do that again after what happened, even with a nice guy like you."

"So I didn't hurt you or make you uncomfortable?"

"I never asked you to stop, did I?" She curls up against the curves of his body. "I feel really close to you now, like we're true husband and wife. I can't imagine doing that with anyone else now. It would be wrong."

"Can you stay just as sweet and old-fashioned as you are? If I come home, I wanna know I'm coming back home to the same old Adicia I fell in love with, not a stranger."

"I'll try my best to be the same as I've always been. I don't think you'll come back to find me in a cult, carrying on with five other guys or another woman, a drug addict, or an abusive wife."

"You promise you'll stay just the same and will wait for me, and you'll never forget me if the worst happens?"

"If the worst happens, and I never find someone to remarry, I'll never forget there was once a guy who loved me just the way I am, who let me know what it feels like to be loved and treated special by a guy."

He kisses the curve of her neck. "That's just what I wanted to hear. You're the best girl I ever had, Adicia. I know nice, sweet, old-fashioned girls still exist, 'cause I was lucky enough to meet you and for you to let me be your fellow."

"And I know nice, sweet, old-fashioned guys still exist, 'cause I was lucky enough to meet you in return. We didn't meet by accident any more than I came running back to your house by accident. For whatever reason, our lives and fates were meant to be joined together, for better or for worse."

*****

Adicia stirs awake when the alarm clock goes off early in the morning. She blearily watches as Ricky pulls on the clothes he brought into the room last night and picks up the bag he packed. It doesn't quite seem real that her newlywed husband is being taken away from her, nor that last night they consummated their convenience marriage a lot sooner than expected.

"Go back to sleep. I don't want you to go to the station and be unable to say goodbye. It's better if we say goodbye here."

"But I wanna go with you. A wife is supposed to see her husband off to war."

"Do you really wanna be there with all the crying wives, mothers, girlfriends, and other people? That might make it even worse for you. Plus I don't think I'd ever be able to let go of you if you went there with me."

"Will you write to me as soon as you get to the training camp?"

"You bet I will, my sweet little treasure."

"I'll write to you every single day, and send you care packages with homemade cookies and brownies. I'll be a good little wifey and hold down the fort for you."

"Do you promise you'll still take me back as your husband if I come home an amputee, blind, deaf, or crippled?"

"You have a really beautiful heart, Ricky. A lot of people with all their senses and limbs intact are blind, deaf, and dumb in their hearts and souls, more so than people with handicaps. I'll accept you just the way you are."

"I'm such a lucky guy to have a girl like you waiting for me." Ricky kneels by the bed and kisses her goodbye, wishing he could stay right here and enjoy his newly consummated marriage instead of having to leave at this early hour and get on a bus going to boot camp. "I love you."

Adicia drifts back off to sleep after he walks out of the room, down the stairs, out of the house, and into a waiting cab taking him to the bus. She has no time to comprehend what Ricky's leaving means for her and Justine. All she's thinking about as she falls back asleep is that she's losing her darling husband, whom she's been starting to fall for and now feels deeply bonded to after last night. She doesn't consider what she'll have to do to pull in enough money to support herself and Justine, that it might take awhile to master driving, or that she's now faced with the task of running a household all by herself at the tender age of eighteen. Nor does she consider what might happen when Allen and Lenore return from vacation. Her one consolation is that perhaps it really is one final test, just like the Pandava brothers had, before her character is deemed worthy once and for all, and she's finally able to enjoy a beautiful happy ending.

Chapter 52: Unexpected Neighbors

"I saw the next door neighbors finally pulling into their driveway last night," Justine says on Friday morning. "Do you think they'll notice the car in our driveway and come to welcome us to the neighborhood? I've heard they do that in smaller towns like this."

"No one else came by with a welcome wagon," Adicia says, still sadly thinking of Ricky on his way to boot camp. "I think they only do that in tiny towns or old books."

"Maybe you're right. But they might introduce themselves. People in smaller towns and cities are supposed to know their neighbors and be friends with 'em."

"I miss Ricky. He's supposed to be here with us, not being taken to boot camp. We can't do much about transportation and me getting a job, most likely, till we find a driving school. I hope they can send the teacher here, 'cause I don't wanna wait till Lucine gets back and beg lessons off her when she's six months pregnant. I doubt I could find a job within walking distance, and I don't wanna rely on taxis and buses now that we're outta the big city."

"I can't believe you did that with Ricky when you don't love him, and so soon after what Seth did. It was one thing yous guys had to get married for convenience, but sleeping together wasn't part of the deal!"

"Do you really think mosta the people in other arranged marriages hold off on consummating their marriages till the feeling's mutual on both sides? They do that first, and the love comes second. Besides, I was starting to fall for him. Now I feel even stronger about him. Once you do that willingly, and you're not being forced, it's like your heart, mind, soul, and body are bonded to that person. At least, that's what I feel. The free love people who run around declaring how enlightened and liberating it is to be promiscuous don't feel like they're pair-bonded for life to all their partners. He was so slow and gentle, since he knew what had happened to me. There was no blood, since I wasn't a physical virgin. He was just as scared as I was, since he'd never done that before. It's nice to find a guy his age who's still a virgin, and who waited till marriage to do that. Not that I think you've gotta be married to do that. Allen and Lenore did that before they were married, but they knew this was the real deal and not just a passing fling."

"Dare I ask if you used anything? You went to Planned Parenthood for the premarital bloodwork and tests, and these days I half-expect them to automatically offer pills to anyone getting married."

"No, we didn't use any birth control. I strongly doubt anything could've happened."

"I hope you're right. That's the last thing we need right now."

Adicia and Justine look at one another when the doorbell rings. They don't know anyone in the neighborhood, and none of the new neighbors have stopped by to say hello. They've greeted them and made small-talk when they pass outside, but haven't come by for tea and cake either. Perhaps the neighbors on the end of the cul-de-sac got curious when they saw the long-unoccupied house suddenly occupied, or maybe their mail has been misdelivered. So long as Ricky's parents haven't come back to harass and abuse them, it might be nice to have a visitor. It would be even better if Ricky himself has come back and this drafting thing has just been a big mistake and misunderstanding.

Adicia opens the door and takes several steps back in astonishment. Allen, a very pregnant Lenore, and their two daughters are right in front of her, looking just as stunned.

"What in the world!" Allen says. "What in the world are you doing in the house next door to us?"

"We didn't even know you'd come up here!" Lenore agrees. "Did you come while we were at Lake George?"

Justine hears their familiar voices and rushes over. "You live in our new neighborhood?"

Lenore hugs both of them. "However you came to be here, I'm so glad you're safe and sound. You won't miss my last birth. It's due in September."

Allen turns around and looks at the dark red Super Beetle in the driveway. "Adicia, when did you learn to drive, and where did you get the money to buy or lease a car?"

"I haven't learnt to drive yet. I've been waiting to find a teacher who'll come to the house, or for you or Lucine to come back from vacation so I can start learning."

"So then how and why did you get a car? Am I about to hear something that'll make me very upset? And how did you know Lucine's on vacation? Did you run into her, and she never told us in the few days our vacations overlapped?"

"How did you get such a nice house?" Lenore asks. "Are you renting a room? Don't tell me you took up squatting."

"The house is paid for in full, as is the car," Adicia says.

"Where in the world did that kinda money come from?" Allen asks. "Boy, I never expected to come home to find my youngest sisters moved into the house next door. Is this legit money you used to pay for all this? This furniture doesn't look cheap either."

"I have enough money in my bank account to afford to live comfortably for awhile. There's plenty of money in there for Justine too."

"Since when did you get a bank account? And how in the world did you already manage to stash so much dough in there you'd be able to support yourselves long-term? Who gave you that kinda money? Is this clean money? Who's your sugar daddy?"

"I don't have a sugar daddy. I'm not that kinda girl."

"Why don't we sit down so we can catch up?" Lenore asks. "We came to meet the new neighbors, and even if we already know them, we can still have a proper visit."

"Would you like something to eat or drink?"

"No, we're fine." Lenore sits on the overstuffed brown leather davenport. "Nice furniture. I wish we had leather upholstery."

Irene crawls onto Adicia's lap and smiles up at her aunt. "We missed you. You missed my fifth birthday last month, but you won't miss my first day of school."

Amelia, captivated by the sparkly sapphire on her aunt's left hand, pulls Adicia's hand closer to her face. "Your ring is pretty."

"Do you like my other ring too, the one with the flowers?" Adicia asks.

Allen stares at Adicia's rings. He grabs her hand away from Amelia so he can examine the rings himself. "Who's been giving you this kinda expensive jewelry, Adicia? I have a sick feeling in my stomach this has something to do with that rich boy Warrick, and if you tell me he's the one who's been plying you with money, houses, cars, jewelry, and other expensive presents, you'll have a hell of a time convincing me not to go give him a piece of my mind for using you like that. You're a respectable girl from a poor and working-class community, not a kept woman in a gilded cage for the entertainment of a limousine liberal who was born with a diamond-encrusted silver spoon in his mouth."

"You can't do or say anything to Ricky, since he left on Thursday morning for boot camp. They drafted him, and he's being forced to go to Vietnam. His number was eighty-eight, and since he withdrew from Columbia, he lost his student deferment." Adicia looks down, overcome by sorrow.

"Wait, that guy was *living* with you? And Justine was here in the house too? Please do not tell me you did anything with him."

"He was drafted?" Lenore asks. "Come over here and sit by me, sweetie."

Adicia gently lifts Irene off her lap and goes over to Lenore, leaning against her. Lenore puts her arm around Adicia and gives Allen a dirty look.

"You should be ashamed of yourself, Allen, for putting your dear little sister and her friend down after you just found out he was drafted. That poor young man could get killed over there, and Adicia and Justine would lose a very good friend. So he has family money to give them. Is it a crime to have a rich friend who willingly helps them out? Most rich people would never consider opening up their pocketbooks to help poor girls!"

"Rich people never help poor people from the goodness of their hearts. At best, some old rich people might start a charity for the less fortunate 'cause they have no heirs, or have cash to burn and won't be around much longer to use it. The classes don't mix for a reason. Warrick has nothing in common with Adicia and Justine. He comes from privilege and isn't from the city; they grew up in somea the worst neighborhoods of Manhattan and had to struggle for everything they got. After the adventure of befriending or dating a girl from the wrong side of the tracks wears off, he'll lose interest and dump her in favor of a rich girl. What do you have in common with this boy, Adicia? You were never raised to accept handouts or charity."

"What about all the meals we ate at the Bowery Mission! You yourself got a loan of three hundred bucks from them when you were just starting out!"

"They're an established mission that goes back almost a hundred years! Don't compare humanitarian mission work with a rich boy deciding he wanted a poor girl for a plaything. Dropping out of college was probably part of his silly youthful rebellion and playing at being onea the people. I bet he really wishes he'd stayed in school now, 'stea-da taking this misguided adventure with you and Justine."

"How did they let you buy a house?" Lenore asks. "Did you have to pretend to be married, or did he move you in here after he already bought the house?"

"Do you wanna tell 'em, or should I?" Justine asks.

"Tell us what?" Allen asks.

"Ricky's my husband," Adicia admits. "We got married the day after my birthday, at the courthouse downtown. The van Niftriks and my friend Marjani Washington came."

Allen buries his head in his hands, too floored to say anything.

"You got *married*, sweetie? How long were you dating him? He was just your friend the last time we saw you. What changed since the end of March?" Lenore looks meaningfully at her daughters. "Why don't you go upstairs and play. This conversation is too mature for yous."

Irene and Amelia pick up the toys they brought over and trot upstairs.

"It's not a love match," Adicia blurts out. With a shaking voice, she gives a recap of the events which led to her running away, and explains how she ended up back with Ricky.

"Your parents were tryna make you marry a wife-beater who murdered his first wife? And they let him rape you? I'm so glad you got far away from all those vultures before they could abuse you further!"

"Well, now I know which guy I should hate more than your rich boy husband," Allen says. "Do you know his address so I can go back to the city and do to him exactly what I did to Ethan?"

"You probably won't need to do the overprotective big brother thing again, 'cause Mother's pressing charges against him for breaking and entering and attempting to assault Tommy," Adicia says. "That's what Ricky's parents told us when they tracked us down a few days ago and tried to convince Ricky to leave me and come home. He showed them the door and chose me."

"What is this guy, a pederast as well as a wife-beater and murderer? What in the hell was he doing with Tommy?"

"He came to our apartment last Friday and said he'd beat me and Tommy to get answers and clues from us if we wouldn't talk on our own," Justine says. "He told Adicia if she wouldn't divorce Ricky and come with him, he'd take me instead. He always wanted a blonde and a virgin, and he said he'd move me in with him and break me in until I turned sixteen and he could marry me."

"Seth grabbed my arms and wouldn't let go," Adicia says. "Ricky flagged down a passing cop car, and he got Seth to let go of me. He gave us a ride back to the van Niftriks. That brute left bruises on my arms. He's in additional trouble from the flyers the van Niftriks put up all around Chelsea. They papered the neighborhood, letting everyone know his pharmacy and grocery store is run by someone who was in the clink for fifteen years for killing his first wife, and about what he did to Tommy and Justine."

"Where did our parents find this prize?" Allen asks.

"Probably the same way they found mosta their other prizes, buying drugs." Adicia nervously twists her wedding ring.

"Did this man touch you, Justine? Should our parents be pressing charges against him for attempting to assault you too?"

Justine closes her eyes and narrates the chain of events which started when Seth came into the apartment on Friday afternoon. Every so often, Adicia chimes in. Both of them make special mention of Tommy's surprise decency, and Justine mentions Zuberi held her hand on the way to Penn Station in spite of his fears of becoming another Emmett Till.

"We're glad you're both safe from that degenerate criminal, but that doesn't explain how Adicia came to be married to the rich boy," Allen says. "Was he her escort when she left the city, and they impulsively decided to tie the knot?"

"Ricky was really unhappy with his controlling, out of touch parents, and he hated city life and Columbia," Adicia says. "He withdrew from the university and got a moving truck. We couldn't travel together without scandal, so he decided we'd get married to put on a respectable appearance. Ours is a marriage of convenience, kinda like an arranged marriage. He's in love with me, I really like him as a friend, we're a very good match, and he took very good care of me. Over time, if he comes home, I think I'll grow to love him the way a wife loves a husband."

"You married a man you don't love? You don't deserve that. You deserve to marry a guy you're madly in love with, not someone you've gotta learn how to love. Arranged marriages went the way of the dinosaurs for a reason. I couldn't imagine having to learn to love Lenore instead of loving her instantly. Don't you want someone you love the way a woman loves a man, not just someone you get along with and have things in common with? Assuming his intentions are sincere, and he won't get bored of his exotic little poor girl novelty and dump you for a rich girl."

"I really like him. He's the only person from the outside world who's ever loved me unconditionally, just the way I am. He was such a gentleman, agreeing to have a celibate marriage with a girl he was in love with. He slept in a different room and promised he'd never lay a hand on me unless I told him I wanted more."

"So your marriage is unconsummated," Allen says with relief. "We can get you an annulment if he gets home alive, and you can both get on with your lives. At least he'll be able to pay you a generous alimony."

"I'm not divorcing Ricky," Adicia says firmly. "I was really starting to fall for him. We spent our last day at a county fair, so our last memories together would be happy ones, instead of spending the whole day heartsick about how he was gonna be ripped away from me."

"What, you'd choose to stay married to a rich boy who comes from such a foreign world, a guy you don't love? Modern people don't have to grow to love their spouses. We have love matches nowadays, unlike our unenlightened ancestors. At least this pretend marriage only lasted a week. Even if you both felt attached and attracted to each other, that'll all end while he's being used as cannon fodder. You might find a boy of your own social class, and he might wake up and realize this was a silly, childish dream. Why don't you write him a Dear John letter and ask to go your separate ways? There will be no hard feelings if you act right now."

"What kind of ill-bred, ungrateful, mean-spirited person do you take me for, Allen? Ricky is my husband and my dear friend, even if I don't feel for him the way he feels for me. I promised I wouldn't leave him or cheat on him while he was away. He's counting on me staying true to him and being the same girl he fell in love with when he comes home. His ordeal will be that much more bearable if he knows his sweet little wifey's waiting for him with open arms and that I'm not taking other men into my heart. Maybe a heartless bitch like Mother would have affairs on a husband away at war, but I'm not like that. Convenience marriage or not, I want to uphold the words of my vow to stay true to Ricky through better or worse, forsaking all others, and to comfort, love, protect, and honor him.”

“So you’ll get it annulled after he comes home from Vietnam? Maybe it is a little cold to divorce or cheat on a guy who’s away at war, even if you don’t love him. I’m sure he’ll fall out of love with you while he’s over there, though, and that you’ll have a change of heart too.”

“He really never did anything physical with you at all?” Lenore asks. “Don’t you have to kiss the bride even at the conclusion of a courthouse wedding?”

“I said I was very shy and private about that, and the judge thought it was really nice to be so old-fashioned and reserved in this day and age,” Adicia says.

“So he hasn’t put the moves on you or tried to seduce you at all?” Allen asks. “Is he having other girls on the side to fulfill his masculine needs, is he secretly homosexual, or is he content to live like a monk in the prime of his youth?”

“Anything we may or may not have done is frankly nonea your business.”

Allen hopes his head isn’t about to explode. “What does that mean? What exactly has he done to you? First base, second base, third base, all the way, what? If you went all the way with him, you can’t get an annulment. You’ll have to go through a divorce, and not all divorces are as quick and easy as Gemma’s.”

“Like I said, nonea your business. You don’t want images of your little sister in bed or making out with a guy, do you? Besides, I’m eighteen now. What I choose to do or not to do is my personal business.”

“What are you saying? Adicia, did you sleep with this guy? If you did, I hope to God you used birth control, ’cause there’s no way of knowing what kinda venereal diseases he mighta had. Rich boys are almost always playboys. You’re not his first or last conquest, believe me.”

“Ricky was a virgin until Wednesday night!” Adicia shouts indignantly. “And his premarital blood test was clean.”

Allen stares at her in disappointment. “Did you just admit you slept with this guy? With that rich boy who I’d bet dollars to doughnuts is using you, or at the very least is a misguided youth in rebellion looking for an exciting new adventure to fool around with till he gets bored or finds another hobby? And so soon after that bastard Seth did what he did? Please tell me I misunderstood what you said and you really meant your rich boy husband got his entry into manhood from a hooker before he left!”

Adicia buries her head against Lenore’s shoulder and starts crying. Lenore gives Allen another dirty look. Her expression becomes even worse when the girls come running at all the shouting.

“Why do you hate Aunt Adicia’s husband so much, Daddy?” Irene asks.

“That’s enough, Allen,” Lenore says. “Hasn’t Adicia suffered enough? Do you have to pour copious amounts of salt onto her open wounds? You should be thanking God she and Justine are both safe and sound from your parents and that horrid criminal, not badgering her about what she chose to do with her husband! Have you forgotten her newlywed husband was ripped away from her yesterday morning? This poor young man could get killed in Vietnam, and our dear, sweet, little Adicia would be a teenage widow!”

“If he survives Vietnam, he’ll still have to survive me when he gets home. He’s not gonna get away with disgracing my kid sister and using her for a plaything. He’ll want a wife from the moneyed world before long, someone who gives a damn about using ten utensils at the same meal and putting them around the plate in a certain order, eating all food with utensils, even watermelon and bacon, giving their kids surnames for first names, and spending their free time making social calls to people with names like Mrs. John Jacob Astor the Ninth and Mr. Kingsley Rockefeller Vanderbilt!”

“I want my husband,” Adicia sobs. “I don’t want the only guy who ever loved me to die in a jungle. He should be safe in my arms now, not riding on a bus to God knows where to endure boot camp before they ship him off to die.”

“Why are you acting like such a bastard, Allen?” Justine asks. “Isn’t Adicia’s happiness more important than your petty need for revenge or being proven right? Ricky’s been nothing but swell to us. He treated Adicia so special, even though she didn’t love him back. You oughta be thanking him on bended knee for protecting her and getting her outta New York safely.”

“He didn’t hafta go and marry her and sleep with her to do that! Nowadays, less and less people give a damn about unmarried people traveling together! They might not let you buy a house together, but they don’t blink an eye at checking into a hotel or getting on a bus or train together! If they cared about old-fashioned appearances, they coulda pretended to be married."

"Lenore, can you make him leave?" Adicia begs.

"Allen, you'd better leave," Lenore orders. "I can't believe how heartless and ridiculous you're being. Why can't you take Adicia's word for it that her husband's an honorable fellow? Even if she did sleep with him, she's a legal adult now, and he's her lawfully-wedded husband. Since when was it so morally wrong and disgusting for a girl to sleep with her own husband?"

"Not just any husband. A rich boy husband who's probably using her."

"I agree an arranged or convenience marriage is very old-fashioned and not what I would've chosen, but if it makes Adicia happy, that should be the end of that discussion. Maybe they'll grow closer together since they didn't start out crazy in love and only seeing each other as exciting dating partners. They've already been through a lot in one week, the kinds of things most newlyweds don't have to go through. Adicia's such a sweet girl, and if her husband really is such a great guy, I think their marriage will be fine if he comes home alive."

"Mrs. Marsenko at the bridal shop said she admires arranged marriage, since her Orthodox brides talk so glowingly about it. Sometimes the strongest, most serious love bonds come when you grow instead of fall in love."

"I don't want my kid sister to have to learn to love anyone. I want you to marry a proper boy you fell in love with, like a normal, modern person."

Lenore points at the door as she continues holding Adicia and rocking her back and forth.

"You're being mean, Daddy," Irene chides him.

Allen sulks as he opens the door. "That rich boy doesn't deserve such a dear, sweet girl. Any feelings she might've developed for him are being wasted. Why don't we have the Ryans over for Thanksgiving or Christmas so she and David can get reacquainted? Wouldn't he be a lovely match for her?"

"David is practically my brother!" Adicia shouts.

"Hey, I think he's cute, but he's too old for me," Justine says. "I don't think he's practically my brother, 'cause he's almost five years older than me. You can wait for me to get old enough if you're that desperate to marry him into the family."

Allen stalks out the door, still reeling at everything he's learnt, coupled with the fact that Lenore is taking Adicia's side against her own husband. Irene and Amelia run to the front windows and watch their father entering their house, slamming the door.

"Allen is gone," Lenore soothes her. "You can tell me the truth, and I won't give up your secret to him. I kept Ernestine and Deirdre's secret. Did you really sleep with Ricky?"

"I hope Allen doesn't hate me. He's been the best big brother I coulda ever asked for, and I'd be heartbroken to lose his love and support when I need it more than ever."

"He still loves you. Sometimes when people love someone so much, they get madder than they might about a total stranger or casual acquaintance, because they're so close to the person and situation. They want what's best for the person, even if the person is telling the truth that something isn't what it looks like. You have to admit this is a pretty far-fetched story, a rich boy falling in love with a poor girl down the street, giving up his life of privilege to run away with her, and entering a celibate, convenience marriage."

"I know it looks strange, but it's not what it seems. Appearances can be deceiving. You know what Emeline says, a lot of people underestimate the quiet ones, and then they turn around and prove themselves full of nifty stuff. Labels should be for shirts, not people. We're people, not stereotypes, assumptions, or judgments."

"Aunt Emeline lives here too," Irene says. "She's an assistant at a library and lives in a neat apartment by herself with her cat George. She'll be super happy to see you and Justine."

"Did Emeline name her cat..."

"Did she ever," Lenore says. "At least she used a cat for a namesake, not a child. She wants to name any future kids after literary characters, so we don't have to worry about kids with celebrity namesakes."

"Emeline's cat was a runt!" Irene says. "She says his namesake was a runt of the litter too, in a way, and she felt a mothering and protecting feeling for him."

"Irene, it's not very nice to call a human being a runt," Lenore gently chides her. "Some people are smaller or younger than others. It doesn't make them inferior."

"Emeline won't be angry at me when she finds out I married

Ricky, will she? Lucine was surprised but not mad when we saw her in the grocery store before he left. She said my happiness was most important."

"I hope Allen eventually comes around. If your Ricky comes home, it'd be too awkward and uncomfortable to live next door to the brother-in-law who hates his guts. Maybe Allen's acting like this 'cause he's never really seen yous guys together and only met Ricky once. If you've only heard about a relationship and haven't observed it in action, sometimes you think the worst things about it, and stuff that sounds really bad on paper turns out to be perfectly reasonable and logical in real life. Have you been intimate? I don't blame you if you did, even if you didn't love him."

"Ricky kissed me for the first time at the fair on Wednesday, at the end of the day, in onea the swan boats in the tunnel of love. When we got home, we consummated our marriage. We were both really nervous, but we did what we had to do. It was really nice. Is it normal to be nervous the first time, even if you like the other person? I've read some romance novels, and no one ever talks about being nervous, scared, or not knowing what they're doing. I knew what you're supposed to do, because of what was done to me before, but I'd never done it willingly."

"Your secret is safe with me, sweetie. It's normal to be nervous the first time, particularly if you've been violated before and never did that willingly. What a beautiful, romantic first time story. It's none of Allen's business what you did with your own husband in the privacy of your own home."

"I wanted him to have that experience in case we never saw each other again, and so he'd have a nice memory to keep him warm at night in the jungle."

"That's perfectly understandable. Do you feel any different afterwards? I felt like I'd just joined the secret grownup club, and felt different all through my being, like now I knew the secret, mysterious grownup knowledge."

"My feelings for Ricky are going crazy. I feel so bonded to him after we did that, like our hearts and souls are bonded together forever. I couldn't imagine wanting to do that with anyone else, or walking away after we shared something so personal."

"That's how I felt too. Sometimes doing that speeds along the process of falling in love with a person you already had feelings for, or it makes you fall in love period. Allen isn't acting very big brotherly if he can't try to understand your feelings and acts like you're a dumb, helpless child who had no say in any of this."

"He won't come over every day to make my life miserable, will he?"

"He's too busy with his two jobs. Allen runs a photography studio out of the attic and works for a catering service, which makes enough money to cover the mortgage. We don't have enough money saved up to rent a building for a bakery."

"Let me give you the money. Allen probably doesn't want anything to do with Ricky's money, but there's enough to cover the cost of a building and start-up equipment and supplies. Ricky hasn't even spent a million dollars since we ran away. There are four million something bucks left."

"You'd really give us money to start our own family bakery, Aunt Adicia?" Irene asks. "Boy, you're really swell."

"I'll talk it over with Allen," Lenore says. "If he accepts the money and the bakery makes a profit, would you consider working there? You could drive to work with Allen. Maybe he'll give you driving lessons."

"I hope so," Adicia says. "At least Allen didn't say he never wanted to talk to me again."

"Allen's a big family man. He might be upset now, but over time, he's gotta come around and accept your marriage. He just needs a little time to come to terms with this situation, and that'll be harder to do when your husband's no longer here to be observed in action. All he's going on is your word against his assumptions."

"Ricky's our Jasper King from the Five Little Peppers series. It made no sense, a rich boy taking so much interest in poor people, becoming their best friend, and prevailing on his sickly old dad to move them all into their mansion, but these things do happen sometimes."

"I believe you, sweetie. You're not a stupid girl, and you never seemed the type to be so desperate for attention from a boy you'd marry the first and only guy who ever showed interest in you. Allen knows it too. Just give him time to accept the situation."

"Would you like tea?" Justine asks. "It'll help you calm down."

"Yes, please," Adicia says.

"You hear that?" Lenore rubs her shoulders. "Tea and then everything will be fine."

"Can you believe Emeline still can't drive at twenty-four?" Adicia asks Justine as they stand in front of her apartment with Lenore on Sunday. "It's easier to believe she's still a virgin."

"Maybe she settled into a pattern of taking the bus and walking," Lenore says. "Or maybe it's a hippie thing about not putting toxins in the air."

Emeline opens the front door a crack and peers out. Her face turns into a giant smile when she sees who her visitors are, and she opens the door all the way.

"Come right in, my darling little sisters!" She pulls first Adicia and then Justine into big bear hugs. "Praise Lord Krishna you found us!"

Adicia and Justine are greeted by the smell of vanilla and coconut incense when they enter her one-bedroom apartment on the first floor. One entire wall in the living room is taken up by a bookshelf almost completely stuffed with books. Along the opposite wall, Emeline has arranged several Buddha figures in various sizes, a medium-sized statue of Ganesha, a small figurine of Krishna playing the flute and standing on lotus petals, several records with display-worthy cover art, a framed poster of The Who, a framed, sepia-tinted reproduction of a photograph of Rudolph Valentino, posters of the Three Stooges and Laurel and Hardy, and taped-up, typewritten pages bearing the text of Charlie Chaplin's speech at the end of *The Great Dictator*, various chapters of *The Tao Te Ching*, assorted quotes from Hermann Hesse, Buddha, Confucius, Voltaire, Rousseau, and *The Bhagavad Gita*, and the late guru Meher Baba's Universal Prayer, O Parvardigar. It's the most bizarre decorating scheme Adicia's ever seen, but she loves Emeline too much to criticize it.

"Georgiekins, we've got visitors. Would you like to meet them?" Emeline bends down and scoops up a small kitten with beautiful smoky-blue eyes, off-white, medium-length fur, and a few gray, black, and orange patches.

"He's cute," Justine says. "Where'd you buy him?"

"He was the runt of his litter, just like his namesake, but we won't say anything that's bad about you, will we, Georgiekins? I took a chance and picked him over the other kittens for sale down the block, 'cause great oaks sprout from tiny acorns. Just lookit what his namesake did after The Beatles broke up. Have you heard the triple album *All Things Must Pass*? I hate the third disc, to be honest, since it's just meandering, endless, pointless jam sessions that only sound a bit better when you're stoned, but the first two discs are brilliant. You can borrow any of my records. Want some tea? I've got a bunch of different types of loose tea, and you can choose whichever you want. I hope you don't mind I don't have any meat to serve yous guys. Come sit down, and we'll start catching up."

Emeline lets George walk around the kitchen table as she gets out a green cast-iron teapot with a dragonfly motif and cups to match. Adicia and Justine nervously pet him, hoping he's friendly and won't scratch or hiss at strangers. They also hope George isn't just the first of many cats and that Emeline won't turn into the stereotype of the librarian and older single woman who accumulates too many cats.

"Can we have chrysanthemum tea?" Adicia asks.

"You certainly can. Japanese legend has it that if you eat or drink of the flower, you'll live a hundred years." Emeline leans over to admire Adicia's rings. "Those are mighty pretty. Who gave them to you?"

"My husband. The sapphire ring's my engagement ring, and the one with the little flowers is the wedding band."

Emeline almost drops the teakettle as she fills it with water. "What! Your *husband*! Is this a guy Mother and Dad forced you to marry, or is he someone you chose? When in the hell did you get married, Adicia? Where is he now?"

"He's probably arrived at boot camp by now." Adicia drifts back to their last night together. "They took him away from me. My sweet Ricky wasn't made to be a soldier."

"Ricky was the swellest brother-in-law ever," Justine says. "You shoulda seen how terrific he was to Adicia."

Emeline looks at the clock. "How much time do yous have? This sounds like it's gonna be a very long story."

"We don't mind staying all day," Adicia says. "Justine and I missed you so much."

"Allen hates him," Justine says. "He said if Ricky survives Vietnam, he'll still have to survive him when he comes home. That's so mean."

"Allen's ten years older than you," Lenore points out. "He's always been more of a substitute father figure than a normal brother. Since he's so much older, he sees and thinks of you as his little kid sister, not an independent, grownup woman."

"Your husband was drafted?" Emeline asks. "Boy, I can tell this isn't a tale that can be told in ten minutes."

Justine and Adicia look askance at the food Emeline sets before them—reheated pancakes made from rice, goat cheese, mushrooms, dark red kidney beans, and green peppers; a large pot of soup made with coconut milk, sweet potatoes, mushrooms, tofu, and carrots; and a salad of chickpeas, diced tomatoes, and avocados. Not having at least a little meat or fish in a main meal is unfathomable.

"Did you know it wasn't all that long ago in this very century that most people didn't eat much meat or dairy? Meat was really expensive, and only very rich people could afford refrigeration. All my hippie friends are starting to get interested in vegetarianism, though I was into this diet since I was eighteen. I've always been ahead of the trends and knew all the best-kept secrets, like Hermann Hesse, Hinduism, vegetarianism, and Buddhism. Now let's hear about what's been going on."

Adicia and Justine slowly start talking, though they're getting tired of having to tell this story over and over again. Emeline repeatedly drops her spoon in shock, and alternately reaches over and squeezes their hands. Several times she exclaims, "Sweet Lord Krishna!" Other times she mutters insult words in German.

"Do you think I'll find a husband that way?" she asks wistfully. "I'll just be minding my own business, and up pops a handsome guy who's got a lot of stuff in common with me? Sarah called it *beshert*, destiny, Fate. At my age, I've kinda started to think if it hasn't happened yet, it's never gonna happen. Maybe it's what God, Krishna, or whoever wants for me, and I'll appreciate him and any kids more 'cause I had to wait so long, but deep down it's a little depressing no guys ever noticed or wanted me in that way."

"You'll find a guy eventually," Lenore says. "Maybe he's so special you can only appreciate him after a long wait."

"I am kinda hard to find a really perfect match for. Not a lot of guys would be interested in someone my age who's completely inexperienced with men, who'd rather read, meditate, and talk philosophy, history, literature, languages, and religion than go to a party, drop acid, or go dancing and drinking. Maybe I'm too deep and serious for my own good."

"Oh, no, Emeline, you deserve a guy who loves you just the way you are," Adicia protests. "Never change anything about yourself. He's gotta be out there somewhere. If I could find Ricky, you can find your own intended. You might be a bit different from other people, but that makes you groovy. You always said you'd rather be one in a million, not one of a million."

Emeline turns to Adicia and Lenore. "I feel like such a baby next to you. Even you're not a real virgin anymore, Adicia. I'm missing out on this big secret, cut off from everyone else in the grownup world."

"Do you feel sad about this often?"

"It comes and goes. Sometimes it's more bearable than others. It'll pass in time, just like all things do given enough time. Even the Universe won't last forever, and I'll find a husband a lot sooner than the Universe will disintegrate."

"Can you help Adicia with learning how to be the mistress of her own house?" Lenore asks. "She and Justine have been getting along, but she's nervous about how she'll have to be the sole breadwinner and head of the household. She's never had to run a household before, as much as she was forced to grow up early for her age."

"It's not so hard when it's only one person, or two of you. I advise you to make mosta your food from scratch. It's healthier, and it saves money, even if it takes more time. It might seem easier, but it really adds up if you buy mostly TV dinners and overprocessed garbage like cereal with too much sugar. I even make my own granola."

"You make *everything* from scratch?" Justine asks.

"Well, not quite everything. I'm not ambitious enough to make my own cheese, yogurt, or ice-cream. And you have to remember to pay all your bills on time. When it's just you in charge, you can't forget about that, and you always hafta make sure there's enough money in the kitty to cover your expenses."

"Oh, I'm awful about that," Lenore admits. "If I could get away with it, I'd stash the envelopes away unopened, 'cause I don't wanna deal with paying bills and forking over our money. I'm kinda glad only Allen works, since that task always falls to him."

"Remember when we first visited the Monsterellis? I still remember the sight of all their clean dishes, pots, pans, and cups sitting in the drainboard and piled all over the stove. Even Mother was horrified, and told Gemma she had a leg up on those people 'cause she was raised to know better basic housekeeping. That looks bad when you have guests who aren't used to such slovenliness."

"I thought they hadn't been ready for company and needed more time to clean up," Adicia says. "That was awful. Even a poor or working-class homemaker takes pride in her home and appearance, and doesn't let dishes sit around and never put 'em away."

"We always put our dishes away after we dry 'em," Justine says. "We also never leave wet towels on the floor or bed, and we put our dirty clothes in the hamper sooner than later. We'll try to do our laundry on time. It's so cool to have a washing machine in our very own house 'steada lugging it all to a laundromat. We'll hafta use our dryer even though it's summer, 'cause we can't figure out how to hang a laundry line without it falling down or being blown over."

"We haven't been here long enough to do laundry, though I've half a mind to burn all our old hand-me-down rags and entirely replace our wardrobes."

"Do it," Emeline urges her. "Use the better ones for cleaning rags or stuff like pillow cases and doll clothes. Mosta your clothes aren't fit to donate to Goodwill or the Salvation Army."

"The dress I wore to my wedding is nice. I'm onea the few brides who can wear her wedding dress again and not look like a fool, since it's a normal dress. I wish I coulda worn a pretty dress with lace and a nicer fabric than cotton, though."

"I'd be more than happy to be your matron of honor if you decide to renew your vows in a real ceremony if Ricky comes home," Lenore says. "Allen could walk you down the aisle, if he comes around by then and realizes you're a grownup now, with your own mind, and that you've chosen your husband, for better or worse, for your own reasons."

"I hope the drill sergeant isn't too mean to him. He's too nice and sensitive to handle getting yelled at, abused, and made fun of by that kinda person. I've heard awful stories about drill sergeants."

"His birthday's only four days after yours," Emeline says. "You have the same Sun sign, Cancer, the crab, the moonchild. Cancer's the most sensitive sign of the zodiac, even more than the other water signs. Earth signs also tend to produce introspective, sensitive people. I'm an earth sign myself, so you probably think I'm patting myself on the back, but I'm just stating a well-known fact of basic astrology."

"I'm a Cancer too," Lenore says. "People born in late June have the sign too."

"What else would you like to know about being in charge of your own household? I must admit I'm terrible at budgeting, but you don't need a lesson in budgeting, since you've got so much dough in the bank. Ricky really is your Jasper, the way he appeared in your life and gave you a real rags to riches experience. Only I hope Ricky doesn't become an insufferably annoying prat who doesn't act like a grownup the way Jasper does in the later books."

"I hope he doesn't." Adicia looks at the floor again.

Emeline pats her arm. "This might not mean much to you, since you're agnostic, but I believe there's a Divine force ruling this world. It makes no sense for you to have come this far, survived so much, been given such a beautiful chance at a happy ending, and have everything destroyed. You'll be with your husband again before you know it. Good people are rewarded and bad people are punished, even if it takes a long time. I useta be like you, not entirely sure I believed in God, or what I believed about him or her, but learning about Krishna really helped me to get a stronger sense of faith. Lord Krishna says to his dear friend Arjuna, when he reveals his true identity at the height of *The Bhagavad Gita,* that he has many names and faces to many different people, but nonea them are wrong, so long as the person has a pure and devout heart and soul. If you wanna view God as science or Nature, that's groovy too. Krishna played many roles during the one hundred twenty-five years of his life, like sneaky little boy, warrior, protector of his village, lover, husband, son, father, dear friend, cowherd, guru. He's not a stern, old, bearded white guy sitting in the clouds and brandishing a scepter."

"I never asked Ricky what his religion was. It doesn't matter now. He's some sort of Protestant, I assume, maybe Episcopalian. I know he's not Catholic."

"How about cleaning the house?" Justine asks. "We never lived in a place this big, and our parents never even owned a cheap vacuum cleaner. They rarely did anything that resembled cleaning. You shoulda been there when they came back from Carlos's trial and broke up our nice Thanksgiving with the Doyles. The stench inside our tenement was awful. I don't think they'd drained the bathwater from the last time they'd been there six months before. It's a wonder we never attracted rats, mice, or roaches."

"Do you have a vacuum cleaner?" Emeline asks. "Or a mop, broom, dust mop, cleaning sponges, anything like that? I assume you've got a couple of garbage cans."

"We've got garbage cans and a toilet plunger and scrubber. I think that's about it," Adicia says. "I don't wanna scrub out a toilet or the bathtub, and it must take forever to vacuum and mop all the floors. I wasn't thinking of that when I picked the house. All I cared about was a real house with tons of space to run around in. We'll need a rake and a shovel too, when the seasons change."

"My landlord does maintenance, but you have to do your own raking and shoveling when you own your home. Raking leaves might not be so bad. Irene and Amelia can jump in the piles of leaves before you bundle 'em up as yard waste."

"I sorta expected Ricky to do the raking and snow shoveling. Those are jobs for a guy, not a girl. And I'm so petite. I don't know if I could handle those tasks. I wanted to sit inside warm and cozy, sipping hot cocoa, waiting for him to come in from the cold."

Lenore smiles at her. "The way you talk about this guy, the way you're acting, and the look in your eyes makes it seem like you miss him and care about him as more than just a close friend. I think you went and fell for him."

Adicia blushes. "I feel a magical connection to him since we slept together. That doesn't mean I'm in love with him. You don't fall in love overnight."

"You can admit it if you are," Emeline says. "There are a lot worse things in this world than a young bride being in love with her husband. Sometimes you realize you're in love with a person, but you were too oblivious to figure it out. There's a lovely line about that at the end of the Chekhov story 'Lady with Lapdog,' about how the truest love was there all along and the narrator hadn't realized it. The final lines talk about how a whole new life is just beginning, though the most complicated part still lies ahead. That'll be you a year from now, when they demob him and release him back to your loving arms. You'll get to begin your love, marriage, and lives all over again, a beautiful new life just starting."

"Why don't we go shopping for cleaning tools and new clothes next weekend?" Lenore suggests. "Not Saturday, since that's Allen's and my sixth anniversary, but Sunday we could go to one of the near-by shopping centers."

"I hope Ricky isn't treated too badly after they demob him, if he comes home," Adicia says, her voice shaking. "I've heard about how some guys were treated when they came home, whether they were drafted or chose the military. Some people spit on 'em, call 'em names, and physically attack them. I hope they give him a change of clothes and don't make him walk around in public in uniform."

"I hope this awful war ends soon," Justine says.

"Everything comes to an end, both good things and bad things," Emeline says. "And everything comes at the right time, not sooner or later. It talks about that in the title track of *All Things Must Pass*. Somea the lyrics reminded me of that High Holidays prayer Sarah told us about, the one where it talks about how everything is fleeting and that we're ultimately nothing more than the cloud that passes, dust in the wind, the dream that flies away. U'Netaneh Tokef, that was the name of the prayer." Emeline smiles. "And yes, I'm well aware that when I talk about stuff like this, it reminds me of why I don't have a fellow yet. Guys don't wanna ask out a woman, at least at this age, who's so serious and deep."

"Even if you don't have a fellow, you've got us," Adicia says. "Yeah, I'll go with you and Lenore next weekend to get new clothes and household equipment. We can make a stab at doing laundry when we come home."

"That doesn't sound very fun," Justine says.

"Grownup life isn't supposed to be all fun and games," Emeline says. "If you don't clean or do laundry, no one else will, and you'll live in a pigsty and go around naked."

***

The next Sunday, Lenore walks next door and gets behind the wheel of Adicia's car, adjusting the seat a little farther back and putting the safety belt lower down so her almost eight months pregnant body can be comfortably accommodated. Adicia slips the checkbook into the bag she bought at the fair, along with some cash and the interim State ID she was issued until the new one comes in the mail, probably around the same time she'll receive her new social security card. As she settles into the backseat with Justine, she takes out her pictures from the photo booth and bites her lower lip to keep from crying. They should've gone out to buy cleaning supplies together. Adicia also feels robbed of the chance to be the sweet little wifey Ricky wanted, since she'll have no choice but to do both male and female tasks—cooking, cleaning, taking out the trash, raking leaves, shoveling snow, plunging toilets, paying bills, avoiding solicitors, doing household repairs. Not wanting to make her workload even bigger, she shelves plans to replace the carpets or put up new wallpaper or paint.

"You wear that thing?" Emeline asks when she gets into the passenger seat. "They're kinda silly."

"Allen would hate it if I got into an accident and lost the baby or went into premature labor. They musta had a good reason for putting these safety belts in the newer cars. They're not just for decoration."

"You're carrying all your weight in the front," Emeline says. "You know what that means."

"Where else would Lenore carry the baby weight, out back?" Justine asks.

"No, I mean mosta her pregnancy weight's concentrated around the very front, not down low, up high, or evenly distributed. An old wives' tale says it's a boy if you carry all your weight in the front."

"We'll find out in September. It might be a third girl. There's nothing wrong with only having girls. Allen was having a tea party with Irene and Amelia when I left the house. I don't know if either of us would know what to do with a boy, since we only know how to parent little girls."

"I thought you wanted Allen to finally have his boy," Justine says.

"It'd be nice if he could have a child in his own image, but I won't knock myself out having more kids than we wanted if we don't get a boy on the third try."

"Lucine thinks she's having a girl," Emeline says. "She picked out the name Simone Juliette. A nice French name for a three-quarters French baby. Dad would probably be pleased if he knew she married a fellow French-American."

"That's pretty," Justine says. "Does she have a boy name?"

"They probably have a backup name stashed away, but they haven't shared it with me."

"Do you know what you'd name your kid, if Ricky comes home and you decide to make a little Carson to celebrate?" Lenore asks, hoping to make Adicia feel better.

"I like the idea of naming a baby after someone. If I weren't so mad at Allen for how he thinks Ricky's using me, I'd give a future son the middle name Allen. Now I'm not so sure he deserves a namesake."

"He's still the same old Allen he's always been. He's just being a typical, overprotective big brother. He'll come around eventually, because he loves his kid sister so much and wants you to be happy."

"I have more important stuff to worry about than picking out names for future kids, but what do you think about Robert? It was the name of the guy who was so nice to me when I washed his windshield. I never forgot how kind he was to me, when he was a millionaire and didn't hafta give any money to a ragged street kid looking like a pathetic little ragdoll."

"How about a girl?" Emeline asks.

"I'd probably wanna name my first daughter after Sarah, though most people would mispronounce it. It has an extra touch of sophistication the way our Sarah pronounced hers, with a long A."

"I think about her a lot too. She was the best substitute mother we ever had. Why couldn't things have been reversed so Sarah could've been our birth mother and our real mother a live-in servant?"

Lenore pulls into a shopping plaza twenty minutes later and steers them into a clothing store. Though it's just an ordinary shop, Adicia and Justine's eyes dance at all the new clothes. They can pitch their old rags and start wearing decent clothes from now on. These clothes have colors that are fresh and bright instead of faded, with the fabrics well-stitched instead of threadbare and with holes worn through. The big fashions are polyester, bell-bottoms, floor-length dresses with high necklines, miniskirts, peasant blouses and skirts, tie-dyed shirts, and frilly blouses. Adicia never dreamt she'd ever wear up-to-date clothes, and feels like buying out the entire store.

"How'd you like these shoes, Adicia?" Justine calls. "They've got really thick, high soles. You could jump up to at least five feet with 'em."

"We can't spend all of Ricky's money on clothes. We need to keep enough saved up for the resta this next year, and clothes aren't as vital as utility bills or food."

"How about picking a dozen outfits each?" Lenore suggests. "When it gets colder, you can get more clothes."

Adicia and Justine pull clothes off the racks until their arms are full. They hand the extras to Lenore and Emeline. Only five pieces of clothing each are allowed into the dressing room at one time, so Lenore and Emeline wait on the bench by the 360° mirror with the rest of the copious clothes. Adicia is very embarrassed and self-conscious when Lenore testily explains to impatient girls and women waiting in line that she's a newlywed who just lost her husband to the draft. The sympathetic looks and whispers are even worse than the glares and muttering.

"This is fun," Justine announces as she struts around in front of the mirror, wearing a midi-length red polyester skirt with little white roses and a ruffled mauve blouse. "It's like playing dress-up. I wish we could do this all day."

"Do you think I look like a man?" Adicia asks as she inspects herself in a pair of dark indigo bell-bottoms that look like Marjani's. "I've never worn pants before."

"Put on the shoes I found! You'll look at least five feet tall!"

Adicia slips on the red platform shoes and feels unsteady at first. They're not as wobbly as high heels, though, and she feels more powerful and superior with several inches added to her height.

"You've come a long way from the Lower East Side and Hell's Kitchen!" Lenore says. "Could you ever have dreamt you'd one day wear modern fashions or have enough money for it?"

"People still live in that neighborhood?" a woman in line asks. "I thought it was just a historic district when people still immigrated."

"It still exists," Adicia says. "It's not quite the same as it was fifty or a hundred years ago, but it's definitely still there."

"Why don't you pick out one really pretty dress to wear when Ricky comes home?" Emeline asks. "Make him fall for you all over again."

"Do you have a picture of your husband?" a girl in line asks.

Adicia reaches into her bag, trying not to fall, and pulls out the pictures from the photo booth and the wedding photos the van Niftriks sent in the mail. She feels like bursting out crying to see her cute husband looking so happy and in love, knowing he's about to be sent into the line of danger.

"He's a nice drink of water. That was just bestial what Nixon did, reinstating the draft. You oughta be modeling clothes for your new husband, not only for your sisters."

She nods, trying to keep her emotions under control.

"As fun as this is, we don't have unlimited time," Lenore reminds them. "You need to pick up cleaning equipment too, and stores close earlier on Sundays."

"What kind of equipment do you need?" an older woman asks.

"A vacuum cleaner, a mop, a broom, a dust mop, and sponges. They just moved into their new house not even a week before he was drafted, and didn't have time to pick up all the stuff they need to run a household. My sweet little sister-in-law has to be both the man and mistress of the house. It's just her and her baby sister."

"I bought my last vacuum at Sears. You can probably find the rest of those things there too. It's not right that a tiny little girl like that should have to shoulder so much burden. Her husband should be taking care of her while she does the easy woman's work like cooking and ironing."

"Thank you," Adicia says numbly.

She and Justine each purchase a dozen tops, ten dresses, ten skirts, ten pairs of socks, three pairs of shoes, including the platform shoes, and two pairs of pants. Adicia hardly believes she's buying pants, but they'll be better for housecleaning than a skirt or dress, and it couldn't hurt to blend in with other modern girls from time to time instead of only wearing skirts and dresses. Emeline also reassures her she's got blouses long enough to cover the crotch, and that the pants are relatively loose-fitting, not skintight.

"You're really a reborn woman!" Lenore tells her as they're walking to Sears. "The Miss Troy who wore hand-me-down rags is no more. You've taken your new identity as Mrs. Carson, a young lady who wears proper, stylish, first-run clothes. I bet you'll feel a lot more confident presiding over your new household when you look so much better. You'd be amazed at how much confidence you get when you look good and feel good about yourself in return."

***

On Adicia's three-week wedding anniversary, August second, Lenore comes over to help her and Justine with hanging up laundry. Irene and Amelia run around in the backyard while their mother and aunts hang up a clothesline and transport laundry baskets full of wet clothes out to the back veranda.

"Can I go inside while you do this?" Adicia begs.

"You won't learn how to hang a line properly if you go inside," Lenore says gently. "Do you feel well?"

"It was hard enough to have to see Ricky's clothes when I sorted them and put 'em in the washer. I don't wanna see 'em hanging on the line too."

"It's just this once. You'll never have to see his clothes again after they're dried. What kind of wife lets her husband's dirty clothes sit around unwashed?"

"You look at his artwork from the fair and the paintings and stuff he brought from home," Justine points out. "And I've seen you looking at his sketchpads and portfolios."

"He was right about being an amateur," Adicia admits. "But I could tell he enjoyed making all those drawings, paintings, and sketches. It's not like he pretended he was skilled or professional enough to be a real artist."

"Maybe he'll draw you when he comes home," Lenore says. "Why don't you show me what you know about hanging laundry. I'd help more if I weren't eight months pregnant."

Justine and Adicia get to work hanging up clothes, towels, and linens, using both clothespins and hangers. They hang them in the order they pull them out of the baskets, each starting at opposite ends of the line. When Adicia notices bedsheets dragging along the ground, she pins the drooping ends up so there's more space underneath. She vaguely remembers how Sarah used to double up their precious few, real bedsheets to minimize dragging, drooping, and falling over.

After they're finished, Adicia notices the middle sagging and tries to readjust the supporting poles with notches carved on the top. Before she knows it, the entire line is drooping, several things have fallen onto the ground along with the poles, and some of the clothes are leaning against a tree. She wants to scream and retreat inside.

"Ten-second rule," Justine says. "Just shake 'em out and brush 'em off. It's not like they fell into a mud puddle or a cat walked on top of 'em."

"You always put the lighter items on the ends, and put more of the heavier items in the middle," Lenore says. "You never want too much tension on the line in the same spots. It inevitably pulls everything down."

"What if we find bird droppings on the clothes when they're done drying?" Adicia asks.

"I'm not a stickler for that kinda cleanliness. Just flick it off and maybe rub extra soap and water on it. You should do your bedding once a week. A mattress pad should be done once every six months, and you should only wash really heavy, bulky things like blankets, quilts, curtains, and comforters once a year, unless they get really dirty, or you start having an allergic reaction and need to wash off the pollen or dust."

Allen comes into the yard pushing a wheelbarrow while Adicia and Justine are picking up the line and rearranging the clothes. Adicia turns away to try to avoid him.

"Have you come back to pour more salt on my wounds?"

"Hey, don't be like that. I came over to give you and Justine a present. Look, I got yous guys a birdfeeder you can hang in a tree, and a starter bag of birdseed. Wouldn't you like to watch birds coming and eating? I also made it so the squirrels won't get at it and steal the birds' food. Squirrels are greedy little bastards."

"That's supposed to make up for putting down my husband, and talking to me like I'm stupid and just thinking with my emotions?"

"Look, I'm not gonna pretend I like him or that I approve of this hasty non-love marriage, but maybe I was a little harsh on you. That was the last thing I expected, that you'd be my new next door neighbor and married to that rich guy I warned you about. Whatever his intentions towards you, and however you feel about him, it's gotta be tough to be drafted. As much as I dislike him, I don't envy the guy. Not all rich boys can get outta being drafted. The last thing I'd wanna do is to make my kid sister cry and make you feel like I hate you."

"So you're gonna leave Adicia alone and not say a word to Ricky if he comes home?" Lenore asks.

"If it keeps the peace between us, I'll bite my tongue as best I can. When you're from a poor and working-class community, you don't have much, but you do have your family. I don't wanna alienate any of my sisters, since it's just us. I won't pretend I like him or your marriage, but I'll hold in my opinion so I don't upset you or make you cry again during what must be a very trying time. I thought about what Lenore said you suggested, and I'll accept some of your Warrick's money to buy a building and bakery equipment. We can call it Treats by the

Troys, and you can work with us if you'd like. I'd cut you a fair deal, but I won't pay you extra just 'cause you're family. What's that fancy word for favoritism when a relative or friend works for you? I think it starts with an N."

"Nepotism," Adicia says.

"Yeah, nepotism. You'd be on our payroll and would get a salary that corresponds with how many hours and days you work, and what kinda tasks you do. It's not like you need to worry about money, since Warrick left you so much, but you don't wanna make a habit of living off only savings. You can't sit at home all day keeping house when Justine's in school. At least Lenore has going on three kids to take care of, and she's not the sole support of the house."

"How about driving lessons, so I can drive myself to work?"

"Of course. Maybe we can go to a gardening store some weekend and look for a birdbath, a hose, and other stuff for the yard. You bought such a nice big house; you might as well enjoy it and make it look as nice as you can."

"But I'm still gonna know you hate Ricky and think I was a fool for marrying him, even if you don't say that out loud."

"I don't know the guy. I only met him the once, and I've never seen yous guys together. Maybe he really is the real deal, maybe he isn't. I can't know that. But whatever I think of him, you'll always be welcome in this family. Us Troys hafta stick together after what we went through. I was chosen to have five kid sisters for whatever reason, and I have to do the brotherly thing and look out for you. I never said I might not change my mind. I don't think I ever could change my mind about this fellow, but stranger things have happened."

"You'd better mean this. I don't want my own brother making this separation more difficult than it already is."

Allen holds out his arms. "Are we friends again? Please?"

Adicia accepts his hug. "You'd better go back to being the same great big brother you've always been, and not just be saying this 'cause you felt guilty."

"My family's the most important thing in the world to me. I'm not gonna throw that away for such a stupid reason. Make no mistake, this does not mean I accept this situation, but complaining about it won't take back what's already done."

"That's a better start than nothing."

"Look, however you got here, and however I feel about your marriage, what's done is done. The most important thing is we're all together again, and in a much better place. We can have family meals, daytrips, and real celebrations of Halloween, Thanksgiving, Christmas, and Easter. How does that sound?"

"I'd do anything to have real holiday celebrations!"

"So this means you're my pal again?"

Adicia looks up at him and gives him one of the few smiles she's had since Ricky went away. "You're the world's best big brother. I'm glad you wanna be my friend too. Yes, I'll forgive you."

"Aunt Adicia's the mistress of the house," Irene says. "If she didn't like you anymore, she could throw you off her property."

"I still can't get used to being the sole mistress of a house. I don't look the part at all, and I have no experience."

"It's just as unlikely you married a rich guy who gave up his family for you, but that happened too," Lenore says. "Nothing ever happens without due cause. Remember that Voltaire line Emeline likes to quote all the time?"

"'All events are linked together in this best of all possible worlds.' Only time will tell just why these particular events were chosen to happen for me and what I'll do with them."

"This looks like a big school." Irene scampers out of the car while holding Amelia's hand. "I hope I don't get lost."

"That's why they're giving us a tour first, so you're not totally surprised and confused when you start school next week," Lenore says. "You'll get to meet the other kids in your class too."

"Kindergarten only lasts half a day," Adicia says. "It won't be too bad if you're only there in the afternoon. You still get to spend your mornings with your mommy and sister."

Allen is negotiating the sale of a building, so it fell to Lenore to register Irene for school and take her to the orientation. Adicia and Justine wanted to go with her to have a chance to get out of the house. On the drive over, Adicia looked through all the postcards and letters from Ricky, wishing she were there with him. Since he arrived, he's been writing every day, telling her as much as he's allowed to, thanking her for the M&M and chocolate chip brownies she sends every week, looking forward to coming home and starting their marriage all over again, describing the other guys in the camp, and telling her over and over how much he loves her. Adicia hasn't been able to bring herself to sign any of her letters "Love." She signs "Regards," "I miss you," "Truly yours," or "I can't wait to see you again."

"Can I bring my new baby brother or sister in for show and tell when it's born?" Irene asks as they walk into the building.

"Maybe your teacher will let me bring the baby in and introduce it to the other kids." Lenore smiles down at her. "You can wait in the hallway while I register."

Adicia and Justine stand against a wall and watch the other incoming kindergarteners filing in, some with siblings, most only with their mothers. Irene watches the other children warily, deciding which ones look like they'd be good friends and which ones she might not like so much. One of the boys looks like a Little Lord Fauntleroy, and several of the girls have overly frilly dresses and patent leather Mary Janes. Adicia, Justine, and Irene think they look like spoilt brats, and that the boy in particular is probably another Tommy in the making.

A little brunette comes out of the office with her mother and a slightly older brother, and looks at Irene shyly. After she hesitates to go forward to talk to any of the other children, her mother bends down and says something to her in a foreign language. Based on the guttural noises and a familiar word here and there, Adicia thinks she must be speaking German. The little girl's mother looks to be in her upper forties, which surprises Adicia, Justine, and their nieces. They're not used to seeing women of that age as mothers of such young children, unless she's like Mrs. Troy and had a whole slew of kids almost nonstop over many years.

Lenore rejoins them, and is also taken aback by how much older this woman is than a typical mother of a kindergartener. Her eyes catch on something on the woman's left forearm, and she stares at it to try to figure out what it is. Lenore looks away in embarrassment once she realizes it's a concentration camp tattoo. This woman probably doesn't appreciate strangers staring at it.

Adicia almost stops breathing when she catches sight of the woman. She turns to Justine and whispers as people continue to gather in the hall. "I almost don't wanna say this out loud, but that woman looks like our Sarah. I'd remember her anywhere."

"You must be seeing things," Justine whispers back. "What would she be doing here? She lives on the Upper West Side. I'd never wanna leave the city if I lived in such a nice neighborhood. I don't even think they have a synagogue in Hudson Falls."

Lenore looks at Adicia in concern when she starts to cry and eases herself into a sitting position. "Sweetie, are you alright? Are you sick, or missing Ricky again?"

"That woman," Adicia whispers. "She looks just like my old nanny. I'm almost a hundred percent sure it's her."

"What in the world would she be doing here? Please don't take any offense, but I think you're so emotional you're imagining things. Sometimes what we think is the truth isn't always the truth, no matter how much we want it."

"The tour's gonna start soon," Justine says. "Do you wanna wait in the car or on a bench? You don't want any of these people to think you're a nutcase 'cause you're crying in public for no reason."

"Didn't Penelope recognize Ulysses after twenty years apart?" Adicia sobs. "I'm telling you, I'm almost a hundred percent sure that's her."

Amelia crawls onto her aunt's lap and makes funny faces at her, trying to cheer her up.

"Pardon me, but can I help you? Do you need fresh air?"

Lenore looks at the older woman, averting her eyes from the tattoo. "My sister-in-law's newlywed husband was ripped away from her last month. He's going to Vietnam in a day or two, after he finishes boot camp. The poor young man was drafted only a week into their marriage."

Adicia stares up at her, sobbing hysterically, uncaring people are staring at her. "Is your name Sarah Katz, are you from Baden-Baden, Germany, and did you spend your first fifteen years in America on the Lower East Side?" she asks in a voice barely above a whisper.

The woman looks at her in amazement. "Have we met?"

"My sister-in-law's name is Adicia Troy," Lenore says, seeing Adicia can't even talk at this point. "The blonde is her baby sister Justine."

Everyone turns and stares as the woman screams, "*Gott in himmel, my babies have finally been returned to me!*" and pulls Adicia up into her arms. Adicia's chest heaves as she feels her surrogate mother's loving arms around her for the first time in ten years. Justine reaches around and hugs her from the side.

"I'll be your *mutter* again, no matter how old you are. I never, ever forgot my dear *kinder* or stopped considering you my babies."

The boy and girl gape, not quite sure what to make of this.

"Are you the family my *mutti* used to be a nanny for?" the boy asks.

"I guess they are," Lenore says, dumbfounded. "You must be Fritz, and your sister must be Nessa."

Sarah stares at Lenore, just as dumbfounded. "How did you know my children's names?"

"Yous guys had the same midwife, Veronica Zoravkov," Justine says. "She brought over a photo album of her past clients, and me, Adicia, and Ernestine recognized your picture and the tattoo on your arm. Veronica said you named your first baby Fritz, and we saw Nessa's birth announcement in the paper. It's groovy you combined your and your husband's last names into a new name for your kids."

"You used a *midwife?*" one of the nearby mothers asks. "I couldn't help overhearing. I thought only primitive women still used them."

"My daughters and Sarah's children were born at home," Lenore says. "This third baby's also gonna enter the world the way Nature intended. Do you have a problem with that?"

"You didn't use a hospital and all the drugs they could give you?" another woman asks. "That's crazy."

"Well, now we know which girls in the class to tell our children to avoid," a third woman says haughtily. "I hate hippies."

"We're not hippies," Lenore calls as the tour starts down the hall without them. "You oughta meet my sister-in-law Emeline if you wanna meet a real hippie."

"Damn hippies," one of the older siblings says in disgust.

"When is your birthday?" Sarah asks Irene. "My Nessa was born June seventh of 1967, during the Six-Day War."

"I was born June sixth of that year. I have my daddy's birthday. He was born on something called D-Day, and I was born on the twenty-third anniversary. My name's Irene."

Sarah smiles at Lenore. "You must be Allen's wife. I suppose he finally got off drugs and stopped drinking, if he's got a respectable wife and family."

"He sure did. My name is Lenore."

"I was born on a special day too," Nessa announces proudly. "I was born the day the Israeli army recaptured the Western Wall and reunited the holy city of Jerusalem. That's why my parents named me Nessa, since it means 'miracle' in Hebrew. My middle name Tzipora is after my *mutti*'s *mutti*."

"What are you doing here?" Adicia finally manages to ask, still holding onto Sarah. "How could you leave a nice neighborhood like the Upper West Side for Hudson Falls of all places? Did you find out Lucine and Emeline live here too? I can't imagine there's a big Jewish community here. It's probably the opposite of Manhattan."

"We drive to a Reform temple in Glens Falls, Beth El. After the big city, I wanted a peaceful, small town. My husband was offered a job in Glens Falls, but we liked the smaller town atmosphere of Hudson Falls more. Didn't I tell you when people are meant to be together, they find a way back to each other, no matter how long it takes?"

"Will you be our substitute mother again? Lenore's been a swell mother figure, but you were always the first, best substitute mother."

"You and your sisters were my babies before I had blood *kinder*." Sarah squeezes her hands. "I'll take care of you like my own flesh and blood. Looks like I'll get to be a substitute grandma too. What's the younger girl's name?"

"I'm Amelia. I'm almost three."

"Her birthday's October eighteenth," Lenore says.

"How come you have numbers written on your arm?" Irene asks.

"Bad guys hurt my *mutti* when she was a teenager," Nessa says. "That number was her name when the bad guys had her in a really bad prison, before she lived in America."

"You have more surrogate grandchildren on the way," Lenore says. "Lucine's due for her first in October, and Gemma's expecting in March."

"Gemma's pregnant?" Justine asks excitedly. "We never knew about that!"

"She just found out. Isn't it swell there are gonna be three cousins born so close together?"

"Is there another tour today?" Justine asks. "We can always catch up later, but we probably can't wait for another tour."

"Can I go to school at home?" Irene asks. "I don't care what the other kids think of me, but I don't want them being mean to me and saying bad stuff about you and Daddy because yous guys do a bunch of stuff like hippies."

Lenore wags her finger good-naturedly. "You, Amelia, and the new baby will all go through proper public schools. I'm not a qualified teacher. Nessa will be your friend. Yous guys can stick together even if all the other kids think you're strange."

"Deirdre and David never went to school, and Deirdre got into a nice college. David's starting college in the fall too."

"They also didn't have birth certificates, social security cards, parents, or a registered address." Lenore turns back to Sarah. "Are you free to come to supper at Adicia's house tonight so we can catch up in private? She and Justine live next door to me and Allen, in one of the strangest coincidences of all time."

Sarah looks down at Fritz and Nessa. "Want to have a special supper at Adicia and Justine's house tonight?"

"What can you cook?" Fritz asks. "And should I call you *Tante* Adicia or think of you more as a big sister?"

"Let's stay on a first-name basis," Adicia says. "I'll cook something special. How do Reform Jews observe kosher again?"

"I don't eat shellfish or pig meat, or mix milk and meat, *mit* a waiting period of three hours between meat and dairy," Sarah says. "Meat from a kosher butcher is optional, and I don't use two sets of dishes."

"Emeline's a vegetarian," Lenore says. "Maybe you should try something she'll be able to eat instead of making her get by on side dishes."

"How does seven sound?" Adicia asks. "I can make peppers stuffed with rice and smaller vegetables, mushrooms stuffed with crushed walnuts and breading, salmon, and a soup with that new-fangled tofu stuff Emeline likes so much. I bought some in case she ever comes over to eat."

"That sounds *wunderbar*. Tell me your address, and we'll be there at seven."

The tour comes back down the hall, almost everyone giving them dirty looks and whispering.

"Would you like your tour now?" the kindergarten teacher asks. "It looks like you hadn't seen each other in a long time, to say the least, so I supposed you wanted time to start catching up."

"Sarah was the nanny of my husband and his sisters a long time ago," Lenore says. "They hadn't seen each other in a good ten years."

"By the way, don't pay any attention to what those other mothers and children said. You might seem unconventional to them, but it's the norm in other parts of the world. Some people are more resistant to change than others. Sometimes it seems like some people slept through the last decade if they still hold on to rigid ideas from a generation or two ago." She leans down to the children. "My name is Ms. Sigurdsson, and you've been assigned to my kindergarten class."

"That's a cool name," Irene says.

"It's Icelandic. Have you ever met a person of Icelandic ancestry before?"

"You're the first," Nessa says.

"I'm Mrs. Troy, and these are my girls Irene and Amelia," Lenore says. "Irene's starting school next month. These are my sisters-in-law Adicia and Justine. Adicia became Mrs. Carson last month."

"And then they took him away from me a week later," Adicia says lifelessly. "Am I being punished because I didn't love him at first, and only realized I loved him after he went away?"

"Her husband's being sent to Vietnam very soon," Lenore whispers to Ms. Sigurdsson. "Only a week into their marriage, he was drafted. At least he had enough money in the bank to take care of her for some time to come, in case the worst happens."

Ms. Sigurdsson pats Adicia on the shoulder. "What a pity. You don't look all that much younger than I am. I'm only twenty-five. Let's all hope your husband is delivered back to you safe and sound when the military's done with him."

"Do you have any pictures of him on you?" Sarah asks. "I'd love to see the guy my sweet little Adicia chose for a husband."

Adicia pulls the envelope of pictures out of her bag and shows Sarah the wedding pictures, the pictures from the photo booth, and a picture Ricky sent her from camp, where he's wearing fatigues and looking very unhappy.

"Very handsome. You'll make beautiful babies together someday."

Adicia blushes.

"Who knows, maybe they already did," Justine teases. "They didn't use birth control when they were intimate the night before he left."

"Justine!" Adicia chides. "You should be old enough to know you don't share such personal information in public!"

"Oh, it's okay, I understand being young," Ms. Sigurdsson says. "I'm not like those people who just finished the first tour." She turns to Sarah. "I'm sorry, I didn't catch your name."

"I'm Ms. Sarah Katz, and these are my children Fritz and Nessa Rosenkatz. One last name, no hyphens. My husband and I combined our names."

Irene and Nessa smile at one another and hold hands as they proceed up the hall. Lenore, Adicia, and Justine hope this is the beginning of a beautiful friendship.

***

Over supper that evening, Sarah, Lucine, Allen, Emeline, Adicia, and Justine catch up on the past ten years, with Lenore, Zachary, and Sarah's husband Henry Rosen periodically chiming in. Irene, Amelia, Fritz, and Nessa are set up around the coffeetable in the living room, and are thrilled Adicia let them drink grape juice in spite of the off-white carpeting. Emeline has brought George, and the kitten explores his new surroundings and lets the children pet him and play with him. He also comes over to Adicia a few times and sits on her lap purring. Emeline tells her animals are very sensitive and can tell when someone's sick, hurt, or in emotional pain, and that they'll do what they can to comfort that distressed person.

Sarah tells the Troys she received her GED in 1963, got her bachelor's degree in childhood education from the School of Education at the City College of New York in 1967, and got her master's degree in the same field in 1970. She met Henry, a fellow German survivor, at a function for non-traditional students in 1964. Henry was a senior at the Grove School of Engineering. They were married within a year, and Fritz was born a year later. Sarah now teaches in a nearby alternative school, where kindergarten through sixth grade cycles in and out of her history classroom throughout the day. Her children aren't in her school, since everyone thought it'd be awkward for them to have their mother for a teacher.

"We're finally back together, the way we belong," Justine says. "I doubt our mother will come up here or find out where we live. No one's gonna ruin our happiness."

"Do you wanna see Gemma again?" Lucine asks. "She's so much more mature and sisterly these days. Our relationship's a good sight friendlier than it was in the past."

"Of course," Sarah says. "I never thought she was beyond redemption just because she was so aloof and spoilt. When will I see Ernestine again?"

"She usually comes up on holidays," Lucine says. "Maybe we can have a big Thanksgiving celebration."

"Ernestine's studying anthropology, Deirdre's studying political science, and their friend Betsy's studying philosophy," Emeline says. "David's going to a two-year school next month. He's studying history, government, and economics. Fiona's going into her sophomore year, and Aoife will be in eighth grade."

"They grew up so fast, didn't they?" Allen asks.

"I'm proud of you, Allen," Sarah says. "I always knew you'd do the right thing and go straight for your sisters. I'm glad to see you're a good husband and *vater*."

"I don't even drink alcohol anymore. Not even socially. At most I have champagne on New Year's Eve, or grape juice. I can't be too careful."

"Even cigarettes he gave up," Adicia says proudly. "I always thought they smelled disgusting, and never got why so many people thought it looked so glamorous."

"Seven out of nine kids getting above their raising isn't bad," Sarah says. "I always knew you were special and wouldn't just accept a fate of poverty and ignorance like your parents."

"Tommy might get above his raising too," Justine says. "He wants to go to college. Very slowly, he's starting to grow up a little. Then it'd be eight outta nine who escaped that cesspool."

"Things still won't be perfect till I get my husband back." Adicia pets George on the head. "I wouldn't be here, reunited with everyone, if it weren't for him."

"He'll come home to you," Sarah promises. "You never expected to see me again, and I turned up right next to you. Good people are always rewarded, and bad people are always punished, no matter how long it takes, and when people are meant to be together, they find their way back to each other the same way they found their way to each other in the first place."

Allen leads Emeline upstairs at 2:00 in the morning on September fifth. "I'm sorry to wake you up and drag you over here at this hour, but Lenore really wanted you to be her labor coach again, and she seems to be going really fast this time."

"How long has she been in labor?"

"She woke up at midnight and felt active labor starting. We thought we'd wait it out and not call the midwife at this ungodly hour, but she feels herself progressing faster than the last two times. I've never given birth, so I take her word for it."

Emeline sets George on the bedroom floor with her nieces and younger sisters, who are determined to stay awake to witness this event. Lenore smiles at Emeline from her position on the bed, propped up among pillows, a plastic sheet underneath her.

"Are you scared something might go wrong and you'll need to go to a hospital?" Justine asks. "This time there isn't a midwife."

"If I could birth ten-pound Irene without any drugs, stitches, or surgery, with back labor the entire time, don't you think I can handle my last labor on my own?" Lenore asks.

"Lucine said she admires what you do, but she doesn't have the guts to do it herself," Adicia says. "I don't know if I could do it either if I ever had a kid. I'm so petite, I might need to have a baby cut out of me."

"Don't you worry about that. Height has nothing to do with pelvic shape and size."

"You want some music?" Emeline asks. "I brought over records again. *All Directions*, by The Temptations; *Music of My Mind*, by Stevie Wonder; *Harvest*, by Neil Young; *Come from the Shadows*, by Joan Baez; and *Long John Silver*, by Jefferson Airplane."

"You're as much of a folkie as Deirdre," Adicia says. "Only you're some kinda mishmash, a hippie-folkie."

"Nothing wrong with that." Emeline puts *Harvest* onto the turntable and takes a seat beside Lenore. "Are you keeping track of how long your contractions are and how far apart they are?"

"They're about a minute each, around three minutes apart. This time it hurts even less than when I had Amelia, but it's going a lot faster than either time before. I won't be surprised if we're holding a baby before dawn breaks."

Emeline rubs her back. "Are you sure you don't want anyone to call the midwife? If she took up that line of work by choice, she should expect to get calls at inconvenient hours and won't mind driving up here. Is this one a former nurse like Mrs. Zoravkov?"

"She retired from nursing in '65 to switch to home-based deliveries," Allen says as Lenore breathes through a contraction. "Like Veronica, she got tired of seeing laboring women doped full of drugs automatically, and couldn't do anything about it since she was only a nurse. Her name's Radana Zupan. She's Slovenian-American."

"What's a Slovenian?" Justine asks. "Is that a tribe of Indian?"

"It's a group of people in Yugoslavia. They haven't had their own independent country in a long time."

"Do you think she's gonna be mad if you call her up after the fact?" Adicia asks. "At the very least, she might be mad she can't collect her money."

"I think she'll understand if the baby came so fast there wasn't time to call her," Allen says. "We should still call her so she can check to make sure the kid's alright, and to see if Lenore needs any stitches or anything."

"You won't get arrested for doing this at home, will you?" Emeline asks.

"Regardless of whether this might be legal or illegal here, most people believe the lie that it was too late to get to the hospital."

Over the course of the next three hours, Lenore walks and crawls around, rocks back and forth, and makes various vocalizations. Emeline thinks once again of Goldmund's revelation that a woman in labor strongly resembles a woman in ecstasy. She alternately wonders if Allen is thinking the same thing as he watches his wife, and if she herself will ever know what either feels like, at the rate she's going. Allen finally decides it might be a good idea to call Radana when Lenore returns to the bed at 5:00 and gets on her hands and knees to start pushing. If Radana hurries, she might be there by 6:00 and get to inspect the baby to make sure it's healthy, whether or not she arrives before the birth.

"Who wants to catch it this time?" Lenore asks in between pushes. "It's coming out of me, whether she's here to oversee it or not."

Allen hangs up the phone. "Are you sure it's coming out that fast? You pushed much longer before."

"Don't question her," Emeline says. "It's her body, and she knows what's going on with it after she's done this twice before."

"But that'd only make it a five-hour labor! Is that even possible?"

"You're choosing *now* to disagree I'm going really fast?" Lenore demands. "Are you catching it or not?"

Allen hurries over to her as she turns around, and freezes when he sees the head coming out. Hoping he remembers how to catch babies, he reaches down to support the head. Allen gently tugs on the head to free the shoulders. Lenore gives one more push to bring the rest of the baby into the world, and then their third child is lying in Allen's arms.

"Allen, you're crying more than the baby!" Emeline says. "Is everything okay?"

"Say something!" Lenore says. "Is our baby okay?"

Allen finally looks over at Lenore, tears still streaming down his face. "Boy, oh boy, we finally got a boy!"

Lenore turns around and lies back down among her nest of pillows as Allen reluctantly hands the baby over to her. He keeps holding onto one of the baby's tiny hands as Lenore slowly examines him to make sure he's got the right amount of fingers and toes and to see what all his unique little features are. Allen continues sobbing like a baby as Lenore starts to nurse their newborn.

"Someone really wanted a boy, didn't he?" Lenore teases him. "I'm glad I was able to oblige you with our last child."

"Do I get to name this one? You promised I'd get to name a boy, and you've named both of the girls. Can I please get a turn now and name my boy?"

Irene and Amelia climb onto the bed and peer into their new brother's face. Adicia and Justine sit on the other end of the bed with Emeline and look at him from a slight distance, not wanting to get too close to Allen, Lenore, and their children during these first personal moments.

"You don't love him more than you love us, do you, Daddy?" Irene asks.

"I love my two little princesses as much as I love my perfect baby boy. Now our family is complete. Three kids, two girls and a boy. Good work, Lenore. You sure found the fastest method of having babies."

"I still have to deliver the placenta. Emeline, can you get a basin, twine, and sterilized scissors?"

Irene and Amelia stare nervously at the placenta that comes out into the basin five minutes later. Emeline ties the twine around the umbilical cord shortly after it stops pulsating, handing the scissors to Allen. His hands shaking, he begins to cut, thankful he went to the bother of taking apart all their scissors to make them left-handed.

"What's his name?" Adicia asks.

"Oliver Leo Troy," Allen announces proudly. "Do you approve of it?"

"Yes, I like it very much," Lenore says.

"Can we call him Ollie for short?" Emeline asks. "I always thought that was a really cute nickname, but maybe I'm biased 'cause I love Laurel and Hardy."

"Barely anyone in this family has a nickname," Allen says, still gazing at the baby. "I never saw the reason for giving a perfectly fine name and then only ever using a shortened form, unless it's too grownup for a little kid, like Joseph or Robert."

"Deirdre might never speak to yous again after she finds out you named him Oliver," Adicia teases. "Oliver Cromwell was a real bastard to the Irish."

"I think she'll know he wasn't named after Cromwell," Lenore says.

"Boy, I'm almost sorry I'm gonna start working soon. I won't be able to help you take care of him during the day."

"You'll still see him every day. We only live next door. I'm sure I'll need plenty of assistance in the evenings and on weekends."

"How about a nice family picture?" Emeline asks.

Allen rushes up to the attic to get a camera with a controlled flash and a tripod. As he's setting it up in the bedroom and darting back into the picture, Emeline holding George on her lap so he won't make any sudden movements to produce a blurry picture, the midwife comes into the house. She stops in her tracks when she sees the baby has already been born.

"He seems fine," Emeline says. "Everything was very smooth and quick. My brother took it worse than Lenore, particularly after he saw it was a boy."

"You're not mad at us, are you?" Justine asks.

"These things happen," Radana says, trying to regain her composure. "Since I'm already here, I might as well check to make sure nothing's wrong."

"His name is Oliver, Oliver Leo Troy," Allen tells her proudly, looking as happy as a cat basking in the sun. "I finally got my boy. There's gonna be another generation of Troys."

After Radana finishes checking Lenore and Oliver, she goes into the kitchen to make breakfast for Lenore. Adicia and Justine follow her, pointing out where everything is and what's available to eat. As they're instructing her, she turns and stares at Adicia in the breaking morning light coming through the windows.

"I didn't get a good look at you upstairs, since most of the light was blocked out. It looks like I might be taking you on as a client too, not just your sister-in-law. When are you due?"

"What?" Adicia asks in shock. "I'm not pregnant! What would make you think that?"

"Your skin. It's called a pregnancy glow. Some people think it's an old wives' tale, but there really is a noticeable glow and blush in the skin of many pregnant women. I've seen it too many times to not notice it when it's right in front of me."

"I didn't use any birth control the one time I slept with my husband, but it's impossible for me to be pregnant!" Adicia hopes Allen can't hear any of this conversation from upstairs, since she doesn't know if his truce with her would end if he suspected she could be pregnant and really did consummate her marriage.

"When was that?"

"It was during the wee hours of July twentieth. I wish I could forget the exact date they took him away from me. They shipped him out to the bloodbath in Vietnam a couple of days ago, and I don't know if I can handle it."

Radana goes over to the calendar and removes the tack affixing it to the wall, flipping back to July. "July twentieth was a Thursday. The last day of August was also a Thursday, and there were six weeks between the two dates. Today's September fifth, Tuesday, only a few days away from seven weeks. My dear child, if I'm not seeing things and you truly are expecting, you'd be almost two months along."

"How could that be possible? I have no symptoms I'm aware of. I don't suspect anything. If you tell any of this to my brother, he'll be very upset. He hates my husband and thinks I never shoulda married him, 'cause we're from different classes."

"When was the date of your last menstrual period, my dear?"

"Sometime in July. I never kept a calendar. I was a very late bloomer and only had my first this January. It's normal to not have it regularly when you first start, and when you're under so much stress, it's also normal to not be so regular."

"Not since *July*?" Justine asks. "You never told that to any of us!"

"Was this before or after your husband left?" Radana asks.

"Before, but that doesn't mean anything," Adicia says.

"You're right that it's normal to be irregular for up to the first five years after menarche and that being under a lot of stress can cause even the healthiest woman to skip. And so far you've only skipped one. Tell you what, if you still haven't menstruated by the end of this month, give me a call, and I'll drive up to check you."

"My brother lives right next door! Even if I believed I were pregnant, he'd wonder what your car's doing at my house! I'm still getting driving lessons and haven't taken my road test, so I couldn't drive myself. Plus I don't know if it's a good idea for a brand new driver to drive that far alone."

"It would not be good if it were true," Justine says. "Adicia doesn't deserve to go through an entire pregnancy and birth all by herself, and no kid deserves to come into the world a potential half-orphan."

"If I were, do you think I'd need a Caesarean?" Adicia whispers. "My husband thought I would if we ever had a kid, since I'm so short and petite."

"A few hundred years ago, many women were under five feet tall, and they all got through natural childbirth without risky, unnecessary surgery," Radana says. "I only transfer my patients for a Caesarean if there's a legit medical emergency, not something so silly as height or build. Caesareans exist to save the lives of mothers and babies, not for convenience or imagined fears with no bearing in medical reality."

"What's taking so long?" Allen calls downstairs. "Lenore's hungry!"

"We'll just be another few minutes. Your sisters were curious about midwifery, and I was answering their questions."

Adicia shrugs off Radana's concerns as best she can as they resume making breakfast. Most women have some sort of symptoms if they're almost two months along, and she's had none. Glowing skin doesn't mean anything, just like a woman with a very large girth isn't necessarily pregnant either.

***

Adicia's first day at the bakery is September seventh, Thursday, the day Justine is picked up by the school bus for her first day of eighth grade. After Allen finishes fussing all over Lenore and Oliver, he picks Adicia up and drives to the new family business twenty minutes away.

"I feel kinda carsick," she says as they pull up to their first stop sign.

"I wish I had peppermints or ginger candy to soothe your stomach. Do you usually get carsick?"

"I haven't ridden in cars enough to know. I've been riding in cars a lot more often lately, but I don't recall feeling particularly queasy before."

"Don't worry, we'll arrive at work soon enough, and you can get fresh air and settle your stomach. Why don't you roll your window down in the meantime?"

Adicia rolls down her window, but is still nauseous. When Allen looks over at her five blocks away from work, her skin has turned gray, and she's clutching her stomach and moving her mouth strangely. Afraid she might ruin his new car, he quickly pulls into a dead-end side street and stops the car.

Adicia pushes open the door, glad she didn't put on the safety belt and can make a fast escape, and rushes towards the nearest garbage can. She's unable to make it there in time, and drops onto her knees, vomiting all over the sidewalk and onto the road. Adicia is mortified her big brother has to see this.

"Was it something you ate for breakfast?"

"I don't know. Maybe I caught a stomach bug from bad water."

"Do you still feel like you've gotta throw up?"

"I'd like a little fresh air before we get back in the car. I don't think I'm so sick I'll have to go back home."

Adicia is even more mortified when several other people walk by as Allen is helping to pull her back up. She immediately turns around and tries to walk up the street with him, pretending she didn't see them.

"Do you need help?"

"My sister got carsick on our way to work. We're gonna walk around for a little bit so she can get fresh air, and then we're getting back in the car."

"Where do you work? If it's close by, it might be better to walk the rest of the way and leave your car here for the time being."

"We're five blocks away. We just opened a new bakery, Treats by the Troys. My wife's gonna work for the bakery too, baking stuff from home and sending it in. She just had our third child on Tuesday morning. I finally got my boy."

One of the women reaches into her purse. "Would you like peppermints, Miss Troy? That's always good for settling an upset stomach."

"That's awfully nice of you. Would you like mints, Adicia?"

"Sure. By the way, I'm not a Troy anymore. I'm Mrs. Carson. Troy was my single name." Adicia fights back the urge to burst out crying in public.

"Are you going to be sick again, Mrs. Carson?" the man in the group asks, seeing her face. "My wife and I were on our way to work with my wife's two friends, but we just live a few houses down. If you'd like, you can come in and sit down till you recover your stomach."

"No, I'm fine. I just miss my husband."

"She got married in July," Allen explains, trying his best to suppress his feelings of dislike towards Ricky. "Her husband was drafted a week into their marriage, and he left for Vietnam last week."

"You poor child," one of the women says. "A frail little girl like you shouldn't be forced to go through something like that."

Adicia nods numbly, very annoyed at how many people immediately cast her into the role of a sympathy case when they hear about what happened to Ricky. She has an identity beyond that of a newlywed wife of a draftee, and she's not so frail if she survived her first eighteen years. She resents only being seen as someone's wife and a frail little woman who looks more like a girl than a woman. Maybe this is why all those radical feminists who are always in the news lately are so angry, since they're tired of being seen as just women, not multifaceted people with their own interests, strengths, and abilities. Not wanting to get a bad reputation with the new neighbors, though, she just smiles and keeps sweet.

Sucking on a peppermint, Adicia gets back into the car with Allen, still humiliated at throwing up in public and being made into a sympathy case for the umpteenth time. She sits silently stewing as Allen drives the remaining five blocks, and only gives polite, cursory greetings to the employees starting to arrive in the parking lot.

Allen unlocks the building and they follow him inside, where he gives schedules and a list of orders and expectations. Adicia has been assigned to alternately work the counter and bake cookies, brownies, and cakes with Allen and several other employees. At least in the kitchen, she won't have to deal with so many strangers and have to smile and pretend to be happy when her heart is breaking, she thinks darkly.

Shortly before Allen is supposed to leave to pick up Irene and drop her off at kindergarten, Adicia bolts from the table where she's mixing a batch of chocolate chip cookie dough and runs into the bathroom, holding her stomach. Allen, who's working the counter, notices her running off, her skin having turned gray again. He hears her vomiting almost as soon as the bathroom door swings shut. Most of the customers pretend they can't hear, trying their best to be polite.

"Are you getting sick?" Allen asks when she comes back out, ashen-faced and walking at a snail's pace. "'Cause if you are, I don't want you to overexert yourself. You can come back home with me, and Lenore will take care of you until Justine gets home."

"No, I'll be fine. I must've caught a stomach bug."

"Do you have any other symptoms, like fever, headache, or a runny nose? You can't work through an illness and risk making yourself sicker, or infecting customers."

"No, I just feel like I have a stomach bug. It'll probably pass by tomorrow."

"If you say so." Allen picks up his car keys from a hook behind the counter and goes out to the parking lot.

Adicia manages to get through the rest of the working day without feeling sick again. When Allen returns, she smiles to reassure him she feels better. She's almost her old self again by the time the bakery closes at 6:00. All the other employees smile as they take their leave, believing as much as Adicia it was a one-off fluke, a run of the mill stomach bug that'll be out of her system in a day or two.

"Would you like to lock up the display cases while I check to make sure all the equipment in the back is turned off?" Allen tosses her the little set of keys for the glass display cases.

While he's in back making sure all the stoves and burners are off, the blenders, mixers, and other electrical equipment have been unplugged, and the refrigerators are still humming away, Adicia fumbles with the keys as she starts lowering the back of the display case containing maple rolls, cinnamon buns, doughnuts, and thumbprint cookies. The next thing Allen knows, thundering footsteps are racing towards the bathroom, followed by the sounds of vomiting.

Adicia is humiliated yet again when she comes out from the bathroom and sees Allen looking at her in concern. The last thing she wants is him thinking she's too sick to work and needs to take a few days off, since she really wants to work and get out of the house. Being a stay-at-home wife with no children is one thing when one's husband is home, but without a man of the house, it's pointless to sit about all day and busy oneself only with boring, mundane housework like ironing, laundry, and cooking.

"Even if this is just a one-day stomach bug, I want you to stay at our house tonight for supper," he announces as he locks up the display cases. "Justine's already over there, and tonight's Lucine's turn to bring food. You can relax on the davenport."

"I'm not an invalid."

"Have I ever let you twist in the wind before? If you still feel queasy tomorrow, you can stay with Lenore and come back to work when you feel a hundred percent again."

Adicia follows him out to the car and mercifully makes it home without another urge to vomit. She's rather fatigued, but not queasy anymore. Once they're in the house, Allen helps her over to the davenport and orders her to lie down while he proceeds to tell everyone about how she threw up thrice today and might have a stomach bug. She darkly wonders how long she'll be considered a charity case even among her own family.

"Why can't Justine and I go home?" she pleads. "Justine can make supper. I'm not taking away the food Lucine brought for only four people."

"We've got extras hanging around. Besides, after what happened today, I don't think you can keep down something as heavy or rich as what we're having. What did you bring again, Lucine?"

"Hamburger Helper's cheeseburger macaroni meal."

"Do you think you have food poisoning, sweetie?" Lenore asks. "Maybe you had spoilt mayonnaise or bad meat?"

"I'll be fine," Adicia tries to insist again as Allen goes to the cupboard for crackers and pulls a bowl of leftover fruit salad out of the refrigerator. "It might just be nerves from having a husband away at war."

"Whatever it is, we're not taking any chances with your health," Allen insists. "You're gonna lie right there, have tea and a light meal, and only go home after your nerves settle. When I come over tomorrow to pick you up, I want you to tell me if you still feel queasy. If you are, I don't want you taxing yourself by going to work when you don't feel right. Understood?"

Adicia nods, though she hates being treated like a helpless child when she's the mistress of her own house. Her brother's trying to look after her the best way he knows how, and she can't fault him for being so overprotective. Still, being cast into the role of victim is getting really old, really fast.

***

When Allen came to pick Adicia up for their second day of work, she felt fine, and got through the entire day without any vomiting. On Saturday, their third day of work, she got sick in the morning, before he picked her up. She was very glad the bakery's Saturday hours are more abbreviated than the weekday hours, so Allen wasn't around to witness it again. Sunday passed without any nausea, but on Monday, she got sick before Allen came over. She felt sick on and off during that day, but managed to hold it in until Allen went to get Irene for school and then again until she was safely home. Throughout the rest of September and into October, her nausea followed much the same pattern, coupled with frequent feelings of fatigue in the middle of the day. Not wanting anyone, particularly not Allen, to know she's been feeling so sick, Adicia has hidden her symptoms from everyone but Justine. The last thing she wants is for anyone to have her committed to a hospital or be made to stay at home instead of working. It's not normal to regularly vomit throughout the day for such a long stretch of time, though she doesn't feel physically weakened, just overly tired and nauseous, sometimes accompanied by a headache. Even Justine hasn't been told the whole truth.

In the back of her mind, Adicia half-wonders if Radana were right when she claimed she spotted a pregnancy glow. She knows about morning sickness from Lenore, and that the very term is a misnomer, since Lenore got sick at non-morning hours as well. She also knows

Lenore felt tired and had headaches, but that could be caused by anything. She continues to attribute her under the weather feelings and so far two missed periods as stress over being separated from Ricky and the upcoming presidential election, coupled with how girls in their first few years after menarche don't have regular cycles yet. To believe anything else would be too much to bear during an already trying time.

By the time Halloween rolls around and Zachary calls Allen at work to let him know he and Lucine are leaving for the hospital to have their baby, Adicia has missed three periods, though she mercifully has stopped throwing up all the time, and is no longer so tired and headachy. She's starting to feel more confident she had those symptoms of illness for a perfectly legitimate, non-pregnancy reason, and that she'll probably menstruate again sometime during November, when things will hopefully start to settle down a little bit. She's really enjoying coming into her own as an independent woman who's mistress of her own house, man or no man, and has begun educating herself more on women's liberation, as Ernestine, Deirdre, and Betsy have suggested in their letters. She's now a proud subscriber to the new magazine *Ms.*, as glad as any of her sisters or friends that there finally exists an in-between title for women who are neither a Miss nor a Mrs. She's also bought Betty Friedan's *The Feminine Mystique*, Simone de Beauvoir's *The Second Sex*, Kate Millett's *Sexual Politics*, Shulamith Firestone's *The Dialectic of Sex*, and Germaine Greer's *The Female Eunuch*.

Though she disagrees with some of these ideas, all these books and magazine articles give her much to think about and challenge her intellectually, force her to critically examine all the forces behind things she's never questioned or wasn't gutsy enough to do more than complain about privately. Adicia doesn't think marriage is slavery and that every single man inherently hates and disrespects women, though she has to admit men like Ricky, Allen, Mr. van Niftrik, and Zuberi aren't in the majority. She's looking forward to staying home and being Ricky's sweet little wifey, but now she's not so sure she wants to jump into that role as soon as he comes home. Adicia could never become a June Cleaver or a Donna Reed, unquestioning a subservient role and never demanding more out of life. Going to a charity function or town party isn't her idea of a fun, fulfilling outlet outside the home, and she'd never dream of doing housework in high heels, pearls, and makeup. Her life as an enlightened, empowered, modern woman would be set back severely if she wound up pregnant at eighteen. She's already an eighteen-year-old bride, but having a baby immediately is almost an automatic guarantor of being shunted into the role of a full-time wife, mother, and homemaker instead of blossoming into her own with her own career.

Allen tosses her his car keys as they leave the bakery a little after 6:00. "Would you like to try driving us home? You've only driven in side streets since you got your permit. Are you ready for road driving?"

"You trust me to drive home?" she asks excitedly.

"You've gotta start somewhere, right?"

Adicia scampers into the driver's seat and puts the keys in the ignition. Allen gives her a look as she starts to back out of the parking lot.

"It's not a law, but I'd feel safer for your sake if you wore your seatbelt. They put those things in there just in case the worst happens, and I'd hate for you to get flung outta the car your first time on the road. Don't take any chances."

Adicia rolls her eyes as she puts the belt on. "It's too tight. What if it decapitates me in an accident?"

"That's extremely unlikely. You'll get used to wearing one before long."

Adicia doesn't believe him, but keeps the tight belt on. She tries to impress him with how calm and confident she is about driving on the road, and makes sure to brake for trick-or-treaters when they get back onto normal streets. During the drive, she feels a funny sensation that seems to come from inside her stomach or abdomen, but the sensations are so subtle, she shrugs them off as food digesting. It's so strange, she wonders if she just imagined it as she pulls into Allen's driveway.

"Aunt Lucine's having her baby!" Irene announces when they come into the house. "That's gotta be the coolest birthday ever, Halloween!"

Irene is a scarecrow with a jack-o-lantern for a head, and Amelia is a strawberry. Lenore made both of their costumes before she gave birth to Oliver, who's in a tiny orange crayon costume.

"Do you think I'm too old to trick-or-treat?" Justine asks. "I never did it before, and I'd be sad to never get that chance. Getting leftover candy isn't the same."

"You're always welcome to go out with us." Allen smiles at her.

"Oh, good, 'cause I bought a costume to wear when we handed

out candy. Can I go next door to change into it?"

"Be our guest," Lenore says. "You deserve to have a fun time on one of the funnest days of the year while you can still get away with it."

Adicia thinks back to the strange sensation she felt in the car, like butterflies gently moving just under the surface of her abdomen. That didn't feel like food digesting normally does, nor did it feel like gas pains. Again she idly wonders if Radana's prediction could be at all true, as much as she'd hate for it to be. There's no question Ricky and not Seth would be the father, since Seth took precautions to avoid a scandal and she got her period after the incident that precipitated her running away. She'd almost want to kill herself if she were pregnant and Seth were the father.

"I guess I'm too old," Adicia says sadly when Justine returns dressed in a pink dress with black and neon blue fairy wings attached to the back. "I don't even have a costume."

"Why don't you try on some of my clothes?" Lenore suggests. "Come upstairs with me, and we'll see if we can't find you a makeshift costume. Most people probably wouldn't peg you for eighteen."

"But who's gonna keep you company while you hand out candy?" Allen asks. "What if you need help with the baby and no one's around?"

"I'm capable of calling for help if your golden only son gets sick," Lenore says as she goes upstairs with Adicia.

Once upstairs, Adicia goes into the walk-in closet and pulls down a few outfits she likes that might reasonably fit her tiny frame. Lenore opens a wooden trunk and pulls out colorful scarves and delicately crocheted shawls. Lenore has an awful lot of hippie- and folkie-looking clothes that might pass for a Gypsy or Bohemian costume.

"I'm six inches taller than you, so they might be a little long, but if anything drags, we can pin it up," Lenore says as she rummages through the trunk for silk stockings. "They won't hang off your bones too much, since I'm only a few sizes bigger than you. I didn't gain any permanent weight from having three kids. I've always lost the baby weight pretty quickly. Veronica told me younger mothers usually snap back to their pre-baby size really fast."

"This one is pretty," Adicia announces as she pulls on a black organza jacket with red roses embroidered on it. "Though this skirt pulls a little across my middle."

Lenore stares at her. "Since when is a size ten too tight for you? I was at least twenty pounds heavier than you last time I checked! I'm usually between a hundred fifteen and a hundred twenty, and you don't even weigh a hundred pounds soaking wet with heavy clothes on!"

"I've been finding somea my clothes a little tight too. I've finally been gaining weight now that I'm no longer on that crummy near-starvation diet."

Lenore takes a good long look at her. "Adicia, have you been stuffing your bra? You've always been so small-busted, I can't help but notice it looks like you've gained an entire cup size."

"Are you saying I'm getting fat?"

"I'm just noticing you look like you've put on more than a couple of pounds. Sometimes we're the last ones to notice we've gained weight. I don't blame you if you've gone overboard since escaping New York. Don't worry, I still think you're a very pretty girl. Weight can always come off the same way it came on."

"I'm less concerned about losing any extra weight than I am about the ugly brown stretch mark that appeared under my navel about a week ago. Have I really gained that much weight that I'd get a stretch mark? Emeline got stretch marks on her breasts and hips when she started developing, but they were pinkish, and there were a lot more than one of 'em." Adicia pulls the skirt down to show Lenore the strange mark on her abdomen. "Do you have any kind of lotion I can rub on it to get rid of it? You must have something you've used for your own stretch marks."

Lenore's jaw drops. After standing speechless for several very long moments, she walks over to the bed and sits down, motioning for Adicia to sit beside her. Adicia hopes she isn't about to tell her she suspects she has cancer.

"When was your last period? I won't tell Allen anything we're saying, since this is private girl talk."

"July, but it's not uncommon for girls to have irregular menses in their first couple of years, and plus it's normal to skip when you're as stressed as I am. I'm positive things are starting to settle down and it'll finally return next month."

"You haven't menstruated since *July*, and it's Halloween now?" Lenore asks in a horrified whisper. "My God, have you told anyone, or did you keep this to yourself and hope it wasn't what it seemed?"

"Your new midwife asked me about it. She had a crazy idea I had a pregnancy glow, but I told her what I just told you. Justine was surprised to find out I hadn't gotten it since July too."

"That brown line is called a linea nigra, and it appears in a number of pregnant women starting in the second trimester. That's not a stretch mark. What about that time you threw up thrice in one day? Was that an isolated incident, or were there more times no one knew about?"

"I threw up about thrice a day about every other day for a bit over a month. I learnt how to hold it in so I wouldn't embarrass myself in front of yous guys or make Allen think I needed to stay home from work. I did it in the mornings before work, in the afternoons when he left to get Irene, and in the evenings after I got home. Justine knew, but I didn't want yous guys to worry about me needlessly."

Lenore sits stunned. "Are there any other symptoms you've had that could be attributed to pregnancy and not just stress, normal weight gain, or an irregular period?"

"I had headaches for awhile, I was really tired in the middle of the day, and my excuses for breasts were a little sore. I'm sure it's nothing. These things happen to everyone for perfectly normal reasons."

"You're pregnant. You've probably been in denial about it 'cause of all the stressful things you've been through lately, or maybe you really do believe these things are caused for other reasons. Dear God, if you made love with Ricky on July twentieth, you'd be past your first trimester by this point. That's too late for an abortion with a reputable doctor willing to break the law. Even if you went to Canada or Europe, I doubt they'd give it to you without a note saying it's therapeutic."

Adicia sits up and puts her hands over her abdomen. "Have you ever had gas pains or felt yourself digesting food in a way that feels like butterflies tickling you right under your skin? I had that funny feeling when I was driving home, but I thought it was a weird thing I mighta imagined, since it was so odd."

Lenore reaches over for the small pocket-sized calendar on the nightstand. "July twentieth is the exact date?"

"We started making out on the nineteenth, but it was after midnight when we went all the way and had intercourse. I wish I didn't remember the exact dates and had my husband here now."

Lenore frantically begins counting through the weeks. "My God,

Adicia, this Thursday's gonna mark fifteen weeks! No wonder you're gaining weight, getting a linea nigra, had morning sickness, fatigue, and headaches, skipped three periods, and are starting to feel a subtle quickening! You're more than halfway through your fourth month! Someone as little as you is gonna have more noticeable weight gain and feel quickening earlier than a woman with more meat on her bones!"

"It's impossible. I can't be pregnant. That'd ruin my plans to be an independent working woman and make my own money. What am I supposed to do if Ricky gets killed and I'd hafta support a kid all on my own? His bank account's gonna run out sooner or later, even if I'm frugal. I couldn't go to college for awhile if I had a kid. If I wanted to be a full-time wife, mother, and homemaker, I'd plan it when I had a husband around to support me and help with kids."

"It doesn't matter what you planned or wanted at this point! What's done is done!" Lenore looks her in the eyes. "Oh, God, is there any chance that awful Seth character could be the father? Do you remember when he raped you?"

"I got home around midnight on July ninth, Sunday, and immediately began packing to run away to Ricky's house. Seth took his disgusting 'test drive' with me on the night of the eighth. Don't worry, my mother insisted he use rubbers so he wouldn't cause a scandal, and I got my period after he raped me. Nothing broke or leaked. I know you're supposed to ovulate after you get your period, even if I have no way of predicting when I was supposed to. I never kept track of it."

"I hope you're right. It'd be too awful if you were carrying a rapist, wife-beater, murderer, ex-convict's baby and not the baby of your loving husband."

Justine knocks on the door. "What's taking this long? Allen wants to know if Adicia's going trick-or-treating with us, or if she decided to stay here and hand out candy with you."

"Oh, nothing, just girl talk," Lenore says. "She'll be right along to join yous guys." She gives Adicia a meaningful look as she peels off the too-tight skirt and pulls on a voluminous size twelve green peasant skirt with an elastic band, from Lenore's pregnancy wardrobe. "As soon as we can, we're gonna take you to Radana in Saratoga, or have her come here when you're playing hooky from work, so we can have what we both suspect confirmed," she whispers. "I can't believe you didn't tell *me* what was going on."

"I'm sorry," Adicia whispers back. "Are you mad at me?"

"I'm surprised and rather hurt, but I'm not angry. I know you had your own reasons for why you were in denial or suspected other things, but you coulda let me know you were having these symptoms."

Irene and Amelia are practically climbing the walls by the time Adicia comes downstairs. Justine hands her a pillowcase to collect candy. Lenore puts on a very good poker face and takes Oliver from Allen, walking them to the door and seeing them off. She shakes her head in disbelief and disappointment as she watches Adicia taking Irene's hand and walking up the street.

Adicia thinks about what Lenore said as they make the rounds of a twenty-block radius, not once letting on what was said in that room upstairs. She doesn't want it to be true, so she's decided it can't be true. The only thing that would make her change her mind would be a positive blood test or a doctor, nurse, or midwife feeling an actual fetus moving. If it's true, she doesn't want to tell Allen for fear of what would become of their truce. She'll have to invest in loose, baggy, oversized clothes so she can hide a potential pregnant form as long as possible. She definitely doesn't want to tell Ricky. He's already unhappy enough, from what he's able to write without being censored. She doesn't want what fragile sense of equilibrium he has in his precarious existence as a draftee airman to be destroyed were he to know he's expecting a child he might never know.

When they get home at 9:00, Adicia and Justine greet Lenore and Oliver and take a seat on the floor with their nieces to tabulate how much candy they got. At eighteen and thirteen, they're just as excited about bringing in a motherlode of candy and spare change and bills as their five- and three-year-old nieces. They roll their eyes at the handful of apples and focus on all the sugar and chocolate confections wrapped in pretty papers and little boxes. Adicia and Justine don't care they're supposed to be "too old" to trick-or-treat, since they were cheated out of this basic childhood pleasure their entire lives. If this is how fun, good, and amazing it is to celebrate Halloween properly, they can barely wait to celebrate Thanksgiving, Christmas, and Easter.

"Remember to brush your teeth," Lenore tells her daughters. "You can only eat four candies tonight. Don't get greedy, or you'll gain too much weight or go through all your candy too fast."

"Do you think they're giving candy to the guys in Ricky's Air Force group?" Adicia asks. "It'd be really sad if they were denied candy. Do you think I can send him some of my candy, or will customs steal it?"

Allen holds back his urge to lecture his sister on just what he thinks of her husband and their marriage. "If you send it to the Air Force base, they'll deliver it safe and sound so long as you fill out the customs form. It's not like you're sending him bombs or guns."

"How come Uncle Ricky was put in the Air Force and not the Army?" Irene asks. "Did he wanna fly a plane and not be on the ground?"

"He had no choice," Adicia says, trying not to sound sad for her niece's sake. "Just about the only troops left there at this point are the Air Force, Marines, and Navy. When Senator McGovern defeats that crone Nixon next week, we'll see an end to all troop activity, and you'll get to meet your handsome uncle."

Allen hates hearing his own child calling Adicia's husband her uncle, but lets it stand to avoid a fight after they just had such a nice time. For Adicia's sake, and because of his opposition to the war in Vietnam, he doesn't wish any harm on his unexpected brother-in-law, but he wonders if flying a plane is more dangerous than shooting at guerrillas from the ground. Being shot down from a plane seems scarier than being shot on ground level.

Justine gets up to answer the phone. Her face turns into one huge smile when she picks up the receiver.

"Who is it?" Allen asks.

"It's Zachary! Lucine just had her baby! Simone Juliette Troy-Martel was born at nine-fifteen at night after an uneventful labor, and she weighs eight pounds, seven ounces." Justine turns back to the phone. "When can we visit?"

"We've got a new cousin!" Irene says. "And she's got two last names! That's twice as nice as having only one!"

"That's confusing," Allen says. "Unless you're royalty, it's kinda silly and pretentious. A lot of last names don't go together well, like pairing a long-winded Polish or Italian name with a simple name like Hall or Jones, or mixing a German name with a Chinese name. What happens when the kids grow up and marry people with double names too? Are they gonna have sixteen names in a couple of generations?"

"We can visit tomorrow!" Justine says. "I can't wait to meet my new niece!"

***

November second, Thursday, Lenore picks up Adicia at the bakery after Justine comes home from school. Emeline is in the back of the car, holding Oliver on her lap.

"We can't wait to give Lucine and the baby our presents!" Justine says. "Now we've got three nieces and one nephew we get to keep!"

"You'll have another niece or nephew in March," Emeline reminds her. "Gemma's baby is only a couple of months away."

"Is someone babysitting Irene and Amelia?" Adicia asks.

"Sarah's husband Henry left work early to pick up Irene, Fritz, and Nessa, and got Amelia so they could all have a playdate. I wanted it to be just us girls, no small children around to overhear anything," Lenore says meaningfully as she looks straight at Adicia.

Adicia has tried to put Lenore's suspicions and assumptions out of her mind, and hopes she doesn't do or say anything embarrassing or revealing in front of Lucine or Emeline. She'd hate for her older sisters to jump all over her and deride her.

When they get to the hospital, they ask at the main desk where the maternity ward is, and then head over to the elevator. Adicia and Justine are so excited they could almost pop on the ride up. They skip down the hall in front of Lenore and Emeline, their hearts loudly thudding as they find Lucine's room number.

"Come meet your new niece!" Lucine calls when she sees their excited faces peering around the door. "Sarah's holding her, but I'm sure she'll give you a turn soon."

"Is it okay if we close the door?" Lenore asks. "There's something rather serious we need to discuss, personal girl talk stuff, and I don't want any nurses or people in the hall to overhear."

"Sure, go ahead. A nurse will knock if she needs to see me."

Adicia sits on the foot of the bed with Justine, smiling at tiny Simone in Sarah's arms and dreading having to face the music.

"How normal would any of you say it is to miss three periods in a row and think that's the most normal thing in the world and not at all possibly related to pregnancy?"

"What?" Emeline asks. "Who is this?"

"Adicia told me on Halloween she hasn't had a period since July."

"Sweet Lord Krishna!" Emeline gasps. "Is this true?"

"It happens!" Adicia continues defending herself. "I only started in January, and a lot of girls skip when they first start. And I've been under a ton of stress 'cause my sweet husband was ripped away from me and sent off to that damn jungle. Stress is a perfectly normal reason to miss it. I'm sure I'll see a red stain sometime this month."

"I didn't have mine for almost two years," Sarah says. "I was starving, and some sort of drugs were in our tea to stop it. It returned in the late summer of 1945."

"You see? Sarah wasn't pregnant when she didn't menstruate for almost two years!"

"I also assume she was a virgin, and anyone would stop having it when she's on a starvation diet," Lenore says.

Adicia sits mortified as Lenore tells them about all the other symptoms. She looks down at the hospital blanket to avoid eye contact with anyone.

"Whose is it?" Lucine finally asks. "Here, why don't you take a turn holding Simone to take your mind off this dilemma?"

Adicia gratefully accepts her baby niece and greedily drinks in her adorable little face, her soft, fresh baby skin, her tiny fingers and toes, the fuzz of hair on her head, her big green eyes, and the folds of her skin.

"Is there any chance that wife-beater Seth could be the father?" Emeline asks. "You can't continue this pregnancy if it belongs to him."

"I know it's Ricky's. That is, if I am pregnant. I got my period after Seth did what he did, and I had to have ovulated sometime within the next ten days."

"Your emotions have been going off the charts in the past few months, even considering you're in love and your newlywed husband just went off to war," Lenore goes on.

"You really love him?" Lucine asks. "The way a woman loves a man, not just the love of a strong friendship?"

"I don't even know anymore if I loved him all along and just couldn't realize it, or if I only properly started falling for him after we were married and then he went away. I liked him, and then I grew to love him."

"Well, you obviously thought enough of him to sleep with him! Knowing how old-fashioned and modest you are, this has gotta be one special guy for you to have even considered doing something so intimate and personal. Don't give me any lines about how you wanted to send him off to war with a special, personal reminder of you and make a man outta him in case he dies. I'm your big sister, and I know you better than almost anyone. You wouldn't give yourself to any guy in that way if you didn't have serious feelings. None of us ever believed in free love, but you in particular are really reserved and old-fashioned, maybe even more than Emeline. You wouldn't let a guy kiss you unless you liked him enough to marry him, and you could only imagine doing such personal stuff if you were married, or a million percent sure you'd get married and would be together forever. Looks like our sweet little Adicia went and fell in love with the unlikeliest of matches."

"If you have it confirmed, are you gonna keep it?" Emeline asks. "Fifteen weeks is a bit late for an abortion, but God knows you've got enough money in the bank to fly to Canada or England."

"Maybe I would in other circumstances, but not now. Not when this could be the only thing to remind me of the only guy who ever loved me unconditionally. Even if Ricky gets shot down or steps on a mine, I'll always have a piece of him, no matter what. I hope it has his beautiful soulful brown eyes. They were the first thing I noticed about him. I always liked brown eyes best, and his are so beautiful and deep, at least a shade darker than mine."

"Wait, now you're finally admitting it's true?" Lenore asks.

"If I can't have my husband back safe and sound in my arms, the next-best thing is to have his child to remind me of him. Maybe, if he does die, I'll remarry another guy someday, but it could never be so pure, beautiful, and sweet as Ricky's unblemished love. I was the only girl he ever loved. His heart was pure, with no pieces of it given away to other girls. He kissed about five other girls, but those weren't kisses of true love. He did and experienced everything for the first time, with a clean slate. Boy, I wish he were here now so I could hold him and kiss him and love him and never let him go."

"You're in love, *liebchen*," Sarah tells her. "Isn't it the most beautiful thing in the world when it comes?"

"It must be really special to marry your first and only love," Emeline says. "Sweet Lord Krishna, it must be even more special to marry your first and only *boyfriend*, to say nothing of the first and only guy who showed romantic interest in you."

"Ricky wasn't my boyfriend. We went right from being just friends, and unrequited love on his side, to man and wife. I made a vow to love him and stay loyal to him, and I'm not gonna turn around and break it now." Adicia hands Simone to Emeline and hops onto Sarah's lap the way she did when she was a little girl.

"My baby is having her own baby," Sarah says proudly as she holds the sobbing Adicia. "If your husband comes back alive, you'll renew your vows as a proper man and wife in love, and I'll walk you down the aisle like your own *mutter*."

Everyone looks up when they hear a knock on the door.

"I'm Lucine's nurse, Allison. May I come in and check her vitals?"

"You sure can," Lucine says. "One of my sisters also needs your services."

Adicia gets off Sarah's lap when the nurse comes into the room, not wanting to embarrass herself in front of a stranger. She watches the nurse checking Lucine's blood pressure, pulse rate, temperature, and respiratory rate. It must be nice to have a baby in a hospital, if only to have a nice private room and a vacation away from home.

"This is my sister Adicia Carson." Lucine points, tripping over Adicia's new name. "She's had a bunch of pregnancy symptoms for awhile, but never told anyone or had it confirmed. She'd be about fifteen weeks. Could you test her?"

"She only wants the blood drawn," Lenore says. "No physical examination, least of all not by a man. We've got that covered by a midwife who used to be a nurse."

Twenty minutes later, the nurse returns with paperwork for Adicia to sign and gets the necessary equipment from a shelf in the closet. Adicia winces when the needle goes into her hand.

"At least we're getting it done this way and not by your midwife," she whispers to Lenore. "That'd be too invasive and embarrassing."

"How do you think the baby's gonna come outta you?" Lenore whispers back. "It comes out the same way it got in!"

Adicia turns as red as a beet. "You don't have to remind me of that!"

"You'll get your results in one to three days," the nurse says. "Would you like to be given your results over the phone, or will you be coming in to have them explained and to set up prenatal care?"

"We already have someone," Lenore repeats. "If my sister-in-law is pregnant and there's a problem, she'll know where to transfer her."

Adicia sits petrified after the nurse leaves. She has no idea how she'll explain this to Allen, since she can't hide a pregnant form forever. She doesn't want Ricky to know right away either. In another lifetime, for another woman, a child conceived of the first union of his or her parents would be considered a miracle, a true child born of love, but not when her husband is thousands of miles away. There's nothing to celebrate, even if it'd be a forever reminder of Ricky if anything happens to him.

***

November 6, the day before the presidential election Adicia and all her friends and family hope will unseat Nixon, the phone rings while Adicia is getting ready for work and Justine is shoveling oatmeal down her throat. With shaking hands, Adicia picks it up.

"May I please speak to Adicia E. Carson?"

"This is she."

"This is Allison Lowell, a nurse at Glens Falls Hospital. Congratulations, Mrs. Carson. You're expecting a blessèd event."

"Oh," she says in a small voice. "That's interesting."

"Did you understand me, Mrs. Carson? I just told you you're pregnant. Most of the first-time mothers I break the news to are very excited."

"My husband's in the Air Force as a draftee in Vietnam. I'm not exactly in the best place to get excited about this news."

"Sorry to hear that. Anyway, good luck with your pregnancy."

Adicia walks next door numbly as Justine goes to meet the bus. Lenore knows from the look on her face, and rushes to give her a hug. Allen is very concerned when he sees Adicia weeping.

"I'm not feeling well," she says, not altogether dishonestly. "I don't know if I can perform well at work today."

"She'll be okay," Lenore tries to reassure him. "I'll make her tea, fruit salad, and graham crackers with strawberry jelly. Adicia can help with taking care of the kids, and she'll feel better by the time you come home."

"I'll try not to use any more sick days for a long time."

"You can use a hundred sick days if you need them. I don't want my kid sister to work through a sickness or a bad day. You girls have fun while I'm at work." Allen picks Oliver up from his purple baby blanket to cuddle and kiss him goodbye.

After Allen has gone, Adicia stumbles over to the davenport and tries to lie down, but quickly sits up rubbing her back in pain. When she tries to lie on her stomach, she sits up just as quickly and uncomfortably. Beaten down in her simple quest to get some rest, she slumps over on her side on the floor, ignoring her nephew's indignant squalls over having so much of his blanket stolen.

"I know you're not thinking of this in a positive light right now, sweetie, but just think, this is a very special gift you'll always have to remind you of your husband, no matter what happens to him. This is a true child of love, and your chance to give a child all the love your own parents never could be bothered to give to you. You'll be such a good mommy, Adicia, and you know I'll help you."

"Why did I gain so much weight already? At the rate I'm going, I'm gonna be over a hundred fifty pounds by the time it's born!"

"Some girls gain the weight early and then taper off. Your body knows what it's doing. Don't pay any attention to doctors who claim it's dangerous to do certain things. Pregnancy and birth were much more natural processes before doctors and hospitals got involved."

"You're having a baby, Aunt Adicia?" Irene asks. "Don't you need a daddy to have a baby?"

"She made her baby before your uncle went off. Can you keep this news a secret from your daddy? Your aunt wants to wait a little while before starting to break the news to everyone else."

"I'll be the best secret-keeper ever!"

Adicia lies on her side listlessly, overwhelmed at the most bittersweet news of her life. Instead of celebrating the impending arrival of a bundle of joy with the man she's realized she loves, she's forced to wonder how she'll go through five more months of pregnancy and labor without her baby's father in sight, how to raise a child alone, and what'll happen to both of them if the worst happens and Ricky never comes home. What should've been a well-deserved happy ending has just turned into even more of a nightmare. If it's true that sometimes one has to go to the lowest, saddest point possible before rising up to the highest, happiest, most beautiful place possible, Adicia hopes she'll be treated to one hell of a happy ever after ending, worth all the agony she's continuing to go through.

"How'd you like to take a road trip to Poughkeepsie to pick up Ernestine and the Ryans?" Allen asks. "Lenore and I thought it'd be nice to have them over for our first real family holiday celebration. We'd like to do this for Christmas too. You and Justine have three spare bedrooms in that big house of yours, and there's another room free in my house. Since you've got such a big dining room, we could have the meal there."

"Isn't that two hours away?"

"It'll be a fun road trip. If you let me ride in your car, I'll give you directions. Lenore and Justine will take my car."

"You'd let me go driving on a longer trip? Does this mean you think I'm ready to take my road test?"

"I think you are. We'll pick a day with good weather, and I'll drive you to the testing site. You're the one who's always talking lately about how you're such a modern, independent woman. Being able to control your own transportation will earn you even more freedom and independence."

"Let's go!" Adicia excitedly jumps up from the davenport and goes to the coat rack for her jacket and the bag she bought at the fair.

Allen so far hasn't thought anything of how Adicia has been wearing a lot of loose, baggy clothes lately. In his eyes, his sister is just another eighteen-year-old in long skirts without fitted waistbands, shapeless dresses, baggy blouses, oversized shirts, and muumuus. He believes her new jacket and shoes are a normal change of wardrobe, not things she bought because of an expanding body and swollen ankles. Adicia is creeping up on the eighteen-week mark and hiding her pregnant shape rather well, though the protrusion is quite clear when she looks in the mirror. Lenore has tried to tell her it'll be worse when Allen finds out later rather than sooner, but Adicia is sure she can keep the secret until she has no choice. If Ricky were here to support her and stand up for their marriage, it'd be so much different. The kind of negative feelings Allen has expressed for Ricky and their marriage will go up tenfold were he to find out she's carrying Ricky's child and therefore linked to him forever.

Justine slips on her jacket and goes next door to help Lenore with getting the kids in the car and preparing something to put in a cooler to eat on the road. Adicia throws a box of granola bars, a box of crackers, and bags of dried fruits, salted roasted pumpkin seeds, nuts, and chocolate chips into her bag and heads out to the car, her head held high. It means a lot to her that Allen trusts her driving enough to let her drive all the way down to Poughkeepsie and back. She really enjoys driving, and now can't imagine how she lived for so many years existing on public transportation. Perhaps living in a big city blinds one to the very real need to know how to drive, and how wonderful it is to have one's own vehicle and the ability to come and go as one pleases, not held hostage to bus or subway schedules.

Adicia waves to Lenore, Justine, and the children as the other car backs out of the driveway, then remembers to put on her safety belt as per Allen's demands for his peace of mind. She still doesn't like seatbelts, and it's a little tight across her midsection, but Allen does have a point about how they were put there for a reason and that it's better to be safe than sorry.

"Was he really good to you?" Allen asks as they approach the exit ramp to Poughkeepsie. "I mean, beyond saying and doing the right things. Any guy can play the part, but a real man puts his money where his mouth is."

"Ricky was such a sweetheart. He cooked for me, went shopping for furniture, electronics, and other household stuff, let me pick mosta 'em, bought me little presents, flagged down that cop when Seth was tryna take me, and got me here safe and sound. He picked me over his stupid parents. Why would a normal guy give up his family money and turn his back on his parents unless he were in love?"

"I'm sure he misses the family money now. As soon as Uncle Sam gets done with him, he'll probably come running back to his parents and beg for forgiveness. Do you still think of him as your friend after he's been away for four months?"

"Whether you approve of it or not, I love him."

"Absence does make the heart grow fonder. You're probably romanticizing him and your unconventional relationship now, but if he comes home, the reality will soon seem a whole lot different. I'm just telling you for your own good."

Adicia tries her best to ignore his lecture and continues following his directions to the Ryans' apartment a little distance outside the Vassar campus. She's proud they've beaten the others by at least a good fifteen minutes. Adicia last caught sight of them in her rearview mirror awhile ago.

"Shall we go on up or wait for the others?" she asks.

"They'll know where we went. A frail little thing like you shouldn't stand around in nippy weather." Allen leads her to the third building on their left, one of five old, indistinguishable, three-story, red brick buildings with wrought-iron patios and sliding glass doors. "They're on the third floor, unit 309."

"No doorman or elevator?"

"They might no longer be squatting, but they don't rake in the kinda money to afford a building with a doorman or elevator. At least the stairs are kept-up, not like those twisted nightmare funhouse stairs we useta have." Allen opens the door and goes up the stairs after her.

Adicia walks a short distance down the hall until she finds 309. A picture of Ernestine, Betsy, and the Ryans is taped to the door. Timidly, she knocks.

"We're coming!" Fiona shouts from the other side of the door.

"Fiona Líobhan Ryan, remember what I told you about always asking who's there?" Deirdre gently chides. "You opened the door to those cultists last week, and I still can't figure out how to dispose of that silly Book of Mormon!"

"It's us, Adicia and Allen. We're not salespeople or missionaries."

Ernestine opens the door. She and Adicia smile huge smiles at one another and hug very tightly, not having seen one another since August 1970. After Ernestine pulls away from her, she holds Adicia at arm's length and looks at her closely.

"You've grown a little bit since we last saw each other! How tall are you now, five feet even?"

"I wish! I was something like four feet eight before, and I've only grown two inches. I'm only five feet in my platform shoes."

"Betsy's here too," Deirdre says. "She's visiting before her bus to New York comes. She's in us girls' room with Aoife, reading her a story. Betsy has very good news regarding that heinous felon your folks were tryna force you to marry."

"Have you been gaining weight?" Ernestine asks. "You were always so tiny, like a living ragdoll, and your clothes often hung off you, but it looks like you've packed on some pounds! Not that there's anything wrong with a woman being over a certain size," she adds quickly.

"I'm eating well for the first time in my life." Adicia doesn't want to confess to her favorite sister about her pregnancy in front of Allen. "If anything, I was underweight before."

"Are Justine, Lenore, and the kids that far behind?" Deirdre asks. "We'd love to give you and Justine the grand tour."

Adicia looks around. A spider plant is on the small kitchen table, and a small bookshelf is next to a television set. Mostly textbooks, feminist, Socialist, Communist, lesbian, and other revolutionary books, and books about Irish mythology, history, politics, and culture, line the shelves. A bunch of posters, taped-up photographs, and typewritten song lyrics take up the rest of the wall. While they wait for the others to arrive, Adicia walks the length of the living room wall to get a closer look at the decorations. Deirdre is still the same person she was when she was simply known as Girl. She has posters of Che Guevara, The Beatles circa 1966, Buddha attaining enlightenment, Karl Marx, Bob Dylan, and an artistic rendering of the Irish goddess Flidais, her favorite goddess. Above the bookshelf, Deirdre has taped several photos from a couple's photography session she and Ernestine had with a photographer friend who wasn't weirded out by a lesbian couple, family photos, the lyrics of "Zor and Zam" and "The Boxer," and the Irish flag.

"Nice work." Adicia thinks it doesn't quite flow as badly as Emeline's strange mishmash of home decoration.

Deirdre is starting to tell the story of how Fiona opened the door to Mormon missionaries last week when Lenore knocks on the door. Aoife dashes out from the bedroom and throws the door open, overcome with excitement at the thought of finally seeing her best friend Justine again for the first time in over two years.

"What a cute baby!" Fiona says. "And look how much the girls have grown!"

"I'm five and Amelia's three," Irene says. "I'm in kindergarten."

"Amelia couldn't even talk when you last saw her, and now she's a chatterbox," Lenore says proudly.

Betsy comes out of the bedroom to hug them. She steps back after she hugs Adicia, feeling a strange, hard protrusion from her midsection. Adicia shakes her head frantically when Betsy opens her mouth to probably ask the obvious question. Ernestine and Deirdre look at them questioningly, not quite sure what just happened.

"Can we have something to eat before we go on the road again?" Justine asks. "It's wasteful to come all the way here and hop right back into the car."

"I make a mean vegetable omelette," David says. "It's never the wrong time of day to enjoy so-called traditional breakfast foods. Anyone else wanna eat?"

"Sure, I'll have some," Lenore says. "It's best to use up as many perishables as you can if you're gonna be outta the house for five days."

Justine smiles up at David, who's now taller than his older sister. "I like your hair. How long are you growing it?"

"I'm not gonna look like a bum. Around my shoulders is long enough for me. Mosta the guys wear their hair long unless they're squares. No offense, Allen."

"My husband wore his hair on the short side," Adicia says. "They still gave him a haircut when he was forced into the military."

"This war had better to hell be ending soon," David grumbles, picking up a dart from a large olive-green ceramic bowl Aoife made in art class. "Help yourselves. Let's see who can get closest to the bull's-eye on that war criminal and murderer." He closes his right eye, aims the dart, and throws it in a trajectory towards a picture of Nixon. "Damn that man. I'm sick to my stomach he was re-elected in a landslide. I thought I was taking part in history by voting him out and being in the first presidential election us eighteen-year-olds could vote in."

"I've got something to show you, Adicia," Betsy says. "Would you like to come into the girls' room with me? You can come too, Ernestine, Deirdre, Fiona."

Adicia follows her and takes a seat on Deirdre's old mattress, which now has an actual bedframe instead of just sitting on the floor. The younger girls' mattress also has a bedframe now. As her eyes drift around the room, she notices Deirdre has hung up papers bearing the lyrics to all the songs on John Lennon's first proper solo album, *Plastic Ono Band*, which came out in 1970. The other walls are taken up by a large map of Ireland, framed prints of Pablo Picasso's *Guernica* and Salvador Dalí's *Landscape with Butterflies*, posters of The Monkees and The Who, and pictures of Julie and the Doyles, Deirdre and Ernestine, and the Ryans with Miss Skoloda in early 1970.

"I'm so grateful to that woman, I promised I'd name my firstborn daughter after her if I have a daughter," Deirdre says. "She made sure we got birth certificates and social security cards, and that I got emancipation and legal guardianship of my siblings. Cecilia Ryan's a really great name."

"How are you gonna have a baby with Ernestine?" Fiona asks. "Two girls can't make a baby."

"We'll inseminate ourselves with a donated sample."

"Speaking of having babies, I swore I felt a pregnancy on you, Adicia," Betsy whispers. "Why didn't you let me ask about it when we were out there?"

Adicia reluctantly takes off her jacket and raises her baggy yellow sweater. The other four girls stare at the by now rather pronounced evidence.

"When did that happen?" Fiona asks.

"Since I'm so small, it looks bigger than it really is. It happened coming up on eighteen weeks ago. You have to promise not to tell Allen. He'll be really mad if he finds out I slept with Ricky, since he hates my husband and our marriage so much."

"So you *did* do things with him!" Betsy says. "I knew you wouldn't be able to resist such a good-looking guy. I wouldn't be able to help myself if I were married to such a fine drink of water."

"It is Ricky's, isn't it?" Ernestine asks in concern. "Seth did what he did not even two weeks before you lost Ricky."

"I know who the father of my child is. I got my normal period after Seth violated me, and I know enough to know you ovulate after your menses are done."

"How's Allen gonna react when he finally finds out?" Deirdre asks. "As much as he hates Ricky for being a rich boy, and as much as he assumes the wrong things about him, he might be even madder at you when he finds out you've been keeping this secret for so long. Unless of course you're planning to step outta town for a spell and give it away."

"I just had it confirmed earlier this month. Lenore was right. I was in deep denial. I had all the usual symptoms, but I chose to attribute them to other things. I might've gone to Canada or Europe for an abortion if Ricky were here, but knowing he might never come home, I feel like I have to keep it. This is my only chance to have a baby by him, a forever reminder of him."

Betsy pulls a photograph out of her handbag. "Look at this, Adicia. Seth being led away from his precious store in handcuffs. My folks and I went over there and picketed a couple of times, along with other people who started picketing after reading all the flyers we put up. He had almost no customers left within a week of our papering Chelsea. I was there the day the cops came and arrested him. I wanted to give you proof he's offa the streets."

"How long was he thrown in jail for?"

"They didn't just hit him up for breaking and entering and attempting to assault Tommy. He also operated his business without a license, was guilty of tax evasion, had no business opening a business period when he was a convicted murderer, was caught selling spoilt meat and passing it off as fresh, and had a whole library of horrifically disgusting pornography featuring underage girls in his house. He also had a lot of drugs all over his house, particularly your mom's favorite, cocaine."

"Wow, what a prize my parents found. He's even worse than Carlos. At least Carlos just never thought things through. I never thought Carlos was deliberately mean or evil, just unthinking and stupid."

David knocks on the door. "You girls want omelettes, or should I put the eggs away?"

"We're fine," Deirdre calls. "We just need to get our suitcases shut and we'll be back out."

On the ride back up to Hudson Falls, Allen lets Adicia drive again, with Ernestine, Deirdre, and Fiona in the backseat. David takes the passenger seat next to Lenore in Allen's car, with Justine and Aoife in the backseat with the girls. Justine holds Oliver on her lap, periodically letting Aoife have a turn. While David rants against Nixon and the Vietnam War, livid that Nixon and Kissinger are enduring till the bitter end instead of ending things and withdrawing all the remaining troops, Justine and Aoife share stories of their respective eighth grade experiences, and Irene talks about kindergarten. In the other car, Deirdre takes up where she left off in her story about how Fiona opened the door to the missionaries.

"Can we talk about something else now?" Adicia pleads after Deirdre seems to have concluded her scathing critique of Mormon history and theology. "How about we talk about what we're gonna eat tomorrow?"

"I'm not so much into Thanksgiving anymore. Indians don't give thanks for anything on that day. That day is a reminder of how the white man stole their culture and land. It's the same reason I never mark Columbus Day. But outta respect for your family and our friendship, I'll be a well-behaved guest and help you share in your celebration, the same way I'd help a Jewish or Hindu friend celebrate their holidays."

"Oh, brother," Allen sighs. "This is gonna be a longer ride than I anticipated."

***

Ernestine and Deirdre have been put up in Ricky's old room, Fiona and Aoife are in the bedroom that had a double mattress put in just in case the need for a guest room arose, and David is on the sofa bed. Adicia finds it a little bit off-putting how Deirdre is giving a whole history lesson on the myth of the first Thanksgiving in the kitchen on Thanksgiving morning. Deirdre is intelligent, so she doesn't doubt it's true, but it's an inappropriate time to share this information. Emeline is meanwhile lamenting how many millions of turkeys have to be slaughtered for this one day.

"That turkey is huge!" Adicia says. "I wonder if it tastes even better than the turkey at the Bowery Mission."

"What do you think our parents and Tommy are doing today?" Ernestine asks. "My guess is Mother dug turkey meat outta a garbage can, or is passing off turkey breast as a proper Thanksgiving feast yet again."

"This is even better than any of our Bowery meals, 'cause this one's in our own home!" Justine says. "I was afraid our dishes would be mismatched, since we don't have twenty dishes all of the same set, but Adicia told me she got two sets of ten in the same pattern at Macy's."

"I don't care if we all eat off a different plate. The most important thing is to be together again. I don't care about silly things like matching dinner sets. Hell, I won't trouble myself with a color scheme when Deirdre and I get married. Everyone will wear what they're comfortable with, and if we use flowers, they'll be whatever colors we choose too."

"Two girls can get married?" Irene asks. "I've never heard of a wedding for two girls."

"We'd like to do it after we graduate," Deirdre says. "Our engagement's understood, though we'll get rings at some point to make it official. I wanna do a Celtic handfasting ceremony. You'll all learn more about it as the time draws nearer."

Adicia looks away as Gemma stops stirring a bowl of chutney to feel her baby kicking. Gemma must only be a month more pregnant than she is, and she's wearing clothes that don't hide her pregnant form. She has a husband by her side, a husband who can feel his child moving and who'll be there in the delivery room. Gemma gets to tell everyone about her pregnancy, and everyone's happy for her. She's announced the names she and Tyrone picked out, Adrienne Nicolette and Julian Emanuel. They'll have a baby shower in early March. A nursery is being set up in their house. Adicia doesn't have the heart to think about baby supplies or names. Not even her own husband knows it, and the customers at the bakery think she's another teenage girl following the baggy, loose-fitting trend, not someone hiding her pregnant form for as long as she knows how. She wishes she too could just stop what she's doing and feel for any little movements within.

"Why are you crying?" Fiona asks. "It's supposed to be a happy holiday. Did Deirdre upset you with her history lesson?"

"No, the history lesson was fine, even if it wasn't the right time or place. I just miss my husband."

"Here." Emeline reaches down for George and places him in Adicia's arms. "Animals make everyone feel better. They have a sixth sense about this stuff. He knows you're in emotional pain and will make you feel better with his special, healing animal energy. Go sit on the davenport, and we'll do the rest in here."

Adicia nods, walking lopsided into the living room with George cradled in her arms. Everyone looks at her with sympathy, which burns her up. They should feel bad for her and move on to seeing her as a whole, multifaceted person with an identity beyond charity case or wife of a draftee. Five-month-old George doesn't treat her like a sad sympathy case. Animals don't judge people or treat them differently based on things like that.

"That poor kid," Gemma says. "Out of all of us sisters, she's the one least-equipped to deal with something so awful. I sometimes wonder how I survived the hell of being married to Francesco, but that's almost like small potatoes next to this. Can someone remind me again why we got involved in Vietnam and why the draft was reinstated?"

"Americans have been systematically brainwashed to believe Socialism and Communism are evil, and that anyone who chooses that political and economic system must be stopped, no matter how much it makes sense in other cultures and how much it resonates with the common working man or woman who's been exploited for years," Deirdre says. "As for the draft, they realized it was an unpopular war and the military ranks weren't being filled as much as they'd been in the last war, which *was* a morally justified war. It was more immoral America stayed neutral as long as it did during that war. They couldn't provide enough men on their own, so they began grabbing as many as they could get. I'm not anti-military, but it oughta be volunteer-only. You should like what you do and have informed consent, not be forced into the military 'cause your president and his advisors wanna fight a losing battle till the bitter end."

"Nixon, Johnson, and Kissinger oughta be tried as war criminals!" Fiona says. "It was all LBJ's idea to escalate our involvement. Kennedy wanted to end it. If he hadn't been shot, we woulda been outta there a long time ago."

"I'd rather go to jail than be drafted," David says. "I made it known loud and clear I'm a conscientious objector when I had to register for that brutal Selective Service. If I'm drafted and they refuse to honor that, I'm going off to prison to stand up for my beliefs."

Adicia lies on the davenport, absentmindedly petting George, until she sees people putting a tablecloth over the large dining room table, a table she never had a chance to use before, and setting the table for twenty places. In the old days, she got very excited and felt her mouth watering when she saw the lavish feast at the Bowery Mission. Now she barely blinks when she sees a huge turkey, orange-apple-cranberry chutney, cranberry sauce, candied yams with pineapple, gravy, mashed potatoes, green beans with mushrooms, vegetable gratin, stuffing, stuffed tomatoes and Portobello mushrooms, salmon with orange slices, applesauce, and Greek salad being borne out to the table. She barely lifts her head when Irene, Fritz, and Nessa show her the centerpieces they made in their art classes. As happy as she is to finally have a real Thanksgiving, it's not as good as it would've been were Ricky here.

"Aren't you coming to the table?" Ernestine asks. "There's more than enough food for everyone."

Adicia removes George from her lap and glumly has a seat. She tries to smile at everyone, though she doesn't feel like smiling.

"Just think, Aunt Adicia, next Thanksgiving will be even better 'cause Uncle Ricky will be home!" Irene says.

"I hope so."

It could always be worse, Adicia thinks as she picks at her turkey and stuffing. Sarah and Henry are the sole survivors of their respective families, while she has five sisters and one good brother, plus a super sister-in-law, two nice brothers-in-law, so far three nieces and a nephew, and the Ryans. Even if she should lose Ricky forever, she'll still have a family that's plenty big, and there will be a bundle of joy in the late spring to hopefully take her mind off of missing Ricky. And she's several hundred miles away from Manhattan, her horrid parents a distant memory and Seth back in prison. Those are all things to be very thankful for.

***

Adicia has been so prostrate with grief over Operation Linebacker II, a brutal bombing campaign involving the Air Force and Navy which began on the eighteenth of December, she hasn't been to work for several days. She hasn't left the house because she's so riveted to the TV, radio, and newspapers. Instead of looking forward to her first real Christmas, she barely gets any sleep, eats almost nothing, and cries her eyes out. More than a few aircraft have been shot down, prisoners have been taken, servicemen have been killed, and Vietnamese civilians have been killed in the Bach Mai Hospital in Hanoi after so-called errant bombs hit one of the wings. For all she knows, Ricky was in one of the planes that was shot down, or he could be among the POWs. It tortures her to know he could've died, or be dying, without knowing she loves him, nor that he fathered a child before he went away. Adicia is now at the twenty-two-week mark, and instead of feeling grateful she's made it past the most precarious part of pregnancy and is heading into the second half and eventual homestretch, she feels only sorrow and pity for the child who may never know his or her father and whose very existence is being treated like a shameful secret.

Saturday, December 23, the bakery closes early, and Allen decides to check on Adicia before going home. She hasn't let him in the house the past few days, and sounded extremely despondent and grief-stricken when he called her on the phone. Justine has told Allen and Lenore that Adicia barely moves other than to get dressed, bathe, eat what little she does, and watch TV or listen to the radio. She's taken to sleeping in Ricky's old bed because Adicia keeps her up all night with loud sobbing and the lights she puts on to read the papers. Adicia hasn't even had the presence of mind to throw on her usual oversized, baggy clothes. She has a stash of normal clothes that fit her nicely in her condition, which she wears when only she and Justine are at home and she doesn't have to worry about revealing her secret. Most maternity clothes are downright awful, not at all pretty or fashionable, so she bought clothes in bigger sizes to accommodate her expanding body.

"Adicia, I'm very concerned about you. I wanted to invite you and Justine to supper tonight. You have to do something to take your mind off of what's going on over there."

Adicia barely stirs from her place on the davenport, uncaring Justine opened the door without asking who was there. She wishes her brother would go back next door and leave her alone in her grief.

"Adicia, can you hear me? It's not healthy for you to sit around moping like this. Why don't we go for a walk to get fresh air?"

Adicia notices Allen walking over to her, and realizes in horror she's wearing clothes outlining her pregnant form rather clearly. In her most animated form in days, she leaps off the davenport and starts running for the stairs.

"Hey, where are you going? You can't run and hide upstairs. You've gotta come outta this bubble sometime."

Adicia stops breathing as Allen grabs her arm gently and turns her around. She closes her eyes in terrified expectation when he gets a good look at her, not waiting to see his facial expression, too scared to think up an explanation for what he's seeing.

"Adicia, are you pregnant? If this is just a lot of excess weight gain, it's an awfully strange place for it all to be centered in!"

She bursts into tears for the umpteenth time in the last few days.

"Who did this to you? Why didn't you tell me sooner? Who else knows? How long have you known? What do you intend to do about this problem? Tell me this bastard's name, and I'll go and break every bone in his body for raping you and knocking you up!"

"She's in her fifth month," Justine reports.

"Is it Seth's? If it is, he'd better thank his lucky stars he's sitting in prison already, 'cause I would've done to him something even worse than what I did to Ethan!"

"Seth was made to use rubbers," she manages to choke out. "I didn't see any breaking or leaking, and I can't believe I'm giving you this much detail. I got my period after he raped me."

"So who did this to you? Why didn't you tell any of us you'd been raped? Were you scared of an illegal abortion or what we might think of you? You're always welcome in this family no matter what, and this wasn't your fault! I'm not gonna throw onea my kid sisters outta my family 'cause she got raped and was knocked up! If you choose to keep it 'steada giving it up for adoption or tryna find a doctor who'll do an abortion this late, that baby will always be welcome in this family too!"

"I know exactly who the father is, but you have to promise you won't be angry at me."

"Why would I be angry at you? You're an innocent victim, not a girl of ill repute who went and slept around!"

"Can we please sit down first?"

Allen walks over to the davenport with her, still reeling from shock and disbelief at what he's discovered. Adicia looks like a scared little rabbit.

"I'm carrying my husband's baby. I wasn't raped. Ricky is the father of my child. He doesn't know I'm pregnant. Lenore, Lucine, Emeline, Justine, the Ryan girls, Betsy, Irene, Ernestine, and Sarah know. I didn't know until early November. I had a lot of symptoms, but was too in denial to put two and two together, even when people told me what they thought was going on."

Allen hangs his head. "So you really did sleep with that rich boy Warrick. We can't do a simple, easy annulment now. This is just great. You're tied to him forever, even after the necessary divorce. He'll have to pay you alimony and child support, and come around to visit. What if his family swoops in and tries to take the child away from you? Once you're divorced from Warrick, you won't have access to the several million bucks in that joint bank account anymore, and you couldn't afford to fight them for custody. At least he didn't knock you up knowingly or on purpose so he'd always have that leverage over you."

"My husband coulda gotten killed in that jungle, and you're still tryna convince me to divorce him? Do you even care I love him, no matter how our marriage started? How are you gonna tell me my feelings are wrong or stupid? Why is it such a crime for a girl to fall in love with her own husband? People in arranged marriages come to love each other all the time. This is no different."

"Rich people have nothing in common with us. Maybe he wanted the adventure of wooing a girl from the wrong side of the tracks, or it was part of an idealistic, youthful rebellion, or he saw you as a charity project, someone he felt sorry for. I'm sure any traces of his crush on you have long since faded since he's been over there. Even if this friendship were sincere, you'll be like strangers if he comes home."

"This child may be the only thing I'll ever have to remind me of my husband! You promised you'd keep your damn trap shut about how much you hate Ricky and how you're so convinced he was using me!"

"That was before I found out he knocked you up right before he left for Vietnam!"

Adicia stands up and points to the door. "If you can't respect my husband and the choice I made to marry him, you can get out of my house. You oughta be ashamed of yourself, Allen, berating me when you know damn well I'm already in a fragile emotional condition, and then finding out I'm pregnant as well. Say what you will about how you think I'm only imagining my feelings for Ricky, but I know this baby was made in love. You were not there in the bed with us to know I was just another notch in the bedpost for him and just acting out of grief or obligation. *I* was the one who told him I wanted to consummate our marriage. He never forced me. He was very hesitant at first."

Lenore comes through the door with the children. Adicia is relieved to see her, and rushes over to her open arms, sobbing hysterically.

"Justine called me while yous guys were arguing and told me to come over. Is this how you react to finding out your dear little sister is pregnant while her husband's in a warzone, Allen? You immediately start lecturing her about how you think her marriage is a mistake and her husband doesn't love her? Adicia needs all our support now more than ever!"

"I hate her husband. I never told her I was gonna pretend I like him or approve of their marriage. He's a rich boy. What does he want with a poor girl from the Lower East Side? His family's been swimming in dough for generations most likely; we're the first generation in our family to get out of that cesspool!"

"In case you're not aware of this, Allen, Adicia's husband gave up everything to be with her. Once that money in his bank account runs down, he'll be on his own like a regular working stiff. His parents tracked them down and berated Adicia and Justine quite horribly, and he stood up for our girls and showed his folks the door. He said he'd contact the cops if they ever came back again. He dropped out of college to run away with her. He writes letters to her every day he's able. He has no blood family support left. This is his family now, like it or not. There's a child coming into this world who may never know his daddy. Do you want that kid to hear his uncle constantly running down his father? How do you think Adicia feels when you talk this way about the man she loves? It doesn't matter how she came to love him or that she didn't start out in love with him. She loves him now, and you're adding to her heartbreak by yelling at her about it. You should be happy Adicia found true love instead of acting like it's the most horrible thing in the world."

"I'd be happy for her to find real love, but not with a rich boy with a silly name like Warrick Grover Carson!"

"He does not go by Warrick! Only his out of touch parents call him that!" Adicia shouts. "If anything happens to him, *I'll* be the one they notify, not his folks! I'm his lawfully-wedded wife and the mother of his child!"

"Daddy, you promised you wouldn't make Aunt Adicia cry again," Irene scolds him. "You're being very mean."

"If it makes you feel any better, I don't wish any ill will on Warrick. I won't rejoice if he's killed in action. That war is immoral, illegal, and unjustified. None of our boys deserves to die there. I hope your divorce goes as quickly and smoothly as possible if he returns, and that he doesn't fight you for custody of this child."

"Get it through your head, Allen! I'm staying with my husband!"

"Who's to say he hasn't gotten over his crush on her over there? He mighta fallen for a military nurse or Vietnamese whore."

"Get him out of my house! I'm not gonna give him Christmas presents if this is how he thinks of me!"

"Allen, if you can't respect your sister's absent husband and treat her respectfully, you can leave," Lenore orders. "If we had a doghouse, you'd be sleeping in it tonight for sure."

"Come on, Daddy, either apologize to Aunt Adicia or leave!" Irene agrees.

"We were having such a nice Christmas season," Adicia mourns. She gazes at her first Christmas tree with vacant eyes. "I wonder if they have Christmas over there when they're in the middle of a bombing campaign. They probably won't let anyone call home for the holiday."

Justine glares at Allen. "Remember how our witch of a mother destroyed what was supposed to be our first real Christmas? You're doing the exact same thing all over again."

In his mind's eye, as clear as though it only happened yesterday, Allen sees their mother banging on the fire escape door and storming inside before unleashing her ridiculous, probably drug-fueled rant. Emeline, Adicia, and Justine looked so beaten-down as they accepted their fate and followed their awful mother into Hell's Kitchen. He'd tried to do everything he'd known how to do to protect them and keep them with him in the safety and peace of the Village. Every time over the succeeding years they'd visited, he felt just as helpless and powerless when they inevitably had to leave and go back to the doom and gloom waiting in their parents' home. After what they went through growing up, he can't afford to burn any bridges, no matter how sick to his stomach he is over Adicia's marriage and pregnancy.

"I'm sorry," he manages to say. "I never meant to make my kid sister cry or upset you so much when you don't need any more upsetting. Whatever I think of that husband of yours, you're family unconditionally, and that baby's gonna be my niece or nephew. You know I'll never stop loving or supporting you, right?"

"Someone who loves and supports his sister unconditionally would never make her cry and run down her husband!"

"It's gonna be even harder for me to do now, but I'll try to keep my mouth shut about this situation. Lenore and I are gonna do all we can to help you with the baby, and I'll take off from work so I can be with you when you give birth. If Warrick comes home, and if he really does wanna stay with you, I'll try to hold my tongue. It's pretty rotten for a kid to hear his uncle putting down his father. If he's a good guy as you insist he is, the kid will pick up on that, just like if he's a rotten egg, the kid will notice that too."

"That's much better behavior," Lenore says. "You talked like a human being and acknowledged her feelings."

"Are we still gonna have a peaceful Christmas?" Justine asks.

"As peaceful as can be given what's happening in Vietnam," Allen says. "Are we friends again, Adicia?"

"I'm giving you one more chance, Allen. You've already gone off on me twice. One more strike and you're out."

"He's going to behave himself," Lenore speaks for her husband. "'Cause if he doesn't, he knows he's gonna be sleeping on the davenport for a very long time."

"I promise you, Adicia. I'm still far from happy about this situation, but out of respect and love for you, I'll keep the peace."

"I'm accepting your apology one last time. If you do this again, I won't accept any more apologies." Adicia reaches over and takes his hands in hers. "Would you like to feel the baby moving?"

He puts his hands on the bulge and smiles when he feels a slight movement. "I bet you're having a boy. You're carrying all your weight out front."

"Whatever it is, I hope it never has to go through any of the stuff we went through. This baby's gonna get all the love I was denied by our parents."

"You'll be holding it in your arms before you know it," Lenore says. "Before it's even a minute old, you'll love it enough to die for it. I can't believe our darling little Adicia's gonna become a mother in four months."

"I won't break our Christmas truce," Allen reiterates.

***

Though Operation Linebacker II is still raging, Adicia has tried to put her mind on happier things now that Ernestine and the Ryans are back. Normal eighteen-year-olds are long past a childlike appreciation of Christmas, but she's unashamedly seeing and doing everything through the eyes of a child. After never putting up a tree, hanging up stockings, baking Christmas goodies, sitting before a roaring fireplace, roasting chestnuts, or waking up early in the morning to an army of presents underneath a tree, she's ecstatic beyond words to finally get to do all this. She has the same sense of joy and wonder she felt back in 1962, when she thought she was going to celebrate her first real Christmas, and when she used to make the big walk to Midtown to gaze at the beautiful toys, decorations, and displays in the shop windows on Fifth Avenue, followed by visiting the immense tree in Rockefeller Center. This is what the spirit of Christmas is supposed to be all about, sort of like what the myth of Santa represents, if she'd ever believed in Santa. One need not believe in Santa to feel joy, peace, and wonder at this time of year.

"I never did this growing up, but I always wanted to," Adicia says after they get back from an early Christmas Eve service at Lucine and Zachary's Episcopal church. "I used to always look so longingly at the pretty gingerbread houses in store windows and wish we could make something so neat."

"Wouldn't it be groovy if we could live in a real gingerbread house?" Fiona asks. "Do you think there's an alternative universe where people live in a fantasy world with gingerbread houses and magic elves and fairies?"

"You're too cute," Ernestine says. "The name Baby really suited you perfectly."

"You could become an architect and design your own house to look like a gingerbread house," Deirdre says.

Adicia frosts the walls and roof together while Justine holds them in place, and Aoife sticks gumdrops and nonpareils around the perimeter of the gingerbread house and the big base plate it's situated on. Ernestine begins strategically frosting the roof and sticking jellybeans and peppermints in a pattern on it.

"Fiona and I are gonna start making the *bûche de Noël*," Deirdre says. "It looks fantastic, and it's so decadent."

"Can I roast chestnuts in the fireplace?" Justine asks.

"I've never used the fireplace before," Adicia says. "I'm scared of starting a fire, in case it spreads and we're left homeless."

"I know a thing or two about how to work a fireplace," David says. "Come with me."

All the girls look askance at Justine as she follows him out of the kitchen to the living room. From the radiant look in her eyes and the little looks she's sneaking at him, it appears thirteen-year-old Justine has a crush on eighteen-year-old David.

"There's no harm in it so long as she only looks," Ernestine finally whispers. "She knows well enough it's massively inappropriate to pursue a potential crush when the guy is five years older than her at her age. What girl hasn't had a fantasy crush on an older guy?"

"My brother knows enough not to mess around with underage girls either," Deirdre agrees. "He's too busy working and going to school to date. He'd rather go to an anti-war protest or demonstration against Nixon than take a girl to the movies or lunch."

"Can we have music while we're baking?" Aoife asks. "Anything but that godawful nonstop Christmas music on the radio. You'd think the normal person woulda gone nuts and thrown the radio out the window ages ago."

"They do go overboard," Fiona says. "I like a lot of the Christmas songs, but not after I've heard 'em fifty times in a week. There's only a couple of 'em I can hear many times, or any time during the year, and not immediately turn the dial on."

"Sure, I brought somea my records," Deirdre says.

"Just don't play that one record you play all the time, the one you liked so much you put the lyrics up all over the walls," Aoife says.

"You mean John's *Plastic Ono Band*? What's wrong with it? It's a very honest record."

"There's too much screaming. Why is he so mad in those songs?"

"It's part of Primal Scream therapy. I recommend it to you too, Adicia. It helps you purge out lingering pain and resentment left over from a crummy childhood, gets it all outta your system and heals you. My favorite song on that record is 'I Found Out.' He so gives the finger to everyone on that song!"

"How does it work?" Adicia asks. "Do you go to a shrink who tells you what to do?"

"You can do it on your own too. Just start screaming out all your pain, anger, and frustration. Better to get it out peacefully through screaming than beating someone up or getting in arguments."

"Please, not now!" Ernestine begs. "Christmas Eve isn't the time or place for Primal Scream therapy!"

"Allen and Lenore might think something bad's going on if they hear Adicia screaming," Fiona agrees.

"And it's probably not good for the baby to hear loud, scary noises," Aoife says.

"Maybe you're right," Deirdre admits. "We'll just play folk music."

"No Dylan, please," Adicia begs as Deirdre starts upstairs for her records. "I respect his talent and message, but his voice still isn't my cup of tea, and he's not the best soundtrack for Christmas baking."

True to her word, Deirdre only brings folk rock albums and her handful of classical records from the free bin at their old favorite record store in Greenwich Village. While Justine roasts chestnuts with Aoife and the other girls bake cookies, *bûche de Noël*, jellyrolls, brownies, chocolate toffee bars, and peanut brittle, the soft sounds of Deirdre's belovèd people's music waft through the house. David steps into the kitchen from time to time to help with baking, but otherwise occupies himself with reading the latest issues of *The People's Weekly World* and grumbling about the state of the world.

"I always liked this song," Adicia says of "Seven o'Clock News/ Silent Night" as they clean up and put away the baked goods at the end of the night, before heading off to sleep.

"Isn't it a crying pity it's just as eerily pertinent at the end of 1972 as it was back in '66?" Deirdre asks as she dumps dirty dishes in the sink. "Only difference is Nixon's heading into his second term in office, and back then he was only a former vice president."

"Peace will finally come when enough people decide they want peace more than war, and that they love life more than death," Fiona says.

As Adicia heads off to bed with Justine, her greatest hope for the coming year is that the beautiful, peaceful message of "Silent Night" will very soon overwhelm the ugly, painful, hateful messages on the nightly 7:00 news. It seems like a faraway dream, but she once thought having all the decent members of her family back together again and escaping from the black hole they grew up in was an idle daydream too. When enough people want something, they find a way to make it happen, even if it takes longer than anyone anticipated.

***

Adicia wakes up at 7:00 on Christmas Day to George's soft paws on her face. She sits up in surprise and sees Emeline sitting on the foot of the bed.

"Merry Christmas, my darling little sisters! How'd you like to go downstairs and open presents with the whole family?"

"How'd you get here?" Justine asks.

"Zachary drove me. We thought it'd be a sweet surprise."

"Of course I'm happy!" Adicia says. "I can't wait to start opening presents!"

She, Justine, and Emeline go down the hall to wake Ernestine and the Ryan girls, and then they go downstairs, Emeline carrying George so he won't get trampled underfoot. When they get to the bottom of the stairs, Justine and Adicia's eyes light up when they see Allen and Lenore's family, Lucine's family, and Gemma and Tyrone. An army of presents wrapped in brightly-colored paper and tied with shiny bows awaits them under the tree, so amply they spill out in all directions. There are also stuffed stockings hung all along the mantel.

"This is awesome!" Justine breathes.

"This is just like we always useta dream of!" Adicia says.

"We decided to come over ahead of your waking up so we could all celebrate together," Allen says. "I hope you forgive me for picking your lock with a safety pin. I still remember how to do that."

"You picked our lock?"

"I forgive you," Justine says. "It's not like you're a burglar."

Gemma stares at Adicia. "When did *that* happen! You don't look much further behind me!"

"I got pregnant in July. I'm due in late April or early May."

"It's Ricky's," Ernestine hastens to tell her. "Adicia didn't tell him yet."

"Well, what are you waiting for?" Gemma asks. "Allen, you're the aspiring photographer. You oughta bring Adicia over to your attic studio and take pregnancy pictures she can send to her husband! Boy, I never woulda dreamt in a million years I'd be pregnant at the same time as my next-youngest sister, since we're twelve years apart."

"I made hot chocolate with my crème Chantilly," Lenore says. "I'll bring it out on trays so we can drink while we open presents."

Adicia and Justine descend on the presents like vultures while Ernestine and Emeline show more restraint, helping to distribute presents and stockings. There are also presents from the van Niftriks, Julie and the Doyles, the Washingtons, the Strausslers, and Sarah's family. This is definitely better than what would've been in store for them back home. Right about now, Tommy must be unwrapping a bunch of toys Mrs. Troy used Mr. Troy's paychecks to pay for, with a stocking stuffed full of candies, chocolates, and oranges also paid for through Mr. Troy's paychecks, no Christmas tree in sight. They probably went to the usual random church last night, and will be having the usual garbage for breakfast, maybe bacon grease on toast with lumpy gray porridge. Part of her wonders if she's been dreaming the past five months, and any minute now she and Justine will wake up, still living above the Strausslers' bakery, Ricky safely up the street in his parents' house, no child growing inside of herself. Then she remembers, if she'd stayed, she would've been married to that vile criminal Seth by now, and might be expecting the child of a brute instead of the child of the man she grew to love and hold as her most dear husband.

"Can we reuse the wrapping paper?" Emeline asks when they finish unwrapping presents several hours later. "It's so wasteful to pay money for it and toss it in the trash just like that. Maybe it can be used in art projects."

"Boy, what fad won't you embrace?" Allen chuckles. "Environmentalism, vegetarianism, the hippie lifestyle, Eastern religions, Yoga, meditation, what's next?"

"I'm genuinely interested in these causes and things. I'd remain interested even if they weren't trendy."

"Can we go sledding on our new sled after breakfast?" Justine asks. "I'm sure it beats going down a hill on a garbage can lid."

"Sure," Allen promises. "We'll have our pick of snowy hills, not like in that run-down East River Park. It won't be as crowded as Central Park either."

"What's for breakfast?" Adicia asks. "Can I help with cooking?"

"You just keep enjoying your first real Christmas," Lucine says. "We'll have Belgian waffles made with walnut batter and topped with strawberries, blueberries, whipped cream, thick maple syrup, and peaches, French toast made with almond batter, bacon, and omelettes of your choice."

"I'll make the omelettes," David says.

"Can you make mine with mushrooms, green peppers, extra eggs, tomatoes, and spinach?" Justine asks, noticing how dreamy he looks with his longer hair.

"You bet, kiddo. You want orange juice, grape juice, or milk with that?"

"Orange juice with no pulp."

"Yeah, pulp is nasty. I'll have it whipped up for you in a jiffy."

Everyone notices Justine staring at him with moony eyes as he disappears into the kitchen. Lenore glares at Allen when she sees him starting to get up.

"Lighten up. She's only thirteen," she whispers. "Most girls her age have crushes on guys they know they'll never have a chance with. Even if he liked her back, he knows they're not at the same place in life at thirteen and eighteen. He'd be a gentleman and wait till she's old enough, just like you did with me."

"This is the best Christmas ever!" Adicia says. "Next year will be even better if Ricky's home!"

"Yes, next year will be even better," Allen manages to say. "The entire family will be together again, and two new members will be celebrating their first Christmas. Your baby's only gonna be a month younger than Gemma's. Who knows, maybe Emeline will have a husband by then."

"Don't hedge any bets," Emeline says, petting George under the chin.

Adicia puts her hands on her bulge. "I feel it kicking. I guess the baby's having a nice Christmas too."

"He sure must be, especially now that he knows he's not being kept a secret anymore," Allen says. "Now why don't we all pose for family pictures?"

***

While Mr. and Mrs. Troy always put up their Christmas tree after the Western Christmas and took it down after Orthodox Christmas, Adicia is starting to think about taking hers down on Orthodox Christmas, which falls on the first Saturday of 1973. She's admiring the lights, colored bulbs, pinecones, birds' nests, strings of popcorn and cranberries, tinsel, and holiday-themed ornaments, wishing she could leave the tree up forever, when she hears the letter carrier putting the mail in the slot.

"Are you gonna get the mail, or should I?" Justine asks. "I think it's okay if we leave the tree up for one more week. I don't wanna rush taking it down immediately after the last part of the holiday season passes. Let's savor it for just a little while more."

"Sure, I'll get it." Adicia walks away from the tree and goes to the closet with the mail chute. "We should get our own mailbox, so we won't hafta go into this dark closet to fetch the mail all the time."

"Can we paint it pretty colors and paint birds and ladybugs on it?"

"Yeah, that'll be fun." Adicia pulls the mail out of the chute, glad none of it fell on the floor so she won't have to squat down in her condition of twenty-four weeks.

She drops the mail on the coffeetable when she comes out of the closet and immediately pitches the junk into the garbage can. Most of their mail is junk mail and utility bills, with the occasional letters from Ernestine, the Ryans, Betsy, Julie, Marjani, and the Strausslers.

"Look at that!" Justine shouts. "It's postmarked Vietnam! We haven't heard anything from Ricky since before Operation Linebacker II began!"

Adicia tears it open with shaking fingers. She starts crying in relief when she sees it's dated December 30, the day after the campaign ended.

"He's okay," she sobs. "He's safe. He survived the battle." Through tear-clouded eyes, she starts reading the letter.

My most darling wife Adicia,

I know how difficult this separation must be on you, and even more so after the battle I was just in, so I'm writing to reassure you I survived and am as safe and sound as I can be in a warzone. It means so much to me that I've got a sweet little wifey waiting patiently for me and that you're staying loyal to me even though ours is a marriage of convenience, not a mutual love match. I'd rather have a wife who's my best friend than someone I can only relate to on a superficial romantic level. I hope absence is making your heart grow fonder and that you'll love me the way a wife loves her husband if I come home. My unending love for you is the one thing that keeps me going and alive. When this is all over, I know I can count on coming home to your sweet, loving arms and giving you all the love I've been longing to give since I've been away. I never thought I could love a girl as much as I love you, especially considering you don't love me in that way and that we were barely together before Uncle Sam called me up. I know you've got what it takes to continue being patient and loyal and saving all your love for me when I return. If you still want me to be your husband, I promise I'll be the best husband you could've asked for. You're the best wife I could've asked for, no matter how we ended up together.

Well, I hope this sets your mind at ease a little bit, knowing I wasn't among the guys who were killed or captured in the recent battle. I hate to think of my sweet little wifey being grief-stricken over the thought that the worst happened. Tell Justine I said hi too, and that I hope she's doing well in school. I hope you all had a good Christmas, though I couldn't be present at our first Christmas as a married couple. Always remember I'll love you until my dying breath.

All my unending love,

Ricky

"So long as there aren't any other major battles, I think he's gonna be okay," Adicia breathes. "But we never can be too sure. It's time to tell him how I feel about him and that he's got a child on the way. He shouldn't have to go to a potential early grave never knowing how very much I've grown to love him or that he'd be leaving behind someone to carry on his bloodline."

"Of course you oughta tell him. I don't want you feeling guilty or beating yourself up if the worst happens and you forever missed that chance to tell him how you feel and that his name will live on."

Adicia goes into the room that was in the process of being made into an office when Ricky was taken away. She pulls out one of the photos Allen took of her on Christmas and writes "Christmas 1972, 22 weeks along" on the back. Then she addresses an envelope and pulls out a pen and paper. She's never considered herself as literary of a person as Emeline, but she hopes Ricky thinks she can string together thoughts and words in a pleasing way.

January 6, 1973, Saturday,

My dear, sweet Ricky,

I was sick at heart over the recent battle you were involved in, but I'm very relieved you're safe and sound. I was tortured over the thought that you might die without knowing I love you. I don't know or care anymore if I loved you all along but didn't want to admit it or couldn't figure it out, or if I grew to love you after we were married. All I know is I love you with everything inside me, and I can't wait for you to come home to me so I can give you all my love in person and never let you go again. There was so much love in my heart for so many years I was longing to give to someone outside of my family and friends, the kind of love that can only be given by a woman to a man. I love you as a friend, a domestic partner, and in a romantic and sexual way. You were the one I waited for my entire life, no matter how unexpected this match was or the unconventional way we ended up as man and wife. I wish I could tell you how much I love you for the first time in person, but I wanted you to know in case the worst happens.

There's also something else I've been keeping from you, but it's another good kind of secret. I'm sure you remember what happened the night before you left. Well, even if the worst does happen, I'll always have a forever reminder of you. See the picture for proof. It does only take one time. The secret recently came out to my brother and oldest sister, so now everyone knows it, and I'm no longer hiding my expanding body in oversized, baggy clothes. Some people think it's a boy because I look like I'm carrying all my weight out front, but that's an old wives' tale. I won't know for sure until late April or early May, when I'm holding our child in my arms. I wish you were here to feel the baby moving and to be with me as I bring our child into this world, but if you come home, there's always a next time. Even if the worst happens, sweetheart, at least you'll know you left behind a child and that your branch of the family tree will live on.

I love you with every breath in my soul,

Adicia

Chapter 57: Bad News

"Us Troys really do run to girls," Justine says as she holds Gemma and Tyrone's new baby, Adrienne Nicolette Duffy-Troy, who was born on March 30. "I bet Adicia's baby will be a girl too, even if she is carrying all the weight out front. That's just an old wives' tale."

"How many weeks are you now, Adicia?" Gemma asks.

"Thirty-seven," she says proudly. "Only a few more weeks to go, and then I'm full-term. I might be holding my own baby by the time the month is up."

"I know you're planning to do it at home like Lenore and Sarah, but if you need to be transferred, maternity wards nowadays are so much better than they used to be. I didn't go drug-free like Lucine, but I wasn't tied down or yelled at either. They gave me a drug that blocked out mosta the pain but didn't knock me out cold or erase my memories. I said I'd sue for malpractice and assault if anyone tried to inject me with that twilight cocktail or tie me up again. All these years later, I can't get over that ass of a doctor who decided he'd like to go out to supper and see a movie with his wife instead of delivering my baby, and how I was given a drug to stall my labor while the almighty doctor was playing. He shoulda entered another profession, or another field of medicine, if he didn't want his schedule interrupted."

Out of the corner of her eye, Adicia sees a strange man in a uniform coming up the cul-de-sac and approaching her door. Her heart sinks when she realizes he must've been sent here to deliver bad news.

"What are you looking at?" Emeline asks.

Adicia points, her throat very dry. Everyone turns to look at the man, assuming the same thing Adicia has, that he can only be here for one reason. When the doorbell rings, no one wants to get up to answer it. They all sit around looking at one another until finally Allen gets up. Whatever he has to say, it's definitely going to ruin their nice weekend.

"Does a Mrs. Warrick Grover Carson live here?"

"My name is Adicia." She chafes at being passively identified as Ricky's wife and not assigned her proper name.

"Mrs. Carson, my name is Colonel Leonard Sullivan, and I'm with the United States Air Force. I have bad news about your husband."

Adicia starts hyperventilating and feels as though she's either going to faint or go into premature labor. Emeline reaches over and takes her hands, squeezing them very tightly.

"As you probably heard, the last troops and non-vital military personnel were withdrawn from Vietnam at the end of last month. Shortly before the withdrawal, your husband was wounded in an ambush while he and some of the other airmen were doing reconnaissance in one of our last sweeps of the area. He was shot seven times."

Adicia wants with everything inside of her to scream, releasing the Primal Screams Deirdre told her about, but she doesn't want to display her emotions like that in front of the officer, who already thinks she's just a flighty woman who doesn't deserve her own identity. Instead she hears herself asking, "Will his body be flown home for burial?"

"Oh, no, your husband isn't dead. He was flown to a military hospital in California after he was found and the Air Force medic treated him. His personal effects were collected from his camp and sent along after he was evacuated. He's been unconscious since the attack, and he's had one surgery so far. Several more surgeries are needed. Don't worry, the Air Force will pay for his medical bills. Sorry to have to break such upsetting news to you in your condition."

"I only have about a month left before it's born," Adicia says lifelessly, barely comforted by the news Ricky is alive and in the safety of the United States. "Will I be able to see him in the hospital?"

"If he regains consciousness and is rehabilitated sufficiently, the hospital staff will probably be able to admit visitors. His condition is so precarious, the only people allowed to see him are doctors, nurses, and the military chaplain."

Lenore puts her arms around Adicia and rocks her back and forth.

"What exactly happened to him? Is he paralyzed or brain damaged?"

The colonel looks at the paper in his hands. "He was shot twice in the right leg, once in the right arm, once in the right shoulder, twice in the chest, and once in the head. Both of the bullets he took to the chest missed his heart by less than an inch and didn't hit any nerves or vital organs, and the shot to the head thankfully wasn't deep or serious enough to cause any predicted brain damage or loss of major senses."

Adicia feels as though her spirit is outside her body. Her entire being is numb, sort of like the hollow feeling she's sometimes had during a fever or bad cold. Surely this happened to another draftee airman. Not to her husband, who once said he'd rather make friends with the Vietnamese than shoot at them sight unseen. It's an abomination he survived Operation Linebacker II only to be shot seven times in an ambush right before the remaining troops were withdrawn.

"Since he only was inducted in July, his term of service isn't up yet, but his injuries make it impossible for him to complete his term of service in a noncombatant capacity in Thailand, where the rest of the Seventh Air Force was transferred. He's been honorably discharged." The colonel opens his briefcase and pulls out a small box. "These belong to your husband, Mrs. Carson, but given his present condition, it was thought best you be given them for safekeeping until he recovers enough to come home. I'm sure he'll be as proud to display them as his country was to give them to him for his brave service."

Adicia is shaking so violently she can't open the box. Lucine reaches over and finally opens it for her. Inside are the Purple Heart medal, a silver oak leaf cluster, and a bronze oak leaf cluster. A Purple Heart and additional oak clusters to mark multiple combat wounds would be an honor if this were the war of their parents' generation. Now it's a tragic, cruel joke, since Ricky never went there voluntarily, and he and everyone in Adicia's family were opposed to United States involvement since the very beginning. He didn't go out of his way to do anything heroic. He was shot in an ambush, not wounded in battle or hand-to-hand combat.

"What are the little leaves for?" Justine asks.

"You get a bronze oak leaf cluster for one or two additional wounds, and a silver cluster for five additional wounds. You should all be very proud of your airman for his brave service to our country." The colonel puts papers on the coffeetable. "This is additional information about the incident and who to contact for more information. Once again, I'm very sorry to have to break such bad news, but you can all rest assured that people who care about our servicemen recognize his heroic conduct."

"One more thing," Adicia manages to choke out when the colonel starts to get up. "I've heard about guys coming home from Vietnam getting spat at, shouted at, and beaten up. Is there a chance that'll happen to my husband if he's discharged in uniform or people see him coming out of a military hospital?"

He shakes his head. "The people who do that are a disgrace. People a generation ago never would've treated veterans like that. If anyone treats your husband with such disrespect after he took seven bullets to defend our country, that's a reflection on them, not on anything your husband did wrong."

Adicia bursts into tears after the colonel has left. Allen and Lenore help her off the davenport and support her as she struggles to climb the stairs and walk to her room, where she collapses onto the bed and puts her hands over her midsection. The baby is kicking furiously, though at least these aren't premature contractions.

"Those dirty, rotten Viet Cong," Allen rants. "I don't exactly have the most positive feelings towards Warrick and your marriage, but I never wished any harm on the boy. I could've taken 'em all on myself if I'd been over there and avenged the wrong done to you. Those awards he got are jokes. You're supposed to get a Purple Heart for bravery in combat, not getting attacked in a war you weren't involved in by choice. I wouldn't blame him if he throws them into a river when he gets home, like other Vietnam vets have done at anti-war protests."

"If either of those two shots to the chest had pierced his heart or any vital organs and nerves, he'd be a dead man! I don't wanna think about what woulda happened had the shot to the head gone deep into the brain!"

Lenore lies next to her and holds her. "This is the worst thing that could happen after you already lost him to the draft, but we'll all be here for you no matter what. That was just wrong this happened so soon before the withdrawal."

"At least Ricky knew I love him and that we're having a baby. He was so over the moon after he found out he fathered a child. He couldn't wait to get home and be a daddy. A girl would've had ballet classes, an immense dollhouse, and all the dolls her room could hold, and a boy would've had all the toys his room could hold, baseball lessons, and scouting. All his buddies in the company congratulated him on knocking me up after only one time. He was so happy to find out I'd fallen for him. He couldn't wait to hear me tell him I love him in person, and said the words would sound even sweeter then."

"Do you think you have what it takes to be the wife of a disabled man? God forbid this happen, but he might come home with memory loss, diminished eyesight, or a limp."

"I'd love my sweet Ricky even more if he came home in a wheelchair or with a disability. He loves me just the way I am, and I promised in my wedding vow to love, support, honor, and comfort him no matter what too."

"I am so sorry this happened to you," Allen says. "You don't deserve this. Haven't you already been dealt enough bad hands since you were born? You deserve a happy ending, not so many false starts on a happy ending."

"My darling Ricky didn't deserve to be shot seven times! Getting shot even once must hurt like hell. What did he ever do to deserve getting so badly hurt? He mighta died instantly if he'd been hit in the heart or neck, or if he'd had a more serious head wound! And now he's unconscious!" She looks up at Allen intensely. "What if he's out of it as long as Carlos was?"

"Everyone's different. Your Warrick might snap back a lot faster. He knows you love him, however misguided I might think that love is. Carlos knew no one loved or supported him. Mother was more upset she'd forever lost onea her extra sources of income and gotten yet another black mark on her joke of a reputation."

"I don't care if he never works again or can't go back to school! I'll go to school myself and get another job! Or I can study business like you did so I can help with running the bakery!"

"I want you at the bakery. It's our family business. You, me, and Lenore. If he's capable of it, and he wants to stay married to you, I'll let your Warrick have a job there too. Maybe he can do simple baking, stock shelves, or make home deliveries."

"He was such a gentle soul. He wouldn't hurt a fly. Those Viet Cong just saw him as an ugly, invading American and hurt him. They didn't care what his political views are or that he's anti-war and wasn't in the military by choice."

Justine comes into the room and sits on the foot of the bed. "Would you like something to eat or drink? You shouldn't let yourself get this upset so close to your due date. You want a healthy baby, and you have to be strong for your baby."

"My baby will be born without knowing its father. It might never know its father. What bull the officer was spouting, about how we should be proud of Ricky for being a hero. Being ambushed doesn't equal being a hero! He wasn't in battle and didn't seek out a dangerous situation!"

"Would you like to throw the medals away, or do you wanna wait for Ricky to come home and do it himself?"

"I don't care what happens to them. Just put them somewhere so I can't see them. The cop who drove us back to the van Niftriks' after Seth tried to kidnap me was wounded in Okinawa in the last war. *That's* a real war hero who deserves a Purple Heart, not a draftee in an immoral war."

Gemma gently knocks on the door, though it's most of the way open. "Is it okay if I come in?"

"Sure, come and join us," Allen says.

Gemma sits on the remaining space on the bed. "Adicia, if you'd like to do something to take your mind offa this, you're welcome to come over and spend a day at my store. I'm off work for awhile after having Adrienne, but I want to stop by next week to check on how things are going in my absence. Lucine wants to come by too. I can give you a tour of the antiques wing, and show you around the bou-tique side. I'll give you a discount if you wanna buy anything."

"Sure, it couldn't hurt. Could I listen to some soft music in the meantime? Can I listen to the song we walked down the aisle to at your wedding, Allen?"

"Sure, I'll bring some records over. You can borrow 'em as long as you want, so long as you give 'em back eventually."

Adicia remains curled up in the fetal position and crying her eyes out while Justine gets tea and graham crackers with honey and Allen goes next door to fetch some records. She wonders how much suffering one person can take in one lifetime, as the tray of food is brought in and Allen puts the record on the turntable. She closes her eyes at the sweet, soothing sounds of "Benedictus," and wishes she could go back in time to July 1966, when she was a bridesmaid and proudly, happily marching down the aisle with her sisters and friends in the happiest year of their lives. Things weren't so easy then either, but they weren't so awful as they've been since Ricky went away. Given the choice, she has no idea which poison she'd prefer, the crummy life in Hell's Kitchen or her adult life with a husband who deeply adores her, even though he hasn't been by her side in almost nine months.

∗∗∗

Monday, April 16, Adicia, Lucine, and baby Simone head off to

Gemma's store in Cambridge. Adicia has had time to process the shock, and now feels able to venture past her comfort zone and do something outside of work, errands, and hanging around the house. She's also starting to feel a bit more cheerful, because her family have been invited to Sarah's first-night Seder tonight. When Sarah worked as a near-slave for Mrs. Troy, she never got to celebrate Passover in the tenement. She always had to go to community events, but now that she has her own family, she's able to celebrate the holiday in her own home, with her own traditions.

"You're as big as a house," Lucine teases as they walk into the store. "Are you sure you're not having twins or triplets?"

"I hope not! Little women like me show the weight gain more, and it just looks really big when it'd look rather normal on an average-sized woman. At least the kid's still inside me. I wouldn't want my baby to see me so upset."

"You should enjoy all the time you have left for the kid to stay baking inside you. When it's ready, it'll come out. Not too soon and not too late."

Gemma stands by a glass display case containing antique china, while all her employees take a break to fawn over Adrienne. She looks up and smiles when she sees her sisters and niece.

"No traffic on the way over?"

"It was a smooth ride," Lucine says. "A very scenic drive. Adicia drove so I could hold Simone on my lap. She's too big now to hold anyone on her lap."

"I love driving. It gives you so much freedom and independence. You take getting around for granted when you grow up in the big city, but then you realize you've gotta learn how to do it for yourself when you move away."

The employees turn to Simone when they see another baby being brought in. Lucine proudly lets them admire her, though she doesn't pass her around. Gemma's employees will have to look and not touch.

"You're all sisters?" the assistant manager asks. "They look so different from you, Gemma."

"Our facial features are similar, even if Gemma's blonde and we're brunettes," Lucine says. "According to our dad, we look very French and take after his side."

Adicia admires the old coins in various baskets on top of the display case opposite the china. "Were somea these coins in use when you were little, Gemma? I recognize somea them from older change, but I'm pretty sure they weren't minted in my lifetime."

"Mercury dimes were used when I was a little kid. The dime with FDR came out when I was four. The Liberty Walking quarters and Buffalo nickels were before even my time, believe it or not. I'm not quite that much older than you."

"Do you have any antique TVs? Emeline says a lot of 'em look like radios or cabinets. A lot of people never know what kinda treasure they've found in the attic. I'd love to have one for my own if you have any, even if it no longer works."

"We can look in the big backroom where mosta the furniture's stored. But you haven't gotten the whole tour around this part of the antiques wing yet. How about checking out these fur coats?"

Adicia runs her hands along a silver fox coat. "It's so soft and pretty. When I'm back at my normal size, I'd love to wear something like this. You can wear them, right? They're not just for display?"

"We sell old flapper hats and antique clothes, and women have worn them for costume parties. Unless the fur's very frayed, I don't see why not. Clothes in the old days were a lot better-made. People wore clothes for a long time and didn't throw 'em out when they got a tear or a strap broke."

"Before he was taken away from me, I thought Ricky would get me a beautiful fur like this for our first Christmas." Adicia's voice breaks. "Maybe he'll get one for me after he recovers."

"I wouldn't be too sure of that if I were you, you little street urchin."

Adicia, Lucine, and Gemma turn around and come face-to-face with Ricky's parents. Mrs. Carson is wearing a hat with fake strawberries, canary feathers, poker chips, and candy corn, and Mr. Carson is wearing a suit that looks like it came straight out of the last century. Both of them look just as ridiculous as always.

"Who the hell are you, and why are you talking so meanly to my little sister?" Lucine demands.

"Oh, you're one of the many other sisters in that overpopulated family from the ghetto? We're Mr. and Mrs. Willoughby Aristotle Carson, Miss Troy's parents-in-law. We received a letter saying Warrick was wounded in Vietnam last month and is being treated in a military hospital in California until further notice. So how about it, Miss Troy?

While he's still unconscious and out of state, you let us take care of all the paperwork that'll end this joke of a marriage," Mrs. Carson says icily. "You forget we know your address. We went up today to try to negotiate the divorce, and we followed you when we saw you heading out of the house."

"That's called stalking!" Gemma says.

"Who's the father? Certainly not my Warrick. You said the marriage was unconsummated, and we know you already whored around with at least two other men before marrying my son. If it is somehow Warrick's baby and you did consummate your marriage in the few days between our last visit and his induction into the Air Force, you'll never be able to keep it. That baby's a Carson, and belongs in our family. We'll take the paperwork over to the hospital and have him sign for a divorce. If we have to, we'll follow you to the hospital and take the baby as soon as it's born. Poor trash like you don't know how to raise kids properly. But of course, that's assuming Warrick's the father. Do you know who the father of this bastard is, or were you planning to trick him into thinking he was the father so he wouldn't divorce you and you could continue using his money, living in his house, and driving his car?"

Gemma raises her hand and slaps Mrs. Carson hard on the face. "How dare you call my sister a whore who doesn't know who fathered her baby and threaten to take her child away from her!"

"If you're the one we heard gave away her firstborn son, you're hardly one to lecture us about proper mothering rights." Mrs. Carson rubs her face. "I suppose they don't teach poor trash like you to respect your elders and to not use physical force against people putting you in your place."

"I gave my birth son to a good couple. The boy will be twelve in June. I never felt a bond to him because I have no memory of his birth and never wanted to be pregnant. Hell, I never wanted to marry my birth son's father, but my parents forced me, and I went through with it so my sacrifice could serve as an example to my five little sisters. Thank God, none of them suffered the same fate I did."

"I'm not divorcing Ricky, and you can have my baby when you tear it from my cold dead hands," Adicia says. "Even if you force yourselves into his room, he'd never sign divorce papers. He loves me too much."

"Oh, Warrick doesn't love you. He was in love with the idea of courting a girl from the wrong side of town. I'm sure his adventure in Vietnam has set him straight for the rest of his life. He'll never try to rebel against his raising ever again. We'll select a nice rich girl for him to marry, a girl who deserves the title of Mrs. Warrick Grover Carson, a girl who'll be a loving stepmother to that kid if Warrick's the father. How many men do you think are candidates?"

"My name is Adicia Éloïse Carson, née Troy. I have a name, and it's not Mrs. Warrick Grover. That's like saying I'm Ricky's wife without using my real name. You're writing me out of existence and passively identifying me through my husband when you refer to me in that way. Given that I've only had consensual sexual relations with one man, your son, and that I menstruated after I was raped by the man my parents were tryna force me to marry, I'm pretty sure Ricky's the father, unless I'm closely related to the Virgin Mary. Oh, and you won't be following me to any hospital, since I'm having my baby in the safety of my own home."

"Isn't that illegal?" Mr. Carson asks. "Did you already blow through all Warrick's money that you couldn't afford a hospital and real doctor? Or do you really want a dead baby that you'd purposely have one without qualified medical personnel? Someone your size would probably need a Caesarean."

"Your son was just shot seven times in Vietnam, and you're busy putting his grieving wife down when she's pregnant with their firstborn child?" Lucine asks. "I guess they never taught you rich people how to act like decent human beings. I met your son once, before he was ripped away from Adicia, and he seemed like a swell guy. Not all people born into money are bastards. When Adicia was nine, a millionaire was super-nice to her and gave her a ten-dollar bill when she washed his windshield. He wasn't born a millionaire, and musta remembered what it felt like to not have that much money. You have no basic sense of decency and human emotions."

"What's your blood type, Miss Troy?" Mrs. Carson blazes on. "We can narrow down who the father might be if we test blood types. Do you have the names of the other possibilities so we can start contacting them?"

"Ricky's the father of my baby! He knows I'm carrying his child! And my title is Mrs. Carson now, not Miss Troy. You can call me Mrs.

Carson all you want, so long as you don't call me Mrs. Warrick Grover Carson."

"If you don't get out of my store this instant, I'm calling the cops," Gemma announces. "Yous guys oughta feel ashamed of yourselves for the horrible things you're saying to my sister. You try being an eighteen-year-old bride who has her husband stolen away from her and then finds out he was shot seven times in a warzone while she's carrying their child."

"I already called the cops, Ms. Duffy-Troy," one of the younger employees announces. "I thought there might be trouble, so I didn't waste any time in calling for help."

"Go ahead and call the police," Mrs. Carson scoffs. "They'll take our side as Warrick's parents. They might even help us with securing a divorce."

"Remember your condition, Adicia," Lucine says as she steers her towards the furniture wing. "You have to keep your emotions under control so you can have a healthy baby and not go into labor too early. Those awful people are just throwing empty threats around. They can't legally take your precious baby away from you. You'll be holding your firstborn in your arms in only a few more weeks. When Ricky gets better and comes home, you'll raise your baby together and give it all the love our parents never gave us. Those people have some nerve bullying you."

"If they want my baby so badly, they can kill me and get it over with, 'cause I'd never turn my baby over to them. I would die for that baby even before it's been born."

"You put our parents to shame. They woulda sold us all for drugs if they could've, and only put in the bare minimum of effort so they wouldn't look bad. The thought of dying for any of us, probably even Tommy, would be foreign to them. A real mother would sacrifice her life for her child, no questions asked."

Gemma smiles when she sees the flashing blue and red lights approaching and the cop car pulling up in her parking lot. She rushes to greet them when they come through the door. Mr. and Mrs. Carson also smile, believing the cops will automatically take their side.

"What seems to be the problem here?"

Gemma turns around and motions to her sisters to come back out. "These vile excuses for life are my second-youngest sister's estranged parents-in-law. They followed her here so they could harass her about ending her marriage against her will."

Adicia pulls herself up to her full height, though she's still not five feet when she stands as straight as possible. "Officers, my name is Adicia Carson. My husband served with the Air Force in Vietnam and was shot seven times last month, shortly before the troops were all withdrawn. He received the Purple Heart for his ordeal. Right now he's unconscious and in a military hospital in California. He's had two surgeries so far and has at least three more coming up. He was shot twice in the right leg, once in the right arm, once in the right shoulder, twice in the chest, and once in the head. I'm only a few weeks away from giving birth to our firstborn child. His parents never approved of him associating with me 'cause we're from different classes, but he picked me over them the last time they came up here to harass us."

"It doesn't matter what that poor trash thinks. We are Warrick's parents," Mrs. Carson says. "I don't even know that's my son's baby. As soon as we can, we're heading out to California to get him to sign divorce papers. I don't care if we have to guide his hand in a signature."

"So let me get this straight," one of the cops says. "Your son, this poor girl's husband and father of her unborn baby, was shot seven times while serving his country, and you're railing against her and scheming to take advantage of your unconscious, severely wounded son? In this country, last time I checked, divorce proceedings have to be initiated by the spouses, not their parents, unless it's an illegal marriage, the parties are underage, or someone's mentally incapacitated. Being unconscious temporarily doesn't count as incapacitated."

"I'd wanna stay with my husband even if he never was rehabilitated one hundred percent," Adicia says. "We're both of legal age. I'm eighteen and he's twenty. Everything was perfectly legal. We were married in the courthouse in downtown New York, had our license signed by a legit judge and two witnesses of legal age, didn't lie on our marriage license, got the required bloodwork, and have never been married before."

"Did you really say you'd guide your son's hand over to a divorce document and sign it while holding his hand for him?" the second cop asks. "That's illegal, and both of them would have every right to press charges against you for such an activity. The signature on a legal document like a divorce paper isn't valid if it were signed under duress, by someone of limited mental capacity, or while drunk or semi-conscious."

Gemma hopes she's sporting her best poker face.

"They also threatened to take my baby away from me, Officers! I'm not handing over my firstborn, or any child of mine, to these awful people to raise! My husband doesn't want to leave me. He was looking forward to having this baby and meeting it when he came home. They said they'd follow me to the hospital and steal it from me there."

"Have you no shame?" the first cop demands of the Carsons. "You'd seriously scheme to steal this poor girl's baby in addition to plotting to arrange an illegal divorce? You could be charged with kidnapping!"

"I know my husband's the father. I'm not a slut. They think I'm trash 'cause my class origins are poor, but their precious East Village was part of *my* family's neighborhood less than ten years ago. I'm proud of being from the Lower East Side, no matter how poor and run-down it is. People there take care of their own and are happy with what little they have. They don't talk trash about people who don't have as much money as they do."

"Child, please. You're from a dumping-ground of poor immigrant trash," Mr. Carson says. "The people in the ghetto didn't get proper jobs, educations, and money since our government wisely stopped admitting so many foreigners. My side of the family has been in this country since the 1740s, and my wife's family has been here since the 1760s. When did your family step off the boat, 1900?"

"My mother's family came from Belgium in the late 1840s, and my dad's family were French Huguenots who came in the 1680s. Looks like I've got deeper American roots than either of you. Almost three hundred years in this country."

"Look, even if your crazy accusations were correct and your son weren't the biological father of this unborn baby, he'd still be the legal father," the second cop says. "When a baby is born to a married couple, and the man had access to his wife at that time, he's the legal father even if he might not be the blood father."

"I know who my baby's father is. I'd stake my life on it. I'm not a whore who sleeps around. My husband's the father."

"Can we get a legal document drawn up so these people don't come around and harass us again?" Lucine asks. "Though we don't live in this city. Only our oldest sister does. We'd have to go to the police station in our town."

"Can you please contact the hospital and tell 'em not to admit these people? I don't want them forcing his signature on a divorce document!"

"Come by later, and we'll take care of a restraining order for both you and the military hospital," the first cop says. "I was in the Air Force in the Korean War. I'll be glad to do a favor for the wife of a fellow airman."

"You oughta be ashamed of yourselves," the second cop says. "You never threaten to take a baby away from its mother. Your son and this girl entered into a consensual, legal marriage and consummated it. You don't have a leg to stand on regarding kidnapping this unborn baby and forcing a divorce."

"I love my husband and want to stay married to him."

"You will remain in your marriage, Mrs. Carson," the first cop reassures her. "No one's going to steal your baby. I can't believe these people are so stupid they'd matter-of-factly admit their plans for such conspiracies in front of two cops."

"She's poor trash from New York City's ghetto! Rich and poor don't mix!" Mrs. Carson shrills. "People always stayed with their own kind until all these radical protestors showed up in the last ten years!"

"Mr. and Mrs. Carson, are you familiar with the Five Little Peppers series?" Lucine asks. "A rich boy on vacation meets a very poor family, and becomes such good friends with them, his crotchety old dad is won over and moves them into his mansion. It turns out the mother's long-lost rich cousin is their benefactor's son-in-law. Everyone lovingly takes these former poor people into their circle and doesn't care about their dirt-poor origins, except their benefactor's mean-spirited, unpleasant cousin. Ricky was for Adicia what Jasper King was for the Five Little Peppers, stepping out of his comfort zone and taking a chance on friendship with someone from such a different social class and world. Isn't it nice to have a rags to riches story and a deus ex machina ending?"

"Right now my life feels more like a Grimms' fairytale," Adicia says glumly. "At least somea those fairytales have eventual happy endings."

"Is that the series with the really annoying youngest kid?" Gemma asks.

"According to Emeline, Phronsie gets better as she gets older," Lucine says. "Mr. and Mrs. Carson, you need to step the hell back and let my sister enjoy her rags to riches story and the fact that she found someone who loves her just the way she is. Ricky will recover eventually, and she'll stand by him no matter what. That's what a loyal, loving wife does, not abandon her husband when awful things happen to him."

Two customers come in the front door and step back when they see the cops.

"Oh, come on in," Gemma urges them. "This is nothing to be concerned about. We had to call for the cops 'cause my sister's estranged parents-in-law showed up and started threatening her. It's all taken care of now, isn't it, Mr. and Mrs. Carson?"

"Yes, it is," the second cop says. "These people are on their way out, or else they'll be run in."

Ricky's parents look indignant and outraged as they march back to their car.

"Well, now that that unpleasant business is behind us, shall we continue taking a tour of my store?" Gemma asks. "After you're done here, you can go to the police station and have a restraining order drawn up."

"You'll have to go to a judge and attend a hearing, but we'll show up as witnesses," the first cop explains. "Since they're not far gone enough to be threatening physical violence, it'd probably be a protective order and not a restraining order. It's basically the same thing, only for different reasons. The paperwork will be available at the courthouse. Usually the trial is brief and is about two weeks after the initial order is granted."

All her life, Adicia heard people railing against cops for how they so often single out poor people and minorities for unfair treatment, since they're not taken as seriously as white men with money, and they don't have the kind of financial resources to stay out of trouble and pay legal fees. If Carlos had been a rich man, he might not be in prison for life, no matter what sorts of illegal activities he did. Now that she's a married woman and no longer in the old neighborhood, people in authority take her more seriously and stand up for her when she's being threatened. She hopes more cops are like these two officers, Officer Brankovic, and the cop who let Allen off with just a warning for fishing in the East River. Though it hurts to deal with the latest tragic hand she's been dealt, it's nice to know people in authority will defend her rights and treat her with respect. She's come a long way from the Lower East Side and Hell's Kitchen, she thinks with bittersweet satisfaction.

Chapter 58: A Bittersweet Birth

May 5, Saturday, Adicia has been feeling funny all day. Not wanting Allen to order her to go home and rest, she's continued to work the counter and help with baking, ignoring the pains emanating from her midsection. She's forty-one weeks along, and Radana said the baby can come anytime now.

As Adicia stirs a bowl of thumbprint cookie batter and Allen mixes orange frosting, she releases the spoon and sinks onto the floor, clutching her stomach. Allen orders another employee to take over for them and rushes to his sister, who's curled up on her side and grimacing.

"Would you like me to drive you home?" he asks. "I'll get Lenore and Emeline to come over to be your support people, though it's probably too soon to call for Radana. Go lie down in the back of your car, and I'll drive you."

"You're leaving your car here?" she gasps.

"I'll have someone swing by to pick it up later. You're past forty weeks, Adicia. You can't write this off as false labor and continue working through it. I'll pay you for maternity leave."

"Why can't we call Radana now?" she begs as Allen struggles to pull her back up.

"Not that I'd know from personal experience, but remembering how it went for Lenore, first labors are usually long. We'll get you home and all settled in, and we'll call whoever you want to be with you."

"I want Ricky to be with me," she says as Allen finally manages to pull her back onto her feet. "Even women in the hospital have their husbands in the waiting room, not thousands of miles away unconscious in a hospital."

"You know that's the one request I can't grant you. Boy, you're heavy at forty-one weeks. You used to never weigh even a hundred soaking wet with heavy clothes on. How much weight did you gain?"

"Fifty pounds, I think. I'm about one-forty now."

The customers look on in concern when Allen emerges, helping Adicia with walking straight. Even the other employees stop what they're doing to gape.

"She'll be fine," Allen says. "I'll be back later today to close up and give orders for Monday. Adicia won't be coming to work for awhile after this, obviously."

"Aren't you the little girl whose husband was wounded in Vietnam?" an older woman asks. "That's such a crying shame that even after he was taken back to this country, he won't be able to be here to see his child being born."

Adicia nods, too much in pain to care yet another person is casting her as a charity case and identifying her only as Ricky's wife.

"Do you still have that protective order, in case your husband's parents show up and try to steal your baby?" a teenage girl asks. "Those people oughta be ashamed of themselves."

"I carry the order in my bag at all times," Adicia says as she continues stumbling out of the bakery with Allen.

Allen unlocks the Super Beetle and helps Adicia lie down on the backseat, then pulls out of the parking lot without putting on his seatbelt. Adicia wishes he'd drive faster, but he keeps insisting it only seems urgent because she's never given birth before. He's never given birth before either, she thinks darkly, and never will. He has no idea what he's talking about, even if he has been present at all three of his children's births.

Justine scurries to open the door when she hears Adicia frantically ringing the doorbell. Her face twists when she sees her favorite sister practically being carried into the house by Allen and collapsing onto the floor.

"Are we supposed to call for help now?" Justine asks.

"For now all we need are Lenore and Emeline," Allen asserts. "Do you have any idea how long your contractions are, Adicia, or how far apart they are?"

"I don't know and I don't care! All I care about is ending this pain as soon as possible!"

Allen goes to the phone to call Lenore and Emeline, then calls Poughkeepsie, remembering Adicia has the kind of money to cover long distance calls. Justine hurries to get pillows and blankets to make the floor comfier.

"Can I have my wedding pictures? Ricky deserves to be here in some form. My baby needs to see its daddy, even if it's just in a picture."

Justine picks up one of the framed pictures from the mantel. Adicia winces when she puts it down near her. As scared and unprepared as she and Ricky were for the convenience marriage they'd just embarked upon at such short notice, at least they were together and relatively happy. Neither of them had any idea that in only one week, they'd be torn apart and have to go through awful ordeals alone, nor that they'd create a child from their unlikely union.

"Here I am, sweetie," she hears Lenore saying. "I'll be right here by your side until the very end."

"Allen's tryna tell me it doesn't really hurt and that we won't need to call Radana until a lot later!"

"Oh, Allen has no idea what he's talking about. He's only a man. It does hurt a lot more the first time, 'cause your body's never experienced this before and you have no idea what to expect. And it usually takes a lot longer the first time. If you do this again, your muscles will be looser and more relaxed, so it'll go faster. Once you've gotten through it with flying colors, you'll feel on top of the world and like you can do anything. You won't be able to believe what you're capable of and how strong you are."

"I hope you're right."

"It helps if you move around, eat, and drink. Some women are in labor for well over twenty-four hours. It oughta be considered abuse to deprive them of all food and drink in a hospital. I woulda stabbed someone if I'd had onea those forty-hour labors and been allowed only ice chips."

"Forty hours?" Adicia asks in terror.

"There's nothing wrong with forty hours if that's how long it takes to get the baby into the world. Some babies take longer than others. You shouldn't try to rush or force it out earlier than it needs to come."

"I wonder what he was thinking of just before he lost consciousness and was being shot seven times," Adicia says wistfully. "He told me over and over if the worst happened, his last thoughts would be of me. He must've been thinking of the baby too."

"Who's gonna catch the baby?" Irene asks.

"We'll decide that when it comes closer to the actual birthing time," Lenore says. "Radana can catch it if you want, but it's even more special if you pull it out yourself, or let a loved one catch it."

"Daddy was the first person to hold me, Amelia, and Oliver," Irene says proudly. "In a hospital, doctors grab you, hold you upside-down, and spank you. That's mean."

"Lucine says no one spanked Simone or held her upside-down," Allen says. "I think they did that when the mothers were drugged for the birth and their babies were often born groggy or not breathing. They used that harsh way to get them to start breathing normally." He pats Adicia's hand. "Would you like me to fetch Emeline?"

"Yes, please. Can Lucine come too?"

"As many people as you want. You make all your own rules here. There's no limit on guests and helpers."

"Just try to relax," Lenore says. "It also helps if you hang out in the bathtub for a little bit, so long as the water isn't too hot and you don't stay in there too long."

"Who's gonna make supper for all yous guys?" Adicia questions. "Is there enough room for so many guests if this lasts overnight?"

"We certainly don't expect you to cook in your condition. You probably won't get any sleep if you're still laboring overnight, and I hope you don't mind if anyone sleeps in your bed."

"My baby's gonna be a Taurus. Just like Emeline. An earth sign, the bull."

"Emeline's gonna bring a stopwatch to know the exact second of birth," Justine says. "She's gonna have a whole astrological chart drawn up for the baby, in both Western and Vedic astrology."

Adicia settles into a relatively comfortable position on the nest of pillows and blankets and periodically moves around. Justine tries to distract her by telling her about what happened in school yesterday, and Lenore rubs her back and shoulders as she rocks back and forth. Even if the pain seems less intense now that she's grown used to the strange new sensations, Adicia still wishes it were already over, or that she could have a labor as relatively pain-free as the ones Lenore had for Amelia and Oliver.

Allen goes to close the bakery at 4:00 and comes back with Lucine, Simone, and Emeline in tow. Adicia reaches her arms out for her sisters as she struggles to breathe through another contraction.

"You're gonna be fine," Lucine tells her as she sets Simone on a blanket. "Just keep thinking all this pain is worth it for what's gonna happen at the end."

"I wish the end were here already!"

"Georgiekins will help you with his special, psychic animal energy,"

Emeline says. "Go over and help Adicia, Georgiekins."

Adicia lets the eleven-month-old cat climb on top of her enlarged midsection and pets him as he purrs contentedly. She stays in that position for the next few hours, in too much pain to get up and walk around or even shift position a little bit. Allen is too upset to see his most sensitive sister in so much pain to think about how angry he was when he found out Ricky got her pregnant. He tries to offer her some of the food the others are having for supper, but she weakly shakes her head, not sure she can keep down anything.

"How long have you been in labor?" Lucine asks, brushing the hair out of her face.

"Mosta the day since I got to work, probably since about eight o'clock. I tried my best to work through the pain, but it got too much to bear."

"Are you tryna beat Dad for best work ethic?" Allen asks. "Even he didn't think he'd get any gold medals for going to work when he was too sick to function!"

"You've only been in labor for about eleven hours so far," Lenore says. "Do you feel your contractions getting stronger, longer, or closer together?"

"All I know is they hurt!"

Adicia shifts into an uncomfortable sitting position when she hears the doorbell ringing. She wants to believe a miracle has happened and Ricky has come home, fully rehabilitated, but she has to settle for second-best when she sees Ernestine, Betsy, and the Ryans.

"Allen made a long-distance call and told us what was happening!" Ernestine says excitedly. "What luck this happened on a weekend so we could be here for you!"

"I thought it'd be far-out to witness a real birth," Betsy says.

"If your kid's born today and not tomorrow, it'll have the same birthday as the great Karl Heinrich Marx," Deirdre announces. "What an awesome, special birthday to share."

"Oh, brother," Allen mutters. "This is gonna be another long visit."

"What, you don't see the wisdom and sense of Marx's teachings? We all started life as members of the long-exploited underclass. The rich and bourgeoisie still exploit the proletariat and the poor. I'll admit somea what he wrote does seem a little dated or silly today, but the heart of his theories are right on the damn money."

"I own my own business now, and I like to think I don't exploit any of my workers. I worked hard to become respectably working-class, and I'm working just as hard on joining the ranks of the lower-middle-class."

"I hope you don't forget your origins on the way up and become just another bourgeois drone who thinks he's hot stuff 'cause he can afford a nice house, a car, and a yearly vacation to the seashore. It's nice to have enough money, but people of our class origins oughta remember where we come from and never take for granted how far up we've come in our station." Deirdre turns to Adicia. "How are you progressing so far? When my mother had Fiona, it was so quiet and peaceful, so smooth, almost like she laid an egg. She didn't scream, moan, breathe funny, or even really push. It was sorta like Fiona birthed herself, no help needed from our mother."

"Is it okay if I write about this for a class I'm taking in women's studies?" Betsy asks. "I wish Vassar would start a whole department for women's studies, but taking classes in the subject will have to do for now. Maybe I'll get my master's degree at onea the schools that offers it."

"I wonder what hurts more, labor or getting shot seven times," Adicia says. "I wonder how many shots he took before he drifted outta his senses. At least he wasn't shot point-blank in the head, and the bullets in the chest both missed his heart."

"That was a really dirty, rotten thing that happened," David agrees. "I can't believe they're still holding draft lotteries after we've been mostly withdrawn. Guys born in our year of birth would be sent next year if the course of the war reverses and troops are sent back there. My number's three hundred twelve, which is probably way too high to risk being called up."

"I thought of you when I saw the draft lottery on TV," Justine says. "I'm glad the Fates assigned you such a high number."

"If I were a man, my number would be seventy-three," Adicia says. "If only Ricky had been my same age or only a year older, this never woulda happened."

"What's done is done," Ernestine says. "You can't help who you fall for." She makes eyes at Deirdre.

"Would you like to watch TV, listen to the radio, or play records?"

Fiona asks.

"Is it still too early to call Radana?" Adicia asks.

"We can't know that unless you start keeping track of your contractions," Lenore tells her gently. "Emeline, give her your stopwatch."

"I don't know how to use a stopwatch."

"Fine, I'll help you with it," Emeline says. "Tell me when you feel one starting and stopping, and I'll do it for you."

Adicia manages to figure out they're about five minutes apart and lasting for about a minute apiece. She slumps against Lenore's chest when Lenore tells her it's still not quite time to call for help.

"Can't she come over and tell me how far I'm stretched inside?"

"You mean how many centimeters the cervix is dilated?" Lenore asks. "You don't need any of those checks as modern doctors would have you believe. It introduces infection, and it might stress you out and stall your labor if you think you're not progressing fast enough."

"If you say so."

"Besides, that's invasive and unnecessary, particularly to women with our histories."

"Please don't play that screaming record," Aoife begs when she sees Deirdre pulling her records out of her large carrying bag. "You and Adicia can listen to all the Primal Screaming you want when I'm not around. It's so harsh and unpleasant."

"He's getting out his issues of abandonment and pain through screaming," Deirdre says. "Would you prefer I play his other solo album, *Imagine*? There are some angry songs on that record too, but it's not at the same level as the first one. My favorite song on it is 'Gimme Some Truth.' It's like 'I Found Out,' where he so gives the finger to everyone. I like 'How Do You Sleep?' too, where it's so obvious he's giving the finger to Paul. But don't tell Julie I said that, since Paul's still her favorite and she actually likes his solo albums. I personally think his solo work stinks, for the most part anyway. It's too trifling and cheesy."

"Boy, oh boy, you were probably onea the few girls who didn't pick her favorite Beatle based on how cute you thought he was," Allen says, hoping he can handle at least another day of the now-adult Deirdre's pontificating and spouting radical philosophy.

"When you pick your favorite based on what's inside and not something dumb and superficial like looks, chances are he'll stay your favorite long-term."

Adicia tries to relax and lie on her side breathing as normally as she can, until the needle gets to the last song on side one, "I Don't Wanna Be a Soldier." The lyrics make her begin sobbing hysterically, and she drops her head onto Emeline's lap, too grief-stricken to notice her contractions anymore. Emeline strokes her hair, and Adicia starts sobbing even more, thinking back to how Ricky stroked her hair and said it was nice and soft, like petting a kitten. Instead of being by her side, he's unconscious, thousands of miles away.

"You wanna see the jokes of medals they gave him?" Justine asks. "I stashed them in the bottom of a closet in onea the empty rooms. I hope he throws them into the river when he gets home!"

"I don't think it's that unreasonable or dumb to get a Purple Heart," Betsy says. "He was doing reconnaissance work and got ambushed. It might not be the same as getting wounded in an actual battle or going outta his way to seek out a potentially dangerous situation, but he was still wounded by the enemy."

"They shouldn't be our enemies," Deirdre says. "The North Vietnamese are our brothers and sisters in struggle. God forbid they chose Communism for themselves. How horrible and unthinkable."

"I don't care what they're like personally!" Adicia shouts. "All I know is they shot my husband seven times and coulda killed him if somea the bullets had hit different places or gone in any deeper! He's lucky to be alive after getting shot in the head!"

"War is a damn shame. If only all warring parties would sit down and break bread together, like they did in the Christmas Truce of 1914, they'd never wanna go back to murdering each other so unthinkingly. The powers that be never allowed anything like that ever again, 'cause the soldiers didn't wanna resume shooting at each other after getting to know each other as friends and people."

"Do you think he got any shots in himself?" Fiona asks. "I assume they teach you how to use a gun in the Air Force, even if mosta the work's in the air."

"I don't know and I don't care!" Adicia sobs.

"Can we please keep the political ranting to ourselves for awhile?" Allen pleads. "Adicia doesn't need that during this particular time."

The hours between nightfall and the morning light seem to last an eternity, as Adicia continues to have painful contractions that won't let her get any sleep. Just as Lenore predicted might happen, her labor has lasted for an entire twenty-four hours and counting. Allen is relieved the baby won't share its birthday with Karl Marx, thus sparing them Deirdre's glowing paeans to the father of Marxism and a rave about how wonderful and special it is to have the same birthday.

"Are you still in pain, Aunt Adicia?" Irene asks during breakfast on Sunday morning. "Even if you're hurting, it's not good to not eat. Food makes you healthier."

"I want Sarah," she moans. "She's the only real mother I've ever had."

"I'll call her," Emeline says. "Maybe we'd also better start thinking about calling Mrs. Zupan."

"You can call her Radana," Lenore says. "She said we could be on a first name basis, though she's old enough to be our mother."

"It seems wrong and disrespectful to call my elders by their first names unless we got to know each other as friends and equals," Emeline says as she goes for the phone.

"Boy, and you're supposed to be the hippie," Allen says. "I thought hippies called everyone by first name and thought it was square to call people Mr., Mrs., and Miss."

"Only old-fashioned types or very young girls still go by Miss," Deirdre corrects him. "The correct title for an unmarried woman or a married woman who kept her name is Ms."

Ernestine tosses Adicia the stopwatch. "Do you think you know how to work this thing on your own by now?"

Adicia measures them as about two minutes apart and lasting one minute each. Lenore hopes her sister-in-law stays in active labor till Radana can come up from Saratoga. Adicia still bears the look of a little ragdoll, looking so tiny, helpless, and frail, in spite of all the burdens she's had to carry on her tiny little shoulders and how much she's grown as a modern, empowered, enlightened, liberated woman.

"They're both on their way," Emeline reports from the phone.

"Can you compare labor pain to something I might've experienced, so I can have a sense of what it feels like?" Fiona asks.

"Try hooking your index fingers around the insides of your cheeks and pulling and pulling until they start to crack and bleed," Lenore says. "That's what I'd compare it to."

Fiona tries this and gives up after about five minutes. "That hurts. You mean I'd have to go through something like that, only about ten times more intense, for as long as Adicia's been having it?"

"Everyone's different," Deirdre says. "Our mother went fast and peaceful when she had you. It was like a chicken squatting down and rising with an egg softly falling away from her body."

"I'd love a labor like that," Adicia says.

"Maybe next time," Lucine promises her.

"I don't know if I want a next time anymore!"

"You'll almost immediately forget the pain," Lenore says. "It's part of a survival mechanism for us women. We have to forget labor pains, or we'd never wanna have a baby again."

Adicia perks up when she sees Sarah coming in twenty minutes later, and crawls over to her, upset she's unable to fit on her lap. She sobs in relief when she feels her old nanny's arms around her and her hands stroking her hair.

"Please don't leave me, Sarah," she begs. "God, if he exists, made a mistake when he was assigning mothers and gave me my birth mother and you only as my nanny."

"Du und deine Schwestern waren meine Kinder bevor ich hatte Kinder biologischen," she whispers to Adicia. "I love Fritz and Nessa as a *mutter* loves her biological *kinder*, but I love you and your sisters as a *mutter* loves *kinder* who are hers through love. You, Emeline, Ernestine, and Justine all said 'Mama' as your first word, and to me, not your blood *mutter*. You, Lucine, Emeline, Ernestine, and Justine are my babies just as much as Fritz and Nessa. I have seven *kinder*, not just two."

"Does that mean you're not my unofficial grandma anymore, since you don't think my daddy's onea your kids?" Irene asks.

"I'm still your grandma. I helped raise your daddy since he was three years old, even if he was never as close to me as your aunts."

Adicia tries her best to keep as calm as possible as her contractions continue at their same strength and pace while she waits for Radana. She feels as though her insides are being ripped apart with a hot knife, and is starting to question the wisdom of going without drugs, at home, with someone whose only training is as a nurse. With any luck, Lenore is right about how she'll feel on top of the world afterwards and that all her doubts about her body's ability to do what it was designed to do will vanish.

Radana finally comes in at noon, while Adicia is crawling along the floor to try to take the pressure off her pelvis and to get the baby to move down faster.

"Have you really been in labor for over twenty-four hours?" she hears a familiar voice asking.

Adicia looks up and smiles in delight when she sees Julie coming in with Radana, carrying a large festive gift bag. "Julie! What are you doing here?"

"Your midwife asked if I'd like to come with her and help onea my best friends while she's having her baby," Julie says. "She says Emeline suggested it."

"Don't worry, I won't tell Julie what you said, Deirdre," Amelia says.

Deirdre turns red. "Apparently you're not old enough to know how to keep secrets."

"It was nothing serious," Fiona says sweetly. "Deirdre just thinks Paul's solo work stinks."

Deirdre gets up and excuses herself, genuinely mortified for one of the few times in her twenty-one years of life.

"Come back here, Deirdre," Julie calls. "That's not a big deal. We all have different tastes in music. On my end, I'm not into John's solo work the way you and Ernestine are. It's too angry and political for me. I like the cheerful stuff you can relax to and not have to think too deeply about. It's not like I'm pretending he writes the deepest and most award-winning songs."

Adicia hugs Julie when she sits next to her. "I'm so glad to see you again. So much has happened to me since I last saw you."

"I bought you and the baby presents." She extends the bag. "I hope the baby gift is okay."

Adicia pulls out a plush rabbit with big floppy ears and off-blonde coloring, and a picture frame made of seashells. "It's just like Justine's bunny, only a different color and with bigger ears! And you remembered how much I loved our trip to Long Island and how I always wanted to do that again when I grew up and had money. I love things related to the beach and the ocean, even if I've only been there once."

"You always useta talk about that book about the stuffed rabbit, and Justine has her own rabbit she's loved the life out of, so I thought it'd be nice if your baby could get its own special stuffed rabbit to love too. You can use the frame to display a nice picture of you and Ricky when he comes home and you can have a real wedding." Julie rubs

Adicia's midsection. "It feels like it's facing head-down, so it's not breech."

Radana stares at her in amazement. "How can you tell that?"

"My mother had a natural delivery with her final pregnancy, boy-girl twins, three years ago. I was with her a lot of times her midwife came over, and I helped with her delivery. The midwife up in Plattsburgh showed me how to feel for the babies' position and explained about things like the stages of labor and how long it can take. It must be really groovy to have a job like that, but I don't know if I'm smart enough for nursing school. They probably don't have any real schools to train women as straight midwives instead of just switching from nurse to midwife."

"What are you studying at Skidmore, my dear?"

"Sociology and music."

"What do you intend to do with your degree?"

"I guess I'll go on and get a master's degree, maybe in social work like Lucine. I wanna help people who grew up disadvantaged and abused like I did. I'm glad girls and women have more rights nowadays. When my parents divorced, the courts wouldn't let my mother keep me and said she was making up horrible lies to try to ruin my father's reputation. Nowadays they might've given me to her and not forced me to stay with an abusive, drug-dealing father."

"You'd be a lovely midwife, Julie." Adicia manages to smile through her pain. "You'd be perfect for women with tragic pasts."

"Why don't you be my assistant?" Radana asks. "Adicia, can Julie catch the baby?"

"Sure, if that's okay with everyone else."

Adicia can barely believe she possesses even a tenth of the strength and patience needed to endure such a long labor. Every hour ticks away at the pace of twenty-four hours, as her pain continues unabated, no matter how often she changes positions and gets into the bathtub. She almost wants to cry from relief when Radana finally tells her she's in transition at 8:00 at night. Though she's been told it's okay to start pushing if she feels like it, it hurts too much to do anything to add to the pain. She desperately wishes she could have even a Tylenol for pain relief. Everyone around her is telling her she's doing a great job and that it won't be very long, but she'll believe that when all the pain is finally over and she's holding a baby in her arms.

The simple, easy, quick, peaceful delivery Deirdre describes Fiona's birth as is still a distant fantasy as she struggles with pushing for the next two hours, almost completely wiped out. She bristles when Radana tells her to take breaks and push more gently.

"Can I please get an aspirin?" she begs between panting breaths. "It's been thirty-six damn hours!"

"I don't think it'll be even one more hour," Radana says. "Would you like to touch your baby's head?"

Julie gently takes her hand and leads it down to the crown of the head emerging, with the amniotic sac covering it. Adicia gasps.

"That's your baby!" Radana says. "It won't be very long now."

Julie gently puts her hands under it when the entire head has emerged. Everyone is smiling at Adicia, though she doesn't quite comprehend she's about to have a baby. It's so surreal. She hears Radana coaching her how to push as the head turns and the shoulders start emerging, but it seems like this is happening to someone else, or as though she's migrated outside her physical body and is floating around in the air somewhere.

"Here he is, here's your little boy!" she hears Julie saying as a moving object is placed on her chest.

Adicia stares down at the tiny little person who just emerged from her body. "Oh my God, I just had a baby!"

"What do you think you were doing over the past thirty-six hours, playing chess?" Ernestine laughs.

Adicia kisses his head and starts examining his tiny fingers and toes through her tear-clouded eyes. Everything is exactly where it should be, and nothing is missing. She's so busy discovering her baby boy, she barely hears Radana instructing her to start pushing again to get the placenta out. She obeys only so it'll get the last part out of the way and enable her to continue drinking in the wonder of her baby and the miracle of life without any further obstacles.

"You did it, little sister," Lucine tells her proudly. "Now you're part of the mommy club."

"You did a great job," Lenore agrees. "And you thought someone of your petite proportions would have to have a Caesarean automatically."

"You had no tearing," Radana says. "I told you a woman's external size has nothing to do with pelvic size and shape."

"Can I keep him?" Adicia asks.

"Of course you can keep him!" Lenore says. "He's yours to keep forever!"

"Ten-fifteen at night and thirty seconds over on May 6, 1973," Emeline announces, holding up the stopwatch. "Your baby has the same birthday as Rudolph Valentino."

Adicia giggles. "Only you would know that, Emeline."

"That's better than sharing his birthday with Karl Marx, like he would've had he been born yesterday," Allen says.

Deirdre rolls her eyes at him. "I'd be proud to share my birthday with Marx."

"What's his name?" Fiona asks, peering over at him. "Boy, he's got really brown eyes."

Adicia picks up the framed picture sitting by her and shows it to the baby. "This is your daddy, sweetheart. He loves both of us very much, though he's unable to be here now. One day, he's gonna come home, and he'll love being your daddy. I'll be the best mommy you ever coulda asked for. I'll give you everything my parents never gave me. You've got great aunts and uncles too, and so many nice cousins."

"He's got the same deep brown eyes as Ricky," Justine observes. "Adicia told you all she knew he was the father!"

"I never doubted it." Adicia kisses his chubby little fists. "I never thought I could love anyone so much when he's not even an hour old yet."

"I wish we didn't have to go back to Poughkeepsie so soon," Ernestine says. "I wanna stay and help with my new nephew as much as I can."

"You didn't tell us his name yet," Fiona reminds her as Radana ties twine around the umbilical cord as it gradually stops pulsating.

Adicia gazes at her son with lovestruck eyes as Lenore cuts the cord. "Robert Allen Rudolph Carson. Robert, after the millionaire who was so kind to me when I washed his windshield; Allen, after the best big brother ever; and Rudolph, since Emeline mentioned he has the same birthday as Valentino, and that's a pretty neat celebrity legend to share a birthday and name with."

"You're giving him onea his middle names after me?" Allen asks. "Even after the less than nice way I talked to you regarding your relationship with Warrick?"

"Blood's thicker than water, and we'll be brother and sister forever. You did everything you could to take care of us, even after Mother took us away from you and Lenore. You've been more of a father figure to me than Dad ever was. Now that I'm a grownup and ten years doesn't seem such a huge age difference anymore, you're my friend too, even after those fights we had."

"Are you having him circumcised?" Fiona asks.

"Of course! It's much cleaner and easier to take care of."

"You should wait until he's eight days old," Sarah tells her. "We always circumcise our boys then because the clotting factor is at its highest, and there's less chance of an accident. I can ask around at my synagogue for a mohel who'll do one for a non-Jewish baby. The way it's done by American pediatricians and obstetricians isn't as humane as how it's done by a mohel."

"Is that even a question?" Allen asks. "I thought everyone did that except over the top hippies."

"I've seen pictures in dirty magazines, and foreskins look nasty," Deirdre says.

"What's a foreskin?" Irene asks.

"This conversation is over," Lenore pronounces.

Adicia continues raptly gazing at him as he starts nursing. "You just keep drinking all you want, baby. You'll always have enough to eat and drink, even if I have to go hungry to feed you."

"What about religion?" Ernestine asks. "Are you having him baptized?"

"I don't know if I believe in God. I don't have any reason to believe I'll become a devout believer after spending my entire life as an agnostic."

"Yeah, you suddenly up and turning religious Christian would be as dumb and outta left field as the bizarre ending of *Anna Karenina*, when Levin suddenly gets religious faith after spending the last eight hundred pages or so as a confirmed agnostic," Emeline says.

Adicia smiles at her, taking her eyes off the baby for a moment. "Emeline, if I do have him made a member of some religion, you're so going to be the godmother. You'd tell him all about great literature, history, world religions, languages, music, art, and everything else under the sun."

"We have classes tomorrow, me, Ernestine, Betsy, and David, and

Fiona and Aoife have school," Deirdre says, standing up. "But we'll be back as soon as we can after school lets out. Radana will drive Julie back to Skidmore."

"Don't worry, I'll stay with you overnight," Lenore says. "You've always got me no matter what."

"We'll have a baby shower for you as soon as we can," Lucine says.

"I'll stay overnight too," Sarah says. "Is it okay if I bless him? I wanted to bless you and your sisters when your *mutter* kicked me out, but I wasn't thinking straight and only realized in hindsight I should've done it."

Adicia reluctantly lets Sarah take him from her. She listens as Sarah says a blessing in Hebrew she vaguely remembers from childhood.

"It's the traditional priestly blessing, Birkat Kohanim. It means 'May God bless you and keep you. May God cause his face to shine upon you and be gracious unto you. May God lift up his face onto you and give you peace.' It was the last thing my parents ever said to me, the last time I saw them."

"I'd like to bless him too, the only way I know how." Adicia gently takes him back and pronounces the words of the song she'll always associate with peace and happiness. "*Benedictus qui venit in nomine Domini,* my precious firstborn child."

Chapter 59: An Eye-Opening Evening

Shortly after the joint birthday for Allen and Irene, who turned twenty-nine and six, respectively, Adicia and Justine are invited next door for supper. Though Adicia prefers to carry Robbie in the baby slings Lenore and Emeline have made, tonight she puts Robbie in the beautiful Victorian-style perambulator Lucine and Zachary gave her, with a navy blue wicker basket carrier and room to hang up a little baby mobile. When they arrive next door, Irene and Amelia immediately rush over to fawn all over Robbie, leaving Allen and Lenore a bit jealous nine-month-old Oliver has lost some of his attention and novelty to his infant cousin.

"You've adapted so naturally to motherhood, as much as you insisted you couldn't be pregnant 'cause it'd mean an end to your plans to be a modern, independent, working woman," Lenore says as they set the table. "It gets easier once you get used to it, no matter how nervous you might be now. After you have more kids, you'll find you're no longer so overprotective, obsessive, and nervous."

"Do you know what his religion is yet?" Irene asks. "I like my Episcopal church. Maybe I can be a priest when I grow up. Nessa wants to be a rabbi when she grows up, since they made the first woman a rabbi last year. Girls can do anything!"

"I can't baptize any kid when I don't know if I believe in God. Either he can make his own choice when he's old enough, or if Ricky cares enough about religion, he can make that decision when he comes home." Adicia quickly snatches Robbie when she sees Amelia struggling to hold him. "I kinda wish he could stay this tiny and adorable forever, even if it means having to deal with diapers forever and never knowing what he wants or needs when he cries."

"This is the easiest stage," Lenore agrees. "Babies mostly sleep at this age, and they don't move or talk back to you. Doesn't it feel humbling to know someone so tiny so completely depends upon you for everything? You're a goddess in his eyes."

"How do they come out so perfectly formed?" Adicia asks in wonder. "If even one little detail is off, it wouldn't be a real baby. Can you imagine if a baby were forming and the eyes or brain were left out?"

Allen leans down to his infant nephew. "How does it feel, little man, knowing you're the only man in the house? You're even younger than I was when I became the man of my house."

"He likes being the king of the castle. He'll probably be onea the few guys in our family if we keep running to girls. I hope he turns out just like you and enjoys being in the minority."

"I'm proud of my harem." Allen grins.

"What's a harem?" Amelia asks.

"It's a big group of women all living together in a special part of a sultan's palace," Lenore says. "They were usually the wives of the sultan. Your daddy's using it in a non-literal sense, to mean a large group of girls and women."

"What's a sultan?"

"Sultan is the title for a king in certain parts of the world."

"Does anyone still have a king besides England?" Irene asks.

"Oh, lots of places. You usually don't study about countries outside Europe, America, and parts of Asia in school. Kings have different titles in different places, like how Japan has an emperor."

Adicia finds it very refreshing Allen and Lenore always talk to their daughters in age-appropriate language and show interest in all their comments and questions. It stung so much whenever her mother routinely told her offspring "Like I care," told them not to talk or ask about such things, or delivered her other common invective, "You talk to me like I give a damn like onea them uppity rich mothers uptown. The only kid I care about is Tommy."

"Isn't it ironic?" Lenore asks as they sit down to eat spinach soufflé, string beans, and lamb chops. "You've been through some horrible things, but maybe there was a higher reason you were put through these tests. You never would've learnt how to stand on your own and be an empowered modern woman otherwise."

"I'm glad you're proud of me. You sound like Emeline when she tells stories about people who are put through rigorous tests as part of a Divine plan, to test their character or give them learning experiences. Even bad events ultimately turn out for the good, though I certainly don't see any sane, humane reason why my Ricky had to get shot seven times."

"He's definitely not gonna come home the same limousine liberal he left as," Allen says. "I don't see how a person can go from being a pampered rich boy to wounded draftee and not have any kinda deep changes in how he looks at life. I bet he won't take anything for granted ever again after this."

"How could he survive being shot that many times?" Justine wonders. "If I were you, Adicia, I'd have more of a reason to not be so agnostic anymore. Something more than dumb luck was responsible for how he survived that many shots, including one to the head."

"All I know is I'm gonna appreciate him even more when he finally comes home. Emeline always said you appreciate your husband more when you had to wait for him and he wasn't automatically handed to you on a silver platter at a young age. It wasn't time for Ricky and I to be together as man and wife. I had to grow to love him back before we could properly begin married life."

Allen puts more string beans on Amelia's plate and ignores the face she makes at the sight of vegetables. "I'm still not a fan of arranged or convenience marriages, but maybe there's more sense to it than I was willing to consider. Lenore and I were a love match, but now I love her in a much deeper way, and we have a more grownup relationship. We've been through too much together to be the same teenage kids who met at the bus stop. Romantic or sexual love shouldn't be the main element in a long-term relationship, since you've got nothing to keep the home fires burning in the tough or boring times."

"We liked each other and had things in common. It's not like we were complete strangers. And I chose to marry him. You didn't see much divorce in the era of arranged marriages, because people were tied together through thick and thin, for better or for worse, and didn't worry about romantic interest or instant compatibility in bed. They made it work because they had to, and they had a stronger love in the long run, even if it wasn't love at first sight or within the first few years."

"Like that song in *Fiddler on the Roof*," Justine says. "Emeline said it was better than most movies or plays at staying basically true to the original book."

"Yeah, while it celebrates and encourages choosing your own spouse, it doesn't discount the place and validity of an arranged marriage where couples grow to love and care about one another just as much as couples who were a love match."

Lenore turns to her infant nephew in the stroller. "Do you know how special and blessed you are?" She smiles at him and lets him grip her left index finger in his tiny fist. "You were born in the caul. That means you're destined for a life of greatness. There's a superstition that a baby born in the caul will do great things in life."

"Deirdre says Fiona was born entirely in the sac of water. She really means it when she says Fiona's birth was like their mother laid an egg. That's a pretty rare thing."

"He's the most special baby ever," Justine says proudly. "Even if he wasn't planned or expected, God or whoever must've really wanted him to be born for whatever reason."

"Well, he wouldn't have been born if it weren't for Allen saving my life all those years ago. Sarah says there's a famous line in the Talmud about how if you save even one person, it's as though you saved the entire world, the same as if you kill one person, it's like you destroyed the whole world. Sometimes I still have nightmares about that fire, and you not getting there in time to save me, Justine, and Giovanni."

"It was nothing doing," Allen tries to brush it off. "I did what I was supposed to do, protect my kid sisters and a helpless baby. You know me. I'd never try to claim credit for being a hero or saving the day."

"Most people would just save themselves like our parents did," Justine says. "You went up to the top two floors to warn people and came back to check for anyone who was trapped by the fire. You even ran back into the burning building to rescue Giovanni."

"You'll be a good substitute father figure for Robbie, won't you, if Ricky doesn't come home for a long time?" Adicia asks.

"Of course I will. The few guys in this family hafta stick together. But I hope for both your sakes that Warrick won't be delayed an extremely long time in that hospital. It can't be easy on a young kid to have a stranger come into his life claiming to be his father. I don't know how older adopted kids manage."

"Allen's gonna be good when Ricky comes home." Lenore gives her husband a warning look. "Whatever he thinks of him or your marriage, he's gonna be a grownup and put your happiness above his desire for trivial revenge or proving some sorta point about how the classes don't mix. It's pretty mean to get into a fight with a guy who was shot seven times."

"Is Uncle Ricky awake again?" Irene asks.

"Last I heard, no. They think he might have a limp 'cause he was shot twice in the same leg, but they don't know if any of his senses will be impacted by the shot to the head." Adicia turns back to her food. "I wouldn't care if he came home deaf, dumb, blind, and crippled, so long as he came home in one piece."

"War stinks." Irene shovels soufflé into her mouth. "I hope they never have another war again anywhere."

After eating a dessert of trifle, Adicia and Justine help Allen with washing and drying the dishes while Lenore gives her children a bath. Before long, Irene will be too old to be bathed or seen naked by her mother, or to bathe with her little sister and baby brother, so Lenore is enjoying all the time she has left of this stage of her firstborn's life. When the dishes are all washed, dried, and put away, Adicia bathes Robbie in the sink, hoping she's impressing Allen by how well she's doing it. She really wants her belovèd big brother to think she's a good mother who knows how to do all the important things right, instead of someone who needs correcting or advising like a helpless child. It means so much to her that Allen's finally grown to see her as a real grownup, her own woman, not just his next-youngest sister and third-youngest sibling who'll forever be little more than a child in an adult body.

Adicia and Justine go upstairs to say goodbye to the girls, now in pajamas and in bed with their stuffed animals. There's no doubt Irene is Lenore's daughter and Amelia is Allen's daughter, Adicia thinks as she goes over to them. There was no half and half going on with either of them when they were created, just like how Giovanni so strongly resembles Gemma and so far Robbie strongly resembles Ricky.

"Will you read us a bedtime story, Aunt Adicia?" Irene begs. "We want something we haven't been read before."

"Go ahead and read to them," Lenore says. "I'll put Oliver to bed. Justine, would you like to help me?"

Adicia gently picks Robbie up out of his stroller and puts him on the bed between herself and the girls while Irene looks through the books on the shelf for a good five minutes. The book she ultimately brings over is very familiar.

"Aunt Emeline got me this for my birthday, but I haven't read it yet. The bunny on the cover reminds me of Aunt Justine's old bunny, and the new bunny Julie got for Robbie."

Adicia takes the book from her. "Emeline read this to me and your aunts Ernestine and Justine when we were little. It was published fifty-one years ago." She opens to the first page and begins reading. "'There was once a velveteen rabbit, and in the beginning he was really splendid....'"

While Adicia is reading, Allen comes by and stands partway in the door to watch and listen. Several times, he notices her blinking away tears, though it's not intended as a sad story. The girls notice their aunt is struggling not to cry at several points too, but Adicia always keeps on with the story and doesn't let herself break down in front of her nieces. To the girls, it's a sweet story about a stuffed toy turning into a real rabbit because his owner loved him so much, not something to cry about. *Maybe she's really weepy because she's just had a baby and her husband is sick*, they think.

"How come you were almost crying, Aunt Adicia?" Irene asks when the story's finished.

"Oh, it's nothing. I always thought it was a bit of a sad story, since it reminds me so much of what my sisters and I went through growing up. You'll never have to go through any of that, of course."

"You mean thinking no one would ever love yous guys besides your family and other friends from the poor side of town? You musta felt like the sad little toys on the Island of Misfit Toys in *Rudolph the Red-Nosed Reindeer*. But you shouldn't be sad anymore, since you're not poor anymore."

"No, we're not. It's really sad to grow up wondering if anyone will ever love you just the way you are, no matter what you look like, where you've been, what's happened to you, or where you're from. Like it says in the story, when someone loves you that much, usually only after you've been put through the wringer, you're Real, and you can't be considered ugly, stupid, or worthless ever again, only to those who don't understand. Once you're Real, you're Real for always, even if the person who made you Real goes away, the way the Skin Horse no longer has the Boy's uncle to play with him."

"You mean sorta like how Uncle Ricky made you Real?"

Adicia nods, blinking away tears again. "Yes, it's exactly like that, sweetheart."

"Don't worry, Aunt Adicia." Irene lays her hand on her aunt's and smiles up at her. "Even if Uncle Ricky never can come home or if he comes home disabled, you've still been made Real by someone who loved you just the way you are. We're all supposed to love each other 'cause we're family, and your old friends are like your family. But it must really be special when an outsider loves you when he doesn't have to or people tell him not to 'cause you're so different. You didn't break when you went through a lot of bad stuff growing up, so you were able to become Real when Uncle Ricky came along. The Skin Horse says you can usually only become Real after a long time and after you've been worn down really hard. It doesn't happen if you break easily."

"I know. None of those things mattered to Ricky, no matter how unlikely it was a guy like him would give the time of day to a girl like me. When two souls are meant to be together, even if it's only for a very short time, a way opens up for them to meet. Now there'll always be a reminder of how very much he loved me and the fact that we were together, however briefly, in your precious baby cousin."

Lenore gently knocks on the door as she comes into the room. "Girls, it's time for bed. You can see your aunt again tomorrow."

Adicia picks Robbie up and gently puts him back into the stroller, then stands aside so Lenore and Allen can tuck their girls into bed. After the girls wave goodnight, she rolls the stroller into the hall and slowly goes down the stairs, Justine acting as a spotter to guard even more closely against any accidents. As they approach the front hallway, Allen catches up to them.

"I'm sorry, but I couldn't help overhearing what you were talking about with Irene. I'm pretty embarrassed my six-year-old daughter can figure out what I was too dumb, blind, or overprotective to figure out in a whole year and a half."

"You mean about how what I had with Ricky was the real thing, as unlikely as it all was?"

"I still think the guy is, or at least used to be, a classic limousine liberal, but that doesn't mean he was incapable of having real feelings for you. A guy who was only interested in using you or who only wanted a friendship or relationship as part of a stupid, youthful rebellion or adventure would never have burnt all his bridges to his parents and his old life, to the extent he ended up shot seven times in Vietnam. You've been through too much, and a true rich snob wouldn't go so much outta his way to befriend and court a poor girl with such a tragic past if he were only after one thing. Anyone from the other side who truly loves you unconditionally, just the way you are, is one in a million. Only people who don't understand would think you're ugly or unworthy. You're Ricky's little velveteen ragdoll."

"Can you please never compare me to a ragdoll ever again?" Adicia asks, as pleased as she is Allen seems like he's finally come around.

"It doesn't matter, remember? Once you're Real, it doesn't matter what you look like, and it can't be undone. Besides, if you were a real ragdoll, you would've turned into a person and not be a doll anymore. You're considered a real person by everyone now, not just a ragged poor girl dressed in hand-me-downs and considered unfit for polite society. I think only your parents-in-law still consider you garbage."

Adicia looks at him hesitantly. "So, this is your long overdue apology?"

"I suppose so. I'll admit it was pretty rotten of me to go at you like an attack dog when you were in such a fragile emotional state. But there's a big age difference between us. When I was eighteen, you were only turning eight. I'd already had all these adult experiences when you were still a little girl, as adult as our growing-up experience forced you to be for your age. Maybe I didn't wanna let go of the idea of you as my sweet, little kid sister, someone who still needed protecting from the bad stuff life tossed at you. It musta never occurred to me that somewhere along the line you became a young woman with her own mind and heart. I owe Warrick a debt of gratitude for how he got you the hell outta that situation with Seth and our parents. It doesn't matter anymore how you ended up married to him or that he had millions of dollars to get stuff like a house and a car for you. You deserve to be set up in a nice house and to get a nice, new car instead of struggling for a long time with just an apartment and no car like I did."

"So this means you'll apologize to Ricky when he finally comes home?"

"I'm man enough to admit when I've been wrong. If your marriage could get through what it's already been through, even without starting off in love, yous guys can get through anything after this. You've probably developed some sorta bond by now that you can't always get from being in love."

"Thank you. Even if Ricky might not come home the same as he left, it's nice to know you'll accept and support my marriage."

Lenore puts her arm around Allen. "Well, it only took long enough. You're finally talking like the guy I remember."

"Better late than never. You really are the best big brother ever."

Adicia is still smiling as she walks home. In spite of all the bad hands she's been dealt, she's glad she's able to count on Allen's love, support, and respect. It took a very long time, but finally their relationship is that of a grownup brother and sister, not a much-older brother forced into the role of substitute father figure to his kid sisters. Even if Ricky is detained in that hospital for another year or more, or if he comes home a much-changed person from his ordeal, she'll always have her brother. It doesn't change their fundamental relationship of big brother and little sister, but after so many years and so many struggles, it's nice to know.

Adicia has hardly been able to sleep all night, since when the dawn breaks, it'll be July 20 again, the one-year anniversary of the day she had to say goodbye to Ricky. The last communication she got from the hospital two weeks ago said he'd completed seven surgeries and was still unconscious. Her nineteenth birthday, their one-year wedding anniversary, and Ricky's twenty-first birthday have all come and gone without the kind of fanfare that would've been due in more ideal circumstances. At times it seems like a long, strange, surreal, twisted, funny dream that happened to someone else. It's hard to believe she of all people summoned enough inner strength to pull through it all with such flying colors. The scared, passive little girl is now a capable, independent mistress and sole support of her household, someone who'll never be bullied, threatened, abused, or bossed around again.

"Do you hear what I hear?" Justine whispers during the night.

"It must be the house settling," Adicia whispers back.

Justine grabs her sister's hands when she hears the creaking noise again. "Someone just broke into our house!"

Adicia's hair stands on end as they hear footsteps coming from downstairs and heading up the staircase. She desperately wishes she'd bought a gun or guard dog in the case of an event like this.

"Should we call the police?" Justine whispers.

"I'll pretend we have a gun and threaten to shoot him. Whatever happens, no one takes my baby unless he kills me first." Adicia looks down at her peacefully sleeping baby, who depends on her to protect him and love him.

Adicia and Justine's hearts stop beating when they hear footsteps coming into their room and a heavy object falling on the floor. Two teenage girls and a two-month-old baby are very vulnerable targets, something no amount of women's liberation will be able to change.

"Stop right now and identity yourself or I'll shoot!" she screams in the most ferocious voice she can muster.

"Now what kind of welcome home is that for a guy who took seven bullets in Vietnam?"

Adicia's heart stops beating again, and she's afraid it might never start again. Her blood runs cold, and she's paralyzed against moving or speaking. This couldn't possibly be what she thinks it is.

"Ricky, is that you?" Justine shouts. "What are you doing here? We didn't know you were coming home or that you'd regained consciousness!"

"What, don't you girls recognize my voice after a year away?"

Justine grabs her rabbit, steps over her nephew and sister, jumps off the bed, and hugs her brother-in-law. "Welcome home! I'd love to stay and catch up with you, but I guess you wanna see Adicia most right now. I'll move to your old bed and let yous guys have this one."

Adicia is now sobbing hysterically, a floodgate having burst deep within herself. All the pent-up emotions she's been forced to deal with for the past year have finally come roaring out in one gigantic release. She forces herself into a sitting position and feels Ricky sitting on her right side. Immediately she feels his arms locked around her and her head becoming wet. She doesn't want to say anything when she finally feels her tongue loosening again, for fear this is all a dream and she'll wake up alone.

"My sweet little wifey waited for me," he says in relief. "You stayed loyal to me the whole time and never moved away, took another guy, or filed for divorce. You didn't start out loving me and didn't have to stick by me, but you did. You're the best girl I ever coulda hoped for, Adicia. I love you so much. No one's ever gonna rip me away from you again. They told me I was honorably discharged after the Viet Cong tried to kill me."

"I love you, Ricky. I love you more than I thought I could love any man. I couldn't wait to tell you in person, and I thought at least you knew I love you when you got hurt. I don't wanna think about what woulda happened if you'd gone to your early grave thinking I didn't love you like a woman loves a man, like a wife loves a husband. How did you survive being shot seven times? And how are you here when you were still unconscious two weeks ago?"

"When I came to, I was told I'd lost so much blood everyone was shocked I was still alive, unconscious or not. Both of the shots I took to the chest missed my heart by less than an inch and didn't hit any nerves or vital organs. I guess I have a really hard head for that shot to have missed any vital brain areas. The doctors and nurses all told me most people who get shot in the head don't survive or are left with permanent disabilities or memory loss. All the time I knew I had to get back to you. Love kept me alive and carried me home to you. There's no other explanation for how I coulda survived taking seven shots, including one to the head, and woken up four months later with almost no permanent complications. They said they'd never seen anyone who just woke up from a coma as though he'd been healed overnight. I had to get home so our baby wouldn't be a half-orphan. I wanted to see my firstborn child." His hands drift to her midsection and feel around in growing confusion and fear. "Adicia, what happened to the baby? Did you lose it after you were told what happened to me?"

Adicia laughs a little. "Are you sure you didn't lose any of your memory when they shot you in the head? I'm not an elephant, Ricky. Humans are only pregnant for between nine and ten months. I gave birth in early May, at forty-one weeks." She reaches over for the lamp switch on the nightstand and carefully picks up Robbie. "Meet your firstborn son."

"We got a boy?" he asks excitedly as he takes the baby from Adicia. "I kinda thought we'd have a girl, since your family runs to girls." He breaks down crying again when he sees the baby stirring awake. "My firstborn son. My boy. He looks like a tiny version of me."

Adicia's heart rends when Robbie begins crying in terror at the stranger holding him. "Don't cry, sweetheart." She takes one of his small hands in hers and looks down at him. "Your mommy is right here. You know your mommy would never let a stranger or bad person touch you unless they killed her first. This is your handsome daddy who waited so long to meet you. He loves you very much and is gonna be the best daddy in the world to you."

"What's his name? I hope you didn't name him Warrick, Jr. I'd hate for such an awful name to be passed on."

"Robert Allen Rudolph Carson, Robbie for short. I named him after the famous guy who was so kind to me when I washed his windshield. Allen is after my brother, and Rudolph is because he has the same birthday as Rudolph Valentino, May sixth. I thought it was pretty cool he shares his birthday with a legendary moviestar, so I gave him the second middle name. I hope you like it."

"I like the name Robert. It's probably the first normal name in my family for a good long while. All the guys, as far back as I know, got either surnames as first names or really pretentious, stuffy names like Theobald and Preston."

Robbie stops crying and reaches his hand out for Ricky's face. He stares at his father and looks very serious for a baby.

"I think he's realizing he looks like you," Adicia says. "It must be like looking into a mirror. I kinda hoped he'd get your beautiful, deep brown eyes so it'd settle any lingering doubts about who was the father. I can't say I blame my family for wondering at first if Seth could've been the father, since the timing was so close, but I got my period after he did what he did, and I was at my ovulation time when we consummated our marriage."

"How could I think about doubting a beautiful baby like this? I can't wait to start spoiling him." He hands Robbie back to Adicia. "He sleeps here?"

"Why not? Allen and Lenore do it. It encourages a natural bond."

"I hope it wasn't too scary when you had the surgery to take him out of you. At least I was unconscious for the seven I had. Don't worry, I still think you're beautiful with a scar across your abdomen. Can I see it? I'll let you see my scars."

"I gave birth to him the natural, old-fashioned way, right here at home, with a thirty-six-hour labor. I didn't need drugs, stitches, or surgery."

Ricky looks at her in disbelief. "Are you serious? A tiny girl like you was able to give birth by herself and didn't need a Caesarean?"

"Yes, I made it through, as painful and difficult as it was. I felt like I could do anything after I did that."

"Wow. I think you're my new hero. I never could've believed a little thing like you could've handled that on her own. You're a lot stronger than I ever thought."

"I'm a lot stronger than you give me credit for. Could a frail little girl have handled everything that's happened in my life?"

"I guess not. We're probably not given more than we can handle. Are you still working?"

"Allen gave me a paid maternity leave. You're welcome to join up in my place. I don't know when I'll go back. I can't bear the thought of leaving Robbie with anyone else, not even Lenore."

"You're still the same old-fashioned girl I left behind," he says in relief. "Don't worry, I'll go to work and support you, Justine, and Robbie. You can continue looking after the baby during the day, at least until he's old enough for school. All day at work I'll be looking forward to coming home to my sweet little wifey and our baby. That's the way it should be. There's nothing wrong with being old-fashioned so long as you're not being forced to do that or unhappy in that role."

"I don't think a woman's place is only in the home. Women and girls have had the short end of the stick for too long. I fully support the goals of radical feminism, but that doesn't mean I'm gonna stop being a loving and supportive wife. I like the fact that you're gonna protect me and take care of me again, as much as I've enjoyed being an independent, empowered, liberated woman."

"I've got no issue with that. By the way, I didn't forget your birthday was last week, the day before our one-year anniversary. I got you presents."

Adicia watches Ricky going into the bag he dropped on the floor when he came into the room and scared the hell out of her and Justine. "How did you get in, and why didn't the hospital tell me you woke up and made an overnight, full recovery?"

"I still had my set of keys, and I wanted to surprise you. It wasn't the kind of surprise I envisioned, since you threatened to shoot me as a robber. Do you really have a gun?"

"No. That was just something I said to sound serious and threatening."

"Here." He hands her a small square box and a wrapped rectangular something that feels like a book. "The small one's for your birthday, and the bigger one's your anniversary present."

"Golly, I'm ashamed I didn't get you anything. Twenty-one is an important birthday."

"Being back with my sweet little wifey is birthday present enough. If you really want, you're welcome to buy me something you think I'd like."

Adicia pulls a necklace out of the small box. "Thank you! This is beautiful, and you remembered my favorite color is dark blue!"

"It's an opal, and it's in the shape of a dove, the symbol of peace. Happy belated nineteenth birthday, my love."

Adicia pulls the wrapping paper off a side-by-side Italian and English edition of *The Divine Comedy*. "Now I don't have any more excuses for not reading this book. From what I'd been told about it, it reminds me of my own life, dropping so low and then slowly starting to ascend to a better place."

"The traditional one-year anniversary gift is paper. I hope you like it. I got the baby a gift too, before I realized he'd been born already." Ricky gets up again and pulls out a soft, dark blue blanket. "I didn't want him to be too cold when winter comes, and it's nice to sleep in something so soft, even if he sleeps here and not in a crib. I'll give Justine her gift tomorrow." He takes his shoes off and tosses them onto the floor. "Why don't you turn the light out so I can enjoy my beautiful wife for the first time in exactly a year?"

"Don't worry, there's almost no chance we'll have a reunion baby," Adicia says as she switches the lamp off. "My menses haven't returned yet, and breastfeeding is ninety-eight percent effective as birth control for at least six months."

"That's enough talking for now, Mrs. Carson," he says before he pulls her back into his arms and kisses her.

This time neither of them are as scared or nervous as they were the night they made Robbie. Their first coupling is rather frantic, to get a year's worth of pent-up sexual energy and frustration out of their systems, followed by five more times at a more relaxed, natural pace. Adicia doesn't care this time if Justine overhears anything, since she's so happy and relieved to be reunited with her husband. Besides, Justine would know she's overhearing an act of love, not like all those times they overheard or walked in on their parents going at it. After they're too exhausted to do anything more, they fall asleep curled up in one another's arms as the first lights of dawn start breaking through the sky, shut out by the curtains and blinds. This time, the breaking dawn doesn't represent an inevitable moment of parting, but the beginning of the rest of their lives.

***

In the morning, Justine goes over to Allen and Lenore's house for breakfast, not wanting to disturb Adicia and Ricky the morning after their reunion. Not finding her coming over anything out of the ordinary, Lenore smiles at her as she takes a seat at the table and adds an extra place setting.

"We're having scrambled eggs and sausage this morning," Lenore says. "Plus orange juice with no pulp. Will Adicia and Robbie be joining us?"

"Adicia probably wants to sleep in today," Justine says vaguely. "She had a long night last night."

Lenore glances over at the calendar. "Well, what do you know. To-day makes it a year exactly since she lost Ricky. She must've been sad all night."

"Yous guys can swing by the bakery and pick up some goodies to make her feel better," Allen suggests as he swigs down orange juice. "I'm glad you're on summer vacation, so someone can hold Robbie while she drives. I don't know how often she'll be able to get out in the car after September. I've seen a really odd, dangerous-looking contrap-tion meant to hold babies in place in the car, and I can't imagine a dot-ing mother like Adicia would put Robbie inside something like that."

"You mean a child safety seat?" Justine asks. "I've seen pictures of a few that didn't look that weird or unsafe, so long as the safety belt's over it."

"Hey, how about we come over to your place for supper tonight?" Lenore asks cheerfully. "Allen and I will make the food, and you just sit back and relax. I'll go over later today to check on her and make sure her mind is taken off this sad anniversary."

"I'm sure her mind is already off of it," Justine says cryptically.

"She might say she's not preoccupied by it, but she's probably still upset by it deep down. I'll go over with chocolate chip butterscotch cookies this afternoon to cheer her up."

Allen heads off to the bathroom to brush his teeth before leaving for work. He notes the blinds are still drawn next door as he goes out to his car, but shrugs it off. He trusts Adicia isn't about to spend the entire day moping in bed, even on the one-year anniversary of the tragedy that befell her. She's too devoted to Robbie to spend all day lying about and doing nothing.

After Allen goes to work, Lenore and Justine make cookies and discuss the growing Watergate scandal, while Irene and Amelia watch *Sesame Street* and *Mister Rogers' Neighborhood* on PBS. From their place on the davenport, the girls notice the blinds and curtains finally opening, first on the second floor and then on the first floor. They think they see a strange man passing by the windows, but they've got to be dreaming, since they surely would've heard someone breaking in. They don't know who'd be visiting Adicia.

"Mommy, is it okay if Aunt Adicia has a friend who's a boy?" Irene asks. "That doesn't mean she's cheating on Uncle Ricky, does it, if she only has a boy visitor and isn't letting him be her boyfriend?"

"What are you talking about?" Lenore asks.

"I thought I saw a strange guy in the house."

"Me too!" Amelia says.

"It's probably nothing," Justine says. "We'll see what's going on when we bring over the cookies. Don't you think we'd hear screams if someone had broken in, or that we would've heard about a new friend by now?"

Lenore wonders if perhaps Adicia finally got so lonely for male companionship she picked up a boyfriend on the side, though it's so unlike her to cheat on a husband who's in a hospital several thousand miles away. Adicia always made it clear she wouldn't seek a divorce no matter what happened, though even the most committed of people sometimes have a change of heart under extreme circumstances.

After the cookies have sufficiently finished cooling and been transferred into tins and a large glass storage container, Lenore and Justine head next door with the girls, Irene proudly pushing Oliver in his stroller. Justine leads them in the front door, wearing her best poker face as Lenore calls for Adicia.

"Do you think she's still sleeping?" Lenore asks in concern when Adicia doesn't answer.

"We saw her walking past the windows with her new friend," Irene says. "Why would she go back to bed in the afternoon when she already got up for the day?"

Lenore tells the girls to stay downstairs with Justine as she goes upstairs and continues to call for Adicia. She isn't in any of the rooms upstairs either, though Lenore finds men's clothes on Adicia's bedroom floor. The bed is unmade. It hardly seems like her sister-in-law to have a one-night stand or casual sex with someone she barely knows. The fact that Robbie sleeps there makes this scenario even more incomprehensible. Adicia would never expose her baby to strange men, or strangers period.

"Why don't we try outside?" Justine calls from downstairs.

Lenore hurries back down the stairs and heads outside with Oliver and the girls, peering around the large backyard until she catches sight of Adicia walking with a strange, tall man holding Robbie. All of them immediately notice the man limping rather badly in his right leg.

"Adicia?" Lenore calls. "Who's your new friend?"

Adicia turns around and rushes to hug Lenore. "God, if he exists, worked a miracle for me and sent my Ricky home last night! Don't you recognize him from his pictures?"

Irene and Amelia break into huge smiles.

"Are you kidding?" Lenore asks. "How in the world did this happen?"

Ricky shakes his head. "I woke up in a hospital and was told it was a miracle I'm alive. I lost so much blood, the field medic couldn't believe I was alive when he found me. When I finally came to, the doctors told me I was good to go, since they couldn't find anything further wrong with me. I had to get home to my beautiful wife and our precious firstborn baby, and I couldn't leave Adicia a teenage widow and our baby a half-orphan who'd never know his father. You must be Lenore. Adicia said you have emerald-green eyes and raven hair."

"Yes, I'm Lenore, Allen's wife. These are my children. Irene's the one who looks like me, Amelia's the middle child, and Oliver's the baby."

"What's wrong with your leg?" Amelia asks.

"Two of the shots I took were to this leg. My leg was in a cast while I was asleep in the hospital. The bone healed funny, the bullets hit a nerve, or the bone wasn't set quickly enough after I was shot."

"You'll be a good girl and won't laugh at your uncle, will you?" Adicia asks. "There's nothing wrong with having a limp. It gives you character, just like scars make the body more interesting."

"We can't wait to have a new uncle living next door!" Irene says. "Mommy and Aunt Justine made you cookies when we thought it was just Aunt Adicia at home."

"Is it okay if Ricky applies for a job at the bakery? If Allen hasn't found anyone to fill my place yet, he could give Ricky my position."

"I hope he holds true to what he said last month, that he's over his stupid opposition to your marriage," Lenore says. "Welcome to our family, by the way."

"Now we have three uncles!" Amelia says.

"Why don't we go over to the bakery right now and ask? Adicia, you can show your husband how well you know how to drive. That is, unless you think you need more time with just the three of you."

"Sure." Adicia smiles. "But Lenore, I have to ask you a question first." She tosses her car keys to Justine.

Irene runs out to the driveway and gets into the passenger seat after Justine unlocks the car and opens the driver's side door. Justine holds Oliver on her lap in the backseat. Amelia keeps looking back and forth between Ricky and Robbie, fascinated by how much they resemble one another.

"This is kinda an awkward question, since you're married to my brother, but would you mind telling me, you know, how I might know if I've had an orgasm?" Adicia whispers.

Lenore grins at her. "Deirdre asked me that question too, and said Ernestine also wanted the information but was too embarrassed to ask me since I'm Allen's wife. Why don't you describe whatever you felt, and I'll tell you if you're on the right track."

"Is it supposed to feel like an intense, aching pressure building up from somewhere deep inside of you, and releasing itself in involuntary body contractions and strange noises?"

"Yes, I think that's what you experienced. Isn't it the most intense feeling in the world?"

"Is it ever," Adicia smiles as they walk out to the car.

When they arrive at the bakery, there are five customers around the counters, and six employees working the counters. Allen is in the back with three other employees. Adicia tries to look as discreet as possible, though she's quickly noticed. She tries to look casual as she picks up a job application on a small table.

"Mrs. Carson, is that tall young man Mr. Carson?" an older woman asks.

"How can you tell?" Adicia asks.

"Like father, like son! I remember you bringing your baby here a couple of times, and that man is your son's spitting image. Isn't it one of God's miracles how little boys so strongly resemble their fathers? That should shut up your miserable in-laws if they come back here and try to say you were unfaithful."

"Is that really your husband?" one the teenage summer employees asks. "When did he come home?"

"Last night," Adicia says. "He's as good as new, except for having a strong limp in his right leg."

"Don't worry about your limp," the older woman says. "My husband was shot four times in the First World War, and he has a limp too. The most important thing is your life. You're a very lucky young man to survive being shot seven times, once in the head, and look as good as you do."

"I came to apply for a job," Ricky says. "Do I need to have an interview with Adicia's brother, or can I fill out the application and drop it off?"

"I'll go ask Mr. Troy," the teenage girl behind the counter says.

Allen comes out a few minutes later and turns white when he sees Ricky. Not wanting to appear like an idiot in front of his employees, family, and customers, he forces himself to say something.

"Welcome home, Warrick. Have you just gotten back?"

"I came in last night." He regards Allen somewhat warily, remembering their last interaction.

"Justine, did you know about this? He came back last *night* and you came over for breakfast like nothing outta the ordinary had happened?"

"I wanted it to be a surprise," Justine says. "Plus they still needed time alone together."

Allen searches for something to say that doesn't sound rehearsed or like he's going on the warpath again. "I'm glad to see you're as fit as a fiddle and done with both the hospital and Vietnam. Welcome to our family. Please don't hold it against me for the way I reacted when I saw you with Adicia last January. I was being an overprotective big brother and just as classist as your parents for thinking a guy like you had to be insincere in his intentions towards a girl like my sister. I took it really badly when I found out Adicia married you, and when I found out she was pregnant by you, but I recognize now this is the real deal, however yous guys ended up together. Love is love, however it happens. I'm man enough to admit when I've been wrong, and I'd like to apologize for misjudging you and your intentions towards Adicia." He extends his hand.

Ricky accepts his handshake. "I'm glad to know you're not trying to be my enemy anymore."

"And remember, if you ever really do mistreat my sister, I know where you live."

"I don't know if I would've bought that house had I known it was right next door to yours, but it was probably all for the best. Adicia and Justine had you and your wife to look out for them. Is it okay if I work here, by the way? Now that I'm home and Adicia has the baby to occupy herself with all day, it's time for me to learn how to be a breadwinner. I don't think I'm going back to school for awhile."

"You sure can. You can take Adicia's place until you're ready to finish your bachelor's degree. It's important you do something to support my sister and your child."

"Can we have a welcome home supper tonight?" Irene asks. "All of us can go over to Aunt Adicia's house and cook for them."

"That sounds like a nice idea. You can go back home and start calling our sisters, Sarah, and the Ryans to invite them over this weekend. Before I get back to work, I have one more thing to ask you, Warrick. I have a photography studio in my attic, and I'd love to give you, Adicia, and Robbie a free family photography session. Are you interested?"

"You bet we are!" Adicia says.

"Can you please not call me Warrick?" Ricky asks. "I hate that name. I don't feel like a Warrick. That's a name for a rich, out of touch snob, not a guy who lives in the real world."

"Okay, I promise," Allen says. "I won't call you Warrick anymore. I'd hate it if people called me Al when I've only ever gone by my full name my entire life."

Adicia feels like she's walking on cloud nine as they head back to the car. No longer is she waiting for the other shoe to drop. This time her happiness is for keeps, no more false starts on a happy ending. Anything that might come up after this will be small potatoes compared to what she's already had to fight through.

***

As promised, on Sunday, Allen sets up his photography studio for a family photography session, with a plain white backdrop instead of one of the more fancy, ornate backdrops he reserves for holidays and children. Adicia feels like a princess as her brother directs them in poses, some with all three of them, some with just the two of them, some looking at one another, some with Ricky's arm around her, some with them holding hands, some with them looking off to the side, but all of them looking like a happy little family. These are the first real photos she's had taken professionally. Now she'll finally have quality-level photographs to display. Maybe one will end up in the seashell frame from Julie.

Allen is struck by how much Ricky looks in love with Adicia and Robbie. He looks the way Allen was told he did in his early days of being in love with Lenore, looking at her as though she were the only person in the room, or the entire world. His eyes, his whole face, positively radiate pure adoration, love, commitment, the kind of look that can't be faked even by the world's best actor. Justine, who's watching in a corner with Lenore and the children, notices it too. Adicia also radiates that look, and it makes all of them very happy to see her looking so happy.

"Why don't you hold the baby for the last shot?" Ricky asks.

"Of course I'll hold my special little man," Adicia says. "I'd never pass up the chance to hold him."

Ricky hands Robbie to her, and Allen proceeds behind the camera again. Allen has just taken the last shot when he realizes he messed up, since Ricky's bad leg gave out. When he looks more closely and listens to what Ricky starts saying, however, he realizes he got the last shot just right.

"I love you, Adicia, and I want you to marry me all over again. That courthouse ceremony wasn't the same as a real wedding, with friends and family, in a nice venue, with a real reception. This time you'd wear a real wedding dress, carry a bouquet, cut a wedding cake, and have a bridal party. Now that we both love each other, in a way you can only love someone after you've been through what we've been through, it seems even more right to redo our wedding and start married life all over again, properly. This time we can take our time and plan a real wedding, send invitations, the works. You're the only girl I wanna be with for the rest of my life, and when the time is right, I want to have more children with you. I want to grow old with you. So will you please marry me all over again and make me the happiest guy in the whole world?"

"Of course I'll marry you again, Ricky!" Adicia says tearfully. "Nothing would make me happier than to have our vows renewed!" She turns to Allen, who's getting a little choked up himself. "Is it okay if I steal 'Benedictus' for my processional song? I always remembered how safe and peaceful I felt while I walked down the aisle to it when I was your bridesmaid."

"Go ahead and do whatever you want for your special day," Allen says. "I'll be more than happy to walk you down the aisle."

"The best things really do come to those who wait, and the rewards are even better when you have to earn your happiness! I can't wait to marry you all over again, my darling!"

"Now *that's* a happy ending!" Justine says.

Epilogue: Finally Dressed in Lace
(May–July 1974)

Diana, my belovèd! The darkness has passed and now the sunshine.
(Penultimate intertitle of *The Sheik*, 1921)

Remember, now, be here now;
As it's not like it was before.
The past, was, be here now.
As it's not like it was before—it was.
("Be Here Now," eighth track on *Living in the Material World*)

"Doesn't it feel funny to be back in this city again?" Adicia asks she steps into Upper East Side Beautiful Brides with Sarah, her sisters, and their friends. "I've been away for two years that seem like forever, and yet everything instantly seems so familiar, as though I never left."

"Last time we were in this store was under much different circumstances," Justine says. "I wanted to punch those bitches for making fun of you. I hope Seth is still in prison and that his mother and adult kids are miserable!"

It's now May 1974, and Adicia and Ricky's vow renewal ceremony will be held on July 12, their second anniversary and the day after Adicia's twentieth birthday. Fifteen-year-old Justine is the maid of honor, Lenore is the matron of honor, and Sarah and Allen will walk Adicia down the aisle. Adicia has nine bridesmaids, not wanting to exclude anyone who's been important to her—Ernestine, Emeline, Lucine, Deirdre, Fiona, Aoife, Betsy, Marjani, and Julie. Irene is a junior bridesmaid, since Adicia couldn't bear the thought of leaving her out of the wedding party. Ricky's groomsmen are Allen, Zachary, David, and Sarah's husband Henry. Giovanni, who'll be thirteen next month, and Matthew, who'll be fourteen in August, are junior groomsmen. Four-year-old Amelia is the flower girl, and Julie's four-year-old half-brother Graham was selected as the ring-bearer. Adicia would've loved for Oliver, who looks like a miniature version of Allen at twenty months old, to take the role, but everyone thought he was a mite too young to handle it.

"The old me woulda been terrified of coming back here and bumping into my folks, but they can never hurt me or boss me around again," Adicia declares as she parks Robbie's stroller in the lobby. "As awful as this sounds, sometimes I think that year-long separation from Ricky was the best thing that ever happened to me, since it finally taught me how to stand on my own two feet and stand up for myself."

"Do I have to wear a fancy dress and makeup?" Deirdre mopes. "Can't I just wear my most formal dress?"

"Boy, even at twenty-two, you're as much of a hell-raiser as always," Ernestine chuckles. "You didn't grow into one bit of a refined lady as you got older. You're not even gonna wear fancy clothes for our big graduation celebration this month?"

"Formal doesn't have to mean fancy. Besides, there's never been anything dainty about me. I wonder if the dumb pamphlets they hand out to junior high girls when they start menstruating nowadays are still loaded with the words 'dainty' and 'daintiness.' Since women's liberation started, I'd hope no one still thinks of girls as dainty little flowers with no desire to be anything but pretty things to look at in gilded cages."

"This time I'm gonna have a real mother helping me look for a wedding dress," Adicia says. "You wouldn't let me try on ugly dresses, would you, Sarah, or approve an orange organza dress?"

"We'll all help you find the most beautiful dress here," Sarah reassures her. "You'll look like a real bride, *mit* pretty lace, a veil, a bouquet, nice shoes, a train if you want, and beautiful material like silk, satin, or chiffon."

Mrs. Marsenko stops abruptly as she comes into the lobby with an assistant. "You! You're back! Whose turn is it to get married against her will to a much-older drug pusher and ex-convict this time?"

Adicia steps forward. "Don't worry, Mrs. Marsenko, we're back for my wedding renewal ceremony. My mother is nowhere in sight. I ran away to avoid the forced marriage my parents wanted, and married the young man I told you about. I grew to love him so much, but a week into our marriage, he was drafted into the Air Force. He was shot seven times shortly before the withdrawal from Vietnam. Four months later, he recovered and came back to me." Adicia picks Robbie up from the stroller. "This is my baby, Robert Allen Rudolph Carson. He turned a year old this month. I got pregnant with him right before my husband left for Vietnam. I'm Mrs. Carson now, not Miss Troy anymore."

Mrs. Marsenko's horrified face changes into a smile of relief. "Well then! I'll be glad to help you find your dream wedding dress and bridal party dresses!" She looks over at Sarah. "I remember you from the first two times that unpleasant Mrs. Troy woman graced my salon, but you weren't here the other two times this family returned. You were some sort of exploited nanny or babysitter, if I remember correctly, with a Hebrew name. Rachel?"

"Sarah. I'm married now, and have two *kinder*. I was an older *mutter* and bride, but at least it happened eventually."

"You've been through enough." Mrs. Marsenko averts her eyes from the number on Sarah's arm. "You deserve a happy life away from that unpleasant woman. Of all the people who've come through my doors over the twenty-five years I've been in business, I have never forgotten Mrs. Troy and her unhappy daughters."

"Our mother's gonna end up all alone and miserable," Justine says. "Word from our old downstairs neighbors the Strausslers is our brother Tommy's going to the State University at Albany with a scholarship he got for being poor. Our mother's in shock that Tommy wants to go to college instead of being happy with a high school diploma and staying in the old neighborhood. She also can't believe he's moving out of the city entirely. Who knows, we might run into him again onea these days and find him more grownup."

"Do you have anything my size in turquoise?" Deirdre asks. "That was the color of my old bridesmaid dress, but it no longer fits."

"You all can start looking through the racks, and your friend will be helped with finding a wedding gown. Remember, I don't buy into any of that nonsense about how only virgins can wear white or ivory, and that a second wedding or a vow renewal only merits a downscale dress. I assume this renewal after only two years is because you didn't have a formal ceremony the first time?"

"It was at the courthouse downtown, performed by a judge," Adicia says. "We only had four guests, and I didn't even get a bouquet. A week later, I lost him for a whole year. We wanted to start over again on the right foot."

"Oh, that's not a real wedding. I don't blame you for wanting to start off fresh with a proper ceremony. You more than deserve it. Come with me and my associate, and we'll have you fitted up in dresses that'll make you look like a proper bride."

"Don't show her any ugly orange gowns this time!" Justine says as Adicia goes off with Mrs. Marsenko and the assistant.

"Only the prettiest, we promise."

As was the case eight years ago, Deirdre stands back looking and feeling confused as everyone else excitedly scours through the racks to find the prettiest dresses in their favorite colors and styles. Ernestine amusedly wonders what she's going to wear to their handfasting wedding ceremony if she's this opposed to putting on fancy clothes on special occasions.

Justine, Aoife, Fiona, Julie, Betsy, and Irene go to the dressing rooms first, each carrying three or four gowns. Justine and Aoife take one room, Julie and Betsy take the second, and Irene and Fiona take the third. Irene thinks it's really nice how a teenager doesn't mind sharing her dressing room with a six-year-old. This beautiful older girl has all the sweetness, kindness, and sensitivity one might expect from someone who went through the first twelve years of her life answering to Baby. Irene smiles at her as Fiona helps her with buttoning up one of the dresses in the back.

While they're modeling their gowns in the lobby, Adicia comes out in the first dress.

"It's too lacy," Emeline declares. "There should be some lace on a wedding gown, and you'd look beautiful in lace, but it looks like it's made of doilies."

"I hope you're not gonna try on any polyester dresses," Ernestine says. "I like my polyester clothes just fine, but it seems wrong for a wedding dress. I can't believe anyone *makes* polyester wedding gowns."

"But do you like the style?" Adicia asks.

"The neckline's a little bit too high, and the sleeves are a bit too long," Lenore says. "Nothing wrong with modesty, but I don't like long sleeves that look like body armor. They should be loose and flowing, or at least not sit right against the skin."

"Do you wanna approve our dresses before you try on another one, Aunt Adicia?" Irene asks.

"Wear whatever you like, as long as it's comfortable and you think it's pretty. Ricky and I aren't having a color scheme, so don't worry about matching. Just no really short skirts or plunging necklines, and sleeves should at least cover the shoulder."

While Adicia tries on the second gown, the first round of bridal attendants make their choices and let Lucine, Emeline, Marjani, Amelia, Lenore, and Ernestine go into the dressing rooms. Lucine and Emeline take one room, Lenore goes with Amelia, and Ernestine goes with Marjani. Nineteen-month-old Simone is fascinated by the brightly-colored dresses, and watches intently as they change in and out of the gowns.

Adicia reappears in an ivory satin gown with no embellishments, rather short sleeves, and a three-foot lace train. Everyone shakes her head.

"It's lovely if what you're going for is simple and laid-back, but I think you'd feel your most beautiful in something a little fancier," Lenore says. "My wedding dress was simple too, but not quite that simple."

"Do you have anything with a splash of color?" Adicia asks. "My favorite color is dark blue, and it'd be nice if my dress showcased my personality."

"I always try my best to make my repeat customers happy," Mrs. Marsenko says. "Why don't you try on the last gown, and we'll see if we might be able to spiffy it up a bit with strategically-placed color."

"Deirdre hasn't even started looking for her dress!" Aoife says.

"I'll wear whatever you have in a groovy color and doesn't make me feel like a lace factory or a cupcake exploded," Deirdre says. "Do you have my previous dress in an adult size? I'm generally a ten or twelve."

"Is everyone decided on what she wants to wear?" Emeline asks.

"I think we are," Ernestine says, still admiring herself in the deep red chiffon gown.

"We've got a lot of colors and shades to work with," Mrs. Marsenko says. "I've always carried gowns in more than just the traditional, subdued colors like pink, light blue, pale green, yellow, and peach. Some ladies don't like pastels, just like some brides don't like white or ivory. There's room for all types in a wedding party."

"Don't worry, Adicia's husband's got a couple million bucks in their joint bank account to cover all this," Fiona says. "He burnt all his bridges to his parents and their family money when he decided to marry her, but he got access to his trust fund before that happened. Her husband's a nice kind of millionaire, not a snob who doesn't care about the little people."

Deirdre carefully inspects the others' dresses. Lucine has violet taffeta, Emeline has light green chiffon, Ernestine has her red dress, Justine has pink rayon, Fiona has yellow organza, Aoife has baby blue chiffon, Julie has purple taffeta, Betsy has medium blue organza, Lenore has dark green satin, Marjani has light red silk, Irene has medium green satin, and Amelia has burgundy silk. Deirdre doesn't know the first thing about the differences between the various fabrics or what the official names of all these colors are. She wouldn't know forest green from olive green or mauve from cranberry if her life depended on it.

"I like this color," she finally announces. "The off-purple one with fabric flowers going down the left side and on the left side of the neckline. That's suitably wild enough for me."

"It's called wildberry," Mrs. Marsenko says. "You can go back and try it on so we can see if we need any tailoring. Your friends have always been lucky here. Most of my customers need at least a little tailoring to make a gown fit like a glove, since bridalwear isn't usually designed the same way as standard sizes in a regular store."

By the time Deirdre comes out in the wildberry dress with decorative fabric roses, Adicia is standing there in the third and final gown. Sarah pulls a veil off the wall and places it on top of Adicia's head, gently lowering it over her face.

"Now you look like a bride," Sarah pronounces.

"I love this one!" Adicia agrees. "I like ivory more than white, and there's just the right amount of lace and beading."

"You look like a princess," Deirdre says. "It sort of looks like Lenore's gown, only without the velvet."

"You do sorta look like a Medieval or Renaissance princess like Lenore," Emeline says.

The sleeves are long and taper off in loose, flowing lace midway between the elbow and wrist; the unembellished skirt extends all the way to the floor; and the bodice is slightly lacy, the lace interspersed with beadwork. Not too fancy and not too plain.

"I know just the thing," Mrs. Marsenko says, carefully inspecting it. "There's just enough room to sew on a ring of dark blue lace around the waist and neckline. That's such minimal work, it can probably be done while you wait here. We have alterations in the basement, but you won't need to go down there and get measured, since they're just putting on extra embellishments, not tailoring it."

"Sure, that'd be most convenient," Adicia says. "We don't live in the city anymore, but we came since we like your salon so much. You've got a really nice selection of dresses, and you and your staff always treated us really nicely."

"Why don't you go and change back into your clothes so we can get the dress fixed?" Lenore asks. "You don't want Ricky to miss you too much."

"Let him miss me," Adicia laughs. "We've already been separated for an entire year; part of one day doesn't mean jack."

While Adicia changes back into her street clothes and puts the dress back on the hanger, Mrs. Marsenko tells the others to bring their dresses to the checkout counter so they can start totaling the bill. Deirdre, satisfied the wildberry dress is the one, quickly changes out of it and has it rung up.

"Can we expect any of you girls to return to this salon when it's your turn to get married?" Mrs. Marsenko asks.

"Maybe, if I ever get married," Emeline says. "But I'm gonna be twenty-six on the fourteenth, and there's no guy in sight. Most people are matched up by this age. I've never even kissed a man. It probably won't happen. I was meant for other things."

"Don't rule out anything, no matter how old you get. Don't believe the lie that you're an old maid if you don't have any boyfriends or male interest by an arbitrary cut-off date. You can still have children for about twenty more years, so there shouldn't be any rush on the biological front either. If you really want a husband, and he's out there for you somewhere, he'll appear in your life when the time is right."

"I don't have a boyfriend either, but I hope I have a fellow by the time I'm Emeline's age," Betsy says.

"I don't have anyone special either," Marjani says.

"Neither do I," Julie says.

"Well, you're modern college girls. I'm glad there's no longer the same obsessive focus on getting your Mrs. degree as there was ten or twenty years ago. You should go to college for an education and the experience of living away from home. If you happen to find your husband while you're there, that's just a side benefit. When I started this business in 1949, I was thirty and doing something very unusual. I'm glad it's no longer considered so strange for a woman to open her own business. I went to school to get an education, not to find Mr. Marsenko." She looks at Ernestine and Deirdre. "How about you two? Any special fellows?"

"We're in a relationship," Ernestine says coyly. "There's gonna be a wedding in the next year or two."

"Both of you have boyfriends?"

"Ernestine and Deirdre are each other's girlfriends!" Amelia pipes up.

"Oh, brother," Ernestine mutters.

"Well, that's certainly different," Mrs. Marsenko says. "I don't suppose there's anything wrong with it if you genuinely have no interest in men."

"Oh, good, you don't think we're mentally ill."

"Why would I think you're mentally ill for being a little different from the others? You're not hurting anybody by having a girlfriend instead of a boyfriend. Such people have always existed. I suppose God had a reason for creating you to be that way."

Adicia comes back out and takes a seat in the lobby, wheeling the stroller with her. Mrs. Marsenko notes the contrast between Adicia and Mrs. Troy. Adicia is smiling at and interacting with her child, no matter how young he is, while Mrs. Troy ignored or snapped at her children as though they were a burden and inconvenience. A first-time mother who isn't even twenty knows more about how to be a good mother than a middle-aged woman with nine kids. She also looks happy and full of life. The seventeen-year-old girl who last came here looked, talked, and acted like a scared little rabbit. Mrs. Marsenko is very glad all the beaten-down girls who first came through her doors in June 1960 are safely away from their toxic parents. The best revenge is living well, and they're now living much better than they did when Mrs. Troy ran the show.

***

"I'm glad July twelfth is a Friday this year," Adicia says as they get ready for the ceremony in a private room of the Unitarian church she and Ricky decided on. "The weekend is just starting, so most people can come. If it was in the middle of the week, we might not have so many people willing to come."

"Friday weddings are nice," Lenore says. "Allen and I were married on a Friday too."

Lucine frowns as she examines herself in the mirror. "I hope this dress doesn't split while we're standing up there. It's too late to have it let out."

"Did you get the wrong size by mistake?" Deirdre asks. "I'm good at sewing. Let me frog the seams, and I'll fix it in a jiffy."

"You'll have to do that for all the rest of my clothes too, since I'm about two months pregnant. I figured it out a week ago. Zachary and I began trying for a second kid in April. I'm twenty-eight, and shouldn't take too much time completing our family."

"Oh, how exciting!" Fiona says. "There'll be a little bit over two years between Simone and this one. That's a nice age difference for siblings. Aoife's twenty-three months younger than me."

"Do you think you'll have another baby anytime soon, Adicia?" Lenore asks. "Robbie's fourteen months old, and we all know how common honeymoon babies are. Irene was a honeymoon baby."

"I don't wanna think about that right now! I like it just being the three of us plus Justine. And I only turned twenty yesterday. There's no rush."

"Does everyone remember what to do?" Emeline asks as they hear the prelude music, "Underture" by The Who, starting.

"I'm going first as the lead bridesmaid, when we hear Mozart's Minuet in C major starting," Ernestine says. "Then you, Lucine, Julie, Deirdre, Fiona, Aoife, Betsy, Marjani, and Irene. Lenore and Justine are gonna walk down together. Amelia, you go after you see little Grahamy going."

"My baby brother is so cute in his little suit and bowtie!" Julie says proudly. She doesn't think to be mortified to have four-year-old siblings at her age. After growing up as an only child, she was more than thrilled to get a little brother and sister at fifteen, with two more on the way.

"How come you need a ring-bearer if yous guys are already married and this is just a renewal?" Irene asks.

"We had them re-dedicated and inscribed," Adicia says. "I'm not wearing mine now, am I?"

"What do your rings say on the inside?" Ernestine asks. "When Deirdre and I have our ceremony, we're gonna have ours say 'Old friends.'"

Adicia wishes she had brain bleach and could get that image and association out of her head, her dearest sister and her best friend sharing their first kiss during that song. "They say *Amor vincit omnia*,' Latin for 'Love conquers all.'"

"I like this song," Emeline says as the ten-minute prelude instrumental runs on. "I've always imagined it recreates the feel of an acid trip. Probably the closest I'll ever get to experiencing an acid trip, since I must be onea the few hippies who never dropped acid. I still smoke pot from time to time, but never acid. I'm scared of having flashbacks years later, or a really bad trip."

"Remember, whatever happens, you can't mess up, 'cause you're already married," Justine says.

Irene goes to the door and peeks out. "All the guests are coming down the hall. I don't think it'll take long for them to get seated, since it's not that big of a crowd. How many guests again?"

"Including our attendants, about sixty," Adicia says.

"I see Betsy's parents, Gemma and Tyrone with Adrienne, Mr. and Mrs. Doyle, Caroline, and Meredith," Aoife reports, going over to stand next to Irene on the other side of the door.

"Who are those people?" Irene asks. "I don't recognize them, and I don't think I've seen them in pictures before."

Adicia creeps up to look, only peering out from the side of the door so no one will see her in her dress before the ceremony. "Oh, that's Mr. and Mrs. Straussler. They offered to cater the dessert buffet."

"No way!" Ernestine shouts. "I would never have believed that if I hadn't seen it with my own eyes! Look who's with the Strausslers!"

"Am I seeing things?" Emeline asks. "What is *he* doing *here*?"

"Who's that?" Irene asks.

"It's our little brother Tommy," Adicia says in shock. "He's eighteen now. He really has finally started growing up after years of our mother treating him like an overgrown baby and spoiling the life outta him."

"Mr. Straussler said Tommy took him up on his offer of shooting lessons," Justine says. "I assume he heard of your ceremony from them."

"I hope this means Mother lost Tommy and has no one left on her side outside of her miserable friends," Lucine says. "It serves her right to lose her precious pet child, her golden prince, and be left all alone at last. Boy, she and Dad are gonna be so miserable with no more buffers left between them. I wonder if they're gonna kill each other. What I wouldn't give to be a fly on the wall now that they're forced to live with just each other."

"Here come the last of the guests," Aoife says. "We oughta start getting ready."

The attendants start picking up the miniature bouquets, which Fiona and Julie spent the morning assembling from irises, marigolds, peonies, cream-colored tulips, and globe amaranths. Adicia picks up her bouquet of purple roses and shamrocks, which Deirdre assembled, and goes to the back of the line. She stands back with Sarah as the groomsmen enter through the side door and her bridal party starts proceeding up the aisle to the sounds of Mozart.

"Are you ready to do this?" Allen whispers as he meets her and Sarah at the end of the hall.

"Remember, you're already married," Sarah says. "The only difference is this time you're having a proper ceremony, and it's about love, devotion, and commitment."

A sense of peace and safety settles over Adicia as she hears the opening notes of "Benedictus," the same way she felt when she was Allen and Lenore's bridesmaid eight years ago. This is the processional she should've had the first time, instead of simply going into an office when her number was called. Though this song is based around a line from the Latin Mass and originally from the Christian Bible, "Blessèd is the one who comes in the name of the Lord" is a very universal, nonsectarian sentiment. There are many paths to and names for the Divine, and none are wrong, so long as the seeker has a pure, devout heart and soul. All truly good people with sincere intentions are unconditionally blessed and welcomed by a benevolent Higher Power, no matter who they are or where they've been.

When they get to the altar, Allen gives Ricky a warning look before taking his place with the other groomsmen, and Sarah takes a seat in the front row with her children. Adicia smiles at her when she pulls Robbie out of the stroller and sets him on her lap. Her son will grow up knowing Sarah as his grandmother, the kind of grandmother who exists through love and not blood.

The Unitarian minister starts with a declaration of intent. "When you first made vows two years ago under less than ideal circumstances, you didn't know where life would take you. You promised to love, honor, comfort, and protect one another for better or worse. In only two years, your life has surely brought you both wonderful blessings and difficult tribulations, things many couples who've been together for an entire lifetime haven't had to go through. Therefore, you've fulfilled your promise to stay true to one another against the odds that might've torn apart many another young couple whose marriage started on such shaky ground. What started out as a convenience marriage has blossomed into a true love match and a strong marital relationship. So, as you come here today to reaffirm your wedding vows, and as you reflect back over the past two years as husband and wife, do you now reaffirm the vows you took on July 12, 1972?"

"Yes, we do," they answer together.

Ricky picks up the paper where he wrote his vows. "Today, after two years of marriage that seem more like a miniature lifetime, I ask you to continue to take me as your husband and your friend. You've stood by my side through sorrow and joy, triumph and defeat, sickness and health, and for this I am so grateful. Adicia, you are my heart, my best friend, my life. Today, before family and friends, I renew my commitment to you under better circumstances. I promise to love and cherish you, comfort and protect you, honor and stay loyal to you, respect you and grow with you for all the days of our lives. This is my solemn vow."

Adicia picks up her vows, glad no one thinks they're cheating by reading them. "On our wedding day, Ricky, I vowed to have you as my husband and to honor, love, comfort, and protect you in sickness and in health, for better or worse, for richer or for poorer. The first year of our marriage tested those vows, but our enduring commitment to one another has prevailed, and I came to love you the way a wife loves a husband. I come here today to make a fresh start, to renew our vows of love, honor, and fidelity, and to reaffirm my love for you. Two years ago, I promised to stand by you for as long as we both should live. I never imagined I'd face losing you so soon, or the depths of despair I'd feel at that prospect. Today, the darkness has passed and the troubled waters have receded, and I'm so happy I get to continue life's journey by your side. Once again, I promise to love you, honor you, comfort you, and protect you, for better or worse, in sickness and in health, for as long as we both shall live. I'm overjoyed today, in the presence of my family and friends, most of whom were missing at our original wedding, to reaffirm my commitment to you, and once again, to promise to love you, honor you, comfort you, and protect you, in sickness and in health, for richer and for poorer, for better and for worse, as long as we both shall live."

After they've read their vows, the selection of readings begins. Deirdre goes up first and reads the same Irish wedding blessing she read at Allen and Lenore's wedding. The second reading is from Lucine, who wanted to include something from the Bible that's suitably nonsectarian for the mostly agnostic Adicia, Ruth 1:16-17.

"'Do not urge me to leave you or turn back from following you; for where you go, I will go, and where you lodge, I will lodge. Your people shall be my people, and your God, my God. Where you die, I will die, and there I will be buried. Thus may the Lord do to me, and worse, if anything but death parts you and me.'"

The third reading is from Lenore, who selected Shakespeare's twenty-ninth sonnet. The sonnet is from the point of view of a man who felt all alone, disgraced, and outcast because he didn't possess a fortune, but then remembered his sweet love and felt better, for the wealth that comes from a true love is more precious than the wealth possessed by kings.

Julie has the fourth reading, an Apache wedding blessing she found in a book from a Native American studies class she took during the fall semester of her sophomore year. "Now you will feel no rain, for each of you will be shelter to the other. Now you will feel no cold, for each of you will be warmth to the other. Now there is no more loneliness for you, for each of you will be companion to the other. Now you are two bodies, but there is only one life before you. Go now to your dwelling place, to enter into the days of your togetherness. And may your days be good and long upon the Earth."

The final reading comes from Emeline. Adicia is grateful a veil is over her face, since she's always been moved to tears by *The Velveteen Rabbit*, particularly the part Emeline is reading, the conversation between the Rabbit and the Skin Horse about what Real is. The process of becoming Real only happens to people, toys, or stuffed animals who don't break easily, and always involves a drastic change from their original perfect form, but none of those things matter to the person who made one Real. Only those who don't understand would consider someone who's Real to be ugly, and once it's happened, it can't be undone. It lasts for always.

Julie's little brother Graham smiles up at Adicia and Ricky as he stands on his tiptoes and holds out the pillow with the newly-inscribed rings. He looks like Matthew, whom Adicia can barely believe is only a month away from fourteen. He's only about a year and a half younger than Justine, but after not having seen him for going on five years, he seems like he's grown a lot more. Several of her sisters and friends laughingly suggested Justine and Matthew can be boyfriend and girlfriend if they go to the same college or attend college in the same town, but Justine insisted Matthew is practically her brother. Meanwhile, Justine continues to sneak little looks at twenty-year-old David, who seems oblivious to her crush on him. Justine doesn't consider him practically her brother. since there are almost five years between them, and they were always at different places in life.

The minister takes the pillow from Graham. "The circle is the symbol of the Sun, the Earth, and the Universe. It is a symbol of holiness, perfection, and peace. This ring is a symbol of unity, with no beginning and no ending, in which your two lives are joined in one unbroken circle. Do you, Warrick Grover Carson, continue to take Adicia Éloïse Carson as your loving wife? Will you continue to love her, honor her, comfort her, and protect her, forsaking all others, for as long as you both shall live?"

"You bet I will."

"Do you, Adicia Éloïse Carson, continue to take Warrick Grover Carson as your loving husband? Will you continue to love him, honor him, comfort him, and protect him, forsaking all others, for as long as you both shall live?"

"Yes, I gladly will." She takes the plain gold band from the pillow, observing how it's over twice the size of her ring. "Ricky, I give you this ring all over again as a token of our abiding love and recommitment to one another."

Ricky picks up Adicia's tiny plumeria ring, marveling at how tiny it is in comparison to his. "Adicia, I give you this ring all over again as a token of our abiding love and recommitment to one another."

"Warrick Grover and Adicia Éloïse Carson, having witnessed the reaffirmation of your vows with all who are assembled here, and by the authority of love itself, I do affirm you have expressed your desire to continue as husband and wife. Ladies and gentlemen, it is my honor to present to you, once again as husband and wife, Warrick Grover Carson and Adicia Éloïse Carson!"

Adicia breathes a sigh of relief that the minister remembered her request for no public kiss at the end of the ceremony. The thought of doing something so personal, private, and intimate with an audience practically makes her break out in hives. They proceed down the aisle arm-in-arm as the recessional song, "Love," from Deirdre's belovèd *Plastic Ono Band*, starts up. Even Aoife gave a thumbs-up to Adicia's choice, since this is one of the few songs on that album that isn't angry and screamy. The attendants walk down after them in pairs.

Once at the head of the receiving line, near the church's botanical and butterfly garden, Adicia giddily takes hugs, handshakes, and congratulations from Gemma and Tyrone, Mr. and Mrs. van Niftrik, Mr. and Mrs. Doyle, Caroline, Meredith, Mr. and Mrs. Washington, Subira, Zuberi, Mr. and Mrs. Straussler, Fritz and Nessa, Father and Mrs. Murphy, her former co-workers from the bakery, and the members of the bridal party. It's a relatively small amount of guests, but having even several score of people who care enough about her to show up for a special, important day is something she never dreamt could happen.

"Is it okay if I give yous guys a present, even if the etiquette says you don't give gifts for a renewal?"

Adicia looks up at Tommy, who stands only a few inches shorter than Ricky's five feet eleven. "Of course you can give us a present, Tommy. Mr. and Mrs. Straussler never told us you'd be coming."

"Our parents think they're taking me up to Albany this weekend to get settled into my dorm early. They were never gonna take me to college orientations or move-in day, so they cared less about checking my story." He hands Adicia a dark blue bag with a metallic shine. "I remembered that's your favorite color. Can I apologize for being such an insufferable little prick for so many years? Mother's gotten really, really goofy, and it made me start thinking about how it's kinda weird a mother would wanna be that close to her teenage son, buy him so many things, and do everything for him like an invalid. She saw nothing wrong or goofy about having conversations with me while I was tryna use the bathroom or bathe. I didn't wanna turn into another Francesco. After the whole truth about Seth came out, she creeped me out even more with how she just shrugged it off like he'd been charged with minor theft or public drunkenness. She was more upset about how he broke into the apartment and tried to beat me. What woman in her right mind would deliberately choose such awful guys for her daughters to marry? She's fifty-one, but she looks closer to seventy-five except for her hair. She's only now starting to go gray."

"What are you gonna study at college, or haven't you decided?" Justine asks.

"I wanna be an engineer. I was never into the liberal arts like you girls, and engineering makes pretty good money."

"Why don't we have a picture of the bride with her little brother?" the photographer suggests. "Then we can take a picture with all eight of the siblings."

"Those are two shots I never thought I'd pose for," Adicia says as Ricky takes the bag from her and steps out of the frame so she and Tommy can stand next to one another and smile for the camera.

"You do realize it takes more effort than an apology and a gift to make up for your first eighteen years," Ernestine tells him as nicely as she can. "You have to demonstrate changed behavior consistently. Deirdre and I are going to the University of Albany in the fall too, for master's degrees, since Vassar doesn't have a graduate track. David's going there too, now that he's got his associate's degree and can transfer to a four-year school. I'll be checking up on you to make sure you're really undergoing a genuine change in behavior and attitude."

"I wish I could join yous," Betsy says. "I'll miss you when I'm at Sarah Lawrence. Maybe someday more colleges will offer master's programs in women's studies."

The photographer has to stand back a bit when he takes the picture of the eight Troy siblings, going in birth order from Gemma to Justine. "This is the biggest family I've ever served as a photographer for. You're not even Catholics or Orthodox Jews!"

"There's one more where the rest of us came from," Gemma calls. "Carlos comes between me and Allen, but he's serving life in prison. You don't wanna know the half of what Carlos did."

Before everyone starts packing up to go to the reception, the photographer asks Ricky and Adicia for one more photo. This is the wedding photo she was cheated out of two years ago, both bride and groom smiling, mutually in love, wearing proper wedding clothes, with a beautiful bouquet, outside on a beautiful day, in a beautiful setting. Right before the photographer snaps the picture, a Monarch butterfly lands on each of them. This is the photo she'll display in the seashell frame from Julie, since the butterfly represents love, good luck, and rebirth, just the things she's so grateful to finally have.

***

"I hope Robbie doesn't mind staying with Allen and Lenore," Adicia frets as she and Ricky set out from their hotel on Monday, Ricky's twenty-second birthday. "It's a good thing Lenore's still nursing Oliver, so she'll be a good old-fashioned wetnurse. I never tasted Tommy's Similac or Justine's Enfamil, but Gemma took a taste of Enfamil when she was Giovanni's only mother. She said it tasted gross and couldn't understand why they didn't come up with something better-tasting if that was all a baby could eat at that age."

"Is that all you can think about on our honeymoon?" Ricky teases. "It's supposed to be a vacation away from real life. Soon enough we'll have to go home and get back to work. Enjoy it while you can."

"Well, I've never left him before in all of his fourteen months of life!"

"He'll do fine. Your family's as attached to him as we are, and won't neglect him or do anything bad. It's not like you left him in the care of your horrid parents or that bizarre family Gemma was married into. I still can't believe her first husband was contentedly living at home till he was thirty-eight."

Adicia stops and breathes in the air. "I never thought I'd have the chance to have a vacation outside America, let alone New York State. Here I thought we'd only have our honeymoon at a nearby beach like Cape Cod or the coast of Maine."

"I know you would've been happy with that, but you deserve more after all you've been through. Italy was the most romantic place I could think of for my beautiful bride. Just wait'll you see where I'm taking you. It's onea the most romantic spots on Earth."

Adicia draws back when she sees a river approaching in the distance. "We're going for a boat ride? I've never ridden in a boat. What if I get seasick or the boat sinks?"

"We're not going for a ride in just any boat. We're going for a ride in a gondola."

The waters of Rio di Palazzo are calm and smooth, though Adicia is still uncertain, particularly when sunset isn't too far off. If there should be turbulent waters or another boat coming at them, the gondolier will never be able to see and do something in time to rectify the situation. Her heart beats very fast as Ricky helps her into the gondola.

"You don't mind engaging in a little public display of affection in front of our gondolier, do you, if he happens to look our way?" he whispers as they take their seats.

"What? I wouldn't do that unless it's too dark for him to see us. You know how I feel about public displays of affection."

"Well, you don't get a choice. You're gonna have to let me kiss you when our gondola goes underneath the bridge that's coming up. You wouldn't deny your husband this one wish on his birthday, would you?"

"Is there a superstition associated with that?"

"It's called the Bridge of Sighs. Lord Byron gave it that the nickname in the last century. He believed convicts got their last sight of the beautiful city of Venice while passing underneath the bridge. That theory isn't historically accurate, but the name stuck."

As the sky fills with the beautiful colors of the setting Sun and the gondola passes underneath the bridge, Ricky leans over and kisses her, the same sweet, gentle way he did at the county fair two years ago. Adicia nervously smiles at him, hoping the gondolier didn't see anything.

"What was that for?"

"The legend says if you kiss your belovèd on a gondola going underneath the Bridge of Sighs at sunset, you'll be together, blissful, and in love forever, and will have a happy, blissful marriage. You want that, don't you? After what we went through, I'm not taking any chances, superstition or not. I wanna be with you forever."

"That's a beautiful legend. There's no one else I wanna spend the rest of my life with."

"On the tunnel of love, you said it was ironic the waters ahead of us were so smooth when in real life they were anything but. Now the waters are smooth in every way."

Adicia snuggles against Ricky. "My life has usually been more like a Grimm's fairytale than a Disney fairytale, but sometimes even the darkest, most twisted fairytale has a happy ending, even for a poor girl from the Lower East Side."

The End

17 July 1993–May 1994 (discontinued original first draft)
18 November 2010–16 February 2011
Edited and revised 2011–2014
Second edition edits January–February 2017
Third edition edits December 2020–July 2021

The Story Behind the Story

Adicia's story was inspired in May 1993, when I heard the story behind The Four Seasons' famous song "Rag Doll." I'd just gotten into Sixties music a few months before, and The Four Seasons had quickly become my favorite band. I became seriously obsessed with that story and the idea of writing an entire novel, loosely based around the lyrics of the song, to give that poor nameless girl a happy ending with a rich boy who loved her just the way she was. The original, discontinued first draft was begun 17 July 1993 and worked on till about May 1994, when the first of the two long files caught a bug and couldn't be opened normally anymore. I was so devastated, I stopped working on the story, though the second of the two files was fine. It ended shortly after Lenore (whose original surname was Lennon) was introduced and the squat had been raided. It may have been cut off around the time Mrs. Troy forces the girls to leave Allen and Lenore. The last scene might've been Tommy's kindergarten graduation or a school play, where he was acting like his usual over the top, mean, spoilt brat self. He was bragging to his indulgent mother about how he was giving the finger and doing lots of other immature stuff to a girl named Georgetta, the class brain.

Sixteen and a half years later, on 18 November 2010, I finally went back from scratch and memory. I'd carried that story around in my head for so many years, even thinking up the character who became Betsy during the long interim. I felt like I'd never be able to forgive myself if I went the rest of my life waiting for those files to be opened again. In the weeks leading up to starting over, I had a number of dreams about that long-ago story. During one of these dreams, the character of Sarah came back to me.

It took three months to write the 397,000-word second first draft, and it was truly one of those times where a book was writing me instead of the other way around. Everything flowed so effortlessly and naturally, particularly after I got past the point where I'd gotten cut off all those years ago, and was no longer relying on misty memory. A few months later, the first of the two original files was miraculously resurrected, and I was so glad I'd started over. There's no way I could've salvaged a decent story by writing around that Grimms' fairytale on acid. It was awful. The only things which stayed the same were the Troy siblings' names and approximate starting ages; the four nameless, squatting siblings whom Ernestine befriends; the characters of Julie (who was originally named Karin) and Lenore; the depressing energy and nightmarish staircase of the Lower East Side tenement; and the general outline. I was also delighted to discover the Bowery Mission, since I remembered Adicia and her sisters eating holiday meals at a soup kitchen in the original. Unlike in the rewrite, they actually did wash dishes there!

A lot of things changed from the original plans and what had gone down in the discontinued original first draft, among them:

Tommy was much more of a spoilt brat, and had a bit of a mean streak. He was too over the top. His slow growth and ultimate redemption were huge but pleasant surprises when I was writing the story anew.

Gemma's first husband was named Giovanni Varracuzza, the baby was Francis, and they moved to Staten Island. Prior to the forced marriage, Gemma had already married her high school boyfriend, with whom she practiced the Beatrice Sparks version of "Satanism" (e.g., sacrificing cats, using Ouija boards, "Our Father who art in Hell"). At one point, Mr. Troy beat her up when he caught her with her husband. After she left Giovanni, she got back with her first husband, whom she'd never divorced. Gemma was also much more of a mean, snooty girl, and disappeared after her big scene when she announced she'd gotten an underhanded divorce and didn't want to raise her baby. The second time around, I grew to like her, and felt real sympathy at her plight. I couldn't write her out so early on or leave her as an aloof princess. Keeping Giovanni around was also unexpected. I felt too attached to him to let him be adopted away, so I gave him to the Murphys and enabled him to remain in the Troys' lives at some level.

The guy Lucine was supposed to marry against her will was a Greek-American named Nikolas Pappadoras, only six years her senior, who already had a girlfriend, Rhonda (Ronnie) Hill. Ronnie was a regular visitor to the squat, where both Emeline and Ernestine had moved to avoid future forced marriages. Nikolas had no plans to dump Ronnie after marrying Lucine, and expected Lucine to accept the fact that he had a live-in mistress. Lucine and Ronnie ended up running away together to escape Nikolas, with the cover story that they were raped and murdered by a guy in a hockey mask, then had their bodies burnt behind the fire escape.

Mrs. Troy was scheming to marry Allen off as well as her daughters, to a Polish woman named Olga Majewski, who later ran off with Nikolas. Allen was in love with a hooker named Kiki (real name Katalin). Then Carlos had his accident, which also seriously injured Kiki and a cab driver (they were trying to carry a taxi that was out of gas, while high on various drugs), and the relationship was over. My original plans had Allen and Lenore getting together not long after she unofficially joined the family, when she was only fifteen. Lenore was smoking pot when they met, and was going to quit drugs like Allen had recently done. (Allen and Lenore's meeting was in homage to the song "Bus Stop.")

Allen, not Carlos, was the unintentional arsonist. He threw his smoking joint and one of Carlos's abandoned, lit cigarettes into a garbage can with oily rags. The fire also happened before Gemma's forced marriage or Sarah's expulsion. My memory was right about Adicia being carried out of harm's way in the wardrobe.

The Troys lived on the twentieth floor of their original tenement, not the eighth, and the superintendent was always coming by to shut off various utilities. There was also that lost tenth sibling, a little boy between Tommy and Justine, who died at several days.

Only the oldest four Troy siblings knew how to read and write, in spite of how they all went to school. Emeline claimed their father only let them take classes he thought were worth paying for, though there's no indication they're at private school. Since when would a private school let parents get away with only paying for their kids to take a few subjects?! Ernestine dropped out of school when she decided to move (not run away) to the squat, and Girl taught her to read.

Girl was a lot further out in left field, expounding upon topics such as planned single parenthood, alternate universes, psychic powers, a universal language, beings from the underworld visiting Earth, sci-fi novels coming true in the near future, and picking and choosing among aspects of all world religions. She and her siblings weren't totally parentless, as their father was the squat's bouncer. They didn't know if they were full siblings, since their father frequently entertained different hookers. There were only fifteen people living there when Ernestine met them, and while it was a safe haven, it wasn't the utopian paradise I later wrote it as. People did drugs, gambled, stole, and used it as a safe house if they were wanted for crimes. Baby calls someone a greenhorn for eating with utensils instead of his hands.

Julie (then called Karin) was a year younger than Adicia, and a psychosomatic mute. She was terrified of people coming after her if she breathed a word about how her parents and Nikolas abused her. To make it even better, she was raped by both her father and Nikolas, was already a drug addict at the tender age of six (pill-popping and glue-sniffing), was frequently attacked when she went to buy her drugs, and was often beaten up, pushed down the stairs, and set on fire by her parents. Adicia, Lucine, Tommy, and Ronnie were in the apartment when Nikolas raped her in another room, in exchange for $355 to buy drugs. Her parents were rarely home, and often came home drunk when they did show up. The only details which stayed the same were that her father was a pedophile and Adicia snuck her to the squat to save her from her home life. The subplot about Julie and Mrs. Doyle being long-separated daughter and mother was entirely a product of the second version.

Adicia didn't think much of Ricky, and was supposed to have a horrible boyfriend named Jack Rogers, who expertly played on her ridiculously low self-esteem. She was going to go back to Ricky's house not because she saw her mother, but because she saw a rapist gang on the horizon. There wasn't much thought or substance put into Ricky or their relationship, though that was the real turning-point of the story and the fulfillment of the happy ending I wanted so badly for that girl. He was a rich boy who was new in town and had a crush on her, and his parents absolutely hated the Troys for being poor. My original plans also had the Carsons moving to the city in 1969, and Ricky being the same age as Adicia. I had to make him two years older because the big plot twist with the draft would only be historically accurate if he were born in 1952, and I wanted to keep the timeline the same.

Adicia originally was going to be forced to sleep with a 35-year-old "man" at age fifteen to be "broken in," because her parents were that sick and evil. I hit upon the idea of her being forced to do that with the degenerate Ethan as part of the storyline of Mrs. Troy embezzling and later being threatened with more jail time if she didn't pay everything back. There was no embezzlement in the original story.

The Troys were going to run out of money, or get even poorer, and be forced to move behind a wall to a ghetto in 1968 or 1969. At that age, I didn't understand that in modern lingo, "ghetto" refers to a really poor, run-down side of town, not a separate, walled-off area. All my envisioned meetings between Adicia and Ricky involved one of them going over this mythical wall separating the haves from the have-nots.

Everything about the original was so dark, dreary, depressing, twisted, over the top. No distinct personalities took shape; everything was too starkly black and white; the prose was excessively purple; the characters weren't natural, realistic, or believable; and I just stumbled into storylines and characters. Probably the best stumbled-upon story-line was Allen quitting his delinquent lifestyle and trying to save his sisters from their wretched home life.

The Epilogue I had planned, for years in the future, was ridiculous too. Allen and Lenore were going to die of LSD flashbacks years after they last used drugs, of course dying so close together because it was "romantic," and Ricky was going to commit suicide after Adicia died of old age, because he didn't want people in Paradise to mistreat her the way she'd been mistreated in her youth. Only from the overactive imagination of a thirteen-year-old!

A number of the last names which appear in this book are from my family tree—Neiman, Spirnak, Hartlein, Wickline, Sviatko. I gave Lenore the middle name and birth surname of my five-greats-grand-mother. One of the last names and one of the first names (not on the same character) were given in memory of an old school friend who passed away in her twenties. Mrs. Doyle's first name, Suzanne, was af-ter The Hollies' song "Sorry Suzanne," and Adicia's middle name was after The Hollies' song "Dear Eloise." I gave the number 515 to Allen's West Village apartment after The Who song "5:15."

Adicia's experience at a rough junior high was largely based on mine, including details such as a very young foreign language teacher who was out of school for many months with a suspected nervous breakdown and a bully who tore down the homeroom/first period flag, kicked it around the room, and threw it out the window with zero con-sequences. I created Marjani as a best friend for her in remembrance of how a lot of the African-American kids at my junior high were a lot nicer to me than some of the white kids. I've always been colorblind, but perhaps they saw in me a fellow outcast, someone different from the others in my own way.

I never planned the unexpected turn Ernestine and Girl/Deirdre's relationship takes, but the farther I got into the story, the more natural and right it seemed. It was the normal next step in their close relationship, irrespective of the fact that they both happen to be women.

Another unexpected, pleasant surprise was the recurring character of Mrs. Marsenko. She was too good not to bring back each time the Troys needed a bridal shop.

One of the Troy sisters was strongly based on myself, albeit with a number of differences. Those who know me very well will probably immediately recognize which one!

About the Author

Carrie-Anne Brownian, who also writes as Ursula Hartlein, was born on the fifth night of Chanukah in 1979. Though a proud native Pittsburgher, she's lived most of her life in Upstate New York and has also lived in Pittsfield and Amherst, Massachusetts.

She earned a bachelor's degree from UMass–Amherst in History and Russian and East European Studies. Her areas of historical expertise are Russian history, the World War II/Shoah era, and 20th century American history. Her ultimate goal is to one day have a Ph.D. in Russian history.

She is the author of *How Kätchen Became Sparky*, set in 1938, the first book in a series set in an unusual Atlantic City neighborhood, and *Movements in the Symphony of 1939*, its sequel, set during 1939. She has also had work published in the anthologies *Campaigner Challenges 2011*; *Overcoming Adversity: An Anthology for Andrew*; *How I Found the Write Path*; *The Insecure Writer's Support Group Guide to Publishing and Beyond*; *The Cat Who Chose Us and Other Cat Stories*; and *Masquerade: Oddly Suited*. Under her other pen name, she is the author of *And Jakob Flew the Fiend Away*, a Bildungsroman set from 1940-46; *And the Lark Arose from Sullen Earth*, its sequel; *You Cannot Kill a Swan: The Love Story of Lyuba and Ivan*, a sweeping saga set from 1917–24; *The Twelfth Time: Lyuba and Ivan on the Rocks*, its sequel, set from 1924–30; *Journey Through a Dark Forest: Lyuba and Ivan in the Age of Anxiety*, a four-volume saga spanning 1933–48; and *And Aleksey Lived*, an alternative historical saga about the greatest Tsar who never ruled.

Colophon

The text of this book was set in Baskerville, a transitional serif typeface designed in the 1750s by John Baskerville, an English printer and type designer. It was intended as a refinement of then-contemporary type-faces now classified as old-style serif. The design was meant to make characters' size and trim more consistent.

The cover and chapter headings are in Journal.